NO PLACE TO CRY

Previous books by Adam Kennedy,
author of *No Place to Cry:*

The Killing Season
Barlow's Kingdom
The Scaffold
Maggie D.
Somebody Else's Wife
The Domino Principle
Love Song
Just like Humphrey Bogart
The Last Decathlon
Debt of Honour
The Domino Vendetta
In a Far Country

NO PLACE TO CRY

The Bradshaw Trilogy

Volume One

Adam Kennedy

St. Martin's Press
New York

NO PLACE TO CRY. Copyright © 1986 by Adam Kennedy. All rights reserved.
Printed in the United States of America. No part of this book may be used or
reproduced in any manner whatsoever without written permission except in the
case of brief quotations embodied in critical articles or reviews. For information, address St. Martin's Press, 175 Fifth Avenue, New York, N.Y. 10010

Library of Congress Cataloging-in-Publication Data

Kennedy, Adam.
      No place to cry / Adam Kennedy.
           p.   cm.
      "A Thomas Dunne book."
      ISBN 0-312-02955-1
      I. Title.
    PS3561.E425N6   1989
    813'. 54—dc19

First published in Great Britain by W.H. Allen & Co., Plc.

10 9 8 7 6 5 4 3 2

This book is dedicated to my daughter, Anne,
to my sons, Regan and Jack,
to my friends, James McGovern and Arthur Hadley,
and to Susan, the best woman I know.

Life is a gift: from the few to the many.
From those who *know* and *have* to those who do not
know and have not.

Amedeo Modigliani

BOOK ONE

Chapter One

1

Among the people who knew Helen Bradshaw best there were few who imagined they knew her well. Indeed, the people who had known her for the longest time were particularly aware that she was an intricate assemblage, a work in progress. Any assumption or conclusion about her, as soon as it was made, ran the risk of being inaccurate. Since she was constantly redefining herself it was impossible, at any given moment, to define her truly.

Able to survive without guarantees, moment-to-moment, Helen accepted herself fully as a creature in transition. In an objective and pragmatic society she allowed herself to live a subjective life. Teaching herself to surrender things she treasured and to tolerate pain that could not be avoided, she developed a genuine faith in tomorrow. And most important she learned how to recognize joy, how to isolate and preserve it, and warm herself with it. She was able, it seemed, to inhabit, very comfortably, her own skin, to live with her own contradictions.

Had she really managed to attain a perfect balance, an easy command of events? Was she unassailable? It seemed so. But underneath her veneer of self-assurance, inside the fortress she had built round herself, sensitive areas were still exposed, lesions from her childhood, wounds that refused to heal.

From her first growing-up awareness, she had sensed a strangeness in her home, in her family, between her parents. Long before she understood it, long before she

3

began to recognize it for what it was, it upset her, kept her unquiet at night, muddled her thinking, forced her to conclude at last that *she* was somehow to blame, that because of *her* something had gone awry between her father and her mother.

Since she was their only child, her parents, together and separately, spent long and attentive hours with her. She was fondled and lovingly cared for, caressed and sung to and made to feel cherished. Before she could feed herself or say clear words she knew the rhythms and the intimate language of love. She developed a strong appetite for it. And it was a hunger that was always gratified.

From an early age, then, sensitized by this abundance of warmth in her own life, she was aware that while her father showed the same tenderness towards his wife as he did towards Helen, he received nothing comparable in return.

Later, Helen sometimes wondered if she had imagined too much, if she had exaggerated the situation in her mind because it served her larger purpose, because it allowed her, under the guise of correcting the emotional imbalance, to turn from her mother to her father; it permitted her to *choose* him, to adore him, and by so doing to punish, in some tangential way, her mother.

Concluding, as she did, that her father was treated carelessly by his wife, Helen truly suffered for him. Persistent pain. At first she had no skills to deal with it, no defences at all. But little by little, piece by piece, she began to put together her own survival kit. As she grew older and wiser, as she saw more and learned more, she added further to her resources, armoured herself and desensitized herself.

Throughout this critical process, her mother served as her laboratory animal. When Helen reached the point, at last, of final disassociation, when, in the name of her father, she felt she had severed all connections between herself and her mother, she concluded, in her fourteen-year-old wisdom, that she was truly separate and protected now, that no one could ever make her suffer as she believed her father had suffered.

4

Thus armed, she glided forward, like a sleek racing shell. Because she appeared undaunted, because she seemed to have no need for either acceptance or approval, both acceptance and approval came easily to her. She had a social grace that comes only to those who attach no importance to it. Seeming never to take herself seriously, she was pursued endlessly by deadly-serious fools who hungered to explain themselves. Having met her once, these same people were anxious always to meet her again so they could explain themselves in greater detail. They saw her as a warm and accessible young woman. They were desperately fond of her and needed to be near her.

Another group, those who believed she was a creature of secret passages and locked rooms, were more wary. They suspected that they were exposing themselves to alien scents and flavours, fast-flying bubbles from a bubble pipe. So they held back.

Among the contradictions, however, there was one undeniable constant about her. Or so her friends believed. However they might quarrel about other elements of her chemistry, all agreed that her father had been the key factor, some said the *only* significant factor in her life. His dying, they said, had altered her permanently.

The people who admired Helen felt Raymond Bradshaw's death had strengthened her, had made her self-reliant and courageous at an early age. Others, who for reasons of their own, admired her less, whispered among themselves that the loss of her father had crippled her, that her dependence on him had been mammoth and unnatural, that she had regarded herself, ever since, as a victim, as someone who had been cruelly sinned against.

They were wrong of course. Both factions. Helen had in no way been strengthened by Raymond's death. Nor had she been crippled by it. She had in fact, been wracked by an agonizing sorrow. And an aching sense of loss. But the sorrow and the loss were tempered somehow by the poisonous anger she felt towards her mother. The heartache was softened by anger and the anger saved her.

That same ugly anger had saved her before. She had

5

come to depend on it. For nine years, from the time her mother left Raymond, till the day of his death, Helen had used that convenient anger as a measuring-rod to make all other traumas seem smaller and less hurtful. Indeed, throughout her life, she continued to feel that the particular moment she realized – she had been eight years old at the time – that her mother had brought her to New York finally and permanently, that they would live there by themselves now while Raymond stayed in Fort Beck, *that* pain, she continued to believe, had been her greatest and deepest one, greater because it seemed never to slacken or disappear, greater even than the final pain of Raymond's death.

Even before her parents' separation, however, before that sudden train journey to New York, Helen had had an out-of-focus relationship with her mother, a gauzy and uncertain connection in which all the mutual sins were those of omission. If it is possible to conclude that a parent and her child could be uneasy and wary in each other's presence, if something resembling mistrust could exist between such a pair, then those were indeed the ingredients that Helen and her mother dealt with day after day.

From infancy, it seemed, Helen had *selected* her father, had imprinted on him like a malamute imprints on its master. Before she could walk she seemed to sense that *their* connection, hers and Raymond's, was deeper than blood, stronger than their remarkable physical resemblance, stronger than anything. Seeing the two of them as compatible animals, four feet stepping in cadence, four eyes that saw the same miracles, and two voices that reported those miracles in like tones, Helen consumed her father and tried in every way to wall off their lives together so no intruder could get in, not even her mother.

An odd and sophisticated tangle, it would seem, for a little girl to create. Like all complexities however, it had had a simple beginning. Staring, day after day, at the magnificence of her mother, the great dark eyes, the black hair piled softly on top of her head, the sculptured facial planes, and the rounded, long-limbed body, Helen, even as a small child, had said to herself, 'I'm not *like* her. I'm

6

nothing at *all* like her. How can my mother be so different from me?'

When she was five years old she said to Raymond, 'I know you're my real father because I look like you and I *am* like you. But is *Mama* my real mother?'

'What a question,' Raymond said. 'What in the world would make you ask a question like that?'

'Because she doesn't look like us. She doesn't look anything at *all* like us.'

'You'll look like her when you're older.'

'No I won't. I don't want to.'

'Why not? She's a beautiful woman. You'll be fortunate if you look like her.'

'No, I won't. She's too *big*. She's too tall and she's too big.'

'No, she isn't. Anna's just a proper size. You may be bigger than *she* is when you grow up.'

'I don't think so. I think I'll be more *your* size. You're just the right size.'

Her father smiled and pulled her up on his lap. 'I don't know how these things get into your head.'

'They don't *get* in. They're just there.'

'Well, don't ever tell your mother what you're telling me. It would hurt her feelings, I expect. You don't want to make her cry, do you?'

'I don't care what she does.'

'Shame on you,' Raymond said. 'You should be ashamed of yourself, talking like that.'

Though it was a tiny family, just Raymond and Anna and Helen, it was complex and mysterious, like all families, and quietly dangerous. Pieces were missing, it lacked a central understanding, a common truth. Instead each member had his or her own truth. Each had separate secrets, each made judgments about the others based on imperfect or inaccurate information filtered through the scrim of their own needs. Helen's feelings towards her mother, for example, had a kind of detachment that was more violent in its way than hatred. Her devotion to her father was so total that it invited disillusion.

7

And the disillusion came, of course. Not long after her father's death. She realized then, circumstances forced the realization, that Raymond, her father, that perfect adored man, had been different, in significant ways, from what she had believed him to be. It was inconceivable to her that he could have practised any deception on her, however small. But he had. The facts were clear.

In her bewilderment she consoled herself with the knowledge that her mother also had been deceived. Carrying it one step further, seeking some absolution for her father, she concluded that her mother, in some way, had been the *cause* of the deception. Something *she* had done or said, something about *her*, had made it necessary.

Thus, in a single stroke, she re-established her sequence of heroes and villains and locked them once again in their proper slots. But all the same her faith in absolutes had been altered.

As she sensed this fact, however, she rejected it. She insisted that her capacity for *trust* was not diminished. She repeated that over and over until she was thoroughly convinced. But her vulnerable inner self kept its own counsel and reached its own conclusions.

2

Anna Bradshaw was born in 1882, five days before Christmas, in Newark, New Jersey. When she was three years old her parents moved to New York City.

Her father's name was Nello Bardoni. Her mother's name was Sophia. She had an older brother, Vinnie, and a baby sister, Rosa.

Nello and his brother, Arturo, were housepainters and cabinet-makers. When they had saved enough money to bring their parents, Victorio and Marcella, to America, they bought a run-down house in Fifth Street on the lower East side so that each of their families, as well as their mother and father, could live there together.

Anna's aunt, her mother's sister, Tullia, and her husband, Vicenzo Mistretta, lived two doors down the street towards First Avenue. Arturo's wife, Evalina, had her twin sister, Eva, just four houses away in the other direction, towards Second Avenue, and her parents, the Mosconis, lived just behind her, connecting back yards, in Sixth Street.

All these names are important because they were important to Anna. It is valuable also, to know where these people lived so it will be clear how Anna lived. Surrounded always by relatives, male and female, young and old, all living close together, crowded together, she wanted no other life and knew no other life. Whenever she turned her head or simply shifted her gaze, she saw someone she loved, somebody who loved *her*.

The Bardoni kitchen was the largest room in the house but because it was always crowded it seemed small. At meal-times it was filled with hungry men and children, eating, drinking and being served by Anna's mother, her grandmother, and her aunts. Between meals the room was crowded with women and young girls like Anna, cleaning up from the last serving and preparing for the next.

All the children in the house belonged to all the adults. Having been passed, since first awareness, from lap to lap, an infant struggling to say his first 'mama' or 'papa' had some difficulty at first knowing who those titles properly belonged to. In Anna's case, both Tullia and Evalina held her and bathed her and scolded her as if she were their own child. And though she never saw her grandmother, Marcella, till she was three years old, Anna sensed, almost from the old woman's first touch, that she belonged to her as surely as she did to her own mother.

Character and industry were not measured, in Anna's neighbourhood, by individuals striking out on their own. Everyone worked, of course, women and children included, at whatever jobs could be had, but the goals were not independence or autonomy or personal achievement. The objective was to bring whatever one could to the family table.

9

All the holidays and their celebrations were family celebrations. Clans would gather, in Brooklyn or Hoboken, in Sullivan Street or wherever Italian families had clustered. Music would start. An accordion or a mandolin or both. And food would begin to appear. On tables in the street, or on the roofs, or spread on the grass in the nearest park. Great wicker jugs of chianti would be opened, and chilled bottles of frascati, and an Italian feast, unlike any other social gathering, would begin. Just as there had been no specific starting time, neither would there be a clear notion in anyone's mind as to when it would end. The sausages and the pasta, it seemed, never ran out, nor did the wine. The musicians seldom tired or lost patience, and the Poles and the Ukrainians in the neighbourhood watched through open windows, their elbows resting on pillows, or sat on folding chairs on their fire escapes and had, it seemed, no impulse to complain about the music or the noise and shouting in the street.

Old men fell asleep on stoops and kerbs, grey-haired women became flirtatious, everyone drank a great deal, and tempers sometimes flared. But those who were accustomed to Italian life in an Italian kitchen saw this street behaviour as a simple magnification of that other daily life. Nothing more. Thundering waves, turbulent tides, then smooth seas suddenly, and light shafts knifing through the clouds. Ebb and flow, night and noon, smile and weep, sick and well, tenderness and violence in equal parts, always on display. All of it public, all of it shared.

When Anna cried and stormed as a child, fumed and wailed and cursed her luck, her grandmother said, 'You are *not* special, Anna. Remember that. In this house you are one of us. No less and no more. But if you *must* be special, just remember that *I* am special, too. So are your mama and papa, and Rosa and Vinnie. We each have a turn. Everyone is permitted to eat from the pot. When you are laughing and turning cartwheels on the grass remember that someone nearby is weeping in a dark room. Nobody picked you to be a happy person or a sad one. You will get some of each as we all do.'

What did this tribal life mean to Anna, this life in a crowd, this seeming rejection of individuality and independent growth, this ownership of everything, this ownership of nothing, this close and tender existence that seemed to encompass life and somehow restrict it, or even deny it, at the same time?

One can only say that as she grew up she questioned nothing. The way she lived was simply the way her people lived, the way the families of all her friends lived. No alternatives were presented to her. She was not aware that other young women had choices that she did not have.

The truth was this. The way she lived, every hour and every day, from her birth till the day she married, existed for her only in its details, in its moments. It never crystallized in her mind as an identifiable, multi-faceted entity, until she was away from it, till she had ceased to live it and be part of it, till she had made another choice.

Then, and only then, not suddenly, not like summer lightning or the shock of familiar perfume in a dark hallway, but painfully and gradually, she came to see what it was she had been exposed to, where she was rooted, how it had formed her, defined her needs and her rewards, conditioned her patterns of joy and disappointment.

From those first moments of truly independent thinking, from the first instant when she isolated what she had known, what she had once had but had no longer, when she measured, in the cold, flat light of plus and minus the expendable against the essential, Anna knew, suddenly and brutally, that she would never know genuine contentment again, not unless she managed somehow to reclaim and re-enter that cocoon she had abandoned, that chaotic, unmanageable but totally fulfilling world she had left.

It is important to understand however, that this longing-back to the flavours and textures of her growing-up years, strong as it was, did not tempt her to turn away from her daughter who was still a baby then. Or from Raymond. In those first years of her marriage, she would not have allowed herself to be so tempted. Her family had not taught her self-indulgence. And even if she had given in

11

somehow, if she had tried to go home with her infant daughter in her arms, she knew that the Bardoni men would have hurried her back uptown to catch the next west-bound train. Without hesitation they would have bundled her off, back to her husband in Illinois.

And of course there was the church, key witness to all transgressions. Anna was a Catholic child in a Catholic world. The nuns taught her in their classes and the priest heard her confession once a week. As a young girl she had no sins to report but she knew she was expected to offer up minor ones in the confessional so she could learn the ways of absolution, so she could see penance and atonement at work. By the time she had actual sins to confess, all of them sins of the heart and the imagination, she was far away from her priest and her parish and had, indeed, to a large degree, fallen away from the church.

For a time she made an effort to raise her daughter as a Catholic. When Raymond took instructions in New York before their marriage, that had been the understanding, his covenant with the church and her family, that their children would be brought up as Catholics. And he never retreated from that agreement. Soon after their arrival in Fort Beck he made inquiries and pointed out to Anna that there was a small Catholic church not far from their house. St. Boniface.

By the following May however, when Helen was born, Anna had become extremely conscious of the fact that Foresby was a Methodist school and Fort Beck itself was a conspicuously Protestant community. Although Helen was christened at St. Boniface, and though Raymond assured his wife that she was free to be as Catholic as she wished and to raise their daughter by the dogma of that faith, Anna began to be self-conscious about her Catholicism. It made her feel conspicuous and alien in their neighbourhood and among the college people with whom they associated. In a pocket of the country that was new and unfamiliar to her, in a very small city, little more than a village, where all idiosyncrasies were highly visible and carefully noted, she was reluctant to call attention to

12

herself, to set herself apart in any way from the women on their block or from the other faculty wives.

Later she realized that she should have felt differently, should have behaved differently, should have made it a specific goal to retain her identity, to be what she was, what she had always been, to be accommodating in some areas but not all, to be herself, to have respect for herself. But no hindsight could alter the fact that she had been not quite eighteen when they came to Fort Beck, not quite nineteen when Helen was born. So wariness and inexperience told her to conform, to adjust, to make herself, as much as possible, like the pale and careful women she saw all around her, their lawns meticulously tended, their window-blinds drawn day and night, their black housemaids washing and ironing, it seemed, every day except Sunday; sheets and towels and undergarments flapped constantly from the lines stretched taut as cables across the wide back yards.

Anna's willingness to compromise, however, her desire to conform, was not a success. The changes she was able to make in herself were so small as to be almost unnoticeable. Sensing this, and being genuinely disturbed by it, she concluded at last that the best solution for her was to stay out of sight as much as possible and when it was *not* possible, to remain silent. But this went wrong too. Among the well-scrubbed and starched ladies of Fort Beck, her shyness was labelled aloofness, her silence inordinate pride.

Her youth, too, was a problem. Many of the women she met were her mother's age. And the ones who were closer to her in years, took pride in looking and behaving as if they were ten years older than they were. And of course, Anna was Italian. The fact of her national origin was not held against her because, having never met an Italian before, the Fort Beck people had had no opportunity to develop a proper prejudice. But they did know, even the people who saw Anna only on her porch or in the dress shops, that she was different, that she looked different, that she was, in almost every way, a radical departure from

13

the tight-corseted ladies one saw normally on the streets of Fort Beck.

Not long after their arrival in Illinois, only a few weeks after their marriage, Raymond, sensing Anna's unease, said, 'Of course you're different from these odd women. They all look like cream scones and they sound like chickens in the garden. But *you* . . . you look like a contessa. Your voice sounds like a cello.'

Raymond was different, too, of course. But he used it to his advantage. He, too, was young. But he had an air of authority that made him seem older. He was able, always, to hold his ground, to take stage. He could do what Anna was unable to do. He could recognize and accept his shortcomings, exhibit them fearlessly, and force other people to accept them, too.

In manners and public decorum, he was an *example*, a paragon of acceptability and respectability. Knowing this about himself, knowing that he projected an impeccable and unassailable façade, he was able to remain, behind that social curtain, as odd and quirky and unpredictable as he liked.

Raymond, quite simply, knew how to deal with people. Appearing to surrender everything, he, in fact, gave up nothing. Behind a selfless manner, he was fully occupied with his own needs and requirements. Not only was he able almost always to have his way, he found, usually, that people were eager to *help* him have it.

3

Quite apart from her struggle to adjust to her new life in a new home, Anna never solved the mystery of her husband. Nor the mystery of the two of them together. When she met Raymond she never expected that they would *be* together. After they were married, she never convinced herself that they would *stay* together, that he would stay with her. Even in their happiest days, when

14

she was able to shut out her doubts, able to ignore her anxieties, when all the contradictory evidence was as strong as it could be, even then she persisted in her belief that she was not a permanent part of his life.

How was it possible? How could the wife of a fine and civilized man have such feelings? She did not know. But the feelings were persistently there and she trusted them.

When she was pregnant, she told herself she would feel different after her child was born, when Raymond and she were no longer just a man and woman together, when they had become a family.

She longed for the first sight of her baby. In her imagination its face was very clear. All the Bardoni babies looked the same. Great round eyes and black hair. In the family albums, the children from one generation to the next seemed almost identical. And Anna's baby, she knew, would be no exception. It would be a living reminder of her own life as a child, a link with that time, with those people, with the cluttered and noisy and beautiful streets of New York.

But Helen, when she arrived, was a duplicate of her father. She bore no resemblance to Anna or her relatives. Even as an infant in her crib she seemed in every way a Bradshaw. The more she grew and developed the more true it became.

This is not to say that Helen was a disappointment to her mother. Anna was wise enough to realize that Helen was not to blame because she bore no resemblance to the Bardonis. She *was* a continuing surprise but Anna did not fault her for that. Quite the contrary. Watching her daughter grow and develop, marking her skills and her grace, Anna increasingly found fault with herself. Listening to her barely school-age daughter as she responded to questions from Raymond and his friends, hearing her display an impressive knowledge of the year before she was born and the years hence, hearing her fix 1900 as the year the first Browning revolver was manufactured, the year that McKinley was re-elected, the year of the first Zeppelin flight, Anna began to feel inferior to her own

15

daughter, cut off from her own child, just as she had come to feel cut off from Raymond. And all this, she sincerely believed, at least in those first years, was because of some shortcoming in her. If some key ingredient was missing, if somehow the wheels had slipped off the rails, it was her fault.

These were not feelings she could properly explain to anyone, least of all to herself. But they persisted nonetheless, and became an unsettling central truth, one that was constantly with her, like a stubborn speck of grit under her eyelid.

Little by little her self-esteem dissolved until at last it disappeared completely. She discovered suddenly that she was unable to make the simplest choice; she avoided the most routine household decision. She concluded that Mrs. Esping, their housekeeper, was in charge of one half of her life while Raymond and Helen administered the other half.

Sensing finally that her foundations were slipping away, fearing that she was near a breakdown, feeling helpless to deal with herself, unable to discuss it with Raymond or anyone else, raw-nerved and sleepless and frightened to death of tomorrow, she ran away to New York one August morning and took her daughter with her. Helen was eight years old. She thought she was making a two-week summer visit to see her grandparents.

Since there was no way she could explain things to her family, Anna told them nothing. She simply stayed on till they realized she wasn't going back. When she tried at last to tell Rosa and her mother how she felt, Rosa asked, 'Did you say all these things to him?'

'No. We didn't talk about it.'

'You mean he wouldn't talk to you?' her mother said.

'It wasn't that,' Anna said. '*I* couldn't talk to *him*.'

When she wrote to Raymond from New York, the letter was unsatisfactory to her as she wrote it and bewildering to him as he read it. When he arrived in New York, however, a few days later, she felt she came as close as she ever could to telling him what she was thinking and feeling. 'It doesn't matter if I love you or if you love me,' she said. 'Love doesn't fix everything. I just can't live with you any more. You're too much for me.'

'That doesn't make sense,' he said. 'It makes no sense at all.'

By then she was crying. 'You're just too *much* for me. Can't you understand that? It's the only way I know how to say it.'

When she first met him, that April in New York, she was astonished when he showed an interest in her. Some instinct told her to beware. He was too striking, too intelligent, too sure. Too much seductive vitality. Too informed. Too persistent. 'He is not for me,' she told herself.

But Raymond persevered. He charmed her parents, her friends, and her relatives. They told her he was a remarkable prize. Still, some animal instinct held her back. At last, however, she knew a decision had to be made. She sat one afternoon in her grandmother's room and told her she had decided not to marry Raymond.

Her grandmother, old and toothless, skin like tobacco, fingers like claws, stubbed her cigarette out in a saucer.

'Did you tell *him*?' she said.

'No. Not yet.'

'Then *tell* him. Why do you tell me?'

'Because I always tell you things,' Anna said.

'Maybe you should tell the priest. If you've been lifting your skirts and giggling with this man you don't want to marry, maybe it's the priest you should be talking to.'

'It's not like that.'

'That's what they all say. That's what *I* used to say.'

'I just wanted to talk to you before I told him.'

Her grandmother slowly shook her head. 'If you want me to make up your mind for you, I won't do it. When a woman wants to cook and clean for a man, when she wants to sleep in his bed and be a mother to his children, she doesn't need a push. The devil himself couldn't stop her. So if you can't make up your mind about this Englishman. . . .'

'He's not English. You always say he's English. He's

from Boston. He told me he was born in Maine but he lives in Boston.'

'He's *English*,' her grandmother said. 'And don't butt in when I'm talking to you. I'm saying if you can't make up your mind, that tells me you've *already* made up your mind. Forget about him.'

'What if I can't?'

'What are we talking about? Do you want him or don't you?'

'I want him, I mean I think I want him, but I'm afraid.'

'Don't think about it. There's nothing to be afraid of. It only hurts the first time.'

'I don't mean *that*. I just mean he's different from us. He's not like anybody I've ever met. I don't even know why he likes me. I don't think I'm good enough for him.'

'Maybe you're not. But that doesn't matter. All that counts is if *he* thinks you're good enough.'

'What if he gets tired of me?'

'He *will*. You can expect it. *All* men get tired of their wives. But not as fast as the wives get tired of *them*.' She got up and poured two small cups of coffee. When she sat down again she said, 'You're a lunatic girl, Anna. All young girls are lunatics. Trying to figure out tomorrow when you haven't got through today yet.' She poured anisette in her coffee and lit a cigarette. 'I was born in 1826. This year we start a new century. Does it matter? Not to me. Some things don't change. And one thing I tell you . . . it is hard for a woman to make a life without a man. If you're very lucky you get a good one. But a bad man is better than no man at all. You have to take a chance on somebody or you'll never *know* bad from good. So that's it, baby-sweet. If you don't want this Englishman who says he's from Boston, *I'll* take him. I could show him a few tricks.'

Anna laughed and her grandmother said, 'You take after your grandfather. Good looks and a lot of craziness under your hat. But that's all right. When you're young and pretty to look at and with a nice behind you're entitled to be a little crazy. The main thing is to have some fun. You've

18

got your whole life to scrub floors and wipe noses and worry about what comes next. You think *you've* got a problem . . . . When you're my age, *nothing* comes next. *That's* a problem.'

They sat there sipping their coffee, sunshine warming the window-panes and making yellow squares on the painted floor. At last her grandmother said, 'Maybe he turns out no good. That's all right. Most men turn out no good. If he's very bad, you talk to your brother and your father about him. They will speak to him. And if he's really mean and ugly, you cut him up some night while he's sleeping. We're from Siena. We don't bend the knee to anybody.'

That night Anna told Raymond she would marry him.

4

A long time after they parted, Anna realized at last what her true feelings had been towards Raymond, what it was that had held her back at the beginning and had grown inside her like a tumour during their marriage. At last it came clear to her, not as an empirical conclusion, but as a kind of uneasy perception. And she believed it though she could not prove it. Not until his death did she realize that her instinct had been correct.

She had never truly trusted him. This is what she came to at last. It was not simply that he was lying to her, though of course he was, it was more accurately a feeling she had, from the beginning, that he was not what he appeared to be.

There had been a false note always, she concluded, something too studied, something concealed behind the veneer, behind the warm cordiality, behind the affection, behind his unquestioned passion for her and his adoration of his daughter; all this, all the capability in his work, the quick mind and the trick of laughing people through their anxieties, all his truly beautiful impulses and qualities seemed less valuable somehow because they were anchored to a foundation less firm than advertised, or to no foundation at all.

Raymond was what he had *chosen* to be, Anna concluded at last, rather than what he *was*. The boy-child who had grown and matured somewhere had been replaced by a physical twin who had been manufactured, a man without living relatives or childhood friends.

Like a creature built in a laboratory Raymond seemed to be made of only the finest parts. But the most important one, sadly, had been left out. Or worn out and not replaced. Anna's instinct was correct. Like a man whose fingerprints have been removed by acid or by plastic surgery, he had managed to conceal his identity even from himself. Since he had succeeded in forgetting who he was, he was able to give away anything *except* himself. *That* gift, it turned out, was not available, not even to him. When he died he simply kept a rendezvous with some vital part of himself that had been dead long since.

5

Raymond Bradshaw was born June 12, 1877, in the north of England, at his family's home, Wingate Fields. His father, Angus, had also been born there, in 1844, as were his father and grandfather before him. Raymond's mother, Louise Dobbs, was born in 1850 in Salisbury and his sister, Clara Bradshaw Causey, was born in 1875.

The Bradshaws had been crofters and shepherds until 1651 when Furman Bradshaw, a soldier who had led one of Cromwell's armies, was rewarded with a handsome grant of grazing land in Northumberland, five hundred hectares that had once belonged to the Duke of Bellingham, a courageous man of principle who opposed Cromwell and lost both his holdings and his head as a result.

Furman, on the death of his first wife, had married Elizabeth Wingate, the spinster daughter and only child of

Richard Wingate, Furman's neighbour to the west, a man whose fields and meadowlands were twice the size of Furman's.

Furman's sons, Pearse and James, also married daughters of the neighbouring gentry, selecting in each case, either by chance or design, families without male issue. By the middle of the eighteenth century, the Bradshaw estates stretched from Hadrian's Wall to Brampton in the west and from Bellingham to Hexham to Haltwhistle in the east.

John, Furman's great grandson, became an enterprising and imaginative wool-merchant and exporter. He built mills in North Riding, owned lead mines in the Yorkshire Dales, and began to buy sites in sections of London that most investors thought were without value but which became, in fact, very valuable indeed.

In 1770, James Cecil, the Sixth Earl of Salisbury, approached John and told him the Royal advisors were prepared to submit his name to the King for inclusion in the peerage unless, of course, John had some objection.

'Of course I could not refuse such an honour if it was offered by my King,' John said. 'But if you, as my old friend, can somehow prevent the offer being *made*, I would consider myself in your debt. The Bradshaws are shepherds and farmers and merchants. While we take pride in our accomplishments, we have humility about our origins. I tell you in confidence that we are content to live like royalty while we remain commoners. Membership of the peerage is not an obligation I wish to put on my children or their children.'

If there could be said to be a critical flaw in the Bradshaw bloodlines, it is, has always been, their propensity for producing lovely and gracious daughters rather more often than male heirs. With a bit of good fortune, however, and a great deal of determination, each generation through the centuries managed to produce, among a legion of girl-children, at least one robust male.

In 1810, for example, when John, in his eighties by then, was still without an heir, his third wife, a timid young woman named Clarissa, quite miraculously provided him

21

with a male child. John, five months later, died triumphant, and a sullen young man named Rennie, who had trained and groomed the Bradshaw carriage horses for five years, returned to Connemara with enough capital to start a stud farm of his own and to marry and start a family he could claim and give his name to.

Angus, Raymond's father, had two brothers, Peter and Robert Dale. But Peter, born in 1840, died in infancy, and Robert Dale, born in 1842, was killed in 1860 in a hunting mishap. So the continuity of the Bradshaws rested squarely on Raymond's mother and father. Their first child, a male, was still-born. Their second, also a male, died of influenza when he was three years old. Then came a daughter, also still-born. And then Raymond's sister, Clara, fat and noisy and healthy.

At last, Raymond was born. Pale and thin he was, fragile and sickly as a child, but tenacious and stubborn all the same, no question about it, destined, it appeared, for survival.

As it turned out however, Raymond, for all his tenacity and energy, was not cut out to manage and sustain the Bradshaw fortunes. Or one should say, not *inclined* to do that work. *Able* to but not at all *willing* to. Or so it seemed to his father. Long before Raymond reached the age of responsibility, Angus began to suspect that his son's interests were far removed from the worlds of animal husbandry, wool trading, and land investments.

Although he never mentioned it to her, Angus blamed his wife, at least in part, for Raymond's far-ranging curiosity. And he was right. Louise was a woman with a marked literary bent. A tireless reader, she also wrote charming sonnets and lyrics herself, and she had kept a journal since she was a schoolgirl. Like many young women of her time, she played the harpsichord as well, and painted delicate watercolours. When she hired a governess, Judith Radei, to look after her son and daughter, she took pains to select a woman whose cultural interests were similar to her own.

The result was that both Clara and Raymond were

22

consumed by a love for books and music and pictures from earliest childhood. When a string quartet was brought in from York or Liverpool to perform in the Bradshaw music room, if a poet was invited to read from his own work, or when the ladies of the county staged pageants or theatricals, Louise's children were always included in the audience.

This is not to say that Raymond was some sort of drawing-room child. He was not. 'Lots of ginger in that boy,' Angus said. 'Enough spunk for three of his size.' He could ride well when he was six and he began to go to meets with his father when he was eight or nine. The gamekeepers taught him to shoot and to handle a fly rod and when he was old enough Angus saw to it that he learned to drink properly.

For all of his own absorption in the agricultural and financial complex he had inherited and then tripled in size and intricacy, and although everyone who knew him was aware of his desire for Raymond to continue that work, some instinct told Angus that the only game he could profitably play with his son was the waiting game.

It was agreed, therefore, that Raymond would read English literature at Christ's College, Cambridge. No mention was made in the family of where exactly he would go from there or what he would do. It was still the nineteenth century, after all, and everyone understood that a young man of means, if he was fortunate enough to be an elder son, or an *only* son, would take over, both as an opportunity and an obligation, the management of the financial affairs of his family. At least Angus understood this and he hoped with time his son would come to understand it too.

Raymond *did* come to understand. Or at least it appeared the process of understanding had begun. By 1897, when he was almost twenty he had completed two years at Cambridge. Trying to look and feel and to seem to strangers as mature and responsible as possible, he affected the dress and behaviour of a man twice his age. Poetry and

23

music continued to dominate his study programme but he had begun to see those passions in different proportion.

He was a wealthy man, he told himself, and he would become, at last, far wealthier, just as his father had done. He would be free to spend his time as he wished, to enjoy the arts, to subsidize them and to practise them as much as his talents would permit. But bit by bit, more and more he came to see that the foundation for this remarkable freedom, his ability to choose freely his routes and his objectives, was the Bradshaw fortune.

Logic and decency, plus his new-found wisdom, told him that he must, when the time came, do his share of the world's work, of his father's work. At twenty, one never questions that there is time for everything. Raymond, certainly, did not question it. He assured himself that he would be able to do it all, the required tasks and the chosen ones, and nothing would suffer.

At this stage, therefore, it appeared that Angus had been correct in his decision to play a waiting game. Without prodding or insistence on his part, Raymond had begun to direct himself to a proper starting gate; he was preparing to compete in a race that would benefit him as well as his family. And of course, he would *win* that race. Any other supposition was out of the question.

This dreaming and planning, however, these all-encompassing aspirations, changed abruptly on his twentieth birthday. On that occasion, early in June, Raymond just home from Cambridge, his parents fêted him with a lavish dinner and dancing party.

It was a soft and enticing evening, bright paper lanterns hanging from the trees, the gardens in early bloom, and an orchestra playing softly on the south portico.

When the guests began to arrive, when Angus and Louise with Clara and her husband, Ned Causey, were greeting people in the main hall, laughing and talking with men and women of the county whom they had known all their lives, Raymond was introduced by his sister to Emily Callison, the wife of Oliver Callison, whose first wife, Agnes, had inherited the Isbell lands. The Callison home,

Maidenstone, formerly the Isbell home, was ten miles to the north of Wingate, across the moors and the limestone crags that rolled like soft waves all the way to the south edge of Scotland and beyond.

From his sister's letters, Raymond knew that Callison, after a proper period of mourning for Agnes, an unhappy woman who had tried unsuccessfully to nourish herself on a diet of sweet biscuits and port wine, had recently remarried. Clara added that although she, herself, did not know Callison well, what she knew of him she didn't like. Raymond, on meeting the man, agreed with her. Observing Callison's heavy lower jaw, his thick, cruel body, his cloudy eyes reflecting no light, appearing not to move in their sockets, Raymond thought him a truly unpleasant man.

But oh, dear God, when he turned and saw Callison's wife, when he looked at Emily for the first time, when she smiled and offered him her hand, what a physical wrench he felt. Not the ache of lust or the gut-contraction of envy or covetousness. His first animal reaction was simply this: such a woman should never be required to submit to such a man as Callison.

Looking at her, Raymond could feel his expression change and he knew that she saw it change. He was convinced that she knew precisely what was in his mind. That thought both embarrassed him and excited him. As he watched her move away towards the music room, Raymond believed that he and Emily had signed a silent and dangerous contract. And she knew it too, he was sure.

But they barely spoke that evening. Like animals afraid of the flame, they stayed on opposite sides of the room, each careful not to watch the other but watching all the same. Although Raymond was desperate to talk to her, to guide her away, to have some gentle words, some sign from her, he was, at the same time, afraid to show his hand, afraid of frightening her perhaps, of killing his chances, afraid to end it before it had begun, to assume too much too quickly, to risk all and to lose.

Also, the hateful Callison never left her side. He stood

25

with his hand at the small of her back like an evil puppeteer, exhibiting her it seemed, posturing like a cock on a railing, smiling his hideous smile, his mouth like a sabre wound, and devouring with his raccoon eyes the young bare-shouldered women who floated past or paused to talk to Emily.

Ned, Raymond's brother-in-law, caught him staring across the room and said, 'She's a lovely young pullet, isn't she? Callison should count himself the most fortunate man in the county. But they say he still beds down with any low-born woman who will have him. Wenches and widows and the wives of servants. The man's a fool.'

Raymond, pretending no interest in the subject, felt his stomach turn over at Ned's words. As the party went on he drank a great deal of wine, trying to blur the images that persisted in his head. But the images remained, clear and ugly.

The evening seemed endless. To make it pass, to distract himself, Raymond functioned as a host non-pareil, dancing with stout women who had moles on their cheeks and warts on their chins, waltzing with their stout perspiring daughters who had been instructed before leaving home to show themselves to best advantage to the young men they encountered, and who did this as well as they knew how by giggling and showing their brown teeth and by thrusting their great udders high against the shirts of their dancing partners.

Raymond also listened tirelessly to the exploits of old soldiers, moustaches bristling and thick tufts of hair in their ears, bright splashes of foreign-service ribbons on the breasts of their tail-coats. He heard tales of corporal punishment in the Sudan and adultery in Singapore, and in one instance had his lower back vigorously massaged by a retired colonel of the horse troops who was longing, it seemed, for an early return to barracks life.

Only twice during the evening did he come near to Emily. The first time, his father was at his side and Raymond tried not to stare at her while Callison, whose cheeks had begun to dapple from the wine, praised his wife with well-liquored enthusiasm. 'A delicate little thing, I'm sure you'd say that. Fragile and dependent. Wouldn't you think so, Angus? Well, that's not the case. Not at all. The fact is, she tyrannizes me. She's Welsh, you know. Caernarvonshire, born and bred. Pretty as a tulip but she must have her way in all things.'

Glancing at Emily, Raymond saw the colour spread slowly upward from her neck to her cheeks. 'Manages the staff with a whip and a stick. And me the same way – never flags nor tires, my fine lady-wife. Up with the dawn every morning. A bit of breakfast and she's off with her dogs and her hunter. All alone, mind you, tilting at the day. You remember my naughty grey stallion, Angus? Well, she's commandeered him as well. Gentled him down and took him for her own. Off across the walls and ledges they go. She rides like a cossack. Off to God knows where in all kinds of weather. Close to midday most days before she's back.'

Angus smiled and said, 'Unless you've changed your habits, Oliver, I expect you're just struggling up from your bed, just ringing for your breakfast tea, when Mrs Callison comes back from her ride.' He bowed to Emily then and steered Raymond away with him. They continued their slow tour of the ballroom, stopping next to greet the Wiswells, an obscenely thin couple, the man with a fringe of silky grey hair around his speckled dome and his wife almost top-heavy, it seemed, with a great basket-shaped mass of henna-red curls blossoming above her knife-blade face.

Their rickety daughter, Arabella, stood beside them, nibbling at her finger-nails when she thought her mother's attention was directed elsewhere and vibrating in some odd and very personal reaction to the rhythms of the orchestra. Taking her fingers out of her mouth then, she said, to no one in particular, 'I have been taught by my nanny that the waltz is the most graceful possible use of the human muscular system.'

Angus looked at his son then in a meaningful way and Raymond whirled Arabella away across the floor, feeling

27

the sharp bones of her vertebrae against his finger-tips and gazing over her angular shoulder at Emily who, with her face slightly averted from her husband, was openly staring at Raymond. Continuing to keep his eyes on Emily with the least interruption possible, he waltzed Arabella relentlessly up and down the floor until she became quite exhausted and had to be guided back to her parents. Had he seen amusement on Emily's face? He could not be sure.

When the guests began leaving to go home, long past midnight, there was some confusion in the cloakroom about Emily's wrap. When Callison stepped away from the foyer with one of the servants to identify and claim the garment, Raymond quickly said to Emily, 'Is it true you ride out every morning?'

'Yes,' she said. 'Every day except the Sabbath.'

'May I ask where you ride?'

'Yes.' She said the word quietly but with force behind it. Insistent and penetrating. 'I ride to the ruined castle on the moors above the Will river. Do you know that place?'

'Yes.'

'I am there by eight in the morning. Nine at the latest.' As she saw Callison returning she smiled and said, 'Every morning except the Sabbath.'

Every day that summer Raymond rode out to meet her. Every morning except Sundays they spent together on the grassy knolls in the dales along the Will and in an abandoned crofter's cottage standing in a grove of oak where the river bends sharply to the east on its way to join the Rede.

Raymond brought food and wine always in his saddle-pouch. They ate and drank and lay together on the thick grass in the cool shade or on the hard-packed earth that was the floor of the crofter's cottage. They lay in each other's arms and talked and dreamed and made plans.

'We must try to be patient,' she said, 'till you reach your majority.' When Raymond told her he could not be patient she said, 'Neither can I but we *must*. If we are not strong and sure in our minds with enough money to make us free we can never win our battle with Oliver. He will never

28

agree to let me go. I must simply leave him. We will disappear like two wild geese. To Italy maybe. Or Switzerland. Or perhaps to America. If we stay here he will kill you. Or he'll kill me. He says he shot a man once in Marseilles. He's proud of it.'

So they worked out their life together. At twenty-one Raymond would have the money left him by his grandfather plus a substantial share of his family's holdings. They would be free, then, he and Emily, to go as far as they liked, to live wherever they chose.

'I have an aunt near Bradford,' Emily said. 'I am allowed to visit her. I will go there as often as I can when you're at university and you'll come up from Cambridge. In between times I will find a way to write to you and you can write to me at my dressmaker's home in Bellingham.'

A week before Raymond was due to return to Cambridge, his father invited him into the library, closed the door behind them, and said, 'You're a man now, Raymond. You are an adult in every way. So I assure you that I find it both inappropriate and distasteful to interfere with your life. But I must. I have decided not to send you back to Cambridge. You will be going to Trinity College in Dublin this year.'

Before Raymond could answer, Angus held up his hand and said, 'Let me finish. Then I will listen to whatever you have to say.' He repositioned himself in his high-backed chair and went on, 'I have known for some time about your situation with Mrs Callison. Her husband knows also. He knows, too, that his wife has made plans to see you after you return to university and he is determined to prevent that. Callison is an excitable man, I'm afraid. I have known him for twenty years. I am not fond of him and I can't honestly say that I respect him, but I've had business dealings with him and I assure you I know him well. When I tell you that he is unstable and dangerous, that he is capable of behaving in a most unpredictable and irresponsible manner, you must believe me. So you see, since you are in this awkward situation, I am forced to intervene. You're my only son, you are precious to your

29

mother and me, and I must protect you in any way that I can.'

Angus listened carefully then as Raymond made it clear that he would not, under any circumstances, go to Dublin and he would not, under any circumstances, give up Emily. When he had clarified and repeated his feelings with all the vehemence he could muster, his father said, 'I'm not surprised at your reaction. If I were in your position I'm sure I would respond in much the same way. But I'm afraid you must accept the fact that you have no choice in this matter. If you are determined to continue this liaison with Mrs Callison, we can not allow you to do so as a resident of Wingate Fields. I'm sure you understand our reasons for that. And I have already said that I will not send you back to Cambridge this autumn. So if you refuse to go to Trinity, all I can do is offer you a beginner's post in our London office. You would be paid an adequate living wage for a single man and you would be gaining valuable experience for the future. And you would be a great distance away from Maidenstone.'

Angus paused then and waited. But Raymond, his face pale with anger, did not answer.

'I'm sure you're very annoyed with me,' his father said. 'I expected that. Since you're an intelligent man, I expect also that you are considering your alternatives. Is that correct?'

'I certainly don't accept the fact that I *have* no alternatives. Everyone has choices.'

'Perhaps you're right,' Angus said. 'But let me explain some of the choices you do *not* have. If you are thinking, for example, that you will be free and independent when you come into your grandfather's legacy next June, let me remind you that I am the executor of that estate, that whatever the language of the various bequests may be, I am the ultimate guardian of those monies. It is clearly stipulated that they are to be released when I sign my name and only then.' He paused, then went on. 'I suspect that money plays a key role in whatever plans you and Mrs Callison have been making. I feel obliged to frustrate those plans in any way I can.' Another pause. 'I hope and I believe that by your next birthday you will have come to your senses. That you will be ready to go forward with your life in a responsible way. With your legacy and your other financial shares at your disposal.'

'I don't need to come to my senses. I know what I'm doing,' Raymond said. 'You say you care about what happens to me. Well *I* care about what happens to Emily. That's *all* I care about.'

'I don't doubt that. And I admire you for it. I'm sure you have strong feelings for Mrs Callison and she for you. All of us face temptation in our lives and many of us yield to it, especially when we're young. But at last we find that the rules of society apply to all. All of us must obey them or suffer the consequences. Mrs Callison made an adult choice when she married Oliver and I suspect she will have to live with that choice. And so must you. If Callison were a reasonable man perhaps some other solution could be found. But he is neither reasonable nor wise. He is, however, vengeful and ruthless and I am determined to protect you from him if I can, whether you want that protection or not.'

When Raymond rode out the following morning and the several mornings after that, Emily was not there, not at the ruined castle, not at the crofter's cottage. After a week, his sister, Clara, took him aside one evening and gave him a small envelope. 'This is for you. One of Mrs Callison's servants brought it this afternoon.'

'I was here. Why didn't I see him?'

'He was instructed to deliver the letter to me.'

When he opened the envelope, Raymond found a short note inside, seemingly written in haste on plain notepaper. No salutation and no signature.

How can I say goodbye in a letter? How can I say goodbye at all? God help us, Raymond. God help *me*. I must be with you and I *can't* be with you. I love you, my dearest, and I always will.

31

'Why didn't you give me this as soon as it came?' he said to Clara.

'I was told to give it to you this evening.'

'I don't give a damn what you were told.'

'It wouldn't have mattered, Raymond. Emily's not at Maidenstone. Callison took her away yesterday.'

'Where did they go?'

'The man didn't know.'

'When are they coming back?'

'He didn't know that either.'

Raymond stood by the window of his sister's sitting-room, immobile as a pillar. There were tears in Clara's eyes. At last she said, 'I'm sorry, Raymond.'

6

Reason told him that his father had acted in his best interests, that he had been genuinely concerned about his son's welfare and his future, perhaps even his safety, but during those grey autumn months in Dublin it was impossible for Raymond to *be* reasonable. Desperately needing an adversary, a target, some specific person he could blame for his misery, his father's face continued to dominate his angry memories.

He answered none of his father's letters and wrote only occasionally to his mother and Clara. The letters he did write contained little information and no sentiment. When Clara wrote that the Callisons had gone to the Continent and would still be there when Raymond came home for his Christmas holiday, he decided not to go. He accepted an invitation from a classmate named Duggan to spend three weeks with him and his family at their home on the Blackwater river, just west of Fermoy.

When he came back to Dublin in January a letter from Emily was waiting in his rooms. It had been sent through the offices of Trinity and was postmarked Florence.

It was his first contact with her for more than five months

but the tone of her letter was as though they had seen each other only the day before. It was emotion-filled and passionate in a way he could not have imagined. The words seemed to have tumbled from her soul with no pen or ink or scented paper in between. At the bottom of the second page she wrote:

> When we first left Maidenstone, Oliver took me to Edinburgh. We stayed there until he knew you had gone to Dublin. I thought we would return home then. But we went to London for some weeks and then he brought me here. By the time we came to Italy I had given up. I thought we had lost everything, you and I. But now suddenly I am fired with hope again. And determination. They cannot keep us apart. They *will* not. We will find a way, I promise you. I'd rather die than try to live without you.

After that first letter he heard from her frequently. She was travelling, it seemed, all across Italy but she was apparently uninterested in where she went or what she saw; her letters spoke only of herself and Raymond, reliving their mornings together that past summer and describing in passionate and indiscreet detail the life they were destined to spend together. Raymond read the letters till they were blurred and worn at the folds and wrote long answers which he knew could never be posted.

As swept along as he was by her words and her dreams, however, and the emotion behind them, he could not forget, in the dark halls of Trinity, during those heavy winter and early spring months in Dublin, the cold finality of the discussion he had had with his father at the end of the previous summer. Needing to believe Emily, desperate to convince himself that they could overcome the obstacles that separated them, he could *not*, no matter how many nights he lay awake trying, solve the riddle, could not stick the ill-joined pieces together in any pattern that promised to deliver what they wanted and needed and longed for, to be simply and peacefully together.

At last, in mid-April, a note came from Le Havre.

We will be at home in a week. Back at Maidenstone.
And I have a delicious plan. I will see you very soon.
I promise.

Two weeks later he heard from her again.

My mother in Wales is ill. I am being allowed to spend
two weeks with her in Caernarvon. You must take the
Dublin-Holyhead Ferry on May 6. I will meet you that
afternoon at the Pembroke Inn in Holyhead. I will be
registered as Mrs Raymond Bradshaw. Do be there,
my darling. Do not, for any reason, disappoint me.

It was a misty crossing from Dublin, but when Raymond
arrived in Holyhead the skies were clear-washed and blue.
Since receiving Emily's last note, his mind had been able
to deal with nothing else. Like a hypnotist's subject, he
had stumbled through his classes and through the streets
of Dublin waiting anxiously for the finger-snap that would
bring him to full consciousness again, knowing as he
waited that only the sight of her, her scent and her touch,
would sweep away the dreary hours, the hopeless and
lonely days and nights that had made up the whole of his
life since the end of the previous summer.
They had experienced, you see, no diminuendo, no
tapering-off or winding-down. Circumstances had forced
them from crescendo to silence. From their final warm and
laughing summer morning together, that last day of all in
the crofter's cottage, they had gone abruptly to nothing.
They had not touched, had not spoken to each other since
that August day. He had heard from her, of course, but
she had received no written or spoken or second-hand
message whatsoever from him. So to Raymond, as the
ferry slid slowly into harbour and positioned itself at the
wharf, the sudden breakthrough of the sun over Holyhead
seemed to be a blessed harbinger, a reminder of summer
past and a promise of summer coming.

The white-haired gentleman at the reception desk of the Pembroke Inn scarcely looked at Raymond when he identified himself. Glancing up from his ledger he said, 'I believe the lady is waiting for you,' and gave him the room number. As Raymond climbed the stairs he had, for the first time, a sense of uneasiness, a tingle of trepidation based on nothing he could identify. His hands were cold suddenly and his stomach muscles tightened. The feeling stayed with him till he actually saw her and touched her, till she opened the door and put her arms around him.

Emily had closed all the shutters. The room was dark except for a soft light by the bed. She was wearing a nightdress with a loose robe over it and her hair fell across her shoulders. Clinging to him with her head against his chest, she said, over and over, 'Oh, God. Oh, my God.'

At last she stood back and said, 'Let me look at you.' Then, 'I can't believe it. You look *younger*. I expected you to look tortured and destroyed and wasted away from missing me so much but instead you look like a beautiful young student just home from a cricket match.'

Raymond stood silent, staring at her, and she said, 'I'm shameless. Is that what you're thinking? I don't offer you tea or suggest a walk by the shore, I simply stand here in my nightdress and offer you myself. But I can't help it, darling. I can't *help* myself. I've missed you so. I've longed for you till my heart hurt. I cried myself to sleep and dreamed about you in every city and town in Italy.'

She turned away from him, then, slipped out of her robe, and got into bed. 'It's a heavenly bed, Raymond. All feathers and goose-down and lovely smooth sheets. Do you realize we've never had a bed before? Only the heather and the sweet hard earth but never a bed in a room where we could close the door on the world. Now we can do it. We have this whole day and night together. Just for the two of us. Then we'll have tomorrow and tomorrow night.'

As she talked he took off his coat, put his cravat and watch-chain on the chest and began to unbutton his waistcoat, his eyes never leaving hers. But suddenly her expression changed and her eyes turned towards the door.

35

They heard a key turning and when Raymond turned to look the knob was turning also.

The door swung open then and Callison, back-lighted from the hall, stood square and solid in the doorway, a strange half-smile on his lips. Stepping forward, he closed the door behind him and locked it. With his back to Raymond and Emily he took off his hat and his great-coat and placed them on a chair. His heavy stick he tilted against the wall beside the chair. Emily, her face very pale suddenly, sat motionless in the bed, the coverlet pulled up to her shoulders.

When Callison turned away from the door, he moved a step closer to the foot of the bed and stood there, his arms folded across his chest.

All the anger, all the hatred and jealousy that had festered inside Raymond these past months began to rise in him now. His eyes ached and his head throbbed.

'Your face is quite crimson,' Callison said. He turned to his wife. 'Your schoolboy is blushing, Emily.'

When Raymond started across the room, Callison moved quickly to meet him, put his hands against his chest and pushed. Raymond stumbled across the foot of the bed and fell backwards on the floor. Callison picked up his heavy stick then, edged towards Raymond and said, 'When I was at school, a naughty student was given a proper caning. I believe that's what's wanted here. When a schoolboy doesn't know his place. . . .'

He swung the stick, but when Raymond scrambled aside it crashed down on a bedside cabinet. Callison raised the stick again then but Raymond picked up a heavy silver candleholder from a high chest against the wall. Callison, turning away, caught its full, hard-cornered weight on his wrist. He staggered back against the wall, his left arm hanging limp, his hand turning away at an awkward angle from his crushed wrist. He stood staring at Raymond, his face grey with pain. Emily spoke then, her voice thin and trembling.

'Please. Don't hurt each other. I'll do whatever you say, Oliver, but please. . . .'

36

Seeming not to hear her, never taking his eyes away from Raymond, he dropped his stick, it clattered to the floor, and his hand went inside his waistcoat. When the pistol was only half visible, not fully cleared from its inside pocket, Raymond slammed hard against Callison and clutched at his arm with both hands. They wrestled along the wall towards the door, half-falling, Callison grunting and cursing, then they stumbled back towards the bed, Raymond never releasing his grip on Callison's wrist.

Sobbing and trembling now, Emily got out of bed and started towards the door. But as she passed the two men, they rolled and lurched against her, tripping and falling, and when they crashed to the floor, the pistol discharged, a flat fire-cracker sound in the room.

Still hanging on to Callison, Raymond dragged him up again, but as they stood upright, Emily slumped suddenly at their feet. She rolled on her back, her eyes staring at the ceiling, a look of pain and surprise in them still, and bright blood pulsed from a wound just below her cheekbone.

Callison sank slowly to the foot of the bed and stared down at her, the pistol slipping from his fingers to the carpet. There were voices in the passage suddenly and someone began to pound on the door. When the pass-key turned in the lock, when the manager from downstairs and two other men edged through the door and stared at Emily's body, not sure, it seemed, how to proceed, not sure if they themselves were in danger, Raymond saw Callison bend and pick up the pistol from the floor. The three men eased apart, out of his path, as he stood up straight and moved towards the door.

Very deliberately then, he walked down the stairs, through the lobby and out into the street, two of the hotel men trailing behind him. He crossed the cobbles to a grassy park just opposite the Pembroke entrance, several riding horses hitched there and carriages pulled up, waiting, at the edge of the grass. He stopped then, just inside the park, and turned back towards the hotel. Standing there, immobile, as people stopped walking on the footpaths and in the park, as they stood alone or in silent groups watching

37

him, he seemed incapable of any sound or movement, his eyes staring straight ahead, his face without expression, his left arm hanging limp at his side.

At the far edge of the park, then, a child began to cry. And as though he had waited for such a signal, Callison raised the pistol to his temple, positioned it precisely there, and fired.

Chapter Two

1

Because he was five years younger than Emily and because Callison was not a respected man in his county, the authorities concluded that Raymond had been an innocent victim in an unfortunate affair. He was censured by no one.

He could find no way, however, to be so easy on himself. He lingered in a private clinic on the outskirts of York for five months. After several weeks of observation and treatment, the doctors said he could be released at any time but still he stayed on in their care.

He refused to return to Wingate Fields. He was unwilling to receive at the clinic any members of his family. The thought of the lovely hills and meadows around Wingate was repugnant to him now; he had no desire to see a familiar face. There was no room in his mind or in his memory for scenes that did not feature Emily.

Every moment they had spent together seemed to be photographically recorded just behind his eyes. With each passing day, those images became brighter and clearer. He saw her everywhere he looked, heard her footsteps and her voice. And clearest of all were those final ugly moments at the Pembroke Inn; those scenes flashed in sequence through his head hundreds of times every day, ending always with her pale face against a background of flowered carpet, blood pulsing slowly from her cheek.

As if those memories were not cruel enough, he received, not long after entering the clinic, an additional thrust. He was told that Emily, when she died, had been expecting a child. This hateful information was almost more agonizing to him than the pain of her death. Like a madman he tried to persuade himself that it was *his* child, tried to mourn that unborn creature as *his* loss. But all the while he knew, no self-deception could alter the fact, that when she met him that day at the door, lovely and still slim in her night-dress, she was carrying Callison's child.

Every trail his imagination followed led him to some barren and awful place. If he had begun to detest Emily, to despise her memory, it would not have been surprising. But no such cleansing transformation took place. No such escape presented itself. Among the thorns and brambles, in the thicket of anger and self-recrimination where he found himself tangled, Emily remained untouched and unsullied.

However much he tortured himself, whatever attempts he made to rework his own instincts and judgments, to rewrite history, he never, not for one second, wished that he and Emily had not met, that they had not spent that delirious summer together. He abhorred the way it had ended; he was frightened and bewildered by the condition in which he now found himself. But he never tried to wish Emily away, to seal off his memory of her.

Raymond was aware of the pain he was causing his family but he felt he had no choice. He could not discuss Emily with them, he could not discuss his condition or his future, nor could he discuss anything else. He could not play the role of warm and loving son and brother, could not pretend that all that had passed was peacefully over now. He was changed permanently. Or so he believed. When he shaved each morning he was surprised that his face looked as it had always looked. He felt as though his grid of instinct, all his intellectual antennae and sensory centres, had been repositioned, like a house in the path of a tornado that has been picked up, turned a few degrees left or right on its foundation, then set down again. The house appears unchanged, nothing torn away or demol-ished, but in fact, the joists and beams are now unreliable, wires are snapped and connections broken, structural integrity has been violated. Pipes must be welded or replaced, cables spliced, and all things fundamental set right before this pile can function again as a dwelling.

How does one explain such ideas and conditions to one's mother or father? Or to a sister? One doesn't. One simply avoids the subject or talks of pleasant things. Visible, physical things. One is polite and communicative and civilized. One makes the best of it.

Raymond knew all this. He had learned his school lessons well. A gentleman does not burden others with his private and painful baggage. He pretends that all is well and will soon be better. He squares his shoulders, clears his throat, stands erect, and continues to function. Such behaviour would have unquestionably simplified Raymond's dilemma; he would surely have behaved in such a manner if he could have done. But he could not. His only choice was isolation; his only survival technique was to sit in his silent white room looking over the clinic's gardens and wait for some internal miracle that would wind him up like the spring on a toy and start him jiggling and jerking forward again.

His parents wrote to him often. So did his sister. Careful, supportive letters. Telling about themselves, the details of their days at Wingate, never referring to his situation, trying to ease him back into their lives, the only kind of life they knew, never acknowledging in their letters, not realizing perhaps, that he had been wrenched away from that pattern, those surroundings, that he would be forced to drift off now in another direction, forced to reshape and redefine himself.

His doctors recognized, even if his family did not, that there was no way to stitch together and reactivate the person he had been, any more than the shed skin of a snake can be magically transformed into a living reptile. The doctors also knew, or sensed, that however skilled their counselling and therapy might be, Raymond's recovery and regeneration would come at last from inside himself. Not from logic or tonics or sense of obligation but from God-knows-what. From some seed, some twinge,

41

some electrical shock in the muscles, some tic or glandular sea-change. A tingling of the scalp perhaps, tension in the neck, stiffness in the ligaments. Or something seen through a window, a familiar scent, or an unfamiliar one, or three crystal notes from a hidden piano.

As it happened, Raymond's key, his impulse to stand up and move away from stasis, came at last, appropriately perhaps, from the source of his agony, from Emily, from something she had said to him. Because all her words and her dreams and plans were with him constantly, piercing his consciousness from all directions like slivers of steel, he was sure that he had re-heard her countless times saying, 'We will go to Italy. Or Switzerland. Or maybe to America,' but the zones of reception had been blocked perhaps, the aperture shrunk too small. Finally, however, one afternoon in late winter, the skies heavy over the clinic garden, he heard her say, very distinctly, 'Or maybe to America.'

He slipped away from the clinic the following week, hired a coach and driver, and was driven to Liverpool. There, at the waterfront, he located a nondescript steamer bound for Boston with interim stops at Dublin and Belfast. It promised to be a slow and tedious voyage, exactly what he needed and wanted.

Although Raymond had told himself many times that his father, and *only* his father, had been the cause of his separation from Emily, he could not, at last, escape the realization that this was not true. He accepted the fact that if he had stayed on at Wingate at the end of that first summer, or if he had returned to Cambridge, or if Emily and he had stolen away to France to live on the cheap in some damp pension in Brittany, whatever they had chosen to do, there would have been no Elysian field for them, no triumph over Callison, no permanent and lovely life that would duplicate and preserve forever those perfumed mornings in the crofter's cottage on the thick-grass banks of the Will. If his time at the clinic had taught him nothing else, it had taught him that. There are, he concluded, no magic boxes, no treasure troves, no garlands for the worthy. Small triumphs are sometimes available, tiny rewards, and short seasons of passion. But there is no such thing as a triumphant, rewarding life, no such thing as enduring love.

As he accepted these conclusions he began to reconsider his assessment of his father. If the loss of Emily had been, somehow, pre-ordained, if his father had played no real role in that tragedy, then Raymond could not, in fairness, continue to hold it against him.

But he *did* hold it against him. Even if his father was not to blame, not solely to blame at any rate, Raymond still *associated* him with the ugly tangle of events that had begun that day in the library of their home when Angus made clear the power he was able to exert over his son, and his future, the power he had to separate him from Emily.

It was inevitable then, that when he decided suddenly to leave England and go to America, he did not tell his father. It never occurred to him to discuss it with Angus or with anyone else in his family. All the same he could not feel good about that decision. There was a tinge of cruelty to it that disturbed him, something vengeful. So, although he could not bring himself to reveal where he was going, neither could he simply disappear without a word. Before his carriage left York for Liverpool he posted a message to Wingate assuring his parents that he was all right, that he was going down to London, and they would hear from him soon. Healing with a lie.

When he was far out on the ocean he rationalized that he had of course done the right thing. The *only* thing possible. It was critically necessary, he told himself, that he begin to take charge of events, that he re-enter boldly his own silhouette. Having made a decision at last it was crucial that he should respect and honour it. To waffle and hesitate was too great a risk.

It was vital, he believed, that he should do what he was doing, that he do *something*, even if it turned out to be the *wrong* thing. He told himself that when he felt more solid on his feet, when his legs were firmly under him, *then* he would contact his family.

As the days passed, then months, and finally, years, Raymond continued to believe that he would, at some time, tell his father where he was and what he was doing. It was a long time before he admitted to himself that the moment, if there had ever been a proper moment, had passed, that no purpose would be served now by reopening the wounds. Taking it a step further he concluded that his principal strength now, his foundation, was his separateness. Only when he had persuaded himself that he came from *nowhere*, only then could he identify himself, only then could he begin to build a personal structure, one he could truly inhabit.

He was ill of course. He was a seriously damaged man. Wallowing in self-deception and desperate for some kind of self-esteem, he came to believe that survival, *his* survival, was everything. So he structured his life accordingly. Years later, when that structure crumbled, scattering debris in all directions, he was shattered and heart-sick but not surprised.

2

Raymond had gone to Boston by chance. But when he saw that city for the first time, after he had prowled its streets and lingered in its public houses, after he had eaten great platters of scrod and sea bass and haddock in its harbour-side restaurants, he realized that no amount of study or planning could have provided him with a better destination. No immigrant, arriving in America at the start of the century, could have hoped for a more benevolent transition.

It was its own city of course, in its situation and its architecture, but in its ambiance and its colour, in its vital and various people, it resembled, in small ways, Cork and Cardiff and Plymouth. Those resemblances, Raymond decided, were most noticeable at the riverside and beside the wharves. But when one went inland to the neighbourhoods and parks, when one visited the schools and libraries and concert halls, there also, one was struck by reminders of England. Even an Englishman's way of speaking went almost unmarked there because on the one hand there was a constant coming and going of the English and the Scots and the Irish; their speech was familiar on the streets and in Boston homes, on all social and economic levels. On the other hand the Boston speech itself, the final product, the sum result of all these mixtures of brogue and nuance, was, Raymond learned, an alien sound to Americans outside Boston.

All the same, even though his way of speaking attracted little attention, even though no one seemed to choose or reject him on evidence of his national origin, he resolved that he would teach himself the sounds and rhythms of this new speech so that wherever he might go in the country he would not be quickly tagged as an outlander.

All this was part of a major conclusion he had reached soon after his arrival in Boston. If he was to put the past months behind him, seal them permanently inside a wall where no one, not even he, himself, could dig them out, if he was to fashion a new and clean life, what was more logical than a total divorcement from England? Once he had laundered his speech patterns so that no trace of Northumberland remained when he spoke, indeed no hint of England, once he had dressed himself like an American, learned regional phrases and a smattering of local history and customs, why should he not then present himself as Raymond Bradshaw of Boston?

Whereas another man in his position might have begun such a transformation by changing his name, this never occurred to Raymond. Self-alteration intrigued him. He found the process fascinating. But destroying himself as a Bradshaw, giving up *that* integral part of himself, was a suicidal gesture he was unwilling to make.

After weeks of study and concentration and careful listening to the speech sounds he heard around him, plus careful practice and drill in his room at night, reading aloud from journals and American novels, he decided to test himself. He left the rooming-house where he had been living and moved across river to another section of the city. When he presented himself to his new landlady as a native Bostonian she said, 'I'd have guessed you came from the old country. Either England or Ireland. One of the two.'

Just then, that first time he presented himself as something he was not, he gave the woman an answer he was to rely on many times later on. 'That's because I've spent a great deal of time in Ireland. I attended university in Dublin.'

Pursuing his private studies of speech and custom and behaviour, Raymond stayed on through the Boston winter, hardly noticing the punishing weather as he methodically re-made himself. Every few weeks now he changed his address, patronized new shops and cafés, made new friends. With each change he could feel that his transformation was becoming more successful. In almost every circumstance he was accepted as a native Bostonian.

He knew the city well by now, its corners and its quirks and its history, knew it far better than many people who had in fact been born and brought up there. He was able to reminisce about eccentric areas and ethnic shopping streets, to point out how they had changed in the past ten or fifteen years. He had become an almanac of anecdote and terrain and local peculiarity. His speech had flattened and slurred to the point where it was seldom noticed at all and almost never identified as the speech of a man from England.

In April he made a visit to New York, his first trip there. Here, he had been told, was a city much less English in character than Boston, inhabited by a motley and polyglot tribe. It would be a true test, he felt, of his turnabout. If he could convince those people that he was a native of their country, then his programme of the past months could be counted a success, a signal to proceed to the next objective, wherever and whatever that might turn out to be.

Although he had become attached to Boston, he could not, since it had been his proving ground, settle there. Too

46

many people knew him for what he had been rather than for what he was determined to be. Nor did he believe that New York would be the answer. Before going there, before his first day there, he was aware that it was the most international of American cities. Even his father's Northumberland friends made annual trips to New York. The passenger travel from Southampton and Bristol and Liverpool was heavy indeed.

New York, therefore, was not the place for him to lose himself. No matter how skilled he became at concealing his roots and his heritage, it was not the ideal spot to weave himself into the American fabric. Somewhere inland, somewhere in the west, he decided, would be better. That was where he expected to end up. In Chicago perhaps. Or St Louis. Or in a smaller city or town, somewhere totally new.

Those final decisions however, Raymond left to the future. When he took the south-bound train to New York that early spring day, his only objective, as stated, was to test himself, to measure himself against new people in a new city.

He stayed in New York for almost four months. When he left at last, early in August, he was married and he had a teaching position at a college in the state of Illinois. He told himself that his life had begun to crystallize, to take on a beautiful and final form.

The skills of deception, however, which he had begun to develop in the Yorkshire clinic, which he had continued to develop during his months in Boston, had turned on him and had become, without his knowledge, skills of self-deception. They were destined, in future, to grow and multiply and tangle themselves together, straining every segment of his future life, changing the texture, the pattern, and the fabric itself till there was scarcely a recognizable fragment left of what he once was or might have been. In losing the pain of that one agonizing year of his life, Raymond lost everything else as well. The cauterizing iron that seared away sections of his memory burned deeper than he willed it. Entire areas of sensibility and

47

response, when he desperately needed them in later years, were no longer there to be used, or offered up, or fed upon. In saving himself, he realized, he had destroyed himself. That realization, when it came home at last, was what killed him. As much as anything else killed him. But nobody knew that except Jesse Clegg. And even he didn't know it until passing time had made it seem almost unimportant.

3

Jesse Clegg was born in Oklahoma City on the twelfth of January, 1897. His father, Thomas, was a musician, a pianist and a banjo player. By the time Jesse was ten years old he had lived in nine different cities, from Spokane to Philadelphia, from Minneapolis to New Orleans.

His mother, Florence, had come from a family of acrobats, the Hanrattys. Along with her mother and father and two brothers she had done a tumbling act in small circuses and second-level variety halls. When she married Thomas Clegg however she retired from acrobatics so she could devote full attention to her husband.

Their first child, Leo, was born in 1890, their daughter, Doris, in 1892. Since travelling was difficult but necessary and money was short, Thomas and Florence decided to limit their family to two children. Nonetheless, five years after Doris was born, Jesse arrived.

As he grew up, Jesse was reminded many times that his birth had altered the course of his father's life. Because agents and bookers knew that Thomas had heavy responsibilities now and an unwieldy family (consensus seemed to be that a musician with a wife and two children could travel freely but one extra child made such flexibility impossible), because they knew he needed steady work and long engagements, usually with hotel orchestras or in city ballrooms, he was in a position of weakness when employment terms were being discussed. He settled almost always for less money than he thought he was worth and he found, in addition, that he was often expected to function as a kind of assistant band manager, a non-musical job he considered degrading.

At last, when Jesse was seven, in 1904, when the family had been out-of-pocket and stranded in St Louis for five weeks, Thomas was offered a fill-in job as host in the roof-top restaurant of the Clifford Hotel there. Humiliated by the prospect but desperate for money, he took the job. 'On a temporary basis,' he told Florence. 'Just till we can tuck some money away and get back to Chicago.'

Two years later, he was still handing out menus in the Clifford dining-room. He never worked as a musician again. When the family returned to Chicago early in 1907, Thomas took a wine waiter's job in the Hotel Sherman. From there he went to the Palmer House as a waiter in the main dining-room. He was a tall and impressive figure in a dinner jacket. That had been his main appeal as a musician and it was, one suspects, one of his major assets as a restaurant man. And though he did enjoy dressing up and though he was conscious of the fact that people were struck by his appearance, all other aspects of restaurant work seemed to make him miserably unhappy in those early years.

For reasons known only to him, however, in 1910, when both Leo and Doris were self-supporting and Florence was working evenings as a cashier at the Humboldt Variety Theatre on North Avenue near where the Cleggs lived, when there was no longer great financial pressure on Thomas, when he was still an erect and vigorous man in his forties, he scoffed at any suggestion that he take up his music again. 'Too late,' he said. 'That's all behind me now.'

By this time he was host and assistant manager of the Stuttgart, a restaurant on Division Street which had begun as a cavernous neighbourhood *bier stube* serving authentic German food to authentic German immigrants but which had been taken up, in 1907, by the north side wealthy after Theodore Roosevelt dined there three nights running and

49

later praised the food extravagantly in interviews in the *Chicago Tribune* and the *New York Herald*.

Soon after Thomas went to work there, Florence said, 'At last your dad has a job he likes.' It was true. He dressed himself with care each afternoon before leaving for work; one could hear him singing as he lathered his face and stropped his razor. After a few weeks at his new job, he grew a handsome moustache which he trimmed with care and stroked with love. 'It's good for business,' he said. 'The customers think I'm a German.'

He was suddenly gentle and kind to Florence and almost affectionate with Jesse. He was, in truth almost unrecognizable to his family. He even retrieved his banjo from a long-locked and stored-away trunk and played it in the parlour on the rare evenings when he was not at the Stuttgart.

After a few months, however, he began to oversee the luncheon business at the restaurant as well as dinner. So he left home at ten in the morning and came home long after midnight. Frequently he did not come home at all. 'We served a large party in the private dining-room and the fools stayed on till four in the morning. So I slept on the sofa in my office.'

Jesse's brother, Leo, always understood the reason for his father's new-found contentment. Doris knew too. The two of them were an intimate triumvirate with their father. Their genetic chains bound them closely. They were confidantes to be sure, *tous les trois*, but they also had a sensory contact that made words unnecessary. So Doris and Leo *knew*, they knew at once about their father and Laura Fenstermacher. Laura had inherited the Stuttgart when her husband, Herbert, died of a stroke brought on, his doctor said, by an excessive passion for his restaurant's food.

Did Florence know also about her husband and Laura? Surely she did. Or at least she guessed. Florence, however, came from a clan of womanizers and scoundrels so perhaps nothing in that line surprised her. Or it is entirely possible that after fifteen or twenty years of sling-shot living she was simply too tired to concern herself with trivial matters like infidelity. Or maybe she didn't care. But whatever their individual schedules of enlightenment about Thomas Clegg's night-time comings and goings, the facts are that everyone in the family knew before Jesse did.

This is not to say that the information, when it finally came to Jesse, was either shocking or surprising. By the time he was fourteen or fifteen, he was acutely aware of his father's leanings; he knew how his mind worked. He was well-schooled in what Thomas referred to as his *modus operandi*. Jesse knew that he drank too much too often and that he was extremely susceptible to available ladies. But none of this affected Jesse. His relationship with his father was so near to non-existent that nothing could damage it.

An odd thing had happened, however, when Jesse was twelve or so. Thinking about it later he realized that it coincided roughly with the time when his father began working at the Stuttgart. To Jesse's surprise, Thomas seemed suddenly to have discovered him. He began to take notice of his son, to draw him aside, to speak to him with what seemed to be affection and concern. Jesse was bewildered; such attention was totally new and foreign in their relationship. Perhaps, he concluded, his father had looked at him one day and discovered that he didn't *know* this youngest of his three children. Or more likely, he had decided that this quiet one, this baseball fanatic, this angular and awkward person who carried home great sacks of books from the public library and then actually *read* them, it may have struck him that this silent stranger in his house didn't *love* him.

There was a contradiction in Thomas Clegg's make-up. For all his independence and anger and self-pity, for all the contempt and even hatred he felt for a great number of his fellows, he was extremely anxious that people should honour and respect him. He was genuinely dismayed when he learned that anyone, an employer, a fellow worker, or a customer, was something less than appreciative of his qualities. And he preferred, of course, to be admired as well as appreciated.

This hunger for approval, Jesse concluded in later years,

51

was certainly what had drawn his father to music. He had become an entertainer because he wanted to please people and thus win their admiration. The restaurant business, once he had accepted it as an inevitability, had given him a similiar role to play. He was able to please people by his appearance and by his manner, by his ability to make them feel that in *this* restaurant, on this particular evening, all would be well. And if anything should go awry, if any single detail was not satisfactory, this suave and well-spoken gentleman, for such he surely was, would certainly put it right.

Jesse also came to believe that his father stayed with his mother not because of his strong feelings for her but because he knew, as sure as the sun, that *she* loved *him*, that she had always loved him, and always *would* love him. In his patchwork life of chancy employment and bouts with alcohol, with women of all descriptions from all walks of life coming and going in his thoughts, in his arms, in his bed, or more accurately, in *their* beds, in all this maze of what-might-have-been and what-should-never-have-been, in the carelessly-woven fabric of his mis-steps, his guilts, his frustrations, Florence was the constant, someone who adored him and admired him for himself, however imperfect that self might prove, time and again, to be.

Thomas also found full approval from Leo and Doris. They thought him a fine fellow; they admired him and hoped in their lives to emulate his reckless notions and his remarkable spirit of self-indulgence. He inspired them in their own nefarious ambitions. Also, he amused them. That, perhaps was more precious than anything. He could always make them laugh. They loved him for that. And he loved them for laughing. It was tangible proof that they loved him.

Jesse, however, was another matter. Was he lined up in the family queue, waiting his signal to bend low and kiss the paternal ring? It appeared that he was not.

So perhaps because of that, Thomas suddenly turned to him, sought him out, and began a full-scale attack on his sensibilities, an attack designed, without question, to make

52

Jesse, once and for all, *his*. His admirer, his disciple, his *son*.

The first skirmishes belonged to Thomas. No doubt of it. First off, he carried the day with surprise. Then with energy and humour and experience. Drawing on all his social expertise he brought Jesse, in no time, to his knees. Or *almost* to his knees. Thomas was, after all, a compelling figure, he *was* Jesse's father, and Jesse had, after all, waited many years to be noticed, to be recognized as something other than an inconvenience or an afterthought.

So he tottered and trembled on the edge. But he did not fall. Thomas, as he had doubtless done on previous occasions, over-played his hand. He went too far, talked too much, persuaded too long and too forcefully, played one too many chorus on his bloody banjo. Fighting for Jesse's full attention he got it, and that was Thomas' downfall. Because Jesse had learned not only to read but to listen. And to understand what he heard. He had taught himself to consider and compare and reflect and make judgments. So he did that. And what he heard from Thomas was many times more disheartening and disappointing than all the neglect had been.

Throughout Jesse's life, Thomas had been a pain and a mystery to him. Now suddenly the father had decided to come forward, to take his son into his arms and into his confidence, and dispel the mystery. When he finished at last, the mystery was indeed gone. All Jesse had left was the pain.

4

The long conversations Thomas had with Jesse dealt primarily with the art of flim-flam. He explained to his son, in intricate detail, how one could manage events, manipulate people, turn them to your purpose and your will. How to be first on and first off the trolley, for example, how to get to the head of any public queue, how to avoid waiting your turn. How to assure yourself a handsome gratuity if you serve the public, how to *avoid* giving gratuities if you are a customer.

In addition, Thomas had an impressive list of devices for fleecing landlords, tailors, and wine merchants. He did not counsel Jesse on how to rob the poor-box in church but he did stress the fact that a church affiliation was a wise move, that there were many ways it could be used to one's commercial advantage.

As he went along, Thomas, to illustrate various points, pointed out to Jesse how well Leo and Doris were doing. Leo, a husky young man of nineteen, had found employment with a gentleman named Seehof who was a tenement landlord and money-lender in the North Avenue-Humboldt area. Leo's job was to drive a fine carriage around the north side of Chicago and collect whatever amounts of money were due Mr Seehof. He wore a grey fedora and a handsome suit, did Leo, and was said to be persuasive in his work. If persuasion was not successful, he grew skilled at getting results by other means. Mr Seehof was impressed. He promoted Leo, put him in charge of his entire collection department, and rewarded him, not with an increase in salary, but with a modest percentage of the monies he managed to collect. This spurred Leo to really remarkable efforts and made Mr Seehof appreciably richer than he had been before.

Leo, of course, prospered also. He moved into an apartment hotel at Lincoln and Fullerton, increased his wardrobe splendidly and made a down payment on an Apperson touring-car. He was well on his way, it seemed, to either wealth or prison and his father was extremely proud of him. At least once a week he said to Jesse, 'Leo has a good attitude. Attitude is everything. That's the key that unlocks the door.'

Doris also had a proper attitude, it seemed. At the age of sixteen she was hired to sell sweets and nuts in the lobby of the Humboldt Variety Theatre where her mother sold admission tickets. Mr Hester, the owner, apparently took a liking to her. When she was seventeen he made her

54

assistant manager of the Humboldt and a few months later he created a job for her in his office downtown. This new position, assisting Mr Hester in the management of all his theatres, required her to keep late hours. Although she still lived at home her family seldom saw her.

'Doris is a fortunate young woman,' her father said. 'Everybody in the entertainment business is well aware of the Hester theatres. When Martin Hester has faith in you, you've got a promising future. No doubt at all about that.'

Jesse's mother, although she seemed to be a gentle and selfless woman, either had the same standards as her husband or she had learned her lessons well from him. She, too, believed that both her elder children were well-launched. 'They're like circus people,' she said. 'They've never been around it but it's in their blood, I guess. Fast on your feet. That's what show business teaches you. It's a scramble, I'll tell you that. Root, hog, or die. That's the slogan. My mother used to tell us, drilled it right into us from the time we were little, "While you're making up your mind whether or not to take the last chop on the plate, somebody else is already *eating* it." "Make your move," my papa used to tell the boys. "There's plenty of time later on to worry about whether or not it was the *right* move." So that's what we learned, all us Hanratty kids. Keep your eyes open. Don't let anybody get the jump on you. We were quick as whippets. Not dishonest but sharp as broken glass. Keeping our heads up, watching for an opening, looking out for number one. Every new town, every new circus lot or theatre had different problems. "You take the town or the town will take you," my oldest brother used to say. He was a tough little mick. No bigger than a minute but he never saw a man he was afraid to tackle, never saw a rumble he'd back away from. It was a fine life if you had the guts for it. You either buckled up to it and took it by the short hair or you had to get out. I'm not a fighter myself, I've got no knack for it, but I got along because I had my folks and my two brothers right there to back me up. All the same I got plenty of knocks. I was happy to give it up and get married when I met your dad.'

55

When Jesse complained to his mother about Leo or Doris, when in his twelve-year-old wisdom he made some moral judgment of them, Florence said, 'They're doing what they have to do, Jesse, just like you will. All of us have to play the cards we're dealt. Even a free lunch ain't free if you don't buy a schooner of beer.'

In Thomas' mouth, pragmatism became not a survival technique but a kind of code. 'When I was your age I didn't listen to anybody either. But let me tell you, I've learned some solid-gold lessons since then. When a man comes to me with a *notion* or an *idea*, I say, "Don't waste my time." But when a man shows me some *results*, when he's accomplished something, when I hear a jingle in his pocket and see a twinkle in his eye, then I know that bozo went up against some tough monkeys and came out on top. That's when I say, "There's a man worth listening to." Because that's the game, Jesse. That's the way it works. Beefsteak in the skillet, whiskey in the bottle, money in your hand. Greenbacks, Jesse. Silver dollars in a stack. That's what counts. And that's *all* that counts. I know you're a great one for books. It tickles your mother because you get high marks in your school work. It tickles me too, I guess. But just keep one thing in your noodle. You won't be sitting in school all your life and when you get out there's a whole new set of rules you'll have to get wise to. I've never seen the book yet that could put beans on your plate or coal in the stove or a warm coat on your back. When I was a snot-nose kid about your age a man told me something that always stuck in my head. He said, "Only two ways I know to get ahead. Either you entertain people or you swindle them." Well, I was an entertainer for quite a few years. You know that. But not any more. Does that mean I'm a swindler now? Of course not. I work hard to make ends meet. But that doesn't mean I haven't learned a trick or two. And the most important thing I've learned is this. . . *power* is everything. That's what it's all about. Stick that in your day-book and think about it and I guarantee you'll come back to me some day and tell me I was a hundred percent right. P-O-W-E-R. Five little letters.

But that's the whole shooting match. The *trouble* is, most of us don't have any power at all to start with. But that's all right. That can be overcome. There's more than one road to town. How does it work, you say? What does a man do when he's on the outside looking in? How does he turn himself from a *nothing* into a *something?* That's the big question. That's maybe the biggest question a man comes up against. Gets asked more often than any other question I can think of. But I've got the answer for you and I hope you'll mark it down because it will change everything for you just like it's finally done for me. And I'll tell you something else. No little bird perched on my shoulder and told me the secret. Nobody wrote it on a piece of paper and slipped it into the pocket of my suit coat. Not a bit of it. The fact is I figured it out for myself. I *learned* it. I looked around me, kept the old eyes and ears open and tried to find out who was eating the cake and who wasn't. When it finally sunk in, I felt like I'd looked out the window and seen a rainbow. It was so simple I couldn't believe I hadn't caught on before.

'The secret is if you don't have any power yourself, no big sum of money to make you important, no respected name, no well-thought-of family, you look around you and you see who *does* have all those things. And when you find *him*, or find *her*, *that's* your answer. Just like plugging a bridge lamp into an empty socket, you *attach* yourself to that person. You find a way to get next to all that power, to tap into the line – so that pretty soon the juice starts to run through your body, the current starts to make your hair stand up and your muscles tingle, and then you know you're *on* to something. You get the feeling you can do things you couldn't do before. Or maybe you *could* do them before but you couldn't get away with them.

'The thing you have to do, the *main* thing, after you've located that person who has the power, is to make yourself useful and necessary, make yourself indispensable. You have to make him think there's something you can do for him that he can't do for himself. When that happens, when that person begins to *need* you, for whatever reason, or

57

begins to *think* he needs you, that means his power is beginning to crackle through the air and pass over to you. The next thing you know, people you never saw before start hanging after you. And that's your first clue. You know then that you've got some real power of your own, that other people smell it even if you hadn't seen it yet in yourself.

'Now you're in business. Now you can move on. You look for a new power source, a bigger one, some new person to fasten on. You keep moving up like that, one rung at a time, and the next thing you know, prizes you never dreamed you could get for yourself start coming to you. People who wouldn't have looked twice at you a year before start inviting you to their homes. Up and up you go. On and on. It's not that you're a different person. You're not smarter or better-looking or richer but all the same, people, *important* people, have started to look at you differently. It's a matter of association. It's not just who you *are*, it's who you *associate* with. It's how people think of you, what category they put you in. You know what I mean?'

Jesse knew exactly what he meant. At least he said he did. Because he'd heard all he wanted to hear. He felt as though he'd stepped into a curtains-drawn room and seen things he wasn't meant to see, heard things that were not intended for his ears. It made him feel guilty in some strange and uncomfortable way, and it made him feel rotten.

It is important to realize, however, that Jesse did not feel superior to his family or his roots. He did not think of himself as a prince among pretenders. Nothing like that. He simply felt separate, shut off somehow, walled away from his parents and from Leo and Doris. And all of his father's efforts to counsel him had only intensified that feeling of separation. Thomas' efforts to make himself clearly understood had made Jesse try desperately to understand him less so that some fragile bond would still be left between them, so that all connecting rods would not be snapped off finally and irreparably.

Thomas, however, for reasons of his own, kept coming back to Jesse; he continued to restate his case, kept searching for new ways to set his son's mind and his values in order, to position him dead-square on the correct path.

At last, Jesse felt only panic and a longing to be by himself, to clear his head, to let his own instincts and intelligence take charge, to set his own course and follow it at his own speed. Everything he was learning at school, everything he responded to in the books he read, was in sharp conflict with the life he saw at home and the views he heard expressed. The measurements, it seemed, were inaccurate, the checks and balances awry, the perspectives poorly drawn, the colours not quite true.

Does this mean, does all of this imply that Jesse was a freak-child who sat in dusty corners trying to construct a philosophy of life or a behaviour system that was distinctly and uniquely his own? Not at all. He was, by nature, an open-faced and cheerful little animal, usually out in the streets, chasing his friends and being chased, throwing snowballs, skating and sliding, fooling around. Nothing he did or felt, either at home or at school or in public, set him apart from his contemporaries. He appeared to be that rarest of all creatures, a normal boy. But all the same he felt unsettled and unquiet, off-stride somehow, uneasy about today and unsure of tomorrow.

He did not blame his parents for these contradictions, for this confusion in his mind; he did not see them as the root cause of it. But at the same time he knew very clearly that they were either unwilling or unable to help him in dispelling it.

5

In 1913, when Jesse was sixteen, he wrote an essay for his high school Economics class in which he defended the 16th amendment to the constitution. That amendment provided for a Federal income tax. His teacher, Roger Leverenz, submitted it to a state-wide essay contest.

Jesse's essay did not win a prize but it did receive a scroll of commendation. And a few weeks later he had a letter from Raymond Bradshaw who had been one of the contest judges; he told Jesse that he had been impressed by his work. He thought it showed clear thinking as well as writing ability. He added that if Jesse planned to attend college, he hoped, when the time came, that he would consider Foresby.

Jesse did not answer the letter. He had no plans and no money to go to college and no encouragement in such matters from his parents. So there was no point, he decided, in thinking about it or writing letters about it. But he kept Bradshaw's letter in his shirt drawer and the name, Raymond Bradshaw, stayed in his head.

Jesse did not believe in predestination. At seventeen, in fact, he had never heard of predestination. Nonetheless, he could not deny that the series of circumstances which led him at last to meet Raymond Bradshaw had something more than the normal element of chance attached to them. When he stood on Bradshaw's doorstep, more than a year after receiving his letter, the clarity of the moment made it seem the final tick of a logical progression.

Later, however, looking back, he failed to see anything logical or inevitable about it. Jesse arrived in Fort Beck one afternoon simply because the south-bound train he was travelling on made a stop there. He stepped off the train, his valise in his hand, for God-knows-what reason. Or so he told himself. But as he stood, moments later, on the platform and watched his train pull out, he knew why he was there. He was going to look up Raymond Bradshaw.

Starting that day and continuing for many years after, Jesse came to believe that Bradshaw was, quite literally, his inventor, that Bradshaw had conceived, designed, and crafted him, set his limbs in motion, and taught him to walk a straight line. Point to point. From one objective to the next. Working it out. Thinking it through. Learning the lessons of self-respect, learning to value one's needs

60

and motives. Forgiving one's weaknesses and transgressions, continuing to move forward. That above all. Staying alive. Keeping the coals glowing.

Later of course Jesse found sharp irony in the fact that he had learned all this from Raymond. At last he realized that Raymond had patiently taught him what he himself could not do. His wisdom, that became so vital to Jesse, was of no use at all to Raymond. In his *head* it rang clear and true, one felt. But in his *life* he could not make it function. He could only pass along to other people the bits of nourishment his own system could not digest or profit from.

The first day they met, that cool afternoon in June, Jesse sat in Raymond's library and recounted, without prompting, every significant fact he knew about himself. He explained that his parents had decided to leave Chicago and move to San Francisco where his father's associates would open a new restaurant. 'A fine opportunity for you to learn the restaurant business,' his father had told him.

'I pretended I was going with them,' Jesse told Raymond, 'but I knew all along I wasn't. I don't want to learn the restaurant business and I don't want to live in California. So first thing this morning I took my San Francisco railroad ticket, rode the street-car down to Union Station and traded the ticket for a one-way trip to Oklahoma City.'

'Why Oklahoma City?' Bradshaw said.

'I was born there.'

'You have friends in Oklahoma?'

'No. We left there when I was two.'

'How about relatives?'

'No relatives either. I just figure Oklahoma's as good a place as any for me to find work and get myself started.'

They had dinner together later, took a slow walk around the grounds of the college, and when they came back to the house, Bradshaw said, 'There won't be any more southbound trains tonight. You'd better stay over in the guest room. We'll have another talk in the morning. Maybe we can figure out something that will be better for you than going to Oklahoma.'

61

The next morning at breakfast Bradshaw said, 'I think you should forget about Oklahoma City. The best way you can spend the next four years is in educating yourself. There'll be plenty of time later for *work*. Now's the time to give yourself something to work *with*. I can fix it so you get some kind of scholarship here at Foresby. You can do odd jobs here at the house to pay for your room and your meals and whatever else you need. If you turn out to be as bright as I think you are, we'll get you a faculty assistant's job in a year or so and then you'll be sitting pretty. After you graduate with a degree in English you'll be able to teach. And if you don't want that I'm sure there'll be lots of other opportunities. The people who graduate here don't have to stumble around looking for employment. What do you think?'

'I don't know what I think.'

'Don't get the idea that I'm handing you the world on a plate. I'm not doing anything for you. I'm just offering you a chance to do something for yourself. How about it?'

'I'd like to try it,' Jesse said.

'Good. There are three bedrooms on the third floor. Take your pick.'

Agnes Esping was Raymond's housekeeper; her husband, Arvid, did the gardening and maintenance work. And there was a hired girl named Edna who came in by the day. Jesse's job was to do whatever the Espings needed him to do. In the spring and summer he did the heavy garden work and in the winter he kept the driveways and paths clear, fired the furnace, and fed the horses and dogs.

He began to feel like a younger brother in a home where no parents resided. Or sometimes it seemed as though the Espings were foster parents to both Raymond and him. But however he labelled or categorized his new situation it was a revelation to him. He was fully occupied, no question about it, with his college work and the work he did to earn his keep, but for the first time he could remember he felt no pressure; he felt as though he had crossed some invisible frontier and taken up residence in a civilized and informed land. Reason and kindness and consideration seemed to be the prevailing standards. No torrents of emotion, no tears, no door slams to climax overwrought scenes. He felt new-born and valuable. His opinions were solicited and listened to. Because he was treated as a responsible adult he became one, almost overnight, it seemed. Many late nights he sat alone in his room, reluctant to turn off the lights and put an end to the day, mesmerized by this new world he had stumbled into, absolutely stunned by his contentment, his excitement, his good fortune.

His relationship with Raymond was the keystone, of course. It was hard to say what their friendship was like. Jesse found it impossible to define even to himself. Between the two of them there had been no time of adjustment, no grinding of gears, no posting of rules or definition of terms. From the beginning Raymond treated Jesse as a contemporary and an equal. He shared his opinions, his prejudices, and his experience, holding back, it seemed, nothing. He never cautioned Jesse not to repeat a confidence, never stopped short, waffled, or held back. His manner told Jesse he was trusted; as a result Jesse became absolutely trustworthy.

Often, at the beginning, Raymond introduced Jesse as his colleague, sometimes following up with the explanation that they were researching a proposed monograph on Piero della Francesca. The first time Raymond said that, Jesse was in the college library the following morning, reading everything he could find there about della Francesca and the fifteenth-century Umbrian school. This was precisely, Jesse figured out later, what Raymond had hoped he would do.

Only a few days after Jesse moved into his house, Raymond showed him photographs of his wife, Anna, and their daughter, Helen. 'They've been living in New York for the past five years. Anna left me when Helen was eight years old. I go to New York to visit them when we have a school holiday or a term break and Helen always spends some weeks here in the summer. She and I are very close. I expect she'll come here to stay when she's a bit older.

I've always wanted her here with me but when she was younger it seemed better for her to be with her mother.'

In a later conversation, Raymond said, 'I told the people here at Foresby that Anna's mother was an invalid and she needed Anna there to look after her. But I don't think many people believed that story. They decided, I'm sure, that Anna left me. And they're right. That's what she did. I never should have taken her away from New York in the first place. It's all she knows. Here in Fort Beck she was like a lost animal in a strange meadow.'

'Couldn't you have taken a job at a New York school?' Jesse asked.

'Perhaps,' Raymond said. 'But I was never sure that Anna *wanted* that. Even if I had followed her to New York . . . well . . . you understand. It's never as simple as it seems.' He smiled. 'Also, you see, I need to live here as much as Anna needs New York. It's my home. The only home I ever expect to have.'

When Jesse said it must be difficult for him to be away from his daughter, Raymond replied, 'Of course it is. But that's what most of us do with our lives. We struggle to get things. Then we lose them somehow and we struggle to get them back. And it keeps going on like that. That's how we occupy ourselves. That's how we fill all those hours between birth and dying.'

Raymond was totally candid, too, or so Jesse believed at the time, about his early life. Born in Portland, Maine, parents drowned in a boating mishap, raised in Damariscotta by his grandparents. 'There was a bit of a legacy from my father. That's why I'm able to live a little better than some of the other faculty people here. There's no continuing money. I don't mean that. I used whatever was left me to buy my home here on this nice bit of property. But the maintaining of it, feeding the mouths, etcetera, is all on my shoulders, all dependent on my silver-tongued lectures on Beowulf and Chaucer and my poetry readings for accessible women's clubs. By that I mean those that I can reach and return from in one evening. For a Saturday or Sunday engagement, of course, I can go farther afield.

64

But I find there's very little interest in poetry on the week-ends. Stronger stuff is wanted then. Something to dilate the pupils and set the pulses racing. Intimate tales of the Barbizon painters, revelations about the Brownings, that sort of fare. But I have no flair for all that. While my colleagues saw the air with their hands, titillate the grey-haired ladies in their whale-bone corsets, and return home with sherry on their breath and fat honorariums in their purses, I have to stick with straight poetry and fruit punch and a few dollars sealed inside a small envelope.'

That first summer Jesse spent in Fort Beck, Helen didn't come for her usual visit with her father. There was an influenza epidemic in New York in the late spring and she had been ill and kept out of school for several weeks. 'Her mother has decided she must do make-up work in summer classes,' Raymond said. 'She says the academy insists on it. So . . . if she can't come here, I will go there.'

The following summer, however, a few days after Jesse completed his first year at Foresby, Helen arrived in Fort Beck. Raymond took Jesse along when he went to meet her at the station. As soon as Helen stepped off the train she put her arms around her father and said, 'I'm home to stay, Raymond. All my clothes and all my books are coming by freight.'

Jesse was struck by how much she resembled her father. The same tawny colouring, the same grace, tall and slender, the facial features irregular but striking, strong white teeth, and lean freckled cheeks. She seemed very much at ease for her years – she was just fourteen that summer – delicate and female, tender and flexible, one felt, but strong-minded, all the same under the tenderness, and with specific limits to the flexibility.

When they shook hands that first day she said to Jesse, 'Raymond thinks you and I will like each other. What do you think?'

'I don't know. I hope so.'

'I hope so, too. How old are you?'

'Eighteen.'

'That's perfect. I need an older brother. Maybe I'll get

65

Raymond to adopt you. Or maybe I'll adopt you myself. Can I do that, Raymond?'

'Not unless we change the laws.'

'Then I guess that's what we'll have to do.'

Late that night, when everyone else was in bed, Raymond and Jesse sat in the library having a brandy.

'Can she really stay here now?' Jesse asked.

'Of course she can.'

'What about her mother?'

'Helen's been with Anna for six years. Now she wants to be here. And God knows I *want* her to be here. I've always wanted her here. I'm sure it will be painful for Anna just as it's been painful for me. But Helen will stay here now.'

'Can't her mother force her to come back to New York? Isn't there some legal way she can do it?'

'She could try, I suppose, but I don't think she will. If parents are separated, when their child reaches a certain age, most courts will allow her to decide where she wants to be. Helen has made up her mind and her mother knows it. This is her home. This is where she belongs.'

A few days after her return, Helen said to Jesse, 'Raymond had a big section cut out of his life. Like an operation without chloroform. I want to make that up to him if I can. I want him to have so much love he'll forget about the bad times. This is going to be a very happy house. You'll see.'

She was right. By the end of that summer, before school began again, she had become the true mistress of her father's house. The gramophone and the player piano were heard more often than before, a telephone was installed in the downstairs hall and a crystal set in Raymond's study. In the kitchen, Helen and Mrs Esping began to experiment with different menus. At least twice a month Helen prepared an Italian meal and every Thursday evening two or three of Raymond's faculty friends were invited for dinner and billiards.

As for Helen and Jesse, they began a friendship that would last throughout their lives. Since they were neither

66

relatives nor lovers, neither blood-lines nor passion held them together. Only mutual trust was the bond. Or so they believed in those early years.

As close as each of them was to Raymond, Helen and Jesse became confidants in a way that did not exclude her father but which was somehow *apart* from him. They told themselves that their private confidences were of the fabric of youth, too fragile and bright-coloured to be of interest to a man like Raymond. At the same time, however, they realized, each of them, that they were gradually constructing a separate haven, its entrances and exits known only to them.

All this was in no sense a conspiracy. It truly was, as they believed, youth speaking to youth. Also, and more importantly, it was the meeting of two kindred souls. In later years, Jesse concluded that the imperfections in each of their childhoods, those inadequacies, some real, some imagined, had left hollows that needed to be filled in and smoothed over. Each of them was able to supply some needed ingredient to the other, some missing piece in the flawed patterns that had been their separate family histories.

Perhaps the finest feature of what came to be a mutual dependency, the thing that helped it to endure and develop through the years was the fact that they never attempted to label or define it. They never discussed how fortunate they were to have stumbled on each other. They never congratulated themselves, never tried to codify whatever it was they had discovered, never tried to prevent it from slipping away. They simply fed on each other, confident that the nourishment would never end. They questioned nothing and expected nothing. So the flavours stayed fresh and sweet and the pitcher never ran dry.

In March of 1917, when Jesse was twenty and Helen nearly sixteen, when he decided to enlist in the army, Helen was the first person he told. War had not yet been declared against Germany; that would come a month later, but the Zimmerman telegram of January 16 had been released to the American press on the first of March and there had been immediate public insistence that war should be declared. When Jesse enlisted he felt it was only a matter of days or weeks before war would be a fact.

He was assigned to Fort Leonard Wood and in August he was sent overseas with an infantry company that was to join the British Fifth Army under General Gough. When they arrived in France, however, in early September, Jesse's company was divided and his group ended up with General Plumer's Second Army which had been taking heavy losses in the third battle of Ypres.

The late summer weather had been wet and miserable but it improved suddenly. Just after September 20, General Douglas Haig, Commander of the British First Army, ordered a new offensive and Plumer's Second moved north against the Germans.

From the first day they hit stiff resistance. On the third day, when they were taking heavy artillery fire, a shell exploded just beyond the edge of Jesse's bunker. His sergeant and two other men were killed instantly and Jesse's left leg was shattered at the knee by a spray of shrapnel.

They moved him back to a field hospital north-east of St Malo and ten days later he was in England, at the surgery centre in Tunbridge Wells, Kent. Early in January, they put him on a hospital ship in a fourteen-vessel convoy heading for New York.

By February 1, Jesse had received his disability discharge at Fort Benjamin Harrison in Indianapolis and was on his way back to Fort Beck. He had graduated *in absentia* the previous June so as soon as Raymond found out he'd been wounded and would be coming back, he persuaded the chairman of the English department to take him on as a teacher of English composition. 'We'll be starting our last quarter soon,' he told Jesse. 'We've a schedule of classes for you then if you like. Or you can wait till the autumn if that suits you better.'

Jesse was angry and disappointed that the war had ended for him. Although he was grateful to be alive, grateful that his injury would leave him with nothing more serious than a stiff knee, he felt, all the same, like a crippled discard.

Because he had been among the very first Americans to go to France, he was also one of the first to return with an injury. In a town the size of Fort Beck that made him both conspicuous and heroic. For Jesse, however, it was painful and difficult to accept praise and testimonial dinners, to be fêted as a returned hero. Because his own estimation of his war record was very low indeed. So he fled. Promising to return in late summer, but not at all sure that he would, he left Fort Beck.

He used his family as an excuse. Having been in only occasional contact with his parents since their move to San Francisco, having lost touch completely, through no fault of his own, with Leo and Doris in Chicago, he had no strong desire to see them, any of them, and he suspected that their feelings were the same; but he explained to Raymond, nonetheless, that he felt obligated to visit his mother and father in California.

The day before he left, Helen said, 'What are you up to? You don't want to see your family. You know that and so do I. Are you just going to wander off and be gloomy somewhere and we'll never see you again?'

'No. Nothing like that. I just feel rotten, that's all. I want to sit on a train and look out the window and feel rotten by myself.'

'You feel like a failure, don't you?'

'That's right,' he said. 'I sure do.'

'You're crazy. You're no failure. You just feel guilty because you're not dead. Isn't that it?'

'I don't know what I feel. *Rotten* is all I know. Every time I see a cocky young guy in a uniform I want to knock him down.'

'You *are* in a mess,' Helen said. 'I guess you'd *better* go off somewhere and catch a fish or get drunk or something. Just don't stay away too long or we'll rent your room to a cannibal.'

That night Jesse and Raymond sat up very late, talking and drinking whisky. 'We might as well make fools of

69

ourselves while we can,' Raymond said. 'Unless I'm badly mistaken the Congress and the temperance lunatics are going to fix it so we won't be drinking spirits much longer. Seems like an odd business for a proper government to concern itself with. If they go ahead with it, I predict they'll *create* more drinkers than they cure. Laws make law-breakers. Especially silly laws. The surest way to preserve Christianity is to pass a law against church services.'

Just before they went upstairs to bed, Raymond said, 'I know you're feeling like a man who misplaced his luggage somewhere and I won't try to talk you out of it. But for what it's worth, just remember this is not some sickness you've invented. It's been around since those little bow-legged cavemen first ganged up to throw rocks at each other. The best way I know to get over feeling bad is to go ahead and feel as bad as you want to till it finally goes away. Just don't let it drag on past September. We need you back here by then.'

6

Jesse had been seventeen years old when he left Chicago. When he arrived in San Francisco and sat, ill at ease, in his parents' apartment, it was four years later. He had no idea as he travelled west towards California what their reunion would be like. And when it was over – they spent just a few hours together – he had conflicting views in his mind as to what had actually taken place and what it meant. Or if it meant anything.

His mother was alone when he got there. It was a spacious apartment in a high street and it was artfully furnished. But it looked as if she lived there alone. As she showed Jesse through the rooms he saw no physical trace of his father's residency.

When Thomas arrived, however, an hour later than the time he had specified on the telephone, he seemed determined to convince Jesse that this was, indeed, his home.

70

'Just had to take a carriage over to the restaurant,' he said, 'to oversee some arrangements for tonight. I don't work the luncheon hours. We hire people for that. But today there was an emergency so they called me.' He glanced at his watch. 'I guess I must have left here just a few minutes before you arrived. Isn't that about right, Florence?'

Florence nodded her head and sipped her lemonade. She was carefully dressed, wearing what seemed to be an expensive frock, and her hair was done up with combs, but she seemed very old to Jesse. Painfully thin. And her skin had an odd colour to it, not cosmetic but not really natural either.

He remembered her as a quiet and submissive woman. She had always been that way. Now she seemed hollow. Made of paper. And fearful, Jesse thought, dropping her eyes when his father looked at her, seeming to shrink when his proprietor's voice filled the parlour of the apartment, sitting rigid as marble when he touched her shoulder or when he bent down to kiss her cheek as he painted for Jesse a bright picture of their contentment together.

The San Francisco restaurant was a conspicuous success, he said. 'We've managed to attract the best clientele, the money people, the old families, from the start. A quality operation, I'm proud to say, from the moment we opened our doors. No expense spared. The finest foodstuffs available and a chef with a grand reputation. And no coloured help or Orientals, even in the kitchen. We pride ourselves on that. Pay a little more to get the best. That's not our motto exactly but it could be. Not quite four years we've been in business here and we've made a reputation that's second to none. Achievement. That's the word for it. Money coming in. *Important* money. And important contacts to be made. Every week I have significant propositions presented to me. Dazzling opportunities. Skyrocket offers. You wouldn't believe me if I listed them for you. But I'm a restaurant man. Known in California as I was in Chicago, as one of the best. That's what I say to these people who want to capture me. I say I'm content to

71

stay in my own field, happy to be able to share in this successful endeavour that Mrs. Fenstermacher and I have worked so hard to put together.'

As he talked, as he paced the parlour with his cigar or struck a pose by the fireplace, Jesse studied him closely, trying to relate to him. Unlike Florence, Thomas seemed unchanged since the last time Jesse had seen him. In some ways he seemed even younger than before. He wore a splendidly tailored suit with a silk cravat held by an emerald pin; his hair and his moustache were carefully shaped and trimmed. Some of the veins in his cheeks and nose were losing their battle with port and cognac and his jawline had softened a bit but all in all he was still a remarkably imposing man.

When Jesse asked about Leo and Doris, Thomas said, 'Disappointments, both of them. Leo quarrelled with Seehof and lost his job and Doris threw away the opportunity she had with Martin Hester's organization. As it was told to me, she let herself become involved with a junior clerk in Hester's office, a *beginner* in business, a young pup without a future, and Hester dismissed them both. We haven't heard a scratch from her in more than two years.'

'We had those picture postcards,' Florence said.

'Almost two years ago, the last one came,' Thomas insisted. 'Mailed from St Louis, that bastard of a town. She said she was on her way to New Orleans. Since then not a word. We don't know where she is. I pray for her every night. I pray she's not gone bad.'

'What about Leo?' Jesse said. 'Where's he?'

'Same old tune. Lost opportunities. Bad judgment. Same as your sister. Last I heard he wrote me a letter, sent it here to the restaurant, and said he was relocating to Detroit. Salvage, he said. Said he'd formed a salvage company with two other men, no names mentioned, gave me the impression that he expected to get rich in a very short time. Since then, not a line. We don't know where he is. I can only hope he's not in some kind of trouble. Lots of problems in the salvage game. Dishonest dealings.

72

Unscrupulous people. Not a place for a young buck to try his wings. Not a good place to prove how clever you are.'

His mother asked Jesse then about his leg and he told her what had happened.

'Will you always have to use a cane?'

'Not according to the doctor who operated on me. Just a few months, he said. It won't ever be brand-new again. He didn't guarantee that. My knee will always be a little stiff, I guess. But I'll be able to walk on it without any trouble. I'll get around fine.'

'Damned shame,' his father said. 'That never would have happened if you'd been out here with me. I could have approached certain people, had some conversations with men who are high up in the political world. You never would have been conscripted. You'd be an experienced restaurant man by now. Well on your way. And you'd have two good legs under you.'

'I wasn't conscripted,' Jesse said. 'I joined up.'

'Well, you wouldn't have made *that* mistake either if you'd been here where I could have advised you and kept you up-to-date on things. Mr Wilson sold this country a tricky bill of goods. Everybody knows that by now. It was bad enough when we were shipping shells and armaments to the British and the French. But it was plain damned criminal for us to send our men over there to fight. We had no business taking sides the way we did. The fact is, our government lied to us. They told us the Germans were the ones who started the fighting when all the time those people were just defending themselves.'

'*Defending themselves?* The Germans? Where'd you get that idea?'

'It's a well-known fact. You must know your history. The French have been attacking Germany for centuries.'

'Maybe they have. But not *this* time.'

'Yes, Jesse. *This* time.' He nodded his head patiently. 'According to *my* information. . . .'

'What information?'

'Mrs Fenstermacher is an educated woman.'

'Who *cares* if she's educated? She's a *German*, for Christ's sakes. She runs a German restaurant for German customers. Don't sit there and tell me about the *Germans*. I was there. If they were *defending* themselves why did they come all the way into Belgium to do it?'

After his father left to go back to the restaurant, Jesse stayed on with his mother for a while. But she had very little to say. It was as though Thomas had carried her voice-box with him when he left. 'I'm very nervous,' she said finally. 'I don't like to see arguments in our family. I hate to hear angry words between a father and son. We all used to be so close and happy. I don't know what went wrong.'

Jesse left San Francisco that evening on a north-bound train. He got off in Susanville and went to visit the family of Bill Klecko, the man who had been his sergeant. He had planned to stop with them for just a few days but they persuaded him to stay longer. 'We want you to stay for as long as you can,' Mr Klecko said.

Bill had built himself a cabin on the river just west of town so Jesse spent most of his time there, swimming in the river, fishing from the bank, and reading the books he had brought with him from San Francisco. He wrote no letters and he read no newspapers. The war seemed far away and Jesse's feelings about it, his role in it, had also begun to fade. The solitary days and weeks slipped past in silence. He heard only bird-sounds and the river rushing by, and cedar branches whispering in the wind.

Two weeks before the school year was due to start, Jesse was back in Fort Beck. He studied the materials Raymond had gathered for him and spent the remaining days before registration preparing a syllabus for each of his courses.

'You threw away your walking-stick,' Helen said.

'Not exactly. I nailed it over the door in that cabin where I spent the summer.'

'So at least you'll know where to find it if you need it.'

'That's right.'

'Are you all right?' she asked then.

'Sure. I'm fine.'

'Don't toss off a quick answer like that. I *know* you. You

weren't fine before. When you left here to go to California you weren't fine at all.'

'That's right,' Jesse said. 'I wasn't. But now I am. I exorcized all my demons and killed every dragon I could find. Now I'm a brand-new shiny creature. Clean socks and faith in the future.'

In addition to his annual enthusiasm about the start of a new school year and the pleasure he felt in having Jesse at home again, Raymond was excited and well-informed about the progress of the war. 'August eighth,' he said. 'That's when they turned it around. Battle of the Somme. The British Fourth took more than twenty thousand prisoners and they killed more than they captured. Even Ludendorff called it, "the black day of the German army" Just wait till he comes up against Pershing's troops. We've got over a million men in France now and more than three hundred, almost *four* hundred naval vessels off the coast. There'll be an armistice before Christmas. I guarantee it. And when that day comes, we'll have the most outrageous party in this house that Fort Beck has ever seen. Champagne will be trucked in from Chicago, Helen will sing her bawdy version of Mademoiselle from Armentieres, and Jesse will dance a jig on his good leg.'

The armistice came as predicted. Well before Christmas. And Raymond's party took place as promised. Great baked hams and roast turkeys were featured, with bowls and platters of vegetables and fruits. Pies and cakes of all descriptions filled one table, flanked with freezer cans of ice-cream. And there were baskets of red wine, chilled tubs of champagne and white wine, cases of whiskey and liqueurs, and barrels of foaming lager lashed to saw-horses in the serving pantry.

Carriages and automobiles arrived, delivering crowds of laughing people. And two slightly delirious couples arrived on tandem bicycles. Women in their best gowns and men in dinner jackets stomped and danced in time to an orchestra playing ragtime at one end of the hallway between the library and the parlour; the dancers screamed and shouted and giggled and kissed each other's husbands

75

and wives while they whirled and jostled back and forth across the dancing space, spilling their drinks and drinking every drop they didn't spill.

At four in the morning the last carriages and automobiles had manoeuvred out of the driveway beside the house, the musicians had packed up their instruments and left, and the first snow of winter had begun to fall in the garden. Raymond stood by the dining-room window, his necktie undone and lipstick stains on his collar, one arm around Helen, the other around Jesse, and said, 'That, my friends, was a fine and outrageous party. *Historic*, it seems to me. *Historic* occasion. Also *hysterical*. And I accept full credit for it in case it's offered. If it's not offered, I *demand* it. Look at me closely. At this moment I am the world's happiest man. Lauded by my friends and envied by my enemies.' He sank down in a high-backed chair facing the window. 'Go to bed, you two. I'm going to sit here in this chair for a while. First I'll count snowflakes and then I will count my blessings.'

When Mrs Esping got up the next morning, Raymond was still there in his chair, still holding his empty brandy glass. At first she thought he was asleep. But the doctor, when he arrived, said he had been dead for five hours.

Chapter Three

1

Raymond had never regretted his decision to leave England. More accurately, he never *allowed* himself to regret it. He believed that he had taken the only turn available to him. He was proud of the fact that as a very young man, as a person with little experience outside his home county, he had thrust himself into an unfamiliar society where he had no friends and no predictable future and had made his way. Apart from his failed marriage which he was able to deal with only by concentrating stubbornly on other matters, apart from that continuing ache, he felt positive about the life he had been able to make for himself and his daughter. He felt connected to his work and to the place where he lived. He felt as if he belonged there.

This is not to say that he had been able to sever all connections with the severe beauty of Northumberland, with Wingate Fields, or with his family. He had not, of course. And as the years passed, as the anger and the heartbreak that had commandeered him and pushed him into a self-imposed exile, as those hot and jagged emotions cooled slowly and lost their dark corners, as he settled into his new life as a teacher, he found, more and more often, that his mind made involuntary trips to the places he had known as a child and as a young man. At first, feeling he was falling into some dangerous reversal, he took elaborate steps to sidetrack his memory. He forced himself to read the most demanding books in his library, heavy and difficult works that required full concentration. Or he did physical labour in his basement work-room. Or he swam in the college pool, lap after lap, or exercised with dumb-bells and Indian clubs in the faculty gymnasium.

Finally, however, as he began to feel rooted in his home and his work, as he related to himself more and more as a father and as a counsellor to young people, he no longer kept such a tight rein on his memory. His fear of looking backward diminished; and at last it disappeared almost totally.

Grudgingly, at first, he permitted himself limited forays into his childhood and his youth, allowed himself to recapture and recreate those seasons in the fields and forests, the family parties, his mother reading aloud to him and Clara or playing the harpsichord in the music room after dinner, Angus and his friends singing drinking songs late at night after the children were in bed. The hunts, the grouse shooting, bathing in the brook that flowed through a thick grove of lime trees down the slope from their house, long strolls across the moors with his school friends, serious talks with Clara about Watteau and Beethoven and the meaning of life.

Whereas his memory, when he first arrived in Boston, had served up only ugliness and frustration and hateful images, now, years later, much of that sadness, many of those unhappy pictures, had dissolved or had been edited away.

He found, at last, that he could even think of Emily, could allow his mind and memory to wander freely without fear of seeing her again as he had last seen her, her sight-less eyes staring upward from her lifeless face. That picture stayed with him, of course, but it rested, for the most part, in his subconscious, surfacing only when he was defenceless, when he was sleeping. There, in the soft dark, all the colours and sounds, the fear and the agony and the nausea flashed as painfully clear as they had that afternoon in Holyhead, torturing him in his bed at night, twisting him into knots that only the morning could untangle.

When daylight came, he was able, through some miracle

78

of self-preservation, to see Emily as she had been the night of his birthday ball, as she had looked through all that shining summer. He managed to recapture, time after time, almost at will, those hours and days they had stolen, managed to turn the pages and savour the moments with no reference whatsoever to the final page of the final chapter.

His feelings towards his father went through a similar change. *Not* similar, really, but as remarkable in its own way. On one level, his condemnation of Angus was unaltered. He believed still that the severity of his father's judgment and the intractability of his position, had, more than any other factor, contributed to the final hopeless and horrid climax to what might have been . . . God knows what might have been. That was one area he did not permit himself to stumble into. He would not allow himself to envision what the future might have become with Emily, he never permitted himself to compare such gauzy projections with what was real and factual and permanent. Had he lived daily with the thought of what he had lost, had he said to himself that his present life was hateful, had he truly believed that all joy and purpose ended when Emily's life ended, then he would certainly have been a poisoned man and his hatred for his father would have continued to grow and spread inside him like a tumour, beyond cure or surgical removal.

But just as he was able at last to remember the lovely and joyous side of his time with Emily, as he was able to dwell on the memories of Wingate Fields and his childhood, of his mother and his sister and his friends, so also did Angus take on a softer outline. The months when their relationship had been dominated, if not totally destroyed, by the fact of Emily, *that* period, that short time, gradually blurred in Raymond's mind, and at last was excised almost entirely. The memories that featured his father came to him from earlier days and they were positive ones. They blended smoothly with that specific collection of flavours and textures and seasons, of food and wine and warm

79

rooms and animal sounds outside the windows that stocked the sense-memory of his growing-up time.

Even when he allowed himself to remember those last contentious sessions with his father he found previously disregarded phrases taking downstage position in his mind. Most often he heard Angus saying, 'Your mother loves you and so do I. It's my duty to protect you if I can, whether you want that protection or not.'

As happens with many young men, the fact and the experience of being a father himself made Raymond understand Angus more clearly, made him less tolerant of his own past attitudes. And his few years with Jesse, which brought him as close as he would ever be to a father-son relationship, was a window into himself that also revealed Angus in a different way.

For many years Raymond never thought about returning to England, never allowed himself to consider it as a possibility. He sensed it was unsafe ground. He was not prepared to risk the identity he had found for himself, not prepared to make a sentimental choice that could possibly unseat him for the rest of his life. And what might it do to Helen? He always came back to her, to how it might influence or affect her.

In her early years before Anna took her away to New York, he had thought of Helen as one with him. Whatever was good and necessary for the father would inevitably be of equal value to the child. Since he had chosen to remove himself from his birthplace, from those blood-ties and comforts and traditions it connoted, since he had made that rupture, that sacrifice, for a principle, then it surely must follow that his rationale and his standards, his judgments of what was possible and valuable, would also be passed along, either genetically or by exposure, to his offspring.

After she came back to him, however, after Helen re-entered his house as a soon-to-be adult, as a smaller female version of himself, but one who made free choices based on her private calculations of plus and minus, one whose code of behaviour, although basically his, had pockets of contradiction and idiosyncrasy and young-woman logic that were very much her own, Raymond, observing her and listening to her, admiring her ability to select and to function, no longer assumed that each of *his* value judgments, past and present, was compatible with Helen's needs, or inevitably beneficial to her.

Following these unfamiliar and unmarked paths, he began to wonder if it was wise or proper for him to separate his daughter forever from her paternal roots. Could his abdication of family be passed along, arbitrarily, to her? Each time he considered that question however, he found the answer more elusive.

It wasn't as though she was *without* relatives. On her mother's side there was an entire vital and whooping clan. Cousins, aunts and uncles, grandparents and every possible combination of in-law and relative.

Raymond genuinely liked Anna's family; he had from the start. Although every facet of their lives was unlike what he had known, fundamentally different in texture and rhythm, he appreciated, from the beginning, their true value. As he admired their unconcerned, hedonistic, moment-to-moment existence, he never questioned that there was solid structure underneath. The fact that they were people who by tradition worked with their hands, who believed that all education beyond grade six was non-productive, who did not question habits and dictums that had been crystallized by their forebears many generations back, these things did not disturb Raymond. He was, after all, a carefully educated and widely-read man, one who was also tolerant and humane. Although he had been reared as a child of privilege he knew from an early age that Northumberland and Cumberland and Yorkshire were but small sections of a small country, that the gentry he knew and was a part of was a very specialized segment of the larger world.

If he had *not* known this, if his mother and his tutors had not taken great pains to teach both him and Clara something of the various natures of the societies they would be living in and the people they would encounter,

81

he would certainly have learned it quickly in Dublin. There he was exposed, almost daily, to levels of privation and poverty that were new to him. His trips to York and Newcastle, and occasionally to Glasgow or to London with his father, had exposed Raymond only to people who were very like the ones he met and knew at home, people who, by and large, charted their own courses and piped their own tunes, who were not victims or targets either by birth or by natural shortcomings or by economic or genetic destiny.

So Dublin had been a revelation. And Boston and New York the same. He had quickly learned, had become convinced, that *all* conclusions about man and his ways are either temporary or mistaken, that the variety is infinite and constantly in flux, that today's theorem is tomorrow's anomaly. This new knowledge, however, that crystallized in his mind only after he had spent some months in America, did not unsettle him. Quite the contrary. It broadened his vision, enlarged his world and his thoughts about it, and sowed seeds of patience and tolerance in him that would continue to grow throughout his lifetime.

So there was nothing judgmental or superior in his attitudes towards Anna's family. They were simply a new experience for him, and a fascinating one. After the sheltered country life of northern England and the mix of intellectualism and schoolboy lunacy that had permeated both Cambridge and Trinity, it was refreshing for him to be exposed suddenly to a noisy, laughing, combative family, many of whom did not speak English and none of whom spoke it properly or clearly but who were, all the same, what they seemed to be, who said what they meant, and who were tolerant of almost anything, it seemed, except slender women and men with small appetites.

Quite the opposite from believing that he was stepping down from his class, marrying beneath him or any such asinine social-category judgment, Raymond was proud to be accepted by Anna's family. If they were immigrants so was he. And a much more recent one. They were an

American family and he was to be included. He felt as though he had made a great leap forward.

A few months later, when he and Anna learned that she would have a child, he said, 'What a good mix. What a fine baby we'll have. A beautiful Italian mother and a mongrel father. A first-rate combination. We'll cause them to rework all the breeding charts.'

As the years passed, however, as he sensed, even before it became obvious, that some personal demon was pursuing Anna, as the life he had envisioned, the idyll in the unfamiliar midlands of a strange country, the cocoon life, isolated from the world by the Boone river, by the walls of hickory and maple and elm trees, oak and black walnut, and by the familiar securities of academic life, bells tolling, musicales and exhibits of silverpoint, faculty teas and student balls; as that life materialized, then began to dissolve, at least at the core, in the most vital area, inside his own home where he lived with his wife and child, or more specifically inside the consciousness of that wife, somewhere in some brain fold, in some inner darkness, as *she* began to slip away, as that key centre of his life began to slide, like a section of clay bank in April flood-time, and later when she was gone and Helen with her, when the two of them were living, permanently it seemed, in the bosom of that warm and electric family he had admired so much, Raymond, without lessening, in self-defence, his admiration for the Bardonis began to feel, nonetheless, that some antidote, some other exposure, some new and fresh viewpoint might now be not only advantageous but necessary. That Helen deserved and needed to be told that there were other sources in her life, other root-fields, that as winning and rewarding as she might find the communal Bardoni chaos, as stimulating, to an eight- or ten-year-old girl, as New York street life might seem after the pastoral lawns of Fort Beck, it might be valuable for her to know that a very different world, structured and informed and traditional and luxurious, was also a part of her genetic inheritance, a foundation-stone of her past, and a key part of her future if she so chose.

When Raymond visited Helen in New York, however, for the first time, just after she had gone there with her mother, he learned that his daughter was neither confused nor divided in her thinking. She had no complaints, then or later, about Anna's family, but she made it clear to her father that New York was not her home, that she did not feel *at* home there, that she wanted to be in Fort Beck with him. At first she assumed that her mother, too, would return finally to Illinois, that they would both go back there together. She didn't realize at the beginning that her choice of place would be, in fact, a choice of parent, a selection of one over the other. But when she *did* realize it, when her mother made it clear to her, when the passage of months, then years, made it even clearer, even then there was no hesitation in her. She wanted to be with her father. And at last, of course, she was.

Once Raymond realized that there was to be no war fought for Helen, that even if such a war *was* implicit in his separation from Anna, he was already the winner, it made it easier to accept the fact that his daughter was temporarily living apart from him. *Temporarily* was the key word. He and Helen discussed it whenever they were together and both of them, together and separately, talked to Anna about it. Everyone understood that Helen, at last, probably before she began high school would live with her father. Anna accepted this thesis because it was somewhere in the future and because she secretly believed it would never happen.

When it *did* happen there was nothing she was able to do about it. She wept a great deal before Helen left and tried to dissuade her by saying uncomplimentary things about Raymond. But those efforts only caused her to lose ground with her daughter. When Anna put her on the train at last, as Helen watched her mother waving from the station platform, she did not have unkind thoughts about her. She felt, in fact, that some bizarre role reversal had taken place, that she was the grown-up, somehow, and her mother was the child. She felt genuine compassion for Anna because she knew her mother was not in control of her hours or her days or her future. She also knew, just as surely, that this was a permanent condition, that she would always be at the mercy of circumstances and events, never sure, at any dawn, what midnight might bring.

Helen loved her mother, but in an unquiet and incomplete way. She felt guilty because she didn't love her more. But she felt no guilt whatsoever about her decision to live with Raymond.

Anna never visited Fort Beck but Raymond saw to it that Helen made at least one trip each year to New York. Each time, however, she stayed for a shorter period of time. When Raymond questioned her about this, the summer she was sixteen, she said, 'You know how I feel. I'll never forgive her for leaving you the way she did. For taking me with her. For forcing you to live here by yourself for six years. I know you don't hold it against her but I *do*. I always will.'

Living with Helen again, being fully occupied with the details of his own life and hers, the impulse to look back towards England, to make contact there, to tell Helen everything about himself that she didn't know, to consider with her the possibilities of going back, of introducing her to his family, of showing her the numberless places he had known as a boy, his discoveries, his lairs and retreats, all these considerations became less specific and pressing. His contentment with the menu of his life, of *their* life together, made him reluctant to change even the slightest seasoning of it. He hesitated to give Helen some new truth, some fresh but surprising element to adjust to. So he said nothing.

All the same, such notions stayed alive in his mind, like fireflies in a glass jar. Especially when Jesse came back from France, and a few months later, when he returned from California; Raymond was struck sharply by the fact that Jesse seemed to be their *only* family, his and Helen's, that they were both strongly attached to him, not for that reason *alone* perhaps, but for *that* reason, all the same, strongly positioned as it was among the other reasons that defined their separate affections for him.

85

For the first time then, since leaving England, Raymond felt a sudden aching *need* to go back to Wingate Fields, to see his mother and Clara. And most pressing of all, to his surprise, he longed to see his father again.

Between the start of the autumn quarter and the day the war ended in Europe, Raymond began to make secret plans for such a trip. It might be months before the sea lanes would be open for passenger travel but until then he and Helen could make their arrangements in detail and exchange letters with his family.

But when should he tell her? The prospect excited him but he kept postponing it. At last, the night of his Armistice Day party, he decided he would tell her on Christmas Day. As he sat in front of the parlour window after the party, watching the snow fall, he rehearsed in his mind the exact words he would use to break the news to her.

2

As angry as he had been with his father, as disconnected from him as he had come to feel, Raymond, when he sailed west from Liverpool that day, had no impulse towards vengeance. Indeed, he believed that his leaving would do greater damage to him than it would do to his family.

The events of the past few months had convinced him that they were not capable of knowing or understanding what he had experienced. He was further persuaded that none of them cared. From those assumptions it was easy for him to say to himself, 'If no one cares about me or my needs, if those are the rules of the game, then I will abide by them. I will look out for myself and they can do the same.'

Since that was his mind-set when he left England and since his mind froze in that position for many months after, one can only imagine what his astonishment would have been if he had known the chaos that resulted from his disappearing from the clinic outside York, if he had known how his family was redefined and continued to be redefined from that day on.

The first shock, the message from the clinic that he had disappeared, was softened next day by the arrival at Wingate Fields of the letter he had posted in York before leaving for Liverpool. Angus and Ned Causey, Clara's husband, left for London at once, Angus assuring Louise that they would be back, and Raymond with them, in ten days.

Louise received several messages from London with reports of their progress but when Angus and Ned came back, almost a month later, Raymond was not with them as promised. 'The police believe he never came to London,' Angus told her.

'Then why on earth would he *tell* us he was going there?'

'Because that's what he wanted us to believe.'

'But why would he want *that*?'

'Because he's very upset still. And because he's angry with me.'

'You can't blame him for that,' she said. 'You handled the whole business badly.'

'That's none of your affair, Louise.'

'Yes, it *is* my affair. He's my only son. You should have dealt directly with that rotten Callison.'

'It's too late to talk about that now.'

'It's not too late to find Raymond. Are you telling me it's too late for that? You should never have sent him off to Dublin like a naughty schoolboy.'

'I did what I thought was best.'

'But it *wasn't* best.' She was weeping now. 'I told you *then* I thought it was an error. Can't you admit you made a mistake?'

'I suggest you try to get hold of yourself, Louise.'

'Where is Raymond now? I just want to know where he is.'

'The police think perhaps he's in Wales. But the chief inspector feels it's more likely he's gone off to Scotland.'

'That means they don't know *where* he is. Any more than *we* do.'

Clara, too, blamed her father for Raymond's disappearance. And when her husband defended Angus, she blamed him also. 'Father was foolish and vindictive. He dealt with the whole matter in a high-handed way. Raymond and Emily had a passion for each other. It was as simple as that. Such things can be dealt with. Perhaps Raymond was foolish but who isn't sometimes? He was a man after all and he should have been treated as a man. But instead he was shipped out of the country. And then, after that dreadful affair in Holyhead he was tucked away in a clinic like a gypsy lunatic.'

'He was ill. You know that. The doctors said he was extremely upset.'

'And so would you be if they stuck you in a bare white room with nothing but a metal bed and a chamber pot.'

'Well he's gone now,' Ned said. 'And nobody knows where to look.'

'What about money? Where did he get money?'

'You know your father released Raymond's legacy ten days after he went into the clinic in Yorkshire. While we were in London we learned he drew on that money a few days before he disappeared. A bank draft was delivered to him by messenger in his room at the clinic.'

It was more than a year later before Sir Charles Tremont, the Bradshaws' London solicitor, was able to convince bank officials that their normal code of client privacy could be breached in a good cause in the instance of Raymond Bradshaw. Examination of his account, however, showed that no withdrawals had been made since that initial one.

When he requested information as to where that first bank draft had been cashed, once again Tremont was rebuffed. Several additional months went by before details were grudgingly provided. The draft had been deposited and drawn on at a bank in Liverpool and, not long after, the rest of the deposit had been transferred on demand by cable to the First Merchant's Bank in Boston.

A few weeks later, when Tremont and Angus arrived in Boston and visited that bank they found that a young man named Raymond Bradshaw had indeed opened an account there. They spoke at length with a bank officer who had serviced the account and who remembered Raymond. But he had not seen him since the account had been closed and the balance handed over in a negotiable bank cheque.

The bank's listed address for Raymond was a letter-box at the Chestnut Street Postal Station. Inquiries there told them only that the box had been unused since the previous April and no forwarding address had been provided.

Months later, long after they had returned to England, Tremont was able to provide Angus with some additional information. The investigations bureau they had engaged in Boston had at last located three people who remembered Raymond Bradshaw: they were a law clerk, a young painter of miniatures and an elderly woman who kept a boarding-house. None of them had known him well, however, and none of them could say where he had gone when he left Boston.

Discussing this disappointing news with Angus, Tremont said, 'It's clear, I think, that Raymond does not *want* to be found. If that continues to be the case, I must, in all candour, report to you that it is very unlikely that we *will* find him. As you can see, even in Boston, where we are certain he spent several months, we have been able to obtain only meagre information. Now we must face the fact that he could be anywhere in America. Or he could be on the Continent for all we know. Or living in a flat in Brighton. It's a discouraging situation. Nothing to be done, it seems, except wait. Perhaps he will be in touch with you at last. Or he may contact some of his Cambridge friends. And of course, we will continue to question the bank people about his account. I think they are sympathetic now to our situation. They assure me that my office will be advised the moment they receive any communication or request for funds from Raymond.'

But Raymond, of course, did not contact his family. Nor did the bank in London report activity in his financial accounts. Beyond that first withdrawal, when he was still in the clinic outside York, those funds remained untouched.

89

For many months both Angus and Ned Causey tried to present an optimistic scenario to Louise and Clara. But Raymond's mother was not deceived. Nor was his sister. At last they stopped asking questions and thus delivered the men from their uneasy inventions of elliptical answers.

The fact that Raymond's name was seldom mentioned, however, did not in any way diminish his disturbing presence. Indeed the fact of the family's silence coupled with their individual awarenesses-that he was somewhere, very much alive, kept him walking the halls and the lawns of Wingate Fields like a spectre. They saw him everywhere they turned. When a silence fell at dinner, each person at table concluded that each other person's thoughts were on Raymond. He became the central figure in their family, the silent leader who dominated by his absence.

The action Raymond had taken, his decision to absent himself totally, to negate his family's existence by abandoning them, to begin and sustain a new life, an isolated and separate life somewhere, God-knows-where, that courage and fearlessness, that disdain, that contempt for the past, for tradition, for consequences, for *them*, became, in their eyes, a kind of ultimate power. By turning his back on his father and the financial structure that *defined* Angus, that in truth defined and delineated the name Bradshaw, Raymond had, in a very real sense, turned historic positives and absolutes into paper toys.

Angus continued to function as before, of course, with authority and wisdom, and ruthlessness when necessary; his instincts and his judgments were honoured and emulated in the world of commerce. He commanded respect as always, was able to instil fear as always. But although his power was undiminished, Angus himself knew that his banner had been stained.

Although he decided and selected and performed as required, he questioned, now, every decision, every action. As he gave his advice and his commands, he heard more often than not, the sound of his voice ordering Raymond away to Dublin, judging, pontificating, obscenely sure in his own mind that *his* instincts were the correct ones. He

90

had been certain, then, certain of everything. But he was certain no more.

For Louise and Clara, their reactions were different in degree but they were, at foundation, similar. Although they seemed blameless in the series of mishaps and misjudgments that had redirected Raymond's life, and though Angus was, by any measure, ultimately culpable, they could not help feeling, each of them, that they could have done more than they did, that they could have *tried* at least to do more, to do things that women must do in a society of males; to cajole, to insist, to question, to withhold approval, to withhold themselves when all else fails. They could have tried harder, they felt, to understand, to empathize. They could have looked at Emily differently. They could have supported and defended her. They could have helped her, seen her not merely as Callison's wilful and adulterous wife but as someone precious and necessary to Raymond.

They could, in short, have made separate judgments, they could have refused to accept the community verdict, they could have lobbied for *time*, for extra consideration, for other solutions. They could have raised their voices and presented minority views, *their* views as women. But they had simply watched and listened and felt ill at ease; they had done nothing. So when Raymond left they felt as if he had left *them*. As a mother and sister they felt abandoned. And that act of abandonment diminished each of them in those family roles. It diminished them also as women. They felt it strongly, each time they thought of him. His absence was a persistent reminder of some hurtful shortcoming in themselves.

3

The fact that Raymond's unhappy love affair, its tragic climax, and his subsequent disappearance had made a permanent scar on his family, should have been no surprise to anyone, not to those family members themselves or to anyone else who knew them and the circumstances involved. There was, however, an additional fact, known only to the people in question. Two individuals who had never *seen* Raymond, who knew his face only from his portrait in the east gallery, namely, Clara's son, Hugh, and her daughter, Nora, had also been powerfully affected by the *fact* of their uncle Raymond. By his absence, by the family's unwillingness to talk about him, and by their neighbours' unwillingness, it seemed, to talk about anything else.

The truth was that the story of Raymond and Emily had become a contemporary legend in Northumberland, a tale that a century earlier would have been set to music and sung as a tavern ballad. All the ingredients were in place, the fair young wife, the evil husband, and the handsome student. Meetings on the moor, trysts by the river, banishment and return, and a grisly finale no poet could improve on. Add to all this the vanished Raymond, wandering God-knew-where across the face of the earth, and the ballad was complete.

Emily and Raymond were mused about and whispered about, admired and envied, mentioned in tandem with the Brownings or with Nelson and his Lady Hamilton. Their story was treasured even more, perhaps, because they were local and identifiable. Callison's home and Wingate Fields were visible sites, still lived-in, the ruined castle by the Will still stood, and the Pembroke Inn at Holyhead was open for business if one was passing through on the way to Dublin.

Available also were Hugh and Nora, as close as one could get to the core of the story, young and vital and attractive themselves, everyday residents in the fateful home of Raymond, key witnesses once-removed, blood links to the legend. By their silence on the subject, by their apparent lack of any information that was not available to all, they made Raymond more intriguing and themselves more mysterious. For they realized, before their parents and grandparents did, that whatever the past and present

92

accomplishments of the Bradshaws, however extensive their lands and honourable their name, they were referred to most often now, as Raymond's family. His absence, his mystery, his romantic identity had become the most evocative identifying feature of the Bradshaws.

Hugh and Nora were conscious always that their absent uncle Raymond was a living element in their lives. As Bradshaws they would have had entrée to any home in their county; as attractive and personable young people they would have quickly become sought after. But as the niece and nephew of Raymond, as links to *him*, they possessed an extra element of desirability and fascination, among their peers without question, but also to people of their parents' generation, many of whom had been personally acquainted with both Raymond and Emily Callison. They told each other that they saw a resemblance to Raymond in both his niece and his nephew, they labelled them as fascinating guests and invited them to their homes as often as they were able or willing to come.

Was there a true resemblance to their uncle? Not physically. Hugh was lean and dark like his father but he had also inherited the clear grey eyes and slightly wicked expression that had made Angus compelling as a young man. Nora, too, it seemed, had strong physical links to the Causeys. She had chestnut-red hair like her grandmother, Mary Causey, pale, almost translucent skin, and her father's brown eyes.

But they both resembled Raymond in one way. Not Raymond as he had been at their age but Raymond as they imagined him, as he had become in their minds, by his act of disappearance. They thought of him as a rake, wild and free, and though they would not have admitted to fashioning themselves after that facet of him, they became, each of them, famously rebellious.

It was as though they carefully studied their parents and grandparents, measured their traditional habits and ideas against something else, they knew not what, and came down firmly on the side of change, of independent

93

thinking, of freedom of thought and action, of rejection of parental supervision.

Their parents, astonished by such behaviour, attempted, in the beginning, to train the children as they themselves had been trained. Starting with affectionate instruction, they moved ahead through calm reason, stern persuasion, bribery, curtailed freedom, withdrawn privileges, mild threats, tears, anger, and every possible variety of punishment, and found at last that absolutely nothing worked.

Hugh, by the age of twenty, was a gambler who cheated, a drunk and a brawler, and a notorious womanizer. No kitchen girl or lady's maid was safe. And there was a persistent rumour that he made midnight visits to at least one novice in the convent outside Rothbury.

He had ridden one of his father's stallions to death, turned over and destroyed numberless traps and carriages, and demolished, on country roads, the first two automobiles the Causeys owned. At nineteen he was cashiered out of the Royal Navy for striking and kicking a superior officer. It required all the skill of Sir Charles Tremont and all the influence of Angus to keep Hugh out of a naval prison.

Nora's pattern of rebellion was of another sort altogether. Or so it seemed. Against the background of her brother's public misbehaviour she seemed to be the essence of a lady. Her eyes, as dark as chocolate, glistened and twinkled and seemed to hide nothing. She spoke well of everyone, appeared always to be gentle and helpful, and behaved generally in a way that made mothers who met her critical of their own less perfect daughters.

Nora's mother, however, realized that she was not, in any way, what she seemed to be. Clara knew, for example, that her daughter had no respect for the truth. She had lied since she learned to speak. She had also pilfered money from her grandfather and jewellery from the homes of her friends. She sincerely believed, it seemed, that her desires and her needs transcended all other circumstances.

It was not simply a matter of selfishness. It was more profound than that. It was, or seemed to be, a true genetic

94

flaw. Blind to any requirements other than her own, she was unable to question her own instincts and unwilling to condemn her own actions. Behind her grace and beauty and a gentle manner that seemed to defer in all situations, she moved forward with the power of the tide.

Before their children were born, Clara and Ned had detailed discussions about parenthood, its rewards and its responsibilities. His upbringing, much like hers, had been, if not strict, at least thoughtfully supervised. Each of them, as young adults, appreciated the guidance and discipline they had experienced as children. They discussed the principles of child-rearing and promised each other that they would be tender and considerate parents. But certain standards, they insisted, would be clarified and maintained whether they had one child, two, or a dozen.

These discussions, however, these vows of purpose and determination took place when Raymond was still at Cambridge, when he was still resident at Wingate Fields, before his fateful birthday ball and all the havoc that came after.

Just as those events culminating in Raymond's disappearance coloured the lives of Angus and Louise and Clara, so also did they dilute Clara's convictions about how to deal with her children. In theory she managed them exactly as she had planned, fairly and firmly. In practice, however, procedures were not at all as projected. Each of them, Ned as well as she, with the shadow of Raymond present always in their home, with the memory of Angus' wrongheaded handling of that situation as clear and meaningful to them as though it had happened only an hour before, each of them, from the start, fought rearguard actions with their children. Hoping that love and tenderness would win the day, telling themselves that strong-willed Hugh and silent and stubborn little Nora would change for the better when they were a few years older, ignoring the steady procession of departing tutors and governesses, they cautioned themselves against being too severe, looked the other way, and hoped for the best. By Hugh's seventh birthday, when his sister was just four, their parents knew that they had lost control.

Ironically, on a level of superficial behaviour, Hugh and Nora seemed to be ideal children, handsome and carefully groomed, quiet and well-mannered, models of social decorum. They did not shout or scream in their rooms or in the corridors, and they did no harm to their pets. They were well-behaved at table, ate and drank what was put before them, and took part in the general adult discussion when it was appropriate. They were affectionate with their grandparents and properly respectful of visiting adults. And they seemed devoted to Ned and Clara. Where, then, was the problem?

The truth was that both children absolutely rejected both the principle and the practice of authority, parental or otherwise. They seemed united, the two of them, in a conspiracy against any force that challenged their right to inner-direct themselves. In another household they might, perhaps, have been brought to heel and made to understand; they might have been properly positioned as responsible members of a civilized unit. But at Wingate, where all four of the resident adults had been rendered tentative and unsure, the stubborn self-rule of its two youngest family members went unchallenged and at last almost unnoticed.

4

It is important to note here that we have dealt, so far, with chiaroscuro only, with underpainting. The household we have described was not a house of horrors peopled by cackling demons. The atmosphere was not one of suspicion and hatred and deception and intrigue.

Conflict, although it existed among the Bradshaws, was not the order of the day. War was not the theme. Neither was vengeance. Nor retribution. The fact was that life at

Wingate Fields was a web of details, most of them familiar, many of them pleasant.

The days, by and large, were a sum of the moments in those days. One had a great and sumptuous breakfast in the east room with sun streaming through the leaded windows. One did one's correspondence then, or dealt with estate affairs in the study, or rode out to visit the cottages, or inspect the herds, or consult with the managers and gamekeepers. Or one did needlework, or planned menus, or consulted with housekeepers and butlers. Or walked in the gardens or rode one's horse for pleasure and exercise until eleven o'clock when a light meal with beverage was provided. A rest then, in one's room and a change of clothing for the women. Then a fine hot meal would be served at one o'clock in the sun room or the garden room or the dining-hall. And on like that, on and on. Cream teas and high teas and light suppers. Or fine dinners with guests and music and decanters of wine on the sideboard. Croquet on the lawns in summer and drives to the villages in open cars. Amateur theatricals and choral singing and dancing and skating and lawn tennis.

All these, as they had always done, remained key parts of the days at Wingate Fields. Love was there still, and kindness, boundless comfort and luxury, and total security, now and for evermore, amen. Great sums of money accumulated. All the time. No cause for trepidation. Nothing to fear but death. And even that, as part of the ancient and cherished fabric, like an eleventh-century tapestry in the great hall, even that seemed, if inevitable, almost quietly and pleasantly so, in such a house in such surroundings, where even wars, if they were fought at all, were fought in foreign fields, far-off, where one might serve and suffer, secure in the knowledge that the meadows of Northumberland would stay as they had always been, that they would be there to return to, green and truly umber, rolling to the north and unchanged.

Did the Bradshaws and the Causeys and their neighbours feel this euphoria about their lives and their lands? Of course not. Correction: many of the old people did feel that way; at least they repeated over and over to themselves that it was the way they felt. But those individuals were truly old and facing death, a great number of them. They welcomed into their minds, and described in scratchy pale voices, only benevolent images. Bound for the world eternal, they were determined to enter it with only praise for the county they came from.

The others, however, those with their lives only half-lived, or less than half, took a harsher view. They demanded more, expected more, and were more critical of what they got. They insisted that each day and each segment of that day deliver to them what they were entitled to or be held forever culpable. In the long view they found no value; like the generations who would follow, they were preoccupied with present time, with the gratification that those moments, those hours, those days, might bring. No years of sacrifice to prepare for a better and more rewarding life beyond. None of that rot. We can only measure and enjoy and pass along what we have, they insisted. Pain is not needed. No anguish is required. Give us this day our daily cake. Preserve our comfort and our traditions. We will show you then how benevolent and appreciative we can be.

An exaggeration? Of course. But with truth at its core. If wealth is a feeling of inner warmth and a solid faith in the future, then few rich people are wealthy. They measure their well-being, as most men do, in terms of their latest disappointment.

The Bradshaws, for better reasons than most, were no exceptions to this practice. As noted, they had weighed every day and every experience in that day, for almost twenty years, alongside their continuing emptiness. No reward could compensate them. No sudden sweet wind could sweep away the fog they had lived in, had hidden themselves in, since Raymond had walked away from the clinic in Yorkshire, posted his final message to them, and disappeared.

It is difficult then, perhaps impossible, to describe their

reaction, to estimate its size or intensity when a card from America arrived telling them Raymond was dead.

Death, among Christians, is never a cause for celebration. And the news of Raymond's death, when it came to Wingate Fields, was shocking indeed. The windows were shuttered, candles lighted, and Angus and Ned and Louise and Clara knelt in the family chapel in their mourning clothes. Even Hugh and Nora bought new and sombre outfits to formalize their participation in the family grief.

At the same time, however, there was, among the Bradshaws, an underlying note of celebration, celebration of the finish of a long span of silence, a time that had been, in itself, a kind of death.

Concluding that Raymond's period of exile had been as bitter and empty for him as his absence from home had been for them, they welcomed the end of it as one secretly welcomes the death of a friend after an ugly and debilitating illness. His family had never found a way to deal with the vacuum of Raymond's absence. His death, on the other hand, final and absolute, was something they could accept.

Death announcements were prepared and printed and sent out across Northumberland, Cumberland, Durham, and North Riding. A formal ceremony was held in the high church at Newcastle-upon-Tyne and the bishop came to Bellingham to deliver a memorial service to the gentry. The church was filled and more than a hundred people stood in the damp January cold outside. A few days later, the Anglican minister from Otterburn performed a service at Wingate Fields for the family and their tenants who had come in by carriage from the cottages scattered across the Bradshaw lands.

At the close of his message of condolence to the family and their servants and tenants, the minister said, 'There can be only sadness when a loved one is taken from us. Joy must wait for other seasons and other occasions. But when an unfortunate life comes to an end, a life that was never allowed to fulfil itself, then we allow ourselves to say, in reverent prayer, "Thank God our son and our brother has found a better world." ' He looked up then and smiled carefully at the Bradshaws. 'On this occasion, *this* family, although their grief is deep and painful, have also received a gift. Along with the bitter news about Raymond came the news that there is a grandchild, that their son was the father of a daughter. So the sorrow of this moment is tempered as God wills it, by the hope that this young woman will soon be here in England with the fine family to which she belongs.'

5

Helen, from her first awareness of their existence, felt only antipathy towards her father's family. If her mother had sinned against Raymond, had made his life awkward and painful and less rewarding than it might otherwise have been, God knows what had taken place in his childhood home, with his parents. Helen's feelings, however, were known to no one but Jesse, because only the two of them, co-trustees of Raymond's private papers, knew the facts, such facts as were there in the locked box he had kept always in his steamer trunk in the attic. To Jesse, Helen said, 'Why would a young man leave his parents and his sister and never see them again, never write to them, never let them know where he'd gone?'

'I left *my* parents,' Jesse said.

'Of course you did. Because they were awful. And I left *my* mother so I could be with my father. But your case, and mine, were different from Raymond's. You *knew* him, better than I did in many ways. He was kind and thoughtful and civilized. His home here meant everything to him. That didn't just *happen*. That instinct didn't *develop* in him all at once. What I mean is his home in England must have been important to him too. So what happened? What could they have done to him? I can't imagine. And I hope I never find out.'

100

Their information about Raymond was meagre. Among his papers they found the passport he had used to come to America, his immigration papers, an old address book, and pages from a diary he had kept at Cambridge. There was also a letter from Clara, written to him when he was at school, telling him she would marry Ned Causey the following autumn. On the engraved letterhead was the address of Wingate Fields. Also in the box were two photographs, one a family picture, Raymond, Clara, and their parents, and the other a young woman in riding costume standing beside a handsome grey stallion. And there was the invitation his parents had sent out on the occasion of Raymond's twentieth birthday.

'Maybe they knew where he was,' Jesse said. 'Maybe they *did* write to him. Maybe he wrote to them.'

'Did you ever see a letter from England delivered here?'

'No. But it could have come to his office at the school.'

'*Why*?' she said. 'There'd be no reason for that. He wouldn't do that just to keep it from *me*.'

She believed that. And she was right, of course. But all the same, whatever the circumstances, whatever his reasoning had been, however valid his double life, the one half kept from his parents and sister, the other half kept from his wife and daughter and everyone who knew him in America, the key fact was that he had kept it from *her*. It disturbed her in a way that she could not describe to anyone, not even to Jesse. Every scenario she constructed to defend her father fell apart in her hands. When she tried to persuade herself that he had not, in fact, deliberately deceived her she could only conclude that he had. When she tried to imagine different sets of circumstances that might require or excuse such deception, the results were invariably unsatisfactory. She was able to make various mismatched pieces fit together, but when she came up against herself and her father, the two of them together, that pure and special unit, everything shared, everything available and free, all channels of communication open, with only a look necessary for complete understanding, when she replayed those memories in her mind, savouring

101

the moments, she could not bring herself to believe, or if believing to accept, this new knowledge that a key element in that closeness had been counterfeit.

God knows his death had shattered her. Stunned and numbed her beyond the normal physical and visual manifestations of heartbreak. She felt as if she were standing to one side observing her house and the people in it during those ugly days, through the vigil, the viewing, the funeral service and the burial, and the parade of sympathetic friends who followed her home from the ceremony for coffee and sandwiches and cakes and pies carried in by the neighbours; observing herself too, concentrating strongly on that slim, black-clad figure, its hair pulled severely back, detesting herself for her ability to walk about and talk and serve coffee, detesting herself for her ability to function.

She knew she was being admired for her control. People were astonished. Many of them expected that when the initial shock had passed, when the house had emptied and the true fact of death, the *absence*, the permanent absence of someone who had always been present, when *that* struck her, they said, when she walked the rooms and hallways alone where she was accustomed to seeing Raymond, *that* time, those moments, would be the test. No one expected, when that after-the-fact loneliness came, that she would not break down.

Helen wanted it to be true. She longed desperately to cry out and collapse and be tucked into her bed in a dark room. But all those acts, those manifestations of grief, had been taken from her. When Jesse had come into her room that morning, Mrs Esping in the doorway behind him, when Helen had seen the tears on his face, when she had watched him struggling to get the words out, she had known. And in that second of knowing she felt tubes and arteries and ligaments being swiftly and neatly clipped inside her; in that same instant she became light and hollow, made of fine paper, as though pins and bits of wire were needed to anchor her, to keep her in her bed, in the room, to keep her from gusting off down Plymouth Street to the river. She didn't feel the anguish she saw on

102

other people's faces. She felt nothing she could express or describe. She simply, on the instant of reading the truth on Jesse's face, felt dead herself.

Later, almost two years later, after she had given birth to a child, she would shed the tears that had not been there to shed when her father died. But those tears, when they came, would be for Raymond. By then she would *know* him, by then she would know more, also, about herself, and only then, as she seemed, in her mind, to see him die a second time, only then, alone in a house in Maine, would she cry for hours without rest or sleep.

After the funeral, days after, when Jesse and Helen had gone through the left-overs of Raymond's life, handled the pieces and the fragments, stroked the sleeves and hat-brims, and slipped oak shoe-trees into the hand-made boots and shoes, when they had dealt with the facts in his locked box, little by little, piece by piece, tried to string them all together and failed, after they had attempted to give each other answers that made sense and failed there, too, when there was nothing left except conclusions that Jesse could not fathom at all and that Helen found difficult to live with, after all the talking and the wondering and the late-night lying awake in their separate rooms and failing still to understand what had motivated Raymond, they ended up with nothing beyond the obvious. Everything floated and dangled and made them cross and edgy, feeling as if something must be done, as if some action must be taken, but not knowing, either of them, what to do.

Jesse said, at last, that whether the prospect was attractive to her or not, he felt that she must try to establish some contact with Raymond's family in England, that it was simple decency and a gesture of respect that she owed her father. She was not obligated to go beyond that but surely she must tell them that Raymond was dead.

Helen was not receptive to that proposal; it made her angry in fact. She would feel like a traitor to her father, she said, if she tried to undo what he had so carefully done over a period of years, if she gave out information that

103

Raymond had been unwilling to give. At last, however, they reached a compromise. Jesse suggested that they simply send a printed card, one of a number supplied by the church at the time of the funeral. On the card was a colour reproduction of the Virgin by Raphael and a quotation from Genesis. In a panel at the bottom, printed in gold, was the birth date of the deceased, also the date of his death, and the date of his funeral and burial.

'I think it's sentimental and hypocritical,' Helen said. 'As far as Raymond was concerned he didn't *have* a family.'

'That's the way it seems *now*,' Jesse said, 'but we can't be sure how he really felt.'

'Well, *I'm* sure, whether you are or not, and I don't want anything to do with those people. If Raymond didn't want them, I don't want them either.'

'Neither do I. I know exactly what you're saying. I don't propose that you write them a personal note or send them your return address. There's no reason for them to know you exist if that's the way you want it.'

'That is *exactly* the way I want it.'

So the card was sent. Mailed to Wingate Fields in a plain envelope with no additional message and no return address. No reply invited and none expected. Even Helen believed at last that they had done the right thing. A simple kindness. A one-time gesture, floating in limbo with no connecting wires, now or in future.

Never having met Angus, however, knowing nothing about him, Helen and Jesse underestimated him. Faced with a challenge, having a problem thrust on him that seemed to have no solution, he was at his best, energized and commanding. Starting with the postmark on the envelope, checking his world maps for the precise location of Fort Beck, noting then its exact distance from Chicago, he instructed his solicitor to contact associates there. If there was a Fort Beck newspaper he wanted them to procure each issue for the week preceding Raymond's funeral. When his son's obituary was found he wanted the entire text cabled to him at his home.

In less than seventy-two hours, he had the information

he wanted. He knew where Raymond had lived for almost twenty years and how he had gained his livelihood. And he knew that there was a Bradshaw granddaughter. He sent a cable to her at once expressing the sorrow of Raymond's family and offering heartfelt sympathy.

'My God,' Helen said to Jesse. 'How did they know about me? How did they know my address?'

'They didn't. They sent it in care of the school.'

'But how did they know he taught at Foresby?' she said. 'Are you sure you didn't tell them when you sent the card?'

'You saw me put it in the envelope. All I sent was the card. You think I'm playing games with you?'

'No. I'm sorry. Of course I don't think that. I just feel . . . I don't know what I feel. *Exposed,* I guess. I feel as though a great horde of people is going to come here in a pirate ship and cook me and eat me.'

'Maybe they feel the same way about you.'

'I hope so. I really don't want to start. . . I don't know what I'm saying. Am I being terrible? You know how I feel. I don't want to be mean but I can't pretend something I don't feel. I know they're blood relatives but I still don't feel as if they're related to *me.* I don't even feel as if they were related to Raymond. Not in a *real* way, the way *I* was. Or the way *you* were. I mean you and he. . . that's the way people are when they care about each other. It's every day. All the time. It's not just sending cables and family records and birth certificates. Am I crazy?'

'Not crazy. Just jumping to conclusions. You can't be sure what they're like.'

'Yes I can. If Raymond didn't want to see them, if they didn't want to see *him.* . . .'

'You can't be certain they didn't want to see him,' Jesse said. 'If they didn't know where he was all these years. . . .'

'It's all the same. If he stayed away it had to be for a good reason. I don't want them making up to me for something rotten they did to him.'

'Don't worry about it. You'll probably never hear from them again.'

But she did hear of course. First a short note came from Clara. She identified herself as Raymond's sister and sent family sympathy to Helen just as Angus had done. She told her about her children, Hugh and Nora.

'My son's a bit older than you. Four years or so. But you and Nora are only a year apart.' She also enclosed a small photograph of herself and Raymond, taken when he was five years old.

'What am I going to do now?' Helen said when she got the letter. 'She sounds like a perfectly nice woman. How can I tell her that I don't want . . . how do you say to somebody that you just want to be left alone?'

'Nobody's trying to tell you what to do. You can do anything you want to. But you're not going to spend the rest of your life sitting in your room with the shades drawn. You know that and so do I. You have more friends than anybody in Fort Beck.'

'I didn't mean that. I just . . . .'

'Don't worry about those people in England. It seems as though they're trying to be nice to you but there's no law that says you have to be nice to them.'

'What are you saying?'

'I'm saying you don't have to answer their letters if you don't feel like it. They'll get tired of writing after a while. If they don't hear from you they'll get the idea. They're not stupid people. I'm sure of that.'

'I just hate to be a pill about it. I ask myself all the time what Raymond would have done. And that makes it easy. Because we know what *he* did. He went his own way and burned his bridges and fiddle-dee-dee.'

'I have a feeling it wasn't as simple as it sounds.'

'You're no help,' she said. 'If you were any help you'd write them a letter and tell them I have a cleft palate and I throw fits every morning after breakfast.'

'I told you before I don't think you should worry about it. Just do what you want to do.'

Sometimes you're a mirror image of Raymond, do you know that? He and I used to have discussions like this. Whenever he thought I was about to do something reckless

106

or selfish he always said I should go ahead and do it if it seemed like a good idea to me. When he said that it was like a signal. A light blinking in the dark. It wasn't so much *what* he said. It was a certain tone. When I heard it I knew I was pointed in the wrong direction.'

'So then you did what daddy wanted you to.'

Helen smiled. 'Not always, but sometimes. We're all brilliant when we look back. Looking ahead is the problem. Besides I can't fool *you*. You were here. Key witness to all my growing pains.'

'I'm *still* having growing pains,' Jesse said. 'So I doubt if yours are over.'

'That's because you're only twenty-one. That's very young for a man. I'll be eighteen before you know it. And that's very grown-up for a woman. My mother was only eighteen when I was born. I could have a baby myself before I'm nineteen.'

'That's a good idea. Why don't you have triplets?'

'I mean it,' she said. 'I *could*.'

'You'd better take another look at your biology book.'

'I don't have to. I'll bet I know as much about biology as you do. I'm not worrying about finding a husband if that's what you mean.'

'Two days ago you told me you were planning to finish college. Unless I'm mistaken you have three and a half years to go.'

'I know *that*,' she said. 'I'm just saying that if a young woman wants to get married she can. Polly Zink's already married and she's only two months older than I am. And Evelyn Johnson's getting married next June on her eighteenth birthday. Besides, you should be encouraging me. The sooner I have a baby, the sooner you'll be a godfather.'

'Just give me a little warning,' Jesse said. 'So I'll have time to buy a new suit.'

'You'll be the first to know.'

'What about your husband? You'd better tell him.'

'I'll tell him *second*. I've known you longer.' She kissed him on the cheek. 'Besides, married people break up sometimes. But not *us*. You're *never* going to get rid of *me*.'

107

During the Christmas school break, when all the Foresby students had gone home to celebrate the holiday with their families, when many of the faculty members, too, had gone off to visit relatives, Jesse had a telephone call one afternoon from Carl Pfrommer, the chairman of the English department. 'I have to go into my office this afternoon. Some correspondence I've neglected. If you're not busy around four, why don't you meet me there. We'll have a little chat.'

Dr Pfrommer's lectures were not highly regarded by his associates. Nor were they stimulating to his students. Failing almost invariably to catch the thematic drift in Milton or Pope or Blake he attempted to compensate, it seemed, with a fanatic devotion to detail. He had taught at Foresby for twenty years and in each school quarter of those years enrolment in his elective courses had become steadily smaller. His colleagues believed that he had been made chairman of his department not as a reward for merit but only because the routine of administrative work would keep him away from the lecture halls. In practice, however, he turned out to be as incompetent as a department head as he had been as a teacher. So the dean of faculty assigned a wise and experienced senior secretary to Pfrommer's office, made her the department assistant and instructed her to handle all of Pfrommer's duties except for ceremonial ones and certain political tasks inside his faculty group, thus allowing him to retain the spirit of authority if not the fact of it.

A master of periphrasis, Dr Pfrommer was famously incapable of coming to the point. His teachers, as well as the few students who were luckless enough to have him as a faculty advisor, knew that one could avoid reprimand or punitive duties simply by leading the conversation far afield, by encouraging Pfrommer to woolgather, to backtrack, to consider every matter from every possible viewpoint until at last, glancing at his watch, he would see that

108

the time allotted for that particular session had passed. He would then bring the meeting to an abrupt close without discussing the topic that had prompted that meeting.

On this afternoon, however, with Jesse, he came quickly to the point. Embarrassed, perhaps, by what he was forced to say, he had decided, it seemed, to put it behind him as quickly as possible.

'The dean of students has asked me to have this meeting with you. He thought it might be a sensitive matter but I disagree. I'm sure it's a problem that you and I can work out in no time at all. I told him that you are a reasonable fellow and that we feel you have a fine future here as an instructor. I'm sure we can make the necessary adjustments with a minimum of fuss.'

When Jesse didn't answer, when he sat across the desk from Pfrommer, his hands in his lap, waiting for some clue to emerge, some hint of what this discussion might entail, when he disregarded several questions that crept into his mind and chose silence instead, he saw that Pfrommer seemed temporarily put off, seemed to want or need some words from Jesse to move him ahead to his main topic. But Jesse remained silent.

'It's simply a matter of residence,' Pfrommer said at last. 'Dean Umbreit agrees with me that once you've taken rooms somewhere else, or a flat of your own perhaps, the situation will be set right.'

'I don't understand,' Jesse said. 'Are you saying I should move out of the Bradshaw house?'

'We are not delivering an ultimatum. Nothing of that sort. I am simply saying that a situation exists, one that you may not even be aware of . . . .'

'No, I guess I'm not aware of it.'

Pfrommer repositioned himself in his chair, rested his forearms on the desk-top, managed a tentative mortician's smile and said, 'We were all aware of your close relationship with Raymond. How old are you now?'

'I'll be twenty-two next Sunday.'

'And you've been here in Fort Beck since . . . .'

'November, 1913. I was almost seventeen.'

109

'I see,' Pfrommer said. 'And Helen. How old is she now?'
'She'll be eighteen in May.'
'All right.' Pfrommer looked out of the window, his finger-tips pressed carefully together. 'This may be an awkward moment after all but let's just push ahead and hope for the best.' He turned back to Jesse. 'Before Raymond's death we had a situation where a faculty member who seemed to be estranged from his wife was living in his home here in Fort Beck with his daughter and a young man who was in many ways like a foster son. Is that an accurate description of the Bradshaw household?'
'I'd say so.'
'Good. Now, however, the situation has changed. We have all lost a dear friend and colleague. An irreplaceable man. And you and Helen, of course, have suffered the greatest loss of all. I'm sure you both feel like a brother and sister who have lost their only parent. The two of you must be very close friends, almost like blood relatives, I imagine.'
'That's right.'
'But the fact is you're *not* blood relatives. You're not related at all.' He paused. 'Don't misunderstand me. I am not describing *my* perceptions of the situation, nor the perceptions of Dean Umbreit. But we must acknowledge that there are such things as public perceptions. We all live in a community and in this case it's a complex one. We have the townspeople, the university people, *and* the students. As administrators we must be aware of all those separate groups. We must try to anticipate and stave off, if possible, anything that will put the school in a bad light.'
'You're not saying . . . I *hope* you're not saying . . . .'
'Let me finish, Jesse.' He paused. '*I* am not making a judgment of any kind. I am simply functioning as an intermediary, trying to bring about an accommodation, trying to clarify matters.' Another pause. 'I used the phrase, *public perception*. Let me get back to that. Whether you like it or not, whether *I* like it or not, it would be possible for someone who doesn't understand the circumstances or the people involved to conclude that a young woman who is

110

a first-year student at Foresby is living in a house alone with a young man who is an instructor at that school.'

'We don't live there alone. You know the Espings. It's their home too.'

'I know that. But many people do not. And even those who *do* might not think of servants as proper chaperones.'

Jesse's voice was very quiet when he answered. 'We don't require a chaperone, Dr Pfrommer. I am a responsible and decent man and Helen is like a sister to me. Any public perception that is unable to recognize that is of no interest to me and I trust it will be of no interest to you or to Dean Umbreit. I do not believe that Helen's school friends or any of my faculty friends see our relationship as anything other than what it is. If you are hinting that you would like me to resign from the faculty . . .'

'No. Of course not . . . .'

'If you are suggesting,' Jesse went on, 'that Helen is a bad moral influence on her fellow students, I can assure you that she will be delighted to transfer to another school at any time. In fact, if she knew about this conversation we're having, you'd have to lock her up to keep her here.'

Pfrommer shook his head. 'I didn't expect this kind of reaction from you. I feel as if I said something I didn't intend.'

'All right. Let's go back to the beginning. You said I should move out of the Bradshaw house and find another place to live. Did you intend *that*?'

'Dr Umbreit and I thought that might be the simplest solution. Perhaps you should talk to him about it.'

'If he wants to see me of course I'll talk to him. But if you tell him that I have no intentions of moving out of the Bradshaw house maybe he'll decide there's no point to such a meeting.'

'We all have a responsibility to Foresby, you know.'

'That's true,' Jesse said. 'And if I am not fulfilling that responsibility, you should dismiss me. But I also have a responsibility to Helen. You're absolutely correct. I am not her blood relative. And I certainly could be no substitute for her father. But I am her friend. I may even be her *best* friend. And I'm certainly not going to walk away from her, only a few weeks after Raymond's death, just because somebody may have a *perception* that two grown-up people, one male and one female, should not live in the same house. If she asked me *why* I was moving out I'd never be able to explain it to her. And I don't think you could either.'

Jesse never managed to blot out that meeting with Carl Pfrommer. Long after he had left Foresby and Fort Beck, when that period and those special values seemed remote and arbitrary to him, when much of the time he had spent there seemed distant and gauzy and, apart from his memories of Raymond and Helen, quite unimportant, he found that he could recreate that interview with Pfrommer at will, reproduce it word for word, every pause and every glance. For many years he believed that his total recall of an incident that at the time had been unpleasant and hateful to him was based on one clear circumstance. It was the first time he had acknowledged, even to himself, that he felt a permanent responsibility for Helen and that he expected himself to be to her what Raymond had been to him.

If this recognition of responsibility and his articulation of it made him feel good about himself, if his outspoken acceptance of a kind of substitute parenthood made him feel suddenly adult and valuable, another facet of that Pfrommer meeting altered forever, in one particular way, his attitude towards Helen, his way of seeing her.

When he returned from Pfrommer's office that afternoon, a heavy, grey day, strangely warm for January, fog moving lazily across the garden beside the house, he found Helen in the library by the fire, curled up on the sofa, pink-cheeked from the heat and half-awake. 'You caught me,' she said. 'Lazy cat by the fire. One eye open and one eye closed. A book in her hand and nothing in her head.'

She asked about his meeting with Pfrommer and he lied to her. 'English department foolishness. Nothing interesting.' But as they sat talking, everything he had heard that afternoon, both the things said and the things implied, played over and over in his head. The implications became specific then in his mind, the fantasy became real and visual.

He had been told that people saw Helen as an appealing young woman and he suddenly saw her that way. He had been told that he and Helen together might be thought of as a *couple*, two people attracted to each other. Jesse, as they talked, sensed that this too, could be true. He felt, that late afternoon, as if he were watching her turn a soft corner from energetic schoolgirl to sleepy young woman.

7

Only after Raymond's death did Jesse realize how chain-connected their lives had become. His work as a teacher, his relationships with students and other faculty people, the entire texture and rhythm of his life in Fort Beck seemed changed. Whole areas that he had accepted and celebrated without question he began now to examine objectively. And he found them wanting. Without the armature of Raymond's judgments and enthusiasms, without that zest and high energy to fuel him, Jesse found, in those first months after Raymond's death, that every morning was a burden, every day a chore.

Even the evening meal which had always been the high point of the day in the Bradshaw house, even *that*, or *especially* that, perhaps, was a daily reminder of emptiness. As close as he and Helen had become in the several years they had known each other, as grateful as each of them was for the presence of the other, there were moments when the longing for Raymond made *any* other company, *all* other companionship, inadequate.

Each of them understood the other's situation and that understanding helped to stabilize them during those lonely months. They treated each other with affection and consideration, asked no questions, and made no demands. But the loneliness persisted.

Later in his life, when his relationship with Helen had

redefined itself, at first in subtle ways and then in ways that neither of them could have envisioned during the sheltered Fort Beck time, when his values and his directions had become deep-rooted at Wingate Fields, when his links with Raymond's family had become disturbing and destructive in ways that he could never have foreseen, he told himself, tried to reassure himself, that the void in his life that had been created by Raymond's death, had turned him, quite logically, he believed, towards Raymond's family in England. Feeling more truly related to Raymond and Helen than he did to his own people, feeling in fact that the Bradshaws *were* his family, it was inevitable, and proper, also an act of kindness, that he should contact them, be in touch with them, and give them information about Raymond and Helen. Who could misunderstand such an impulse or disavow such an action? The answer to that question was clear in his mind. He knew that Helen, if she had known what he was up to, would have both questioned and disavowed. So he didn't tell her.

He and Helen assumed that the Bradshaws would stop writing to her if they had no answers to their letters. They miscalculated. Letters from Louise Bradshaw and from Clara arrived on a regular basis; and occasionally there was a more formal note from Angus. At first Helen read the letters as soon as they came. Then she began to leave them on the hall table without opening them. At last she said to Jesse, 'I wish they'd stop writing to me. It makes me feel strange. They sound like perfectly decent people but I thought they'd realize by now that I don't want to . . . that I don't have any desire to . . . you know what I mean. They're like strangers to me. Just because we have the same name . . . what does *that* mean? Why do they persist?'

'They probably think you're still upset about Raymond.'

'I *am*. I always will be.'

'I'm sure they believe they'll hear from you finally.'

'But they *won't*,' she said. 'If Raymond didn't want them, *I* don't want them. *You* understand that, don't you?'

Jesse nodded. 'Of course I do. But I also think you may change your mind later on.'

114

'Why would I?'

'I don't know. People do change their minds.'

'Not me,' she said. 'Not about this.'

'Then I guess you'll have to write to them and tell them you don't want them to write you any more.'

'I don't plan to do that either. Since they're still sending everything in care of the school, I thought maybe you'd speak to the mail clerk and ask him to send the letters back to England when they come.'

'Are you sure that's what you want?'

'I'm sure.'

Jesse spoke to the Foresby mail clerk but he didn't instruct him to return the letters to England. He said, 'If any more letters come to Miss Bradshaw in care of the school just put them in my box at the faculty building. I'll take them home to her.'

The letters continued to come. Jesse read each one carefully and then placed it in a folder in his desk drawer. At last, early in February, three months after Raymond's death, he wrote a short letter in reply. He addressed it to Angus Bradshaw and family. He identified himself as a close friend and colleague of Raymond and wrote further that he was a sort of unofficial guardian to Helen. He described her and praised her and said that though she had been remarkably brave about her father's death it continued to upset her. 'She has gone ahead with her class work at the university but apart from that has kept very much to herself. Raymond had not told her about his family in England so she has needed time to absorb this new information and to adjust herself to the fact of close relatives she had not previously been aware of. I tell you all this so you will understand why you have had no answer to your kind letters. Helen is a confused young woman just now. Until she is in firmer control of herself I think it would be better perhaps if she did not hear from you. I trust this is a temporary circumstance and I hope she will be willing to contact you herself after a bit more time has passed. I will certainly encourage her to do that. In the

115

meantime if I can be of help or if there's any further information I can provide, please feel free to call on me.'

As he sent off the letter, Jesse assured himself that he was performing a selfless act, not precisely what Helen had wanted, but achieving the same ends. He told himself further that this would undoubtedly stop the flow of mail, that the Bradshaws would perhaps acknowledge his note but beyond that they would have no reason to write to him.

This last, however, he did not believe. He hoped they *would* write. For reasons that were not clear to him he was most anxious to be in contact with them, to meet them if he could, to *know* them. Not because it would benefit him in any way. But because some instinct told him it would complete a circle that had begun to be sketched out when he received that long-past letter from Raymond praising his schoolboy essay. Thus explaining himself to himself, he felt totally exonerated. Later in life, however, especially when he was drunk or despondent, he accused himself of an entirely different set of motives. Time after time he tried to measure the damage he had done to Helen, and to himself, by writing that single letter.

8

In the continuing letters from Wingate Fields, there was, now that they were written to a person who wrote back, a warmer tone, a stronger sense of communication, and an unending flow of information. Now they knew *their* letters were received and read, knew they had made contact, if not with Raymond's daughter at least with an informed surrogate.

Jesse, starting out with the feeling that he was betraying, although in a well-meaning way, Helen's trust, was reserved in his responses, sending one letter for every three received, and in that letter giving little specific information, withholding details, however innocent, about

116

Raymond and Helen, but furnishing abundant facts, a few at a time, about himself.

The result was that Angus and Louise and Clara and Ned and Nora and Hugh came to *know* Jesse, or to feel that they did. True, he was primarily a conduit to Helen but he began also, and very quickly, to have a value of his own. Their curiosity about him was expressed in such polite and civilized terms that it began to resemble affection.

These letters to Jesse, carefully written on heavy paper with an engraving of the gateway to Wingate Fields at the top of the page, came from Angus and Louise and Clara, sometimes all together as though they had been written on a Sunday, after the morning meal, perhaps, and other times, one letter a week, or two, or occasionally, only a letter every fortnight. But the flow, whatever the frequency, was constant and the underlying message never-changing. 'You must come visit us here at Wingate Fields and bring our Helen with you.'

Their individual letters were distinctive and almost thematic, as though a stern schoolmaster had told each of them, Angus and Louise and Clara, what their subjects should be. Angus, trying to be humble and disarming, but feeling ill at ease in both those categories, took refuge where he felt secure, in listing his triumphs of the previous week, in discussing the effects of the new world peace on the price of mutton and hides, in bewailing labour unrest in the mills, in questioning French motives in their trade with the British, and in lauding New Zealand as the wool centre of the future. As a leitmotif he often counted grouse shot and poachers apprehended or praised a particularly fine slice of beef he had been served in York or Newcastle.

To Louise, it seemed, had been assigned the job of describing the splendours of Wingate, in a modest and decorous manner of course. She did not mention the names of painters whose work hung in the great hall, cite the age of the tapestries there, or stipulate which salon featured Louis Quinze and which Louis Quatorze. She tended to concentrate on repairs that were needed, draperies that

117

wanted mending, new slate for the hearth, fresh gilt for the carved ceiling in the music room, and new parquet in the morning-room where the rain had seeped in under the French doors. Her letters, filled with details of parlour and pantry and dining-salon were like a snug and comfortable nap on a soft sofa, logs burning in the grate, the scents of coffee and fresh-baked loaves in the air. Cut flowers filled all the vases in Louise's letters, port-filled decanters glowed red in the candlelight. Sheets were crisp and cool, towels were heavy, scones were sweet and crusty, cream thick and yellow, tea hot and strong. No sickness, no death or distemper in the barns or stables, no insect bites or influenza in the house. No cancelled appointments, no broken promises, no plans gone awry. With no impulse to deceive, with no desire to misrepresent to Jesse the quality of their life at Wingate, she simply described it as she wished it to be, including repeating, and elaborating on the things that gave her joy and giving no space whatso-ever, either in her mind or in her letters, to things that spelled disappointment or bad tidings. If the spirit of truth was flawed in her reports of life among the Bradshaws she was careful to ensure that there should be no specific *untruth* included. Having found a vision she could live with she kept her eyes firmly fixed just there, determined to avoid the distasteful and the unchangeable.

Angus and Louise were fired by a need to retrieve some living portion of Raymond by capturing his daughter; they felt there might be some absolution for them if they could deliver to her some of what they had failed to give their son. Material things, certainly, but more important, atten-tion and caring. Those were the motives behind their letters, at first to Helen and then to Jesse, making contact with this newly discovered granddaughter and luring her home, by whatever means, to Wingate Fields.

Clara's objectives, however, were quite different. She was curious, of course, about Helen and, like her parents, was anxious to see her and know her, but her emotional focus was still on Raymond. Having concluded long since that she would never know what had become of him, where he had gone, and what sort of life he had chosen for himself, having told herself that the twenty-odd years since she'd seen him last were forever lost to her, she was desperate to know, now that it seemed some channels of information had reopened, everything she *could* know about him. Her own history, she felt, was ragged and incomplete unless she could somehow stick together a more exact synopsis of his.

Jesse's emergence, therefore, was particularly welcome and promising to her. Here, she felt, was a source of information that could be rich indeed. A male friend of Raymond's, she concluded, even one young enough to be his son, might have insights and observations that would be very different from those of her brother's daughter. Consequently she was delighted to be able to direct her letters to this specific, identifiable man.

Hoping to instil in Jesse a feeling of acceptance and familial ease, hoping to stimulate a free exchange of information, she provided in her letters to him a detailed history of Raymond's childhood and adolescence, his life at school and at home. She found as she wrote that her pen truly activated her mind. Long-forgotten memories and experiences and conversations with her brother came back to her with a clarity that was astonishing. Raymond came to life for her again in a way she would never have believed possible. And as he began to occupy her thoughts more and more, her need to find the missing pieces, to know what he had become after he left England, became increasingly intense.

Jesse's letters, however, though warm and responsive, were frustrating in their lack of the details she craved. Longing for a face-to-face meeting with him, it was she who insisted to her parents that when Helen came to see them, if she could at last be persuaded to come, Jesse must of course be invited, too.

It was Clara, also, who suggested to Nora that perhaps both Helen and Jesse would like to hear from members of the family who were closer to their own age. To her surprise Nora responded positively and a few days later

119

she sent off a chatty letter to Jesse enclosing what she believed to be an especially flattering photograph of herself.

Although Nora was flirtatious by nature as well as by choice, she did not envision Jesse as a potential suitor. Like her mother, however, she was eager to learn whatever she could about Raymond, and like Clara, she had concluded that having Jesse on the premises, having a chance to talk to him when he was at ease and at home at Wingate, was her best chance to piece together a more complete study of her romantic and elusive uncle.

So, although she was instinctively seductive, she had no such impulse towards Jesse; the inclusion of her photograph was not intended as an enticement to him. On the other hand she had learned in her nineteen years that she had natural gifts which, when subtly utilized, could cause people, particularly male people, to alter their courses, to change their minds, to behave quite differently at a given moment from the way they had behaved just moments before. So if someone had said to her that her letters to Jesse, filled with energy and laughter and lightly-scented irresponsibility, if someone had told her that such letters, along with her photograph, might suggest to a suggestible young man that she would be an interesting person to meet, she would undoubtedly have smiled and said, not demurely at all, 'Of course.'

9

Early in May of 1919, five weeks before the spring term at Foresby would end, Jesse was notified by the dean of the faculty that his teaching contract would not be renewed for the following school year. When he told Helen she said, 'I don't believe it. Raymond said you were the best young man on the faculty. What reason did they give you?'

'No reason. Dean Umbreit said they have no complaints

about my work and they would recommend me enthusi-
astically to any other college.'

'That doesn't make sense. What did Pfrommer say?'

'Nothing to me. But he told Dave Savidge that school
fees are going up and they expect enrolment to be down.
Also, two of his teachers who were working in Washington
for the War Department are coming back in September. So
someone had to be terminated.'

It never occurred to him to tell Helen about his earlier
meeting with Pfrommer. He knew without question that
his dismissal stemmed from that confrontation but he saw
no purpose that would be served by sharing that knowledge with her.

'You don't seem very upset about it,' she said.

'I'm not.'

'Well, *I* am. I'm mad as hell. I feel like marching straight
over to the President's office.'

'I wouldn't like it if you did that.'

'Why not?'

'Because in the first place it wouldn't do any good, and
in the second place even if it *did* some good, even if they
asked me to stay, I wouldn't do it.'

'Why not? You're a teacher. You have to teach
somewhere.'

'No, I don't,' he said. 'I'm not even sure I *am* a teacher.
Raymond was a teacher. He thought it was the greatest
thing a man could do. And in his case he was right. But I
can't do what *he* did. I think I'd go crazy saying the same
things year after year to a new bunch of faces.'

'I've never heard you talk like this before.'

'That's because I haven't talked like this before. I was a
teacher because Raymond was a teacher. If he was still
here I'm sure I'd feel different. But he's *not*. And I don't
have a job here even if I wanted it. So I have to think about
other things.'

'*What* other things?'

'I don't know. I might try the newspaper business. Or
look for a job in advertising. They say that's going to be a
big field for people who know how to spell and put the

121

commas where they belong. You know me. I'm a cracker-jack. I'll get along one way or the other.'

'You're a cracker-jack, all right.' There were tears in her eyes suddenly.

'What's the matter with you?' he said.

'What do you think's the matter? I'm sitting here talking to a stranger. That's what's the matter. Six years ago, almost six years ago, you got off a train here in Fort Beck. Now you're going to get on another train and leave. Is that what you're saying? Everything matter-of-fact. Bread and butter on a plate. If you can't work here you'll just go get a job someplace else.'

'I don't have much choice.'

'What about me?' she said. 'What choice do *I* have? I know you don't owe me anything. But we're friends, aren't we? If *you're* not my friend, who *is*?'

'I'm not planning to disappear. I didn't mean that.'

'I don't know what else you'd call it. If you're in Chicago or St Louis or Kansas City and I'm still steaming along here in this cow-pasture town . . . .'

'You're going to finish school, aren't you?'

'I guess I am,' she said. 'But there are schools all over the place. Unless you're planning to work in some jungle, there should be a college close by.'

'What about your house here?'

'What about it? I'll rent it or sell it or burn it,' she said. Then, 'I don't mean that. I love this house. I don't think I'll ever sell it. But it doesn't *own* me. I don't expect to sit here on the veranda for the rest of my days guarding my real estate.'

As they talked he knew he had bungled things badly. Trying to avoid a topic that he knew would at last have to be faced he had gone far afield, said or implied things he hadn't meant and failed to say things that had to be said.

The fact was he had not expected to lose his teaching job. In spite of the audacious front he put up for Helen it had never occurred to him that he might leave Fort Beck before she finished school. He felt an obligation to her; the feelings between Jesse and Raymond had been duplicated between him and Helen.

He remembered often the day they had met, the afternoon she got off the train from New York and calmly told Raymond she had come home to stay. He saw that same resolve in her manner now. But all the same, whatever his attachment to Helen, their attachment to each other, there were practical considerations to be dealt with. There were countless questions that Jesse had no answers for.

And always, just at his elbow, were the Bradshaws. He told himself over and over that they were not a factor in any decisions he made about himself. Nor were they concerned with him, he felt, however warm and friendly their letters had become. Indeed, they had painted a group portrait of themselves that was quite astounding in both its candour and its detail. Without knowing the particulars, Jesse sensed that Raymond's departure had seriously disrupted his family. He sensed also that there was a humility about them now, particularly in the case of Angus, that had not always been there, a need to make amends. There was a note of desperation in their fervour to make contact with him and Helen, to find some way, *any* way, to fill in those lonely spaces of time and lost opportunity. All their letters, even the saucy ones from Nora, bespoke kindness and accommodation and generosity. 'What can we do?' seemed to be stencilled between the carefully written lines. Implicit also was a secondary message. 'We can do *anything* we want to.' For all the other things, major and minor, that Jesse had come to realize about Raymond's people, the principal fact was that they were a family of great wealth. When he sensed it originally and when he knew it at last as an absolute truth it made him unquiet.

He repeated to himself like a catechism that whatever the extent of the Bradshaw resources it had nothing whatsoever to do with him. It could certainly, however, have a great deal to do with Helen if she allowed herself to be taken into her father's family. It would make her, he suspected, from her first embrace of her grandfather, a flagrantly wealthy young woman. Although no such desire

123

was made explicit in their letters he sensed a strong need, on all their parts, to place some gleaming coronet of blood connection and family riches on her neat small head if only she would step down from a fine carriage some English morning and identify herself to them.

Jesse, however, in these circumstances, felt like a kind of family retainer, trained for a specific task, encouraged to perform that job well and on demand, but to remain always outside the circle. And he expected nothing more. He was stern with himself on this subject. If Helen, by chance, should decide to re-enter the Bradshaw family it would be her choice and only hers. He would not persuade her or influence her. And even if she were somehow persuaded or influenced by him, it would be, without question, inadvertent. There would be no thought in his mind of any gain for himself.

Without his teaching job, however, with no specific plans for the future, he began suddenly to see things differently. Telling himself that a teacher of English literature owed it to himself to visit the land of Wordsworth and Byron, Keats and Chaucer and Shelley, to expose himself to English customs and culture, telling himself further that such an opportunity might never present itself again, he decided to accept the Bradshaws' invitation to spend the summer with them in Northumberland.

10

When Jesse handed over to Helen the packet of letters and photographs, postal cards and newspaper clippings he had received from the Bradshaws in the past several months, she said: 'Maybe my brain isn't working properly, but I don't understand. When you knew I didn't want to be in touch with Raymond's family why would you go to the trouble of carrying on this flood of correspondence with them?' She lifted the tied bundle and studied it. 'There must be thirty letters here.'

'Not quite.'

'Did you answer all these?'

'No,' Jesse said. 'They wrote much more often to me than I wrote to them.'

'But why did you want to write at all? That's what stops me.'

'I didn't plan to. But their letters to you kept coming to the school and I felt sorry for them. So I wrote them a note, trying to explain in a nice way that you . . . I didn't say that you didn't want to have anything to do with them but I made it clear that they shouldn't expect you to answer their letters. So then they started writing to *me*.'

'And you wrote back?'

'I told you. I felt sorry for them. I still feel sorry for them.'

'Well, I don't,' Helen said.

'No one said you should. I'm not trying to tell you how *you* should feel. I'm just trying to give them the benefit of the doubt.'

'It doesn't sound that way to me. It sounds as if you've already decided they're splendid people. Are you really serious about going there?'

'Sure, I'm serious. They sent two steamship tickets. You'll find them in an envelope with the rest of the mail. There's a sailing from New York June twelfth.'

'Not for me there isn't. They can't buy me with a steamship ticket.'

'They can't buy me either,' Jesse said. 'They're not even trying to. I think they're curious to know what we know about Raymond. And I'm curious to know about them. I felt more connected to your dad than I do to my own family so I think it's natural that I want to see where he came from and what kind of people he grew up with.'

'Well it's not natural for me. I know all I need to know. And I'm not going to visit them. Not this summer or any other time.'

'I know you're not,' he said. 'I never expected you to go. And they don't expect you either.'

'Then why did they send me a ticket?'

125

'They didn't send it to you. They sent it to me. They said I could bring a friend with me if I wanted to. You can read the letter yourself. They seem to know how you feel.'

'What did you tell them about me?' Helen said then.

'I didn't tell them anything. Except in that first letter I wrote. I told them you were upset about Raymond's death and you felt strange about finding out you had relatives in England that you'd never even heard of.'

Helen put the packet of letters on the table beside her. 'You should have a fine time. You'll have the whole summer to discuss my quirks and peculiarities.'

'What's the matter with you?'

'Nothing. It's the truth, isn't it?'

'Of course it's not the truth. I won't discuss you at all if you tell me not to. I'm much more interested in finding out what I can about Raymond.'

'I'm surprised you didn't find out everything there was to know from these letters.'

'I did find out quite a bit. Especially from his sister. But I want to know more. And I want to see where he grew up.'

Helen studied him carefully and said nothing. Then, 'Maybe you'll like it so much there you'll just decide to stay on. Maybe they'll give you your own little lamb to raise. You can send me the wool and I'll knit you a blanket.'

'You're really mad at me, aren't you?'

'No. Why should I be mad at you?'

'I don't know,' he said. 'But you are.'

'No. I'm not. I just can't figure you out. That's all. I'm sitting here listening to you and it all sounds made-up to me. Fairy tales.'

'Why would I lie to you?'

'I don't mean you're lying,' she said. 'I just think maybe you're not telling *yourself* the truth. I always thought I knew you better than I know anybody. Now I'm not so sure.'

'About what?'

'About *all* this. About everything we're talking about. All of a sudden you're best friends with some family you

126

don't even know. All of a sudden you're off on a ship to spend the summer in some house you've never seen. Wingate Fields. What kind of place is that?'

'I don't *know*,' Jesse said. 'That's the point. I didn't say there was no selfish motive involved. I'm a ding-dong kid from Chicago. Almost everything I know, almost everything I've *seen*, came from the books I've read. Crossing the Atlantic in a troop ship is not a terrific way to travel but it gave me a hint of what it must be like to go on a different kind of ship. All I saw of France was mud and blood and craziness but it made me curious to see the rest of it. And the same with England. What I saw of that country was through train windows or hospital windows but that was enough to hook me. I want to see more. When I open an envelope and find a steamship ticket, free passage to England and back, I don't start making a list of reasons why I *can't* go. All I think of is why I *should* go, how much I *want* to go. I don't know where I'll be five years from now. I don't even know what I'll be doing. But one thing I don't want to be doing is kicking myself in the pants because I was too dumb or too cautious to take an opportunity that was dropped in my hands like a ripe peach.'

That night, sitting up in her room, Helen read, slowly and carefully, all the letters Jesse had given her. She studied the photographs and county maps and informative pamphlets about Cumberland and Northumberland and Durham. At last she turned off the lamp and lay in the darkness, listening to the night sounds from the garden under her window and trying to organize into some acceptable pattern the tangle of conflict and contradiction that lay quiescent and immovable at the centre of her consciousness. She slept, then lay awake again, slept fitfully for a few minutes, then came totally awake. She turned on her lamp and read again all the letters from England, knowing as she did it, as she sat finally and watched the first light defining the shapes of furniture in her room, that there were no answers or solutions for her there in those letters, that the reason for her concern lay elsewhere.

127

That morning at breakfast she told Jesse she thought it was a fine idea after all for him to go to England. 'You'd be foolish *not* to go.' And then she said, 'And so would I. I'm going with you.'

11

Concentrating, as we have till now, on the major themes and considerations of Helen's life, there is a risk that she may seem to be other than she is, that she will appear to be, perhaps, a one-cell animal of an unfamiliar species, obsessed and vengeful by turn, abnormally concerned with her own destiny and her own directions.

That she was an unusually reflective and perceptive young woman, there is no doubt. She was quick to spot imperfections in herself and others. And an innate sense of order that had been passed along to her from some genetic God-knows-where made her uncomfortable with such flaws.

From early childhood she had an impulse to *fix* things, to set things right. Her exposure to the come-and-go relationship between Raymond and Anna intensified, unquestionably, that impulse. Since she cared about them and her relation to them and since she was wise enough to realize that unmended fractures are destined to heal imperfectly, since she knew that the baggage of her childhood and youth would travel with her throughout her life, she became keenly conscious of the main avenues she would travel, two of which, certainly, were symbolized by her mother and father. As she went along, she promised herself she would repair as many of the pot-holes and wash-outs as possible.

If one of the hallmarks of Helen's age group was a fierce concentration on today that eliminated serious consideration of either yesterday or tomorrow, then Helen was conspicuously atypical. She had a sense of history, not the text-book kind, the careful cataloguing of names and dates,

128

and events, but a feeling, almost primal in nature, that things past and future are connected, that accidents are seldom accidental. She knew that the most random wind-blown seedling shakes itself free from a stationary parent plant and that it will inevitably take root in some receptive soil of its own and start another cycle of errant seedlings.

Thus, because she was thoughtful and seemed wise for her age, she appeared to be firmly anchored. If one is susceptible to the medieval concept of *old souls* inhabiting young bodies, then Helen would perhaps have been properly placed in such a group. But for all of her solid foundation, in spite of her truly splendid sense of order, she was a curiously off-centre young woman.

Two weeks before she and Jesse were to leave for New York to board the ship that would take them to England, as they sat on the porch swing looking out across the back garden, Helen said, 'I probably shouldn't tell you this but I have an odd feeling about this trip.'

'How do you mean, *odd*?'

'I don't know. That's why I used such a vague word. I just feel . . . I don't know . . . how does a child in a dark room feel?'

'Different from you, I'm sure. You're just nervous because you're doing something you've never done before,' Jesse said. 'Going someplace you've never been . . . .'

'I don't think so. It's more than that.'

'You didn't let me finish. Of course it's more than that. It's like jumping into the Boone river in April. Difficult to do but not so bad once you're in the water. In two or three weeks you're going to have a brand-new family. Not brand-new exactly but new to you. That's enough to give anybody the tremblies.'

'I know what you mean, but it's not *that*. I mean it *is* that, but not *just* that. Raymond taught me some good rules. He said you can cope with almost anything once you've defined it. It's the shadowy stuff. The midnight noises in the attic. Those are the things that . . . you know what I'm trying to say?'

129

'No. And neither do you. A month from now you'll forget we ever had this conversation.'

'I hope so,' she said. 'Last night I dreamed I was doing a swan dive off the high platform and when I was in the air I looked down and saw there was no water in the pool.'

'Everybody has bad dreams.'

'Not me. I dream about rabbits eating lettuce. And dogs sleeping in front of the fireplace. You know me. I can turn almost anything into good news. But now I'm scared. I feel the way I did when Raymond died. As if I'm made out of crêpe paper and little orange sticks. If somebody lights a match I'll be gone in a second. I mean it. If I'm alive ten years from now. . . .'

'God, you *are* morbid today.'

'I'm sorry. I didn't mean *if* I'm alive. I just meant . . . I feel as if ten years from now I'll be saying to myself that if I hadn't made this trip, everything would have been different. Not just different . . . *better.*'

After a long moment he said, 'Then maybe we shouldn't go.'

'No. I didn't mean that. I'm babbling too much. I don't want to spoil things for you.'

'You said you were scared. I've never seen you scared of anything.'

She turned and looked at him. Then she said, 'You're right. For a minute I forgot. I'm *not* scared of anything. I am the powerful Katrinka.' She smiled. 'I wrestle Kodiak bears and crocodiles, sleep on a bed of spikes and dance barefoot on hot coals. I am indestructible.'

'Maybe we should stay here. We'll go on picnics and catch catfish and think clean thoughts. We can tell the Bradshaws we have a bad case of the Chinese *bot.*'

'Not *me,*' she laughed. 'No bot for me. We're *going,* Mr Jesse. And we will conquer England. We will be the biggest event of the season in . . . what's that place?'

'Northumberland.'

'We will be the toast of Northumberland, *je t'assure.*'

So the window opened. Then it closed. In that moment when she turned to look at him she came close to telling

130

him the most central truth she knew about herself, that she was frightened of everything, that every day produced a new freshet of fear inside her, that all her life, for as long as she could remember, she had felt that way and she could see no end to it.

When Jesse said to her 'I've never seen you scared of anything,' he described the impression she left wherever she went. Like a man with a stammer who struggles to become an orator, she had overcome, not her weakness, but all outward manifestations of it. Piece by piece she had fashioned an impressive survival kit, had covered herself with what seemed to be impenetrable chain-mail. No rejection, no disappointment, no rebuff unsettled her.

Even if one suspected that behind her easy self-assurance, there was a soft and appropriate centre of vulnerability, no one, not her mother or Raymond, none of her school friends or teachers, not even Jesse, suspected that she was *totally* vulnerable, that her admired qualities of resilience and self-reliance had been created or cultivated to mask what she considered a terrifying weakness. The entire structure of her public image – positive actions, confident responses, conspicuous achievements – all this had been engineered as carefully as a fortress and for the same purpose, to *protect* her, to surround her with a wall of energy and honour and excellence that would discourage criticism or attack.

Helen had been extremely successful in fashioning this elaborate structure; it had become, at last, a part of her. Technique had become reflex, contrivance and invention had become instinct. Even *she* sometimes believed, as those who knew her believed, that she was actually what she seemed to be, a gracious and stable, complete and unassailable person.

The serpent of fear, however, was not deceived. He lay coiled and sleeping inside her, secure in his ability to rouse himself and feed on her whenever he was hungry.

BOOK TWO

Chapter Four

1

However strong and specific her original reluctance had been towards a continuing correspondence or worse still, a face-to-face relationship with the Bradshaws, whatever her trepidations had been when Jesse proposed the trip to England, Helen found, as the departure day came near, that her curiosity and her sense of excitement, her anticipation of an experience that would be totally new to her, had begun to diminish her original negative feelings.

This excitement stayed with her through all the stages of their journey – the train trip from Chicago to New York, the ocean voyage itself a fresh and foreign adventure that nothing in her previous life had prepared her for – another train trip from Southampton to London, and after a night's stay in the station hotel, the final leg, by train again, north through Bedford, Leicester, Nottingham, York and Newcastle, and on to Morpeth. From there, then, by automobile, north and west to Wingate Fields.

Through every stage of this trip, her eyes and ears, all her senses, were fully occupied and stimulated by a pageant of newness, by colours and scents and flavours and textures that were unfamiliar and thrilling. But what would the ending be? When they reached their destination at last, when the doors opened and closed behind them and they found themselves, she and Jesse, at the end of the journey, boxed in and closely studied, when every detail of their physical and intellectual selves would be subject to perusal and inspection and silent judgments, how would she adjust to that, how would she handle it, what inner resources could she draw on, who could she turn to in a house of strangers who happened to be also her sudden relatives?

One thing she was sure of, as sure as she could be of anything. There would be endless questions about Raymond; there would certainly be no end to his family's curiosity about his time in America, how he had lived and where, what his days had been like, what *her* life had been like with him. And she would be expected also to be curious, to inquire about his boyhood and young manhood. She anticipated an endless back-and-forth flow of information and reminiscence about Raymond.

When she had first become aware of her father's family in England, when she was sensitive just after his death to what she deemed the deception about his life and his background, she wanted no such alien information, was anxious, in fact, *not* to have it. She was determined that *her* Raymond Bradshaw would be the only one. Now, however, now that she had accepted and in a sense ratified his other life by her agreement to visit Northumberland, she found that she also was eager for information and more than willing to supply it herself, to answer questions, show photographs, and search her memory for whatever scraps and remnants she could find which might give some joy and sense of completion to Raymond's mother and father and sister and perhaps, also, to her.

In short, in her own mind, with no pressure from anyone, she had capitulated to the situation, had turned away from her own needs and chosen to be and do the best she could to help quilt together the pieces of family fabric that Raymond had torn apart when he left England twenty years before.

Wingate Fields, the physical place, the approach, the long curving drive through corridors of ancient oaks, the endless meadows and orchards on all sides and the lavender hills to the north, were all that she had been led to expect from the letters and photographs she and Jesse had received.

At the same time, the house itself was something she could not possibly have envisioned. More spacious and extensive. More lavish and splendid. But warm and used and comfortable at the same time, all problems worked out generations before, all the household machinery functioning smoothly, each person, whether servant or master, keenly aware of his role, his functions and his responsibilities, content with his prescribed share of the estate labours, solid and sure in all his tasks. One sensed no disturbances below stairs, no contention or threatening voices. There was a spirit of community, of common traditions, values and work habits. And a striking atmosphere of order.

When they arrived, Helen and Jesse were not made to feel that special arrangements or provisions had been made for their coming. This was simply because no such arrangements were necessary. All services and comforts were a part of the house rhythm, all schedules of meals and work and recreation and leisure had been established and formalized through numberless generations. Once Mrs Bradshaw and her housekeeper had selected rooms for the guests and those rooms had been prepared, once their luggage had been carried in and unpacked, the daily and hourly routine of the house went forward as usual, altered only by the required number of extra places at table.

Wingate Fields, like the other great houses of the county, had, it seemed, an almost infinite capacity to accommodate. New sets of requirements, new tastes in food and linen, new sleeping and waking habits were stirred matter-of-factly into the pot-au-feu of the household. All gears meshed quietly and smoothly with no break in service, no loss of forward speed.

The residents of Wingate Fields, Angus and Louise, as well as their tributary Causeys, were skilled, each of them, in the arts of hospitality. If they seemed to go their individual ways after a genial and pleasantly organized welcoming session in the library, that, too was a part of custom. One allows one's guests to settle in, to get their bearings, to put themselves properly together before gathering again for a cream tea or drinks in the reception room

137

just off the dining-hall. It was a Bradshaw credo that their guests were required to conform in only the most general way. No surrender of independence or personal idiosyncrasy was necessary.

All this was welcomed by Helen. She had been afraid of being overdirected, too specifically or constantly entertained. Both she and Jesse were surprised to find that for the first several days, contrary to what they had anticipated, they were left, except for meal-times, quite to themselves. When they did come together for drinks or tea or at table, however, the atmosphere was splendidly cordial and warm, sometimes quite festive in character. Angus, a robust man of seventy-five, who for all his physical presence and sense of command seemed more a listener than a speaker, gave some hint of the family's position in relation to their guests in a toast that one suspected had been carefully written out and memorized.

Holding his glass up, having taken an unassailable position before the fireplace, and fixing Helen and Jesse in turn with an overpowering smile, he said, 'We welcome you again. We welcomed you upon your arrival and we will continue to welcome you and celebrate your presence for whatever length of time you are willing to share our home. It is truly your home too. Please know that. We consider you members of our family. You, Helen, by the most direct and precious blood connection, and you, Jesse, by our choice. We feel that Raymond regarded you as something between a son and a friend and we are proud to accept whatever share of that relationship you are willing to give us. We want you to feel at ease and to enjoy whatever we are able to provide. Your only obligation to us is that you should make your time in this house as pleasureful as you can. If being here is in any way as rewarding for you as *having* you here is rewarding for us, then it will be a fine summer, indeed, for us all. We want you to come to know us, each of us, the Bradshaws and the Causeys, in a natural, family way. So we will not try to organize you or educate you in the customs and quirks of Northumberland. We are all at your disposal, singly or

138

in groups, and as the days go by, we look forward, each of us, to spending many happy hours with each of *you*.'

Thus the tone was set. Whether that had been the intention of Angus' toast or not it did outline procedures in a way that seemed beneficial to everyone. The spectre of awkward group activities, of balls and parties and community gatherings was put to rest. No one would be placed on display or made to perform in any set of circumstances that might be either uncomfortable or embarrassing. In short, Helen and Jesse were free to do as they wished, go where they wished, and *be* what they wished.

Furthermore, Helen soon discovered that her exchanges of information about Raymond were to be other than imagined. There was in fact, certainly at the beginning of her stay, what seemed to be a kind of unspoken pact, a silent provision that his name would not be spoken at all except in the most general way. Louise, for example, *never* spoke to Helen, as two confiding people together, about Raymond. Nor did Angus, except on the occasion some weeks after her arrival when he took her for a fine luncheon, just the two of them, at a seventeenth-century inn in Newcastle and explained to her in detail the dimensions of her personal wealth.

In fact, during the three months she spent at Wingate Fields, only Clara and Nora spoke to her, in more intimate detail, about Raymond; only those two, especially Clara, made clear to her, at last, why Raymond had gone to America; and only those two, particularly Nora, seemed hungry for details about his life there.

Helen knew, however, because Clara told her, that Louise and Angus were also eager to know whatever they could find out about their son, that they hounded her to repeat carefully each grain of information she had gleaned from Helen. But they were unable, for reasons known only to themselves – some strange sense of honour or privacy or guilt perhaps – to speak directly to their granddaughter about their son, either to tell what they knew or to find out what they did not know.

Clara spent long hours with Jesse also, as did Nora,

patiently supplying missing pieces to him and hearing in return, details about Raymond that only Jesse knew. These facts, too, were passed along to Angus and Louise who were no more open with Jesse, on the subject of their son, than they were with Helen. Nora also told everything she learned to Hugh, who, like his grandparents, chose to be neither a primary source nor a direct recipient of information about Raymond.

Helen and Jesse, of course, as they strolled across the moors or sat on stone benches in the garden, diligently compared notes, withholding nothing from each other, until they came to feel, at last, that they had moved past the vernissage, and the portrait of Raymond was now complete. The afternoon when they decided, each of them, that the last area of the picture had finally been brushed in, Helen said, 'God, I feel awful. I can't tell you how miserable I feel. The more I find out the sadder it gets. He must have been the unhappiest man who ever lived.'

'Not at all,' Jesse said. 'You're looking through the wrong end of the telescope. You can't measure somebody's life by just looking at the bad stuff.'

'Raymond's life was all bad stuff.'

'No, it wasn't. It was bad and good. That's what *everybody* gets.'

'What was good about it?'

'You're not dumb, Helen. Use your head. If you think life is nothing but happy endings you're going to have a lot of surprises. Everybody *ends up* with nothing. It's what you get hold of along the way that matters. Raymond had a great childhood, a terrific education, he spent his work life doing something he loved doing, something he thought was important. He had a daughter he adored. He slept well every night. He loved to eat. He loved to drink. He loved horses and dogs and throwing a baseball in the back yard . . . .'

'What does all that have to do . . .'

'It has everything to do with it,' Jesse said. 'That's all there *is*. Raymond was *alive*. That's what I'm telling you. He *lived* his life. So some bad things happened to him.

140

That doesn't mean he had a miserable time of it. Nothing like it. You'll be lucky if you get half as much out of your life as Raymond got out of his.'

'I don't know what you're talking about.'

'I know you don't. But I like you anyway.'

'I don't want to die when I'm forty-one,' she said.

'Nobody does. But it's not as bad as being dead all your life. When Raymond was my age he'd been crazy in love with two women . . . .'

'You mean *one* woman.'

'No, I don't,' Jesse said. 'I mean *two*. You think just because your mother and dad broke up that means it was never any good to start with?'

'Oh, I guess he must have liked her at the beginning . . . .'

'Not just at the beginning. For a long time. And maybe right up to the end. Didn't you ever wonder why Raymond never got married again? He was only thirty-one when your mother left him.'

'Raymond wasn't dumb enough to love somebody who didn't love him.'

'What does that mean? *Everybody* loves somebody who doesn't love *them*.'

'Not me,' Helen said.

'Good for you. Maybe you'll be lucky.' He pulled her close to him, put his arms around her and kissed her on the forehead. 'Today is July the tenth, nineteen-nineteen. Twenty years from today let's have this conversation again. We'll see how you feel about it then.'

'In twenty years I'll be an old lady.'

'We'll talk about *that*, too. I'll say, "How does it feel to be an old lady of thirty-eight?" And we'll see what you have to say.'

'You think you're very smart and grown-up, don't you?'

'No. Not very smart and not very grown-up. But I know when I'm lucky.'

'You feel lucky now?' she said.

'I certainly do. Don't you?'

141

'You know I don't. I feel like I don't know where I'm going.'

'Who does? It's all surprises, Helen.'

'I don't believe that for a minute. And neither do you.'

'Oh, yes I do,' Jesse said. 'It's the only thing I'm really sure of.'

'I like to *plan* things, look ahead and figure things out. I mean I want to be in control of my life.'

'Everybody *wants* that. But nobody works it out that way. Nobody *I* know. And nobody *you* know either.'

'Well, *I'm* going to.'

Jesse held up three fingers and smiled. 'What does *that* mean?' Helen asked.

'Topic number three,' he said. 'That makes three things we have to talk about when we sit down for this meeting we're going to have in twenty years. Three big questions I'll ask you then. Have you ever loved anybody who didn't love you back, do you think of yourself as an old lady, and are you in full control of your life?'

'You know something?' she said. 'You're really a pain.'

'I wouldn't be surprised.'

2

It is a truism of animal behaviour that even the most docile creature can become a killer when his terrain is threatened, when his space is taken from him, when his cage becomes too crowded. Animals sense, it seems, that each new animal, even of one's own species, is a competitor, an intruder who is to be treated with suspicion and if necessary, punished with violence or death.

All histories of the human animal indicate that they are subject to the same tensions and pressures and are liable to react in the same violent manner when a castle or a cubicle that they have considered their own province is suddenly occupied by one or more alien bodies.

It would not have been surprising, therefore, however

142

benevolent the intentions, if the addition of Helen and Jesse to the mix of two ageing Bradshaws and four wildly varied adult Causeys had produced unforeseen frictions and aversions.

The fact that Helen *was* their blood relative, one fully-grown but never-before-seen, *that* fact in itself, their urging her to visit them notwithstanding, might have been a cause of discomfort and awkwardness. Her resemblance to Raymond could have been an upsetting factor or there could have been a silent disappointment that she did not resemble him *more*, either in appearance or in temperament. Within the confines of a family unit, a habit of dress, a style of coiffure, or the monotonous cadence of a particular voice can begin to colour all the other judgments of the person to whom that attribute is attached. There might have been a slow-to-surface resentment of the fact that Helen had refused for months to answer their letters or to acknowledge their existence as Raymond's family and hers. On arrival she could have been thought common or plain or too proud. Her Italian blood could have been thought to be a poor mix with the blood of the Bradshaws. All sorts of deficiencies and inadequacies, real or imagined, could have been silently fastened to her image by her new-discovered family.

Jesse was even more subject to potential disfavour. Without a blood relationship to give him stature and a reason for being, he could have been truly without either shield or armour. His relationship to Raymond could have been misconstrued in all sorts of ways. Likewise his relationship to Helen. Many of his actions and motives were subject to question. Why would a young man who was not in fact an orphan, choose to become one? Why would he allow himself to become a kind of foster child? Should his account of his service in the war be believed? Was a stiff knee or what seemed to be a stiff knee truly evidence of a battlefield injury? And as much as they had welcomed, at the time, his letters to them, why, in retrospect had *he* chosen to correspond with them when in fact it was Helen they were anxious to contact? Although they

143

were aware that his motives had been described as selfless, that he had wanted only to be a temporary bridge between them and Helen until she was ready and able to see the situation in proper balance, they might, all the same, have come to question those motives. Although they had provided the steamship ticket that had brought him to England, at least one of them might have quarrelled with his quick willingness to use it. Although their offers of hospitality had been forceful and attractive, they could have questioned his eagerness to accept. Even his friendliness and affability could have been held suspect. Was it possible that he liked them, all of them, as much as he seemed to? And if not, why did he pretend? What motive could he have?

In fact and in practice, none of these potential lesions and discomforts took place. Perhaps, in part, because of the social ground rules that Angus seemed to have put down in his toast of welcome, but more probably because the residents of Wingate were, by nature, more separate than cohesive, more inclined than most families to live their disparate lives, albeit under a common roof; because each of them made individual contacts with either Helen or Jesse and engaged in individual conversations, each of them also made separate judgments and assessments.

This is not to say that Nora and Hugh never exchanged confidences or that Clara's views were unknown to Ned or to Louise, but by and large, the accepted family habits obtained. Each of them kept, for the most part, his or her own counsel; they made choices based on their individual standards. There was, in their home, seldom a consensus; there was no such thing as a *family* decision or a group choice. Each of them chose or decided for themselves and implemented their decisions in whatever style best suited them.

So it was in their relations with Helen and Jesse. All of them made their own judgments, incorporating various shades of acceptance and denial, and tended to keep the results to themselves. The conclusions, however, for the most part, were positive ones. Each of the Bradshaws and the Causeys tended to approve of Helen and Jesse just as Helen and Jesse approved of each of them. No aversions surfaced, no arguments took place, and each relationship seemed free to languish or develop as it might choose.

As her letters had indicated, Clara was the true centre of the clan, both by nature and by choice. This had always been the case. Even as a young girl she had interceded between her parents and her brother. When he defied his tutor or offended their nanny, it was Clara who served as liaison, who presented each adversary's case to the other. She was thought, even then, to be fair and even-handed although all parties understood, and seemed to accept the circumstance, that whatever rivalries existed between the two children they always closed ranks when threatened by an adult or an outsider. Clara, in such situations, was particularly inclined to make judgments that favoured Raymond.

When she had her own children she continued her role of philosopher queen, explaining Hugh and Nora to Ned, and explaining Ned to his son and daughter. And there was the continuing task of advising tolerance to Angus and patience to Ned. Angus, for whom a day never passed that he didn't curse his ill fortune because the Bradshaw line would end when he died, secretly considered Ned a disappointment. 'He can't see beyond tomorrow,' he told Louise. 'That might be all right if he had courage. But he has no courage either. Still he's all we have. And after Ned comes Hugh. God help us.'

Ned, even though he didn't know Angus' assessment of him, suspected that something was amiss. Complaining to Clara, he attributed it to her father's age. 'He's not himself. It must be that he's failing somehow. Veins tightening up on him, that sort of thing. Can't delegate authority, you see. That's the size of it. Keeps me away from the business in London as though I was fit for nothing but stable chores. I've had a hand in managing the lands here and all the tenants and the sheep farmers for twenty years. I know that end of it as well as I know my own name. But he still looks over my shoulder as if I were the last boy hired.

145

Damned tiresome, I'll tell you that. Rotten way to treat a person.'

Clara's role had been particularly crucial after Raymond's disappearance. Feeling the loss more profoundly perhaps than any member of the family, it fell to her, nonetheless, to console and reassure, to buoy up the hopes of her parents long past the point when she herself had lost hope, to place a positive sheen on every surface, to see around corners, to try to persuade each person, in their turn, that the blame, if indeed there was *any* blame to be assigned, was not theirs. She truly held the house and its occupants together in those slow and painful months up till the time when Angus came back from his Boston search. After that there was no role for her to play, no room for reassurance, no place for any kindness except silence. She watched her mother and father pull back slowly into the darkness and knew that beyond her ability to function as before, at least on the surface, with the servants, with her children, with her clubs and charities, she could do nothing for them.

Nothing touched her, crippled her, wounded her, however, as much as the sense of her own failure towards Raymond. Of all people, she realized too late, she was the one who should have been his ally, right or wrong. No matter what the difficulties. She was the only one who could have made real contact with him, the only one in the family who had easy access also to Emily, and most important, she was without question, the only living soul who might possibly have influenced Angus; the only one who had the will and the guile to make him think twice, to reconsider, even perhaps to reverse himself, to change his mind. But she had done nothing. Totally immersed in her own affairs, in her own marriage, in her husband, but most of all in her fascination with herself as a newly emerged adult, as a bride, as the mistress of her own life, she had done nothing to help Raymond. She had sat, like a lady in a wide hat at a cricket match, and waited for the final score to be posted.

So to Clara, the prospect of meeting Helen, of coming to know her, of being her aunt and her friend, was a

146

welcome opportunity to redeem herself. If her sins of omission could be atoned for she was determined that they would be.

From their first moments together, she and Helen were drawn to each other. Just as Helen saw something of Raymond in his sister, Clara saw in Helen all that was left in the world of her brother. She was wise enough to relate to Helen, not as she would have normally to someone her daughter's age, but as a *woman*, as she would have related to someone closer to her own age. Helen responded to this and the two women met in the centre, somewhere halfway between Clara's forty-three years and Helen's eighteen.

In the unstructured pattern of coming and going that Angus had recommended and which was indeed the prevalent rhythm at Wingate, only Clara and Helen established a routine which brought them together at least once every day. They walked together, took long drives together, and sat in the morning-room after breakfast doing needlepoint. They talked and laughed like long-separated sisters who had a limited time together before some circumstance would separate them again.

It was Clara, key witness to Raymond's pleasures and follies, who told Helen the story of his childhood and youth, filling in details that she had only indicated in her letters. Without a preconceived plan, without knowing, in fact, before meeting Helen, *what* she would say to her, how *much* she would say, or *how* she would say it, she allowed the subject, as the days went by, to find *her*, let the facts and the fun, the surprises and the foolishness of Raymond's growing up unfold at its own pace.

And when it came to the unhappy termination of Raymond's time at Wingate Fields, when his history had been recounted up to the date of his twentieth birthday and the party that marked that occasion, it was Clara, of course, who carefully told Helen all there was to tell about Raymond and Emily, how Angus had tried to separate them permanently but had failed, and how it had all ended at last in the Pembroke Inn at Holyhead.

As Helen took up the story from that point, telling as

147

much as she was able about Raymond's life in America, including the past he had fabricated, as the two women exchanged information about brother and father, as they put together an almost complete, three-dimensional portrait that had been unavailable to either of them before they began to talk together, they established at the same time a bond between themselves.

Just as Clara fought against any impulse to compare Helen with Nora, so did Helen never allow herself to wish that she might have had such a mother. All the same these thoughts rustled about in each of their brains and could not be totally stifled. The fact was that these two women had, from the start, an elemental contact, a kind of connection of the spirit, that could not be ignored. They quite simply *understood* each other, *liked* each other, enjoyed each other's presence. Some common genetic colour scheme existed in each of them; they were two lovely panels of a triptych of which the third section had been Raymond.

Any lingering reservations Helen might have had about her decision to come to England vanished totally as she came to know Clara. Because of her she felt at home at Wingate Fields. Because of her, Helen's connections with Angus and Louise and Ned, and with Nora, became smoother and stronger. Only with Hugh did she have no rapport at all. Hardly any conversation or contact. At family gatherings he sat, dark and silent, his eyes on the glass in his hand or fixed on some spot in the middle distance, never making eye contact with her, never joining in the general conversation.

If they met by chance in the house or in the gardens, and it happened very seldom, Hugh was cordial but solemn, almost mute, and always most anxious to be on his way. Within two weeks of her arrival Helen had concluded that he felt some resentment towards her or that he simply disliked her. If she had been told then that when she left Wingate Fields, suddenly and unannounced, very much as her father had done, it would be, at least in part, because of Hugh, she would have thought of that as an impossibility.

But she did leave, with no word to Jesse, near the sultry end of August, delivered herself to Liverpool, as Raymond had done, and booked passage on the first steamer departing for America.

Convinced that she had no other choice, wedged into what seemed to be an escape-proof corner, she did, under the circumstances, all she *could* do. Feeling abandoned by Jesse, angry with him in a way she had never imagined she *could* be, she had no qualms about leaving him behind, about making plans that did not include him. In fact, the notion that her leaving might cause him some discomfort did not disturb her at all. Quite the contrary, it gave her a kind of vengeful pleasure that was a new experience for her. Knowing nothing heretofore of male and female combat she found herself suddenly in two very different battles, one with Jesse, the other with herself. As she stood on the ship's deck, watching Liverpool harbour grow dim to the east, she felt she had lost badly in one battle but had won perhaps a moral triumph in the other.

3

Early in the summer, long before Helen's sudden flight, when she and Jesse were just beginning to know and be known by the Bradshaws and the Causeys, there was no hint of what was to come, no indication at all, it seemed, that anything other than *politesse* and good fellowship would prevail. In this summer meeting of family members, eight adults, all but one of them connected to at least one of the others by blood-lines, in a benevolent situation untainted by vengeance, passion or commerce there was no possibility, it seemed, for turbulence or despair or even substantial surprise.

This is not to imply that these weeks that concern us, from June to early September, ended in bloodshed or adultery or arson. No such theatrical events transpired. But all the same, stones were dropped in still ponds, winds changed direction, and each of the eight people who spent those days at Wingate Fields, either as performer or as witness, discovered, either just then or a bit later, that there were subtle new turns now in all the paths and lanes they knew, new gradings on the slopes, alteration in the stream beds. What had been would still be, of course, in some ways, and what would be would surely have strong and visible links to what had gone before. But each of them knew the best of what had been would never really be again. Never precisely and never totally. Two strangers had entered the household or, in reverse, two people had entered a strange household, and when they left it, they would leave it changed. And they would be changed themselves.

It is unfair, inaccurate also perhaps, to say that one impulse, one action, or one person served as the firing mechanism, that everything that followed was somehow a result of that single person's cosmic path. But all the same, as one sorts through the emotional evidence, it is difficult to ignore the fact of Nora, almost impossible not to conclude that though she was certainly not responsible for all the changing tides of that summer, hers was the impulse that caused the first currents to move beneath the surface.

In retrospect, everything she felt and did was, if not inevitable, at least understandable. Although Nora was very knowing for her years, she was, after all, only nineteen and all her adult conclusions had been founded on local experience. She was a daughter of the gentry, a child of the county, socially adept in her own milieu, a cherished and sought-after young woman in her own corner of Northumberland. But she was acutely aware that there was a vast field of action, a great community of deft and graceful people who lived wonderfully self-indulgent lives in beautifully sculptured cities she had never seen.

London, of course, she *had* seen. In her lifetime she had visited it perhaps a dozen times. But always as a daughter, as a chaperoned young lady in the company of her parents, visiting places that interested them or places that were thought to be enlightening or educational for her and her

150

brother. Patiently she had suffered the National Gallery, the Albert Hall, and the British Museum, longing all the while for the supper clubs, hotel grills and ballrooms, the names of which she had memorized after reading about them in the illustrated papers that Hugh pilfered from the servants' pantry.

Paris and Rome and New York also bubbled in her imagination. She knew numberless superficial and not quite respectable details about many cities like Deauville and St Moritz and Lugano where aimless people went to be frivolous together. All of these places were filed in her mind as future inevitabilities. But her immediate goal was London.

Among the families she knew, Nora had been the first young woman to cut her hair. She had done it herself after seeing just such a cut in an illustrated fashion paper. Her father had been shocked and her grandparents had been scandalized but she had ridden out the storm, flashing her shorn and shaggy locks like a coronet, delighted to be pointed out and labelled dangerous, sunning herself warmly in the admiration of her girl friends, confident that her new appearance brought her, somehow, a step closer to London.

But a year had gone past, her hair had grown out and had been recut many times, and other young women had followed her example; short hair was no longer either a novelty or a scandal in Northumberland. And still Nora languished in her family's house, rode her horse recklessly, drove her roadster dangerously, and behaved indiscreetly with at least two of her brother's friends. But London was as far away as ever. 'Plenty of time for you to go to London and act like a fool after you're married,' her father said.

Once she persuaded Hugh to take her with him to London and twice she made it all the way by herself. But each time her father, as soon as she was missed, called ahead and had her intercepted as she got off the train at the Great Northern terminus. Chaperoned by a woman from the Bradshaw London offices, she was brought directly home, back to Wingate Fields.

151

At last, grudgingly, she came to accept her father's judgment as the truth. She would never get to London to stay, would never sample that delicious life until her husband took her there. With this in mind, three months before Helen and Jesse arrived in England, Nora allowed herself to become engaged to Edmund Bick, a friend of her brother who knew her well, who drank even more recklessly than Hugh did, but who, when he was sober, truly adored Nora.

Clara thought it was a sorry match, believed that Edmund was one-dimensional and potentially cruel, but hoped for the best. Knowing her daughter's weaknesses and proclivities, Clara did not believe that marriage would serve her but she hoped it would at least distract her for a time. Hugh, to everyone's surprise, opposed the engagement. He became impossibly drunk the night it was announced and threatened, just before he passed out in the entrance hall, to punish Edmund with his riding-crop. 'I don't understand you,' Nora said to him when he woke up the following afternoon, whimpering for a whiskey and soda, 'Edmund's your best friend.'

'Yes, he is. But that doesn't mean I want him in the family. If you want to thrash about with him in his touring car that's up to you, I suppose. But don't do something *really* immoral by *marrying* the man. He's capable of being a bloody fool and he'll make you bloody miserable.'

'If he's such a fool, how can he . . . .'

'How can he be my friend? That's a child's question. Fools make the very best friends. They never disappoint you. You expect nothing and you *get* nothing. On the other hand they are eternally grateful to you because you *tolerate* them. Show me a better recipe than that for friendship.'

'You're frightful, Hugh,' she said. But she laughed as she said it. 'And you're growing worse every day. I pity the woman who marries you.'

'So do I. She'll be leading her geese to a poor market.'

When Nora had begun writing to Jesse in America with a concentration that was unlike her, her mother suspected that, in spite of her recently announced engagement, she

152

was permitting herself additional options. Knowing her daughter to be both reckless and impatient, Clara would not have been surprised, on Jesse's arrival, especially when he turned out to be amenable, civilized, and pleasant to look at, would not have been surprised at all if Nora had behaved outrageously, if she had carried him away to the forest forthwith in her jaunty roadster.

When Nora presented herself as a proper maiden, as the unwed, untarnished daughter of the manor, Clara was pleased but astonished. With shining hair and well-scrubbed cheeks, wearing her most girlish frocks, Nora glided about, poured tea, played the piano sweetly when asked, and deferred to everyone, including Jocko, the family spaniel, a creature she had previously despised. Having not been warned about his sister's proposed transformation, Hugh pulled her aside one morning after she had been particularly cloying and unrecognizable at breakfast and said, 'What the hell has come over you? You're disgusting.'

'Don't spoil my fun,' she giggled. 'I'm having a frolic. I'm being *good*.'

The truth was she had decided to feel her way. In spite of the quite acceptable quality of Jesse's letters she was not sure what she might encounter when he appeared in person. He might turn out to be a tiresome academic or a frontier misfit or God-knows-what. But just in case he was something splendid she decided she should appear to be something other than herself until she was sure of her ground. If he proved to be hopeless she would revert at once to type. If, however, he seemed worth cultivation and pruning, if he responded to her – and it never occurred to her that he would not – she would gradually reveal herself, shedding one veil at a time, until he came to know that she was something quite unlike the pretty little Causey daughter and Bradshaw grandchild he had met on his arrival.

Nora did not, however, expect to be disappointed. It is hard to imagine what combination of physical misfortunes and character flaws Jesse would have had to present in order to discourage her. She had, in a very real sense, in spite of what she told herself, prejudged him and found him acceptable, all based on one simple circumstance. He was an *outsider*. He had *been* somewhere. From his letters she knew he had seen Chicago and New York and San Francisco. He had gone to France and fought in a war. He had been wounded and survived. He had freedom of movement, for God's sake, *that* most appealing of all conditions, the thing she needed and longed for most ardently. He was a different person from a different country, far-off and exciting and strange. In her society and that of her family, in their county, all one's friends were lifetime friends, all the names and faces were familiar to a fault.

It was characteristic of the gentry that they were rooted to the land; they thought their home acres were not only the finest and most beautiful and bountiful place to be, they were the *only* place to be. Pleasure was to be found at home. Only commerce would take a man to London or to the Continent or to America. And for his family there was no reason whatever to leave the estate except perhaps to visit a neighbouring estate. All bounty was there and at home, all comfort, all family, all pleasure. Only the known and familiar were acceptable. Families of less than fifty years residence in the county, and they were rare indeed, were still considered transient and untried.

These community icons, however, were totally unacceptable to Nora. Such values and standards she associated with another century. She had an indescribable hunger for tomorrow. Only the new or even the *prospect* of the new were stimulating to her. And Jesse, whatever else he might turn out to be, would be *new*.

Then, of course, there was the link with Raymond. Next to meeting Raymond himself, looking at him, listening to his voice, and touching him, Nora could envision nothing more provocative, more fulfilling, than having the chance to see and know this man who *had* known him, had spent long hours with him, had lived in his home.

When she thought about Raymond, and she certainly

154

did that, almost every day, the details of his entwinement with Emily always came first and lingered longest. Those months, those events, those follies *defined* them and they would continue to for as long as people lived who knew the facts or who knew someone who knew them. Nora had fed on the romance and heartbreak of Raymond and his tragedy since she was eight years old. The photographs and mementoes, the stories and rumours and speculations were finger-tip familiar to her, but always fresh somehow. And just as all those elements defined Raymond, her relationship to him, she felt, defined *her*. Having no true access to his values or his feelings, she believed, nonetheless, that she did have such access; she felt as though she had perused his private diaries – and peered inside his soul where no one else could see. She did not believe in communications from the dead to the living but if she had held such beliefs she would certainly have expected to have daily conversations with Raymond.

As she grew up, as the sensual aspects of Raymond's legend were not totally replaced, but were diffused somewhat by the emergence of those elements in her own life; as she *became* what she had for so long fantasized about, Raymond took over a different role for her. The fact of his affair with Emily seemed less important than what it had stimulated him to do. He had *escaped* – magic word to Nora – he had buttoned himself tight inside himself, cut connections with everything he had sprung from, all he had known and experienced up to then, and raced off into the darkness, never looking back, longing back, or coming back.

This image became clear and specific in Nora's consciousness. It became, in fact, the more she railed internally against the strictures of Wingate Fields, the central image of her day-to-day existence.

Trying to plot her course, planning endlessly her own escape, wishing to God she were a man, she referred constantly to Raymond, tried to draw parallels between his circumstances and her own; failing that, she simply cursed her lack of courage and looked for solutions outside herself.

Her engagement to Edmund had been an attempt at such a solution and she held on to it like a crucial card in a game of whist. But it was a card she expected never to play.

Of all the members of her family, it was Nora who was most keyed up about the arrival of Helen and Jesse. Linking the event to her own frustrations in ways that made no sense even to her, she had magnified and hand-coloured the proceedings to such an extent that they had, at least for her, totally lost their original purpose and definition.

Helen, for example, had been almost completely painted out of Nora's projections. She was seen as a female cousin and nothing more. Suffering from what she thought of as a surfeit of family, Nora was not enthusiastic about the addition of still one more, particularly a young woman near her own age.

Jesse, however, as we have seen, was another matter. Nora's curiosity about him was enormous and her hopes were high. But when he arrived at last, when he stepped down from the car on the gravel outside the south portico, she was disappointed. Not in what she saw but in what she failed to see. In his clothing which was conservative and almost British in appearance and in his manner which seemed careful and quiet and well-bred, she saw nothing at all that was strange or foreign or unusual. No high energy visible. No signs of stubbornness or anger. Not a hint of rebellion apparent in his nature. Except for his speech, he could have been a young neighbour who had driven over from his family home in Haltwhistle to spend a pleasant country afternoon. He was, or appeared to be, the thing that Nora abhorred most of all . . . *proper*.

What she had forgotten, of course, was that she herself had temporarily made herself over for the occasion, had made *herself* seem proper also. It was only after she abandoned that masquerade, when after the first few days she gave up her flower-girl manner and her milkmaid frocks and went back gradually to her own chic and often daring wardrobe, when she re-entered her own skin and became her own iconoclastic who-gives-a-damn self, that she got a truer picture of Jesse.

156

By then, he had put on a tweed lounge suit and had pulled back noticeably from the ultra-polite, rather formal mien she had observed on his arrival. He seemed taller, suddenly, and lankier, his hair was often tousled, and his speech, as he relaxed, became more distinctly American mid-west. 'He looks a bit like those cowboys we saw in the cinema in Newcastle,' Hugh said one afternoon. 'Put a big hat on him and a coil of rope in his hand and he'd pass as a proper wild west actor.'

Jesse looked nothing like an actor, of course, neither the cowboy type nor any other. There was, in fact, nothing remarkable about his appearance. He was not even remarkably plain. But he had flat cheeks, and long legs and though Hugh's vision of him was off the mark it gave Nora an image she needed, something to help her see him as fresh and unusual and exciting, to help her regain the enthusiasm she had felt before he arrived.

Once she had made the necessary readjustments, once she had altered her first impression of him she found that *nothing* about him displeased her. His quiet manner became for her a model of masculine behaviour, his uneven features and wilful hair seemed far more attractive to her than the chiselled beauty of Edmund Bick.

So Nora's decision was made. She would choose Jesse. To what end she was not certain. How it would start, what exactly might transpire and how it would either end or develop she did not know. Nor did she know how she would deal with Edmund. Or how she would deal with Jesse, when he inquired about Edmund. She simply knew that the obstacles which had existed in her mind had been dissolved or removed. She saw before her a succulent summer with a new and unknown man in residence in her house.

Although her instincts were, and had always been, predatory, her manner gave little hint of that. Young as she was, she had been hungrily interested in men since the age of fifteen and perhaps because of that interest, in addition to her unusual off-the-mark beauty, men had been interested in *her*.

157

Her instinct had told her, and experience had proved it, that however strong her impulse to pursue, it was absolutely necessary that she turn and flee. And if that flight went unnoticed, one must reappear, then flee again. And continue to flee until the quarry turned pursuer.

She had no intention of modifying this technique in any way. Considering Jesse, however, she realized that there were additional factors to cope with. For one thing, he was a guest of her parents and grandparents. Perhaps that would inhibit him. Also, as noted, there was Edmund. She had no plan to abandon Edmund until the proper time came, if indeed it *ever* came. So care must be taken and deftness employed. She decided at last to deal with Jesse's reluctance only when that reluctance surfaced.

In matters of passion, Nora, like her brother, was not given to patience. She did not consider it a virtue. In fleeing, she contrived to be pursued and, when pursued, caught. With Jesse, however, though it rankled, she was forced to admit that a more deliberate rhythm was required. So she resolved to become his friend, to befriend him, to flee, as it were, in a stationary position, to be seen as a discontented young woman who was not available and to become by some circuitous process available at last. An act of God. A stroke of lightning. A surprise to them both.

In addition to the factors we have examined, Nora, in her pursuit of Jesse, was fuelled by another consideration. Her apathy towards Helen, the vaguely negative and dimly-focused feelings she'd had when her cousin was several thousand miles away, turned, once they'd met, to something more specific.

Nora made no secret of her preference for the company of men. It was family lore that since babyhood she had preferred the attentions of Angus and Ned to those of Louise and Clara, and Hugh was, without question, her most intimate friend. But all the same, women liked her. There was something about her light-hearted irresponsibility that they found intriguing. Some of the women of the county were not absolutely sure they respected her and some of them cautioned their daughters not to emulate her, but almost all of them, in one way or another, envied her. Even those who did not covet her freedom could not help admiring the way she assumed it and flew it above her head like a scarlet banner.

Although she was bound to her family as were all the young women of her station and although that bondage, as we have seen, was painful to her, among the women she knew, other than her mother and her grandmother, she never referred to it. She preferred people to believe that she was as wildly free as she seemed.

Also, in a community where people, women especially, were brought up to speak harshly of no one, Nora had a famously liberated mouth. She did not use profanity or blasphemous language. She was more subtle than that. She had managed, as early as the age of sixteen, to turn gentle character assassination into a fine art. She ticked off the flaws and foibles of other women's husbands in a flippant way that they themselves would have not dared but which made them laugh till the tears came.

Although she was a gifted mimic and satirist she leavened every remark and observation with a good humour that dulled the barb and diluted the poison. Whenever she sensed that she had gone too far she was quick to take refuge in self-deprecation, to say things about herself and her own failings that were far more outrageous than her comments about others had been; thus she exonerated and endeared herself at one stroke.

It was true that she had few truly intimate women friends. But there were no women of her acquaintance who did not invite her and none who did not mention to friends that she *had* been invited and had accepted the invitation. Even her romantic peccadillos were more envied than censured. Anyone who criticized this area of her life was quickly reminded that she had never been seen to cast a sidelong glance at another woman's husband or the fiancés of any of her friends. 'There's a bit of lunacy about Nora,' one of her mother's friends said, 'but all the same she has her own standards. I suspect we'll see many young women

159

like her in the next few years. The war has changed us all and our young people most profoundly.'

So Nora's reaction to Helen was not an automatic one. In fact it didn't crystallize at once. Not at all. The period of time that passed between the arrival of Helen and Jesse and the day when Nora turned right round and decided that he was a garland worth wearing was the precise amount of time it took her to decide that she was not uncontrollably fond of Helen.

Did she suspect that the two of them, for all their brother and sister camaraderie, might be, in fact, something other than they seemed? Of course she did. But since she had been *told* something else, she felt guiltless as she studied Jesse carefully and planned his summer in her mind.

If Nora's interest in Jesse was, or seemed to be, dispassionate and calculating, her brother Hugh's reaction to Helen was cut from a totally different bolt of cloth. Had he been a different sort of person, one whose feelings were more visible, any attentive onlooker would have concluded, without hesitation, that this dark and surly young man had been unmistakably smitten. If his features had mirrored the unfamiliar sensation he felt at the pit of his stomach he would have become, undoubtedly, a figure of either fun or pity.

Hugh, like Nora, had based all his judgments on a small area of experience. The men and women he had known in his twenty-two years seemed to fit neatly into one of less than half a dozen familiar categories. Surprise did not typify the social milieu he had grown up in, departures from the norm were neither encouraged nor applauded.

Mating, also, was severely circumscribed. A few of the sons and daughters of Northumberland did marry outside the county but very few. Occasionally a second or third son who had no claim on his father's lands would bring a wife home from North Riding or Cheshire but the elder sons almost always found their wives among the local gentry. In such cases her dowry would be land; it need not be adjacent to the acreage of the groom's family, but if it was she was a particularly good choice for wife.

160

Such traditions meant that a young man, by the age of sixteen, had almost certainly met his future wife; he had probably known her, through various county social events, since he was ten or even younger. This is not to say that he had no marital choices. He did. But of any given vintage there were rarely more than half a dozen young women, often fewer, whose economic and personal qualifications made them marriage candidates for the well-placed elder son of a substantial family. When the time came for such a young man to marry the list had usually narrowed, because of natural selection, attrition, or intricate inter-family negotiations.

The suspense, therefore, for someone like Hugh, was minimal. Although he accepted very few strictures from either Angus or his father, he knew that his financial future, which to him meant the freedom to live in an extravagant manner with no effort expended, was at least partially dependent on his marrying advantageously, probably a young woman who had been selected for him. In his particular case, he suspected that it would be Patricia Goodpastor, Victoria Weeks, or Mary Elizabeth Cecil. As far as Hugh was concerned they were interchangeable, one as good as the next. This judgment, although cynical, was also factual. These three, as well as the other young women of the county, certainly the ones whose families were acceptable to Hugh's family, did indeed resemble each other. They had all been brought up in like circumstances, had received similar educations, and lived in family surroundings which were so like as to be duplicates. From constant exposure to each other and to few other people, their tastes in clothing, their speech and their mannerisms seemed identical. Although their separate genetic heritages might have been expected to make them physically distinctive, the fact was that their affectations, their gait, their rhythms and gestures were so similar that they began at last, by the age of eighteen or nineteen, to truly look alike, act alike, and *be* alike.

It is likely that Hugh's attitudes towards women and his behaviour towards them was connected, in a very direct

161

way, with this stiff and sterile sameness that seemed to characterize the women he had been exposed to since childhood. He did not, however, include his mother or Nora in this group. His admiration for them, in fact, made it even more difficult for him to admire the lesser females of his acquaintance.

His reputation, therefore, as a rake and a womanizer, was earned, to a large degree, outside the social climate he had grown up in and into which he would certainly marry. There had been, of course, whispers about his visits to a certain widow. And Patricia Goodpastor's aunt who was generally known to be unhappy in her marriage to an arthritic and alcoholic tyrant, had confessed to several of her friends that she had received Hugh in her summerhouse.

Apart from these limited forays however, Hugh, when confined to his home territory, behaved admirably. Although he was considered a threat to the county maidens, a fact which titillated the maidens in question, in practice he treated them in a gentlemanly manner which was either exemplary or disappointing, depending on whose viewpoint was solicited. He behaved this way not because he was a gentleman but because those particular young ladies were boring to him, more boring than he could begin to describe.

Like many men with choices, both before his time and since, he found his entertainment elsewhere, far afield, away from the nest. From the age of sixteen he cultivated a taste for harlots, tavern women, and young serving girls. They existed in abundance, he found, for men of a certain age with certain appetites, especially if those men were personable, if they drove fine carriages or motorcars, and carried a full purse.

It was not simply a question of paying for his pleasure and being done with it. He genuinely enjoyed the company of these lesser creatures. They were all the products of hard circumstances but apart from that common feature, they were as unlike as women could be. By the standards he knew their speech was atrocious but the words they

162

spoke, the expressions they used, the ways they revealed themselves, were personal and unusual.

They were not self-conscious about accepting money. In a world swollen with commerce they had only one commodity to sell, and having chosen that course they put it out of their minds, it seemed. Once an arrangement was made and a deal was struck, no further thought was given to it. From that point forward, it was a structured social engagement, each party intent on having an absolutely glorious and memorable romp. 'It's one thing if a gentleman wants to give me a bit of money. My hand's as quick as the next girl's. But if he don't show me a jolly time, he'll have to hand his silver to some other dolly the next time round. A good-time girl is one thing. A common whore is another sort altogether.'

As unlike as these girls were in their appearance, in their ages, in spirit, in religion, in the range of their past misfortunes, they shared one tantalizing trait. They laughed. They were laughers. In the world that Hugh came from laughter was rationed, held suspect somehow. Polite laughter was expected after polite jokes, young girls giggled nervously, and men, in their smokers or billiard rooms, laughed derisively at political figures or at a rival's failed business venture; very occasionally, if a particularly outrageous or ribald joke was told, a genuine shout of laughter could be heard through the heavy oak doors. But uncontrolled laughter was thought to be as tasteless as anything else that was uncontrolled. Once one left small childhood and began classes, laughter was no longer considered a legitimate expression of joy. Like conversation in a public reading-room it brought hostile stares and hushing noises.

These friends of Hugh, however, these pink-cheeked, ale-quaffing sparrows and waifs, seemed to survive on laughter. They laughed at the past and the present, at good fortune and bad. Walking, sitting, dancing, drinking, in bed or at table, they found things to laugh about. They laughed at themselves, at life itself, and thus made it better than it was. When they laughed at Hugh it was a new

163

experience for him; at last when he began to understand this new language they taught him to laugh at himself. This young man who prided himself on his cold grey eyes and his expressionless face, who was noted for his frown, occasionally fell into a frothy pond of laughter, of senseless hilarity for its own sake. It unsettled him, made him uncomfortable, and at the same time gave him the greatest, unnameable delight he had known in his life. But it was something he felt he could not carry home. Like the trans-ports of opium, one had to go to the place where that pleasure was made available. Only there in the dim light and the moist heat were such dreams to be had.

For all his rebellion, then, Hugh remained, at the time of Jesse's and Helen's arrival, as compartmentalized and restrained as the society he told himself he was rebelling against. He was a child of privilege and it had made indel-ible marks on him as it does on all those who are so cursed. Though he scoffed at his wealth, he depended on it. Though he pretended to detest the values of his family and their friends he fully intended to marry an acceptable woman with similar values, bring her to Wingate Fields and spend the rest of his days there. With regular side-trips of course, to places where laughter could be heard. And when all else failed, as it surely would, his cut-glass decanters of whiskey would see him through.

So there he was, at the age of twenty-two. He knew himself; for all his flaws and his needs, he knew how the flaws could be concealed and the needs gratified. For an imperfect world he had fashioned an imperfect philosophy. But it pleased and gratified him as much as anything pleased him. Like an ugly, ill-trained but sturdy riding horse, it would serve him, he felt, keep him moving, get him through. Carrying with him a surfeit of self-satisfaction and not a shred of contentment, he was that most common of God's creatures, a man forging strongly ahead on the wrong road, all his problems solved, all his choices made. No detours contemplated, no advice sought or welcomed.

What likelihood might there be that such a man, so elaborately wrong-headed and determined to stay that

164

way, a man so dependent on the permanence and reliability of each of his survival categories, could be nudged off course and caused to question himself, could in the matter of a few days dare to venture, if only in his own thoughts, that perhaps it wasn't inevitable that one must settle for a bit of this and a bit of that, that it might be possible to put everything together, have it all, under one's own roof, that maybe, by some miracle, a particular person, a particular woman, could catch up all his wayward strands and knit him firmly together.

These fantasies, this craziness, did not overpower Hugh the moment he saw Helen step down from the car. At that time he only admitted to himself that she was not what he had expected. But as the days passed, as he watched her, listened to her talk, and heard her free-floating American laugh from all corners of the house, he knew without question that many things he knew he wanted but had never seen before had indeed come together in this one eighteen-year-old woman. Tiny private souvenirs he carried in his mind, the finest qualities of a dozen different women, he saw or imagined he saw repeated in Helen, small things that could not be described or codified but which had meaning for him.

Never having experienced a non-physical, truly loving impulse towards a specific woman, having always been, at least to some degree, an objective observer, he lost now all vestiges of objectivity and allowed his senses and his desires and his imagination to lead him wherever they chose. The ensuing few days were the most ecstatic period of his life. Without speaking to Helen except in the most matter-of-fact way, without their walking together or touching, he experienced what seemed to him a lifetime of wishes granted and needs fulfilled.

For much of this time Hugh took his meals in his rooms, sat there drinking by himself, and lived, in his imagination, a rich, full life. At last he went to bed and slept for twenty-four hours. When he woke up, he dressed without shaving, walked downstairs, crossed the gravel path to

165

the garages, backed his car out, and drove west towards Newcastle.

At the foot of the stairs, in the reception hall, he had passed Helen; they passed close enough to touch. But he didn't look at her or speak to her.

4

Both Helen and Jesse, before they had learned, bit by bit, what had taken place prior to Raymond's departure for America, both of them had assumed, they had in fact discussed it, that there was a father-son conflict somewhere at the bottom of things. Youth versus authority. The brief, rather terse letters Angus had written to them in Fort Beck tended to bear this out. So they suspected that he would be the difficult hurdle, the thorny patch in the Bradshaw family. Although they knew too little about any of the family members to be eager to meet them, they were least eager, they concluded, to meet Angus.

Their first meeting with him did nothing to contradict those earlier suspicions. He was not an unattractive man, quite the contrary. He was rough-hewn and square-rigged, looking more like a prosperous buccaneer than a captain of commerce. But he had strong presence, unmistakable authority, and one sensed great energy behind his restrained speech and composed manner. Although he was visibly secure and at ease in his own reception rooms, in his dining-hall, or strolling through the gardens, he gave no impression of a man who demanded tribute. Watching him with his family there was no feeling that he ruled by fear. At table he did not insist on leading the conversation. He was, in fact, more inclined to listen than to speak, and was thus something of a surprise to both Helen and Jesse.

'Something about him frightened me at first,' Helen said. 'I guess I was expecting someone like Raymond; but they look nothing alike. Clara says both she and Raymond resemble their grandmother, Angus' mother. But whatever

166

I may have expected, it hasn't happened. He's *careful* with me. Almost timid. I haven't been five minutes alone with him.'

'It's hard for him to unbend,' Jesse said.

'That's right. But I like him anyway. I like him a lot. And before I leave here I'm going to tell him so. I know he has a lot of power and money and everything but I'm sure he's like me in one respect. I'll wager he lies awake half the night.'

'Is that what you do?'

'You should know. You've heard me complain about it often enough. I fret about everything that went wrong during the day. Then I worry about what might go wrong tomorrow.'

'Sufficient to the day . . . .'

'Don't tell me,' she said. 'I've heard that a thousand times. Anyway . . . now that I know more about what happened between him and Raymond, instead of blaming him, I feel sorry for him. He's like an old lion, trailing along behind the other lions. They fear him maybe, he may be the strongest lion of them all, but they don't love him. Or if they do he doesn't know it.'

'I resented him like hell at first,' Jesse said. 'Because of Raymond, I guess. But after I'd spent some time with him, after you'd told me everything Clara said, I felt different. I decided he's a captive like everybody else. And more so than most. If Raymond wanted to get even with him when he ran off the way he did, he certainly got the job done. He turned Angus inside out. He can't even say Raymond's name, can't ask the simplest question about him. He's hanging by his finger-nails and I feel sorry for him. He talks to me about the hunt and shooting grouse and I start wishing I could ride and shoot birds so I could make an impression on him. Isn't that odd? We were both ready to hate him. Now I'm just hoping *he'll* like *me*.'

For his part, Angus was as smitten with Helen as Hugh was. Like electricity shooting through him, he saw, suddenly a young woman who closely resembled both his mother and his son. But that resemblance gave him less

167

pleasure than pain. Looking in her eyes at their first meeting he saw Raymond looking back at him, saw the same stubborn strength there, heard Raymond's voice saying 'I'll never go to Dublin.'

For the first few days he avoided Helen except at table, fearing some rejection or abuse which logic and common sense told him would probably never come. The fantasy, however, drove him to stay in his bunker, covered with whatever protective colouration he could devise, waiting for his courage to return, giving himself time to become accustomed to this gracious young woman who continued to look at him with his son's eyes.

Eager to please her somehow, to atone if atonement was required, desperate for her to like him, but still unable to manage a private meeting with her, two people sitting face to face discussing pertinent matters, he took refuge in his public-man costume and said, in a toast at dinner, some of the things he was feeling.

'Once again we salute our guests . . . our son's friend, Mr Clegg, and our most welcome granddaughter. The short time you both have been here makes us all the more anxious that you should stay for a long visit. In fact, let's not use that word, "visit", lest you think of yourselves as *visitors*. We fondly hope that you will see yourselves as *residents* here. If you must leave for a time you must think of *that* trip as a *visit* from which you will return quickly to Wingate Fields.'

The inclusion of Jesse in all his gestures of hospitality and family affection to Helen was more than social grace on Angus' part. He did not, either consciously or subconsciously, substitute Jesse for Raymond, no such story-book transposition took place in his mind, but it was not lost on him that Jesse's age and his stage of development were very close to what Raymond's had been when Angus had seen him last.

Angus discovered, soon after Jesse's arrival, that he could talk to him, that they had a common language or if not that, a mutual flexibility that permitted each of them to make some sense out of the other's interests and activities.

168

Having long since abandoned hope of making any rewarding connection with either Ned or Hugh he was delighted to find that he had an articulate and informed man under his roof.

Jesse drank well, also, another characteristic that Angus admired. Both Ned and Hugh drank tirelessly but not well. The one grew flushed and garrulous, the other sullen and silent. Angus had known Brewster Causey, Ned's father, for many years and he too had been a disastrous drinker, combative and pugnacious, although he was an inept fighter, and apt also to offer his attentions to other men's wives. After a ball or a dinner-party, when guests began to leave, Brewster was usually found, dead asleep, in some upstairs bedroom. Almost always he left by the back entrance assisted discreetly by a servant. When he died of a rotted liver, he was barely fifty years old. While neither Ned nor Hugh drank in the self-destructive style of Brewster, they seemed, nonetheless, to have inherited a diluted strain of his weakness.

Jesse, however, was of another genus altogether. With him, it seemed, liquor played its proper role, as a social lubricant, as a companion to conversation. He seemed to enjoy his hours in Angus' study as much as Angus did.

Though he felt solid and at home in all matters financial and commercial, Angus hesitated, all the same, to discuss Helen's inheritance with her. Before the two of them made their day trip to Newcastle Angus did a rehearsal of the relevant material for Jesse.

'You're an observant person, Jesse. For a man your age you seem to have a solid notion about how the world works. I have enjoyed our discussions. I think I have profited from them and I'd like to think that you have also. I have been candid with you about many things, including the Bradshaw business and agricultural interests. The family has been at work for a long time and as I've told you we've enjoyed good fortune. We all like to believe that we rise only by our own efforts but that is a fiction. Some of us are more fortunate to start with. Some of us have a leg up. For more than two hundred years the Bradshaws have had a specific programme to secure the futures of their children. When I reached my majority I came into a large sum of money for my own use. This in addition to a considerable share of all the Bradshaw holdings. My own children, when they came of age, also had their proper shares turned over to them. And Helen, when she is twenty-one, will benefit in the same way. For now, however, because of Raymond's death, she is entitled to everything that was his, the legacy he received at twenty-one which has now tripled in size, plus his share of Bradshaw Enterprises which I have administered for him for all the years since he left. As you can see, Helen, since the day Raymond died, has been an extremely wealthy young woman. And when she is twenty-one, as I have said, her fortune will more than double. Is she aware of this?'

'We've never discussed it,' Jesse said. 'I don't think she's aware of it at all.'

'Will it be a shock to her?'

'A surprise perhaps but I don't think it will shock her. She's not much impressed by money. It was never important to Raymond and I don't think it's very important to her.'

Angus nodded his head. 'I know it wasn't important to Raymond. He withdrew ten thousand pounds before he left for America and that was the last bank withdrawal he ever made. It baffles me. I can't imagine that he lived very comfortably on his income as an academic.'

'Actually, he lived extremely well. He had a fine home and many friends and he loved to have them with him in his house.'

'He was a determined young man,' Angus said. 'He must have used the money he brought from England to buy his home in America. And beyond that he paid his way with his income from teaching. That cut him off totally from his family and that's what he wanted most, I expect. Damned shame the way things turned out.'

At the end of this conversation about the Bradshaw finances and their relevance to Helen, Angus suggested

170

that perhaps it would be wise if the details, as Angus had explained then, came to her directly from Jesse.

'Since she hardly knows me,' he said. 'I thought perhaps it's a piece of news she might like to hear from you. You seem to be her best friend and since this is a circumstance that could make some change in her life . . . .'

'No, I don't think so,' Jesse said. 'I mean it *is* a family matter, isn't it? And since you're Raymond's father and Helen's grandfather, I think it's something the two of you should handle together.'

So the journey to Newcastle was arranged. When Helen was told about it, when she learned that Angus would take her off for a day, she said to Jesse, 'What's this all about? We've scarcely spent five minutes alone together since I arrived, and now we're off on a day trip. Just the two of us. Am I to be scolded or will he buy me a new toy?'

'Neither, I should think. He's an old-fashioned man. He's trying to show you around a bit and give you a treat, I expect. You won't be bored, I promise you. He's an interesting man to talk with.'

'I wish I had your social courage,' she said then. 'You're not afraid of anything. These are my relatives but you know them better than I do. Outside of Clara . . . .'

'She's the best,' Jesse said. 'She's the prize of the clan.'

'I think so. But I can't really compare because she's the only one I've spent much time with. Mrs Bradshaw tries to be nice but it's all very stiff. If she ever put her arms around me and gave me a serious hug, I'd faint. As for Clara's husband, he's always just arriving or just leaving. And Hugh . . . I don't know what to make of him. Is he friendly to you?'

'We drink together sometimes but that doesn't mean anything. Hugh will drink with anybody. He reminds me of a piece of fruit that stayed too long in the sun. Not rotten yet but getting there.'

'Nora thinks he's grand. She says all the women in the county are in love with him.'

'How do you like *her*?' Jesse said.

'I don't know what to make of her either. One minute

171

she treats me like a long-lost sister and the next thing I know she's behaving as if *she* had just come back from a world cruise and *I'm* the little waif from the workhouse. But I think she's awfully attractive, don't you?'

'She looks all right, I guess. I've never seen anybody like her, if that's what you mean.'

'Ahhh,' Helen said.

'What does that mean?'

'That means you like her.'

'No, it doesn't. It just means I've never seen anybody like her. She's like her brother. Nobody ever said no to her. I pity the man who marries her.'

'You mean Edmund. We met him. That's who she's supposed to marry.'

'Then I pity *him*.'

'If she's so impossible why do you spend so much time with her?' Helen said then.

'Just trying to be nice,' Jesse said.

The following afternoon when Helen came back from her day with Angus, she went looking for Jesse. But he'd gone riding with Nora and Hugh. The three of them had supper at the inn in the village and came home after dark. It was the following morning after breakfast before Helen could get Jesse alone.

'How was your trip to Newcastle?' he asked.

'You know how it was,' she said. 'You knew all about it and you didn't tell me.'

Jesse grinned. 'How does it feel to be so rich?'

'I don't feel rich. I feel stunned.'

'I guess you'll change your whole life now. Get new friends. Buy a pet leopard, sell the house in Fort Beck.'

'You're a crumb. Why didn't you tell me?'

'He's *your* grandfather. I thought you should get the news from him.'

'I guess you're right, but it certainly seemed strange. That's almost all we talked about. The money. I mean *he* talked and I just listened mostly, with my mouth open. He acted as if he was afraid he'd hurt my feelings. He was almost apologetic, like he wants me to like him and he's afraid I won't.'

'Did you give him a kiss and say, "Thank you, Grandpa?" '

She shook her head. 'We never got that informal. It was sort of like a guided tour through the fields of Northumberland and the Bradshaw money. Nothing very personal about it.'

'That's what's wrong with money. That's why it wrecks people.'

'It won't wreck me.'

'We'll see.'

'Besides, it's not just *my* money. It's yours, too. I wouldn't even be here if it weren't for you. *We're* the ones who are related. You and me. Raymond and you and me. That's the only family I feel connected to. Not these English Bradshaws, no matter how nice they are to us. I'm *not* going to get new friends or a leopard. And we don't ever want to sell the Fort Beck house, do we?'

'That depends on what you plan to do with yourself,' Jesse said.

'No, it doesn't. It depends on what *you're* going to do. Remember the conversation we had before we left home?'

'I remember.'

'So?'

'So nothing. When I get home I'll be looking for a job. That's all I know.'

'Are you sure you're not planning to stay here?'

'Why would I do that?' he said.

'I don't know. You tell *me*.'

'I just told you. I'm going back when you do.'

'That's what I thought. But Mr Bradshaw had a different idea. He thought you might be staying here. He thinks Nora has her eye on you. Does she?'

'Not that I know of. Besides she's engaged.'

'Everybody knows that. But it doesn't seem to bother her. She has plenty of time for you. And you have plenty of time for her.'

'Like I said, I'm trying to be nice.'

173

'I know. I heard you say that. But I'm not sure that's the answer.'

Jesse smiled and put his hand on her cheek. 'You're not turning into a possessive female, are you?'

'I don't know. Maybe I am. I know I wouldn't like to see you make a silly mistake.'

'*You're* my silly mistake,' he said. 'Here I am tied down to a nervous girl who can't decide if she's my mother or my sister.'

'I'm not nervous. Besides, I didn't bring up the subject. Mr Bradshaw did.'

'What did he say exactly?'

'I don't remember the precise words. But he likes you. He likes you a lot. I think he'd like to keep *both* of us around. He just said something to the effect . . . I told you I don't remember the words . . . he said he thinks you may have some serious ideas about her.'

'Why would he think that?' Jesse said.

'Because the two of you are prancing around together and giggling in corners most of the time.'

'Is that what he said?'

'No. *I* said that. He didn't say anything negative about her if that's what you mean. But he left me with the impression that he doesn't think she's a *femme serieuse*.'

'Well . . .' Jesse said. 'She'll grow up, I guess. Like everybody else. She's only nineteen.'

'The other thing he said was that she's very old for nineteen.'

5

Other than Raymond himself, only Clara had read the letters he received from Emily Callison during the months he was in Dublin. He had carried them with him in his satchel when he went to meet her at Holyhead; when his father brought him home to Wingate Fields after Emily's death he gave them to Clara and told her to hide them.

174

Clara had no thought of reading the letters. She knew who had written them, she guessed that they were extremely personal, and in any case, she had no impulse to relive that portion of her brother's grief.

She had concealed them in a third-floor niche that only she and Raymond knew of, a cubicle they had used as children to hide their treasures. It was not a part of the house that Clara, or anyone else, visited very often so she seldom saw the compact bundle of envelopes wrapped in a square of oilskin. But the little parcel, the memory of it, remained vivid in her mind.

Only after Raymond had been away for more than ten years, when the family had withered, when her life with Ned, too, had become what it was destined to be rather than what she had hoped it might be, only then, finding herself living more and more with memories of her brother, unwilling to accept the fact that she would never see him again, desperate for some glint of hope, some clue that might perhaps point an arrow to where he had gone, only then did she retrieve the letters one day, lock herself in her upstairs sitting-room, and slowly read them through.

Seeming as though they had been written only the day before, their pages filled with passion and longing, the letters disturbed Clara and saddened her. She had never read anything so openly sensual. She was not shocked or offended; quite the contrary. But new insights tumbled, one after the other, through her consciousness. She saw Raymond, of course, in a different way from before, she felt the raw power of the attachment he and Emily had experienced, and she saw her own life in a colder light than she ever had before.

Although all the letters were from one person, without replies, there was no mistaking the frantic mutuality of their relationship, no way of misreading the joy it had brought them. However short their time together, however painful and ugly its end, they had been, for that one lunatic summer, truly transported. Each time Clara re-read the letters, and having read them once, she read them often, she came away with a strong positive impression. She

175

knew that, faced with the same impossible choices again, both Raymond and Emily would have chosen, without hesitation, exactly as they had before.

When she first began talking with Helen, it never occurred to Clara to share those letters with her. Just as she had never considered showing them to her parents or to Ned, she thought that Raymond's daughter was perhaps the last person who should be permitted to enter this most personal and erotic chamber of his life. Nothing would be served, she felt, nothing would be gained.

When she and Helen, however, reached a plateau of empathy and understanding, when they reached it so quickly, she began to have second thoughts about the letters. She told herself that this young woman, emotionally mature for her years, would see the letters as *she* had seen them, would feel that they supplied the last missing piece in the puzzle of her father. She would know him at last as he had been as a young man, little older than she herself was. And if there should be any shock or misunderstanding, Clara would be there to supply a prologue and an epilogue, to leaven the mix, to protect Helen from a wrong reading.

Having thus persuaded herself, Clara continued to hesitate, continued to review her logic for signs of error. Each time, however, she reached the same conclusion, that it must be done, and each time she found reason for postponement, or finding *no* reason, postponed anyway. At last, impatient with herself for her lack of courage, six weeks after Helen's arrival in England, she told her about the letters, told her of all the considerations she had reviewed in her mind, and asked her if she wanted to read them.

'I don't know,' Helen said. 'It seems so strange and faraway. So much time has passed. That woman dead for so many years and Raymond dead now – what do you think?'

'I'm not sure. It was a problem for me, trying to decide if I should tell you the letters existed. Finally, it seemed to me it was only fair that you should know. But if you don't want to reopen a closed book, I can understand that. As

176

I've told you, I waited a long time myself before I read them. So take as much time as you like. But if you decide you'd rather *not* read them, I think they should be destroyed. I would hate it if anyone else stumbled on them.'

Perhaps the knowledge that the letters would be destroyed if she chose *not* to read them helped Helen to make up her mind. Or perhaps Clara's attitude and the things she said stimulated Helen's curiosity. But she told herself, when she sat locked in her room at last, the packet of envelopes on the table beside her, that it was perhaps the final chapter in her search for the truth about her father and it could not be ignored; it was a decision, she felt, that had been made for her, one that she must not reverse because of failed courage or fear of pain.

For many years after, indeed throughout her life, Helen, like a kitten with a ball of wool, worried and toyed with that long-past decision. She knew, without question, that those hours spent alone, reading and re-reading Emily's letters to Raymond, had altered her, had changed some of her attitudes towards her father, and almost all her attitudes towards herself. Feeling that she had switched somehow from a spectator to a participant, it was as though she had been carried across the threshold of her child's room with its books and toys and pleasant memories, into a dim-lit adult's bedroom. Seeing Raymond through Emily's eyes made him seem an altogether different creature, not flawed or diminished, but mysterious and transformed, a familiar and beloved actor made unrecognizable by a change in costume and *maquillage*.

This is not to say that Helen, at eighteen, was a sheltered and ingenuous child with no knowledge of the winds of life that whirled about her. She was, in fact, and had always been, both perceptive and curious, an ardent student of human behaviour, foibles and failings included. She had studied medical books in the library, had whispered with her girl friends and shared forbidden novels with them. She knew that men and women were bound together by many cords other than parenthood, that there was joy to be had, as well, and mutual fulfilment. She had been courted by young men her own age within the strictures of Fort Beck society, and she knew as everyone did, the two or three girls in town who ignored those strictures. But to a large degree, it was a time when young people, men as well as women, had their first taste of shared passion on their wedding nights.

In Helen's case, of course, she had had exposures beyond Fort Beck. As a young girl in New York, living with her mother among the Bardonis, she had experienced a living diorama of physical love in all its bright variety. The touching, the kiss, the embrace, the caress, were a part of their days, as ever-present and necessary as chianti or manicotti.

In the various family households Helen moved through, visited or stayed the night in, emotions of all sizes and colours were on energetic display. An attempt to produce a society diametrically opposite to that of Fort Beck could have developed none more deliciously different than that of the Bardonis. And Helen, alert and inquisitive, all her senses recording and transcribing, had been square in the centre of that life.

So she had been schooled, no question of it, more thoroughly than many young women her age. In addition, after returning to Illinois, she had had her father and Jesse, both of whom treated her always as an adult with an adult's mind, capable of absorbing adult information. There was no discussion she was not allowed to hear, no subject she was not invited to comment upon, no school gossip or scandal she was not made privy to. Raymond's theory, often expressed, was that most people become what they are expected to become. He expected Helen to be tough enough to take the blows, tender enough to suffer, and intelligent enough never to feel sorry for herself. He expected her to be mature in responsibility, young in pleasure, and stubborn enough to make her own decisions.

She had always known what Raymond sought for her. It duplicated what she expected of herself. And after his death, when she no longer had him there as a measuring-

178

stick or sounding-board, when she had to assess her own strengths and weaknesses, she was encouraged. She had no feeling that she would bring off great accomplishments in her life, but she felt, all the same, that she was *prepared*, in a way that Raymond had wanted her to be, that the foundation stones were all in place and the girders set, that her father had done that greatest thing a parent can do for a child, prepared her to function on her own, taught her that she could live alone and not die from it. He had left her feeling like a properly engineered product, a functioning mechanism; she was not at all sure where she was going but she felt prepared for the journey.

It was with that kind of self-assurance that Helen began to read Emily's letters. Within an hour, however, less than halfway through the envelopes, her stomach felt strangely hollow and chilled. She stood up and walked to the window looking out across the garden. Taking deep breaths she felt her heart thumping in her chest. Turning away from the window, then, she drank a glass of water and lay down on her bed with her eyes closed, trying to put what she had read, at least for a moment, out of her mind. She was tempted to give the letters back to Clara without finishing them but she knew as the thought came to her that she would not and *could* not do that.

As she continued to read the letters, as she became an unquiet witness to Raymond's passion, carefully described by Emily on hotel stationery, Helen sat there in her quiet room and saw him slowly change from a warm father figure in a Norfolk jacket to a young lion on the grass by the river Will.

Reading Emily's detailed listing of her own body's sensations, seeing *her* there too, fearless and frenetic under the sky, Helen felt a sea change begin inside herself. Trying hard not to visualize what she was reading, struggling to curb her imagination, to depersonalize the words and the images, she failed. She saw it all. The hills above the moors, the ruined castle and the two horses grazing, the river rushing in its channel, and two naked bodies, tangled together in the soft shade beside the water.

179

During the next several days, as she read and re-read the letters, telling herself that familiarity with those impassioned words and images would at last render them ordinary, she also told herself, over and over, that it was physiologically and psychologically impossible, however close the connection she felt with Raymond, that these specific and erotic revelations could in any way affect *her*, that they could bring *her* to life in a new way, that those evoked images could stay fresh before her eyes when she was away from her room, away from the letters locked in her satchel, that her physical self could be awakened so suddenly, her skin sensitized, her body damp and fevered under her summer dress.

When Clara showed her a photograph of Emily it only intensified Helen's waking nightmares. Now the faces and the bodies were even clearer and more specific. They took refuge in her subconscious and began to appear in her dreams, acting out always some section of one of Emily's letters. Then, suddenly, Helen began to see herself in these tableaux. Barely recognizable sometimes, but it was her face, all the same, on Emily's body. And other faces, too, on Raymond's body. Strange composite faces usually, but never Raymond's face. When she did recognize a man's face, a young man from Fort Beck, or a teacher from Foresby, or someone she had seen, or met, since coming to England, she pretended not to notice, pretended it was all abstract and crazy and had nothing to do with her or with the men whose faces she saw in the night.

After a few days had passed she returned the letters to Clara and they burned them one by one in the grate in her bedroom. Helen did not tell her that she had kept one of the letters, had hidden it in her passport case for reasons that were unclear to her. Nor did Clara confide that she also had held back one letter when she delivered the packet to Helen.

Watching the fine old stationery curl and blacken in the flames, turn to ash and float up into the chimney, Helen, taking refuge in whatever voodoo rite she could conjure up, persuaded herself that an exorcism was taking place.

180

The letters would no longer occupy her mind or occupy *her*. The transferral process would stop. She would no longer *take part*, would no longer see herself as a secondary protagonist in that far-off episode. She would re-enter, now, the rhythm of her own life, go forward at her own pace, find her own sensual homestead when she was ready. Neither Emily, nor Raymond, nor anyone, would seep inside her and *drive* her to be something other than what she was, not till she *chose*, not till *she* decided.

But the dreams did not end. And the waking obsessions did not disappear. Defying Helen's will, they asserted their own will. Trying to fight them off, she only made matters worse, made the struggle more intense. Determined to control her thoughts, to cleanse her mind, to replace whatever was there with words and pictures of her own choosing, she failed completely. The things she was determined to destroy stayed fully alive from the sheer energy of her determination. As she identified her victims and targeted them, that process stamped them, and made them permanent, like bright and fresh tattoos on her brain.

Tormented and guilt-ridden, she began to feel as if her carefully-hidden thoughts were visible to everyone, especially to Angus and Ned and Hugh and Jesse. Having never sinned, she felt, nonetheless, like a sinner. And like all sinners, she believed that her sins were obvious, that she revealed herself at every turn, that her innermost crimes and secrets were public chattels.

Her behaviour began to change. Frightened of being herself, feeling ill at ease with her normal, quite admirable persona, not trusting that balanced, good-humoured young woman, she turned herself quite suddenly into what could best be described as a commentator. At table or whenever the social requirements of the day put her in sustained contact with one or more members of the household, she contrived to avoid perceptive observation by forcing herself into a role that was not her true one.

On these occasions she led the conversation. More precisely, she was the conversation. Leaving little space for either questions or answers, she prattled on, touching

181

all fields of knowledge and opinion from the cuisine of Abruzzi to the blood flaws of the Hapsburgs. Since her information was considerable and since she was displaying a facet of herself that was as new to the Bradshaws and the Causeys as it was to her, they were fascinated by her performance and never attempted to steer her back to the real self she was trying so hard to conceal.

Her alternative gambit was to stand or sit, depending on the circumstances, with cast-down eyes until someone asked if she felt all right. She would then reply that she had a touch of quinsy and thought it best not to tax her voice, or that she had looked too long into the direct sunlight and was now resting her eyes. In her frenzy she believed that any ruse which allowed her to avoid eye contact, which prevented other eyes from peering into her soul, would protect her.

In later years, remembering this behaviour, Helen found it both idiotic and amusing, thought of it as an imagined crisis. An eighteen-year-old girl eager to move ahead into womanhood but fearful of taking the first step. Failing to accept the fact that she had undergone a true and profound emotional experience, looking back on her torment, she mis-read it, as completely as she had when it was happening.

It was true that Helen had been thrust suddenly into a recognition of her sexual self and that if it had not happened then, under those circumstances, it would have happened later under different circumstances. But it is also true that other forces were at work. Just as her giving birth to a child would release a storm of grief inside her which she had not allowed to break at the time Raymond died, so also was this period very closely connected to his death. The revelation of his love for Emily, a physical love that was a new element in Helen's portrait of him, brought him back to life for her in a way that startled and shocked her. It was not that she saw him suddenly as *her* lover. She did not. For all their intimacy and physical tenderness, he was always her father to her. And just that. None of her sexual fantasies featured Raymond. Not then and not later.

So there were two fields of energy at work in the turbulent days following Helen's reading of Emily's letters – her father came to life again, and she herself came to life with an abruptness she could not accept. Longing to talk to someone, someone earthbound and sensible, she turned to Clara. But even with her the words would not come. All the things that disturbed her and kept her sleepless were so blurred in shape and definition that she could not possibly put them into words, not for Clara, not even for herself.

A few weeks before she would have turned to Jesse. But now he seemed to have gone diaphanous. He divided his time, as much as she could tell, between Angus and Nora. And both those relationships were somehow disturbing to Helen. Even Clara was mystified by what seemed to have become a close bond between her father and Jesse. The first week in August they went off to London together for six days. They were seen talking earnestly together when they climbed into the car to be driven to the railway station and they were no less earnest, though visibly less sober, when they returned to Wingate Fields the following Saturday.

'What was the big trip to London all about?' Helen asked Jesse the day after he came home.

'Nothing special.'

'Just trying to be nice?'

He smiled and said, 'That's right.'

About his comings and goings with Nora there was less mystery. Where previously they had been laughing and flirtatious around the house, they were now more formal on the one hand and less visible on the other. When one of them was missing, the other was usually unaccounted for also, clear proof to a practised eye that their relationship had proceeded to a more private plateau. Their frequent departures and arrivals in Nora's sleek roadster tended to confirm such a conclusion. Also, Edmund Bick was never seen now around the premises and his name was rarely mentioned.

183

'I guess you know what you're doing,' Helen said to Jesse. 'At least I hope you know what you're doing.'

'How's that?'

'You know how's that. I'm talking about Miss Nora. Did she capture you? Are you captured now?'

'Not me,' he said. 'She's our cousin. I love her like a cousin.'

'You're acting pretty cocky lately.'

'I love you like a sister and Nora like a cousin.'

'Very cocky, if you ask me.'

Raymond had always told Helen, 'Never take your troubles to bed with you,' and she had followed that advice, had, at least, tried to follow it. But not at Wingate Fields, not in the heat of August. She read in her room until very late each night, didn't get into bed till she was exhausted. But still she couldn't sleep. Or worse, she went to sleep at once and was awake thirty minutes later. She tried drinking a glass of wine from the decanter on her table, tried several glasses of wine, felt lovely and light-headed but still not sleepy. So she read again, sometimes till the very early sun of midsummer edged above the trees in the deer park. Often she dressed herself then, slipped quietly out of her room, went downstairs, and took a solitary walk before breakfast.

One such morning, if there had been any question in her mind about Jesse and Nora, that question got a firm answer. As she eased out of her bedroom door into the corridor, Nora backed out of Jesse's room, two doors down, and closed the door behind her. She walked towards Helen then, hair tousled, barefoot, and wearing a man's dressing-gown. Smiling sweetly and sweeping past, heading for her own room in the south wing, she said, 'Somebody has to put out the tabby cat. This morning it was my turn.'

That morning Helen walked in the fields for a long time, till she knew breakfast would be over. As she turned back towards the house she felt quite alone. And far from home.

History tells us that obvious conclusions and easy assumptions prove, almost always, to be neither obvious nor easy. Complexity is the only characteristic that all men share. No other tendency or behaviour trait is truly common. The study of humankind must recognize as a basic principle that broad generalizations will not do, that each creature is a separate study, that at last only *his* conclusions about *himself* are valid ones, that one's true interior landscape is never visible from the outside. And if it were to become briefly visible only a shaman or a gypsy would be likely to see it. The attentions of the priest and the psychologist and the sociologist would surely be focused elsewhere. Science and religion bestow their richest rewards on scientists and zealots.

In Helen's case, the obvious conclusion, the easy assumption, would have been that sometime in the past, during her growing-up years, she had chosen Jesse for herself. All protestations of brotherhood and sisterhood to the contrary, she believed secretly that they would be together, that they would live together, have children, and complete a circle that would seem to have been preordained.

Why not? No one who knew them could have quarrelled with the rightness of such a joining. All the elements were in place. They were friends certainly. More than that, they were lashed together, and had always been, by their love for Raymond. He had, in a very real way, reared them both. Their tastes and values were his. Bartok was his. And Mozart and Mondrian and Uccello. They shared a vocabulary and a frame of reference all of which had come to them, in one way or another, from Raymond.

They knew each other and loved each other. What could be more right and logical than that they should *continue* to love each other, that this eighteen-year-old woman and this twenty-two-year-old man should redefine their feelings for each other and tumble smoothly into the permanent relationship that fate, and Raymond perhaps, seemed to have envisioned for them.

A persuasive case. But flawed. The logic of such a future was absolutely powerless against the actual emotional cords that held Helen and Jesse together. The fiction of their being blood relatives, brother and sister, children of Raymond, had long since ceased to be a fiction for them. Having spent those excellent years together as a family, with Raymond as its head, all that experience plus their feelings for each other rejected any notion that they should label themselves as anything other than family.

Any such deviation would have diminished Raymond, would have made their whole triumvirate seem less important and solid and joyful than it was. Although it was never articulated between them, Jesse and Helen surely felt, after Raymond's death, that they had a responsibility to preserve what was left. And what was left, his principal legacy, was their relationship, the two of them, as they had been, with Raymond still suspended somewhere between, still real and alive in some ways but unable to adjust to a fundamental change in what had been, unable to give his blessings, from beyond the grave, to some dramatically altered relationship between his daughter and Jesse.

Helen's reaction, then, to what she saw as abrupt changes in Jesse, was not what it seemed to be. She did not see his liaison with Nora as a violation of her rights of possession. She was not jealous of her cousin. She had been witness to Jesse's previous romances with certain young women in Fort Beck. Raymond's teasing him about those adventures had been a frequent theme in their dinner conversations. Raymond's remarks such as, 'She's a perfect chicken for a hay-ride or a sleigh-ride but don't bring her home to roost,' were familiar to Helen. Listening to her father's extended and often ribald advice to Jesse about how he should go about choosing a mate, there had never been any doubt in her mind that he would, in fact, choose or be chosen one day, he would marry, and 'I'll be an

186

aunt.' But *that*, in her mind, was in the future. Not now. Not this soon.

It would have been easy for her to deposit all responsibility for her unrest at Nora's feet but Helen knew that the feeling had begun much earlier, before she left Fort Beck. Her first intimations of abandonment, her suspicions that Jesse, for whatever reasons, was preparing to set out by himself, were rooted there. What had seemed to be her easy acceptance of the journey to England had actually been triggered by her almost certain conviction that if she did not go, he would go without her. So she had simply packed her bags and sailed with him, smiling, cheerful, and apprehensive.

In her quandary and confusion, however, over Emily's letters, she was reminded again of what seemed to be her changed role in relation to Jesse. Desperately needing an ally, having never been without one since meeting him, she felt suddenly that he was unavailable, that he had drifted off, that his concentration was elsewhere. His long, cloistered meetings with Angus, and his comings and goings with Nora she saw as symptoms of that new distance between him and her, not as causes.

7

Helen and Jesse had planned to return to New York the last week in August. Ten days before their departure date, Jesse said, 'How would you feel about staying on here for another month?'

'I'd feel as if I were wearing out my welcome.'

'No, no. That's no problem. They *want* us to stay. You know that.'

'The summer's over, Jesse. We've been here long enough.'

'Another month won't matter.'

'It matters to me,' Helen said. 'Is all this about you and Nora? Are you planning to get married or something?'

'No.'

'No what?'

'No, we're not getting married.'

'Does she know that?'

'Of course she knows it. We've never even talked about getting married.'

'Gee, mister, what *do* you talk about?'

'Don't be cute,' he said. Then, 'Actually, we talk about you. She says her brother is, how shall I put it, rather impressed with you.'

'She's mistaken. I've never said twenty words to him at one time. Nor he to me.'

'Still water runs deep.'

'Don't change the subject,' she said. 'What's so important that we have to stay here another month?'

'I didn't say we *had* to stay. At least *you* don't. If you want to get back for the fall semester, I'll meet you in Fort Beck in a month or so.'

'Am I allowed to ask what's keeping you here if it's not Nora?'

'You remember that monograph that Raymond and I were going to write?'

'About della Francesca? That was a joke, Jesse. Just something Raymond used to say at parties.'

'Well, it wasn't a joke to me. I've been talking to Angus about it and he thinks it's a fine idea. He wants me to go ahead with it and if it works out, I might do a whole series on Italian painters.'

'You don't know anything about Italian painters.'

Jesse smiled. 'That's true. But don't tell Angus. He's willing to give me a stipend so I can pull this thing together. That's why I need to stay another month. I'll have to go down to London and do some research in the libraries there. And in the National Gallery. Then I'll write it up when we're back in Fort Beck.'

Helen said yes to their delayed departure because she could find no good excuse for saying no. But she had misgivings. Although there was great joy at dinner that night when Angus announced they would extend their visit, and a magnum of champagne was carried to the table to celebrate the occasion, she could not help feeling that she had become an innocent accomplice in some conspiracy she knew nothing about. But she laughed and chattered through dinner, returned joy with joy, and drank a great deal more champagne than she had ever drunk before on a single occasion.

In the time remaining before Jesse was to leave for London, Helen rode daily, played tennis and croquet on the lawn, had long conversations with everyone except Ned and Hugh, helped Mrs Bradshaw with her flower arrangements, and drank a generous amount of wine with every meal.

She was delighted to find that the wine helped her sleep. Not all through the night. But if she had several glasses with dinner and a few sips of port after, she was sometimes able to sleep till three in the morning.

For the rest of the night, however, the trolls and demons who had pursued her through the past weeks continued to sit in the corners of her room, silent and ominous, their eyes flashing in the darkness.

She saw Jesse every day for at least a few minutes but they talked together now like two guests at a large party, two strangers who, having just been introduced, were not certain they had got the names straight from the hostess. Or so it seemed to Helen.

She did not, however, totally trust her own reactions. Not just then. Feeling at one moment as though her anxieties were manufactured and at the next moment as if all her absolutes were dissolving in her hands, judging Jesse as blameless on the one hand and then deciding that he had lost all resemblance to the person she knew, branding herself first as fool, then as victim, she danced along the edge of uncertainty and waited for some new insight or announcement to tell her what might come next.

On the last night before Jesse's departure, once again there was champagne on the table. But there was an uncharacteristic silence during the meal as though certain people knew what to expect and the others only sensed

189

that they could expect *something*. Whatever their individual feelings, however, everyone drank a great deal of wine.

At last, as dessert came to the sideboard and the champagne was opened, Angus stood up importantly at the head of the table. It was clear from his expression that if a secret had indeed been carried into the dining-hall, Angus was the one who possessed it. He held up his glass and said: 'First I drink to all those present. God bless us and keep us.' He drank, everyone drank with him, and the servants refilled all the glasses. 'Everyone who knows me is aware of the fact that I am not an inspired conversationalist. I feel, however, that I have no peer as a toastmaster. I was seventy-five years old this past April. My grandfather prodded me to make my first toast when I was fourteen and I've been at it ever since. But tonight I expect to outdo myself. Tonight we have an occasion for twofold celebration. After two short announcements, one by Ned Causey, the other by myself, it will be plain to everyone, I believe, that this is a singular night for the Bradshaw family.'

Nodding to Ned, then, Angus sat down. Ned arose, flushed and self-important from his late afternoon gin and his evening claret, lifted his glass and said, 'By way of announcement, speaking for my lady wife and myself, speaking with the greatest possible pride and joy, I propose this toast . . .' he turned towards Nora, '. . . to my cherished daughter.' He drank, all drank with him, the glasses again were refilled, and Ned continued, turning this time towards Jesse. 'And to our new-found friend from America. My wife and I are delighted to announce that during the holiday season, on Twelfth Night to be precise, Nora and Jesse will be married here in the chapel at Wingate Fields.'

There was a little flutter of applause around the table, Nora sang out, 'Here's to the blushing bride,' and another toast was drunk. Then Angus took stage once more at the head of the table while Ned, his face quite crimson now, sat down.

'This wedding will give us a true occasion for

celebration,' Angus said. 'So also will the news that I'm about to announce. To all but two people at this table what I have to say will come as a surprise but to each of us it will represent, I am certain, a most welcome addition to our lives.'

Taking a white envelope from the inside pocket of his coat he said, 'These papers were delivered to me just today. Sent up from our solicitor's office in London. They testify that as of the third of August this year, our American friend, Jesse Clegg, has become Jesse Bradshaw. We have officially and lovingly adopted him as our son.'

No gasps were heard at the table, no sounds of panic or dismay. There was, rather, a total and empty silence. No one moved or spoke.

'Since the death of Raymond, our only son, we, as his parent and as guardian of the Bradshaw name and legacy, have been faced with a prospect that has threatened our lineage several times before . . . no male heir to carry on our name and our traditions. Since time and God's choices have eroded all possibility of our having a natural male child, what better solution than this, that a young man who was like a son to our son, who is like a brother to our new granddaughter, and who will now be husband to our daughter's child, should also be our son.' He turned to face Jesse. 'I salute you now as a Bradshaw. May this action benefit you as fully as it will surely benefit us.' He raised his glass to drink and all drank with him.

8

If Helen had felt confused and abandoned before, she now felt betrayed. And she felt a cold anger towards Jesse that she would never have believed possible.

Following the dinner-table announcements, however, she had lifted her glass with apparent gusto through all of Angus' series of toasts. No hint of dismay showed on her

191

face. She smiled till her jaws ached and added her laughter to the general joy.

When everyone left the dining-hall at last, just before she went up to her room, Helen managed a final deception. She kissed Nora on the cheek and said, 'What a lovely bride you'll be.' To Jesse, who faced her with all the aplomb of a man caught stealing from a poor-box, she said, in words pitched only for his ears, 'What a sly fellow you are.'

Moments later, in her room alone, she drew a warm bath, took off her gown, got into the tub, and let her thoughts run free. But all roads led back to Jesse.

Why had he set out on such an intricate trail of deceit? There was no reason why he shouldn't marry Nora or anyone else if that's what he wanted to do, no reason on earth why he shouldn't be adopted by Angus Bradshaw if they both agreed to it. But why would he feel it necessary to keep everything from Helen? What purpose did such secrecy serve? Why would he agree to the notion, or insist on it, perhaps, that she should learn about these personal and life-shaping facts in such an impersonal way, like a child listening through her window to the town crier.

She had been excluded, she felt, in a way that was almost vengeful. Lying motionless in her scented bath-water she seized on that word. It *was* vengeful. An act of vengeance. But why? For what reason?

She stayed in the bath for a long time, till the house had gone dead silent. No footsteps, no servants' voices or door closings. Pushing through her original anger, forcing herself to reason and remember, she organized her thoughts, cooled her emotions, and tried to find a rational path through what seemed to be a thicket of contradictions.

Like a student preparing a thesis, she made mental lists of incidents and conversations that had taken place between the time of Raymond's death and her departure with Jesse for England. She weighed and balanced, considered and reconsidered, selected and rejected, concentrated till her head ached.

When she got out of the bath, she dried and powdered

192

herself, put on a light silk dressing-gown, and sat in a velvet chair looking out across the gardens. The day had been heavy and hot but now a breeze stirred the lime trees outside and cooled her skin under the delicate silk.

Sitting there in her quiet room, only an occasional night-bird breaking the silence, she came at last to a conclusion, came to what she believed was the only possible conclusion. Jesse had shut her out because he felt he had to. He could not risk revealing to her that nothing had been chance. There had been conscious design behind it all.

Sometime between the moment when they discovered in Raymond's papers his connection with the Bradshaws of Wingate Fields, sometime between then and Jesse's announcement to Helen that they had been asked to come to England, he had made a solitary decision. The secrecy had begun then. Some previously unrevealed facet in his make-up had taken charge, had told him that here was a chance for him, while playing the role of friend and benefactor, to better himself, to enrich himself, to be, perhaps, something he had never been, something he had never dared, even, to aspire to. Jesse had gone to England as a privateer and had captured a booty far greater than anything he had imagined.

As it all spun out slowly and irrevocably in her mind, Helen could not believe it. But at last she could believe nothing else. It shocked her and sickened her, made her feel like an accomplice, and made her, thus, feel estranged not only from the new Jesse she had revealed, but also from herself. As agonizing as her search for an explanation had been, some key to the turn-around in his behaviour, her *finding* the explanation, even *suspecting* that she had at last uncovered the answer to all the questions that tormented her, that completion of the circle truly sickened and deflated her.

The darkness that shortly before had been soft and comforting seemed threatening to her now, suffocating and heavy. Her pursuit of Jesse, her indictment and conviction of him, reversed itself suddenly and she saw *herself*

193

convicted. Her own guilt, though more difficult to define, was suddenly very real to her. Identifying hitherto unseen flaws in Jesse had caused her to question herself. She found herself, all at once, without a centre. Too much had changed too quickly. Key supports had tottered. Her unshakeable confidence in tomorrow had dissolved.

Crumpled there in the lonely darkness, she wished she could cry. But she could not. Her mouth felt dry suddenly and her eyes burned. The skin across her forehead and her cheekbones seemed as tight as stretched vellum.

At last she stood up and paced around the room. The curtains had stopped stirring; the air seemed unbearably dense and moist. She walked back and forth from corner to corner, around the bed and to the windows, her arms straight at her sides now.

Passing the window, her cheeks flushed and warm, the garden below looked cool and fresh to her. She crossed the room, opened her bedroom door, stepped out into the corridor, and walked down the carpeted passage towards the staircase, passing Jesse's door, several vacant bedrooms, then the door to Hugh's room, just before she turned towards the great stairs leading down to the entrance hall.

At the top of the stairs she stopped; she stood there in the darkness for a long frozen moment, then she turned and walked back the way she had come. She opened Hugh's bedroom door, stepped inside, and closed the door behind her.

Chapter Five

1

Three days after his arrival in London, Jesse received a letter from Nora. Four days after that a second letter arrived, telling him that Helen had gone home to America. The following morning Jesse took the express train to Newcastle.

'She told us she had already written to you there in London. I'm sure you know by now that she has gone.' So Nora had written. But no letter from Helen had arrived.

When Nora met him at the railway station in Newcastle she had little information about Helen.

'It's nothing to be disturbed about, darling. She simply told my mother that she's going back to finish school. I can't see that it affects you one way or the other. The truth is I'm rather pleased about it. Not that she isn't a pleasant girl, and she *is* my cousin, but I couldn't help feeling she was keeping watch over you a bit more than was required.'

She took Jesse's arm as they walked through the station. 'Now that your chaperone's gone off, perhaps we'll get married sooner than planned. Why should we wait till Christmas? Why not October? Beautiful autumn days then. We could make it the fourth of October. That's my grandmother's birthday. She'd be delighted if we got married then.'

'Do you know what ship she sailed on?' Jesse asked.

'I have a frightful memory for such things. I've warned you of that.'

'You must have heard Clara mention it. You said she went with her to Liverpool.'

'I suppose I did,' Nora said. 'Seems to me it was the Royal Something-or-other. The *Royal William* perhaps. Is there a steamship by that name?'

Jesse located a cable office inside the station and sent off a message to Helen on board the *Royal William*.

Are you all right? Why the sudden departure? I'm worried about you. Cable reply to Wingate.

'I think I'm getting a bit jealous,' Nora said as she manoeuvred her roadster out of the station's car park. 'The day you arrived at Wingate Fields I wondered if there might not be something bubbling between you and Helen. Now you've started me wondering all over again.'

'Don't be silly,' Jesse said. 'I brought Helen over here and I had planned to take her back. I feel responsible for her.'

'She's a grown-up young woman, darling. Only a year younger than me. You certainly think I'm grown-up, don't you?'

'No question about that.'

'You're not complaining are you? If you'd like me to be different I can behave in all sorts of different ways.'

'I'm not complaining. I like you fine the way you are.'

'Am I perfect then?'

'That's the exact word for you,' he said. 'Perfect. Perfectly awful. Perfectly rotten. And very spoiled.'

'I think you mean it.'

'I always say what I mean.'

'So do I,' she said. 'And I say you're a dreadful tease. You deserve to be jilted. If ever a man deserved to be jilted, it's you.'

'Why not? There's always your faithful Edmund standing by. Edmund Bick at the ready.'

'And you've your baby Helen. Why deny it?'

Jesse, when he answered, had lost the rhythm of the banter. 'I can't understand why she'd go off like that.'

196

At Wingate Fields, Jesse found that everyone seemed unconcerned about Helen's sudden departure. They were sorry to see her go, of course, but they had known all along that she was serious about her schooling.

'We thought perhaps when you decided to stay on that Helen might do the same. And I think she did consider it,' Clara said. 'She certainly seemed to have mixed feelings about going. She wept when I left her at the ship. So did I. I became awfully attached to Helen and I shall miss her terribly, all our chats and gossips together.'

'I was just surprised,' Jesse said, 'that she left so quickly without saying anything to me.'

'She did write you a note, I think. But she posted it, she said, just before she boarded the ship. So you wouldn't get it till after she'd gone. She was most anxious not to spoil any of your plans. Didn't want you to interrupt what you were doing because of her.'

'When did she make up her mind? When did you find out she was leaving?'

'Just the day before. She'd asked one of the servants to send a wire to the steamship office and as soon as she received confirmation she told me about it, asked me to make the journey to Liverpool with her. Of course I was delighted to do it.'

'Liverpool,' Jesse said. 'That's where you said Raymond left from.'

'That's true. But we mustn't jump to conclusions about that. Liverpool is simply our closest port. Most of the county people leave from there if they're taking any sort of a sea voyage.'

'I'm surprised she didn't tell someone her plans beforehand.'

'She could have done, of course. But pernaps she wanted to wait until she was sure of her departure. Also, I hadn't seen much of her those last days before she left.'

'Why was that?'

'She didn't feel well. Took her meals in her room,' Clara smiled. 'I didn't feel awfully bright myself. None of us did. We overdid it a bit with the champagne, I'm afraid, that

197

night before you left for London. But . . . there was a great
deal to celebrate, wasn't there? When Father begins one of
his evenings of toasts and tributes it's a poor time to practise temperance.'

'Was she feeling better by the time you left for
Liverpool?'

'Oh yes. Fully recovered, I expect. More quiet than usual,
and seeming a bit pale in the car, but not complaining
about a headache or anything of that sort. We drank a bit
of wine, in fact, in her stateroom, before I left the steamer.'

Angus, too, had apparently expected Helen to leave, or
if he had not expected it, was at least prepared for it.

'Disappointed, of course,' he said to Jesse. 'Damned
disappointed to see her go. She's a winning child. Has a
charming way about her. And a backbone to go with it. I
admire that. I admire *her*. Felt very close to her in just those
few weeks. Nothing I would have liked better than if she'd
decided to stay on. But . . . she's off now. Gone to finish
her schooling and there's no argument to be made with
that choice. She'll be back soon, I expect. Next summer at
the latest. I made her promise me that much.' He paused.
'But if she doesn't come then, we'll just wait till she *can*
come.' He paused again. 'If you're thinking the old man
has learned his lesson I have to tell you you're only half
right. When I *want* something, I still want it as much as I
ever did. And I'm prepared to do whatever I can to get it.
That's my nature, Jesse. Good or bad, I have to live with
it. But I know something now that I *didn't* know for many
years. Just because a man *wants* something, just because
he works and schemes to get it, doesn't guarantee, by any
means, that it's going to come to him.'

After four days had passed and Helen had made no
reply to the cable from Jesse, he decided to follow her to
America. When he explained to Angus that he wanted to
make sure she was safely home and settled into the routine
of school life, the old man said, 'Of course you do. We've
all remarked that you have a protective attitude towards
Helen and we respect you for it. We're very fond of you,
Jesse. All of us are. And we hope you're fond of us. We're

proud that you're a Bradshaw now. But I hope you will think of that as an advantage and not an obligation. Whatever we have given you or will give you in future is given freely. No conditions. No strings attached, as they say. If we can help you to have a greater range of choices in your life, more freedom to function, we will be delighted about that. But it is still *your* life to handle as you see fit. My wife believes that I'm trying to atone for my bad judgment with Raymond, that I am trying to erase those mistakes by giving you some of the things I was never able to give him. Perhaps she's right. But I like to think that what we are able to do for you is less important than what you will now be able to do for yourself.'

Nora's reaction, when Jesse told her he would be leaving within a week for New York, was in no way as gracious as he had hoped. There was, in fact, no grace at all in her attitude.

'That's a lot of rot, Jesse, and you know it. Helen doesn't need to be tucked up at night or led to her classes each day. You've told me yourself she has her own house with a staff to take care of it. Do you expect me to believe that she also needs you there to feed her porridge in the morning?'

'It's not a requirement that I be there. She hasn't asked me to come. It's just something I want to do. It's not that long since Raymond died . . . .'

'It will soon be a year.'

'. . . and she's never lived in that house by herself,' Jesse went on. 'I think I should be there to ease her into it.'

'Ease her into *what*?'

'You know what I'm saying.'

'I know what you *think* you're saying but it makes no sense to me. How long do you estimate this errand of mercy will last?'

'A few weeks, I suppose. End of October or middle of November I should be heading back.'

'But you can't be certain, can you? If my delicate cousin has sleepless nights or develops a skin rash you might very well be delayed.'

199

'What's the matter with you?' Jesse said. 'Why are you acting like this?'

'I'm not acting any way at all. I was wondering if we should consider some alternative dates for our wedding. It could be quite awkward if our guests gather on Twelfth Night and someone has to explain that you're still in Illinois, making a coddled egg each morning for baby Helen.'

'Go to hell, Nora.'

'Why are you angry with *me*? *I'm* the one who should be angry. I'm not running off with Edmund Bick. It's you who's doing the running off.'

'What the hell has Edmund Bick got to do with it?'

'Nothing perhaps. But if we're going to set up multiple households, if you're planning to spend your life travelling back and forth between Helen in America and Nora in England, then I'll need someone to console me, won't I, when you're not here to do it?'

'Does your mind really work that way,' Jesse said, 'or are you simply trying to make me angry? You and Bick were engaged to be married after what seems to have been a long and happy courtship. Are you trying to draw a parallel between that relationship and the one that exists between me and Helen?'

'Why not?'

'Because it's idiotic.'

'Perhaps it is and perhaps it isn't. But whatever you tell *me*, whatever you tell yourself, I don't see the two of you as barefoot children splashing your innocent little toes in the paddling pool. I think Helen left here because she's jealous of me. Otherwise why *would* she leave without telling you? As soon as my father announced that we planned to be married she started making plans to leave.'

'You're mistaken.'

'I don't think so,' Nora said. 'And why didn't *you* tell her about us? If she's like a sister to you, why didn't *you* tell *her*? When my father made the announcement, Helen was the only one who seemed truly surprised.'

'I know that. I *should* have told her. That was a mistake.'

200

'So now you have to follow her home and explain your-self. Mend your fences, so to speak.'

Jesse sat looking at her for a long moment. Then he said:

'I'm going for the reasons I told you. And only for those reasons. If you can't accept that, then . . . .'

'Then you're going anyway. No matter what I say.'

'Of course not. If my going had anything to do with you and me, if I thought it would affect us in some way . . . .'

'Don't you think it *will* affect us?'

'Of course not. I'll be gone for a few weeks. Then I'll be back. And that will be that.'

It was Nora's turn now, to be silent. At last she said, 'What if I told you that *I* am jealous of *her*, that I have been since the day you arrived, when I saw you get out of the car together?'

'You're *not* saying that, are you?'

'What else *could* I be saying? I thought you and she were *together*, the way you and I are together now. I *still* think that.'

'Why would I lie about it?' Jesse said. 'You didn't lie to me about Edmund. Why would I lie to you about Helen?'

'Because you're a man. Men always lie about such things. If they *have*, they say they *haven't*. If they *haven't* they want everyone to believe they *have*. It's the nature of the brute.'

'Not this brute. I've told you the truth before. I'm telling you the truth *now*.'

'What if I told you this is something more than a silly argument to me?' she said then. 'What if I said it means a great deal to me for you to stay on here? What if I asked you to cancel your trip for my sake?'

'You wouldn't ask me that.'

'Yes, I would. I *am* asking you that.'

'Unless there was a good reason, I'd have to say no.'

'I said it means a great deal to me. Isn't that a good reason?'

'It's a reason for you, I suppose. It's a reason to have things your own way. But it's no good reason for me not to go.'

'Do you expect me to pretend this conversation never took place?'

'Of course not. Why should you pretend anything? We have a difference of opinion, that's all. It's not the first time and I'm sure it won't be the last.'

In the remaining days before Jesse left for Liverpool to board the ship to take him to New York, it was as though Nora had forgotten their conversation about Helen. She was more warmly attentive to Jesse than ever. It was as though she believed that the fact of their announced engagement gave them more freedom than before and she seemed determined to take advantage of it. She still made a pretence of sleeping in her own room at night but it was not an elaborate pretence. The servants were not deceived certainly. Nor was her mother. Her father pretended to be deceived but was not.

In addition to her affection she gave Jesse every other possible help and support, hovering at his elbow like a gracious combination of governess and valet. She helped him pack after seeing to it that every sock and handkerchief had been laundered and pressed, each button secured, all his boots cleaned and polished, hit hats brushed and blocked. And she oversaw personally the details of his journey to Liverpool.

When he left that last morning, when the family gathered outside to see him into the car, she became almost demure, a kind of reprise of the performance she had given when Jesse and Helen arrived. As though in deference to the sensibilities of her family she kissed him decorously on the cheek, whispered, 'I'll miss you terribly,' and stood erect between her mother and father as the car door closed behind him.

As she watched the car roll away down the long drive through the oak trees there were tears in her eyes, and what appeared to be an expression of genuine sadness on her face. Her true feelings however were a complex mixture of resentment and anger and jealousy. And a determination to have, on some near-future occasion, a proper accounting.

If we were to assume that Helen had *fled* from Wingate Fields, we would be mistaken. It is true that she experienced, as we have seen, a time of torment after learning about Jesse's adoption and his forthcoming marriage. A case could undoubtedly be made that she had taken refuge in Hugh's room, in his bed, to escape herself, to rid herself of the confusion and mixed feelings that she was unable to resolve.

Following this line of reasoning, knowing something, knowing a great deal in fact, about Helen's background and character, it would be easy to conclude that the next step for her would be humiliation, a sense of shame about what she had done; she had remained in her room as Clara had reported, feigning illness, because she could not face the prospect of sitting at the family table as though nothing had happened. Such, however, was not the case. Far from feeling humiliated or ashamed, Helen felt, to her surprise, triumphant. She had followed an impulse, something rare for her, had made a dangerous choice, and had survived it.

This is not to say that her physical awakening, her free gift of herself to Hugh, had redefined her, had suddenly allowed herself to see herself in a new way, had transformed her from an intelligent but inexperienced young woman into a sensual forest creature. Not at all. Like many young women the act of love was less startling and rewarding to her than her decision to commit it.

It was that decision, that emotional breakthrough, that stayed with her, that made her see herself differently in the looking-glass, that kept her in solitude in her room lest she lose her new-found sense of self, that sudden awareness of her ability to navigate her own course, to move ahead in a solitary way, to *be*, to *exist*, to make choices, to make mistakes, and remain not only stable but buoyant.

Her decision to leave, then, was in no way an escape; nor was it, as it might have been, a vengeful flight from

Jesse. It was, in its way, a positive action, a need to preserve her new-found sense, if not of importance, at least of independence, or if not that, the first intimations of the *possibilities* of true independence, of some sense of strength and resolve inside herself that she had never been aware of before.

Because, heretofore, she had keyed her decisions and her values to the messages she received from her mind, because she had been carefully structured, had prided herself always on her ability to follow a line from impulse through decision to action and on ahead to results and consequences and from there to either self-criticism or reward, she was, inevitably, conscious of how things might end, and how that ending would affect her. She was determined always to be rewarded rather than punished, eager to make choices that would make negative results either impossible or unlikely.

Now, however, this most central of all her anxieties suddenly left her. She did not ask herself if any of the servants had seen her enter or leave Hugh's room or if anyone had heard them while they were together. Nor did she suffer with the thought that Hugh might tell someone. Knowing very little about men apart from Raymond and Jesse and knowing almost nothing of Hugh, she believed that he would *certainly* tell someone; he might, in fact, tell a great many people. But that seemed unimportant to her during those final days at Wingate.

None of us who are knowing and sophisticated, who are widely-travelled and who think well of ourselves, none of us worldly-wise souls believe any longer, if indeed we ever did so believe, that a single event can turn our courses sharply to either the right or the left or along one of the other various diagonals. We choose to believe that many twists of the wheel must be made before a craft can be turned completely round, and it's true, of course, or at least it tends to be true. Holocaust and cataclysm indeed exist and they have cataclysmic effects on people's lives. But the numbers of those lives are comparatively few. Most of us are the sum of our days rather than the over-sized,

204

brightly painted rendering of the effect of one remarkable day or of one significant, heart-stopping incident taking place on that day.

Helen surely belonged to that larger group and would have been quick to admit it. But as a lifelong student of herself she would have insisted, if only silently, that there *are* corners along the way, that those corners are either turned or turned away from, and that many circumstances, if not dramatically altered, are nonetheless, thereafter, altered. In that context a foolish action, even a regrettable one, can have a memorable and permanent effect, can stimulate or stifle forever the function of the acting force.

So it was with Helen. Without taking a great inductive leap into the unknown, without trying to construct a philosophy of conduct after observing a drop of water on an oak leaf, she simply felt that having acted independently in a way that was totally foreign to her, she was now forever capable of independent action. Later she would be able to add to her credo and make it 'independent action without fear'. But that would come later. More accurately it would come and go. But throughout her life when she felt she was suffering from failed courage, she referred back to that single turning, seemingly senseless and unwilled, that short trip from the head of the Bradshaws' great staircase, through the upstairs corridor to the doorway of Hugh's room.

On board ship, she stayed in her stateroom just as she had kept to her room those last days at Wingate. She took breakfast in her bed, then dressed carefully and walked for half an hour on the deck, after which she returned to her quarters and stayed there, going to the deck again only in the early evening when the other passengers were at dinner, when the deck was hers alone.

Apart from her meals and those short walks round the deck she avoided any semblance of a daily routine. She read sometimes, silly novels from the ship's library, she wrote long letters to each member of the Bradshaw and Causey families, and even longer letters to some of her school friends. And she listened to a portable victrola Clara had bought for her in a shop in Liverpool. Ragtime records and senseless tunes from New York musical comedies.

Much of the time, however, she sat quietly on a chaise longue just beside one of her portholes, thinking and dreaming, enjoying her sense of self; it was a feeling she had experienced only once before, when she had left New York and journeyed by train, by herself, to Fort Beck. Her return to her father. Then she had been too young, too excited and filled with trepidation to let the feeling come to full tide. But now she relished it, luxuriated in it like warm foam, let it wash over her, lull her to sleep, and gently waken her again. She reviewed in her mind all the talks she'd had with Clara and the single conversation she'd had with Hugh, the two of them sitting in the library just after breakfast the day she left for Liverpool.

And she thought often of Jesse. Strange thoughts. Not the anger she'd felt before. None of that sense of betrayal and abandonment. Something elusive rather. Something new to her, something akin to the way she had felt the day she left her mother at the railway station in New York. Something final.

3

For all his feigned bewilderment about Helen's departure from England, Jesse was neither surprised by the news she had gone nor at a loss to understand her reasons for going. He knew he had treated her badly. In those three months he had done serious, perhaps irreparable, damage to what had been a foundation relationship in his life. He knew that. As he crossed the ocean towards New York he reviewed the events that had taken place since Raymond's death. Making no effort to exonerate himself, he examined his motives and his actions with relentless honesty, laid bare all his sins of judgment and omission and tried to construct a case that he could present to Helen when he saw her.

206

He knew it would not be easy. He had seen in her expression, the night before he left Wingate to go to London, that she had passed judgment on him, indicted him, and convicted him. But until he heard that she had gone back to America, he chose to ignore what his eyes had told him.

Trying to anticipate the questions he would face when he saw her, trying to construct in his mind a rationale that would support him, that would make him less hateful to her, trying to fashion a step-by-step review of what he had thought and what he had hoped for, knowing that self-deception and subterfuge would not serve him well, he concluded at last that only simple honesty would do. He would have to tell her that he had been seduced by the life he had anticipated at Wingate Fields and totally captured by what he had found there. To be included in such easy splendour for one summer had had an hypnotic effect on him. The slow realization then that he could become a permanent part of that world, of that ease and grace and comfort, had acted on him like morphine. It was as though he had stood to one side, observed his own behaviour, abhorred it, but was unable to do anything about it.

After his disembarkation in New York, he crossed the country on a train; through the mountains and forests of Pennsylvania and the flat green fields of Ohio and Indiana, he felt as though he was re-entering his own body. It seemed unreal to him that his name had been legally changed, that he was pledged to marry a young woman whom he scarcely knew and specifically mistrusted, and that his future had been provided for in a manner that he would never have thought possible. Only when he got off the train in Fort Beck, when he walked through the summer streets, the boughs of giant elm trees forming a canopy over his head, only then did he begin to see himself whole again. He told himself he was unchanged, that if he chose he could put that sumptuous summer far behind him, and go on with his life as before, as Jesse Clegg, an unemployed instructor of English who walked with a slight

207

limp. He told himself all this, liked the sound of it, and for a short time almost believed it. And he was convinced he could make Helen believe it.

Everything was pointed towards Helen. All his ruminations and self-examinations were directed towards the moment when they would sit down in Raymond's library and talk themselves back to where they had been six months before.

He had examined all exigencies, he felt, had prepared an answer, an honest answer, to all questions. Once he had admitted his carelessness and his guilt, once they had gone on from there, he knew that everything could be solved, that Helen, having returned to Fort Beck, would find she was her old self, just as he had; she would be reasonable and forgiving.

The one thing Jesse had not considered, it had, in fact, never occurred to him, was that she wouldn't be there when he arrived. He had never questioned that she was going home, as she had said, to enrol in school. But when he walked into Raymond's house, it was empty. The Espings, according to the neighbours, had driven to Minnesota for the funeral of a relative,.and there was no indication that Helen had come home or was expected.

When the Espings returned three days later they showed Jesse their last bit of news from Helen, a postcard mailed from England late in July with no mention of any plans she had made for returning to Fort Beck.

4

Helen had expected to go directly home from New York. But the last two days of the crossing had been unpleasant. Grey and overcast skies, the ocean swollen and churning, the ship rolling from side to side, the furniture in the dining-salon lashed in place, dishes rattling, serving pans clattering to the floor, wine glasses breaking. Inside her stateroom, with the porthole covers closed and no horizon line to stabilize her, Helen had followed her steward's advice, had eaten lightly but regularly, had felt lightheaded, but had not been ill.

She was not, however, upon arriving in New York, eager to go immediately from the rolling motion of an ocean liner to the lurching and swaying of a passenger train. Deciding to accustom herself to solid ground for a few days, she booked a suite in a hotel just beside Central Park, and settled in.

Before she left Wingate Fields, Angus had supplied her with a thick packet of pound notes, a letter of credit for her London account, and a personal note to the manager of Barclays Bank in New York City. 'You needn't go to the bank. Simply telephone the manager and he will send someone to you.'

She called the bank the second morning she was in the city and an hour later Mr Winters, a grey-haired gentleman wearing a severe dark suit and pince-nez spectacles, came to call on her. 'We will have these pound notes changed to U.S. currency and returned to you. And we will set up a checking account for you in this branch as well as our Chicago branch. We are also issuing a new letter of credit which will be honoured at any bank. And . . .' he took a card-case from his waistcoat pocket' . . . here is my address and telephone number. And my home telephone number as well. Since I will personally supervise your accounts, you must feel free to call on me at any time.'

A few months earlier, Helen would have taken no pleasure from this new-found wealth. It would have made her self-conscious. She would have felt like an impostor. Now, suddenly, she simply accepted it, attached no great importance to it, and began to enjoy it. Not the money itself, not the fact of it or the feel of it, not the power to buy or sell, but simply the fun of it. Having been assured that there was, or soon would be, more money in her name than she would ever be able to spend, she had no desire to spend as much as she could. Considering her new and splendid affluence, she didn't exult. She simply smiled.

After strolling though the September streets of the city,

she bought two new frocks which closely resembled her old frocks, had her hair bobbed, bought a striking hat, and spent long hours in the art museums. She attended matinee performances of *Apple Blossoms* and *Irene* and bought a just-published copy of *The Moon and Sixpence*. She read newspaper articles about liberated women and letters to the editor attacking shingled hair and shortened skirts and she concluded as she ate her dinner each night in a quiet corner of the hotel dining-room, that she was indeed a fortunate young woman, that her age, her present state of mind, and the vibrant temper of the times had all come together in a most harmonious fashion, that lovely broad avenues were stretching out before her.

She did not telephone her mother because each day she told herself she would undoubtedly leave New York and go home to Fort Beck. Also, she was selfish suddenly about what she thought of as her new identity. She didn't want to share it, didn't dare to take that risk. If she was to be the resolute creature she hoped to be, that she sensed she had begun to be, it was necessary for her to learn to act resolutely, to wall herself off when necessary, to guard her territory. Just now it was essential for her to protect the gains she had made, her ability to choose and reject, to take the risks, and suffer the consequences. She was not prepared, for Anna's sake, to slip back into her thirteen-year-old self and be displayed among the Bardonis. Nor was she prepared to relive the details of Raymond's death, to answer a thousand well-meaning but hurtful questions.

Nonetheless, because her residual guilt when she thought of Anna never completely left her, she continued to tell herself that if she stayed on in New York she would certainly make contact with her. But the days turned into weeks; at last nearly two months had passed. Helen decided that she *must* see her mother now. But not until she was feeling better.

She was not actually ill. She felt strong, had a decent appetite and she took long walks every day in the crisp autumn air, but the light-headed feeling she had developed on the ship, the occasional weakness in her knees and

queasiness in her stomach caused her at last to request a
visit from Dr Hendricks, the hotel physician.

'You seem remarkably healthy to me,' he said. 'But if
you're uncomfortable, come into my office and we'll do
some simple tests. Perhaps it's winter coming on. The body
plays strange tricks on us sometimes when the seasons
change.'

The following day she did visit the doctor and two days
after that his nurse called and asked her to come in again
to discuss her test results. When she sat down in his office
the doctor said, 'As I told you the first day I examined you,
you are a remarkably healthy young woman.'

'Then why do I feel the way I do?'

'Quite normal under the circumstances, Mrs Bradshaw.
You're going to have a child.'

In the next hour, as she walked down Fifth Avenue, all
the way to Forty-second street, then back to her hotel, a
torrent of emotions bubbled through her, each one of them
tinged with elation. Until elation, at last, was *all* she felt.
Although the doctor's words, professional and dispassionate, had been a shock to her, although she had felt
the warm blood in her cheeks and a sudden sensation of
chill at her hands and feet, she could not, in truth, say that
she was surprised. She had sensed, these past weeks, that
she was somehow transformed. She had thought it was
psychical change, altered attitudes, new insights, new
courage. She felt she had suddenly taken charge of her
life. She still believed those things, thought all those
changes had indeed taken place and were permanent. But
now she knew, knew for certain, that she was altered
physically, internally, that all the subtle messages her body
had been sending had not been simply signals from her
psyche.

For the rest of that day every fantasy and fairy tale of
parenthood that she had heard of or read about, and a
few that were completely original with her, occupied her
senses. She floated through the streets and the shops, a
young woman with a secret, but at the same time she was

211

convinced that any eyes that turned to her knew what her secret was.

Back at the hotel she undressed and studied herself in her full-length mirror, searching for changes, for signs that would make her physically authentic. Surely when she felt so emotionally full of herself, so rounded and complete, surely some evidence of that condition, would be visible to her. But try as she might, straining her eyes and her imagination, she saw the same reflection she always saw in the glass, a slender and tawny young woman, ivory skin and softly formed, long lovely legs and delicate hands and feet. There was beauty there, certainly, and radiance. But no visible evidence of the far countries her consciousness had taken her to.

She dressed herself in a new and striking gown before she went downstairs to dinner. To mark the occasion, she drank champagne. She felt blessed and bountiful. But before she had finished her meal, longing to share her excitement with someone, she realized she was unable to do that. All her solitary impulses of the past few weeks, all the pleasures she had found in being alone, began suddenly to lose their appeal as she realized it was no longer a choice, that circumstances had forced her into a rhythm which up to now had been deliciously voluntary. Where all had been positive and glowing before she began to encounter questions now for which she had no answers. As she lay in her bed later she realized that the only two people she might have confided in, Jesse and Clara, could not be confided in now.

5

In circumstances where another young woman might have felt anger or resentment towards the man who was responsible for her dilemma, Helen felt nothing but compassion for Hugh. She felt she had treated him badly and it bothered her conscience. For all his sullen manner he had behaved towards her with kindness and tenderness.

When he managed at last to talk to her, when he led her into his grandfather's library only a short time before she was to leave for Liverpool, she thought he seemed years younger than he had before, direct and guileless and vulnerable.

'Why are you leaving?' he asked.

'It's my schooling. I must get back to start my autumn semester.'

'That can't be the reason.'

She laughed. 'Of course it is. What other reason could there be?'

'There are fine schools here,' he said. 'Why couldn't you go to school here?'

'I could, I suppose. But it never occurred to me. I think it's simpler for me to finish at Foresby where I started.'

'*Simpler*?'

'Yes, I think so.'

He looked at her for a long moment. At last he said, 'Why have you locked yourself in your room these past few days?'

'I wouldn't say I've been locked in exactly. I wasn't feeling so well. Too much champagne, I expect. I'm not a sophisticated drinker.'

'That was the reason? You didn't feel well?'

'That's right. Not sick. Just not well.'

'Your maid told my man you were quite well and happy. She said you ate all your meals and seemed in excellent health.'

'It's not nice to contradict me . . . .'

'I'm not trying to be nice. I'm trying to find out why I haven't seen you, why you deliberately stayed away from me.'

'I didn't . . . .'

'Of course you did.'

'Why are you so angry?' she said.

'If *I* made a *fool* of you, *you* would be angry.'

'But I'm not . . . I didn't . . . .' She stopped.

213

He sat looking at her. 'Why don't you finish your sentence? I would be very interested to hear what you were starting to say.'

Helen didn't answer. Hugh walked to the drinks table and poured himself a brandy. He stood behind his chair, then, and looked down at her.

'Why did you come to my room?'

'What do you mean?'

'What do you think I mean? It's a simple question. You must remember that you came to my room the other night and stayed till the sun came up. I simply asked why you did that.'

'I don't know.'

He moved round his chair and sat down. 'I haven't met many people from America. I suppose they're very different from us. Would you say that's true?'

'I don't know.'

'You're not an experienced woman . . . is that what you're saying?'

'Why are you questioning me like this?' she said. 'You *know* I'm not experienced. I don't know anything about *anything*.' She stood up then and walked towards the wide doors leading to the hallway. She stopped there without opening the door. Hugh sat in his chair watching her. Finally she turned and came back. 'I'm sorry,' she said. 'I know you must think I'm crazy. But if you expect me to make sense out of something that *doesn't* make sense, I can't do it. Can't we just leave it the way it is?'

'Of course we can. We can say you were walking in your sleep. Or you had a bad dream and you were frightened. Or perhaps it was simply an impulse. Something that happens on a hot summer night. Spur of the moment. I can accept any of those possibilities.'

'Why do we have to put a label on it?'

'We don't. I'm a promiscuous man. Somebody must have told you I have a chancy reputation. Fast and loose with the ladies of the county. That's the tone of it, I believe. A different woman in every village. Have you heard that?'

She smiled. 'Something like that.'

214

'It's not completely true,' he said, 'but it tends to be true. I don't question people's motives and I ask them not to question mine. But in this case I believed that the circumstances were different.' He drank from his glass and set it down on the table beside his chair. 'Perhaps what I mean is that I would *like* them to be different. Nothing I can think of would please me more.' He stood up then and moved not towards her but a few steps away. He smiled. 'God knows what it would do to my reputation if it became known that Hugh Bradshaw had become smitten with a young woman who had no interest in him at all . . . .'

'I didn't mean that . . .' Helen began but Hugh held up his hand and went on.

'It would be an irresistible piece of gossip. It would sweep across the county like a gorse fire. Rejecting all the fine ladies of Northumberland, and some who are not so fine, the young Mr Bradshaw has been done in by someone he could never hope to claim, his lovely cousin from America.'

'I'm sorry.'

'Don't be sorry. I'm not wounded. I'm disappointed. And I am beginning to feel lonely in a way that is quite new to me. But I assure you that all these feelings will go away. By the time I'm ninety years old I will certainly have forgotten that I ever loved you.' He walked to the door then and turned back to look at her. 'If you promise not to tell anyone how foolish I've been, I promise that I won't tell how truly lovely and remarkable *you* are.'

Later in the morning, as she and Clara drove off towards Liverpool, the family and the staff waving to them from the steps, Clara said, 'I must apologize for Hugh. He drove off an hour ago, headed for Edinburgh. Said he plans to marry there and produce a dozen children.'

'Is he serious?'

'Hugh is never serious. Seldom charming, often unreliable, and never serious. If he weren't my son I'm sure I'd fall in love with him.'

215

If Helen had avoided a meeting with her mother before, her impulse, after learning she was pregnant, was to postpone such a meeting indefinitely. Instead, she visited Dr Hendricks again. They talked in his office for almost two hours. And the following morning she went to see Reverend Galston at the First Presbyterian Church on lower Fifth Avenue.

That afternoon she wrote a long letter to Clara telling her she had postponed returning to school and had decided instead to travel to the west coast and Canada; she gave her New York bank address as the place where her mail could be sent, care of Harold Winters. The next morning she checked out of her hotel and was driven to the railway station where she took a train to Portland, Maine; the day after her arrival there she kept her appointment with the Reverend Jack Kilwinning.

'As you know, Reverend Galston called me about you and I said we would be happy to help you if we can. I'm sure you feel self-conscious about your situation. Most of our young women do. But only at the beginning. We don't make moral judgments here. Our concern is for the present welfare of the mother and the future welfare of the child.'

He glanced down at a printed form on his desk-top. 'I have here the basic information you've given us. You are eighteen years old, in good health, and your doctor in New York believes your baby will be born near the end of May next year.'

'That's correct.'

'You are not married and there is no possibility that you will be married to the father of your child. Is that also correct?'

'Yes.'

'We do not insist that you give us the father's name but there are certain facts we need to know, that our doctors need to know, to make the child's medical history as complete as possible.'

'I understand.' Helen had told Dr Hendricks and Rev. Galston in New York as much as she was able to tell about Hugh. She had omitted the fact that they were first cousins and she had falsely stated that he was already married. She gave that same information to Rev. Kilwinning. 'He is twenty-two years old,' she said. 'He is a British citizen who lives in England and as far as I know, he is in excellent health. He is about six feet tall, weighs a hundred and sixty pounds, I would guess, has dark hair and grey eyes.'

'Any childhood diseases that you know of?'

'I'm sorry. I would have no way of knowing that.'

'His parents are still living, I assume.'

'Yes,' she said. 'And his grandparents. They are a sturdy family.'

'Now we come to rather a personal question. So that we can anticipate, and avoid if possible, any future claim on your child, we need to know what members of your family know about your condition.'

'No one knows.'

'No one at all? Not even the young man?'

'No one. Only Dr Hendricks, Reverend Galston, and yourself.'

'As you can imagine,' Reverend Kilwinning said then, 'many of the young women who come to us are in difficult financial circumstances. Their families are often either unable or unwilling to help them. In addition to the prenatal care that we provide, they need to be housed and cared for while they await the births of their children. I assume from my talk with Reverend Galston that your circumstances are rather different from that.'

'That's right, I came here because no one knows me in Portland and because I feel it's essential that my child's birth be kept a secret, but more important than that, Reverend Galston convinced me that you will find a wonderful home for the baby.'

Kilwinning nodded. 'That's our main function.' He took off his reading glasses, closed the folder on his desk-top, and sat back in his chair. 'As I have said we are concerned with the welfare of the mother *and* the child. We also feel

217

obliged to protect the rights of the adopting parents. We insist on even-handed and humane treatment of all the people we deal with, including infants who are not yet born and adoptive parents who may not yet be known to us. We do not function as an orphanage or a foundling home. Prospective parents are not permitted to come here, visit our nurseries, and select whatever child pleases their eyes. The parents do not *select; we* select. All the infants who are adopted through our organization have been placed with adoptive parents three months before they are born. And the matching process, matching what we know of the child's background with the information we have been provided by each set of prospective parents, has begun some time before that.

'As Reverend Galston told you, we sign no contract with the young women who come to us for help. We allow for a change of heart through the major course of the pregnancy. But three months before the baby is due we have a thorough counselling session with the expectant mother. If none of her circumstances have changed, if she still wishes us to find a home for her child, then our foundation becomes the interim legal guardian of her baby, the papers to become effective at the moment of birth. I'm sure you understand that we could not perform the service we do if we had no such structure to protect us and the people we deal with.'

'Do any of the young women change their minds after they've given birth?'

'Of course they do. We're dealing with human beings. And each case is handled in the fairest way possible. But the circumstances that cause young women to come to us are seldom changed by the birth of the child.'

In that meeting and subsequent ones, the details of the foundation's responsibility to Helen and her responsibility to it were made clear. She learned that the organization was funded by donations from church groups and from concerned individuals. It accepted money from neither the mothers nor from the couples who would adopt the children. It was also made clear to her that she would never

218

see her child. It would be taken directly from the delivery room to the nursery and cared for there by the nurses, usually for a three-month period. At that time it was released to the new parents.

'You will be told only the sex of the child and if it is a strong and normal baby. We've learned that the less information the mothers have the easier it is for them to avoid a painful emotional reaction after they've left us and gone back to wherever they came from. And needless to say, all our adoption records are sealed. The new parents will know nothing about you and you will know nothing about them. We recommend that the child be told he or she is adopted when they are old enough to understand such things but that of course is a matter for the parents to decide. And under no circumstances do we open our files to either party, either before or after the adoption process is completed. If that seems cruel and arbitrary, I assure you we have found it is the greatest act of kindness we are able to perform.'

7

If Jesse and Helen had gone to Wingate Fields on a premeditated mission of vengeance, if they had gone, with daggers in their teeth, to pillage and sack, they could not have wreaked greater havoc than they did. Although that summer had seemed to be a pleasant and civilized joining of family members, no specific aversions or conflicts evident, it had ended badly. With the exception of Ned Causey, whose anxieties were internal and permanent, each other person in the household felt diminished, somehow, by Helen's abrupt departure, and by Jesse's following her a week later. Their sudden absence made painfully clear how quiet the Wingate corridors had been before they came, how silent the dinner table, how dreary and familiar each detail of the Bradshaw lives had been and would become again now that they were left with just themselves.

Even the long postponed sense of completion they had felt as they learned, bit by bit, about Raymond, even *that* paled and seemed unreal somehow when the faces and voices of the first-hand messengers were no longer seen or heard. Whatever they had brought with them, whatever morsels of energy and information had been provided, all of it seemed to have been bundled up and taken away when they left. Although the Bradshaws knew well, and understood, the reasons for Helen's leaving, and Jesse's, they still could not help feeling they had been discarded.

It was not a group reaction, of course. It was not their custom to react or function as a unit. Nor did they, for the most part, confide in each other. The household motto appeared to be: The greater the anguish, the greater the silence. That autumn and winter at Wingate Fields was silent indeed.

If this should seem to be a poetic conceit, something too rhapsodic to be real, it is important to remember how high their hopes had been, each of them, how critical to their lives, to their separate relationships with Raymond, they had expected Helen's visit to be. She would complete a pattern that had for so long been incomplete in each of their minds. She would cause the machinery to cough and the gears to grind together. She would fill a void.

All this she did, of course, she and Jesse together. If nothing else they were new and unfamiliar. But they also brought vitality and quick movement into an atmosphere that seemed sometimes to be populated most tellingly by the portraits of ancestors in the gallery, the carefully chiselled marble busts, and the suits of armour in dim corners. Helen and Jesse stirred the dust, changed the patterns of conversation, admired objects that no one had noticed for generations, asked questions that had never been asked before, and generally altered the rhythm of the house and grounds in a most unpredictable and delightful way.

Just as each family member had participated differently

220

in their presence, each had specific and private reactions to their absence. Angus, whose continuing activities and travel, whose always-filled day-book and general high level of self-esteem would have been thought to be guards against almost any sort of qualitative rearrangement, even he, he more than the others, in fact, was thrown off-stride by the sudden absence of Jesse and Helen. Jesse in particular.

Most of Angus' labours, as well as his pleasures, had been shared with other men, many of whom resembled him, if not in physical characteristics, certainly in their standards, their habits, their dress, and their love of sport. In fact, he quite openly sought the business association and social companionship of men in whom he saw, or imagined he saw, a likeness to himself. In matters of commerce, for example, he trusted only ruthless men. 'I can do business with a roughneck or a cut-throat. I like a bit of rough and tumble in the board room. But show me a soft-spoken gentleman in a lavender tie and I will keep my hand firmly on my purse. And on my private parts as well.'

He had been brought up to believe that a first-rate wife was a necessity but a fine male friend was a gift. He had at least half a dozen cronies who knew details about his thinking and his values which his wife had no knowledge of at all. Angus and Louise lived together but did not confide in each other. They knew their marital duties and fulfilled them conscientiously in much the same way that he engineered the family business and she managed the household. But any notions of mutual self-revelation or true psychic intimacy would have bewildered and humiliated them.

This bonding between men was characteristic of Angus' time and place. It coloured all family and community life and had for many centuries. It explained, at least in part, a man's obsessive need to have a male child and his wife's sense of guilt if she was unable to provide such a child.

It was a matter of property, of course, the necessity for passing real goods along from male to male. But it was

221

more than that. It was the need to have a male companion, a business associate, a man to ride with and shoot with and drink with who was also one's heir, someone who could be taught, little by little, everything his father had learned.

To men like Angus who were accustomed to quantitative thinking, to measuring in metric tons and thousand-acre land masses, there was an unfamiliar qualitative thrill to having a friend and confidant who was your son. It was one of the very few valuable things whose value could not be measured. It was a kind of immortality, as close to that state as any wool merchant or mine owner was likely to get.

Angus' loss of Raymond, then, had been a multi-faceted one. Without a son, a man must grow old by himself with no replica beside him to remind him of how things once were. And Angus, more arrogant and self-aware than most men, more conscious of his strengths, more angry with his weaknesses, was particularly agonized to see his heroic face and woodsman's body deteriorate, feature by feature, and to know that no one stood nearby to support him in his life or succeed him after his death.

As we have said however, he did not deceive himself that Jesse was Raymond reborn. No such fantasies were welcome in Angus' rock-bound system of values. Nor did his adoption of Jesse convince him that he had replaced by legal fiat what fate and his own foolishness, and now death, had taken away from him. Just as his doctors, in the past ten years, had begun to patch him together, so was Angus trying to do what he could with what was left. Instead of a son he would have a stepson. Instead of Raymond, he would have a friend of Raymond. And at worst, by befriending Jesse, by providing for him, by accommodating him and truly caring about him, he would feel some of that warmth returned, perhaps. Jesse would never *be* his true son or replace his son but he would be a permanent entity in his life.

For all his assurances to Jesse that he must not feel obligated to him, for all his insistence that Jesse was free

222

to go where he wished, to be and do as he liked, Angus, in truth, wanted only one thing. He wanted Jesse to stay at Wingate Fields. When he left, when the family smiled and waved him away from the portico above the west drive, Angus stood staunch in the centre of the group, smiling his lion's smile. But inside he felt tentative suddenly. And very old.

Louise, who for reasons of her own had made little effort to become intimate with either Jesse or Helen, seemed, of all the family members, least affected by their departure and by their absence. Having abandoned hope long since, having taken refuge in the mechanics of her life, in making lists, in counting objects, in giving instructions, in hearing grievances from the staff, she told herself that by becoming a sort of social engineer she could avoid exposing the internal, more sensitive areas of herself.

To a large degree she was successful. Aspiring to a kind of numbness of the spirit, she had achieved it. Never hoping for a lovely harvest, never truly expecting a pleasure or a reward, she had managed to avoid disappointment and disillusion. By this process however, she also desensitized herself to the pleasures that *did* come her way. By continually anticipating the worst she fell into a pattern where the best and worst became indistinguishable. In protecting herself from pain she totally removed herself from the arena of joy.

When she learned for example, that Jesse and Helen would come to visit Wingate Fields, she had reached a private conclusion that it would be a disappointment. Just as she managed the affairs of her household, however, so also had she made her contribution to the months-long campaign of correspondence that was designed to lure their granddaughter home to them. When it was discussed among the family, she projected always a positive tone. But her feelings were far from positive.

Although Louise had long believed that Raymond was dead, the actual news of his death when it came was more hurtful to her than to anyone else. She kept the hurt to

223

herself, of course, as she did most things that mattered, but her grief, and at last her anger, throbbed inside her.

She was sympathetic, had always been sympathetic and had fully understood Raymond's attitude towards Angus. Like Clara, she was critical of herself for not having functioned better at the time, but all the same there was no doubt that Angus had been the architect of Raymond's misfortune; the false moves had been his.

Raymond's departure then, his ostracism of his father, seemed, to Louise, an almost poetic reprise of his earlier banishment to Dublin. She believed he hated Angus and the reasons for such hatred were clear. But, dear God, why would he *hate* her? Why would he place her in Coventry along with his father? When he had been gone for only a few months she answered that question by telling herself he was dead. She began by believing it was a possibility and concluded soon after that it was a certainty.

The news that Raymond was only recently dead, that she had been separated from him for twenty years, not by death, but by abandonment, by his conscious refusal to have any contact with her, not just with Angus but with *her* as well, this news had truly undone her. Until at last she defended herself and her innocence with anger. She could only conclude that the things he had gone through had twisted Raymond's sense of truth in such a way that he was no longer himself, was not able to remember accurately or make proper judgments. Or he had become so careless and cruel that he included her in his hatred of Angus. Such conclusions made her feel ill-served. And angry.

Feeling that Raymond had cast her aside, Louise was less than enthusiastic about the coming of Jesse and Helen. She felt no need for further information. She had, in effect, closed the book. Feeling cast aside, she could envision no fresh facts that would dispel that feeling. As noted, however, she *pretended*, both before Helen and Jesse arrived, and during their stay at Wingate Fields. Functioning properly and fully as hostess she managed to keep herself, to a large degree, to herself, sharing her true thoughts with no one.

Even the announcement that Angus had adopted Jesse and the further announcement that Jesse would marry her granddaughter did little to alter the negative mind-set Louise had chosen. She insisted to herself that all would come to naught, that nothing could reopen the book and force her to deal yet again with Raymond's mysterious and unfair treatment of her.

When Helen left suddenly with Jesse close behind her, Louise saw it as a vindication of her views. The seer had seen clearly. Following her instincts she had gracefully avoided her guests. Knowing they were transient and temporary, suspecting that they were as unreliable as Raymond had turned out to be, she had protected herself. Their departure proved to her that she had judged them accurately and had behaved correctly.

This period of self-congratulation, however, was short-lived. When they had been gone little more than a week, she caught herself listening for them. Twice she reprimanded the kitchen staff for not setting their places at table. By the time two weeks had gone by she admitted to herself that she missed them, missed them both, and wished they were back. Thinking about their reasons for leaving, she checked with Clara to be sure she had those reasons clear in her head, and concluded at last that they undoubtedly had other reasons as well. Finally she admitted to herself that it must have been her fault, they had gone because of something *she* had done or failed to do.

8

Nora believed that all relationships between human beings began as a contest, changed gradually from one sort of struggle to another, and ended usually in a different sort of contest altogether. Her senses were carefully tuned to

225

the sounds of battle, to its smells and vibrations. No intimations of conflict escaped her. She found traces of it, in fact, where no conflict existed. In her nineteen years she had become unbelievably specialized. She was a remarkable contestant, not because of superior skill or experience, but because she was constantly battle-ready, smiling and alert, with all weapons at hand. And with an unerring instinct for the high ground.

Men, of course, had been her principal adversaries. And against such competition she was convinced she had never lost a skirmish. Primarily, she admitted, because fortune had been kind to her when she was truly young and inexperienced, before her instincts and her observations had had the opportunity to mix and crystallize into a method and a philosophy, before she had managed to make herself invulnerable and unassailable. Her good fortune had been that the young men she had encountered, if *encounter* is the proper word, when she was just old enough for such exposures, were chaps who for whatever reasons did not cause her to respond. Or perhaps one should say that even when responding, she never lost her objectivity, never surrendered her powers of observation. She was perfectly willing, often eager, to lose control, but she was never in danger of losing *herself*.

Learning quickly the advantage that accrues to a person who manages, in an emotional circumstance, to remain unemotional, she vowed to herself that what had begun as good fortune would become, in her hands, a programme. She would always think in terms of objectives, she decided. She would identify the areas of resistance and then negate them one by one, staying always in balance, always sure, putting no forces in the field that she was not able to sacrifice, and most important, she would maintain detachment, keep herself cool and balanced always, her eyes clearly focused on her own needs.

This is not to say that Nora was, by nature, a dispassionate young woman. She was not. But knowing herself and believing very strongly that she understood the game at hand, she determined early on that in any situation

226

of passion or high emotions she would always prevail if hers was the lesser passion, if her emotions were the least turbulent. In her years since childhood she had followed this rule and it had not failed her. Like the traveller with a carefully-studied road map she felt secure and solid about future journeys.

As we have seen, she applied her best experience in these matters to Jesse. After wondering at first if he was worth the bother, deciding for a time that he was not, and concluding at last that he might after all be able to solve problems, provide answers, and take her to the horizons where she needed desperately to go, daring to believe that he might even turn out to be something quite wonderful, she took him by the hand and led him into the garden.

As the summer passed along, as they had a truly enjoyable time together, as pieces fell into place and at last a date for marriage was set and made public, Nora never questioned that everything would proceed according to plan, *her* plan, that all events would occur on their proper dates, that rooms would be bathed with light when she touched the nearest switch, and that very soon she would be in London or Venice or God-knows-where with a proper and presentable husband. Country life would be far behind her. Wingate Fields, safe and predictable and indescribably insular, would become what it deserved to be, a place to visit on odd holidays.

Against this hand-painted scrim of fond hopes and fierce longing, it is easy to imagine Nora's disappointment when Jesse announced that he was leaving at once for New York. She did not see it as a major detour. She did not question that he would return as quickly as he said he would, late October or early November. Nothing she had planned would be altered or delayed. But his departure, all the same, gave her uneasiness about the future. Jesse's independent decision about going and his refusal to consider her objections or to change his plans for her sake gave her a sudden new identity in relation to him, one that she had not chosen and one that she in no way enjoyed. It was

227

foreign to her. It lessened her self-confidence and threatened to alter her inner-directed rhythm.

Thus it was that she played a loving and conciliatory role with him those last days before he left for Liverpool and New York. As we have seen, however, as she watched him go, she was planning ahead. She promised herself that she would find ways to discourage such independent actions in future. After Twelfth Night, after their wedding, she would lovingly clarify and he would lovingly understand the way their life together was lovingly destined to be.

Her insistence to him that she had questioned his relationship to Helen from the start, that she had labelled it as something quite apart from its surface presentation, her feigned jealousy of her cousin, was in fact, more ploy than fact. If Helen had not existed, Nora would probably have created her. One of the tools in her seduction kit was her belief that no man can resist the notion that he is caught between two women, that he is the single golden male in a pride of lions, that a specific competition has been engaged with him as the only prize, that blood will be shed, if necessary, to best the adversary.

Foolishness? Perhaps. But not in Nora's experience. She had mastered the art of creating, then destroying, nonexistent rivals, all to the purpose of generating or embellishing the ego of the man in question. Once she had made contact with that particular male centre she could, she felt, stimulate whatever response might serve her purpose.

Nora was additionally bolstered, as far as Jesse was concerned, by her belief that Helen, even if there *had* been something between them, was no match for her. They were as different, she felt, as two young women could be, and though Nora did not see herself as a choice assemblage of all female attributes, a woman whom no man could resist, she did believe that any man who interested *her* would not be a man who would be taken with Helen.

So Nora was, for the most part, relaxed and sanguine, watching Jesse wave from the car window as he set off for Liverpool; she knew that she had been bested in a minor skirmish but she had no doubt about her ability to prevail when the sustained engagement would begin, when all her bowmen and lancers were in position, when Jesse was back at Wingate Fields, and Twelfth Night was past.

She was on a pinnacle, then, that day in early September when Jesse left. She had contrived to position herself on a high crag indeed. So her fall, when it came, was a long one. At the end of the second week in December, she did something she hadn't done since she was a child. She went to her mother for help. Sitting in Clara's upstairs parlour, heavy rain outside, a wind from the west punishing the great trees that ringed the gardens; she began to weep. 'What shall I do?' she said. 'What can I possibly do?'

'I think we shall have to make some changes. Postpone matters a bit. We'll schedule the wedding for springtime when the weather is pretty. How would you like a garden ceremony? We could do it in May if you'd like. On your birthday perhaps.'

'Let's not deceive each other, Mother. There's not going to be a wedding. You know that and so do I.'

'No, I *don't* know that. I've read Jesse's letters. He's written to me and your grandfather as well as to you. I don't think he wants to postpone the wedding any more than you do.'

'Then why isn't he here?'

'I think he's explained that. You understand the situation.'

'No, I don't understand it. I don't understand it at all. He told us he was going to America to spend some weeks there with Baby Helen . . . .'

'Why do you call her that? She's your cousin, Nora. And she's a fine young woman.'

'She's a baby. She wants spoon-feeding, it seems to me. She wants constant attention and fresh nappies.'

'She's had a difficult time.'

'Everyone has a difficult time,' Nora said. 'A grown-up person reacts in one way and a baby reacts quite differently. Can you tell me what she's doing?'

'I think she's trying to get hold of herself.'

229

'What does that mean? She left here as if she was on fire. Had to get back to university on a specific day or the earth would stop. And what does she do? She doesn't even go home. She decides to travel for a few months or a few years or for her lifetime maybe. I mean it, Mother. She's a baby. Crying to be noticed. Throwing her toys on the carpet. And all the while Jesse is sitting in Fort Beck waiting for her to come home so he can help her adjust to living in her own house. It's like a play written by a lunatic. If *she's* not there, why does *he* have to be there? And where is she, anyway? Is she living in a bank vault? She says she's travelling but all her letters are postmarked New York and when you write to her you must write to her bank there. Also, *wherever* she is, she doesn't write to Jesse. Or if she does he doesn't mention it. He just says he has to wait till she comes back. I don't understand it. And you don't understand it either.'

'I don't understand *you* sometimes,' Clara said. 'And Hugh is often a total mystery to me. But that doesn't change the way I *feel* about you.'

'We're not talking about me and Hugh. We're talking about Jesse.'

'I'm talking about tolerance,' Clara said. 'And patience. Just because you have strong feelings about something . . . .'

'Strong feelings? Of course I have strong feelings. I'm supposed to be married in less than a month and it seems the groom will be a little late. A few months late, in fact. Or maybe he won't make it at all. What would you do if you were me? How would you feel?'

'I'd feel dreadful,' Clara said. 'I would be frightfully disappointed. But I would try to understand. . . .'

'I've tried that already. And it doesn't work. Because I *don't* understand. I *can't* understand. And neither can you. I know you're trying to make me feel better but the whole thing makes no more sense to you than it does to me. Isn't that a fact?'

'I believe it's an awkward time for Jesse.'

'Why? You said it was difficult for Helen. Now it's

awkward for Jesse. How would you describe *my* situation? What do you think it's like for me.'

'Don't misunderstand me, Nora. I think I know exactly how you feel. I wish I could wave a wand and put it right for you. But I can't. I can't even give you sensible advice. None of us wants sensible advice anyway when we're angry or our feelings are hurt. All I can tell you is what I tell myself. Try to have patience. You'll need plenty of patience after you're married and have children. Maybe this is a good time to practise.'

Nora sat with her hands in her lap watching the rain slash against the window. 'Just tell me one thing,' she said then. '*Why* is it so difficult or awkward for Jesse? *Why* does he think he has to sit there in that house waiting for her to come home? What in the *world* is that all about?'

'I don't know. I'll admit I don't understand it. But that doesn't mean it isn't real for *him.*'

'What *is* it that's so real? That's where I go aground. What is it he must say to her that he couldn't have said this past summer?'

'I don't know. I just know the two of them are very close. Maybe they've had a misunderstanding and it needs to be sorted out.'

'Maybe Baby Helen isn't pleased because he's decided to marry me.'

'Why would she object to that?'

'I don't know. Why is she living in a bank vault?'

Clara smiled. 'You are the most unusual young woman I know. I am very fortunate to have such a lovely and fanatic daughter.'

'I'm not fanatic enough. I should get on a steamer, go to America, and deliver myself to his doorstep. "Since you can't come to me," I'll tell him, "I have come to you." What do you think of *that* idea?'

'I don't know. I'd have to give it some thought.'

'Don't bother. I've already thought of it. And it's a bad idea. If I'm to be jilted I would prefer not be told face-to-face on Jesse's doorstep. I suppose I shall find a way to

231

live with it when it happens but I do not look forward to the moment when the news is broken to me.'

'That's absurd, Nora. There's no such thing in Jesse's mind. Nothing like that is going to happen.'

'Oh yes it is. That's exactly what's going to happen.' She smiled. 'If I'm not careful.'

The Twelfth Night wedding did not take place of course. On the eighteenth December, Nora and Hugh took the train to Scotland to shop for Christmas gifts for their parents and grandparents and to attend a holiday ball at a great house just north of Kintore on the river Don. Two days later, Nora and Edmund Bick were married by a district judge in his chambers in Aberdeen.

9

Helen's child was born on Thursday, March 18, 1920, at one-thirty in the morning. He arrived nine weeks early and was a tiny infant, weighing less than four pounds. The doctor who came to her room after the delivery said, 'He's a little bit of a thing but apart from that he seems perfectly normal.'

'Thank you,' Helen said. 'I'm glad.' She wanted to ask a thousand questions and she had the feeling that this particular doctor, if she *had* asked, would talk to her freely, would tell her whatever she wanted to know about the baby. But she had carefully prepared herself for these moments. She simply said, 'Thank you very much. I appreciate your coming to tell me.'

Her pregnancy had been remarkably easy. She had been physically active, had walked several miles each day, and had carefully adhered to her prescribed diet. As a result she gained only fourteen pounds; when she left the hospital three days after the baby was born she was only five pounds above her normal weight. She wore a snug dress under her winter coat and drove her own car from Portland to the house she had rented near Damariscotta.

232

Since the baby had arrived ahead of schedule, Helen had several months left on her lease. All the same, as she drove north from Portland she told herself it would be wise for her to pack up and leave as soon as it was convenient for her, as soon as she felt like travelling.

Apart from maternity clothes, a few kitchen things, and some warm sweaters, wool hats and parkas and boots which had got her through the winter, she had bought almost nothing during her months in Maine. Her car had been leased from a Packard dealer in Lewiston so that would go back to him as soon as she was ready to leave. Except for one additional valise and her warm coat she expected to depart carrying no more luggage than she had on arrival.

Her packing, then, was a simple matter. But as the days passed, she found herself unpacking and repacking day after day. It was always carefully thought out. Each time she had a specific objective in her mind, a reason why she must start again. But at last she could no longer deceive herself. She stood one mid-morning, the white winter sun reflecting off the sea behind the huge rocks where the waves broke, felt the sun's heat burning through the glass and warming her cheeks, studied, for what seemed to be the thousandth time, the neat stacks of clothing and toilet articles and books alongside her pieces of luggage, and began to cry.

She sat in a deep chair with the sun on her face and her hands limp in her lap; like a mute witness, she felt as though she was observing, rather than producing, the tears that came from her eyes. It was as though she had waited forever for this silent and solitary time, as though she had kept this rendezvous with sorrow, had held everything back till some signal told her that *this* moment, if not the *perfect* moment, was the best one she would ever have, that everything proper and studied and thoughtful about her, all her reserve and *politesse*, could now be put aside. She could dive as deep as she chose, stay under as long as she was able, explore every subterranean grotto of grief she could find. She could lie on her bed, pace the floor,

233

soak in her bath, prowl the midnight beach, and cry until there was no more crying left, sob for her tiny, early-born son, for the loss of Jesse and all he had meant to her, and most of all for Raymond, at last for him, for what he had been, when he was alive, and for the cold vacuum he had created by dying.

Some jungle wisdom told her she had fallen into a pool that was deeper and blacker than anything she had known, and that one could survive it only by surrendering to it. She sensed that this ugly, almost orgasmic revelation of her capacity for grief had been triggered by some control centre that was foreign to her, that she had no choice but to let it take her where it might until that same force chose to release her, to put her down like a child, pat her gently, and let her sleep.

At last it happened. One late afternoon, she rolled into a ball like a soft dog in winter, pulled a coat over her and went to sleep on the couch that faced the stone fireplace. When she woke up finally it was early evening of the next day and she was in her bed, still wearing her clothes but with the blankets pulled over her. She had no memory of moving from the couch to the bed.

Looking at her pale cheeks and swollen eyes, she did not conclude that she was a changed creature cut off from where she'd come from and unsure of where she would go. No such poetic conclusions seized her. She did not feel in any way, exorcized or transformed. But she knew she had seen a face at the window and the face had been unmistakably hers, that she had slipped outside herself and taken a complex journey.

With no desire to repeat that journey, and with no notion of how she could proceed even if she *did* need to repeat it, she was conscious, all the same, that, whatever it was, whatever it had been, it was precious and vital to her, it would always stay with her, would haunt her and frighten her, sustain her and shore her up, console and challenge and define her for the rest of her life.

234

Before she left Damariscotta, Helen wrote a note to her mother.

I am anxious to see you. It's been too long. I will be in New York for a week starting May fifth.
All my love,
Helen

Throughout her pregnancy, through those autumn and winter months in Maine Helen had been baffled by Anna's almost constant presence in her thoughts. She refused to accept the simplistic explanation that her own impending motherhood had touched some sensor inside her and had caused Anna to appear. But accept it or not, the reality of her mother was inescapable. It was, however, a changed reality. In all the years since she was eight, her judgments of Anna had been anchored in the period *after* she left Raymond. Now Helen found herself bringing the earlier years into focus, when she had been a little girl.

She found much that was warm and lovely in those memories: fresh images of Raymond, and an endless number of things to love and admire in her mother. Just as her adoration of Raymond had survived the revelation that he was in fact a different and more complex man than she had thought him to be, so did she begin to regard Anna as something other than the woman who had abandoned her father. Helen could see that her mother too, had been deceived, and even if she hadn't known it, she must have sensed it; it must have been a factor in the series of circumstances that had persuaded her, at last, to leave him, to leave Fort Beck, and go back to New York.

Having operated previously from the premise that her father was perfect and her mother less than perfect, Helen, in her new wisdom, suspected that everyone was imperfect, herself included, and that objective judgments,

however fair and carefully arrived at, have nothing whatsoever to do with love.

Even before going to Maine, before she began to think
of herself as a mother and was drawn by such thoughts
into thinking of her own mother, during the summer weeks
she spent at Wingate Fields, she often caught pictures of
Anna flashing through her mind. Her conversations with
Clara and the development of that warm relationship were
a part of the process, no question of it. Her enjoyment of
those warm aunt-and-niece colloquies made her wonder if
such pleasures were permanently unavailable to her and
Anna or if they had been unavailable only because she had
assumed they were.

Reaching no conclusions, damning neither herself nor
Anna, she continued to examine the evidence and she
began to see her mother in an increasingly favourable light;
she began to look forward to seeing her again, to making
a new connection, a more direct connection, not through
Raymond, or around Raymond, but simply between Anna
and herself.

As we have seen, however, her state of mind when she
arrived in New York from England was not conducive to
new beginnings. The final events of the final days she had
spent in Wingate still occupied her totally. The alternating
currents of self-doubt and self-confidence that coursed
through her, colliding sometimes in the pit of her stomach,
made her temporarily unfit, she felt, for the company of
others, particularly Anna. When that meeting took place
she wanted to be able to give it full concentration.

Later, spending long hours alone in the house in Maine,
noting her symptoms and body changes, reading at length
about how she should nurture herself and care for herself
and reading, too, all the books and magazines she could
find about infant care, knowing as she read and reread and
memorized that these were rules and dictums she would
not be able to test, information she would not be allowed
to implement; as she spent those silent days by herself,
she remembered in detail the very different atmosphere
that had surrounded an expectant mother in the Bardoni

households. Only the act of conception and the moment of birth were private efforts there. Everything else was communal. When a woman was pregnant her entire household, it appeared, developed symptoms. Everyone had first-hand experience in midwifing, nursing, and infant care. Differences of viewpoint were settled by seniority or lung power. But the principal point that Helen remembered was that it was a *living* subject. It was *discussed* and examined, thoroughly and constantly. It was a part of the family's life.

As a young girl, Helen had misunderstood the process she was witnessing. She assumed that expectant mothers wanted privacy and gentility, that it was an experience to be shared between a man and a woman, no other relatives invited, no other opinions or experiences needed. In Maine, however, with only her occasional check-ups in Portland to break the solitary pattern, she had fantasies, sometimes, as she sat by the fireplace sipping tea. She imagined she heard cars stopping in the road outside and the babble of Italian voices. Then the door would thump open and half a dozen women of all ages would sweep through the short hallway and into the large, open room where she sat, carrying food and pans and cutlery, footbaths, balls of wool, and knitting needles, great loaves of crusty bread and jugs of chianti. The image made her smile, made her solitude more bearable and more lonely all in one stroke.

Most of all, she needed to talk. She needed to make clear to someone what she was doing and why she was doing it. Longing most of all to understand, to explain herself to herself, she knew it could not be done in solitude. It could not be simply written down or thought through. It had to be spoken, expressed, to someone who would understand, who would not pass judgment, someone who would listen and sympathize, and give support. Helen had never needed that kind of reassurance before, had never questioned herself so profoundly, had never truly understood that blood-link, that kinship that binds a daughter to her mother, a mother to her child.

237

Now, however, once the thought had possessed her, it wouldn't let go. In a matter of weeks she had transformed Anna, had changed the impulse to talk to her into an obsession. She saw it as a final and necessary step in her absolution. Knowing she had had no choice, *feeling* that, very strongly and consistently, she needed, all the same, to have someone, *anyone*, tell her she had done the right thing. But primarily she needed to hear Anna say it.

Having decided that she would be completely open with her mother, that she would tell her everything as simply and candidly as she knew how, she reviewed the sequence of events in her mind and decided she could present her case well and sympathetically up until the final act. How could she tell Anna or anyone, that she had never looked at her baby, that she had agreed to that arrangement in advance, that she had simply dressed herself, left the hospital, and had gone home. End of chapter, end of story.

What had driven her? What had motivated her? Helen knew the answer. She certainly knew the emotional climate that answer had sprung from. But how could she make it clear and understandable and defensible to Anna? Helen wrestled with it and rehearsed it in her mind, as though she was speaking to her mother.

I'm not ashamed of what happened. Perhaps I was crazy to throw myself at Hugh the way I did. And perhaps I was foolish when I decided that I would go ahead and have the baby, all by myself, without telling anyone. But, God, I so wanted to have that little child. Those months when I waited for him to be born were the most important months and days of my life. I don't mean I was happy all the time. I wasn't. Sometimes I was tortured. But I felt . . . I can't describe it. I felt the way a woman's meant to feel, I guess. I didn't think then about how it would end, I wouldn't let myself think about the agreement I'd made. I just sat there like a lazy cat, smiling inside and patting my stomach and thinking about the miracle I was about to perform, thinking how my life had changed, how *I* had changed

238

in just a few short months. There was a bird-feeder outside my window. Some birds stay in Maine all winter, did you know that? Little brown birds, and speckled ones, their feathers ruffled from the wind. I used to watch those tough little sweethearts, all courage and perseverance, and beautiful in their scruffy way, and I thought, if they can survive these winters, then a human being can do anything. *I can do anything.* But I was wrong. I couldn't keep my own baby. I signed a paper that would let him go and become somebody else. With a new name and strangers for parents. I let him go because I couldn't help myself. I was scared. But it's not like you think. I wasn't afraid for people to find out I'd had a baby when I wasn't married. And I wouldn't have been afraid to raise him by myself. I could have done that. I know I could have. So it wasn't selfishness or a lack of courage. It was just . . . if you want to know why I was scared, it was . . . it was because I was afraid he wouldn't be *normal*, that he wouldn't be *right*. You know what I mean? The baby's father is Raymond's nephew, his sister's child. Hugh's my first cousin. Nobody knows for *sure* what that can mean. But nobody thinks it's a wise chance to take. Nearly everybody believes that some really bad things can happen. Crazy overlaps of tendencies and characteristics.

I found some medical books in the Portland library and if I hadn't been scared before I was certainly scared after I read them and saw the pictures. I mean what does a person do with a poor little creature like that? How do you live with yourself if you let something like that happen? Even it it's not your fault.

If I'd been completely honest, I would have told the people at the Foundation the truth, but I was afraid. What was I afraid of? I'm not sure. Afraid they'd think I was a terrible, immoral woman, I suppose. Afraid they wouldn't help me. I thought that if something *did* go wrong, if the baby was . . . I thought they'd know what to do, whereas if I was alone . . . I don't know.

239

Anyway, the most beautiful words I've ever heard were when the doctor came into my room and said the baby was perfectly normal and healthy. At that moment I wanted to get up and run into the nursery and steal him. But I was still afraid. No matter what the doctor told me, I was scared.

When she called her mother's telephone number in New York, a woman's voice said, 'Anna's not here. She works every day at Rattner's on Second Avenue.'

'What time does she get home?'

'Late sometimes. Besides she doesn't live here any more. They've got their own place on St Mark's and First. Is this Helen?'

'Yes, it is. Who's this?'

There was a pause. Then the woman went on. 'Anna said you might call here. If you want to see her she's got some time off between the lunch trade and early dinner. Between three and four-thirty, she said she could talk to you.'

'Do you have her home telephone number?'

'No, I don't. She said you should come to Rattner's.'

If Helen had imagined that this telephone conversation was indicative of the kind of reception she would get from Anna, if she had believed that their meeting would be grey and accusatory perhaps, especially after the confession she planned to make, she would have been mistaken on both counts.

Anna, it turned out, was working as a restaurant hostess and it was clear from the first moment Helen saw her that some circumstance in her life had brought about a change in her. She wore a conservative grey frock with a white collar and her hair was piled strikingly on top of her head. She wore little make-up but there was high colour in her cheeks that Helen had not seen there before. She had also gained a certain amount of weight but it was becoming to her and her ankles were quite beautiful below a skirt that would have been scandalous in Fort Beck but which had recently become fashionable in New York and London.

Since Raymond's death almost eighteen months before, Helen had had almost no contact with Anna. She suspected that was the reason for the abrupt conversation she had with the unidentified woman on the telephone. And she fully expected, and felt she deserved, some recriminations and searching questions from her mother. No such pattern developed however. From Anna's opening remarks it became clear that she had no desire to dwell in the past. Nor was she interested in any impulse of Helen's to apologize or confess her wrong-doings. On the contrary, Anna seemed almost exclusively concerned with furnishing information about herself.

'Will you look at me? Did you ever imagine I could be so plump? My mother loves it. All my relatives love it. Italians say a woman after she reaches thirty must decide in favour of her face or her behind. If she wants to have a pretty face, she must eat and enjoy herself and be content with a big bottom.'

'You don't have a big bottom,' Helen said. 'You look wonderful.'

'Hard work and good food. They work me to death here. I'm at the door at ten in the morning and I'm lucky if I'm home by ten at night. But I feel fine, kid. I feel the best I've ever felt. I'll be thirty-eight years old in December and I feel like I'm eighteen.'

'I thought maybe you were mad at me. Whoever I talked to on the phone this morning wasn't very friendly.'

'That's Rosa. She's mad at the world.'

'I know I haven't written much or anything. I wouldn't blame you if you were mad at me. I had some crazy ideas in my head and I was feeling pretty awful after Raymond died.'

'I guess you were. It's a shame he died so young. I couldn't believe it when I heard from you.'

'It's not right that I didn't come to see you,' Helen said. 'I'm sure that's why your family's mad at me. And I should have written.'

'You don't have to say you're sorry to me, Helen. I'm your mom. And I'm not perfect either. If you and I start

241

apologizing to each other we might not get finished till Saturday.'

'I've never seen you like this,' Helen said.

'How do you mean?'

'I don't know. You're just different.'

'Better or worse?'

'Better, I think. You act like you're happy.'

'Good for me.'

'I used to think you were sad a lot.'

'I *was* sad a lot. I must have been a great picture for a kid like you to look at. But I'm not sad now.'

'I've been in England,' Helen said then. 'I was visiting Raymond's relatives. It turned out he wasn't American after all. At least he wasn't born here.'

'That's funny,' Anna said. 'The first time my grandmother met him she said he was English. I used to get very angry with her but she always said, "I know an Englishman when I see one." '

'I found out quite a bit about him. Some things I thought you'd probably like to know . . . .'

'I don't think so.'

'I don't mean bad things,' Helen said.

'Bad *or* good, I don't think it's any of my business now. I'm sure Raymond had good reasons for pretending to be something he wasn't but they're not important any more.'

'Some of them *are* important. There was a great deal of money involved. And since you and he were still married when he died . . . .'

'No, we weren't. We hadn't been married since I left him. Not really. If I hadn't been raised a Catholic, if your dad and I hadn't been married in the church we would have been divorced a long time ago.'

'That doesn't matter. You're still entitled.'

Anna shook her head. 'I'm entitled to nothing. If there's some money for you I'm glad to hear it but it would bother me a lot to get involved with something like that.'

'You wouldn't have to work so hard.'

'Maybe not. But I *like* to work. Everybody in my family works. You know that. All the people I know who are

242

looking for a hand-out end up miserable. I even felt funny about accepting Raymond's life insurance money when it came but the man said I had no choice. I was the beneficiary and that's all there was to it. Five thousand dollars. I'd never seen so much money in my life. I put it in a savings bank and haven't touched it since. If you ever need money . . . .'

Helen shook her head. 'I was going to say the same thing to you.'

'I don't need anything. I'm fine. Whatever you got from Raymond and his family, that's yours to use and enjoy. Young women your age are going to have lots of chances now that women never had before. Things are really changing, they're changing fast, and you should take advantage of it. Make a good life for yourself. My mama thinks the world is going to hell but I told her it's just going to be different, that's all. When I was your age, when I married Raymond, I was scared of my shadow. And I felt like that for a long time. It seemed like there was a set of rules for everything. Whenever I turned around I felt like I was breaking some law. It's taken me a long time to get over it but I don't feel like that any more. If I'm lucky I could live forty or fifty more years and I don't want to waste that time. I want to enjoy myself. I can't spend my whole life worrying about whether I'm doing the right thing. I just want to make sure I do *something*.'

'What do you think you'll do?'

Anna smiled. 'I've already *done* a few things,' she said. Then, 'I'm sorry we couldn't have had this talk before but I didn't know how to get in touch with you. After Raymond died I wore black for a year and I lit a candle for him every morning at St Ignatius. My family thought I was crazy to be in mourning for a man I hadn't lived with for more than nine years but I felt it was the right thing to do so I did it. But after my mourning period was over and I'd put away my black dresses and my veil, early in December last year, I got married. I've been married to a very nice man for five months and six days.' She studied Helen's face and waited for a reaction. 'Are you surprised?'

243

'I guess I am. I thought . . . I don't know what I thought.'

'I'll tell you what *I* thought,' Anna said. 'I thought I'd get grey hair and spend the rest of my life in your grandmother's kitchen, cooking linguini and osso buco and taking care of my nieces and nephews. I always felt guilty about Raymond and you, never thought I'd been very good at being a wife or a mother. So I didn't have much interest in trying again. After you left and went back to Fort Beck I didn't have much interest in anything. But during those months I wore black I spent a lot of time in church. And I spent a lot more time in my room at home, thinking about things and trying to figure out what I'd done that was so wrong. Finally I decided it hadn't been my fault. It hadn't been anybody's fault. Two people choose each other and it doesn't work out. It's sad but it happens. Raymond and I were too different. We came from different worlds. One of us should have been smart enough to see it. But neither of us did. So we made a mistake. And you were the one who had to suffer for it.'

'I don't feel that way,' Helen said. 'I don't blame anybody for anything.'

'You used to blame *me*. You told me so.'

'I know I did. And I'm sorry for that. Things look different to me now.'

'They look different to me, too. That's what I've been trying to tell you. I looked around at all my women relatives, all married to Italian men. Men from the neighbourhood, people they'd known all their lives. They scream and fight and threaten to leave each other, but they don't do it. They stay together because they're *alike*. They *know* the same things and *need* the same things. When I took off my mourning clothes I knew that if I ever *did* get married again, it would be a man from the neighbourhood.'

'Is that what you did?'

Anna smiled. 'I sure did. A month later. You remember Joe Buscatore?'

'Vinnie's friend?'

'That's right. My brother's best friend. He's been underfoot in our house for as long as I can remember. Six years

244

younger than me. For years Vinnie's been saying, "Joe's waiting for *you*, Anna. Ain't going to marry anybody else till he's damned sure he can't have you." The family used to joke about it. When Raymond and I got married, Joe was only twelve years old but Vinnie said he drank two bottles of verdicchio and was drunk and sick for three days. I saw him every day after I moved back here from Fort Beck but I never really *looked* at him till a year after your father died. Then I *looked* at him. He forced me to. He said, "I've been waiting a long time, Anna. And I'm not twelve years old any more!" I told him I was too old for him and he said "That's right. And I still can't drink verdicchio. But if you overlook my flaws, I'll overlook yours."

As she travelled from New York to Illinois, Helen went over her meeting with Anna, reconstructed it in sharp detail in her memory, tried to sort through her reactions to see how her feelings towards her mother had changed or if they had changed at all. No matter what position she took, no matter what adjustments she made or tried to make, one thing was certain. The woman she had spent almost two hours with in a corner booth of a Second Avenue restaurant was so different from the Anna she had known all her life as to be almost unrecognizable. True, she was not physically changed. Her features and proportions, indeed all her characteristics and mannerisms were as Helen remembered them. But apart from these visible things, nothing remained the same. Anna was like a landmark ante-bellum building, an historical treasure whose exterior had been preserved by law but whose interior had been entirely removed and replaced by new timbers, fresh lath and plaster, elegant woodwork and floors, carefully painted walls, and fine furniture, each element perfectly crafted but bearing little resemblance to what the previous interior had been.

Unquestionably, Anna had become an altered woman. Helen now saw humour and courage and a hint of recklessness in her where before she had felt that pessimism was the key colour, complemented or contrasted with sombre tones of fear and caution. Realizing that she knew this redone version of her mother only slightly, concluding further that she would very likely never come to know her well, she decided, all the same, that she liked this woman better, felt connected to her and related to her. Having passed the age when she needed the comfort and guidance of a mother she felt as if she had at last made contact with an imperfect but positive female who was also very much, for the first time, perhaps, her mother.

The irony would not go away. Having longed for an opportunity to confide in Anna, to talk at length about her own sins and poor judgments believing that this was the one person she could tell what she had needed for months to tell someone, Helen had found their roles surprisingly and completely reversed. She had felt like a parent hearing her daughter's romantic confessions.

Anna's description of Joe, of the small apartment they had rebuilt and painted and furnished, of the gifts he had bought her, the meals she had cooked, their ferry rides to Staten Island where they hoped to buy a small house, all these high-key, bright-coloured pictures were too positive and dominant and filled with joy and hope. There was no room left for Helen's sad little story, no place to slide in that dim, black-and-white snapshot of misfortune and doubt and self-criticism. How could she present her plea for understanding, her *mea culpa*, her reasons for abandoning her never-seen child, to a handsome and vigorous woman whose fondest hope, it seemed, and whose clear expectation, was to have a house filled with children. 'Joe would like to have six kids. And so would I. My grandmother had five babies after she was forty. And two after she was fifty. And *her* mother the same. It runs in our family. And Joe's family too. I don't think you'll be an only child for very long. With any luck and a lot of candles lit at St Ignatius you could end up with half a dozen little brothers and sisters. Sticky fingers and bare bottoms all over the place.'

Before she left New York, Helen sent a wire to Jesse telling him when she would arrive in Fort Beck. As she looked out of the window of her compartment and listened to the click of the train wheels she wondered how it would be, what they would talk about. Nearly ten months since they'd seen each other; but the length of time was less significant, she felt, than the circumstances of her leaving England and her frame of mind when she left. She did not regret her actions at that time. She suspected that under similar circumstances she would behave in the same way again. On the other hand, whatever her convictions, however clearly she remembered her departure and the why of it, it had taken a more abstract form for her now. She had been carelessly dealt with, she was still convinced of that, but now that some time had passed, Jesse seemed less flagrantly the villain. It made no sense to her, separating the action from the actor, but she did it, in her mind, all the same. Measuring the time she had known Jesse against the comparatively short time they had spent in England, trying hard to understand the temptations and pressures he had been exposed to there, she came down on the side of tolerance and forgiveness; she concluded that whatever anger and bewilderment she had felt when she left Wingate Fields it was not something that should be given permanent life; it should not be allowed to continue. Her total relationship with Jesse was more important than any single section of it. This, she decided, was a first principle and she was sure that Jesse felt, or would come to feel, the same.

A more serious problem, she decided, was, or might be, the length of time that had passed since she had returned to America. In all that time, until she sent him the wire from New York, she had not been in touch with Jesse. From the day she found out she was expecting a baby she could not bring herself to write to him. It was one thing to send off letters to Clara and Angus describing her travels in Canada and the western part of the United States, all the details copied from travel books and vacation folders, it was quite another thing to foist such stories on Jesse. She could not bring herself to lie to him. Nor could she tell him the truth about where she was or why she was there. So she didn't contact him at all. The enormity of the secret she was forced to hide made this silence seem not only logical but absolutely necessary. To Jesse, however, she knew it must have seemed quite different.

In addition to the cable he had sent to her ship as she crossed from Liverpool to New York, she had heard from him three times. Two letters had come to her in New York and one, several weeks later, to Maine, all forwarded to her by Mr Winters at the bank, her bank address having been sent on to Jesse by Clara. In his third letter, Jesse had said –

It seems that I'm not going to hear from you. If that is the case then I won't write again. I have no idea what you're up to or what's rattling about in your head but whatever it is, I wish you luck with it.

After that letter, Helen decided that perhaps Jesse would not be in Fort Beck by the time she was able to go there. But each letter from Clara made what seemed to be casual mention of the fact that he was indeed still there, the last such message having arrived just before she left Damariscotta to see Anna in New York.

Helen was reasonably certain then that Jesse would be there when she arrived. She was also confident that she would be able to bandage whatever wounds he might have sustained from what appeared to be her neglect. She believed she was as important, *enfin*, in his life-scheme as he was in hers, that he would come to realize that if he had not already, and the wreckage they had scattered around them in England could be patched together again and made to float.

Her arrival at the Fort Beck station however, was not encouraging. Jesse wasn't there. Nor was he there to meet her at home. 'He had to be in Springfield,' Mrs Esping told her. 'He'll be back very late.'

Helen waited up till midnight but he didn't come home. Next morning at breakfast, Mrs Esping said, 'He rang up first thing this morning. Had to stay over in Springfield. Says he'll try to get home by supper-time.'

Once again, however, Helen had dinner alone. She sat up late reading the Springfield paper and listening to some of Raymond's old records on her victrola. She waited till nearly midnight. Then she went upstairs to bed. Sometime later she was awakened by the sound of a car pulling into the driveway under her window. The engine shut off. Two car doors opened and closed and she heard Jesse's voice, then a woman's voice, and footsteps walking away down the gravel drive. She listened for the sound of the downstairs door but she heard nothing. At last she went to sleep again.

Jesse did not appear for either breakfast or lunch. It was mid-afternoon before he and Helen sat down in Raymond's library for the reunion she had envisaged for months. The conversation, however, did not flow easily. Jesse seemed quiet. And cautious. He was thinner than she had ever seen him and his limp seemed more pronounced

'You look tired,' Helen said.

'I am.'

'Mrs Esping says you're on the run all the time. Are you working?'

'I keep busy,' he said.

'I mean are you teaching?'

'No, I'm not.'

They sat quietly in the big, cool room, not looking at each other, each of them waiting, it seemed, for the other to speak. Finally she said, 'I was hoping you'd be at the station when I got here. Did you get the wire I sent?'

He nodded. 'I had to be in Springfield.'

Another silence. Then, 'I've never seen you like this,' she said. 'What's the matter with you? Am I supposed to say I'm sorry. Is that it? Do you want me to apologize because I left England without telling you? Well, I can't apologize for that. I was mad as hell at you then and I'd do the same thing again. What do you think of that?'

'It doesn't surprise me.'

'God, you're maddening,' she said. 'You sit there like a buddha, a very skinny buddha. You're too thin, do you know that? Don't you ever eat?' When he didn't answer, she went on, 'All right, I know you're mad at me. And maybe I deserve it. Maybe I should have got in touch with you when I knew you were back in Fort Beck. But I didn't. So what are we going to do about it? Maybe you should have done some things *you* didn't do. I had my reasons and I guess you had yours. When I left England I didn't care if I never saw you again. I felt as if I'd been auctioned off. So I decided . . . .'

'What did you decide?'

'I don't know,' she said.

'Yes, you do. You decided to teach me a lesson. You knew I came back here just to see you, to spend some time with you before I had to go back to England. But for some half-cocked reasons of your own you decided to disappear. If I was concerned about you, you apparently wanted to make sure that I had something to be concerned about. You took off on your Cook's tour to God-knows-where.'

'No, I didn't. I didn't go anywhere. I was in one place from September till just a little while ago. I was in Maine all that time.'

'Then why all the made-up magic lantern tour? Why all those travel-folder letters to Clara?'

'I felt silly about that. But I didn't want her to know where I was because I knew she'd tell you. And I wasn't ready to see you yet.'

'But now you're ready.'

'If I weren't, I wouldn't be here.'

'What makes you think I'm ready?' he said.

'I know you've been waiting here for me to come home.'

'No, I haven't. I was when I first got here. That's why I came back. But once I saw what you were up to, when you didn't bother to answer the letters I sent you, I started making other plans.'

250

'Was that one of your other plans I heard talking down in the driveway last night?'

He smiled. 'No. Mid came a little later.'

'Mid?'

'Mildred Quigley. People call her Mid. She's a chemistry instructor at Foresby. Very bright. She rented the Bergmann house across the street. Bergmann's on sabbatical.'

'How convenient.'

'Yes, it is.'

'I trust she's superior in every way to Nora.'

'She's a nice young woman. I've never compared her to Nora or anybody else.'

'I hope you don't blame me because your marriage to Nora didn't happen,' Helen said then.

'I don't blame anybody for that. It probably wouldn't have worked out anyway.'

'That really stunned me,' Helen said. 'I couldn't imagine you two together.'

'Nothing mysterious about it. She liked me and I liked her.'

'Then why didn't you . . . .'

'She decided it wasn't a good idea, I guess. And after she married somebody else I decided the same thing.'

'If you want my opinion . . . .'

'I don't,' he said.

'Since we're being rude to each other, I'll give it to you anyway. I think you're *lucky* she married somebody else.'

'Is that what you think?'

'Yes, it is. It's good you got away from there. The whole atmosphere, the way those people live, the way they *think*, is no good for you. It's no good for me either.'

'It may not be good for you,' he said, 'but it's good for *me*. I *like* the way they live. I like it a lot. I like everything about it.'

'You just like the easy life. You got used to it. You got used to people polishing your boots and pouring your coffee.'

'You're right,' he said, 'I *do* like that. I like the money and I like the comfort. I like it all.'

'Then you should be happy. You have all the money you want; you can live wherever you want to and pay for all the servants you need. You don't have to hang around Wingate Fields.'

'You missed the point, Helen. I *want* to hang around there. Two weeks from now I'm going back there.'

'Why, for God's sake?'

'Because I think of it as my home. And besides, I feel an obligation to go back.'

'Why? Because your name's Bradshaw now?'

'No. Because I think I owe it to Angus to be there and spend some time with him. He wanted a son and now he's got one. I may not be the real thing but I expect to do what I can for him as long as he's alive.'

'That's a long time,' Helen said. 'He'll live to be a hundred.'

'No, he won't.'

'What do you mean?'

'I mean he's sick. He's wearing out.'

'Does he know it?'

'Of course he knows it. Nobody keeps secrets from Angus.'

'I'm sorry,' Helen said.

'So am I. But he hasn't exactly wasted his life. He's used every minute of it, made a great record for himself.'

'And that's what *you're* going to do? Learn the wool business, figure out how to buy land cheap and sell it dear. Are you planning to learn everything Angus can teach you?'

'No, I'm not. And he doesn't expect me to. But I hope to learn enough so I can be some help to Clara. She's the brains of the family after Angus goes.'

'Sounds like you'll have a lot of free time on your hands. Maybe you and Nora can take some long drives together in her roadster.'

'What's the matter with you? Nora's not a little sugar angel on top of a cake. Everybody knows that. But she's not all terrible either.'

'I think she's trashy.'

252

'Do you think I'm trashy?'

'No.'

'Why not? I was about to marry her.'

'That's because she had you hypnotized.'

'I wasn't hypnotized. I made up my own mind.'

'But you changed it,' Helen said. 'You didn't marry her.'

'It wasn't my fault.'

'I don't believe that. If she hadn't married Edmund I still don't think you'd have married her.'

'Let me ask you a question,' Jesse said then. 'If you'd decided you wanted to marry Hugh, how do you think I would have reacted?'

Helen felt the blood rush to her face. 'Why would you say something like that?'

'It seems like a fair question to me.'

'Are you saying there was something between me and Hugh?'

'That's not the point,' Jesse said.

'Yes, it *is* the point. If you're implying that . . . .'

'I'm not implying anything. I just said *if*. And since you don't want to answer, *I* will. If you'd told me you were going to marry Hugh, I'd have told you I wasn't crazy about him but it was up to you to choose any man you want.'

'Did Nora say something out of the way about Hugh and me?'

'No. What are you so jumpy about? Nobody ever saw you say a civil word to him. And he goes for days without talking to anybody.'

'I can't stand it when people gossip or imply nasty things about other people.'

'Neither can I,' he said.

Whatever they may have planned to say to each other, whatever objections and resentments they expected to present, and whatever defences, it all trickled away somehow. They arrived not at accommodation or peace or understanding or forgiveness but rather at an impasse. All threads of argument and investigation seemed to tangle together. Words continued to come out but they were

253

shored up less and less by conviction. Like mourners at a graveside they seemed to have arrived too late. Nothing to be done beyond dropping a handful of dirt into the dark hole and walking downslope to the waiting carriage.

In the days before Jesse left for New York to board the steamer that would take him to England, they were friendly and cordial to each other, managing a pale facsimile of what their relationship had been a year earlier, before they had gone east together to explore the mysteries of Raymond's family. Everything they discussed now and their manner of discussing it was reasonable. When Helen said, 'I might as well sell this house. I don't think I'll ever live in Fort Beck again,' Jesse said, 'In that case I guess it doesn't make sense to hang on to it.' When he said, 'I always expect to work. I'm not the type to sit around doing nothing,' she said, 'No, you're certainly not.' When he went on to say, 'I'm not sure I have the gift to be a writer but I think I could be *helpful* to writers. Perhaps publish a little magazine, that sort of thing,' she said, 'That's a fine idea. Lots of little magazines springing up now.' And when she said, 'I want to see the west. I'm particularly interested in Santa Fe and Taos. The Indian silverwork fascinates me,' he said. 'You should open a little shop maybe. Sell just the very best things. I think you'd be good at that.'

When he left they embraced at the railway station and told each other how much they would be missed. Two days after he departed she left Chicago on a train going west. She was stunned and saddened that she had seemed to give up so easily something that had been so precious to her. She wondered what it was in her that had allowed it to happen. Jesse, on his way to New York, had questioned himself in the same way. Like Helen, he had found no answers.

254

Chapter Six

1

When Nora and Edmund were married in Aberdeen she knew of course that she was acting in haste. Under hard questioning she might have conceded that there was madness as well as haste in her decision. But any hesitation or misgivings she may have felt were cancelled out by her conviction that she had regained control. As we have seen in the conversation she had with Clara, Nora had been truly dismayed by the situation with Jesse. The belief she expressed to her mother that he had no intention of marrying her, either on Twelfth Night or at any other time, was not as disturbing to her – she wasn't, in fact, as convinced of that fact as she pretended to be – not nearly so disturbing as the flash of stubbornness and independence he had suddenly displayed. This is not to say that if he had returned to England in early November as promised she would have rejected him. She would not have. But all the same, the strength of purpose he had shown would have made her a wary bride. Nora's value system where it concerned her continuing relationship with a man made no provision for give-and-take. She sincerely believed, and experience had supported that belief, that *her* being in command of any such situation was a biological and psychological imperative. The fact that she had been reared in a male-dominated atmosphere made her all the more intent on reversing those poles of power in her own life.

Nora never deceived herself for a moment about the

255

comparative desirability of Edmund and Jesse. Jesse was her choice. But if he was to be a problem, if all decisions were to be routed through him, if the sabre was to be in *his* hand, then the sooner she escaped the better. Better to deal with the familiar dullness of Edmund than the unpredictability of Jesse, stimulating and exciting as that might turn out to be. In settling for her second choice, she told herself over and over, she had been wise.

There was another reward for her in marrying Edmund. As she spoke the responses of the ceremony she was thrilled by the realization that she was creating a scandal, one that would be marked outside her own county, indeed as far away as London, where some of the announcements had gone, inviting carefully selected people to the ceremony that would wed her to Jesse. What a delicious and outrageous surprise it would be when all those guests discovered that the bride had made other arrangements, that she had secretly planned and carried out her own version of the marital rite, changing the date, changing the location, and most important of all, capriciously and light-heartedly changing the identity of the bridegroom, substituting a gentleman, everyone would surely assume, better suited to her purpose.

Furthermore, not only was she choosing a young man who knew her well, one who knew from experience the lengths to which she would go to have her requirements met, she was entering the lists with an opponent who in his previous tilting with her had never known victory. He had watched her mark her territories and had accepted those boundaries without a struggle. He was a conquered prince, permitted to keep crown and sceptre, but relieved of all his weapons. In addition, she felt now that she could expect gratitude from Edmund as well as affection and obeisance. Because she had publicly and flagrantly *selected* him. Having first humiliated him by rejection, by choosing another suitor for fiancé, she had then healed those wounds by turning her back on Jesse and labelling Edmund the better man by her marriage to him.

Having thus put behind her the disappointment she had

256

felt about Jesse, Nora, on her return from Aberdeen, as she supervised the packing of her things to be conveyed some sixty miles west to the Bick estate, was in high spirits indeed. And their wedding trip, a slow journey through the Loire valley followed by two weeks in Paris and a month in London, seemed to her an intoxicating preview of what her future life would be. In London, a gentleman from her father's offices accompanied them to Mayfair and Knightsbridge to look at various residential properties that were available for freehold acquisition. Although Edmund did not take the lead in these viewings, he stood by and nodded his head in a way that seemed to indicate acquiescence.

In the furniture salons, too, and in the houses in St James's that displayed certified antiques, he seemed, if not enthusiastic, certainly interested. And he was surprisingly deft, Nora observed, in discussing financial matters with these dealers.

She was pleasantly surprised, too, to discover that Edmund had friends wherever they went. At Boulestin's, or the Silver Slipper, or Grafton Galleries, customers and staff greeted him by name. And even in Paris, at the Grand Ecart and Boeuf sur le Toit, he found friends. As Nora studied him, handsome and very much at ease in his evening clothes, she decided that she was truly in love with him, that he seemed to sense the kind of vital life she wanted and needed, that she had dreamed of since she was a child, and he was determined to provide it for her.

As they left London and headed north towards Cumberland, she was planning ahead for their next trip to London and beyond that to the time, not later than April, she felt, when they would move there, establish permanent residence, and become fixtures in the clubs and restaurants and cabarets that delighted her so.

As she gradually settled into her new home, however, known simply as Bick House, the exhilaration she had felt on leaving London, the excitement and hope for the future, grew fainter each day as she found herself occupied with the supervision of a large staff and the demands of Abraham, Edmund's father.

Abraham was a particular problem. A widower for many years, he had become accustomed to the attentions of his sister, Alma, who had come north from Sussex to look after him and his household soon after the death of Edmund's mother.

A dry, seemingly bloodless woman, pale and angular, Alma had administered the affairs of Bick House with military precision. She had been a scourge to the staff and to any tradesmen who came into contact with her but she had seen to the needs of Abraham and his son with an almost frightening devotion, had coddled both of them like pre-school children and had, in the process, made them totally dependent on her and the staff, all of whom were instructed to drop whatever they were doing to answer any call, day or night, from the master or his son.

Edmund was persuaded that he was a chosen person who should not, indeed *must* not do anything for himself. And Abraham, who suffered from mild attacks of gout and chronic indolence, became convinced that he was a helpless soul. He accepted Alma's diagnosis of his condition as well as her insistence that he must be confined to either bed or chair and waited on hand and foot. Occasionally he jumped up to chase a startled servant girl around his bedroom or to attack one or the other of his dogs with a stick but by and large he was dealt with as an invalid and was content to accept that role. He was content also to accept his sister as his nurse, his advisor and his lackey, as an irreplaceable element in his confined life.

It is almost impossible to describe, then, the impact that was made on Bick House by the news of Edmund's marriage. Alma began to pack her things an hour after she was told. When Abraham's manservant told him that the mistress had ordered the car to take her to Carlisle at four that afternoon, he bounded up from his chair and trotted down the corridor to his sister's apartment. He found her fully dressed, including her bonnet, and fully in charge. Valises and trunks and packing-cases were strewn about her rooms and half a dozen servants were filling and closing them.

As soon as Abraham entered her sitting-room, Alma said, 'I know why you're here so before you speak let me tell you you're wasting your breath.' Ignoring the presence of the servants, continuing, however, her direction of the packing procedures, she continued, also in full voice, her admonitions to Abraham. 'A house can have but one mistress and *I* have been the mistress of Bick House for twenty years.'

'So you have,' Abraham said. 'And you still are.'

Ploughing ahead as though he hadn't spoken, she said, 'I've been fully exposed to Edmund's generation. I've seen the young women we've entertained here through the years and I've heard them speak. And I say they are a disappointing lot. I know no other way to put it. A great supply of opinions and theories in their small round heads but not a whit of experience or judgment. And if I may say so, in front of God and my staff, young Miss Causey, Miss Nora Causey is the worst of them all. Stuck on herself in a way that I haven't seen before. Full of her own importance. And careless about her behaviour, if you know what I mean. When she jilted Edmund and her father announced that she would marry that American person, I told your son it was the most fortunate day of his life. And I believed it. I *still* believe it. But it appears that the young woman in question has had a change of heart. And Edmund has been foolish enough to be taken in by her. So I wish you well. You'll have her on your hands now and welcome to her. But for me, I'll have none of it. From now on I'll be in Pulborough, back with my cousins where I belong. They were right, it turns out. They said you would turn me away at last.'

'You're not turned away,' Abraham said. 'You've been here twenty years and I'm anxious for you to stay on. And I know Edmund wants you here.'

'Ahhh,' she said. 'If he *does*, then he's made a sorry mistake.'

259

'He's a young man, Alma. He's got a right to get married.'

'So he has. Just as I've got a right to go back to Pulborough. And that's precisely where I'm going.'

'If you stay, I promise you nothing will be changed.'

'You're wrong there, Abraham. I promise *you* that *everything* will be changed. I said it before and I say it again. A house can have but one mistress.'

So she departed as scheduled, leaving behind her a joyous staff and a dejected Abraham. By the time Edmund and Nora returned from their wedding trip two months later, the staff, though still joyous, had become remarkably disorganized and Abraham had gone from dejection to resentment to anger. Edmund also had been angry. 'Damned awkward, Aunt Alma's running off like that,' he said to Nora. 'But I'm sure you'll have things in running order in no time.'

Showing a brand of patience that was surprising even to her, Nora gave full time for several weeks to the problems of the household, established her presence and her authority with the staff, dismissed several malcontents, and hired replacements. She even managed a civil, if not particularly cordial rapport with Abraham who, missing the daily ministrations of Alma, had grown quickly bored with his quiescent role and was on his feet again, stamping through the house, visiting the stables, driving round to the tenant cottages, and shouting orders from breakfast till bedtime to whatever staff member wandered within earshot.

Nora's patience, however, did not extend to Edmund. She found his easy acceptance of her new role detestable. He came and went, announcing neither his departures nor his arrivals. He drank with his cronies in the nearest public house and drank with his father in the drawing-room. He was in all ways cordial and kind to her, and attentive in their bed, but he bore little resemblance to the man who had courted her or the young husband who had proudly displayed her in Paris and London. He seemed by turn, the carousing friend of her brother, Hugh, and a younger version of Abraham, feet firmly planted in the soil of Cumberland, comfortable in his house, secure in his values, riding with pride the perimeters of his estate but taking no interest in the world beyond.

Nora was seized at first by disbelief, then by frustration, and at last by anger. During the period of frustration she tried without success to explain her state of mind to Edmund. But late one night in May, five months after their marriage, using her anger like a broadsword, she captured his full attention. 'I would like to point out to you,' she said, 'that I am not your lunatic Aunt Alma. I am not her replacement in this house and I am not to be thought of as someone who resembles her in any way whatsoever.'

'Alma? Why in the world would I confuse you with her?'

'I don't know. But you have done. And so has your rude and impossible father.'

'Oh, come now. No need for that.'

'Oh yes. There is a definite need for that. If you believed, if you or your intolerable father believed, that you were marrying a county lass whose fondest ambition was to oversee cooks and washerwomen, plan menus and order new bed linen, if *either* of you thought that our marriage contract was in fact an employment contract for someone who would be able to function as head nurse, hostess, and housekeeper from that day forward, then I want to tell you that you were seriously and monumentally mistaken. You, of all people. You know me as well as anyone does. Did you imagine that I would be transformed by a marriage ceremony, by a stupid ring on my finger?'

'I don't know what you're getting at,' Edmund said. 'You're really upset, aren't you?'

'No. I *was* really upset. Now I'm really angry.'

'I know it's been a bit sticky trying to take over from Alma. But it seems to me you've been quite successful at it.'

'Go to hell.'

'Now what have I said?'

'I don't *want* to be quite successful at it. It is *not* my life's ambition to be the mistress of Bick House.'

261

'But you *are* the mistress here. Just as your mother is the mistress of Wingate. Certain jobs have to be done . . . .'

'Edmund, I warn you, if you start to lecture me about my duties as a wife, I will scream so loud that everyone in this dreary house will sit straight up in bed.'

'I must say I don't like your tone of voice.'

'Good. At least I've got your attention.'

'I don't like it at all,' he went on.

'Good. Now let's discuss what *I* don't like. I do not like being classified, by you or your impossible father, as the mistress of Bick House. I find no honour in the title or the work, no glory in being the only unpaid servant on the staff. So as of this moment, with all due respect to you and the great surly Abraham, I tender my resignation. I suggest that you hire a truly expert and experienced lady or gentleman to replace Aunt Alma, and *me*. And I will return to the full-time job of being mistress of myself.'

'Seems odd to me. But I'll talk to my father if you like.'

'I'm not married to your father, thank God. I'm married to *you*. And I am not asking for permission to ride my pony. I am *informing* you in the privacy of our bedroom that as of now I am no longer functioning as your father's nanny, as the secretary of the exchequer, as the overseer of the upstairs maids or as the inspiration of the kitchen staff. I was twenty years old two weeks ago and I've just declared myself a redundant employee.'

Edmund studied her for a moment. 'Are you sure you feel quite well?'

'I feel quite marvellous. I feel the best I've felt since we left London.'

He smiled then and made an effort to lighten things up a bit. 'I'm afraid you've gone a bit dotty on me.'

'Very possible.'

'I've never heard of a wife who didn't want to be mistress of her own house. Does that mean you'll want your own bedroom soon?'

'Not bloody likely.'

'Since you're giving up your other marital duties, I thought perhaps . . . .'

262

'I don't *have* any marital duties,' she said. 'I have marital privileges just as you do. If I find them turning into duties then I expect we'll have a chat about *that*.'

'You seem damned wilful all of a sudden.'

'I've always been wilful,' she said, 'You should know that better than anyone. If you thought I would change my stripes the day we got married, then this seems an appropriate time to say I did not. I am the same person you have always known. With the same faults and the same desires.'

'But if you don't want to be mistress of Bick House . . . .'

'I don't want to be mistress of *any* house. I don't want to be *anything* I've ever been or anything I've seen. Don't you know that about me? I don't know what I want. But I'm determined to find out.'

'That's pretty much the way we all feel. We're all trying . . . .'

'Don't preach to me. It's *not* the way we all feel. Because I know exactly what I *don't* want. I didn't want to stay in Northumberland and I don't want to spend my life in Cumberland either. I don't want to be a fat lady of the county and see the same faces year after year, go to the same parties, hear the same stories repeated a hundred times. I want to be where things are happening. And you *know* that's what I want. I thought you wanted it too. If you *don't*, why were we talking to estate agents in London? Why were we visiting furniture salons and asking the prices of antique sofas? Was that just a way to fill the time between luncheon and the theatre?'

'Not exactly. I've always known you have a yen for London. I don't mind it myself. I like to have a run at the cabarets and the music halls every now and again. Get out the evening clothes and dash about in a taxi half the night. Once or twice a year . . . .'

'It's not just *that*,' she said. 'I don't want to stumble into the city for a frolic like a country bumpkin on holiday. I want to *live* there. I want to be a *part* of that life.'

'How could we do that?'

'How could we *not*? Are you pretending you've never

263

heard me talk like this before? We've talked about it many times.'

'*Talk* is one thing. We all talk rot sometimes. A few drinks and we're off to America in a canoe. But when we think it over, the home county looks pretty good.'

'Not to me it doesn't. It *does* not and it *will* not. If you believe that I was simply changing my address from one great pile of stone in Northumberland to another great pile of stone in Cumberland, then you simply haven't been paying attention. I will *not* live my life as a county matron while you trot off to shoot sad little birds or chase a fox across the fields. I have no intentions of living such a life and I *won't* live such a life.'

The situation was not resolved that night of course. Nor was it resolved in many subsequent discussions. Nora continued to be forceful and demanding and Edmund continued to listen. But little by little he developed his own plan of attack. He decided that by feigning surrender he would triumph. Compromising a bit at a time he slowly allowed himself to be won over. But only in principle. He agreed at last that they should plan to live in London but he insisted that they must proceed in a businesslike manner. Alma, or someone equally capable and devoted to his father, would have to be persuaded to take over the household management, the estate manager would have to be persuaded to look after what had previously been Edmund's responsibilities, and most important, there would have to be a period of transition during which Abraham could become accustomed to the idea. 'It's a major step,' Edmund said, 'and it must be carefully handled. No dashing off half-cocked. If we are to do it, let's do it properly.'

Even Nora, impatient as she was to discover Babylon, could see the wisdom of Edmund's position. But as they made their secret plans, she saw also that as each problem was solved, as she and Edmund found what they hoped would be a solution, half a dozen new obstacles presented themselves. Edmund, a shrewd fellow behind his county exterior, became unbelievably sophisticated at managing

264

events, at listing and creating problems, at leading her into one impasse after another; he made countless concessions that only led to further difficulties.

Time after time, in exasperation, Nora wailed, 'Let's just go. Can't we just pack up and *leave?*' Always, in reply, Edmund said, 'That's what *I* would like to do. But we can't do it, can we? I mean we have to be decent about this. We want to be able to live with ourselves.'

'I can live with myself,' she said. 'What I can't do is live *here.*'

'It won't be forever. I promise you that. Just a bit more time to lay the proper groundwork and we'll be off and running.'

By midsummer Nora realized she was being manipulated. She told Edmund she was going to London the first week in September. 'Not just for a visit, not just for a drive round with estate agents. I am going to remain there. If you feel you can't come then, I hope you will come along later, but I am definitely going to live in London either with you or without you.'

A few days later she found she was expecting a child. As she sat weeping in her room, frustrated and angry, she knew without being told, by Edmund or anyone, that London was as far away as before.

2

Clara was aware from the beginning that Nora had chosen an impossible course for herself. When she tried to discuss it with Ned he said, 'She's been given in to all her life. We didn't do a proper job of training her. Or her brother either for that matter. I was just as humiliated as you were when she ran off and married as she did. Damned foolishness. I thought. Still think that. Careless thing to do. Downright cruel to poor old Jesse. Bouncing him about like that. But on the other hand, now that the deed is done, I think she's well off with Edmund . . . .'

'*You* may think that,' Clara said, 'but she certainly doesn't.'

'Nora doesn't know *what* she thinks. Or what she wants either. I suspect she's one of those badly organized women who will always want what she doesn't have. On the other hand, what she lacks in judgment, she's made up for in luck. Edmund's a young man she's known all her life. Friend of Hugh and all that. Friend to all of us. He's her sort. Maybe she's having a sticky time of it just now but she'll come round. Once her baby is born she'll see things in a different light. No more chasing shadows. She'll come down to earth in a hurry then, settle right down and be a proper wife and mother.'

Throughout her married life, Clara had listened to such pronouncements from Ned and had marvelled at his ability to mis-read every human situation. His instinct was to clutch for the nearest available rule; if there *was* none he created one. Faced with a problem, his instinct was not to solve it but to find some way either to avoid it or dismiss it. As a consequence he lumbered through his days like an itinerant tinker, all sorts of unrepaired pots and pans hanging about his person, clanking as he walked, and all manner of broken tools dangling from his belt needing to be replaced.

Reluctant or unwilling to deal with the issue at hand, Ned's instinct, in all circumstances, was to create an elaborate scenario that would absolve him of all responsibility before the fact and all blame after. He was quick to discover what he thought were the principal flaws in others; his rationale seemed to be that as those shortcomings caused his adversaries to capsize and sink, *he* would then rise like a cork on water.

Ned's chief asset in his own mind was his air of authority. Nonsense and wisdom were given precisely the same readings in his public pronouncements. Quick to speak, eager to share his opinions, he believed that his version of the truth should be made public as quickly as possible after it crystallized in his mind. Although he was hyper-sensitive to any criticism of himself he felt that other mortals should

266

suffer all judgments as long as they were presented in a forthright manner and with honourable intentions.

He had consistently been critical of Clara, for example, for what he called her 'lack of standards'. 'I know you enjoy a fine reputation for kindness and fairness,' he said, 'and it makes me proud when people speak well of you. I like to think that *I* am fair-minded as well. But I am less tolerant than you are of fools and mischief-makers. I believe that we are all accountable for our actions. Therefore we mustn't be surprised when someone brings us to account. I try to be neither judgmental nor vindictive but on the other hand I see no benefit in praising a nincompoop or tolerating a scoundrel.'

Although he had been fully involved in the rearing of Nora and Hugh, particularly in their early years when he could still deceive himself that they were paying attention, he had gradually, as they grew up, shifted the responsibility for their upbringing to shoulders other than his own. He was not foolhardy enough to blame Clara so he selected anonymous culprits, people whom he had employed and who, therefore, in his mind, had no rights of rebuttal.

'A chancy and undependable lot,' he said, 'the governesses and tutors one can find these days.' Admitting to no shortcomings in the final product that could, in any way, be attributed to him, he nonetheless found substantial fault with the process and with some of the stages his children had passed through on their way to maturity. 'My son could have become a rascal and a lie-about if he'd followed the guide-lines of certain incompetent tutors he was exposed to. All highly-praised fellows mind you, recommendations from the finest families. But failures on the job. Not up to the mark in any way. Foppish for one thing. Sycophants for another. It is not the job of a teacher to curry favour with his pupil, to teach a young man what he *wants* to learn rather than what he *should* be taught. Nor is it the job of a governess to pander to the fears and insecurities of her charges and to reward their disobedience with extra portions of trifle.'

About Nora he said simply, 'Only her blood-lines and

267

special attention from her parents prevented her from becoming a truly wilful and self-serving young woman. The people who were engaged to teach her guided her badly and I condemn them for it.'

In such statements, Ned was able to demolish publicly all governesses and tutors who had been in his hire and to voice privately his assessment and disapproval of his own children. In fact Clara believed that his labelling of Hugh as a rascal and a lie-about had in some way inspired their son to be just that. Nora, however, her mother felt, was genetically destined to be wilful and self-serving, with or without her father's help.

Because she and her husband were cut from very different cloth, Clara never allowed herself to be as judgmental of Ned as he was of others. Although her intelligence was keen and her perceptions clear, although she was difficult to deceive, she found no satisfaction is listing the shortcomings of other people, in fastening on their weakest traits or greatest vulnerabilities. She chose to think of Ned as a disappointed man, someone whose ambitions had exceeded his abilities to attain them. His inability to admit he was wrong had prevented him, almost always, from being right. If an ethical archer, on missing his target, puts all blame on himself, Ned was unable to blame anything other than the arrow. Earlier in their marriage Clara had continued to love him even after she ceased to respect him. But later the love had stopped too.

About her mother, Clara was baffled. Louise had always been a restrained woman, bound by rules and restrictions, even in her love of the arts. Where she had seemed most free, in her music, she had in fact been most confined. Clara came to believe that the hard lines and inflexibility of those strict bars of music, cross-hatched with vertical notes, had been a kind of security for Louise, something severe and final to hide behind. She had tried, Clara was convinced, to guide her children to a sense of freedom that was unavailable to her. And she had succeeded, particularly in Raymond's case, to a degree that had frightened her.

Clara realized that her mother's mind had begun to go, had slowly thinned itself out and lost contact with critical reference points. What Clara could not know was whether her mother had willed that condition, had accepted it, or had actively created it as one final safety barrier to hide behind.

Nor could Clara see her father clearly. Try as she might, love him as she did, she could not get past the symbolic paternal image she remembered from childhood, could not get inside or behind what he *presented*, could find no chance or impulse or accident in him. But she did not agree in any way with Ned's judgment. 'Angus is what he seems to be and that's all he is. It's all to do with money and victory. Any victory is a good one. *Any* defeat is a disgrace. If he'd been a soldier, he'd have burned every village he marched through. Win all the battles, rape all the women, capture the gold. *That's* Angus.'

As she thought about her family, and she thought about them constantly, as she reviewed their defeats and disappointments, Clara felt like the fortunate, gilded one. Having reached for so little she felt she had realized the most. Having failed to succeed at anything significant, she had also avoided abject failure. In a family of self-deceivers and tragedians she felt, more each year, like a witness. Watching them surge and storm around her she had come to feel like an emotional dustbin, collecting the weeping, wailing memorabilia of their errant lives. Even Nora and Hugh, so young and beautiful and wild, their whole futures stretched out ahead, had a scent of doom about them. Heavy bass notes in the legato, anguish behind the make-up.

In this climate of disappointment, Helen and Jesse had seemed new and fresh, unburdened by the emotional trappings of numberless generations of Bradshaws. Seeing them every day and talking to them had made Clara feel better about herself. For a short time she had hoped that such an infusion of energy might revitalize the entire household, that these visitors might bring her family to life in a new way. She saw encouraging signs: the relationship

269

that developed between Angus and Jesse and the close connection from the start between herself and Helen. The affair that developed between Nora and Jesse, on the other hand, both surprised Clara and made her uneasy. By the time their engagement was announced, however, she had forced herself to conclude that though they seemed to her an unlikely combination there was more good to it than bad. And Angus' adoption of Jesse she saw as a master stroke, an almost miraculous gift her father had made to himself, and one, it seemed, that was of equal benefit to Jesse.

By the end of summer, Clara, like Angus, had come to believe that Helen and Jesse were truly at Wingate to stay. She hoped things would move along bit by bit, day by day, until at last, as though by general agreement, it would be understood that these emissaries from Raymond had settled in and had become permanent members of the household.

Paradoxically, then, it was Clara, the positive one, who believed when they left, Helen first and Jesse not long after, that they would not return. As Angus, Nora at the beginning, and even Louise, accepted the fact of Helen's school obligations and Jesse's obligations to Helen, as they told themselves and each other that both of these pilgrims would return to Wingate, Clara told herself that they had come and gone and would *not* return. She did not pretend to understand their reasons but she detected a sense of panic in their separate departures that left her with misgivings.

When Helen wrote to her and continued to write to her she was surprised. When she tried to console Nora, when she told her that Jesse would of course return for their wedding she did not believe it for a moment. Trying to understand what had happened and how she felt about it she could only conclude that it was part of a pattern that had begun long before with Raymond's departure, that this new series of departures was somehow just a reprise of that original heartbreak.

Such mystical excursions were not a part of Clara's

nature; she was more inclined to deal in specifics, in cause and effect. But in all matters connected with Raymond, reason, it seemed, did not apply. When evidence was scarce and relevant experience also was in short supply, one theory was as good as another. A flight of fancy could prove as valid as an equation.

Those months after Helen's departure, then, and Jesse's, were grey months, indeed, for Clara, and the chaos and confusion that followed Nora's surprise marriage only exacerbated her discomfort. Hugh had disappeared to his hunting estate, recently acquired in northern Scotland. Nora was writing unquiet letters from Bick House, Angus was spending more and more time in London and drinking too much brandy when he was at home, Louise had begun to give disturbing and contradictory instructions to the staff and was often seen in the drawing-room or the garden in her nightdress, and Ned was more consumed than ever by a paranoia he could not assuage and angers he could not identify.

Functioning like a supervising nurse in this clinic of emotional cripples, Clara began to feel as if she too, were developing odd symptoms, impossible to diagnose and difficult to treat. As she took over all the household duties that had once been managed by Louise, as Angus called on her more and more for consultations about family business, as her hours with Ned became, increasingly, the meetings between a psychiatrist and her patient, she found herself staring through windows in the daytime and staring at the ceiling at night, longing for some human contacts that might exist for themselves, some conversations that did not begin with a problem and strive for a solution, some laughter, some joy.

When the letter from Jesse arrived saying he would return late in June, saying he was coming for an indefinite time, to live at Wingate Fields, to *be* there, to do his work on the premises, to help if he could, to be a family member in fact as well as in name, when all this blessed information came to Clara in one precious letter, she felt as though

271

she had glanced through her window and seen something remarkably lovely outside.

3

Through all her silence and separateness since leaving Wingate, since saying goodbye to Clara in her stateroom on the steamer in Liverpool harbour, in all that time, with the choices she'd been forced to make, the problems she had dealt with, through all those days of indecision and anxiety and guilt, Helen felt persistent dissatisfaction with herself for what she saw as her careless treatment of Clara. She agonized over the fact that the person she most needed to confide in was the one person she could not possibly confide in. Or so she had convinced herself. She couldn't tell Clara her feelings about Jesse, not because they were shocking or forbidden but because they were so totally unclear in her own mind, so baffling to her.

She hadn't been able to say how she felt about Jesse's scheduled marriage to Nora because she didn't know how she felt about that either. Jealousy was not a factor. She was sure of that. But she was equally sure that a careful observer of her departure from England would have *assumed* she was jealous of Nora. Regardless, it was not a topic for candid discussion with the bride's mother.

Nor could she talk to Clara about Hugh. Or the baby. Or her lonely decision *about* the baby. Out of bounds, all those matters. Not easily explained. Not easily understood. At the same time she realized that if any woman she knew, any *person*, could understand her dilemma, then surely Clara could. So she had been tempted a thousand times to drop the barriers and tell her, to write it all down, send it off, and to hell with the consequences. But she hadn't done it because she *could* not.

Sometimes, reading Clara's letters, Helen had the feeling that she knew, or surmised, much more than she revealed. At the beginning, she made almost no reference to Nora's forthcoming marriage to Jesse, and after she had gone off and married Edmund, she mentioned that, too, as little as possible. Also, her comments about Jesse were spare and circumspect. She mentioned, of course, that he had followed Helen to America and from time to time she referred to the fact that he was still in Fort Beck but she never went below surface information nor tried to solicit any facts about him from Helen. For her part, Helen never revealed in her letters to Clara whether or not she wrote to Jesse.

Since Clara's letters, as well as Helen's, dealt, to a large degree, with surface details – they were, in fact, reminiscent of the earlier letters Louise had written when Jesse and Helen were still in Fort Beck – they revealed very little about her thoughts or feelings or the intricate family politics among the Bradshaws and the Causeys. She wrote a great deal about estate matters, about Ned's dealings with their tenant growers, gamekeepers and sheep farmers, about the ebb and flow of the wool and hide markets, and the effects of the weather on the lambing season. Much also about Angus' machinations, both locally and in London, but always positive things, no indications of character flaws, errors in judgment, or business losses. Her letters, in fact, like Helen's, gave a high-gloss picture of her days. Cerulean skies, fresh linen, and smiles on all faces.

To Helen's surprise, Clara wrote most openly and warmly about Hugh. At first this alarmed her, made her suspect that Clara either knew or suspected there was or had been some link between Helen and her son. But subsequent letters, persuaded Helen that Clara had no inkling of what had transpired.

She wrote about Hugh almost as though he was a fifteen-year-old boy whom Helen had never met. The rake, the profligate, the womanizer and public-house habitué did not exist in his mother's letters. Her letters, in fact, revealed a warmth towards Hugh that Helen had never observed when she saw them together. His presence in the drawing-room or in the garden or at table had always seemed to put his parents and grandparents on the alert, as though

273

his most recent outrageous act had made them wary about what the next one might be. His silence, his infrequent participation in the general conversation, seemed only to intensify that wariness. Without looking at him, they all seemed to be *aware* of him, seldom making eye contact but letting their eyes wander, rather, and quite frequently, to a spot just to the right or left of his head. He was *included*, in a general way, but never challenged, like a family dog who is generously fed but never petted.

Only Nora flew in the face of what seemed to be family practice. She chattered gaily to Hugh whenever he was nearby: at dinner sometimes she talked *only* to him, in a light-hearted, semi-abstract way. The subjects of her discourse and her ways of expressing them seemed often to exist in some private meadow where only she and Hugh had walked. He seldom interrupted Nora's monologues; he listened attentively, nodded occasionally, and looked at her with a warmth which, as far as Helen could tell, was reserved only for his sister. The rest of the family he seemed to treat politely but with disdain. In his mother's letters, however, even his shortcomings were described with affection.

We hear all too seldom from Hugh. And we see him only rarely. As I wrote to you before, he had an opportunity to buy a shooting estate in Scotland. It's in Sutherland, in the mountains, far in the north. He moved there in January, just after Nora and Edmund were married, and says he expects to stay on in Scotland.

None of us have visited him yet. It's a long journey and it's beastly cold there in winter, but Father knew the previous owner and shot stag there on several occasions. He says it's one of the great hunting estates in Britain but he's incensed, I think, at the idea of Hugh's owning a thousand acres just for sport. Not a sheep from one boundary to the next, he says. Only streams and mountains and forests. And fields of hay for the horses.

274

It's been a strange experience having a child like Hugh. Even when he was tiny, before he could walk or talk, I always felt as if he had a secret. I still feel that way. And I am convinced it's a secret he will never divulge. Mothers, however, often have faulty insight in relation to their own children, so perhaps I've been mistaken about him.

He always had such a serious face, such a hard expression for a small boy. When he was tiny and I nursed him he used to stare at me in the most unsettling way. Almost vengeful, I thought then. I'd see engravings of poor children in workhouses, ill-fed and badly clothed, and those little pinched faces had expressions that looked very much like Hugh's. I didn't understand it then and I don't understand it now. As a young mother it made me feel frightfully guilty. I felt as though my son desperately needed something I was unable to provide. But now I think . . . I don't know what I think. I suppose Hugh is just a unique mix of traits and quirks as all of us are, all those strains and blood-lines mixed and spliced together and producing a mysterious and original human being.

Helen reread Clara's letters many times, especially, she found, the letters about Hugh. Since she knew almost nothing about him, she was curious to know his mother's views.

Thinking of herself as the mother of a child she would never know, a child fathered by a man she also didn't know, it was as though a key section of Helen's life had taken place in limbo, in the unfamiliar dark. One part of her was content to leave it there, to seal it off, put it out of her mind and go forward. But another stubborn part struggled to keep the past alive. Consequently, Helen dwelt on those months in Maine more than she had expected to. She was surprised to discover that the baby she had never seen was more real to her than Hugh was.

Hugh, she concluded, had been an isolated character,

275

one who had entered and departed without logic or planning. Before those few hours in his room she had had no feeling for him, and afterwards . . . she wasn't sure. She could never clarify for herself how she had felt afterwards. As we have seen there had been a sensation of something very like triumph but this, she knew, had been, in truth, a matter of herself in relation to herself, a statement of her freedom from fear, an evidence of her courage to function. She had committed an act of love but it had been, more accurately, an act of independence, a gesture of freedom that required a partner.

With another man she might have felt shame. With Hugh she did not. Whereas under different circumstances she might have been disturbed by the thought of being just one among his many adventures, in this instance she was not. Since the impulse had been hers, she could not be classified as a conquest. And since it was not an unusual experience for him, he could in no way be considered a victim. She told herself, in other words, what she wanted and needed to believe; all other possibilities and ramifications were neatly excised. Thus there was no need for endless examination of Hugh, no need for reflection or information, no purpose to it.

As time passed, however, as she found herself thinking about her son, wondering about him, what he looked like, what he would grow up to *be* like, and as she read Clara's references to Hugh in her letters, Helen could no longer keep him locked away as she had previously done. He might exist for her only in relation to her child but that existence was real and permanent whether she liked it or not. So at last she kept him alive willingly because he helped her to visualize her son, helped make the game of imagination more specific. Studying baby pictures in the rotogravure sections of newspapers she was able to look for resemblances not only to herself or to Raymond but to Hugh as well. He was admitted into the game.

In Clara's anecdotes of behaviour, Helen looked for characteristics, tried to determine what had been transferred to Hugh from Angus and Louise and Ned and Clara

276

and what in turn he might have passed along to her child. Always, of course, she chose the best qualities, the best combinations of feature and trait, to structure the appearance and character of the real-life make-believe son who accompanied her now wherever she went.

We must not assume, however, that this absentee motherhood was an unpleasant experience for Helen. Quite the contrary. Realizing early on, soon after she left Maine, that she couldn't wall off and put behind her totally, even if she wanted to, that significant year, she decided that she would welcome it as an integral part of her life, something to cherish, not something to shrink back from or avoid. It would be a positive memory for her. She would make it so. She would envisage an infant and watch him grow, and be, in her heart, a mother to him. She would not diminish him, or herself, with tears and regrets and might-have-beens. She had made difficult choices. She had done the best she knew how to do. And she promised herself she would never try to redo it.

Clara, in her letters, never failed to mention that Helen was wanted back, and expected back, at Wingate Fields. 'We know you have things to do now and we all applaud your energy and curiosity, but don't forget us. To us, this is your home as much as ours and we want you to use it that way. Come for a short while or a long while or forever. Just don't stay too long away.'

Helen did not know how to respond to these loving invitations. She could not tell the truth. She couldn't say, 'You're mistaken. I have *nothing* important to do. I'm just finding ways to kill time.' Nor could she tell her what precisely was keeping her away from Wingate. She only knew that she had no desire to go there, had no plans to go there. But she didn't know why, had no specific reasons to give to Clara, and was not sure in her own mind if there *were* such reasons.

At last, however, knowing that she had to tell Clara something, she wrote, 'As much as I long to see you again, and Angus and Louise and all your family, the thought of going back to England, at least just now, is very upsetting

277

to me. Why do I feel that way? I can't explain it in any sensible way. All I can say, the only possible reason for my feeling the way I do, is that I am constantly reminded of Raymond when I'm there. I'm always reminded of him anyway, but *there*, where he grew up, it overpowers me. I'm sure the feeling will go away, finally. At least the association of my sadness with Northumberland will grow fainter. It *has* to, doesn't it? But for now, please be patient with me and try to understand.'

As Helen read over what she had written, she realized that it was true. Having set out to create a believable falsehood she had instead told the truth. She even managed to persuade herself that it was the *whole* truth.

4

Helen had told Jesse about her meeting with her mother in New York, had told him, at any rate, the superficial details of that meeting, where it had taken place, how Anna had looked, the fact that she had married again. When Jesse arrived in New York to spend three days there before his ship to England would depart, he went almost at once, for reasons that were unclear to him, to Rattner's restaurant on the lower east side. As Anna showed him to a table, he felt strangely uneasy, as though he was being unfair by refusing to identify himself to someone about whom he knew so much. As he walked behind her, as she seated him, smiled, and handed him a menu, he could feel the blood in his cheeks. He quickly looked away till he felt her move off. Then, pretending to study the bill of fare, he watched her across the room, like a stranger peering into lighted windows.

Having never seen Anna with Raymond, nor with Helen, it was impossible for Jesse to transfer this handsome smiling woman from the brightly-lit restaurant where she seemed magnificently at home, difficult for him to make this graceful, striding public hostess into Raymond's wife

278

or Helen's mother. Perfectly suited to her surroundings, she gave off no evidence of previous or future lives. She seemed all of a wonderful piece, living fully and completely in the moment. Appearing younger, years younger, than Jesse had expected, she resembled, only very slightly, the woman whose photographs he had seen in Raymond's picture albums. Nor did he detect any hint of the dependent and insecure woman he had manufactured in his mind, working with the scraps of information he had picked up through the years from Raymond and Helen. On the contrary, the woman he watched from his table seemed capable of dealing with whatever obstacle might present itself.

Jesse came to Rattner's at least once a day while he was in New York. One day he had both luncheon and dinner there. Each time he told himself that he would make himself known to Anna but each time, as she approached him, smiling, he allowed himself to be led across the room and seated and he said nothing. On his last visit to the restaurant, the evening before his morning sailing, she was not there.

Jesse ate a larger dinner than he had planned, ordered several courses and then sat with his tea for more than an hour after he'd finished eating, but Anna did not appear. As the taxi drove him back uptown to his hotel he wondered if she had known all along who he was, if she had recognized him perhaps from some snapshot that Helen might have sent her. Kept awake by the tea, lying in his hotel bed staring at the ceiling, he decided at last that he would visit Rattner's the following day, have the taxi stop there en route to the steamship departure sheds; he would go into the restaurant, then, and tell her who he was.

When morning came, however, when he'd finished breakfast in his rooms, and seen his luggage loaded in the car, he went directly to the ship and sat in his stateroom drinking until sailing time.

It was an unquiet voyage for him. Pacing the promenade deck, sitting in the ship's lounge or in the bar, he found himself dwelling on his flaws and failures. It was a pattern he had fallen into in recent months. Beginning with his return to Fort Beck from Northumberland he had found himself, day after day, listing his sins against others and against himself. At first he resisted, tried to turn his thinking around; concentrating, as much as he was able, on positive things, he struggled to restore his faith in himself, to re-establish his self-esteem. But at last he stopped beating against the current and allowed himself to be sucked under. He began to find a kind of joy in discovering his past errors and misjudgments, in remembering wrong turns and self-serving choices.

Trying to recall in detail various criticisms he had heard of himself and failing to find the penetrating material he sought, he began an intricate process of invention. Listing the people who knew him best, ignoring their past kindnesses and encouragements to him, he concentrated on what he imagined to be their *true* feelings about him, their secret assessments of his failings. Sitting in a chair in the library or lying in bed at night he trained himself to hear the voices he knew so well, carefully speaking words and sentences they had in fact never spoken, revealing thoughts and evaluations that came not from their own minds but from Jesse's.

'Pride and arrogance,' his father said. 'Worse than tuberculosis. Almost always incurable. And you've got a bad case, Jesse. You can't accept anything as a fact unless it's proved to you. I'm your father but when I talk to you, you have the look in your eye of a man who's being fleeced. On the other hand, you'll take the word of a thirty-dollar-a-week schoolteacher as if it was the gospel. Or if you see something printed in a book, *any* book, you'll learn it by heart and swear it's the God's truth. Maybe you'll end up as the world's smartest man but even then you won't know everything. There's always somebody who can teach you something you *don't* know. Till you accept that fact you won't ever be worth a damn.'

His mother said, 'You think you're better than your own family. You look down on us. I don't know what kind of ideas you have in your head or where they come from but just remember something. Nothing you learn on the outside is ever as good for you as what you get from your own flesh and blood. Maybe you can turn away from your own people but you can't change what you are. "Judge not that ye be not judged." Stick that in your hat, young man. That's something you'd better remember.'

'You're not fooling me,' his brother Leo said. 'You can pull the wool over Mom and Dad's eyes but not mine. All this running around with a book in your hand, trying to get the best marks of anybody in your class. What does that mean? I'll tell you what it means. You're looking for someplace to hide. Trying to keep yourself out of the rough and tumble. Because you're scared. You were scared silly when you were six years old and you're still scared. You don't want to stand up to anybody. Don't want to get your hat knocked off. You're a big lily, Jesse. You'll be hiding behind somebody's skirts all your life.'

'You've missed the most important truth about teaching,' Dr Pfrommer said. 'You seem to feel there would be no school without the teacher. The fact is there would be no school without the students. The students are our reason for being here. We exist and have importance only as we relate to them. We are simply a conduit of knowledge. We are not here to be admired or catered to. It is not our mission to entertain or build monuments to ourselves. Or to win popularity polls in the student newspaper. Ours is a selfless profession and you, Mr Clegg, are anything but selfless.'

'I think you're perfect,' Mid Quigley said. 'You look nice, you smell nice, and you're a sweet man in bed. You're smart and you're kind and you don't spend all of your time proving yourself. You can make a mistake without falling apart. I expect almost any woman would be delighted to have a man like you around. At least for a little while. But then she might want to find out more about you than you're willing to tell, she might want to unlock some of those little doors. And that can't be done. So you're a treasure for anybody who wants *part* of a perfect man. But as far as I'm concerned I would rather have *all* of an imperfect man.'

'I never deceived myself,' Angus said, 'that you are anything other than what you appear to be. Just after I met you I said to myself, "This young fellow is an *arriviste*, an adventurer." I'm not even sure you know that about yourself but it's true, nonetheless. It is also true that all victims are not defenceless or unwilling. I, for example, was by no means an unwilling victim. You served my needs just as I, undoubtedly, have served yours. My perception of you, my feeling that I know you better than you would, perhaps, like to be known, in no way lessens my affection for you. Seeing something of myself in you doesn't win you my respect but it assures you of my acceptance.'

'Now that I've had a chance to think about it,' Nora said, 'I see that I didn't lose you to baby Helen but to Angus. You made a commitment to *me* before he made a commitment to *you*. But once you became Angus' son, there was no need for you to be Nora's husband. It became, in fact, almost incestuous. I would have been marrying my own uncle. You would have bedded with your own niece. My grandfather would have become my father-in-law, my mother would have become my sister-in-law, and my brother would be my nephew. As we toasted your adoption and our engagement that night, I knew without question, as I became pleasantly swiggled, that our marriage-to-be had become a marriage that-would-never-be. I had become flamingly unnecessary.'

'From the start,' Raymond said, 'I thought you were a fascinating chap. All sorts of surprises in your mind, unusual viewpoints, an ability to *accept* a concept without fully understanding it. A tolerance for ideas even when you didn't agree with them. Damned unusual, I thought. I never thought of you as a potential genius. Not even as a first-rate intelligence perhaps. But I believed the basic ingredients were all in place, that there was a potential for creative thought and a happy balance of intellect and instinct. As I knew you better, however, as I came to accept you as I would a family member, as I loved you more, I

282

admired you less. But the fascination persisted. I discovered at last that your mind is like a blotter, able to soak up an astounding amount of information and pass it along without really thinking about it. You have a talent too, I found, for telling people what they want to hear, for taking on the protective colouration of the area, of *any* area, where you happen to find yourself. You are capable of being, in other words, whatever the circumstance dictates, capable also of deceiving yourself that you are acting from conviction rather than convenience. Your talent for self-deception, it turns out, is your principal talent.'

Helen said, 'I love you, Jesse. I'm not *in* love with you but I love you and I always have since the first day we met in the Fort Beck railway station. But I don't *like* you very much and I don't know why. Perhaps it's because you're capable of surprising me more than I like to be surprised. In all that open friendliness of yours, there's too much mystery. Behind the candour, too many secrets. As I say all this, as I remember all the wonderful times and how much you meant to Raymond, I'm biting my tongue. But I know you're edging away from me and you have been, little by little, ever since Raymond died. So there's nothing I can do except to let you go.'

As he listened to these voices, as the words he put into their mouths played persistently in his ears, Jesse, depending on his mood, chose certain statements as truth and rejected others as products of his own imagination. Tuesday's truth could become Wednesday's falsehood. He had selected a self-examination device that allowed him to be critical of himself and to, somehow, at the same time, escape self-condemnation. By mixing fact and fantasy and straining it through the personalities of other people he was able to fuse the real and the unreal in a way that kept him free of true reality and any pain that might accompany it. Everything remained relative and flexible and intangible.

One specific, however, he could not avoid. As he headed towards England and Wingate Fields he knew that he was making the trip because he *needed* to. He needed particular surroundings and people to relate to; had he been an actor,

283

his talent would have been for *reaction*. Unable to define himself in limbo, he had reached a point in his life, like it or not, where he *needed* to be defined. He needed circumstances and conflicts and adversaries. And he needed approval. He needed to be seen and heard if he was to see or hear himself, needed to be assured each day that he was alive and relevant.

5

The Wingate Fields that Jesse returned to seemed different from the place he and Helen had first seen a year before. The grounds and buildings were unchanged, of course, and the routine of the household was as smooth and controlled as ever, but there was a stillness and a lack of vitality in the reception rooms and the hallways that made them seem foreign indeed. The number of residents had been reduced by one-third, and if one included Louise who almost never came downstairs now, by one-half. Hugh had permanently located himself in Scotland and Nora was at Bick House. 'I can't tempt myself,' she wrote to her mother. 'If I came to Wingate as often as I would like I would *never* be here in Cumberland.'

The dinner table was now set for three. Angus, Clara and Ned. And on many occasions neither Angus nor Ned were there. Warned by his doctors to cut his drinking to one glass per night, Angus had responded by tripling his hours at the nearby public house. And Ned, as often as not, accompanied him there. Although they were barely civil to each other when they were sober, they grew almost affectionate after an evening of drinking.

Far from feeling abandoned on those nights when she was alone, Clara welcomed them. She came to love the cavernous quiet of the dining-hall, candles on the long table, her single place set at the farthest end from the serving pantries, no sound at all except the careful footsteps of the servants moving towards her, then receding

284

in the soft dark, faint clinks of silver on china and crystal decanter on crystal glass, and candles guttering faintly on the sideboard. It made her feel whole, and very young somehow.

For all of her adult life, the evening meal had been a constant reminder of Clara's responsibilities. Each face she saw at table represented, for her, an unfinished task of some sort, something she had failed to do for Louise or Angus or Ned or Hugh or Nora, or something she had done or said to one of them which she would like to expand on or alter or take back altogether.

It had become also, that evening meal, a pageant of deterioration. Each week, it seemed, she could see the changes in Angus and Louise. And in Ned, too, whose internal beast was consuming him at a rate totally out of keeping with his age: Hugh and Nora, of course, did not sag or discolour or deteriorate. They seemed to grow more beautiful each day. But gradually, through the years, Clara had seen all innocence leave their faces. Their eyes shone in the candlelight, wet and large, the pupils dark and round as if they had been dilated, faint blue shadows under them, their cheeks so bright they seemed fevered, and their lips as red and swollen as ripe fruit. Their faces seemed punished by passion and self indulgence.

Clara was forty-five years old that summer of 1920. Unlike many women her age who have seen their marriages turned stale and tiresome and their children grown and gone, she not only accepted her hours alone, she looked forward to them. She felt as though she had found herself again, as though she had re-entered a favourite room after a long time away. She began to take joy in indulging small pleasures, using her time carelessly if she wished, squandering an entire day on occasion. Dressing as she liked, taking her meals when she chose to, riding alone across the moors, driving to the village in her trap or all the way to the coast, if she liked, in her open car.

Clara was in no sense a woman who tried to compete with young women of her daughter's generation. She took

285

pride in her appearance, dressed well, and remained slender. She looked and felt much younger than her actual age and was delighted that she did, but she was content to be *naturally* attractive, she did not inspect herself daily for signs of deterioration; the sight of a grey hair on her brush did not cause her to believe that life had ended. Instinct told her that youth had its roots in some internal spring, that positive feelings about herself and freedom from anxiety were greater beauty aids than any cream or lotion or hair colouring. In short, she was in control and in balance. In a household that was characterized by chaos and disintegration, Clara prevailed and functioned. In an atmosphere where people seemed driven to feed on each other, she took sustenance from herself.

Despite this new-found sense of autonomy, however, or perhaps because of it, Clara was delighted by the news that Jesse was returning to Wingate. She knew it would have a therapeutic effect on Angus, perhaps even on Louise. She knew it would revitalize a house that had gone dull and silent. And it meant there would be someone now for her to talk to, to relate to, someone whose horizons stretched beyond the stone walls of Northumberland, someone whose eyes and ears and finger-tips still sent fresh messages to his brain.

On Jesse's first day back, he and Clara sat in the summer-house at the back of the garden and talked for the entire afternoon. She told him in detail about Angus and Louise and Hugh and Nora. And Jesse told her what he could about Helen. 'She's not going back to college. She has some impulse to educate herself. She's going to travel here and there around the country. She wants to see places and cities and meet people. And I think she plans to work at various jobs. Three years or so she expects to devote to this project.'

'And then what?'

'She'll be twenty-two in May of that year. She tells me she expects to get married that summer.'

'Who will she marry?'

'That remains to be seen. Someone new, she says. Someone she hasn't met yet.'

Clara smiled. 'I'm always fascinated by young people who lay out their futures like a road map. They decide precisely when they will marry while they're still in the junior school, how many children they will have and what sex they will be, where they will travel to celebrate their silver anniversary and what sort of coffin they would like to be buried in. How simple it would be if our lives could be arranged like that, if we could stitch them together like a quilt. And how tiresome. Only when you're very young do you believe that everything can be predicted and planned for, that the pieces can all be locked together so they'll never come unstuck. But little by little you discover that what we deal with mostly are surprises. Unpredictable circumstances and crazy unsolvable problems. Most of our lives are spent repairing things. Closing seams and putting on patches. We start out believing that the chores and hardships make our lives difficult and we end up with the knowledge that those awkward, thorny, inconvenient things *are* life. They keep us going. Without them we'd all die of boredom at the age of twenty.'

'That's what I told Helen,' Jesse said. 'But she didn't want to hear.'

'I suppose we all have to work it out for ourselves. One person's experience isn't worth tuppence to somebody else. Helen will have a lot of fun. That's the main thing. And she'll learn what she needs to learn. And then maybe she'll be ready to come back to England. She's a lovely girl and I miss her.'

When she asked Jesse what he had done in Fort Beck through the autumn and winter when he was waiting for Helen to come back, he laughed and said, 'I'd like to tell you I accomplished a lot. Hard work and big projects. But the fact is I managed to do very little. It wasn't for lack of thinking about it. I had plans all right. But they didn't come to much. I ended up spending most of my time feeling guilty and drinking a lot of whiskey. Half of the country couldn't wait for the Eighteenth Amendment to

287

take effect and the other half was drunk. Drinking all they could while there was still something to drink.'

'Seems like an odd thing for a government to do.'

'That's what Raymond used to say.'

'If they tried it in England, we'd have riots in all the streets. Old ladies carrying banners.'

'In Chicago they're saying there'll be just as much beer and whiskey as ever. All of it illegal. That means the government won't collect their liquor taxes. Once the Treasury Department adds up how much income they're losing, they'll do away with prohibition. At least that's what people are saying.'

Clara was candid and thorough as they discussed the family. 'Angus worries me sick,' she said. 'He seems to have declared war against his doctors and the whole of medical science. Any advice, any prescription, any caution, he totally ignores. More than ignoring it, he turns it around. When he is advised to sleep more, he sleeps less. When he is given a list of foods he should avoid, he eats *only* those foods, and he drinks now *sans arrêt*, from the moment he's awakened with tea and brandy till the final noggin he tosses off as he tumbles into bed at night.'

'Won't he listen to you?'

'I'm the only person he *will* listen to. He listens carefully whenever I lecture him, nods his head and seems to be memorizing every word I say. He puts his arms around me and says, "You're my salvation, Clara. We'd have to close up shop if it weren't for you. You keep us on the proper path." But it's all for naught. His words are agreeable. He seems to be the soul of cooperation and good intentions. But his habits never change.'

'Why is he behaving like that?'

'God, how I wish I knew. He's angry, I expect. Bloody angry at getting old, at not being able to do the things he used to do. But he doesn't know what it is to stand still. Angus only knows one tempo . . . full speed. His only defence is to attack. That's his defiance and his security. Always has been. His remedy for over-indulgence is *more* indulgence. When he knows he's overworked he simply

288

works harder. If I really push him and keep after him and scold him terribly he says, "I've got to live my life, Clara. I wasn't made to sit about and wait." He's not an easy man to understand, of course, and never has been, but I think he means that he has to follow the course he's always taken. And perhaps he's right. All I know is that I love him and admire him and I want him to live forever. But I know he won't.'

'Maybe he's worried about your mother,' Jesse said.

'I don't think so. He sees through her, just as I do. Mother sincerely believes, each night when she goes to sleep, that she'll be dead before morning. But the fact is, she's in splendid health. Our doctor says she has the physical constitution of a woman of forty. And unlike Angus, she seems damned determined to preserve it, even though she insists it's a day-to-day proposition for her. She eats carefully and sleeps ten hours every night. But still she's persuaded herself she'll never reach seventy.'

'How old is she?'

'She'll be seventy-two in October. The real problem, of course, is her mind. It's going. And rather quickly, I'm afraid. Since last year at this time there's been an unbeliev-able change in her. But she insists that her thoughts have never been clearer. She says she can remember every moment of her life. Tells anyone who will listen that she can repeat verbatim conversations that took place fifty years ago. But the fact is she can't remember her own name. Calls herself Juliana. That's the name of her older sister who died in childbirth. She calls Angus Benjamin. That was her uncle's name.'

'She called me Raymond this morning when Angus took me upstairs to see her.'

'Of course,' Clara said. 'As often as not she calls me Angela and she often calls Nora Margaret. And Hugh, she pretends not to remember at all. Calls him, "that nice young man from America".'

On that first afternoon they spent together, Clara made no mention of Nora and neither did Jesse. Nor did they speak of her in the days that followed. At last, after he'd

289

been in England for more than a week, after he'd spent several hours each day with Clara, he said to her, 'Do you realize you haven't mentioned Nora?'

'Haven't I?'

'No, you haven't.'

'Neither have you. Neither one of us has mentioned her.'

'That's right,' Jesse said.

'I wasn't sure how you felt. How you feel now, I mean. It was all such an awkward business.'

'Yes, it must have been.'

'For all of us, I mean,' Clara said. 'For you as well.'

'Yes.'

'I can't tell you how astonished we were. So I can imagine how surprised you must have been.'

'I *wasn't* surprised actually. Nora and I had discussed things quite thoroughly before I left. I knew she wasn't pleased about my going back to America just then.'

'She had some notion that she was being jilted.'

'I know she did,' Jesse said. 'But I had no such intention.'

'That's what I told her. So she went ahead with all the wedding details, allowed *us* to go ahead with our really quite lavish plans. Her father was determined to make her wedding a spectacular affair. And Nora participated in all the planning. I've never understood it. She must have known all along that she didn't intend to go through with it.'

'I'm sure it was my fault. When I told her I had to delay my return from America, when I said that the wedding would have to be postponed for a bit . . . .'

'Do you think so?' Clara said. 'I'm not sure.'

'Well, it doesn't matter now. She's married Edmund and I'm sure they'll make a good life together. Angus told me she's expecting a baby.'

'Yes. Late in October, the doctor says.'

Jesse grinned. 'So you'll be a grandmother and I'll be a great-uncle and everyone will live happily ever after.'

Clara studied him. 'I was afraid it might be painful for you, coming back here.'

'Not at all. It was painful being away.'

'I mean because of Nora.'

'I know what you mean. But that's all in the past. I meant what I said. I wish her well and I hope she'll be happy.'

'I can't decide whether you're a very grown-up young man . . . .'

'Not grown-up at all, I'm afraid.'

'. . . or if you never truly expected things to work out between you and Nora.'

'Let me put it this way,' Jesse said. 'I *wanted* things to work out. I expected them to. But I knew that Nora was unpredictable. How shall I say it? I come from a family of unpredictable people. I've always known that some of us are more reliable than others. Am I saying something unkind about your daughter?'

'Quite the contrary. I think you describe her in the kindest possible way.'

Jesse smiled again. 'I did not come back to Wingate to break up Nora's marriage. I came because I wanted to be here. And because I feel that I'm welcome here.'

'That is an understatement.' Clara paused for a moment as though trying to decide whether she had said precisely what she intended. Then, slowly, she added, 'I speak for everyone. We are all delighted to have you back. And since I'm old enough to be your mother perhaps I can be flirtatious and say that *I* am particularly delighted.'

6

Nora's first reaction when she learned that Jesse had returned to Wingate Fields, her first emotion, was one of exhilaration. This was followed by exasperation and then by anger. At each separate stage she was unsure of how she felt or, more accurately, *why* she felt as she did. She was astonished to find that she felt anything at all. After her marriage to Edmund she had eliminated Jesse from her thinking. In her mind she had publicly rejected him, had

291

chosen another course for herself, and that was that. She had triumphed. Jesse had lost. He was across the Atlantic and she was in Cumberland, married and expecting a child. The fact that her marriage was a strangely unquiet one and the fact that she did not look forward to motherhood were circumstances she did not consider when she thought of Jesse.

Since learning of her pregnancy, Nora had not gone out of her way to be kind to Edmund. She had, in truth, treated him shabbily. But he appeared not to notice. Or perhaps he had concluded that the best way to deal with his petulant wife was to *pretend* he didn't notice. In any case, the result was the same. When she refused to take any role whatsoever in administering the affairs of Bick House, Edmund simply drove into Carlisle and engaged an experienced couple to oversee the household. When Nora dismissed her personal maid and brought over two servant girls from Wingate he thought it was a fine idea. When she was rude to his father he took her side before the servants and privately assuaged his angry parent by persuading him that such behaviour was not uncommon among expectant mothers.

When her mother wrote to her about Jesse's arrival, Nora did not tell Edmund. Waiting for her first reactions to thrash about in her mind and settle down a bit, she told herself that the presence of her former fiancé might be of some value to her after all. If she could be properly adroit Edmund might be led to believe that Jesse was a threat to his marriage, at which point Nora might tearfully ask, 'Can't we go away somewhere so he won't be tempted to . . . I mean he's a part of my family now. I can't ignore him. We must go to Wingate and we must invite him here. But if we were in London . . . .'

Edmund, however, scuttled these tentative plans. One day he said, 'I've just had a letter from Hugh. He says he's heard from your mother and it seems your American friend and adopted uncle has returned to Wingate. I'm surprised your mother hasn't invited us over for a family reunion.'

'Perhaps she thinks you don't want to see him.'

'Why not? I liked him when we met last year. Seemed like a decent fellow. Nothing at all like some of those American fools I've met in London. Why wouldn't I want to see him?'

'I don't know. Bad blood perhaps. It's not exactly a secret that Jesse and I were . . . .'

'Oh, for God's sake. That's all in the past. Over and done with. I'm not that sort and you know it. I wasn't exactly a choirboy myself before we were married. I'm not likely to go all stiff-necked because you had a fiancé before you married me. Not my style at all. If anything I'd expect the shoe to be on the other foot. Here we are, married and chuckling with a wee child on the way and he's back at Wingate Fields doing God-knows-what. It must be a dreary place with you and Hugh gone away.'

'Dreary? Wingate? A funeral at Wingate is more jolly than Christmas at Bick House.'

'Shame on you,' Edmund said. 'Don't let the servants hear you. They love it here. They'll think you've gone dotty.'

'If they think I'm dotty, it's because I *stay* here. It's the only convalescent home I've seen where nobody is ill.'

Edmund laughed. 'A day will come when I will remind you that you said that and you will say I'm lying.'

'A day will come when I'm mouldering in a coffin, too. But in the meantime I would like to see something other than this ugly house, I'd like to eat something tastier than a joint of mutton, I'd like to hear some sound besides your father hawking and spitting into his spittoon.'

Refusing, as he always did, to enter the lists with her, Edmund smiled and said, 'What a naughty little monster you are. You mustn't lose those qualities after you're a mother. It would be a pity if you turned into a dowd, sitting by the fire and doing needlework.'

'What sort of remark is that?'

'We've all seen it happen. A bright and lovely young woman has a baby and suddenly it seems as though all life has been drained out of her. Transferred to the child. She loses interest in everything except the little one. Takes

293

on a bit of weight usually and wears her hair in a snug bun.'

'I think you've lost your mind.'

'Have I?'

'It seems so. I'm only twenty years old. If I made a list of everything I want to do in my life, it would be too heavy to carry.'

'Good for you,' Edmund said. 'Moving ahead.'

'You're playing some sort of game with me and I'm not sure what it is.'

'No game at all. I'm simply looking out for your interests. I'd hate to see you lose your ginger and start to wear brown dresses and lace caps just because you've become a mother.'

'No chance of that, Mr Bick. No chance at all.'

Three weeks later she went to Wingate Fields to spend a few days, taking with her her finest gowns and a carefully rehearsed mien of radiance and contentment.

'I'm sure I must be the world's happiest woman,' she told Jesse. 'If I'd known how nice it is to be married, I would have married when I was ten.'

'You're lucky. In America, they expect 150,000 divorces next year, in Germany over 40,000. The war switched everything around they say.'

'Not here. Less than four thousand divorces in Britain last year. Steady as a rock. That's us. Solid values. God, mother, and the King.' She looked at him. 'Why are you smiling like a sleepy cat?'

'I don't recognize you,' Jesse said.

'I don't look so different, do I? I'm in my fourth month and I haven't gained an ounce. I have a very progressive doctor. He wants me to gain only the baby's weight plus seven pounds. He's promised I'll be able to come home from hospital in whatever dress fits me most closely.'

'You look very well. More beautiful than ever. Maybe you're a born mother, one of those women who's destined to have a baby every year.'

Nora caught herself before she said what came quickly

to her mind. Instead she answered, 'I just might do that. I'm sure I'll be very good at it.'

'I'm sure you will.'

'Edmund says he expects my children will be wild and beautiful and unruly.'

'Like their mother.'

'Is that what you think of me?'

'I'm not sure. But I suspect it's what you think of yourself.'

'You think you know me quite well, don't you?'

'Not at all. I know very little about you,' Jesse said.

'But we were almost married.'

'That's true. *Almost.*'

'Were you angry when you found out I'd married Edmund?'

'Not exactly. I was disappointed.'

'But not sad or upset?'

Jesse nodded. 'Sad, upset, and disappointed.'

'So was I,' she said, 'but it looks as if it turned out for the best.'

'I hope so. How *is* Edmund, by the way?'

'He's divinely happy.'

'And *you're* divinely happy.'

'That's right. We are both divinely happy.'

'So life in Cumberland pleases you,' Jesse said.

'I can't imagine that any place could be nicer.'

'I got the impression from Clara that you weren't too fond of it at the beginning.'

'What did she tell you?' Nora said quickly.

'Nothing specific. It was just an impression I got. Maybe I imagined it.'

'You must have done. Bick House is the grandest estate in our county. The gardens and the house itself have been absolutely *perfected* through the years. Every convenience one could imagine has been included It has the splendour of a castle and the comfort of a cottage.'

'I can't wait to see it,' Jesse said. 'Will you invite me?'

'Of course. But not just yet. You see, there *is* a bit of a problem with Edmund.'

'Oh?'

'About you, I mean. He's knows, of course, that there was something going on between *us*. As you undoubtedly remember, I broke off with him to become engaged to you . . . .'

'But he won out in the end.'

'Yes, he did. That's what I say to him. But all the same there is some tension. You understand.'

'Of course I do,' Jesse said. 'I'm surprised he let you come over here by yourself under the circumstances.'

'That's the way he is. He never says no to me. He knew I wanted to see my mother so he had no hesitation about my coming. Sometimes I think that all he wants to do is please *me*.'

'A story-book marriage,' Jesse murmured.

'What?'

'I said you are very fortunate.'

'Yes, I am. I know how fortunate I am. When I think . . .'

'. . . how it might have been if you'd married me?'

'No. I didn't mean that.'

'But things did turn out for the best, didn't they?'

'For *me* they did.'

'That's what I mean,' he said. 'They turned out well for *you*.'

'Everything is perfect for me.'

'That's marvellous.'

'And everything seems to be perfect for you.'

'That's the word for it,' he said. 'Perfect.'

'You'll be staying here for a while?'

'Permanently. I'm here for good.'

'How lovely. We'll have to find you a nice county girl. Someone to keep you amused.'

'That's a good idea. We'll have to work on that.'

The day she was leaving to go back to Cumberland, they talked again in the breakfast room. 'Tell me about your father-in-law. Clara says he lives there at Bick House with you.'

'Yes, he does.'

'You get on well with him?'

296

'Very well. He's a kind person. Gracious. Eager to be of help. But at the same time he keeps to himself. Makes no demands on anyone. Doesn't want to be a burden to me or to Edmund. He's awfully fond of Edmund. Keeps telling him it's *his* house now. Generous and kind. That's how I'd describe him. He treats me as though I was his own daughter.'

'How extraordinary. What an ideal situation for you. It sounds as though you won't be so eager to travel now. Not so anxious to be in London and Paris and Monte Carlo. No need to wander, is there, when one has everything at home? I'm sure when the baby comes you'll be as much a stay-at-home as any other young wife.'

'Not at all,' she said. 'Edmund agrees with me that our children should not dominate our lives. We expect to have a house in London before the year is out. We're in constant contact with an estate agent who is looking out for us. And once that falls into place, we'll spend a great deal of time there. Also we will certainly spend several months each year on the Continent. Edmund has many friends in France and Switzerland and Italy. Angus says, "The only reason for not getting what you want is not *knowing* what you want." That, quite definitely, is not *my* problem. I *know* what I want.'

After a moment, Jesse said, 'You really *do* know, don't you?'

'Of course I do. Don't you?'

'Not at all. I haven't the faintest idea. I wish I did have.'

As she sat in the back of Edmund's touring car being driven home to Cumberland, she felt that she had presented herself exactly as planned, that she had made all the points she had hoped to make. Had clearly defined herself as a triumphant young woman. But she felt no sense of triumph. She believed, rather, that she had somehow made a fool of herself, that her euphoria had been so total it had lacked credibility. Surely Jesse, who had sat quietly studying her and listening to her, had not been deceived. And even if he had been, the cloth of fantasy she had woven had given *her* no pleasure. Each

297

fabrication about her life and her marriage had only reminded her, and sharply, how very different her real situation was. She did not allow herself to wish that she had waited for Jesse. She did not permit a re-examination of that matter, did not attempt to hypothesize whether their marriage would in fact have taken place if she had not married Edmund. But, all the same, she could not forget, having seen Jesse again, what that previous summer with him had been like, the plans they had made, their hours together in the dark. At first, half-reclining in the rear seat of the car, she attempted to push such thoughts from her mind. But at last she relaxed, felt the sun through the window on her cheek, and lost herself in disturbing memories.

When she stepped down from the car at Bick House, she saw that one of Edmund's dogs had fouled the driveway. And when she entered the house the first sound she heard was Abraham hacking and spitting in the library.

7

'You've been a proper rascal, Raymond,' Louise said. 'You've been very naughty.' Jesse was sitting alone with her, late morning, in her drawing-room upstairs. Louise had requested the meeting.

When Clara brought him in, Louise had said to her, 'No, no, young lady. I won't have you here defending your brother. He's been a scamp and I intend to give him a talking to. You just run along and leave this young fellow to me.'

After a slow look at Jesse, Clara had said, 'Whatever you wish, Mother.' Then, to Jesse, 'I'm afraid you're on your own, Raymond. If you want my advice, I suggest you simply listen and nod your head. Even Father says there's no way to dissuade our mother once she's decided to have her say.'

As soon as Clara was out of the room, Louise said, 'I'm

disappointed in you, Raymond, and so is your father. We have high hopes for you as I'm sure you know. Fond expectations.' She paused as if to let that preamble sink in. Then, 'But recent reports about your conduct have made us uneasy. Your father believes you should be punished but I disagree with him. I told him you have always been a bright boy and I believed I could reason with you. Your father's experience in the stables and the dog run are not what's needed in this instance. Whatever his success at training a jumper or teaching a hound to fetch I believe that *I* have better instincts for moulding the character of a child.' She paused. 'I see you are nodding your head. At least you *seem* to be nodding your head so we will assume that you agree with me.'

Feeling ill at ease, not sure at all what role, if any, he should attempt to take on in this little playlet of false chronology and mistaken identity, Jesse chose simplicity. He tried to look properly guilty of something, he knew not what, and smiled. Louise repositioned herself in her chair, seemed reassured, and said, 'Now, let's examine some of these transgressions as they have been reported to me. First, let's consider your nanny, Mrs Lockett. Nanny, as you surely realize, is an unusual woman. She has lived with us since your sister was born and we are fortunate to have her. Having been in service for more than thirty years, she has wide experience in caring for privileged children. In addition to that, she is genuinely fond of you and Clara. And *loyal* to you. *Protective*, in the most admirable way. It would never occur to Nanny, for example, to carry tales of your misbehaviour to either your father or me. She feels that your training is in her hands and she never attempts to pass *her* responsibilities along to your parents.

'There are other witnesses in our household, however, who are quite willing to come to me with things they have seen and heard. Without going into greater detail let me say only that I am certain my information is correct. Let me remind you further that if you are unwilling or unable to profit from my advice to you, I will simply pass you

299

along to your father who will, unquestionably, be able to command your full attention, one way or the other.'

Fixing Jesse with a steady look she let that veiled threat hover between them for a long moment before she continued, 'My mother always said to me, "A word to the wise is sufficient," and I hope that in this instance, *that* will be true. My words are these: Nanny must be treated, at all times, with respect and kindness. She is not to be a target of any sort. No pranks at her expense and no careless language. You are to behave like the gentleman you are expected to be. One day you will be the master of Wingate Fields and that fact should be always at the back of your mind. You are not a Newcastle urchin or a gamekeeper's child. You will never live in a crofter's cottage. You will be a man with immense responsibilities and you must prepare yourself, starting from this moment, by being a responsible boy. Do you understand?'

Stunned by the unreality of what he was witnessing, Jesse sat mute, unwilling to speak, anxious not to extend the charade by seeming to participate in it. But silence, in this instance, would not get him through. Louise set down her tea-cup with a clatter and said, 'Speak up, child. Don't simply sit there and stare at me as though I was talking to you in Swahili. I asked you if you understood what I've been saying. *Do* you understand what is expected of you?'

Still frozen in a role he had neither selected nor rehearsed, Jesse tried for an expression of acquiescence, but he managed only a sickly smile.

'I won't *have* it,' Louise said. 'I asked you if you understood me and I expect an answer. Do you understand?'

Fighting an impulse to stand and leave the room, Jesse linked his fingers together in his lap, stared at a spot on the wall twenty feet past Louise's head, and said, in a voice that sounded foreign to him, 'Yes.'

'Good,' she said. 'Good and *good*.'

Her face went empty then as though she'd lost the thread of her thought. She turned her head towards the window and looked out across the garden; she sat immobile, her profile turned to Jesse, the light from outside filtering through the trees and the bluish panes of the window and making a soft, shifting pattern on her face. When she turned back to Jesse at last her cheeks glistened with tears. 'You must forgive Angus for what he's done to you. You must try to forgive him. He thought if he could . . . he believed if he sent you away. . . oh, my God, when I think of it . . . when I see . . . when I look at you and see what it's done to you . . . .'

She stood up abruptly, seemed to pull back inside herself, and walked stiffly across the room to a small table where several crystal decanters and half a dozen glasses clustered on a silver tray. Pouring herself a glass of sherry she moved back to her chair and sat down. She sipped from her glass thoughtfully, then set it on the table beside her chair and turned again to Jesse. 'Two further matters,' she said, 'two examples of your careless conduct. The first concerns your tutor, Mr Lampley. While he praises your sister both for her manners and her attention to her studies, he makes quite a different report about you. Careless work, he says. And often no work at all. Poor concentration and listless behaviour. It won't do, Raymond. We took great pains to find Mr Lampley. Your father offered him a handsome bit of money to come to us, to tutor you and your sister. So please understand that we will not allow you to waste Mr Lampley's time nor to squander your educational opportunities through your own indolence. Your father and I want you to understand that you are to do everything your tutor requires of you, that you are to do it thoroughly, on time, and with good spirit. No more scribbling or drawing in your books, no saucy remarks to Mr Lampley, and absolutely *no* more cruel teasing of your sister. There is no place for cruelty in this house. We are kind to each other; we are kind to our staff. We *must* be kind to each other or we have no value. And it goes without saying that a young gentleman must be kind and protective to the female members of his family, particularly to his sister. Remember that. You're nine years old now. Old enough to understand your obligations and discharge them.'

301

There was a soft silence then, in the room. Louise changed focus again. Her eyes wandered. As Jesse watched her, her face lost colour and her features softened. She did not weep as she had before but her eyes, as she looked at him, appeared to have a film over them. She seemed to have difficulty in speaking and her voice when she spoke at last, sounded raw and husky.

'I don't know how to begin,' she said. 'You're twenty years old. Able to make your own choices and decisions, able to function in whatever world you select for yourself. We see you so seldom, only on holidays, so we don't have that everyday contact that we once had. I am still your mother and I'll always be. But you don't need a mother now. At least you don't require a mother in the way you once did. When I used to scold you or lecture you there was always a purpose to it. There was something I felt I should teach you, something you needed to learn. But now you're learning different lessons. As you should. From other teachers. From strangers who can take you to places where I've never been. You have a different expression on your face. It's the look of a man. When I search for the little boy I knew he's not there any longer. Nor do I want him to be. But all the same I miss him. You'll find out for yourself, before too long, what it's like to be a parent. It's not all love and warmth and sentiment and noble intentions as we're led to believe. It's a difficult and demanding job. In one sense it's over before you want it to be and in another sense it never ends. For a mother it's the most rewarding thing in her life. And the most heartbreaking. Part of her never wants to let go of this person she has created and another part of her knows that if she has done a proper job as a parent her child will be not only willing but eager to leave his childhood home and find a world of his own. How can it be so? How can a child who is properly brought up be eager to leave his parents while one whose parents have bungled the job is unwilling or unable to leave the house he grew up in? I don't know the answer. I only know that it happens. So I'm delighted to see you happy at Cambridge with your friends, filled with energy and plans, eager for life, confident about the future. I know how you feel because I was your age once. Nothing can go wrong when you're twenty. Life is infinite and all problems have quick solutions. Indeed, no problems are recognized *unless* they have quick solutions. It is truly a season of glory. The days are long and the nights never end.'

She picked up her glass again and sipped from it. When she set it down, she said, 'I must forget for the moment that you are a man and speak to you as I did when you were a small boy. I remember I used to tell you that an unintentional hurt is just as painful as one that comes from malice. An accidentally discharged weapon is just as deadly as one that is deliberately aimed and fired.'

She paused then like a person who has approached her main topic by the most circuitous possible route but who can now delay no longer. At last she said, 'I'm sure you know what I'm leading up to. Although it has been little discussed, it has been a principal force in this household for many weeks. It has hovered about our heads like a swarm of insects.' She looked at her half-empty glass, stared at it for a long moment but did not pick it up. Still looking at the glass, her eyes averted from Jesse's, she said, 'You must know that you cannot continue with Emily Callison. You must realize that such a situation must come to a stop. I know that Angus has discussed this with you and I know how you reacted. But I hope you will come to see things differently. It is most important for you to understand that your father and I are not making a moral judgment. We know that human beings are fallible. You are young. Emily Callison is young. We understand. We do not want to chastise you or punish you for what you have done. We simply want you to understand that it must end now . . . before it's too late. Your father can still control the situation as it is now. But only if you are able to control yourself, only if you . . . .'

Like an actress gone cold on her lines, she went suddenly mute. And as before, her face lost colour and seemed to crumble. And as she had before, she began to weep, her face half-turned from Jesse, looking down at her hands in

303

her lap, her fingers twitching, her handkerchief rolled into a tight ball.

Finally, she spoke again, very softly, her voice scarcely audible. 'If you would only speak to me. If you would try to forgive me. I know I should have done more. I should have tried . . . I don't know what I *could* have done but surely I . . . surely someone could have done *something* to make things better, to make things different. Nothing could have been worse than the way it all turned out. Anything would be better than the way things are now. Two people dead and one . . . oh, God, how I wish I'd been wiser or stronger. How I detest myself when I see you sitting here like this. Like a stranger. Looking like my son but resembling yourself in no other way. I know how tortured and hurt you are. Can't you see that I'm tortured too? Can't you please *try*? Won't you make an effort? Don't destroy yourself and take all of us with you. Please, Raymond . . . please.'

She covered her face with her hands. When Jesse said, 'Mrs Bradshaw . . .' she didn't answer. He stood looking down at her for several moments. Then he crossed the room to the door and let himself out.

8

In the three years after she left Fort Beck and began her wandering programme of self-education, Helen achieved, in her own mind, everything she had set out to do. Realizing at the start that she was freeing herself from any discipline other than her own, she vowed, nonetheless, not to discipline herself. Having spent her life inside family environments she was now determined to expose herself to a world of strangers. She would arrive without introductions or recommendations or blood-ties and she would make her way.

She never questioned her survival skills. She questioned, in fact, none of her impulses. Knowing she was perfectly able, if she wished, to travel like a fine lady on a grand tour, she rejected that notion from the start. At the same time she had no desire to live like a beggar, to subject herself to hunger or privation just to prove a point. She had no hesitation about using her letters of credit if it seemed wise. But by and large she expected to support herself, to live on her earnings.

She anticipated that she would have no difficulty in finding work. And she did not. Perhaps because she was not in desperate straits, because she brought no sense of panic or anxiety into her employment interviews she was almost always engaged for the jobs she sought. She was attractive and personable and intelligent. And she had been well-educated. She was, in fact, over-qualified for most of the jobs she held. She accepted these jobs because she knew, as her prospective employers did not, that she would stay for only three or four months, six months at the most. Her project, as she thought of it, involved multiple locations, exposure to the greatest possible number of people and work situations.

In a period when it was not unusual for young women to work sixty hours in a week, Helen specified in all her job interviews that she was able to work only half that schedule. Because she seemed to be a war widow, because she wore a wedding-ring and a mourning band on her sleeve, her employers, more often than not, were willing to accommodate her need for free time.

The mourning band and the ring had been suggested by Jesse. 'If you're planning to move around the country on trains, it's a sensible thing to do. You know yourself you don't see a great number of women travelling alone. And very few as young and pretty as you are. So you have to protect yourself, build a little wall around yourself. You don't have to say anything. Better if you don't. The black band will say it all for you.'

It had worked. On trains and everywhere else she went. She had seen hundreds of pairs of eyes glance from her face to the band on her arm. For the most part people drew their own conclusions, and asked no questions. Those who *did* ask questions met only silence. Only a few times was she forced to say, 'I can't talk about it.'

There was no real pattern to her changes of location. She did not block off sections or states on the map and visit them in some order. Quite the contrary. She sling-shotted back and forth, up and down, through the country, stimulated each time by something as insignificant as a newspaper item, a chance remark, a town mentioned in a book, or a travel advertisement.

During the three, almost four years, of her exploration of the country Helen spent varying periods of time in Missoula, Montana, Round Rock, Texas, Gatlinburg, Tennessee, Lafayette, Indiana, Laurel and Greenville, Mississippi, Red Wing, Minnesota, Ottumwa, Iowa, Taos, and Santa Fe.

She learned early on that all large cities resemble each other, if not in appearance at least in the quality of life there. Consequently, she spent much of her time in lesser cities or in small towns where individuality and idiosyncrasy abounded and where regional and ethnic differences were more pronounced, where the language had local rhythms and unfamiliar expressions.

She felt at ease in these smaller communities and though she stood out more sharply as a stranger she found a climate of acceptance there that she did not feel in the great cities. In Greenville or Gatlinburg or Ottumwa she truly felt like a young woman on her own, supporting herself, content to live in whatever accommodations her wages would provide. With the exception of a three-month work stint in San Francisco, a month in Salt Lake City and six weeks in Miami, she came to large cities only as a visitor.

In Denver and Dallas and St Louis, in Cincinnati and Minneapolis and New Orleans, in Washington, D.C. and Atlanta she threw off her working-girl role and lived in hotels, in unself-conscious luxury. After months in a boarding-house or a country inn or in an upstairs bedroom of a private home in a poor street, she welcomed these changes.

Having thought always that she was dependent by nature, that she required daily contact with someone she loved who also loved her, with a Raymond or a Jesse, she discovered that her true instincts were quite the reverse of this. She found herself approaching each new town or city with an excitement she could not explain. Having believed that fear of the unknown is a constant, she found now that *only* the unknown was thrilling to her. Stepping down from a Pullman car in the depot of a strange town where she knew no one became the keenest exhilaration she could imagine.

Finding a place to work and a place to live, making friends, insinuating herself into the life of the community, beginning to *understand* that life, all these things were challenges to her, challenges that gave her real pleasure. Feeling as though she was re-inventing herself each time she moved on, feeling as though all her emotional baggage was piled together and burned when she left wherever she had lived for a number of months, she began to develop a new faith in her own resources, in her ability to adjust and survive and make do.

In the dark moments that come to anyone who lives in furnished rooms, she began to fear that her eagerness for the new and untried and unfamiliar might turn on her, might switch from a positive to a negative, might change her into a migrant, someone who *must* be on the move, a person who runs from the familiar only because it *is* familiar, who avoids friendship and at last fears it. She dealt with this anxiety most often, by simply putting it out of her mind. When she was unable to do that, she got up, left her room, and walked through the streets until she was too tired to think and too sleepy to condemn herself.

In various towns and cities, she worked as a waitress, as a book-keeper, as a cashier, as a salesgirl at Woolworth's, as a ticket-seller in a cinema box-office, as a file clerk at a college in Colorado and as a receptionist in a newspaper office. She was a mother's helper for six months and a short-order cook in Kansas for three. And she worked as a teacher's assistant in Lexington, Kentucky.

She rejected no reasonable job. She took pride in her new-found ability to take the shape of whatever container

307

she was poured into. As she checked the help-wanted columns in each new community or as she questioned waitresses or librarians or shopkeepers in towns that were too small to have a newspaper, she found, after the first few months, that she was particularly attracted to jobs that were unfamiliar to her. She was eager always to try new work in a different atmosphere.

She became expert at measuring character, at pinpointing the strengths and weaknesses and peculiarities of the people she would be working with. She learned when to be silent and when to assert herself. She learned who must be obeyed, who must be flattered, and who must be avoided. She discovered that it was impossible to earn the respect of certain employers and that others gave their respect only to employees who made it clear in one way or another that they would accept no shoddy treatment, no abuse, and no unfairness. The people who were willing to take off their work aprons and walk out of the door at any moment were the people whose jobs were most secure.

As important as these work experiences were to her, as enlightened as she felt from her constant exposure to people whose backgrounds and aspirations were different from her own, as flexible and tolerant as she felt herself becoming from this continuing contact with the new and unfamiliar, her greatest benefits were derived from her non-working hours, from her time alone, exploring unfamiliar streets and local stores and museums, browsing through village libraries or reading at home in her room.

In October of 1923, in a letter to Jesse she wrote:

You'd be proud of me, I think, if you saw how I spend my time. Without being a bore about it, I try not to be frivolous, try not to squander the hours and the days on foolishness. Mostly I try to find connections between different areas that at first glance seem to have no connection at all. I look for the common threads in literature and history and politics and painting, try to see the central concerns and concepts that are repeated in truly outstanding work. Is there a

308

common ingredient, for example, in Gide and Santayana and Gigli, in Elgar and Jung and Aldous Huxley? My thesis is that *all* true excellence is related. All people who create something new and valuable or something that is simply unique, all those strange and quirky individuals have something very striking in common.

Some of the things that have enlightened and startled me are: *Character and Opinion in the United States, Three Soldiers, Women in Love, Love of Three Oranges,* and anything painted by Munch. Also, *Jacob's Room, Human Nature and Conduct, Ulysses, The Waste Land, The Ego and the Id, King Oliver* and Jelly Roll Morton. I'm a little bit in love with Douglas Fairbanks and very much in love with E.E. Cummings.

She did not write often to Jesse nor did she receive frequent letters from him. But she wrote regularly to Clara. And very occasionally to Nora who less occasionally replied, usually with a picture postcard apologizing for her shortcomings as a correspondent.

In July 1921 Anna gave birth to a daughter, Maria, and her second daughter, Christina, was born just over a year later. In January 1924 she had a son, Paul.

Not long after word came to her about Paul's birth, Helen left Elkins, West Virginia, where she had been living and went north to New York to visit her mother. From there she went to Maine. This time she stayed in Hedrick with a man named Bud Feaster and his wife, Opal. They gave her a snug third-floor room with a window looking across the snow fields to the harbour. When she went to Portland for her meetings with Dr Kilwinning, Opal drove her there and back.

Early in May of 1924, Helen went back to Illinois. She had decided it would be fitting for her to celebrate her twenty-third birthday in her house in Fort Beck. Travelling west on the train she made elaborate plans for a birthday dinner. She would invite all of her school mates who were still in Fort Beck and some of Raymond's faculty friends

309

from Foresby. It was also time, she concluded, to begin thinking of a more permanent location for herself. She favoured New York or San Francisco. But she also began to think that London might be a fine place to live. When she got off the train in Fort Beck her head was filled with plans and possibilities.

As her birthday approached however, she decided against a party. When the day came she had lunch in the kitchen with Mr and Mrs Esping. There was a small yellow cake with four blue candles on it.

After lunch, explaining that she didn't feel well, Helen spent the rest of the day and that evening in her room, trying to decide where she would go next. She concluded at last that for the moment it would be pleasant to stay where she was. She pretended not to notice that the old anxieties she thought she had conquered still sat in her room with her.

BOOK THREE

Chapter Seven

1

On the third day of September in 1924, Helen was married. She was twenty-three years old. Her husband, Frank Wilson, was twenty-five. He would be twenty-six the following December.

Because she had told no one about her plans, everyone who knew her was surprised. Helen herself was a bit surprised. Frank Wilson was not surprised at all. He had proposed to Helen three days after they met, almost fourteen months before. 'I think we should get married,' he said. 'What do you think?'

Astonished, taken aback, not knowing what to say, she had laughed and said nothing. 'I'm serious,' he said. 'I expect to be very successful and very rich before I'm thirty. I want to have a wife and a family and be retired when I'm forty.'

'That's the most romantic thing anyone's ever said to me.' She made a face when she said it.

'I'm sorry. This is the first time I've ever proposed to anyone. I guess I'm not very good at it. But I'll get better.'

'I feel as if you're trying to sell me a life insurance policy.'

'If I were doing that, you'd have said yes already. I'm very good at selling insurance.' He smiled. 'You don't have to give me an answer right now. I'll give you thirty seconds.' He looked at his watch, then looked up at her. 'Now . . . how about it?'

'How about what?'

'We've got a question on the table. I asked you to marry me.'

'No, you didn't. You simply made a light-hearted remark on the general subject of marriage. Not to be taken seriously.'

'Then I'll rephrase it,' he said. 'I seriously want to marry you. I seriously would like *you* to marry *me.*'

'You're not serious. Just saying the word, *seriously.* . . . .'

'I'm very serious. I'm a deadly serious young fellow.'

'But I don't even *know* you.'

'Of course you don't,' he said. 'And I don't know *you.* But I'm willing to take you on faith.'

'Does that mean I should take *you* on faith?'

'Why not? All contracts are based on faith. The legal language is just a formality to codify that faith.'

'That may be true,' Helen said. 'I know it's referred to as a marriage *contract* but I've never thought of it that way somehow.'

'How do *you* think of it?'

'Differently.'

'Tell me,' he said.

'I can't.'

'Sure you can. Make an effort.'

'I mean when I finally choose someone, when somebody chooses *me*, I'm sure it will be . . . .'

'*What?*'

'I don't know exactly. But certainly different from this conversation *we're* having.'

'More romantic?'

'I guess so.'

'Not so much talk about logic and more talk about *love.* Is that it?'

'Not just *talk* about it. Some feeling that . . . .'

'Let me ask you a question,' he said. 'If I told you right now that I'm in love with you, what would you say?'

'I'd say you don't even *know* me.'

'You're right. But I like what I *do* know about you. And what I'm saying is . . . I'm saying I want to know *everything* about you and I want you to know everything about me.

And once we do, however long that takes, I think I'll love you and I think you'll love me and we'll get married. You're laughing again. What did I say now?'

'It's *everything* you say. You're the strangest young man I've ever met. I feel as if this is an elaborate riddle and any minute you're going to give me the answer.'

'*You're* the one who's supposed to give the answer. I'm asking the question and you're the one . . . .'

'You're really *mad*.'

'Not at all. I'm absolutely sane and serious.'

'All right,' she said then. 'I will pretend that I think you're serious and give you a serious answer.'

'Perfect.'

'I am leaving for Cincinnati in two days. From there I don't know where I'm going. All I know is that I have the next year or eighteen months of my life all mapped out . . . .'

'So do I,' he said. 'I'm moving to Chicago next month.'

'So there you are,' she said.

'You have things to do and so do I,' he went on. 'I didn't mean that we should get married this minute. We'll write to each other and I'll send you nice presents and flattering photographs of myself and I'll come to see you wherever you are. And you'll come to Chicago to see me when you can. We'll get to know each other. I'll take you to meet my folks. We'll have some cuckoo times together, go to the circus, see some plays in Chicago, and look at pictures in the art museum. And first thing you know we'll start to miss each other when we're not together. And then we'll get married. How does that sound?'

'It sounds ridiculous. You make me feel like a wind-up toy.'

'Not you. Nothing mechanical about *you*. You're a beautiful girl and you're smart enough to know that your best bet is to marry a plain, serious guy like me.'

'You're not *serious*,' she said. 'You're crazy.'

'That's better. Crazy is even better than serious. But I'm *serious* too.'

Years later, when Helen tried to describe Frank to Clara,

315

tried to explain how he was, she said, 'He was all self-confidence. That's the thing that struck me first about him. He truly believed that *nothing* could defeat him. It was like the central truth of his existence. At first I hated it. I couldn't believe it was real, couldn't imagine that *anyone* could be so absolutely *sure* that things would turn out just right. It was bravado, I decided. Nothing real or valid about it at all. But little by little, as I knew him better, I saw that he really was what he seemed to be, that he truly was unafraid, that he saw no reason why he shouldn't dare and try and move ahead in whatever direction appealed to him, following whatever road he came to.'

Two days after his proposal, leaving the city in central Indiana where she had met him, travelling south-east by train towards Cincinnati, her dialogues with Frank Wilson seemed unreal to her. She felt sure she would never see him again; there was no thought in her mind that his fantasies about their future together would come true. As she reviewed those dialogues, as the flat green fields slipped past outside her train window some part of her believed still, that it was some intricate word game at which he was particularly skilled, some charade he had practised many times before and would surely practise again.

Feeling as she did, it seemed senseless for her to stay in contact with him. She told herself she would write just a short note to thank him for his kindness to her and to wish him well in Chicago. When she wrote, however, a week after her arrival in Cincinnati, she described in detail her impressions of the city and the new job she had found. What was to have been a short note became a three-page letter. Telling herself that she did not want to begin an extended correspondence she decided not to give him her address in Cincinnati. But just before she dropped the letter into a post-box, she wrote her return address on the back of the envelope.

Two weeks later, just before his move to Chicago, Frank came down by train from Lafayette and spent the weekend in Cincinnati. He stayed at the Netherland Plaza and they danced and had dinner there. They also took long walks,

316

attended a Haydn concert, visited the art museum, and talked. More accurately, he talked and Helen listened. He had a dazzling supply of information on almost any subject and she was content to listen.

'The world of finance,' he said, 'has three legs. Banking, insurance, and real estate. No manufacturing involved, no distribution, no merchandising. We're talking simply about the science of money. Engineering it, moving it around. I decided a long time ago that the best way to make money is to be *involved* with money, to work with it, to understand it, to speak the language.'

'Of course you feel that way,' Helen said. 'Your father is a banker. And your uncle too.'

'Not true. They're *not* bankers. Not by *my* definition. They're book-keepers, custodians of other people's life savings. They're cautious and conservative and frightened to death.'

'What are they frightened of?'

'God knows. Afraid to take a chance, I suppose. Afraid to be successful. Afraid to be rich.'

'Owning a bank sounds pretty successful to me.'

'That's what everyone thinks. But that's because people don't know what's involved. They don't know that a great banker has to be creative just like anyone else who's creative.'

'But not reckless,' Helen said.

'Why not? We have to be reckless sometimes. You can't tremble and shake just because you're risking other people's money. The whole idea of banking is a risk. Any time you hand over your hard-earned cash to a stranger you're taking a chance. If it was *really* safe to put your money in a bank there wouldn't be any reason for them to use words like *security* and *trust* and *fidelity* when they're picking names for themselves. Nobody really trusts banks or bankers. They just accept the idea that their money is safer in a big marble building than it is under the mattress. Or in a coffee can in the pantry. But it's not. If a banker's any good he takes investment risks and if it's your money he's investing there's always a chance you could lose it.'

317

'I don't think I'll put money in *your* bank.'

'I don't blame you,' he said. 'Most people would feel the same way you do. But that's all right because banking doesn't interest me anyway. Not as an end in itself. I just need to know how to talk to bankers. That's why I spent two years working in banks, first with my dad, then in Indianapolis at the Farmers and Merchants. When I found out everything I needed to know I quit and got myself a job in the insurance business. That's what I was doing in Lafayette. Talked Midwest Mutual into letting me open a branch there. I did something they'd never done before. Sold insurance to the students at Purdue. Wrote hundreds of policies without ever leaving the campus. Then I branched out. On the other side of the river. In the business part of town. I wrote every kind of policy Midwest Mutual had on their list and I invented a few they didn't have. In fourteen months my little office in Lafayette took in more money than any office in the state except for Indianapolis. I had them goggle-eyed, ready to offer me the moon. When I told them I was quitting to go to Chicago and work in real estate I thought they'd have an attack. First they couldn't believe it. Then when it finally soaked in, they got mad as hell. But I just kept smiling and told them how much I appreciated the opportunity they'd given me. Then I waltzed out the door. When you know what you're after it doesn't matter if people think you're crazy. If *nobody* thinks you're crazy then you're really in trouble. At least that's the way I look at it.'

In the year that followed, events fell into line much as Frank had predicted they would. He and Helen wrote to each other and they saw each other whenever he was able to come to wherever she was. She did *not*, however, go to Chicago to see him and she did not meet his parents. But she thought of him often, as he had said she would, and she missed seeing him when a longer-than-usual period of time went by without his coming to visit her. At no time, however, did she imagine that their relationship, whatever name she put to it, was likely to grow into something else. She was tender and affectionate with him as she had been with Jesse but it was an affection that showed no signs of turning into passion or love or anything other than the fragile and polite little thing that it was.

For his part, Frank seemed to have forgotten that he had proposed marriage to her months before. He treated her with kindness and consideration and as he began to make progress in his career assault against Chicago, with remarkable generosity. Knowing nothing of her financial situation, he constantly sent her gifts, most of them practical ones, that he felt she might need or want. He never questioned her about her family, never asked her why she changed employment as often as she did or why she moved, without apparent reason, from one town, from one state, to another. He knew only that her father was dead, that he had been a teacher, and that her mother had remarried and was living in New York.

Helen was surprised, particularly in view of his earlier attitude, that he made no demands on her, exacted no promises, showed no signs of jealousy, never tried to discover how her free time was spent when he was not around. He seemed to be as content with their arrangement as she was. He never mentioned marriage again and never referred to the future. On the other hand he kept her fully informed about his business ventures, discussed them with her in detail, asked her advice, and when she had an opinion, paid attention to it, even as she insisted that she knew nothing whatsoever about his problems or their solutions.

'Of course you do,' he said. 'Common sense. That's the most uncommon thing there is. In our offices we have a dozen experts. Each of them knows his own little area of real estate operations, each has a pocket of expertise, but none of them can see the whole picture. If they could, they'd be in business for themselves. They'd be as successful as I'm going to be.'

Although they seemed frozen, in many ways, at the exact spot where they had made original contact, Helen was pleasantly surprised, each time she saw him again, to find that her original feelings for him still obtained. His

319

intelligence, his energy, and that endless self-confidence continued to fascinate her. Frank had that strange something that all great performers have. He was watchable. He was interesting to look at. His face hid no secrets. Whatever was inside his head at a given moment became instantly vocal and visual. He brought the same vitality to every subject that seized him. If he had been a single-cell creature with only business and money to define him, Helen, who cared nothing for such matters, would certainly have turned quickly away. But when he explained, in informed detail, how one could distinguish between two cubist paintings, one by Braque, the other by Picasso, two works that seemed to be identical, she was aware of something unfolding that was too good to miss. On the subject of trolls in Norway he was equally well versed. Also on the private life of George V, the childhood of Mary Pickford, and the flaws of the Gatling gun. He believed that *Aida* could not be performed properly unless elephants were brought on stage and he was convinced that the Wright brothers' contribution to aviation had been negligible. These were not opinions. They were convictions. 'It's my curse,' he said. 'I can't just *talk*. I have to *persuade*.'

After Helen left England, after her ultimate return to Fort Beck and her unsatisfactory reunion with Jesse, his subsequent departure in one direction and hers in another, it would have been understandable if she had decided to lose herself in the first romantic situation she encountered, placing her hand in some dependable masculine hand. This, however, was not her intention. Not at all. And even if it had been she would surely have decided that it would be madness to allow herself to duplicate, to try, in even the smallest way, to duplicate, either Raymond or Jesse. She would surely have said to her private gods, 'Please don't let me fall in with someone I *admire*. I don't want to *admire* a man. I'm not sure what I *do* want, but I know it's not *that*.'

Ironically, however, that is what she came to. Although Frank was as far removed as one can imagine from the angular leanness of Raymond and Jesse, also from any other young man who had caught Helen's eye during her school years, although his stocky build and thin dark hair, his brashness, and his impulse to dominate seemed to guarantee that no lasting contact would be established between the two of them, such a contact *was*, in fact, established and maintained. She found at last that she *did* without question, *admire* him and depend on him.

Since *his* feelings, the longer they knew each other, seemed to match hers she had no reason to believe that her friendship with Frank would become anything other than a friendship. He would play, she believed, somewhat the same role in relation to her that Jesse had played. It was an involvement she hadn't sought and one she wasn't sure how to deal with; but she was unwilling to discard it.

Seeing clearly the amorphous and passionless situation she was in, recognizing it for what it was, how was it that she suddenly found herself married? It is impossible to say. Impossible for an observer. And it was also impossible for Helen herself.

As previously noted, when she returned to Fort Beck in the early summer of 1924, Helen told herself that after a brief stay there, drawing on her nomadic experience of the past three years, she would select a city that pleased her – New York or San Francisco, or Denver perhaps – take up residence there, and waltz on with her life. But she didn't follow that route. Instead, at the end of the summer, she went with Frank to his parents' home in Logansport, Indiana; they were married there in the garden beside the only private swimming-pool in that part of the state.

2

How do we deal with Hugh Causey? He cannot be dismissed or forgotten. Nor is it fair to imply that at some point he came bursting forth from his isolation in Scotland to re-enter his family's life. Or Helen's life. Because he did not. Having exiled himself, he was content, it seemed, to remain in exile.

On the other hand we must not assume that in his seemingly hedonistic life, Helen had no importance. We know, from his final conversation with her before she left Wingate to return to America that he was anxious for her to stay in England, and that he was suddenly willing, in a manner that was unusual for him, to reveal his feelings and display his vulnerability.

It would be false to assume, however, that Hugh's self-banishment to Scotland was in any way connected with Helen. It was not. It was, in fact, a move that had been in his mind for a long time, something involving only *himself*. Having only the filmiest notion of what he *wanted*, he was very specific, at least in his secret thoughts, about what he did *not* want. In some schoolboy text he had read: 'It is not difficult to obtain the things you *want* from life if you can simply avoid the things you *don't* want.'

It had become Hugh's credo and he began to follow it as closely as he was able to follow any rule. He concluded, for example, that he did not want or need the ducal authority that Angus enjoyed. He had no lust for power, no hunger to amass wealth or property. He was appreciative of the freedom his money gave him but he had no wish to spend his days increasing that wealth. Nor did the manager's role that his father had assumed appeal to him. Having shunned his duties as son and grandson, Hugh had no intention of becoming an administrative son-in-law, of falling into the dull routine of his wife's family whoever that wife might turn out to be.

Hugh felt, in short, that he had exhausted all the pleasures of his home county. He had no enthusiasm for the future responsibilities that seemed to loom ahead of him. So he chose to absent himself. In Scotland, he discovered, he had no family tradition or honour either to uphold or besmirch. He could choose his companions and be chosen by them without family considerations or even family awareness. Feeling no need for acceptance *he* would be free to accept whomever he chose with no regard to their blood-lines, their social pedigrees or any other Northumberland standards.

He would also be free to be alone. Contrary to the convictions of everyone who knew him, all of whom thought him to be a gregarious fellow, Hugh was, at foundation, a solitary. Another schoolboy dictum he remembered, this one from a class on literary themes: 'He who lives to himself will be left to himself.' It seemed true to him. At least, he wanted it to be true.

Hugh loved to ride, for example, was an expert horseman, but did not enjoy riding to the hunt, did not like the costumes, the crowd, or the ceremony. Nor did he like a shooting party, group orgies in a brothel, or long carousing evenings with a dozen friends in a public house. More and more often he found himself riding out alone, shooting alone, walking by himself across moors, and drinking alone in his rooms.

He approached the solitude of his hunting estate, then, not with trepidation but with pleasure. He engaged a staff that reflected his inclinations. Heavy on gamekeepers and gillies, gardeners and grooms and stable boys, but a minimal domestic staff inside the main house. To his manservant, Alfred, who selected and hired the other servants, Hugh said, 'Let's not have a great troop of people rattling about. A good cook and half a dozen hard-working locals should be enough to keep the place in order.'

This is to say that he had a specific vision of the life he would live in Scotland. It was not a hermit's existence he envisioned. He had no wish to forego the pleasures of female companionship, of gambling, or dancing. He expected to attend concerts and plays, to make trips to Glasgow and Edinburgh and London but he wanted all such choices and decisions to be his and only his. He needed to be in charge of himself, to choose, to select, to reject, to make private judgments based solely on his own whims or standards.

Since projected Utopias often turn out to be distasteful places, it would not have been surprising if Hugh's haven by the Oykel had failed to provide what he felt he needed.

Men who hunger for silence can find themselves suddenly desperate for the noise of a petrol engine; a misanthrope has been known to walk for miles to look at a face he detests. A man who understands his fellows is a saint. A man who understands himself is a god.

Hugh, however, was wise enough to know what he wanted and fortunate enough to want it still after he possessed it. From the moment he moved into his vast stone house and stood in its great hall looking up at its vaulted ceiling he was content in a way that was new to him. Having spent his days, for as long as he could remember, in rebellion, having chosen irresponsibility as his *raison d'être*, he found himself suddenly, with nothing to rebel against and with a great deal to be responsible for.

No man changes in a second. There are no instant perceptions that transform us. No one sheds his skin like a serpent and slithers into the warm sunlight as a totally altered creature. Nor did any such miracles happen to Hugh. The following change, however, did, very gradually, take place. Certain facets of his inner machinery, particular elements and tendencies and genetic traits that had lain dormant in him through most of his childhood and youth, rose, bit by bit, to the surface and in the process caused certain other less attractive features, many of which had been his distinguishing marks, to fade or subside or submerge, to seem, at last, to have disappeared altogether.

Like his sister, he had been moulded by conflict, or by his anticipation of conflict and resistance; the sudden absence of those elements in his new and solitary existence caused him to be subtly re-worked.

It all took place so simply and smoothly, the process fuelled by such ordinary events and adjustments, that he felt no discomfort or changed rhythm. The sensation was one of relief rather. A man wearing many sweaters and waistcoats and jackets and all the greatcoats that can be draped across his shoulders, a person who is stifled by the warmth and almost totally immobilized by the weight of those garments, is forced to shuffle through his days thus clothed, is not allowed to remove one item of the clothing

324

that weighs him down. Then at last he is released, permitted to take off as much of his burdensome clothing as he wishes, encouraged to strip himself to the skin if he likes, to do whatever he needs to do to free himself, to breathe, to move, to run.

Although Hugh's decision to live alone in Scotland was in no way triggered by his feelings about Helen, this new life he had chosen began to bring her, all the same, into sharper focus. He found her, very often, in his thoughts.

They had spent very little time together when she was at Wingate Fields; he knew almost nothing about her. Because they had spoken so seldom and so briefly there was no store of comment or viewpoint or opinion for him to draw on. He could visualize her and refer to the snapshots of her that Clara had taken; he had, in fact, taken one such picture of her to a commercial photographer in Inverness, had it enlarged and placed in a silver frame. He kept it in a cabinet with his dress shirts, looked at it frequently, and thus kept her physical presence very much before him. But he could not make her speak, even in his imagination. He knew too little, had witnessed too little, had heard too little.

His mother, however, as though she sensed his situation – she knew, in fact, nothing at all about what had transpired between Hugh and Helen and how it had affected him – relayed to him, in frequent letters, all the information she had about Helen. He was always up-to-date as regards her present location, what she was doing, and what her most recent report to Clara had been. He found it a poor substitute for being in contact with her himself but it did give him information and current details to supplement her photographic likeness and to make him feel that his connection to her was somehow living and current.

He began, after some months, to jot down questions that he would ask Helen when they met again. He did not tell himself when or how this would take place, did not try to envision the outcome of their seeing each other again, but he quietly assumed it would happen.

In addition to the questions he planned to ask her, he

325

made up a list of things he proposed to tell her: detailed descriptions of his house and his lands, the lawns and the plantings and the gardens, the long walks he took in fine weather, the drives to Aberdeen or Edinburgh, excursions to the Isle of Skye and South Uist.

Gradually, then, the letters from Clara began to seem like letters from Helen. He copied out the portions that related to her and kept these separate from Clara's letters. And eventually, many months after he had last seen Helen, he began to write to her. His careful notes and lists he now incorporated in long letters.

These letters were not posted, of course. They were kept in the cabinet with her photograph. But just as he assumed that they would meet again under some circumstances, he also assumed that sometime in the near future he would indeed write to her, would post the letter, and she would answer him.

It is important here to realize that we are not witnessing the gradual breakdown of a man who has lived too long in his own company. Although Hugh's imaginary connection to Helen had become a continuing part of his life, perhaps even a vital part of it, it was in no way an obsession. It did not dominate him. The key to the matter was that his thoughts of Helen gave him only pleasure. No mist of gloom hovered over him as he read Clara's letters or as he composed replies. The fact that his letters were not posted in no way altered them and in no way determined his frame of mind as he composed them. He was simply a young man writing to a young woman in another country. He presumed nothing and demanded nothing; he did not burden her with passion and unrequited love. His feelings towards her were quite proper. If Raymond had risen from the grave to ask Hugh's intentions towards his daughter he would have been convinced that those intentions were conservative and honourable.

Finally, almost four years after he had last seen Helen, knowing from his mother that she had returned to her home in Illinois, Hugh booked passage for America on a liner that would leave Liverpool in early September. Not

326

allowing himself to imagine what the result of his trip would be, not even daring to think of it as a journey with a specific objective, he, nonetheless, occupied himself that entire summer with the refurbishment of his home. A squad of painters and decorators and upholsterers came from Aberdeen and were quickly replaced by a like squad from Edinburgh who gave way after two weeks to a supercilious but enormously qualified group from London.

As the decor and furnishings and carpets became richer, as some of the massive chairs and couches were replaced by more precious specimens, Alfred found it necessary also to augment his domestic staff. The house, which had always been splendid, became, now, indescribably grand and sumptuous.

Hugh, also, was substantially redone. He shaved his two-year-old beard and side-whiskers. His tailor came from York to run up new suits and jackets and formal wear that would present him properly during the trip to America and would serve him well when he returned home.

For weeks, Hugh had worried over the letter he would send to Helen announcing his coming. He was determined that the tone of it should be just right. But none of his attempts pleased him. When he tried a long letter, he felt he had said too much. The short ones seemed abrupt. At last, as the time grew near when his ship would leave, he concluded that a cable, because of its forced brevity and its impersonal quality, would be the best solution. Two days before he was to leave for Liverpool, as he sat in the library trying to compose a proper cable message, his man came to him with the daily post. In a letter from Clara was the announcement of Helen's marriage to Frank Wilson.

3

Edmund's assumptions that motherhood would transform Nora and change her into a selfless person were incorrect. Her protestations that *nothing* could change her, that her sense of self could not possibly be turned over to an infant any more than she had surrendered it to her husband, were also off the mark. The birth of her daughter had a strong impact on her. Her research about child-bearing, the reading, the questioning, the long conversations with Clara and with other women she knew who had children, had prepared her well, had taught her all that one could learn short of the actual birth experience. After a peaceful and almost enjoyable pregnancy she had entered the hospital in Carlisle without fear or anxiety. She had an abbreviated period of labour and a swift delivery. Everything unfolded almost painlessly as if she had willed it so. And indeed she had. The fact of childbirth, the physical act, had wrought no great change in her.

The condition of motherhood, however, was quite another matter. She was delighted, first of all, that her child was a girl. She told herself that these were not simply vengeful feelings towards Edmund but all the same, after his months of prediction, sounding very much like insistence, that they would have a son, there was a kind of joy in seeing the asinine expressions of disappointment on his face and Abraham's. The anger she felt because they seemed to have lost interest already in a child who was only a few hours old was tempered by the realization that her daughter would surely be left to *her*, to counsel and bring up as she saw fit. Beating back Abraham's insistence that the little girl must be named Cynthia, the name of her grandmother, Nora named her Valerie. 'An odd damned name if you ask me,' Edmund grumbled. '*Valère*,' Nora said. 'It means to be *strong*. She'll be a strong young woman. I'll see to that.'

Any hopes Nora might have had for her marriage disappeared altogether during the months of her pregnancy. Whatever his other shortcomings, Edmund had always been kind to her. Through their courtship and the early weeks of their marriage he had been gracious and deferential. Whatever her feelings about *him* at any given moment, he had never given her reason to question his devotion to her.

Once it was established however, that she was expecting a child, once those maternal locks had snapped shut around her wrists and ankles, Edmund lost, almost over-night it seemed, his gift of *politesse*. He became, in her mind, that most hateful of all eventualities, a younger version of his father.

It was as though a secret meeting had been held between father and son and she had been reclassified. Transported below stairs into a lesser category. The catechism of motherhood, of madonna and child, was lovingly repeated. The dogma was observed. But the process of their con-verting her from vital young woman of the house to expectant mother had removed all her distinguishing characteristics, at least in the view of father and son, had stilled her voice, cancelled her vote, and blurred the whorls of her finger-tips. Having experienced grievous difficulty in their attempts to squeeze her into the tight slots labelled *wife* and *daughter-in-law*, they exulted now, it seemed, in the assistance that nature had given them. They professed to see in her eyes, as soon as her condition was known, what the French call *sensualité maternelle*. Soon the world would be witness to her swollen breasts, her changed gait, the widened hips and great stomach. The physical truth about her would be her *only* truth. Her rebellion would subside, anger would turn to gentleness, and son and father would reclaim their rightful places of power in the household.

Even in the servants she detected a changed attitude. They were kind, of course, and they managed a softness in their eyes and in their voices when they spoke to her. But it was a tone that is reserved, by most of us, for words spoken to pets and invalids, the malformed, the crippled, and the dying.

'What in the name of God is happening here?' she said to Edmund when she first became conscious of the changed atmosphere that had taken over the household. 'I'm not a leper or a lunatic. I'm just a woman who's going to have a baby.'

329

'Special circumstances,' he smiled. 'Special treatment for special people.'

'I don't *need* special treatment. And I don't *want* it. I don't expect I shall ever need it. But *if* I do, it's a long way down the road. Seven months at least. I'm barely two months pregnant, for God's sake.'

'Can't be too careful.'

'I don't want to be careful,' she wailed. 'I don't want people looking at me as if I'm an animal in the zoo or staring at my stomach to see if it's popped out yet. I will not be coddled and categorized. I am not a baby factory. I'm the same person I was a year ago and I'm exactly the same person I'll be a year from now.'

'Can't be sure of that, can we?' Edmund said. 'We all change a bit as we nip along. Nature's plan.'

'I don't give a damn about nature's plan. We're not talking about rules or trends or customs. We're talking about me.'

'Don't think I don't sympathize . . . .'

'I don't *want* sympathy. Haven't you heard a single word I've been saying?'

'Of course I have. And I understand. Chemical changes and all that. Father said that my mother . . . .'

'Edmund, I am not interested in what idiotic Abraham said. I am also not interested in discussing your mother's symptoms. I am not interested in *anything* you have to say until you stop treating me like a brood mare who'll stand content as long as she has fresh hay in her stall.'

When Edmund repeated this conversation to his father, Abraham said, 'They're all the same. Skittish and nervous when they're first in the family way. Give her a few weeks and she'll gentle down. She'll sit by the fire and do her needlework and start to feel proud of herself. And once the baby's come, this fractious little wife of yours will stop fighting the bit. She'll grow up in a hurry then. There's nothing like a wee child to turn a wild young girl into a sensible woman.'

He was wrong, of course, about Nora. No such transformation took place. Her post-natal behaviour was, in fact, quite the opposite of what Abraham had predicted. With Valerie in her arms, Nora withdrew even further from the mainstream of the Bick household. Moving herself and her child, a nurse, a manservant, and two maids into the west wing, she set up a small fiefdom there, took all her meals in those rooms, and admitted Edmund and Abraham only when it was convenient for her.

To her husband, who had begun to court her again once Valerie was born, who was most anxious that she should re-enter their bed-chamber in the east wing, she smiled sweetly and said she was not in good health. 'The doctor says it would not be wise for me to have another child so soon.'

Edmund protested, pouted, and ranted but he made no progress. He and Abraham held frequent war councils in the billiard room after dinner. They agreed that it was absurd for them to be manipulated by Nora. Neither of them had ever heard of such behaviour. 'It's as though she's set up a fortress in our own house,' Abraham said. 'What kind of wife is she? You have to make an appointment to see her. Damned foolishness. A man has to be *invited* to visit his own child. We'll put an end to that. I guarantee it.'

They did not, however, put an end to anything. Short of the use of force, they found there was no pressure they could bring to bear, no persuasion they could use, that would alter the set of circumstances Nora had forced on them. Knowing they should act quickly, before time and habit had codified the behaviour pattern she had established, they fussed and fumbled and found themselves unable to act at all. At last, when even the most conservative members of the household staff had come to accept the arrangement of a firmly but peacefully divided house, Edmund and his father also accepted it. This is not to say that they accepted or condoned the concept. They were simply forced to live with the reality.

Considering her inclinations and her previous record of self-service, it would have surprised no one who knew her if Nora had been an inattentive parent. There was certainly

331

no strong bond between her and Edmund and she made no secret of the fact that her pregnancy had been unexpected and unwelcome. In practice, however, to everyone's astonishment, she was an exemplary mother. If someone had asked her the reasons for this, she would undoubtedly have said, 'I *enjoy* it. I enjoy my daughter. I like her and I love her and she amuses me. I expect that she will be my very best friend as soon as she's old enough to serve tea.' When Hugh on one of his rare visits home pointed out that Nora was inordinately attached to Valerie only because the child was an exact replica of her, Nora replied, 'That's not fair. I would love her even if she looked like her father.' Then she smiled and said, 'God forbid.'

'From what Edmund tells me you don't see him often enough to *know* what he looks like.'

'That's true. But I have an excellent memory.'

'I'm glad *I'm* not married to you.'

'Ahhh, but I would be a devoted and admirable wife if I were married to someone as strange and wonderful as you.'

'Isn't Edmund strange and wonderful?'

'He is odd but not strange, bizarre but not wonderful. Mostly he is a dull and predictable person, growing duller and more predictable by the moment.'

'Father thinks he's a fine chap. Thinks he's too easy on you. Thinks Edmund should assert himself as your husband and master of the house.'

'Father is mistaken on all counts. And not for the first time. Surely he doesn't imagine that *he* is the master of *his* house. I would place him at about fourth in command. After Angus, Mother, and Louise.'

'He also believes that you may be about to do something foolish.'

'He's wrong again. I already *did* something foolish. What I am *liable* to do is something *sensible*. But not just now. At the moment I am fully occupied with my excellent daughter. When she's a bit older, two or three, perhaps, when she's able to give me valuable advice, then I'll decide,

332

the two of us will decide, Valerie and I together, what our next move will be.'

4

The persona that Jesse presented to the world, and to himself as much as he was able to accept it, was one of peace and resolve, strength and good humour. He had concluded, not long after he came to live with Raymond, that it was important for a man to *appear* to be what he wanted and needed to be. Thereafter, by careful observation and by self-discipline he had managed to mimic the behaviour patterns and social rhythms of the few men he'd met who had attained levels he aspired to. He convinced himself that the *appearance* of achievement would speed him on his way to true achievement. He shamelessly and skilfully put the cart before the horse and presented himself, in all situations, as a secure and productive man.

Productivity was a key word in his lexicon. Sensing no electrical charge of genius inside himself, he was wise enough to know that he would have to work much harder than a gifted man would, that his only route towards the pinnacles he envisioned was through industry, through trial and error, through labour.

He had responded well to the disciplines of academic life. When schedules and deadlines and work sheets were placed before him he excelled. 'You're basically insecure,' Raymond had told him. 'That's why you work so hard. You want people to like you.' Jesse saw it differently. He believed that he could do a great many things and do them well as long as he was *told* what to do. If demands were made on him, he was capable of meeting those demands. When he not only had to do the work but to decide what exactly that work should be, how it should be done, and at what tempo, he was inclined to flounder and lose speed.

Having decided that he had a problem he compounded it by concentrating on the problem itself rather than its

333

solution. He was capable of sitting for long periods of time, giving his full attention to the various facets of his make-up that seemed to stand between him and a maximum effort. He also liked to discuss it in great detail, find a pair of sympathetic ears and perform a thorough dissection of the work ethic and his relation to it.

Mid Quigley, however, the instructor at Foresby whom he had met and spent long hours with, sleeping and waking, during the months after he had returned from England and was waiting for Helen to come back to Fort Beck, although she was truly fond of him and respected his intelligence, had no patience at all with his discussions of his work. What it should not be, what it should be, and why it seemed to be so difficult for him to get at it.

'I've decided we all have a particular rhythm of work,' he said, 'whether we like it or not. If you study the biographies of exceptionally productive men you find that some of them worked at a punishing rate, day and night, while others who did work of equal value, were more spasmodic. Long periods of inactivity sometimes followed by intense days of work. Some psychologists say that periods of inactivity are as productive as work periods. I tend to believe that.'

'You tend to believe that,' Mid told him, 'because it makes you feel better about yourself. My experience is that inactivity generally produces nothing except more inactivity. Just because Isaac Newton took a nap under a tree and an apple fell on his head doesn't mean that sleeping in the daytime will bring about scientific revelations. In your case the reason you don't feel you're accomplishing anything is because there's nothing in particular you want to accomplish.'

'What does that mean?'

'Just what it sounds like. People work for one of two reasons. Either they *have* to work to support themselves or they really *want* to work. Your case falls someplace in the cracks in between. You have enough money so you don't *have* to work. But you don't really *want* to work either. You just feel that you *should* work. It's some sort of guilt pattern.

334

You think you should *want* to work but you're not sure what you should work *at* so you work very hard at thinking about it. What you ought to do is count your blessings, think clean thoughts, make an annual gift to the charity of your choice, help support your favourite bootlegger, and enjoy yourself.'

When he showed her the preliminary work he'd done on the della Francesca monograph, she sat up late one night reading it over. The next morning at breakfast she asked, 'Do you want me to tell you how wonderful you are or do you want me to tell you the truth?'

'When you put it that way, I think I'll settle for being wonderful.'

'No, you won't. I'm not planning to crucify you. You've done some honest work. But the cold fact of the matter is that there's nothing new to be said about della Francesca. And if there were I'm not sure that you're the man to say it. I mean what can anyone say about the fifteenth century? Uccello was a genius. So were Donatello and della Francesca. But the pictures and the sculptures tell the whole story. There are no footnotes to greatness. Except for fools who like to read footnotes. When something is truly brilliant all anybody can say is, *"My God!"* Then you stumble outside into the sunshine and you know you'll never be quite the same again.'

'You're talking about romance,' Jesse said. 'I'm talking about *information*. People need to *know* things.'

'No, they don't. They just think they do. There's no biographical titbits about da Vinci that will change The Last Supper. All the facts are useless.'

'Then how can people learn?'

'They *can't*. It's not a learning process. In painting only painters know what's good. And sometimes they don't know either. Most of us only know what we're told. And what we're told is foolishness. Did you ever hear some idiot spinster lecturing in a museum? They're trying to describe a rainstorm to a man who's never been wet. It's a worthless activity. Just a way to kill time in the afternoon. It's really a sociology problem. We tell ourselves that every-

335

thing that's great and beautiful must be great and beautiful to everybody. It's not true and it never has been true. Most of us are plain ordinary people. We like plain ordinary things. We don't want to be kept awake by revolutionary ideas. The structure of a sonnet means nothing to us, and Venus de Milo is just a naked lady with her arms broken off.'

'Are you saying that nobody can write about art or music or literature?'

'No. I'm saying most of us *shouldn't* write about it. But if we're going to, we should write about something that hasn't already been bled dry by a thousand hacks. If you want to write about an artist, you should write about my father.'

'Is he a painter?'

'No. He's a sculptor. I mean in his head he's a sculptor. In his heart. In real everyday life he's a carpenter. Not a cabinet-maker. A plain construction carpenter. A rough carpenter, they call it. He hammers boards together. Builds concrete forms and scaffolding and fences to keep thieves out. But that's just to feed his family and buy gas for his truck. In his own mind, in his *gut*, he's an artist. That's what fires him and keeps him percolating.'

'What sort of work does he do?'

'I told you. He's a carpenter.'

'I mean what about his sculpture? What's it like?'

'It's like nothing you've ever seen. It's rotten. He's all passion and no skill. He hacks away at great logs and blocks of cedar. He saw photographs of a figure of Christ by a sculptor named Zadkine a few years ago and it drove him crazy.'

'Did he like it or hate it?'

'He loved it. He worships it. It haunts him. It's all angles and tortured shapes. It's what he wants to do but can't. He's a lovely man and he's absolutely driven by what he's trying to do but it's hopeless. He's not an artist and he'll never be an artist but he can't stop trying.'

'Why did you say I should write about him?'

'I didn't mean that. Not literally. Or maybe I did. In a

way he's a kind of symbol of what's happened to painting and sculpture. It's all blown apart in the last twenty years or so. The big talents, the really gifted people, the men of genius aren't satisfied to make replicas of what they see. Not any more. It's not enough to hold a mirror up to nature. Artists are exploring *themselves* now, not just the world around them. If your friend della Francesca were alive today, he'd paint very differently. So would Rembrandt or Vermeer. Craft isn't enough. Skill and technique won't do it. This will be the most explosive century in the history of art. It started with the impressionists and now there's no end in sight. The artist has become more important than the subject. The power, the guts, the paint itself, the painter himself . . . that's what it's all about now. My poor father senses all this. He revels in it. He knows he's found his perfect time in history. But his hands betray him. His eyes won't take him where he wants to go. They *can't*. He simply doesn't have the vision. Doesn't have that instant link between conception and action, between seeing and doing. There's no electricity in him. And none in the hacked-out sculptures he does. He *burns* to do good work. He's consumed by it. He says, "If I'm not an artist, I'm *nothing*." But he's *not* an artist, not a sculptor, and he never will be. He started too late. Or perhaps he should never have started at all. It's ironic and it's sad. *Without* what he has, no one can begin to be a serious artist, but when there's nothing else . . . when there's only desire and passion, that won't make it happen either.'

'You lost me,' Jesse said. 'Is there some message in this for me?'

'Not really. My crazy old papa is reaching for the stars when all the time he knows he can't even touch the tree-tops. You're too smart for that. And too conservative. I'd be surprised to see you go after something you didn't think you could get. You're not a buccaneer, Jesse, my darling. But you're not a merchant either. You're a wire-walker. Very good at keeping your balance but never quite sure which edge of the canyon you want to run to. But that's all right. Don't worry about it. Some people get born with a golden light shining on them and unless I'm badly mistaken you're one of those creatures. You may not get what you *think* you want, you may not even *know* what you want, but somehow or other you'll be provided for. People will love you and admire you and look after you. You'll keep all your teeth and never get fat and you'll die in your sleep at the age of a hundred and two with a sweet smile on your kisser.'

Mid, in the time that she was with Jesse, made no effort to mould him or direct him. Sensing that he was eager, almost desperate sometimes, to be led and guided, she held back. 'I'm not smart enough to tell you what to do or what not to do,' she told him. 'I've got my hands full with my own silly decisions. Any time my shoes match and I don't have lipstick on my teeth, I figure I'm having a good day. I'm my father's girl, earthbound and slow-witted. I'm generous and warm-hearted and I make a great corn pudding. But when *that's* said, it's *all* said.'

All the same, in those months, Jesse explored some avenues that were new to him. He wrote a number of book reviews for the Springfield newspaper, he had two short critical pieces accepted by a quarterly in Chicago, and he put in long hours as a kind of ex-officio faculty advisor to the student literary magazine at Foresby. Mid, claiming no share in these activities, said, 'I am merely a supportive witness.' But she did provide a foundation of common sense that kept him moving forward. And she gave him a piece of advice that stayed with him from then on, two pieces of advice in fact. When he complained about his inability to remember certain vital facts about one subject or another, she said, 'Who cares? Don't worry about it. Never use your brain as a filing cabinet. Most people mistake a good memory for intelligence but the fact is, almost all those strange creatures who spend their lives recording facts and statistics, have very chancy minds. Even if they do have a respectable brain, there's no time to use it. They're too busy memorizing foolishness.'

When he complained about the enormity of a project he was considering she said, 'The secret is to think small. You

338

can only drive one nail at a time, take one step, write one sentence. The bigger the job the more necessary it is to tackle it moment to moment, one little unit at a time.'

Like a squirrel gathering nuts, Jesse stored away such scraps of wisdom and observation. He told himself he was creating a portable ambiance of work for himself, one he could take with him wherever he went. He envisioned himself as a disciplined solitary worker, keeping regular hours, turning out a predetermined amount of work each day. Projects came and went in his head like butterflies, each one more exciting and provocative than the last.

After returning to Wingate Fields he discussed his work plans at some length with Angus. And in even greater detail with Clara. Quite apart from her affection for Jesse, she was stimulated by the thought of having a critical scholar at work on the premises, an active mind searching and probing and bringing an air of vitality to the household. Eager to be helpful and supportive, she saw to it that a handsome suite of rooms facing the south gardens was refitted to accommodate Jesse's needs. Adjoining his spacious bedroom and its adjacent sitting-room, she converted an additional bedroom into a large office and library. She further instructed the staff that Jesse's work schedule might require him to take his meals at odd hours. Proper adjustments, therefore, would have to be made.

More important, Clara spent long hours with him, listening to detailed descriptions of various projects he was considering and offering suggestions when they seemed appropriate. Since she felt that encouragement was the best contribution she could make she was seldom critical of Jesse's proposals. His idea, for example, of doing a series of nature pieces to be called Northumberland Afternoons was a marvellous notion, she thought. She agreed with him also that a strong case could be made for Edward Munch's influence on Die Blauer Vier, and that Juan Gris was the quintessential cubist. She did not share his enthusiasm for Schönberg, did not truly believe that a thematic link could be established between Ivan Bunin and John Galsworthy. But whenever her reactions were either

339

lukewarm or negative she kept them to herself. She listened with enthusiasm and curiosity as Jesse discussed and expounded and examined his choices day after day. She was a perfect audience. She never insisted that he go beyond discussion, never asked to see physical evidence that his plans and schemes were, in fact, being transferred to paper. As he dismissed one project after another after weeks or months of exploring it, she pretended to believe that he was functioning sensibly, that there was no point in finishing something if it seemed to be unworthy of the time and effort needed. She pretended to believe that Jesse was simply proceeding carefully and that sooner or later, when he came upon a worthwhile subject, he would give it his total energies and full concentration.

Angus, however, was not deceived. Both his instinct and his experience told him when a man was truly productive. He could spot self-delusion as clearly as he could see a wine stain on a white tablecloth. But just as he had made allowances for his own children and grandchildren so also did he not demand that Jesse should be something he was apparently unable to be. Angus liked him and respected him and, more important, he accepted him. He was a decent and attractive young man who was able to behave in a civilized manner and Angus required no more.

Ned Causey, however, was less tolerant. He had been cautious from the start about Jesse, had not been pleased about his liaison with Nora, and had been bitterly resentful of his close relationship with Angus and the adoption that had resulted. Unable to delineate precisely how that act of adoption had diminished him, Ned could not help feeling, all the same, that he had somehow been vandalized. He took great pains, however, not to reveal his feelings to Jesse or to Angus or to anyone except Clara. But for her ears he was disturbingly explicit. 'It baffles me,' he said, 'to see undeserving people rewarded time after time.'

'Jesse's not undeserving,' Clara said. 'He's a fine young man. I think we're fortunate to have him in the family.'

'Of course *you* think that. It's clear to one and all from the time you devote to him. Anyone would imagine you're his governess to see the trouble you take with him. Long conversations day after day. Deciding the fate of the world, I'm sure. Or planning what recommendations you two will make to Angus about the future of the Bradshaw holdings. What a charade.'

'Are you saying I'm not capable of advising Angus? I've been doing it now for more than twenty years. Do you feel that I'm incompetent?'

'No. I don't feel that. I think you know the ins and outs as well as Angus does. But I can't say the same for your foundling brother, Angus' adopted son.'

'You'd be surprised,' Clara said. 'Jesse has a good head. When a set of circumstances is presented, when it's clear to him what the choices are, he can make a proper decision as well as anybody else.'

'As well as *I* could. I expect that's what you're saying.'

'No, I'm not saying that. I know very well what you can do. I believe you can do anything you set your mind to. I think you'd be a real asset to the business and I've told Angus that. But he won't have it. It's nothing against you.'

'It's not, eh? What would you call it then?'

'You know how Angus is. It's Bradshaw money, he says, and it should be handled by Bradshaws.'

'Our young Mr Jesse is a long way from being a Bradshaw.'

'No, he's not,' Clara said. 'He's a Bradshaw now just as much as *I* am. In name and in fact. I know you resent that but you might as well get used to it. He's here to stay.'

'Here in the family or here in the house?'

'Both, I should think. I believe he's very much at home here. As he should be.'

'Seems damned odd to me. A young buck his age cuddling up to the fire like a spaniel. Seldom leaves the house. No life of his own. Shows no interest at all in the young women of the county.'

'Can't blame him for that, can we? They're a sorry crop.'

'There's nothing sorry about Alice Carmichael if you ask me. Or the Goodpastor girl. And even Nora thinks Louisa

341

Tharp is stunning. I don't know what our Mister Jesse is after if he can't take an interest in those young women.'

'Maybe he's not after anything,' Clara said. 'He's awfully keen on his work. I imagine he doesn't have a lot of time for social doings.'

'He always seems to have time to loll about and have a good chat with you.'

'I'm glad he does. I enjoy talking to him.'

'Of course you do. That's clear to see.'

'Do you have some objection . . . .'

'Not at all. Would it matter if I did?' When Clara didn't answer he went on, 'I only brought it up apropos his so-called work. It's many months now he's been back here and I've seen no evidence of his industry. Have you?'

'Of course I have. His mind never stops. He has one idea after another.'

'I'm sure he does,' Ned said. He took a cigar out of his case and lit it. 'Are you sure he's not having a bit of fun with one of the servant girls? Perhaps that's why he sticks so close to home. It wouldn't surprise me if that little ginger-haired girl had caught his eye. What's her name then?'

'I don't know. What *is* her name?'

'Damned if I know. Priscilla, I think.'

'Oh yes,' Clara said. 'Priscilla.' She smiled. 'I would think it more likely that Priscilla would have caught *your* eye. I understand her uncle is a publican in Bellingham. They say she helps him out there sometimes on her days off from us.'

'It's news to me,' Ned said.

'I thought you might have seen her there.'

'Are you trying to get me off the subject of Jesse?'

'Not at all. Why would I do that?'

'I'm not sure,' he said. Then, 'I hesitate to ask you this. I wouldn't want to offend you in any way. But is it possible that your adopted brother has something more than a brotherly interest in you?'

'Since I'll soon be fifty years old,' she said, 'perhaps he sees me as a mother.'

342

'I think not. Nobody sees you as a mother, not even your own children.'

'Go to hell, Ned.'

'No offence intended. I just meant that you're damned attractive and you know it. You could pass for thirty-five any time you chose to.'

'Not likely.'

'I'm not implying that you might be smitten with *him*. I'm simply bringing to your attention that he could very well be a bit taken with you.'

'If I am being admonished, I find it outrageous. If I am being cautioned, I find it humiliating. Whatever your intentions I think this is a topic we should not explore any further. I will try to forget that you ever brought it up and I suggest you do the same. If I should ever repeat this conversation to Angus . . . .'

'Why would you want to do that?'

'I *don't* want to do that. But if I *did*, if for some reason I *should*, I'm sure you would be exposed to some facets of my father that you have never been aware of up to now.'

'If you think . . . .'

'Shhhh,' she said. 'I *told* you what I think. I think you should drink more than usual tonight and erase this conversation totally from your mind. If you *don't*, if it *ever* comes up again, I cannot describe to you how suddenly and permanently your life could be altered.'

5

Nora did not, as she had promised herself, take complete charge of her life on Valerie's second birthday. She told herself it was not fair to her daughter to uproot her at such a critical age, to carry her off to unfamiliar surroundings. New sounds, new rooms, new faces. So she stayed on at Bick House.

She would have been quick to deny that motherhood had changed her, and it was true that her basic desires were as strong as they had ever been, her yearning to break away from the region where she had grown up, her need to taste the unfamiliar and sample the exotic. But she had learned also, from her daily routine with the baby, that parenthood is a mosaic of a thousand tiny disappointments, frustrations, and sacrifices. For the first time in memory she found herself adjusting to schedules and rhythms and demands that were not her own, that did not benefit or serve *her* in any way. At least not at the beginning. But slowly the benefits began to come clear to her. Living on the isolated island she had fashioned for herself in a wing of Bick House, she played a larger role than she would have had to in Valerie's upbringing. Because she chose to, of course, but also because there was little else for her to do. Since everything was provided for her, there was nothing to compete for, no barriers to topple, no conflicting person to struggle with. So Valerie became, at one, Nora's problem and her joy. Watching her grow and learn and develop, hearing her begin to speak, watching her toddle, Nora, for the first time, felt pride in someone other than herself. In the beginning it confused her, made her question her own armature. But gradually she came to believe that her close and tender relationship with her daughter, that new role, was not a replacement or an alteration of what she had always been, the self she had identified with and taken pride in, but an adjunct somehow, a new growth, something added. Rather than seeing Valerie as a restriction, as a barrier to keep her from the life she had envisioned for herself, Nora began to look at the little girl as striking evidence of her own ability to deal with new elements in her life, to meet new challenges, to take them on and continue to move ahead.

She did not, by the act of motherhood, come of age. She did not become a selfless person. But she found, to her amazement, that there are spoils that do not have to be won in battle. She saw things simply come to her. Warm, rewarding things. As she measured these things, as she began to find pleasures that were small and peaceful and totally new to her, she in no way lost sight of the golden horizons she had always yearned for.

Although she still thought of Edmund and his father as the leaders of a band of Mongols riding shaggy ponies, although she told herself many times each day that her life and that of her daughter would not truly begin until all thoughts of Bick House had been washed from their memories, her confidence in the future and the warm physical joy she got from her days and nights with her child gave her a kind of patience that was akin to the warm bath she soaked in every late afternoon. It was temporary and pleasant and sweet-smelling, and most important it was a preamble to the evening, to the pleasures and joys and mysteries that could unfold in a woman's life between that moment when she stepped out of the warm water to be wrapped in a soft towel, and the moment, hours later, when she would slip into her bed and fall asleep, her brain still dancing, her skin still tingling with the thousands of glittering sensations that had made up her evening. So it would be when she, at last, left Cumberland, she told herself. The new beginning would be, if anything, sweeter and more electric for having been so deliciously postponed.

When her moment came, however, when the day she had so long planned for arrived, when she told Edmund, in the kindest and most considerate way she could manage, that she was going away and taking Valerie with her, that she was no longer able to be married to him, she stimulated a reaction for which she was totally unprepared.

'You may go any time you wish,' he said. 'And the sooner the better. I will drive you to the station myself. If you can leave in an hour I'll have the car waiting just outside in the east drive.'

'Don't be ridiculous. I'm not trying to create a public situation. I think we should proceed in a civilized manner. We have Valerie to think of. We don't want to make a fuss. There's no need for us to humiliate each other.'

'I shouldn't worry about that too much if I were you. If you haven't been humiliated by the way we've been living in the past few years then I'm sure that nothing we say or do now will humiliate you.'

'I don't understand what you mean.'

'Of course you don't.'

She studied him carefully. 'I don't know what you're up to but whatever it is, I don't like it.'

'Like it or not. It's all the same to me. I stopped trying to please you a long time ago.'

'I don't remember that you *ever* tried to please me.'

'I'm sure you don't. Since you're totally occupied with pleasing yourself it must be difficult for you to notice anyone else's efforts.'

'You're really trying to be cruel, aren't you?'

'No. I'm simply telling you the truth.'

'Your version of the truth doesn't interest me.'

'Of course not,' he said. 'Why should it?'

'You're being hateful and I'm surprised. I expected you to be reasonable about this. It can't be unexpected. We haven't had a blissful relationship.'

'*Blissful*? Was that the word you used?'

'Yes. You heard what I said. Blissful.'

'You're right. It hasn't been blissful.'

'I can't imagine that you would like to go on living the way we have since Valerie was born.'

'You're right,' he said. 'I haven't liked it at all. As I recall, I've told you that on numerous occasions.'

'Well, that's all past now. Now you'll be free to choose a wife who'll be more satisfactory than I've been.'

'I think not.'

'Then you can live the bachelor life. I suspect you would prefer that in any case.'

'Let's just say that I'm accustomed to it. I have grown particularly accustomed to it since I've been married.'

'I salute you. If you're about to tell me about your successes with the ladies of the county, please spare me.'

'I shall.'

'I'm sure they'll be delighted to learn that you're free and available again.'

346

'I'm *not* free and available,' he said. 'We're still married. I have a wife and a child.'

'Only for the moment. What do you think we've been talking about?'

'We've been talking about your departure. I understood you to say you're leaving.'

'And you said you were delighted to hear it.'

'I am. Relieved and delighted.'

'That means you won't object?'

'Not at all.'

'Don't be so smug and aggravating, Edmund. I'm not just running home for a week with my mother. I want to take charge of my life again.'

'It seems to me you've been in complete charge of your life all along.'

'You know what I'm saying. Don't pretend you don't. I want to be free. I want a divorce.'

'Oh, now . . . that's a new development.'

'No, it isn't. What do you suppose we've been discussing?'

'It hasn't been a discussion exactly,' he said. 'More of an announcement. You announced that you were leaving me, leaving Bick House, and leaving your daughter . . . .'

'I'm not leaving Valerie. What in the world gave you that idea? She's coming with me.'

'I see. You want me to give you a divorce so you can wander off somewhere and take Valerie with you.'

'Do you expect me to leave her behind?'

'Do you expect me to let her go?'

'A moment ago you said . . . .'

'I said *you* are free to leave any time you choose to go. But I did not agree to a divorce and I did not agree to give up my daughter. This is her home and this is where she belongs.'

'She belongs with me,' Nora said. 'I'm her mother. I've devoted myself to her. You *know* that.'

'That's true. I *do* know that. Can you think of any other reason that would have persuaded me to tolerate the way of life you've forced on me? However ridiculous and

347

humiliating *our* living arrangements were I was able to tell myself that Valerie was being properly cared for.'

'Exactly,' Nora said. 'I never tried to keep you away from her. You saw her whenever you wished. I was always cordial to you when she was present. She never heard me say an unkind thing about you. She chatters on about you all the time. She adores you.'

'And I adore her,' Edmund said. He was silent then as though he felt that nothing he might add would further clarify his position.

The silence disarmed Nora. When she told him, 'Whatever you say or do, it won't change how I feel,' he said nothing. She began to weep then and said, 'Don't make me miserable. I have a right to a different life, don't I? I'm not angry with you. I don't *blame* you. We just made a mistake, that's all.' Still he didn't answer. When she dried her tears, however, when she squared her shoulders and said, 'I'm not a prisoner here. You can't lock me up and keep me if I don't want to stay,' he replied, 'I didn't mean it when I said I was eager for you to go. I've been angry with you many times these past few years and I've said things I didn't intend. But my feelings for you are what they've always been. What I want, what I've *always* wanted, is for us to live together as we did before Valerie was born. If I seemed inflexible to you then, I'm sorry. I knew you hated living here but I thought you'd come to like it. I thought the idea of our packing up and moving ourselves to London was foolishness. But I don't feel that way now. I'm willing to do whatever I have to if it will keep us together.'

'Oh, Edmund. It's too late. I'm sorry but it's just too late for all that. I just need to . . . .'

'I know. That's what I thought you'd say.' Then he said, 'I have no intention of trying to keep you here when you don't want to stay. But you must understand one thing. You must believe me when I tell you that I will not give up Valerie. I have every right to keep her and I intend to do it.'

'You think if she stays here, I'll stay too. Isn't that what you think?'

'I have no idea *what* you'll do. I've never known what to expect from you. I only know that I am determined to keep my daughter with me whether you stay or not.'

Curbing her anger and her frustration, stimulated by what she would decide later had been a spark of almost divine inspiration, Nora, after a long moment of silence, smiled and said, 'I can't give her up either, Edmund. So I expect we'll have to try it your way. If we're both willing to compromise a bit, perhaps we can have a life together after all. Why don't we think about it for a while, each of us, and when we're in a different frame of mind, maybe we'll go away for a few days, have a chance to talk and spend some time together. In the meantime I promise not to do anything foolish.'

As she had anticipated, Edmund was clearly in favour of such a programme. He accepted, without question, the objectives she proposed as well as her indefinite and uncertain timetable. On the following day, however, her maid brought her a message from the chauffeur saying it had been necessary to take Nora's car to a garage in Carlisle for a substantial engine overhaul. Wallace, the chauffeur, did *not* disclose that he had been further instructed to take Mrs Bick and her daughter on no car journeys that had not been approved by her husband. When Nora learned of these restrictions a few days later she countered by seeking Edmund out in his study. 'I've decided where we should go on our little trip,' she said. 'Why don't we take the train to Inverness and spend a week in that hotel we like so much. Maybe Hugh will come down from Sutherland and we can have a proper reunion. Drink and smoke and tell naughty stories.'

'When would you like to go?'

'Around the twentieth of next month perhaps. How does that sound?'

Before she left the room she put her arms around him and kissed him. 'I think we've been very foolish,' she said. 'I've really missed you.'

At the door she turned and said, 'If you're not too busy next Wednesday, why don't you plan a little outing with Valerie? I've asked Wallace to drive me over to Wingate that day. Angus gets very cross with me when I stay away too long. I'll stay the night and come back the next afternoon.'

'Maybe Valerie and I should come with you.'

'I'd *love* that,' Nora said quickly. Then, 'But I'm afraid she's not very happy on long car trips. Or short trips either for that matter. Also, I promised her you might take her up-country so she can see the wee lambs. She's very excited about that.'

As a schoolgirl, Nora had excelled in county theatricals. She had rehearsed tirelessly, had carefully researched her costumes and her make-up and the style in which she should wear her hair. Her energy and dedication had over-powered the limp young women and stumbling amateur males she performed with. She had seemed, in their eyes, to attack her roles in a manner that was almost unladylike. One stupefied young girl had stammered helplessly to her mother, 'It's hateful. She's *exhausting*. She's like a real actress.'

It had been, of course, a competition for her, a kind of battle where there would be clear winners and losers. She had no sense of the play, no thought of the cast as an ensemble. She saw it quite simply as *her* play performed before *her* audience. It was an opportunity to be selfish and outrageous, to outdo and outmanoeuvre her fellow performers and be applauded. She adored every moment of it; by combining her delicate translucent beauty with an aggressive, rapacious manner that was hypnotic in its intensity, she was thought to be much more gifted than she actually was.

Some of that surge of energy and competitive fire she had used in preparing a role, she felt racing through her again as she was driven across the moors and dales from Bick House to Wingate Fields. She had carefully prepared her case, clarified her charges and indictments, and memo-rized her key speeches. In the car, with the side-curtains drawn, she rehearsed it all silently in her mind. When they were perhaps twenty minutes away from her family's house, Wallace heard her speaking indistinctly in the back seat behind the glass dividing pane. When he handed her out of the car in her grandfather's driveway, when Angus came down the steps to meet her, she was weeping uncontrollably.

She had taken pains to arrive when she knew her parents would be away from the house, Ned at a business meeting in Morpeth and her mother at a charity luncheon in the vicarage at Bellingham. She intended to do her performance only once and she was determined that the audience should be Angus and only Angus.

Her instincts had been correct. Her grandfather had been shocked to see her in such a state. He had taken her into the library, forced her to sip some brandy, and had tried to calm her. But his concern and loving attentions only seemed to intensify her sobbing. Fully ten minutes passed before she was able to quiet herself, to straighten up in her chair and start to speak. Her first words were, 'I can't tell you. I'm too ashamed. It's too awful.'

'Yes you can,' Angus said. 'Just take your time.'

They sat in the library for more than an hour. She wept and trembled but she kept talking. Angus sat facing her, like a stone figure, and listened. At last he rang for his wife's personal maid. 'Take my granddaughter to her room. See her comfortably into bed and give her a sleeping draught.' To Nora he said, 'I want you to have a good rest now. And you're not to concern yourself about anything. I will take charge of these matters and I assure you it will all come round as you wish it. Don't discuss it with your mother or with anyone else. You and I will see this thing through.'

As soon as Nora went upstairs, Angus placed a call to Charles Tremont at his home in Kent. They talked for almost an hour. When he rang off, Angus phoned the bishop of the Anglican cathedral in Newcastle and made an appointment to meet him in two days' time. Then he sat heavily and motionless behind the great desk in his study, his eyes looking straight ahead, his mind plotting the comeuppance of Edmund Bick.

Nora returned to Bick House the following day as planned, feeling cleansed and pure and diaphanous. When Edmund met her outside the house he said, 'I'm very glad to see you.'

'Thank you. It's nice to be home.'

'How is Angus?'

'Angus,' she said, 'is extremely well. You could never imagine how wonderful Angus is.'

The next three weeks were perhaps the happiest time of Edmund's married life, not for what they provided but for what they gave promise of providing. Nora had begun to have dinner with him and Abraham again; she brought a gracious charm to their table that was new and totally irresistible even to Abraham. It was as though her long period of isolation in the far corridors of the house had never taken place. She spoke only of today and tomorrow. All previous tensions and recriminations seemed to have been forgotten. And *her* forgetting them set a tone that Edmund was unable to ignore. Remembering only what served his highest purpose he saw her again as he had when they were engaged to be married. He found that he was totally concentrated now on Inverness and beyond. He saw, he was absolutely certain that he saw, true devotion in her eyes. She listened when he spoke, and seemed genuinely amused when he said something that was meant to be amusing. Also she began to take note of what cravat he wore with what shirt and to make droll suggestions as to how he could improve his appearance. This, to Edmund, was a fond reminder of how they had once been, how *she* had been in relation to him, and it convinced him, more than any other piece of evidence or behaviour *could* have convinced him that wherever she had gone and for whatever reasons, she had decided at last to come back.

When Nora pointed out that it would be nice if they had new luggage for their trip to Inverness, Edmund agreed. 'I had a notice in the post from your leather man in Carlisle,' she said. 'He has some softer bags, Italian leather.

They sound attractive. Lighter weight than our other cases.'

Mid-morning, two days before they were due to leave for Inverness, Edmund drove into Carlisle to fetch the new luggage. Less than an hour after his departure, a grey limousine and a smaller official car pulled into the driveway at Bick House. Angus and Sir Charles Tremont stepped down from the limousine. A local constable and an officer of the district court got out of the other car. As Angus led the way up the steps to the main entrance, Nora and Valerie, dressed for travel and accompanied by Valerie's governess, came out through a side door, crossed a corner of the garden, and got into the grey car.

Abraham, summoned by his butler, came down the great hall to the entrance foyer. When he saw Angus he said, 'What a fine surprise. We don't see you as often as we'd like.'

'This is not a social call,' Angus said. 'These gentlemen will speak for me.'

The constable, grey at the temples and deep-chested, steady-voiced and sure of his role, said to Abraham, 'We've had a complaint that two people are being held here against their will. Mrs Nora Causey Dick and her daughter, Valerie.'

Before Abraham could make a reply, the officer of the court, a thin, sour-looking young fellow in a dark suit, his bowler in one hand, stepped forward with a document in his other hand and said, 'Pending a detailed investigation of certain allegations, the district court has made Angus Bradshaw the temporary guardian of Mrs Bick and her daughter.'

'What's this all about, Angus?'

'My granddaughter and her child are waiting outside in my car. I'm taking them with me to Wingate Fields.'

'What about Edmund? Can't you wait till he comes home? What will I tell my son?'

'Tell him the truth,' Angus said. 'Tell him exactly what these two men have told you. And tell him I say he's a

353

rotten bastard. I look forward to telling him that to his face.'

'By God, Angus,' Abraham said. 'You'd better watch what you're saying.'

'I've said exactly what I believe and I'll say it in court when the time comes.'

Tremont spoke up then, his voice quiet and soothing but armatured with authority. 'I am Sir Charles Tremont. I am the legal representative of the Bradshaw family. I will be at Wingate Fields during the weekend. If your son's solicitor would like to contact me there I would be happy to arrange a meeting with him. Or he can reach me later at my office in London.'

'I don't know about any solicitor. But you'll certainly hear from my son. You can be sure of that.'

'The sooner the better,' Angus said.

'Damned funny business, it seems to me,' Abraham said, 'when you can come round here with a scrap of paper and kidnap a man's wife and daughter.'

The officer of the court responded quickly. 'I would advise you not to make disparaging remarks about official actions. When you study those papers I've delivered to you, you will see that Edmund Bick faces possible criminal charges. He would be wise to be cautious indeed in his reactions to this matter.'

6

Two days later, Edmund sat in Angus' study at Wingate Fields, Angus across the desk from him and Tremont just to his left in a high-backed wing chair. The curtains were drawn; the room seemed grey and chilly. No one smoked. No drinks or tea had been served. The silence was heavy and ominous.

At last Tremont said, 'I can understand your dismay. It's an awkward situation for you. That's why I thought it would be wise for you to bring your solicitor.'

'I don't need a solicitor,' Edmund said. '*I* haven't done anything. You people carry off my wife and child and now you tell me I may have to defend myself in court.'

Tremont indicated a folder of papers on the table beside him. 'Let's be very clear about this. Mr Bradshaw and I have found you guilty of nothing. All that is a matter for the courts. Mr Bradshaw's concern, and *mine*, is for the well-being of Nora and her daughter.'

'*Well-being*? You're talking about *my* wife and *my* daughter. What do you imagine . . . .'

Tremont held up his hand. 'Please. Let me finish. In a strict legal sense, the decision to press these charges will rest with your wife. I will be candid with you. I don't believe that any purpose would be served by exposing this material in open court and I have so informed your wife. But she is angry and frightened, for herself and her daughter, and she wants to have things set right once and for all.'

'What is she frightened of?' Edmund asked.

'You know damned well what she's frightened of,' Angus said. 'You've heard what she testified to in her affidavit.'

'You don't believe that rot, do you?'

'Are you saying Nora's a liar?'

'I don't know what I'm saying, but if she swore that I have mistreated her, then that's a lie.'

'If there's lying being done it's not Nora who's doing it.'

'Let's not let this get out of hand,' Tremont said. He turned to Edmund. 'I can understand your being upset, Mr Bick. But it's important for you to remember that Mr Bradshaw is not your adversary. Nor am I. If your wife decides to proceed against you, if the court, after examining these affidavits and depositions chooses to prosecute, it will be in their hands. I am interceding on Mr Bradshaw's behalf, functioning more as a family friend than as legal counsel, because we think it would be preferable, for the child's sake, for your wife's sake, and certainly for your sake, too, if this distasteful material . . . .'

355

'It's distasteful because it's all contrived,' Edmund said. 'Not a word of it is true.'

'I've heard about all I want to hear,' Angus said.

'What the hell are you so upset about?' Edmund said. 'I'm the one who's being outmanoeuvred, not *you*.'

'You've outmanoeuvred yourself, you rotten bastard.' Angus stood up behind his desk, pink with anger. 'You and that father of yours. You both should be taken out and whipped.'

'Angus,' Tremont cut in. 'We're getting into a situation that doesn't benefit any of us. If you want me to continue here I think it would be wise if I talked to Mr Bick alone. This is an emotional problem at best. Let's not make it worse than it is.'

'I'll not have this damned fool drive me out of my own study.'

'No one is driving you anywhere, Angus. I am simply trying to function in everyone's best interests and I'm asking you to let me do that.'

After a black silence, his eyes still fixed on Edmund, Angus said to Tremont, 'I'll be in the drawing-room.' When the door closed behind him, Edmund said, 'I've known that man since I was twelve years old. I can't understand what's happening. Does he really believe those things about me? Do *you* believe them?'

'It's not my job to believe or disbelieve. I have to look at both sides and try to decide what the court will believe. Not what is *true* but what is believable. We're all adults. We know that wives have been known to lie about their husbands. For the sake of argument, let's assume that Nora *is* lying. But why would those servant girls lie?'

'Because she told them to.'

'That's possible. But in court, if your position is that three people are lying about you and those three people say *you're* lying also, you can see that makes matters difficult. And in a case like this where your wife is simply trying to establish that there is a moral tone in your home which is not conducive to the proper upbringing of a young

356

girl, even if there is only *doubt* in the minds of the court it could work against you.'

'I don't understand all that,' Edmund said. 'All I know is what's just and proper. Or what seems that way to me. The only course I can see is to contest any divorce action and to fight for the custody of my daughter.'

'I applaud you for that. But the primary issue here is neither one of divorce nor of custody. If your wife proceeds against you and the court decides in her favour you would not be allowed custody of Valerie under *any* circumstances. Even if Nora agreed at some future time to *let* you have your daughter, the court would not permit it.'

'We'll see about that.'

'You'll see that I'm right.'

After a long moment Edmund said, 'I know you're on the Bradshaws' side in this . . . .'

'Not strictly true. I am trying to make things better rather than worse. Better for all concerned.'

'Then tell me how things can get better for me.'

'I'm not certain they can. But let's go over the ground again and see what we can discover. I will summarize your position as well as Nora's and see if there is an opportunity for compromise.'

'My position is very simple. Nora's my wife and I want to stay married to her. If that's impossible then I want to have custody of Valerie.'

'That seems simple enough. Nora's wishes, on the surface, seem equally simple. She does not want to live with you any longer and she wants her daughter to be with her. Knowing that you won't let Valerie go without a struggle, she has decided to go to court and reveal the reasons for your failed marriage. She is not anxious to do this but, like you, she is determined to have custody of the child.' He glanced down again at the papers on the table by his chair. 'Now,' he continued, 'what is the nature of her complaint against you? Not very pleasant, I'm afraid. In this attested deposition she has stated that you have unusual needs and desires, that you forced her to perform unnatural acts. When she resisted or refused, you used

357

physical force, and on several occasions, struck her. Her servants stated that they saw clear evidence of these attacks. They said also that in the year preceding Valerie's birth when you and Nora were still living together as man and wife that Nora was constantly depressed and upset and she wept a great deal. They said the gossip among the servants was that you were unfaithful to your wife even in those early months of your marriage. Nora says that she established a separate menage, if you will, in your home, not because she no longer cared for you but because she was determined not to give in to . . . I'm quoting her now . . . "his bizarre animal instincts". Also she was physically afraid of you, she says. Afraid you would strike her. For the sake of the child she tried to maintain some semblance of a proper marriage but she decided at last that it would never work, that the moral climate of Bick House was not a proper place to bring up her daughter. And here we have a further complication. If we are to believe the servant girls, as well as these other stories which Angus tells me are common knowledge in your county, your father does not have a spotless reputation. Is that true?'

'What does my father have to do with it?'

'A great deal, I'm afraid. He is still the master of your house. And it is that house and the standards which exist there that are at question. If it is brought out that your father is the sort of man who seduces servant girls, if that has been his practice for many years, such a circumstance does not exactly strengthen your case. Are you aware of these things about your father?'

'I'm aware that such stories are told about him.'

'Do you see that his reputation could be used against you?'

'I see that someone has gone to great pains to make a case against me.'

'You deny all of Nora's statements then?'

'They're totally untrue. The principal ones I will not even discuss. Her allegation that I struck her, that she is physically afraid of me, is absurd. Nora's not afraid of anyone.'

358

'So there we are,' Tremont said. 'Where we began. At an impasse, I'm afraid.'

'What if we go to court and the court decides against me?'

'The worst that could happen is that you could get a sentence for either battery or moral turpitude.'

'And if I win?'

'I'm afraid you *can't* win. You can't force Nora to live with you and you can't keep her from divorcing you. And when she does you can be sure that all the material from the court procedure will be reviewed again when custody talks begin.'

'Then I lose either way? Is that what you're saying?'

'A mother always has an advantage in a custody struggle. And in Nora's case I understand she's been an excellent mother.'

'That's true.'

'It's a tight fit whatever you decide.'

'It seems to me,' Edmund said, 'as if there's nothing *for* me to decide. Nora can take me to court and tell any lies she chooses to or she can divorce me and get custody of Valerie by telling the same lies.'

Tremont studied him carefully. Finally he said, 'I'm going to say something to you in the strictest confidence. I'm not ethically bound to silence since I am not serving here in a professional capacity. But all the same my first loyalties are to Angus and his family.'

'I understand that.'

'I have not been told this in so many words but it is my understanding that Nora would prefer to destroy those affidavits. For her daughter's sake as well as her own sense of decency she would prefer that such material should never be made public. Either in open court or in a divorce proceeding.'

'Then what have we been talking about?'

'Don't misunderstand me,' Tremont said. 'I didn't say she *won't* use it. I said she would prefer not to. If you are amenable I think she would choose another solution.'

'What other solution is there?'

'If I can report to Angus that you believe a public struggle would not benefit anyone, if you are willing to go home and leave this in my hands, I can promise you that within a month, six weeks at the most, you will be notified that your marriage to Nora has been annulled.'

'Annulled? That's impossible.'

Tremont smiled. 'The Lord moves in mysterious ways.'

'But we've been married for six years. We have a child.'

'I know that. And so does the Church. But we have been assured by the bishop that there will be no problem.'

'Does that mean he knows what's in those depositions?'

'Yes. I'm afraid he does.'

'My God . . . .'

'It's embarrassing for you, I know,' Tremont said. 'But not half as embarrassing, I should think, as a court procedure could prove to be.'

'My daughter's future, how all this could affect her, is much more important to me than protecting my own reputation.'

'Of course it is. As it should be. But it seems to me, the circumstances being what they are, that if *you* suffer public humiliation *she* is very apt to suffer, too, sooner or later.' He paused, then went on. 'Let me counsel you if I may. First, do you believe that another solicitor, if he were aware of all the facts we have discussed . . . .'

'Not facts. Allegations.'

'Of course. But with the same power to do mischief. Do you believe that your family solicitor would advise you to go into court and sue for custody of your daughter?'

'I don't know.'

'I don't know either. Not for certain. But I *do* know that no solicitor *I* know would so advise you. I believe you would be told, as *I* am telling you, that by risking all you could lose all. Not only could you fail to win custody of Valerie, you might be denied access to her altogether.'

'How could they do that?'

'If they were persuaded by these charges of moral turpitude, if they conclude that you are an improper parent, anything is possible. Many courts can be over-zealous

360

when they feel they are protecting a child.' He paused again, walked to the window, then turned back. 'Let me put it to you this way. If you concede that there's no possibility of your continuing your marriage with Nora, if you concede further that it appears unlikely that any court would grant Valerie's custody to you, then it would appear that your objective should be to maintain the best possible relationship with your daughter, to have the widest possible range of access rights.'

'It's not likely that Nora will be willing to grant me anything.'

'On the contrary. If I tell her you are willing to support the annulment process, I assure you that she will be most generous in permitting an arrangement that will allow you to spend reasonable time with your daughter.'

'Having seen those affidavits I wouldn't trust any promise she would make.'

'Then I ask you to trust me. I will intercede for you to this extent. You and I will sit here and put together a strict calendar of visitation, one that you approve of. I will then explain to Angus and Nora that your acceptance of the annulment hinges on their acceptance of the access provisions. Does that sound fair to you?'

'Nothing sounds fair to me.'

'I understand that. But fair or not, I suspect it's the best compromise you will be able to effect.'

An hour later, Tremont sat in the drawing-room with Angus. Angus studied the sheet of paper Tremont had given him with its carefully written notes and dates. When he looked up he said, 'Seems damned generous to me. Nora won't like it, I promise you.'

'Nora must compromise whether she likes it or not. If she tried to go into court with those affidavits, any skilful barrister would crucify her. And God knows what those two little servant girls would say under severe questioning.'

'*He* doesn't want to go into court either,' Angus said. 'I'm sure of that.'

'That's correct. I convinced him it was not in his best

361

interests. And I *promised* him those rights of access to his daughter.'

Angus looked at the paper again, then at Tremont. 'I suppose it does no harm to *promise*, does it?'

'Let's be clear about this, Angus. You asked me to help out in this matter and I agreed. But not, as you will recall, without some hesitation. I explained to you that if this became a court matter I would not participate in any way. I volunteered to function only as a dispassionate intermediary. But my personal code of ethics still applies. In exchange for something *you* want, I promised Edmund Bick something *he* wants. It was more than a promise. It was a guarantee. And it must be honoured.'

Angus looked uncomfortable. Finally he said, 'Well, I suppose I'm agreeable. But the final decision is up to Nora.'

'I'm afraid not, Angus. I took on this untidy task as a personal service to you. I have managed to deal with Edmund. Now I expect *you* to deal with Nora.'

Seven weeks later, Angus was notified that the marriage between Nora and Edmund had been annulled. Nora was not on hand to receive the news. She was in Paris supervising the decoration of an apartment she had recently purchased at the edge of the Bois du Boulogne. Nor was Edmund at Bick House. He had gone to Norway for a brief holiday with his daughter.

Chapter Eight

1

When Nora's child was born, just six months after the birth of Helen's baby in Maine, Helen, when she had the news, in a letter from Clara, wrote a return note at once saying how delighted she was to hear that Nora had a daughter. In July of the following year when her own mother, Anna, gave birth to a daughter, Maria, and when a little more than a year later, she had a second daughter, Christina, Helen told herself that she was equally delighted. In January of 1924, however, when Anna's son, Paul, was born, Helen was suddenly and painfully aware that her own son was nearly four years old now.

No matter how hard she concentrated on her daily activities, whatever techniques she used to distract herself, to focus on other matters, she found herself staring at small children in the street. And when she was alone she stared at blank walls and besieged herself with questions for which she had no answers.

She had never looked upon her wanderings around the country as a form of therapy. It had not been her intention to lose herself in unfamiliar places, new jobs, and a constantly changing mural of faces. But whatever she had intended, she could not deny that the ever-changing texture of her days had fully occupied her, had distracted her, had kept her thoughts, for the most part, in the present, had not allowed her to question herself, to make value judgments of past actions that could not, now, be altered.

She refused to acknowledge that Anna's growing family could in any way alter her own estimation of herself, she refused to make a connection between her mother's situation and her own. But Helen could not escape the fact that Anna's giving birth to a son had stimulated a reaction in her that was far more profound than simple joy. And hurtful in a way that bore no resemblance whatsoever to joy.

She wrote to her mother at once, of course, told her how anxious she was to come to New York and see her new sisters and, now, her brother. But she was not eager to go. Although she did not admit it to herself, she was afraid to go. But she did not permit herself to question her feelings directly. She simply occupied herself with her normal work and survival tasks, filled her days and evenings with action and activity, and by so doing, demonstrated to herself that it was impossible to take the time to journey to New York.

As the days went by, however, her unrest seemed to intensify. It manifested itself, not by focusing on Anna's growing brood of children, but by leap-frogging back to the four-years-ago time in Maine. All that unquiet, anxiety-ridden period came clearly into focus again, cluttered Helen's days and kept her sleepless at night. At last she concluded that she was being punished, or more accurately, was punishing herself for behaving like a child.

The logical thing to do, she decided, was also the *best* thing for her to do. She would simply go to visit her mother, spend some time with her, and be as helpful as she could. By forgetting about herself and her dilemmas, by seeing Anna's children, by holding them, by performing in an unselfish, grown-up manner, she would set things straight in her mind, she would see things as they were. She would share in Anna's contentment and stop seeing it as a threat to her own.

The visit was everything Helen had hoped it would be. The frame house in a small Italian community at the far end of Staten Island, last stop on the narrow-gauge railway line, was as far removed from the chaos of New York City, from the tenement-like apartments of the lower East side of Manhattan, as one could imagine. Anna's house had a front garden and a fenced yard with a dog and three cats at the rear. 'In the summer I have beautiful flowers out front. Geraniums and petunias and pansies and asters, growing like weeds. Every bright colour you can imagine. And in the back we grow tomatoes and lettuce and cabbage and radishes and turnips and kale. Joe loves our garden. He works there every evening in the summer. And he has his workshop in the basement with all his tools so he can build cabinets and tables for his customers right here at home and deliver them when he's finished.'

The day Helen arrived in New York there was a snow-storm. Great soft flakes began to fall late in the afternoon as she and Joe drove in his truck from the station to the ferry terminal at the south tip of Manhattan and as they stood at the rail of the ferry trying to see the Statue of Liberty and Ellis Island and Staten Island through the screen of snow.

'The paper says we're in for it,' Joe said, as they drove off the ferry at St George and turned towards the south-west tip of the island. 'The weather report this morning said we could have a foot of the stuff. At least a foot. Could be a record-breaker. It's all right with me. We've got two ton of coal in the bin and I've got enough work on hand to keep me busy for a month.'

Any trepidations Helen had about her trip, any reservations she had felt about visiting her mother, disappeared quickly once she was inside the house that Joe and Anna had bought. When she came out of the snow and the cold, through the back door and into the kitchen, she experienced an immediate sensation of warmth and kindness.

Nearly half of the ground floor had been converted to a kitchen. A great gas range stood in one corner facing a gigantic ice-box on the opposite wall with a double sink beside it. A round table dominated the centre of the space and ill-matched chairs stood everywhere. Two great pots and an enamel-finish coffee-pot steamed on the stove. Smells of fresh-baked bread, oregano, onions, meat sauce, and coffee seemed to come from all corners of the room.

365

Italian love-songs floated in from a radio in the next room. Two-year-old Maria was laughing hysterically in her playpen by the stove and one-year-old Christina was screaming with either frustration or anger in her high chair beside the table. The infant Paul was being bathed in the sink and the dog, Lorenzo, exhibiting no physical characteristics to match the splendour of his name, was barking shrilly from the doorway leading into the parlour. 'Welcome to the asylum,' Anna called out. Holding her dripping son loosely under one arm, she hugged Helen with the other arm and kissed her on both cheeks. 'Your room's at the top of the stairs. You can't miss it. It has a blue door and it's the only uncluttered place in the house.'

Afterwards, whenever she thought about those ten days she spent with her mother, she particularly remembered the snow, a soft screen of flakes falling day and night, piling up outside the windows like tons of cotton-wool, turning the neighbourhood into white cushioned silence. Helen felt no intrusions from the outside world, past or present. Indeed it seemed, during those days, that no such world existed.

The snow seemed to have a quieting effect on the children as well. Lorenzo, nervous and high-strung and frightened of everything, was sent to the basement where the white mounds outside the windows couldn't puzzle him and set him off into fits of barking. 'He likes the sound of the power saw,' Joe said. 'It settles him down. And he likes a rest from the children. The basement's a good change for him.'

It was a floating sensation, Helen felt. All silent and protected, she and Anna in a white cocoon, talking and working together, always in the kitchen. From breakfast till bedtime it seemed, busy from morning till night, cooking, cleaning, and doing the washing. Washing clothes endlessly. 'Joe has a cousin who runs a commercial laundry. He found us a second-hand industrial-size washer and dryer. And thank God he did. Three children in nappies is surely not what the Lord intended for me. Or for any woman. I thought Maria would be trained by now but

366

she's a stubborn little wretch. And now, I think, she's had a setback. She wants to be like her younger sister. God help us if they both decide they want to be like little Paul. I'll still be washing nappies when my hair's as white as those snow-banks outside.'

In the three years since Helen had seen her last, Anna had changed remarkably. 'I'm forty-two years old,' she said, 'and I look it. Hair as grey as a pigeon and a bottom as big as my mother's. It started as soon as I left Rattner's, when I found out Maria was on the way and I stopped working. Six months later I was the size of a house and by the time the baby was born, I'd gone grey. But I don't mind. Joe still likes me, I guess. At least he says he does. He's got his three kids so he's happy. And I've got *him* so *I'm* happy.'

If Helen had feared she would be stifled under a blanket of sentiment and home-grown emotions, she experienced no such thing. Anna, on the contrary, seemed almost matter-of-fact when they discussed the fabric of her life.

'I'm a lucky woman,' she said. 'I know that. I could have spent the rest of my life selling buttons in the five and ten. Or handing out menus at Rattner's till I got varicose veins from cruising back and forth across that marble floor. But instead here I am with a nice house of my own, a good husband who treats me decently, and three healthy babies. So what more could a woman my age want? Nothing, I guess. At least there's nothing else *I* want. But at the same time I don't kid myself that I stuck my hand in the crystal bowl and came up with the silver doughnut. I know what's ahead. I mean I don't know *exactly* what's ahead but I don't expect a free ride. I look at my little kid, Paul, I mean, the newest one, and I say to myself, "When he's eighteen, I'll be sixty." All right. That's not the end of the world. Plenty of eighteen-year-olds have sixty-year-old mothers, don't they? Or maybe they don't. Like I say, one way or the other, it's not the end of the world. But it's something to think about. I mean I'm not old now. I don't think of myself as *old*. Not for a minute. But I know when a teenage kid looks at me in the grocery store, he's saying to himself,

"*That's* an old lady." So I can't help asking myself what kind of a mother I'll be later on. I said I don't feel old and I don't. But if I told you I feel the same as I did ten years ago or as I did *twenty* years ago, I'd be lying to you. Worse than that, I'd be lying to myself. I mean we're all victims of the calendar. The clock keeps ticking and the water drips. And every once in a while you say to yourself, "Wait a minute. I took a great big piece of cake on my plate. Am I going to be able to handle it or not?" It's something to think about. At least *I* think about it. All the time.'

The night before Helen's visit was to end she sat in the parlour with her mother sipping coffee and amaretto, all three of the children asleep and Joe working late in his workshop in the basement.

'You hear him singing down there?' Anna said. 'They say all Italians can sing. Not Joe. I mean he *loves* to sing. He sings all the time. But it's not a pretty sound and he knows it. He says, "What can I do? I'm a happy guy. I open my mouth and I sing. I'm not Caruso. I'm a cabinet-maker. I sing because I feel good. If it comes out bad it doesn't matter." '

'I've never seen anybody like him,' Helen said.

'How do you mean?'

'It's like he has control of everything. Everything's in working order. A lot of men I've met seem to feel as though the world's at war with them. Not Joe.'

Anna laughed. 'Joe's a *liker*. He likes his work, he loves his house, he loves me and all his brothers and sisters, and he's crazy about his children. I think we talked about this the last time I saw you. Joe's idea of a proper-size family is ten or twelve kids. If you think he's happy now you should see him when I'm in a family way. He's like a little boy at Christmas time. When we bought this house I thought we'd be better off with something smaller and easier to take care of but Joe said, "We need the space. Kids take up a lot of room." '

'Do you think you'll have more children?'

'Don't ask me,' Anna said. 'I wouldn't be surprised.'

'You've had three in four years. Isn't that . . . you know what I mean.'

Anna smiled. 'The doctors say it's a terrible idea. The priest says something else. And Joe thinks it's marvellous. It depends on who you talk to.'

'What *does* your doctor say?'

'My doctor's a tough Italian lady who left the church. Or maybe the church left her. She thinks I'm crazy. She says, "If you were twenty years old I'd think you were a lunatic. At *your* age I'm sure of it." '

'But what do *you* think?'

'I don't think about it. Joe and I are good Catholics. We know what the church teaches. And I knew from the start how Joe felt about having a family. Also I know how strict he is about the church. I can't dictate to him. I wouldn't if I could. We're very very happy together. So I just live my life a day at a time and take what comes. My mother says, "God will decide when it's time for you to stop having babies." I've decided that's as good a way to look at it as any.'

'No matter what the doctor says?'

'You can't listen to everybody, Helen. If you did you'd go crazy. I'm with Joe twenty-four hours a day, seven days a week. I see my doctor two or three times a year. Figure it out.'

'Never mind the doctor then. How do *you* feel about it?'

Anna sipped her coffee. Then she smiled at Helen and said, 'I think I'm the luckiest woman I know. I read in the papers every day about the *new* woman, one who is completely in charge of her life. That sounds terrible to me. My life is in charge of *me*. I like it that way. I'm perfectly willing to accept whatever cards I'm dealt. That's what we all do, anyway. Whether we admit it or not.'

Helen lay awake very late that night, staring into the darkness, hearing Paul cry occasionally, hearing Anna get up to feed him or console him. But mostly she was cushioned by silence, the snow still heavy on the tree branches outside her window, the streets and lawns padded with thick white layers.

369

Helen was not disturbed by her sleeplessness. She felt, in fact, strangely peaceful. Ten days in her mother's kitchen had not transformed her. She had not seen all her questions answered or her problems solved. No golden highway had opened before her. By all measurable evaluations she was the same person she had always been, indecisive on the one hand, relentless and angry on the other. On any rating scale she could devise she would have found herself, on that particular night, unsatisfactory.

Why then, did she feel so triumphant? Light and buoyant and euphoric. Warm in her bed and managing to function, she felt, without reference to her shortcomings, real or imagined. She was not able to tell herself that nothing mattered. But she was able to believe that *many* things did not matter, that all of her dragons need not be slain. They could simply be bypassed and ignored and allowed to die natural and respectable deaths somewhere outside her field of vision.

She did not allow herself, during that soft night, to imagine how this new euphoria would manifest itself, how she would convert it to action or if, indeed, she would take any action at all. During the next few days, however, she concluded that perhaps the action, or the decision for that action, had preceded her feelings of peace and had in truth brought about those feelings.

The action, when it came about, the morning she left Anna's house, was precise and satisfying. When Joe delivered her and her bags to the railway station in Manhattan, she went inside and bought a ticket to Portland, Maine. Before she boarded the train she wrote a note to Frank Wilson in Chicago.

If you don't hear from me for a bit, don't worry. I'll be on trains and buses and generally on the move.

When she arrived in Portland, however, and telephoned Dr Kilwinning, he seemed reluctant to meet her, explaining that his board of directors were arriving the following day for a three-day conference. 'Immediately following that I

370

must go to Montreal for a series of meetings there.' When Helen persisted he made an appointment to see her on a Wednesday three weeks hence. An hour later she was on a bus, heading north to Hedrick.

That winter was a fierce one in Maine. And late January was the most severe period of the entire winter. By late February, however, although snow was still drifted high and the temperature was below freezing, the road between Hedrick and Portland was open at least three days out of five. On the day that Helen was scheduled to have her talk with Kilwinning, the weather was cold and clear and driving was not hazardous. She arrived at Kilwinning's office ten minutes early.

'I wasn't sure if you would remember me,' she said as she sat down in front of his desk.

'I see a great number of young women in the course of a year. But we checked your file after you telephoned me a few weeks ago and then of course I remembered.'

'I had a little boy,' she said. 'March 18, 1920. Almost four years ago now.'

'Yes. I saw that when I went through your file.' He paused as if he expected her to speak. At last he asked, 'What can I do for you, Miss . . . is it still Miss Bradshaw?'

'Yes. I'm not married. I've been . . . I guess you could say I've been completing my education.'

'I see.'

Another pause. He studied her carefully. She thought she saw a flicker of impatience in his expression. 'I don't know how to begin,' she said. 'I don't know what to say.'

'Maybe I can help you. I assume you've come to see me about your child.'

'No,' she said quickly. 'I mean it's not what you may think. I don't want to be a bother or cause anyone any trouble.'

'Of course not.'

'I don't want you to think that I'm some kind of nervous wreck. You don't have to be afraid I'm going to cry and wail and make a fool of myself.'

371

'Just tell me what you want exactly and we'll try to go on from there.'

'It's not that I *want* something,' she said. 'I remember that you explained your procedures to me very carefully. You made everything extremely clear.'

'That's my principal duty. It's absolutely critical that we all understand each other.'

'Of course. I realize that. I understood you perfectly. What I didn't understand was myself. I knew there was a situation, a problem that had to be solved, and I came to you for help. I thought it all through carefully and I concluded that I was doing the only thing I *could* do. I knew it would be painful for me and it was. So I told myself the pain would finally go away. But it didn't. If it had I wouldn't be sitting here now.' She paused, seemed to be considering what she would say next. Then, 'The fact is . . . I can't forget about my child. I can't get him out of my mind.'

'That doesn't surprise me.'

'For the past four years I've done everything I could think of to occupy my mind, to distract myself. And there were times when I thought it was working. Times when I told myself that the memories were getting fainter, that eventually . . . but nothing changed. Nothing *has* changed and I don't think it ever will. So I had to come to you. I know you probably won't be willing to help me. Maybe you *can't*. But if you *won't* or if you *can't* . . . .'

'What is it you want me to do?'

'I need to see my child. I can't bear not knowing if he's all right, what he looks like, if he's well taken care of.'

'You want me to tell you where your son is so you can visit him . . . is that it?'

'You won't do that, will you?'

'I *can't* do that and you know it.'

'I don't want to cause trouble,' Helen said. 'I don't want to disrupt his life or take him away from the people who adopted him. I just have to *see* him.'

'I'm sure you realize that many young women have sat

372

precisely where you're sitting and made the same request you're making.'

'And you've said no.'

'I have no choice.'

'But what harm could come from my simply *seeing* him, if he didn't know who I was?'

'Are you telling yourself that if you stood across the street and watched a little boy you'd never seen before playing in his front yard, that you'd be satisfied?'

'No, I'm *not* saying that. It would kill me. But it would be better than this vacuum I'm living in now.'

'Are you saying that you could simply go home then, forget where he lived, and never try to make contact with him again?'

'Yes. I *am* saying that. At least I would have seen him once. I would know his name and what town he lived in.'

'Four years ago you convinced yourself you could give up your child. Now you've convinced yourself you could see him once, know how to get in touch with him, but never do it. Does that seem logical to you? It doesn't to me. If I were in your position *I* could not do that. My wife, I am sure, in such a position, could not do it either. It's simply too much to expect of a human being. Certainly too much for anyone to expect of a parent.'

'You don't *know* me,' Helen said.

'Of course I don't. Nor do you know yourself. None of us do. Four years ago you didn't expect to be sitting here as you are today. Isn't that true?'

'Yes, but . . . .'

'The only protection we have in this operation is secrecy. It protects *you*. It protects your child. It protects the adoptive parents. That secrecy cannot be violated. It has never been violated in the almost twenty years I've been here and as long as I'm here it never will be. You must have known I would say that.'

'I knew it but I didn't want to believe it.' She stood up and walked to the window, looked outside at the snow for a long moment, then turned back. 'Isn't there anything you can tell me? Don't you have any snapshots in your

373

files? Don't you take an infant picture when a child is born? What harm could *that* do if I just saw a picture of him?'

'We have no pictures. Once the adoption is completed the infant picture is turned over to the new parents. We keep only the child's footprint.'

'Can't I see *that?*'

'I'm afraid not. That would serve no purpose whatsoever and you must know it.'

'If you have *any* pictures in your file, if the people he's with have sent any snapshots, what harm would there be in my seeing those? Just looking at them for a minute and handing them back to you?'

'There *are* no such pictures. For the first five years the parents send us written reports on the child's development. And every two years one of our regional people pays a visit to the house to see the child. But there are no photographs.'

Helen came back to her chair and sat down. 'I want you to know that I understand your position. I know *why* you have to keep everything from me. But *you* must understand that it's tearing me apart. If I ask you for one *small* thing, something that won't violate your rules of secrecy, would you try to stretch things a little bit? Since I can't be told anything significant about my son, will you please at least give me something insignificant, something harmless?'

'I can't promise. What are you thinking of?'

'Those reports that the parents send. . . or the report that your regional person sends in . . . .'

'No one is allowed to see those reports,' he said.

'I don't want to *see* them. Can't you just read me a few lines from one of them, leaving out all the names and places? Just something personal about the boy. If you think for a minute before you say no, you'll see it can't possibly do any harm. And it would mean such a great deal to me.'

'That's a request no one has ever made before.'

'Please . . . I would be so grateful.'

He sat looking at her for a long moment. Then he stood up, walked across his office, and left by a side door. A draught of cold air came into the room as the door opened

374

and closed. Helen stood up, put on her coat and crossed the room. She stood there with her legs touching the warm radiator and looked out of the window. She could see her car parked in the cleared space beside the building.

After what seemed to her an interminable time, Dr Kilwinning came back into the office, carrying a single sheet of paper. He sat down behind his desk and she quickly returned to the chair facing him. 'This report was filed four months ago,' he said. Then he adjusted his glasses and began to read. 'The boy is now three and one half years old. He has brown hair and blue eyes and is a healthy active child of average size for his age. He eats well and sleeps well and is affectionate with his parents and his pets. He has an Airedale dog and two calico cats and is very anxious to have a pony when he's older. He has been taken several times to see cowboy movies and they made a strong impression on him. He draws many pictures of cowboys and horses. He seems to draw very well for a little boy.'

When Dr Kilwinning put the page down and looked up at Helen she was smiling but there were tears on her cheeks. 'Don't mind me,' she said. 'I'm crazy. You just made me so happy, I . . . . you don't know how much this means to me. You just painted a picture that will stay with me till I fall over.'

'I can't say I'm as happy about it as you are.'

She dabbed at her eyes with her handkerchief. 'You should be. You've done a great kindness and no one has been harmed in the process. You'll never know what a gift you've given me.'

They both stood up then and he started around his desk to show her to the door. She stopped him by holding out her hand and shaking his. 'May I ask you for one more thing?'

'I think I've gone about as far as I'm able to go.'

'Can you tell me his first name?'

'Out of the question.'

'Just his *first* name. That would tell me no more than the report you read me. No one can be identified by a first name alone. We all share our first names with thousands of people.'

'You're a very persuasive young woman but I have to say no.'

'Then lie to me,' she said.

'Beg pardon?'

'I mean just tell me a name that *could* be his name. Say it as if it *is* his name and I will believe it. Just say the first boy's name that comes into your head. Or tell me his real name and pretend you've made it up. Only *you* will know the truth. And I'll have a *name* in my mind.'

He walked her across the office to the door. Just before he opened it, he said, 'His name is Floyd.'

As she walked down the corridor to the foyer, Helen said to herself, '*Floyd*. Floyd Bradshaw. What a fine name.'

2

On April 19, 1929, Angus Bradshaw was eighty-five years old. That night Clara produced a great banquet in his honour, the most lavish party Wingate Fields had seen since Raymond's birthday ball more than thirty years earlier. Hugh came down from Scotland, Nora and Valerie arrived from France and two hundred guests from Cumberland and Northumberland and London joined the family for dinner in the great hall.

Advised by his doctor to sleep late on the festive day, to conserve his energies for the pleasures of the long evening ahead, Angus appeared in the upstairs corridor that morning an hour earlier than usual, woke Jesse on his way downstairs, and whisked him along to the breakfast room where they shared a breakfast of porridge and kippers, eggs with bacon and sausage, stewed fruit, soda bread and tea.

'We're slipping away, you and I,' Angus said. 'Into the car and off across the moors. Too damned much commotion for me here today. We'll take your car and angle across to Blythe or Newbeggin, then follow the sea up to North Sunderland or Bamburgh, stopping for a drop here and there when we see a likely public house. And on the way home we'll have a midday feast at the establishment of my old friend, Clive Pritchett. He'll lay out a few roast birds for us and pour you a claret as soft and lovely as a maiden's throat.'

When Jesse reminded him of the banquet that evening, Angus said, 'It's not a day for wisdom or restraint. Celebration is the keynote. When a man is eighty-five it is not a time for caution. Three score and ten the Old Testament promised me. Well, so far I've stolen fifteen more. A bonus, Jesse. And not for careful living, I promise you. On my headstone will be carved the legend — "Here lies a reckless rooster".'

It was a cool and blustery day, gusty winds and high clouds racing as they drove east to the sea and then north along its edge. Short fierce showers came down till midmorning, each lasting a few minutes only, washing the sky wide and clear blue then till the next screen of clouds blew through and brought another squall.

'This is the kind of weather I appreciate,' Angus said. 'A perfect day for my *fête*. God save us from a world of sunny days. I prefer the world in action. All the good stuff comes from conflict; show me a man who longs for peace and quiet and I'll show you a scoundrel. A chap who ceases to test himself has taken the first step towards selecting his grave-site. God knows I've made my share of mistakes but I wouldn't take back a single one. A man without scars is no man at all.'

As we have observed earlier, Angus was not, by nature or inclination, a conversationalist. To a large degree he was convinced that an exchange of opinions was a waste of time. Once a subject came into focus or a problem was identified, his instinct told him it should be disposed of. His business life had taught him that discussion was rarely a strong foundation for decision. He believed that firm choices were more valuable than interminable searches for the single correct course. While his competitors pondered,

377

he took action. 'If I make a mistake in judgment, I can correct it. But there is no way of correcting the folly of indecision. A man who thinks too much, no matter how clever he is, will eventually lose to some scruffy fellow who knows how to take action. Intelligence and courage are a fine combination in a man. But if he has to choose one and forego the other, the wise chap retains his courage.'

It was no accident then that Angus' skills of articulation were reserved almost exclusively for business situations, where something was at stake, where there was a task that needed to be done. 'Social conversation puts me directly to sleep. It's like fishing without a hook. One says what one imagines some idiotic stranger wants to hear. People who go to dinner-parties every night of the week have only one goal. They must not offend anyone or they won't be invited back. They must be liked by all and spoken well of to the hostess. What rot! All the people *I* respect don't give a damn what anybody thinks of them. If you want to know why all politicians are worthless, we've hit on the reason. The poor damned fools *must* be popular. *Everyone* must be keen on them or they can't win an office. And once they've painted out all their blemishes and flattened out all their views so they're acceptable, once they've been voted into one job or another, *then* they have to make sure that all the other lackey office-holders adore them too. They must be popular with their peers. Otherwise they will be unable to function. What a dreary life. How ironic that we should imagine ourselves well-served or properly governed by such eviscerated men.'

Early in their marriage Louise had remarked, 'Angus is more apt to lecture than he is to converse.' He agreed. 'I simply say what I believe about a subject and then I'm ready for another topic. Or silence. I'm not really interested in dissenting opinions unless they come from a wise person. I only know three or four such men and I never see them at social affairs. And if I do they're as silent as I am.'

Only a memorable occasion, some significant family event which seemed to require an elaborate toast or congratulatory comments could alter Angus' normal social silence and cause him to hold forth. This occasion, his eighty-fifth birthday, seemed to be such a time. As Jesse drove, all the way north to Bamburgh and then home again, and as they stopped west of Rothbury at Clive Pritchett's inn for roast partridge, Stilton, and an unending flow of fine claret, Angus covered in detail, it seemed, all his fields of interest and expertise, like a man with gold scissors snipping out cuttings from the pages of his history and his thought and stringing them on a bright wire just at reading level.

'People say that when a man feels the world is going to hell, that's the first sign of old age. *I* say when a man doesn't *notice* that the world is going to hell, *that's* the first sign of lunacy. The war was at fault, I suppose. Unstrung a lot of reasonable people. Got them out of their normal patterns of thinking and living and left them high and dry. It became fashionable even among bright people to trash away all the best standards and smash the icons. But they neglected to put anything in their place. Any fool who believes that problems will solve themselves has *his* biggest problem in that single erroneous belief. Let's take the world of finance something I know quite a bit about. Every charwoman in London has become an investor. The waiter who brings drinks in my club in St James's is buying on margin. A man can't possibly lose, they say. You sign your name, seal the bargain with all the pounds you can scratch together, then lie back and wait for the surge of general prosperity to make you wealthy. What arrogance! What tragedy is about to fall on these foolish souls. All of the Bradshaw assets have been pulled back and invested in property and the most conservative bonds. I know that you and Nora and Hugh have done the same thing with your monies. I salute you for following my lead. You will not be sorry. My bank has also been instructed to properly protect Helen's holdings. Many of my associates think I'm overly cautious. *I* say there is a financial crisis of unimagined proportions just ahead. And it will fall most heavily where the speculation is the greatest, in the financial centres of America.'

As they sipped their port after the midday meal, Clive Pritchett joined them at table and Angus included him in his attempts to pull together the tattered remnants of life as he saw it. 'Where do you imagine we're heading, Clive? Has the petrol engine changed us fundamentally and permanently? I suspect it has. We'll undoubtedly become a world of tinkers now. The Ford company alone produced more than fifteen million cars last year. And now that Lindbergh and that Earhart woman have flown the Atlantic the airship business will soon be a principal mode of transport. I've no doubt of it. A zeppelin will take you to New York as simply as a railway train takes you from Newcastle to London. And God knows what kind of wars we'll be fighting now. Our government has allocated nearly a hundred and twenty million for defence spending next year. Did you know that? Nearly twenty million for the Air Force alone. So you see where we're heading. I suspect that our philosophers and clergymen will be replaced by engineers now. By scientists and technology experts. Nothing is more fascinating to the average human being than watching an engine turn over. Nothing captures his imagination like the operation of a machine, the principles of which are totally foreign to him. Einstein is a god now to people who cannot spell simple words or add up a column of figures. Perhaps that is the key to it all. As the world learns to function faster and better, as it becomes swifter and shinier and more complex, each of us will understand it less and less. Until at last we won't be able to understand it at all. We will simply accept whatever is provided, call it progress, and be satisfied to enjoy it or make money from it. What do you think, Pritchett?'

'I think you're damned gloomy for a man who's celebrating his birthday today.'

'Not gloomy at all. I've gobbled up eighty-five years. You're the ones who should be gloomy, you and Jesse here. I'm only *talking* about what's coming. You chaps will have to see it happen. You'll have to suffer through it whatever it turns out to be. While I'll be peacefully herding sheep in the pastures of the Lord.'

'Or stoking a nice coke fire,' Pritchett said, 'in the other place.'

'That's right,' Angus said. 'Waiting for old friends like you to show up for a pig roast. Or perhaps they roast publicans down there.'

As they drove towards home, the afternoon sky gone totally grey and heavy now, Angus dozed off. As Jesse looked at him, slumped heavily in the corner of the seat, he was sharply conscious of how fond he was of the old man, how close he felt to him, how truly related. He reached over and adjusted the car rug which had begun to slip off Angus' legs. He'd never seen him asleep before, had never seen him in any way vulnerable. With his eyes closed and his chin slumped forward on his chest he looked truly old and at the same time like a great blocky child.

A bit later, his full attention on the narrow road ahead, Jesse was not aware that Angus had opened his eyes. He heard his voice suddenly. 'I met Herbert Hoover a few years ago. Did I tell you that?'

'No, I don't think so.'

'What do you think of him?'

'I don't know. Didn't make much of a study of him, I'm afraid, before the election.'

'I met him twice actually,' Angus said. 'After the war when he was heading an organization that was sending food to Europe. Feeding displaced people and war victims, that sort of thing. Did a damned fine job of it, they say.'

'Did you have a chance to talk to him?'

'Not the first time. But the second time we chatted for ten minutes or so. I did most of the talking, as I remember it.'

'Did you like him then?'

'No, I didn't. Didn't trust him. Don't trust a man who looks you in the eye and seems to be memorizing every word you say. He stared at me as if he was trying to see past my eyes, directly into my brain, nodding his head like a marionette at everything I said.'

381

'What were you saying?'

'Damned if I know. And I don't think he knew either. It was just a trick he'd learned. Something politicians do. Especially a man who's temporarily out of office. They concentrate so hard on listening that you know they've not heard a bloody word.'

'What did he have to say?'

'Nothing that I can remember. I don't think he said a word. Just listened. He reminded me of a book-keeper, a man who keeps accounts. All starched and polished and buttoned up tight. Every hair in place. I don't trust book-keepers. Any man who spends his life scratching numbers into a ledger . . . .'

'I think Hoover was trained as an architect.'

'To me he's a book-keeper. I make it a rule never to promote a book-keeper. I don't trust them to make management decisions. Don't think they're capable of handling money. I wouldn't hire Hoover for *any* position other than adding up columns of figures. I promise you he'll make a sorry president.'

'He can't be much worse than the last one we had.'

'Of course he can. That's one thing about office-holders. Just when you think you've seen the worst, a shoddier one comes along to take his place.'

'How old would you take me for?' Angus asked then, 'if you didn't know me.'

'I *know* how old you are. Everybody does. You tell everyone you talk to.'

'That's true. I'm proud of it. If a man stays on his feet for eighty-five years, that's something to advertise. But that's not what I'm talking about. If you'd just met me today and you *didn't* know my age, how old would you say I am?'

'Not eighty-five, I know that.'

'Don't try to compliment me. I don't need compliments.'

'Sure you do,' Jesse said. 'Everybody likes compliments.'

'Not me. I like a nice vigorous insult. And if the man who says it is angry, I like it even better. Then I know he's sincere. Add up all the bad things people have said about

382

you and you'll know everything important about yourself. Compliments are just repetitions of the lies we tell ourselves. Not worth a damn.'

Jesse smiled and looked over at him. 'I'd say you look about seventy-five. Except when you're angry. Then you look as old as God. About two thousand years old.'

'That's it. You're getting the hang of it. You keep talking like that and you'll make me proud I adopted you.' As soon as he spoke the words, when Jesse glanced at him, Angus said, 'I didn't mean that. I take it back. That's not something I care to joke about.'

They had reached the crown of the hills above Wingate Fields and started the long descent to the gate when Angus said, 'I saw you and Nora having a walk in the garden yesterday. "A handsome couple," I said to myself.'

Jesse grinned. 'We're not a couple. I think of her as my niece.'

'And she thinks of you as her uncle. Is that it?'

'I can't guarantee it. Mostly we think of each other as friends.'

'I know you see her when you go to Paris. Do you think she likes that life?'

'It certainly seems that way to me. What do you think?'

'How would I know? I'm the head of the family. Nobody tells *me* the truth. They tell me what they think is good for me. When I was a younger man, everybody came to me with their troubles. Now all I hear is sunshine and sugar buns. Everybody takes their troubles to Clara. If Nora has problems I'm sure she does the same thing.'

'What makes you think she has problems?'

'I *don't* think that. I'm just asking questions. When Ned and Clara went to see her in January he told me he thought she'd had enough freedom and irresponsibility to last her for a while. He thinks she may leave Paris.'

'That's news to me,' Jesse said. 'When I've seen her there. . . .'

'Ned thinks she wants to get married again.'

'That doesn't surprise me. I'm surprised she's waited

383

this long. She's young and beautiful. It seems to me she can do whatever she wants to.'

'Ned had some notion that you and Nora might be planning to get married.'

After a moment, Jesse said, 'What gave him that idea?'

'I don't know exactly. He knows you see each other from time to time.'

'Not that often.'

'I suppose Ned thinks,' Angus went on, 'that since you were engaged to be married at one time . . . .'

'That seems like a long time ago.'

'Nora's only twenty-eight years old. At that age, five years is like five minutes.'

'How about nine years?' Jesse said.

'That's *nine* minutes.'

When he turned his car into the garage and switched off the ignition, Jesse turned to Angus and said, 'I think you're trying to find out something from me and I'm not sure what I'm meant to say.'

'You're not *required* to say anything. I'm just a curious old bird.'

'You want to know about me and Nora. But there's really nothing to say.'

'I realize that. You made that clear.'

'I know I did. But I also know you don't believe me.'

'Of course I do.'

'Let me put it this way,' Jesse said then. 'What if I said we *have* made some plans, that we *are* planning to get married?'

'*Have* you made plans?'

'No. I was asking *what if?*'

'I would give you my blessing, of course. But I can't imagine the two of you coming to ask my permission.'

'Why not? You're my adopted father. She's your granddaughter.'

Angus sat very straight in his seat, his eyes fixed on the windscreen of Jesse's car.

'You're not answering,' Jesse said. 'That's an answer in itself.'

384

'As I understood it, it was only a hypothetical question.'

'Then give me a hypothetical answer.'

After a long moment, Angus said, 'Let me put it this way. You and I have a special relationship. You are my son and you're *not* my son. You are my dear friend and you have been for ten years now but you are more than a friend. Clara is my daughter, my oldest child. I am closer to her than I am to my wife. But I feel equally related and connected to you. I told you once that you owe me nothing. I say it again. I cannot say it forcefully enough . . . .'

'But . . . .' Jesse said.

'But what?'

'You didn't finish what you were saying.'

'Yes. I believe I did.'

Jesse sat looking at him. Finally he said, 'I think we'd better go inside. You have to get yourself spiffed up for your fracas tonight.' He put his hand on the car door but Angus made no motion to get out. Instead he said, 'I would be lying to you if I tried to pretend that your presence here hasn't been important to me. I like to think that you came back from America, at least in part, because you knew it would mean a lot to me. And it has.' He paused. 'Of course I would not stand in the way of your being married. When you do I hope you would bring your wife here to live . . . .'

'You're telling me you don't want me to marry Nora. Isn't that right?'

'I said nothing of the sort.'

'I know you didn't. But you expect me to understand and I do.'

'I have no right to select a wife for you. And if I had such a right I would not exercise it. If you told me that you and Nora want to be married I would announce it at the banquet tonight with the greatest joy and pride.'

'Thank you. I'm sure you would.'

'I mean it,' Angus said.

'I know you do. But there's nothing to announce. As you said, it was just a hypothetical question.'

385

Very late that night, long after the banquet had ended and the great house had at last gone silent, Nora came to Jesse's rooms. As they lay in his bed, her head on his shoulder, she said, 'My brain is going round and round.'

'Too much champagne.'

'I used to believe there was no such thing as too much champagne, no such thing as a surfeit of pleasure.'

'And now?'

'I still believe it but my head tells me otherwise. I have not inherited my grandfather's constitution.'

'He led the celebration,' Jesse said. 'There's no question about that. He obviously meant it when he said, "I intend to set a bad example for all those present." '

'He has a hollow leg. And so do you, my dear. Didn't you tell me that the two of you were drinking all afternoon as well?'

'Morning *and* afternoon,' Jesse said.

'Two gay blades on a spree, was it? Pinching the girls and telling naughty stories of sexual conquest.'

'Nothing like that. We were quite serious and philosophical actually. *I* was serious and Angus was philosophical. For the most part he talked and I listened.'

'Seems proper to me,' she said. 'Did he counsel you about your sins?'

'Not exactly.'

'Do you think he knows about us?'

'I'm not sure what he knows. Your father told him he thinks we plan to get married.'

'You and I? Where did he get that notion?'

'You'd better ask your father,' Jesse said.

'I'm sure Ned thinks I'm being a hussy in Paris. He'd like to see me married to anyone.'

'How about Clara?'

'She's silent on the subject. Doesn't pry into my life at all. Afraid of what she'd find out perhaps. She'd be shocked to discover how proper I am. Very surprised, I'm sure, to learn that I save all my favours for you.'

'Don't exaggerate. It doesn't become you.'

'You don't believe me?'

'Of course not.'

'Then I'll put it another way. If you were more available I would save all my favours for you. As it is . . . .'

'I know how it is.'

'If you would simply tear yourself away from this mausoleum and come and live in Paris we could have a fine life. We could do anything we want.' Then, 'What did Angus have to say on the subject?'

'What subject?'

'You and me.'

'He was circumspect,' Jesse said.

'Angus? Doesn't sound like him at all. You mean he said nothing about *me*?'

'Nothing specific.'

'He didn't admire me after my break-up with Edmund. I'm sure of that.'

'Why not? He thought Edmund was a boob.'

'That's true. But all the same he felt I treated him badly.'

'And you did,' Jesse said.

'Exactly. And I would do it again. Only I would do it sooner. I do not believe that self-imposed suffering is a mark of character or high resolve.' She turned over in the bed. 'God, I feel strange and awful. Do you think I'm going to be sick?'

'It's possible.'

'What shall I do?'

'Get up and rinse your face and hands in cold water. And there's a vial of capsules by the sink. Take one of those.'

She sat up on the edge of the bed. 'So you're going to drug me, is that it? So you can use me in some deplorable way.'

'It's a good thought,' he said, 'but I don't think you're quite up to it tonight.'

'Somehow I've handled you badly.' She leaned over and kissed him. 'I've let you get the upper hand.' She got up and made her way in the half-light to the bathroom. When she came back a few minutes later she lay close against him in the bed. 'At least the room stopped spinning. But now I can't keep my eyes open.'

'That's good. Go to sleep.'

She lay very still. He could feel her regular breathing against his skin and her steady heartbeat. He thought she was sleeping. But she spoke then, very softly. 'We don't care what *anybody* thinks, do we, Jesse? We don't have to fit ourselves into some jelly mould and do what people expect of us. We can do whatever we want to, can't we? We can just have a lovely time and be ourselves . . . .'

4

In the autumn of 1925, as she neared the end of the first year of her marriage to Frank Wilson, Helen was assaulted by two heart-rending events. In late October she gave birth to a still-born baby and three weeks later, just before Thanksgiving, she received a telegram from New York telling her that her mother had died in childbirth.

Either happening would have wounded her cruelly. The two in tandem were crippling. And the effects were intensified by her *refusal* to be crippled, by her refusal to recognize her wounds. Pulling her pain inside and concealing it, she gave it a cancerous life of its own.

In some ways she felt that two exclamation marks had been put to the guilt she had lived with since her wedding day. Since she had never had the courage to examine or define it, it had been a featureless guilt but it had been no less present and no less painful.

Never allowing herself to stitch together the circumstances that had preceded her marriage, she had never linked her visit to Anna in Staten Island, the subsequent time in Maine, her interview with Dr Kilwinning, and her unsettling birthday and early summer months in Fort Beck; she had never added up the integers into an inevitable sum. Her refusal to face the mathematical truth had made it less true. She could tell herself that an irresistible impulse had seized her and persuaded her, had propelled her, irresistibly, into marriage.

It is also possible that had she dealt directly with the addition and its sum she would neither have believed nor accepted the result. Too simplistic, she might have told herself, too primitive and structural, not taking into account any of the subtleties and intricacies of her make-up. 'I am not a one-cell animal,' she might very well have said. 'I am not a bell-trained brute. I have powers to reason and adjust that can alter or forestall what seem to be inevitabilities.'

Whatever pattern of obfuscation or self-delusion she might have chosen to follow, however, it is unlikely that she would have out-distanced or outmanoeuvred the persistent voice of her conscience. There was an absolute involved and Helen sensed it. In her mind she *knew* it. She had flown to Frank Wilson for help, to provide a solution to problems she was unable to solve herself, she had redefined him to fit her needs, had persuaded herself that he was the man, of all men, who seemed designed for her, and she for him. In one particular lonely moment, sitting in her room in Fort Beck, she had concluded that marriage, after all, was her principal objective, a life shared with one carefully chosen man. In that same moment she had selected Frank. Ignoring her true objective which was to create a life for herself like the one she had witnessed in Staten Island, she also pretended that she felt no need to replace the child she had given away in Maine.

It would be ingenuous to presume that none of these contradictions and dualities were in her mind as she repeated marriage vows in the garden of Frank's parents. There seemed to be no language in the ceremony that accurately described her own marital intentions. Since nothing in her previous life had prepared her for dissembling and artifice, she felt, in her maiden's gown, cradling her white and pure bouquet, like a fraud. As she smiled at all those open faces in the reception line she suspected

389

that they, for all the warmth of their good wishes, knew at a glance that she was a fraud, that she had married not for love but for God knows what reasons of her own.

Because she sensed that she was unable to supply the most important element in her marriage contract, she was determined to atone for that deficiency by being an exemplary wife in all other respects. Because she knew she was intelligent and kind and because she truly was fond of Frank, she was determined to behave in such a way that he would never suffer from what she was unable to bring to their union.

She began by capturing his family. Within forty-eight hours of her arrival in their home they were willing to be bound and gagged by Helen, carried off in the night, and held for ransom. They considered Frank a fortunate fellow indeed and by the day of the ceremony at least two of his relatives, cousins from Minneapolis, were asking each other if Frank was good enough for her.

At the reception following the ceremony, Helen widened her sights and targeted on all those present. She waltzed with balding arthritic gentlemen who waltzed badly and she discussed needlepoint with their wheezy wives. She found, indeed, and quickly, some point of connection with each guest in the garden. Not for the joy of acceptance by people she had never seen before and would perhaps never see again, but for the pride she saw on Frank's face. It was clear that he believed he had made the greatest sale of his career. As she struggled to present the embodiment of something she did not truly feel it was evident that for him no such struggle was necessary.

On their honeymoon trip to St Louis, Helen was a passionate and responsive bride. Through his business connections in Chicago, Frank had been put in contact with the most distinguished bootlegger in Missouri. Each day two bottles of authentic champagne were delivered to their suite, carefully concealed in a box of long-stemmed roses. Each morning after she put the roses into a vase, the hotel maid carried away yesterday's empty bottles in the flower carton.

'What a sinful life,' Helen said. 'Will we live like this in Chicago?'

'Exactly,' Frank said. 'Only there we have our own bootlegger. He came with the apartment.'

The day before they left St Louis to take a train to Chicago, Helen wrote a note to Clara.

Hallelujah – I'm married! Are you surprised? *I* am. It was a sudden decision but a very happy one. We have been friends for quite a long time – Frank is his name – now we're more than friends. He's a fine and unusual man. I can't wait for you to meet him. I think I have poor qualifications as a wife but I am going to be as perfect at it as I'm able to be. Please give everyone the news, particularly Jesse. Tell him I'll write to him soon. And tell him I'm outrageously happy.

'We must be very rich,' she said when she saw their apartment in Chicago. 'Are we rich?'

'No,' Frank said. 'We are elegantly *prosperous*. Planning very soon to be rich.'

She had told him, before their marriage, of her own financial situation, had explained in detail her relationship to the Bradshaws in Northumberland, and had showed him the statements of her holdings. His reaction surprised her. 'What a long face,' she said. 'You look as if someone had just given you sad news.'

'I'm surprised. That's all.'

'That's not surprise I see on your face. It's dejection.'

'I want to get everything for you,' he said. 'Now I find out you already *have* everything.'

'No, I don't. I don't have *anything*. I just have a lot of money.'

'That's what I mean.'

'But it's not real,' she said. 'It's like play money. I never think about it. I hardly ever use any of it. You know how I've lived since you met me. That's the *real* me, not some financial statement that comes every month from New York. I just told you about it the way you tell me about

391

your projects, the things you're working on, the buildings going up, the land you're trying to sell or buy. *You* want to share everything with *me*, don't you?'

'Sure, I do.'

'Well, I feel the same way. This silly money I told you about is yours as much as it's mine.'

'That's what bothers me. I don't want it to be.'

'Why not? You've told me from the start that money was the key to everything you want to do.'

'That's right. It is. But not *that* money. Not somebody else's money. I'm trying to build something. I'm testing myself. It's like putting up a building. One floor at a time. That's the fun. Starting from nowhere and ending up where you want to be.'

'Rich when you're thirty, retired when you're forty,' she said.

'That's it. That's what I'm after. I don't want to be rich just because my wife is.'

'Then we'll pretend I'm poor. If I am desperately hungry for a caviar sandwich or if I can't survive without a sable coat I'll come to you for the money.'

'That's what I want you to do.'

In a letter to Jesse a few weeks after her marriage, Helen wrote:

I think I'm a chameleon. I'm at home in Chicago as though I was born here. Taking on the protective colouration of the community. I keep reminding myself that this is *your* town, where you grew up before you abandoned it for the splendours of Fort Beck. Too bad you're not here to show me around. All I know so far is the Loop and the near north side where we live. A view of the lake and everything.

My husband (quaint word) must be the busiest man in this city. He apparently requires almost no sleep. Very late to bed. Up and out early in the morning. I sometimes meet him for lunch. And we manage to have dinner together almost every evening. But it's usually in a restaurant and often with architects or bankers or real-estate developers. He seems to do business twenty-four hours a day, seven days a week.

But it's exciting. There's a great building boom in Chicago and Frank is right in the centre of it. He's a *wunderkind*, they say. And I am a wunderkind's wife. I don't get much chance to use my brilliant cooking skills but I'm redecorating our apartment and learning something about business politics. Volunteering for charity work and having lunch with the wives of Frank's associates and clients. He says I'm good at it. I hope so. We have a box at the opera, I know the galleries at the Art Institute by heart, and the head waiters at Adolph's and the Pump Room know my name. I'm a success! I'm *splendid!*

She was anxious for Jesse to know that she was exhilarated and fulfilled by her new life but all the same her representation of it to him was not an exaggeration. She was truly excited and thrilled and challenged. In her efforts to convince Frank that she was everything he thought her to be, in her determination to match his energy with a complementary vigour of her own, she succeeded in persuading herself as she persuaded him. She began to believe that the details were enough, that the movement and the words and the trappings were a substitute for the whole and might at last either create it or replace it. Objective correlative. Provide the proper circumstances and behaviour and the true emotion will follow. Swept along by her ardent, positive, and tireless husband and by her own desire to *be* swept along, she convinced herself at last that she had indeed become what conscience had told her she could not. She felt that by sheer will and concentration she had transformed and elevated herself.

In the springtime, when she knew, without question, that she would have a baby it was like a golden gift to her, definitive proof that she had made proper choices, had begun to follow new and unselfish routes in her life and was being rewarded. Years later, in the early thirties, when she met Clara in New York, Helen remembered those months, that spring and summer and early autumn of 1925, as an indescribably glorious time.

'It wasn't just that I was expecting a baby, although that was certainly a key part of the way I felt. It wasn't just that sense of power that a woman feels, that primitive thrill of bringing a new person into existence. In my case it was an even larger and grander kind of self-hypnosis. I felt singled-out and marvellously special. Everything I saw or touched or smelled seemed extraordinary to me. I can still remember specific meals I ate during those months, particular passages of particular symphonies I heard. I can close my eyes and see every inch of that beautiful Van Gogh landscape at the Institute, almost entirely green but seeming somehow to incorporate every possible gradation of every known colour. I was incredibly sensitized. Missing nothing. The days seemed endless and deliriously intricate. I was smothered by details and I felt as though I was absorbing and recording every one of them. I remember standing at my bedroom window in the morning after Frank had gone off to his office, standing there in my negligee, looking out across the lake and thinking, 'It's all too beautiful and sweet-smelling and throbbing and pulsing with promise.' It really overwhelmed me. Everything overwhelmed me. I was like an addict. Addicted to the splendour of myself and my life and the world around me, catatonic with wonder and hope. It sounds maniacal, I know. And it was, I suppose. If one can be deranged by joy, then I was certainly in such a condition. Flowers blooming inside my head, the sea pounding in my veins, and the sun hot in my stomach. It makes me tremble just to remember those days. I had a brush in either hand and I was redecorating the world, painting rosy cheeks on everyone I saw. And Frank, who was a kind, loving man needing no embellishment whatsoever, I elevated to the level of God-dom. There was no fine physical trait or character attribute that I didn't ascribe to him. In those months he was the strongest and wisest, the most beautiful and passionate creature alive. If I'd had *any* wisdom, any restraint, even a shred of common sense, I would have known, *something* would have told me, that I was preparing myself for chaos. But no such glint of sanity disturbed my fantasies. I blundered ahead through the days, congratulating myself, blessing myself, *loving* myself, living in a moonstruck world that I had created, of which *I* was the only inhabitant. *Reality* was a word that had left my vocabulary. So when it all came apart suddenly, when it flooded over me, when I lost my baby and my mother in a space of three weeks, I lost everything. And for a long time I felt as though I'd lost myself.'

5

It is easy to make assumptions about Jesse. But they would surely be either inaccurate or incomplete. His own assumptions about himself, for example, were often untrue. He felt he was indecisive, that he lacked direction and initiative. And he was haunted by the suspicion that he was, at heart, an opportunist, waiting silently in the shadows for some piece of good fortune to present itself. No day passed that he didn't remember his father's dictum about success. 'Position yourself near the power. Use it to your advantage. When you've exhausted one power source, move along to the next one.' He had detested those words every time he'd heard them and he detested himself when he suspected that he was his father's true child, that many of his own actions and allegiances were direct results of an adherence to his father's hateful philsophy. For all his admiration of Raymond, his genuine love for him, he told himself, when he was being particularly self-critical, that he, Jesse, had used him, that a disinterested observer, on examining the details of that relationship, would have concluded that Raymond had given far more than he received and that Jesse had planned it that way, had planned to profit.

Had he used Helen, too? He felt a case could certainly be made for such a conclusion. Also he knew from her own statements that Nora believed he had used *her*. And what about Mid Quigley? And Clara? Although his friendship with her was unlike any other he had known and although he could not accuse himself of seeking advantage from that close and rewarding relationship, he knew, without question, that he had come to depend on Clara, and she on him; though he had not engineered the situation, he very much enjoyed it and relied on it.

One could say, and perhaps with a great deal of accuracy, that if Jesse had been required to rise early each morning and go to some office or classroom or other work place, if he had been forced to concentrate his thoughts and his physical energies, to devote a great number of his waking hours to earning a living, he would have had much less time to dwell on his imagined deficiencies and shortcomings. But the fact was that he *did* have a great deal of free time, his time in fact was totally his own, and he spent more of it in self-criticism than in self-congratulation. And very often he returned to the suspicion that he was parasitic, either by nature or by habit, that he instinctively solved his problems by finding someone, often a woman, to solve them for him.

He suffered no such doubts or self-recriminations, however, where Angus was concerned. In what would seem the most obvious illustration of his benefiting from a personal association, Jesse believed that he had given, in this instance, as good as he had received. If anything, he felt that his contribution to their contract might well have been the major one, that *he* might have found emotional stability and financial security by following any one of a number of other courses but that Angus would perhaps have *never* encountered another young man he wished to take into his house and his family as a son. This is not to say that Jesse's gratitude was not real and continuing. It was. But he was aware of the same gratitude coming to him from Angus. And he felt he deserved it.

Jesse knew also, as surely as he knew anything, that there was nothing Angus could ask of him that he would not be willing to give. Their bond went far deeper than the adoption contract. Jesse felt an attachment and a loyalty to Angus that he had never felt to his own parents and he knew that he held a special place in the old man's affection and esteem that Angus' own family members did not share.

For all his tireless self-examination and the self-condemnation that often resulted, Jesse surprisingly, was not aware of the principal ingredient that dominated his character. Had it been pointed out to him he would most certainly have questioned it. It is nonetheless true that if Jesse possessed one foundation element it was decency. He had become alienated from his own family because of it and his response to Raymond, his decision to follow his advice and guidance, to accept his friendship, had been a direct reaction to that same sense of decency. But Jesse seemed unaware of it.

During one of his long conversations with Clara, he said, 'I'm like a house without a dustbin. I can't get rid of my emotional rubbish. Everything stays with me. Many people, I think, have cyclical lives. In one period they have certain interests, certain activities, certain friends. A few years later, or even a few *months* later, everything is changed. New habits, a new address, a whole new circle of friends. And it goes on like that. A new life every few years. Like a reptile shedding its skin. Start over. Start fresh. Wipe the slate clear and become somebody else. A new job, a new wife, a new car. I *can't* do that. Once I connect to something or somebody, I'm stuck. I feel responsible for people I haven't seen for years. I don't think I'd recognize my brother if he walked through the door but no day passes that I don't fret about him. And my sister too. And my peculiar parents. My life's not a straight line or even a crooked one. It's all a loop. Like a laundry line on pulleys. You keep pulling and the same things keep coming back to you, over and over. New shirts and drawers from time to time. But the old ones, faded and worn-out, are still there, too. Needing to be taken care of. Needing to be considered and watched over. One time when I was six or seven years old, my mother heard me talking to a pair of my socks that were full of holes. Totally worn-out. I was *apologizing* to them because she'd told me I had to throw them away. She thought it was extremely funny and told my father about it. But he didn't laugh. "Who talks to clothing?" he said. "Only a demented person apologizes to a pair of socks." He's probably right. But I haven't changed. I can't let anything go.'

His father, for example, seemed to be in his mind constantly. Sometimes for hours at a time. As Jesse sat at his beautiful desk in the handsome office Clara had provided, pen in hand, a block of paper in front of him, his father, oftentimes, lectured at length, pontificated and held forth. Or his mother, looking sad and tired and put-upon, recited kitchen truisms. His sister and brother, Doris and Leo, were also frequent guest speakers in his mind, and Raymond made daily appearances. Most frequently, however, it was Helen, or Clara, or Mid Quigley, who spoke to him, always in the present time, vital and fresh, and dealing, each of them, with current subjects, staying alive, as he had said, inhabiting his days, pointing out to him by their words or sometimes only by their presence, his shortcomings and failures, keeping his present uncomfortably linked to his past, reminding him that self-deception is a fool's activity, that someone always knows the truth about you even if you've managed to evade it yourself.

To someone with Jesse's particular mind-set, to a man who constantly keeps his fingers tangled in the past, repetition is a principal theme. People enter and exit. But most often, they *re-enter*. The prevalent atmosphere is one of *reprise*. One accepts it and at last comes to welcome it. The familiar becomes appealing and at last *only* the familiar is appealing. Carried to its extreme, one can be seduced only by what one knows. Past intimacy, and *only* that, stimulates present passion.

Was it this that pulled Nora and Jesse together after she left Edmund? From Jesse's standpoint it most certainly was a contributing factor. It provided, at the very least, a sympathetic subsoil. But still another factor was at work.

For each of them. Rejection. Nora had believed she was jilted when Jesse left for America and Jesse had *known* he was rejected, specifically, and publicly, when, without bothering to break her engagement to him, she married Edmund. If it is true that an injured lover can only be healed by an act of love, that in itself, that principle alone, would have folded Jesse and Nora lovingly together again. But they each had, in addition, a vengeful motive. Not flagrant but persistent. If Helen was the thief who seemed, in Nora's mind, to have stolen Jesse away and if Edmund was, in Jesse's mind, the beneficiary of Jesse's break-up with Nora, then it was inevitable that a sense of order, if nothing else, demanded that those two spoilers be punished, erased from the tableau, pushed back into history, symbolically assassinated in a warm bed to which they had not been invited, where they had been, in fact, replaced, each by a rival.

Too intricate and Jacobean? Perhaps. But not nearly so hazardous a speculation as the one that says Jesse and Nora simply came together again because it was pleasant and convenient. No such bland and comfortable answer will serve. Not for Jesse. And certainly not for Nora. Their reunion, however simple and classic its execution, had not been simple at all, we can be sure, in its conception.

For all the pressures and secrecies and anxieties that had characterized their original time together, their rediscovery of each other was calm and comfortable. Telling themselves and each other that nothing was at stake, that there were no requirements to be met by either party, they came together as friends, as two people who knew the best, and perhaps the worst, of each other, but were not dismayed by that knowledge. They became true confidants as well as lovers. 'We are now passionate friends,' Nora said.

Having sworn neither fealty nor eternal devotion, they were bound by no contract or formal allegiance; they felt free to discuss their former lovers with each other and they did so. They felt free also to divulge their most intimate feelings and opinions. Nora assured him, for example, that she was not interested in marriage. 'Not just now at any

399

rate,' she said, 'and perhaps not ever. There are certain menus one need not sample twice.' As though it was clear to anyone who knew him that *he* felt no need to marry, Jesse saw no reason even to discuss the matter.

In those last years of that self-serving decade, when values and standards were turned around just for the joy of watching them spin, when many young women strove not just to *be* liberated or to *appear* liberated, but to be, each of them, the very cutting edge of liberation, Nora, with little effort, seemed to epitomize what the entire commotion was about. She was gorgeous and reckless, dependent on no one, free to do or not to do as she chose. She had cut herself loose from her family, her husband, and her country. She had established herself in Paris and she lived there with her daughter and their servants in a luxurious, flower-filled home which was hers alone. Men were welcome at her home but none were required. She plotted the course of her days and set the cadence to be followed, altering both the course and the cadence whenever the impulse struck her. She had friends and enemies, lovers and rivals, cats and dogs and a splendid golden parrot. She drove her blue roadster through the streets of Neuilly and St Cloud and was chauffeured in her town car to the opera and the ballet.

In the midst of all this joy and self-indulgence, having realized her ambition, the dream she had nurtured since childhood, was she, in truth, miserably disillusioned and lonely and unhappy? Of course not. Her life was everything she had hoped it would be. It was better, in fact, because in the process of setting herself free, of making all her own choices and decisions and mistakes, making them gleefully, all by herself, she discovered, like a painter with his colours, that it was the *process* that gave her joy, that freedom to go where she chose and come home when she wanted was sometimes enough. Deciding *not* to attend a gala or a soiree or a vernissage could sometimes give her as much pleasure as going.

She did not, of course, lead a reclusive life. Nothing of the sort. But on the other hand she did not entice men

400

away from their wives; she did not permit herself to be passed about from one eligible male to the next. She could not be *selected*. If one was to succeed with Nora Causey – she recaptured her maiden name after the annnulment – there was only one tactic to follow. One simply waited, made oneself pleasantly conspicuous, and hoped that *she* would choose *you*. When a disappointed suitor said to her, 'Why are you so difficult?' she replied, 'I'm not difficult at all. I'm *impossible*. But only for you, Monsieur. If you have to pursue me it is already too late. When I see someone I want, I pursue.'

This was the social attitude she presented. It amused her friends and it amused her. But it was not an insight into the quality of her life. In fact she was often alone. That is to say that although she was extremely visible socially, the men at her side were most often intelligent or distinguished gentlemen who were content simply to function as her escort, to fetch her at her home and deliver her there when the evening was over.

Although in her heart, Nora was promiscuous, in practice she was selective. Whatever her physical desires she had too much pride and too much vanity to allow herself to be thought easy or common, to be a topic of sexual conversation, to be gossiped about or compared with other young women.

There was also the matter of her ego, her quite remarkable sense of self. She valued herself too much to fling herself about, to offer herself up. She took herself seriously and expected to *be* taken seriously. Only serious suitors need apply. But here was the paradox. She did not *want* a serious suitor. She did not want a husband or a lover-in-residence or any kind of long-term *ami*. Her credo seemed to be, 'If you don't take me seriously, I'm not interested. And if you *do* take me seriously, I'm *really* not interested.'

One should not assume, however, that she floated through her Paris years like an apple-cheeked convent girl. She did not. But she shared herself only with men who were as concerned with privacy as she was, often older men, from Lyons or Bordeaux or Basle, men who respected

401

her and understood her and had no need to boast about her, except perhaps to their mistresses in their home cities. Under no circumstances did these men ever escort her to social functions. Nor did they come to her home. She simply met them, they spent the evening together, and she returned home in a taxi, a proper lady who had spent a quiet evening with lady friends.

As indicated, however, these were only incidents in Nora's life. They were not the pattern of it. At first they had importance because they were evidence to her of her ability to choose. But that importance diminished gradually and when Jesse's trips to Paris became more frequent her jokes about 'saving her favours for him' became the truth. She took great pains, however, to keep that fact from him just as he concealed the fact that his trips to Paris were not for the elaborate reasons he gave, not for research or for meetings with fellow writers, but simply to see *her*, to lunch with her at Fouquet's, to walk in the Tuileries, and to spend long afternoons with her in his hotel bedroom with its half-shuttered windows looking out across the Etoile.

They spent time with Valerie, also. At the Jardin des Plantes and the zoo at Vincennes. And they watched numberless performances, the three of them, at the puppet theatre in the Luxembourg gardens. Valerie referred to him as, 'Mr Jesse, mon oncle', and accepted him as a loving and permanent member of their small family group.

At Wingate Fields, however, as the new liaison between Jesse and Nora was seen to develop, they handled it by seeming to ignore it. Among themselves they pretended it did not exist. Clara and Nora, who discussed everything together, did not discuss Jesse. Louise, through her network of informants among the staff, was aware that when Nora came to visit Wingate she slept with her head on Jesse's pillow. Louise muttered and complained to Angus about this but since she seemed convinced that Jesse was, in fact, either Raymond or Hugh, Angus simply left the room when she brought the matter up.

For his part, Angus was mute on the subject. His only

reference to it was when he mentioned it during his discussion with Jesse on the day of his birthday celebration. Even then, as we have seen, although Jesse felt he understood the thrust of Angus' remarks, those remarks were, in fact both vague and contradictory, and Angus, while making them, seemed uneasy and indecisive.

Just as Angus refused to discuss the situation with Louise, Clara refused to discuss it with Ned. When he persisted she said, 'They are adults, they are friends, and they are members of the same family. That's all I know and that's all I care to know. I will not gossip about my daughter and my brother.'

'He's no more your brother than the man who curries my mare is my grandfather.'

'I know you keep insisting that Jesse is not a Bradshaw. But he *is*, whatever you may say, and has been for some years now. Angus thinks of him as his son and I think of him as my brother. And legally he is indeed just that.'

'I don't care a damn about what's legal. I'm talking about what's *right*.'

'As I recall, at one time you thought he'd be a fine son-in-law.'

'Nonsense. I didn't approve then and I don't approve now.'

Clara smiled. 'But it doesn't matter whether you approve or not. Nora's an adult and has been for a long time. She'll soon be thirty years old.'

'She's still my daughter and I feel responsible for her.'

'Have you told her that?'

'Not in so many words. But I expect to.'

'May I eavesdrop when you speak to her?'

'It's not amusing, Clara. You may feel that your job as a mother has ended but I will be a father to both my children for as long as I'm alive.'

Ned had no intention, of course, of speaking to Nora. Direct confrontation was not his style. He preferred the manner of Iago. A suggestion dropped here. A doubt planted there. Tangential. Oblique. He was capable of constructing a bomb but was physiologically unable to

403

detonate it. His resentment of Jesse, however, which, finding no outlet, had continued to grow inside him, was truly a source of unending torment. It seemed to him that this loose and easy interloper had clogged all his arteries, had invaded every area of his life. He had captured Angus, had gained his love and respect with no apparent effort. He had hypnotized Clara, it seemed. She thought him gifted and worthwhile and charming. And now, once again, he had slipped into Nora's bed or had somehow persuaded her to slip into his. Like a free-booter from some western outpost, Jesse had come to Wingate Fields to rape and pillage, and no one had challenged him. On the contrary he had been loved and fêted and rewarded.

Ned's indignation overcame, at last, his cowardice, and he did speak to Nora. She simply stared at him. Then she smiled, kissed him on the cheek, and said, 'You're really sweet, Daddy. You're a darling man.'

'Didn't you hear what I said?' Ned mistook her show of affection for weakness and it gave him the courage to storm ahead.

'Of course I heard you,' she said. 'But I'm not quite sure what sort of an answer I'm expected to make.'

'I'm hoping you'll behave sensibly and do as I ask.'

'I'm not certain I understand what you're asking.'

'I made it quite clear. I'm talking about Jesse. I'm asking you to give him up.'

'How can I do *that*? He's my uncle.'

'He's no such damned thing. That's just some charade that he and your grandfather are playing.'

'But if Angus calls him his son and Mother calls him brother how can I not think of him as my uncle? Don't you consider him your brother-in-law?'

'I most certainly do not. And please do not change the subject.'

'Did I miss something?' she said. 'Perhaps I don't know what the subject *is*.'

'*Jesse* is the subject. And your liaison with him.'

'My what?'

'What?' he said.

'You said my . . . did you say *liaison?*'

'Yes, I did.'

'I can't believe it. No one uses that word any longer.'

'Whatever word they use, I'm saying it has to stop.'

'*What* has to stop?'

'This *thing* . . . this arrangement between you and Jesse.'

'Shame on you,' she said then.

'I beg your pardon.'

'I said, I'm ashamed of you. Does Mother know you're talking to me like this?'

'No. Why should . . . .'

'Well, I'm going to tell her,' Nora said. Then, 'Does Angus know?'

'What difference does *that* make?'

'It makes a great deal of difference. I need to know if you're acting as a spokesman for the family or if this is just some strange notion of yours.'

'It's not a strange notion.'

'Yes, it is. That's precisely what it is. And I'm shocked. I'm going to speak to my mother and tell her the dreadful things you've said to me. Next I'm going to speak to Angus and Jesse. Then maybe we'll get this sorted out.'

'This is not a matter for general family discussion,' he said.

'It isn't? Then why are we *having* a discussion?'

'What I'm saying is that this is a private talk. Between a father and his daughter.'

'I see,' Nora said. 'That means you don't want Mother and Angus to know what you're saying to me. Is that it?'

Suddenly Ned felt as though he'd lost control of the situation. He fumbled for his cigarette case and said, 'It seems to me this is something we can settle between ourselves.'

'Well, I don't agree.' Nora stood up. 'You've hurt my feelings. I don't remember your ever doing that before. You're accusing me of doing something I haven't done. I'm hurt and I'm embarrassed and I'm damned angry.' She turned and walked out of the room.

She went directly to the morning-room and found Clara

405

and Jesse there. Closing the doors behind her she sat down with them and had a cup of tea. She made no reference to her talk with Ned. Rather she told them a series of hilarious anecdotes about two ageing sisters in Clichy. One of them stuttered and the other was half-deaf. She laughed very hard at the stories and Jesse and Clara laughed too. Nora wanted to be sure that wherever he was in the house, Ned would hear them laughing together.

6

There are few people, modest as they may be about their other accomplishments or their general wisdom, who do not think themselves expert on the subject of marriage. Even individuals who have never, themselves, married are convinced, most of them, that by some process of observation or osmosis they have absorbed all there is to know about that vast and intricate field. Sensible people have been heard to say that it is actually preferable, if one is to advise or console a person whose life is in chaos because of a failed marriage, for the advisor to be a dispassionate observer and theoretician who has not himself been scarred or temporarily deranged by such an experience. Under close questioning these same people do *not* suggest that a non-swimmer should attempt to conquer the English Channel.

This may seem to suggest that only a man or woman who has been married at least once can be knowledgeable about the process. If this were true, then a person who had married five or six times would be a sage and the old black gentleman in South Carolina who is known to have had twenty-two wives would surely be canonized in the temples of matrimony. The unfortunate truth is that repetition does not appear to bring enlightenment. Just as a mother of thirteen children, if she is candid, will attest that her last-born was as great a puzzle to her as the first had been, so also will a much-married lady almost invariably admit that marriage, *any* marriage, is a mystery.

Previous experience is of no value. To the ceremony one can bring only faith and courage and a prayer that at least some remnants of either that faith or that courage will survive. Although we see, all around us, evidence that marriage can be endured and even enjoyed, no sensible person believes it can be understood or explained.

When a marriage ends, particularly a marriage between two young and promising people, the number of experts increases threefold. Almost anyone, even people who have never met the two individuals involved, after a short briefing, can usually tell you the precise reason for the break-up. If prodded, they will tell you which partner was chiefly at fault and predict which of the two will be the first to remarry. When a divorce occurs, only the couple involved seem truly bewildered, both by the action itself and the factors that brought it about. All others are sanguine and sure.

One popular thesis, which millions of people believe they, themselves, first articulated, is that the seeds of all marital estrangements were sown on the wedding day or before. Carried further, the message seems to be that people who separate, whether it's after five months or thirty-four years, probably should not have married in the first place.

Another theory is that people who marry simply do not understand marriage. They do not, in the vernacular, know what they're getting into. The assumption seems to be that once they've *learned* what they're into, they immediately get out of it.

We are told, also, that only people who know each other well should marry. Another school says that only strangers should marry, that *mystery*, particularly during the first years, is all that keeps two people together. Common interests are thought by some to be a requirement. Others believe that disparate individuals stand the best chance of staying together. And what about children? Are they a necessity for a permanent joining or do they destroy more marriages than they save? All the available answers fit all the recurring questions. And the waltz continues.

When Helen and Frank admitted at last, first to themselves and then publicly, that whatever they had planned for and reached for, however close they had come or however disastrously they had failed, when all had gone limp and they stood with their hands at their sides and admitted it was over, that it *had* to be over, they were stunned, each of them, but not surprised. Nor, strangely, were some of their friends surprised. 'It looked too perfect. There had to be something wrong.'

A great number of people came to that conclusion or some approximation of it. No one had a dramatic theory or a shocking explanation. It had seemed to be a neat and peaceful and civilized joining so no one imagined that their separation would be anything but neat and peaceful and civilized. No one expected that Helen would accuse her husband of infidelity or cruelty or lack of generosity. Nor would he brand her as a spendthrift. Neither would complain of neglect in the marriage bed. Possibly they would not discuss their situation at all. They would simply separate and divorce, one of them would perhaps move to another city, the tides would continue to flow and recede on schedule, and life in Chicago would go on. Truly significant matters like buying on margin, finding a reliable bootlegger to replace the one who had been shot in Dearborn Street, and motoring to South Bend for the Purdue-Notre Dame game would come to the fore again.

But what answers did Helen and Frank give each other? And what did they tell themselves? They told each other nothing. That is to say there was no need for announcements or accusations or apologies. It was the summer of 1930. They had known each other for more than seven years and had been married for almost six of those years. It was not a case where two people share the same experience but have totally different perceptions of it. Each of them had realized what was happening to them as it happened. The fact that they did not discuss it made it no less real. Long after they suspected their situation was hopeless, they pretended not to notice. Because they were decent people they tried to persuade themselves that if the

408

units could be handled properly, if the events of each day could be sensitively managed, that perhaps the accumulation of those perfectly polished slivers of time and circumstance could be moulded into a larger assemblage that was equally satisfactory. If all the moving parts were carefully tooled how could the resulting machine fail to function? The *whole* must, necessarily, be a sum of its parts. Or so they reasoned. But the formula was not a true one. As though they were trying to paste pictures in a book while a powerful electric fan oscillated beside them, they sat together, through those months and years, and watched the pieces swirl about.

When the process was over, when the disintegration was complete, or when it had at least, clearly *defined* itself as disintegration, they were able, each of them, to read the signs at almost the same time, to share the blame, to close the book, without *referring* to blame, and to believe, or at least pretend to believe, that the result could not have been other than it was. Like close relatives at a graveside they seemed to realize that only kindness was appropriate now. Unruffled by either passion or resentment, they simply *presided* over the last months of their marriage. They lived together, ate together, and slept together through all the separation details and the arrangements for the divorce. When everything was in order, both in the lawyers' portfolios and in the minds of Helen and Frank, when she left to go to New York, he drove her downtown to Union Station, kissed her goodbye on the platform and stood there chatting with her through the window of her drawing-room till the train pulled out.

Just as there is a legion of marriage theorists, there is also a great body of opinion that maintains there is no such thing as a civilized divorce. 'If the marriage was worth a damn to start with,' the credo reads, 'if the people really cared about each other and lusted for each other, if they truly *believed* they would be together for life, then there's no possibility of diluting *that* to a bland post-divorce friendship.'

If that is true, and if it's not true it should be, then

perhaps what we have seen as the dissolution of Helen's marriage to Frank is proof that it was not constructed of the purest and staunchest materials to start with. It is worth noting, however, that for all their kindness to each other, for all their consistent choices of reason over self-exoneration, they did not, when they parted, that final morning at the train, make any reference to the future. They did not promise to write or ask to be written to. No mention of occasional meetings or token gifts to be sent on holidays. They simply kissed and said goodbye. They fully expected never to see each other again.

What does all this mean then? What *can* it really mean? Underneath the consideration and politesse was there hatred bubbling, rancour and resentment and unspoken accusations? The answer seems to be not in how they behaved, not in the things they said to each other, but in what they said, each of them, to themselves.

We have seen Frank only in relation to Helen as he courted her and persuaded her and deferred to her. Throughout their marriage he deferred to her, not because she demanded it but because he chose to. If we were to conclude, however, from that choice that he was, in any sense, a weak man, that he cast himself, from habit or by instinct, in a subservient role, we would be making a gross error.

Frank's confidence in his business ability, for example, was in no way misplaced. If he had been asked to analyse that gift he would have said, 'I'm a reactor. I go on instinct. If a man wants tough, I go tough. I can get down in the mud. I *like* it down there. But I can also sell your grandmother a fly-swatter. Mostly, I try to be nice if somebody's nice to *me*. If they're *not*, if they want to play some other game, then I'll play *that* way. I'm agreeable. It's my nature. I'm a pretty nifty fighter too. But I'm like all the other fighters I know. I'd rather *not* fight if I don't have to. I don't want to hurt anybody.'

From the first days of their marriage, from the moment, in fact, when it was understood between them that they *would* marry, Frank had believed that he had the major role

410

to play, that the responsibility for their happiness was primarily his. These convictions did not stem from arrogance or from some belief that the male partner must be in charge of all events. Nor was it simply a projection of his business thinking into his personal life. The fact was that he sensed from the start that there were reasons behind Helen's sudden decision to marry him that he would probably never know. It had, in truth, been a surprise to him when she had summoned him to Fort Beck that sultry July, embraced him warmly when he got off the train, and told him that evening that she would marry him.

After she went to New York to see her mother, and during the following months, Frank heard almost nothing from her. He began to suspect that this was her way of telling him that their relationship of the past eighteen months, whatever name one chose to put to it, was over. For all his energy and enthusiasm, Frank was a realist. He had never deceived himself that Helen's attitude towards him had gone beyond affectionate acceptance. She allowed herself to be pursued, she liked him, enjoyed him, and appreciated the attention he gave her, but try as he might, he could discover no electricity between them. Certainly there was none crackling from her to him. Having inspected the property she seemed to have no interest in acquiring it.

Frank's attitude changed, of course, as their marriage date approached, during that festive time, and in the weeks after the ceremony when they had taken up residence in Chicago. Because their *situation* had changed. And because Helen herself had changed remarkably. She had folded softly and sweetly into their life together in a way that would have eliminated the doubts and reservations in the mind of any husband. When Frank remarked about this she said, 'Of course I've changed. Once I'd made up my mind about us, once I *knew*, everything was different. Before we were a *maybe*. Now we are a definite *certainty*.'

All the same Frank persisted in his private belief that although contracts had been signed and deeds handed over, his role of persuasion and reward would never end.

411

And he liked it that way. He felt like a fortunate man, indeed. In all departments of his life. But particularly in his marriage. The sweetness of his nature, which he kept carefully concealed in most of his business dealings, he lavished generously on his wife. He planned for her, gave her presents, cared for her, and entertained her. He took nothing for granted. 'You make me feel as if we'd just met,' she said, 'and you're about to propose marriage.' 'Good,' he said. 'That's the way you should feel.'

He refused to travel without her, he made no plans that did not include her. Even his business day was scheduled to accommodate whatever free time she might have during the day. 'I'm courting you,' he told her. 'If you don't like it, you'd better tell me. Because, otherwise, that's the way it's going to be.'

She *did* like it, of course. She knew he was an unusual husband and she did her best to respond in kind. As she had written to Clara, she was determined to be the best she was able to be, determined to *give* her share and *do* her share. And in the first buoyant year of their marriage she did all those things she had set out to do, did more than she had ever imagined she was capable of, truly gave of herself, surrendered herself, became quite another creature altogether.

Frank never allowed himself to conclude that the fact of the still-born child, that single event, had totally redirected the course of everything for him and Helen. Nor would he blame the death of her mother for the changes that took place. Helen consoled him, in fact, about the dead child as much as he consoled her. And although he had never met Anna, he shared that grief with his wife. They told each other, over and over, that no cataclysm could destroy them, that they would compensate and adjust and go their way. 'And we'll have a houseful of children, no doubt about that.'

But there were no children. Just that one poor dead thing. And none after that. But this, too, this failure to produce a family had not, in Frank's mind, been the cause, the reason, the clue to what would come later. They had discussed it, calmly and often, he and Helen. 'I promise you I will not develop a baby obsession,' she said. 'I will not turn into some pitiful nervous creature with a thermometer in one hand and a calendar in the other. We will live our lives and have some fun and be grateful for whatever kids we have, whether it's three or half a dozen.'

They handled everything correctly. They said the proper words to each other, thought the right thoughts, and did the right things. At last, when they had been childless for five years, they were able to say to each other, 'What if we *don't* have a family? It's not the end of the world. We're happy together. That's what matters. We can come and go, travel when we want to, and do what we like. It's nice to have kids but it's not *everything.*'

Thus they consoled each other. But no one was deceived. This does not mean, however, that Frank was not correct. Perhaps it was not, after all, so one-plus-one as it seemed; it was not simply the problem of a childless marriage. Perhaps the fact that an atmosphere of failure developed, that this one very visible and particular failure became, or seemed to become, a *condition*, perhaps that was the key to the puzzle that Frank was never able to solve. Perhaps their marriage died, not from a wound, but from suffocation.

Whatever the stimulus, however, whatever they were able to decide or conclude later about the reasons for their separation, when the time came, the debris of disintegration, at the end, was scattered all around them. Meals eaten in silence, averted eyes, cancelled appointments. It was as though a powdery dust had settled softly over every bright surface. The wine had turned and the food lacked seasoning; one partner slept all the time, the other not at all. And the ashtrays overflowed.

There was little to discuss at the end. They simply looked at each other and they knew. They couldn't be bright and capable any longer. Not together. There was just enough vitality left to fuel their guilt and disenchantment.

Chapter Nine

1

Through the centuries, the Bradshaws, like a river fed by hidden springs and freshets, had moved always forward, diverted at times by the currents of history, buffeted and drenched and partially submerged, but surviving, *enfin*, all change and cataclysm, remaining miraculously intact. Sometimes it appeared that they *prevailed* over difficult circumstances. At other times they seemed simply to ignore the eddies and treacherous currents; they triumphed in spite of the dangers, in spite of themselves.

In 1930, for example, when social disturbance and economic chaos seemed unavoidable, the Bradshaws, thanks in large part to Angus' foresight, kept a steady course and lost no ground. As others floundered, Angus found new ways to profit. Using the family wealth like a weapon, he invested far and wide, in Belgium and Australia and New Zealand, in America and Canada and South Africa. Wherever anxious and desperate people were selling, he bought. Sheep stations, wheat fields, cattle ranches. And great blocks of downtown property in cities such as Auckland, Melbourne and Johannesburg. Clara and Jesse, working with the London staff, became extremely clever at spotting property opportunities and then making quick, or very deliberate, acquisitions, that tempo dictated by their judgment of the sellers' need and urgency. By 1934, Angus was able to boast that in a period of world crisis, the Bradshaw holdings had tripled in real value with an estimated tenfold

414

increase in ultimate worth. 'I'm a survivor,' he boasted. 'When the world needs a bath I sell soap.'

As their economic foundations held firm, however, many other aspects of their lives in that critical year, 1930, seemed to be changing, not in the gradual ways they had become accustomed to, not simply the process of making adjustments and compromises, not those familiar rhythms at all. Rather, each of their lives, from Angus, the eldest, to Helen, the youngest, seemed to make an abrupt turn. Separations took place, and new joinings. But the principal changes seemed to be internal ones, personal choices, individuals coming to terms with themselves, charting new courses, finding new trails, and destroying, in some cases, each bridge they crossed.

It is a common occurrence, in a family unit, for the behaviour of one individual to set up a chain of events that will affect each person in that unit. One stone falls in the pond and the ripples touch every shore. One person acts and all the others *react*. This, however, as noted, was not the pattern of the Bradshaws in 1930. Their problems, it seemed, were not family problems, their solutions were not group solutions. Rather, each individual seemed to be moving away from centre, away from Wingate Fields, sinking new roots, forging fresh identities. It was as though some silent signal had been given and each of them had responded.

Angus, for example, as though he had been stimulated by the world financial crisis, as though the disaster he saw all around had energized him, took on, in his eighty-sixth year, a hugely expanded schedule of duties. He began to travel almost constantly. Telling himself that his acquisition of property in other countries necessitated his examination of those properties, he kept a sheaf of train and steamer timetables at the ready on his desk-top; in a typical six-month period he was four months abroad, one month in London, and the remaining four weeks at Wingate Fields. On many of his trips, Clara accompanied him. She was accustomed to hearing him say, as they dined in Mexico City or sat in a coffee-house in Milan, 'What a fool I've been. How I've squandered my life. I feel as if I'm just now beginning to *know* something, to realize a bit about how the world works. Such an insular life we live in Northumberland. Cloistered and cut off. Over-indulged and under-exposed. If I were a man of twenty I would make different choices from those I made before. No question of that. No doubt at all that I would gladly give up a lot just for a chance to roam about and see what the world consists of. We're too preoccupied, all of us, with the familiar and the comfortable, determined to spend our lives with *friends*. What a mistake. The unfamiliar is our best teacher. Much more to be learned from strangers. I like porridge and kippers and mutton as much as I always have but, by God, it's exciting to be in places where such meals are not to be had for any price. I think I've uncovered a strain of the gypsy in me. Late in life I've found it. And maybe I'm lucky for that. But I don't think so. I've seen so little and learned so little and there's so bloody much left that I'll never get around to. It's a cruel and greedy world we live in. Starvation in every corner. Inequality and neglect. But what a splendid place it is, all the same. And the more I see of it, the more splendid it becomes. When I was a young man, just married to your mother, I thought the greatest gift life could give me would be the privilege of dying in my fine old bed at Wingate, just as my father and my grandfather did before me. But now I've changed my point of view. *Now*, if I'm blessed, I will die on the deck of a great ship, heading west, the horizon all white and gold and mysterious, with places and people I've never seen just beyond it waiting to be discovered.'

'You're very romatic,' Clara said. 'I didn't realize I had such a romantic father.'

'I'm romantic all right but not in the way you imagine. I've spent my life pursuing money, getting hold of it, and then trying to keep it. That's the most romantically sense-less activity a man can devise. All those financiers who jumped out of windows in New York last year were victims of a romantic misconception. They'd devoted their lives to money. Told themselves they were dealing with something

416

finite and permanent. When it turned out to be spun sugar, when it melted and ran down their shirt-fronts and dripped on their silk cravats, *they* melted, too.'

What about Louise then? What does an elderly wife do, a dependent and fragile woman, when her husband, a man in his eighties who has been her companion for more than sixty years, abruptly changes the rhythm of his life and becomes in a period of weeks everything he had never been, turning away, in the process, from much that he *had* been. How does she adjust to only occasional meetings with this man she had seen, taken meals with, and shared her bed with, for all of her adult life? Not exactly as one might have imagined.

The fact was that Louise had begun to detach herself from Wingate Fields and the life there some time before Angus began his programme of extended travel. Her separation from her home had begun, not with a thunderclap, but in a gradual way. Responding to a request from church leaders in Newcastle she helped to organize a Charity in aid of unemployed ex-soldiers and their families, providing food and clothing and arranging for housing in particularly grave cases. Enlisted originally as a sponsor and as a fund-raiser among the Northumberland gentry, Louise soon became involved in all aspects of the Charity. As unemployment increased, however, as the churches realized that the problem would soon become a financial burden far beyond their resources, she forged ahead and at last took on the entire operation herself. She attacked the churches then, accused them of abandoning their own project. She passed out handbills, spoke on street corners and staged demonstrations.

Expecting that she would be resisted by Angus and Clara, Louise was pleased to discover that they supported her. This is not to say that they were in sympathy with all of her activities which became, early on, controversial as well as charitable, or that they approved of some of her associates, but in general her family was delighted to see her rise up from the almost comatose condition into which she had slipped.

417

'I'm astonished,' Clara said to Angus. 'I didn't think such a change was possible.'

'I don't think it *is* possible, but it's a splendid tonic for her for as long as it lasts. I talked to Dr Leeks about it and he said the more she does, the more she'll be *able* to do. He thinks we should turn her loose and give her her head and that's what I intend to do.'

2

Perhaps it cannot be truly said that any particular year, or any month or day of any year, could be pinpointed and labelled a watershed moment in the continuing *angst* of Ned Causey. No positive development, no moment of joy seems to have deterred him in his determined downhill slide. From his first day at Wingate Fields following his marriage to Clara he seems to have branded himself an outsider. No contrary evidence could turn him away from his conclusion that he was an abandoned and neglected man, allowed to serve certain functions as husband and father and son-in-law but never truly valued or appreciated for himself. Close examination would have shown that his life at Wingate very closely resembled his previous history with his own family, with his parents, his two brothers, and his sisters. There, too, in that house, he had been ignored and undervalued. No one had praised him or encouraged him. No one had thought him acceptable. Or so he persuaded himself.

After he left his parents' home, however, after his marriage to Clara, Ned was shrewd enough not to pass along to the Bradshaws these complaints about his relatives. Except to Clara. He explained to her in detail how he had been mistreated. He painted the shortcomings and evils and cruelties of his family in Dickensian earth colours, dredged up moments and incidents and memories that stretched from his days as a toddler to the morning of his marriage.

418

Clara, who had met all the members of the Causey family and thought them excellent people, was astonished to hear Ned's revelations about them. Because she was in love with her young husband, however, she felt all his wounds as if they were her own; she altered her judgments of his family to match Ned's and found it difficult to be civil to them for the first few months after her marriage. The fact that she was unable to detect in his relatives the characteristics Ned attributed to them only made them seem more hateful to her. 'Of course they won't allow you to see them as I see them,' Ned explained. 'They're a clever lot.'

Although she had no inclination to question Ned's facts or his feelings, although she had no doubt about her primary loyalties, little by little, Clara began to see, as he complained to her about his treatment at the hands of Angus, that his anguish was all of a piece. His complaints about the lack of respect he had received from his own family and was receiving now from hers were, in truth, a reflection of his own estimation of himself. When she tried to suggest this to him, however, he reacted angrily.

'What rot. I expect something better from you. Is that a statement you've heard your father make? If so, it proves my point. I'm sure he feels guilty because he's given me so little responsibility. But I guarantee you, the flaw is not in me. I am well aware of my own capabilities. There's no lack of confidence in *me*. You can be sure of that.'

Ned would not admit to himself, or perhaps was unable to so admit, that Clara's recognition of his central flaw was in no way a condemnation. She was tender and compassionate by nature, did not demand perfection in anyone, least of all in her husband, and would have been eager, in those early years, to intercede for him with Angus. But Ned's stubborn profession of superiority, his insistence on playing the martyr when another role would have better profited him, made it difficult, and at last impossible, for her to guide him or advise him in any way. He was particularly resentful of any assistance offered by Clara and at last came to feel that far from being his ally, it was she who blocked the path between him and Angus,

419

she who kept him from the decision tables and the planning rooms. He envied her and she knew it and it was that ill-concealed envy, as much as anything, that began to pull their marriage apart.

After more than thirty years at Wingate, all of that time spent under the same roof with Angus, after many nights of drinking, hours spent together, their tongues loosened by claret and stout and brandy, how was it that Ned had never spoken of his discontent, had never complained to his father-in-law about what he considered to be his second-rate treatment? Why had he growled unceasingly to Clara and never to Angus? It was a question Ned never asked himself because he abhorred the answer. The truth was that he was deathly afraid of the old man, totally unable, even when drunk, to question or contradict him, to take any sort of adversary position whatsoever. It was not a rational fear, it was not a question of acts and consequences, it was simply a blind emotion, the serf's fear of the master.

Why, then, after all those years of what he considered subservience, did Ned finally pull himself together and voice his complex grievances to Angus? What motivation did he find, in February of 1930, that he had never found before? It is impossible to say. Surely he had become accustomed by then to his repetitive and compartmentalized duties. Surely he had come to accept the circumstance that when an investment decision was imminent, it was not Ned's counsel Angus sought, but Clara's. And the hateful inclusion of Jesse which had taken place more than ten years earlier still tortured Ned.

One would assume, however, that Ned's outrage would have subsided by now, that he would have made whatever adjustments were necessary, that if he was not content he would be resigned. Angus certainly assumed that. As he listened to his son-in-law's detailed recital of dissatisfaction that February afternoon in his study, he felt that his surprise must surely be visible on his face. At last he said, 'I'm astounded, Ned. All these years without a whisper of complaint from you. And now, all of a sudden . . . .'

'You must have realized that I was not contented.'

'No, I must say I did not. You've managed our lands here and our tenants and our livestock, handled the accounts and kept things ship-shape and it never occurred to me that you felt, as you've just said to me, that you were undervalued or improperly used. I'm sure you agree with me that what you've been doing is a full-time effort. Are you saying that you have a great deal of free time to handle other duties?'

'I feel that I am capable of handling more important matters.'

'I'm certain you are,' Angus said, 'but I'm not quite sure what sort of thing you're referring to.'

'The larger picture,' Ned replied. 'Investments, acquisitions, land development. That sort of thing.'

'I see.'

'Management decisions. Planning for the future. Taking on the big problems. The major issues.'

'Are you saying that you'd like to go down to London and work with our people there?'

'Oh, no. I don't think that's the answer. They get their orders from you here at Wingate after all. This is where the key decisions are made.'

Angus smiled. 'And you would like to make those decisions.'

'I think I'm capable of it. But for now I would simply like to participate in the process.'

'Have you discussed this with Clara?'

'Not precisely. I feel it's a matter between the two of us, as senior members of the family.'

'That may have been true at one time. But now Clara has taken over a great share of the responsibility. I count heavily on her and Jesse and it's Jesse we'll have to rely on at last. He's the young blood. He's the only link we have with the future.'

'You're telling me there's no place for me. Is that it?'

'Nothing of the kind. You play an important role here, whether you think so or not. It would be difficult to replace

421

you. But sooner or later we all have to give over. How old are you now, Ned?'

'I'll be fifty-eight in July.'

'And I'll be eighty-six in April. I can't remember when I was your age and you can't imagine you'll ever be the age I am now. Compared with me, you're a young buck but all the same you'll soon be sixty. That's a time when most gentlemen are planning ways to spend more time with their dogs and their fishing-rods.'

'I don't give a damn for that and neither did you at my age.'

'That's true,' Angus said, 'but I'm a pirate. It's what I've always been. You're another sort of person altogether and you should be happy for it.'

That evening when he told Clara about his meeting with Angus, Ned said, 'He turned me away as if I were a schoolboy applying for a clerk's position. He dismissed me. Sent me packing. Back to my crofters and sheep farmers. I was tempted to tell him . . . .'

'What?' Clara said.

'I almost told him I have no further interest in those duties. I may still tell him that.'

'I wish you would. You're not an employee, after all. Why should you spend your time at something you dislike? We'll find someone else to supervise the land and the tenants.'

'And what will I do then?'

'Whatever you like,' she said. 'Do nothing. There's no need for you to work. There never has been. Enjoy yourself. Ride and hunt. That's what most of the men in the county do.'

'And when you go down to London with Angus and Jesse for your investment meetings would I be invited?'

'You're always welcome to come along. You know that.'

Ned nodded. 'Only for the trip, however. Not for the meetings. I would be allowed to see a matinee or visit the zoo or spend the afternoon at my club. Isn't that correct?'

'No one tells you what to do, Ned.'

'Perhaps not. But it is always made clear what I am *not*

422

to do. I am not to enter certain chambers and take part in certain dialogues. Among the Bradshaw princes I am a consort, a man without privileges.'

'That's ridiculous.'

'I agree with you,' he said, 'but it's also true.'

'I can't believe,' Clara told him, 'that you are still upsetting yourself about things that cannot be changed. For more than thirty years I've been hearing the same complaints from you. To many people you must seem to be a man who has everything. But you want something more. You want something unattainable. You want to be Angus.'

'Nothing of the sort.'

'It's true. From the time Raymond disappeared, you've been possessed by the thought that you were the heir apparent, that you would sit at Angus' side and take his place when he died. What other reason could you have for hating Jesse the way you do?'

'I didn't like him from the moment I saw him.'

'That's not true. When you thought he was going to marry Nora you had no reservations at all.'

Ned shook his head. 'I always thought he was an opportunist and I still think that.'

'Maybe you did and maybe you do but you certainly made no objection to that marriage. Only when Angus announced that he had adopted Jesse . . . .'

'I was angry. I admit it. I felt as if I was the only one who hadn't been told.'

'Not true. Nora didn't know. Hugh didn't know. And Helen didn't know . . . .'

'*You* knew,' he said.

'Yes, I did.'

'And *you* didn't tell me.'

'Because Angus asked me not to. Apart from him and Jesse, only Louise and I knew.'

'I should have been told.'

'You *were* told. That night at dinner when Angus told everyone else.'

'I'll never know how Angus was taken in.'

423

'We've discussed this before,' Clara said. 'I don't want to go over it all again.'

'Why not?'

'Because I'll get a terrible headache.'

'Have we reached the point where nothing negative can be said about your American cowboy?'

'You can say whatever you like. But I prefer not to sit here and listen.'

'A sensitive subject, is it?'

'Not at all. And even if it were, I would surely have built up scar tissue by now. Jesse has been your favourite target for the past ten years. I can't imagine that you have something new to say about him that I haven't heard before.'

'You may be surprised then. Because I do indeed have some fresh observations about him.'

'I am genuinely not interested.'

'That may be true. But on the other hand you may be fascinated by what I'm about to say. It concerns your daughter as well as you.'

'Are you going to say that you know things about him that I don't know? Because if you are . . . .'

'I would never presume to be as knowledgeable about him as you are. I've never doubted that your tête-à-têtes in the morning-room involved a great exchange of biographical information. But I would like to suggest that none of us is ever *totally* informed about another individual.'

'If you've managed to uncover some gossip . . . .'

'No gossip,' Ned said. 'Simply an observation.' He took out his cigar case, selected a cigar, and lit it. 'What would your reaction be if I told you that Jesse is a bigamist?'

'Is that the revelation you spoke of?'

'What would your reaction be?'

'I expect I would yawn. Might even drop off to sleep.'

'I don't believe that,' Ned said. 'But no matter. Because what I'm referring to is not bigamy in the legal sense.'

'Is there another kind?'

'Oh, yes. I should think so. A very particular sort, it seems to me.' He studied his cigar for a long moment.

'You mentioned that I've talked about Jesse quite often these past years. It's true. That's because I think about him a lot. He's always been a puzzle to me. Still is in many ways. I've never admired him. I've never pretended I do. But lately I've begun to believe he's a shrewd chap. Far more clever than I had supposed.'

'I told you I've heard all this before.'

'I don't think so. I'm not going to discuss whether or not he mesmerized your father. I will concede that Angus was so anxious to have a son that the adoption notion may have come from him and not from Jesse. I think it's unlikely but I will concede it nonetheless.'

'I'm sure Jesse would appreciate that.'

'I think of myself as a thoughtful man,' he went on. 'I really do try to learn the reasons for things. I need to understand. And if that brings a certain amount of torment then I'm inclined to accept it. What I was about to say about Jesse, for example, is not something that gives me joy. But it does bring me some satisfaction. I feel as if I've solved a difficult puzzle. Not all of it. But a particular sticky part.' He paused. 'You remember, I'm sure, that I've commented several times on the fact that Jesse has shown no interest in marriage. Whatever his other shortcomings he seems a normal and vigorous man and it has continued to surprise me that he hasn't selected a wife. A permanent home, a loving woman who shares your bed, shares your life, and provides you with children. I've asked myself over and over why Jesse appears to be different from other men, why he would be willing to forego the pleasures and rewards that are so important to most of us. I've pondered it for almost as long as I've known him, certainly for all the time since he came back here, since he's been a permanent resident at Wingate Fields. Then one day it came to me. The answer simply presented itself and it was so clear and obvious that I was astounded I hadn't thought of it before. I realized that Jesse hasn't given up *anything*. He enjoys, in fact, *all* the pleasures of marriage. A sense of permanence, affection, passion, and emotional security. He is even permitted the joys of parenthood without any of the

425

responsibilities. And not with one woman but with two. He divides himself between a lovely young woman and her equally lovely mother.'

Clara sat frozen in her chair, staring at him, her face suddenly very pale. At last, in a penetrating whisper, she said, 'How *dare* you . . . .'

'Don't misunderstand me,' he said quickly. 'I am not implying that anything improper exists between you and Jesse. I am simply describing a *condition*. And as far as you're concerned I believe that condition is only in his mind. I have not taken this roundabout course to accuse you of adultery. Nothing could be further from my mind. Such a thought has never entered my head. As we both know, our daughter has taken over those duties. She has provided Jesse with a marriage bed. Since her relationship with him preceded her marriage to Edmund and since it was established again *after* her annulment, we have to assume that it is satisfactory to each of them. But particularly to Jesse. He comes and goes at will between here and Paris, something like a steamship captain, I should think. Nora provides him with a home where we must assume he is treated with affection and respect. And since he is legally her uncle, his presence need not be offensive to anyone's sense of propriety. You will agree with me, I'm sure, that Jesse, when he is in France, enjoys all the privileges of marriage while he is burdened with none of its restrictions or responsibilities. As an added benefit, he is able to function as a kind of ersatz parent to Valerie. As we have seen firsthand the child adores him, calls him *uncle* but relates to him in all ways as a daughter to her father.'

'That's not true. She visits Edmund on a regular basis. She knows very clearly who her father is.'

'Of course she does. But all the same she is *devoted* to Jesse. Just as her mother is. And just as *you* are.'

'Have you quite finished?'

'Not at all,' Ned said. 'Just partly finished. We have examined only half of Jesse's rewarding life. His life abroad. When he returns here to Wingate, he has, one

426

would think, an equally benevolent time of it. He is truly the master here, second only to Angus. But since Angus defers to him in all matters, Jesse is, in fact, the master of Wingate Fields.'

'He doesn't think of himself that way. I can assure you of that.'

'Perhaps not. I'm sure he's become accustomed to the golden goblet, to winning without competing. But however he regards himself it's clear that, apart from me, no one in this house finds fault with him. He is treated, on all sides, with care and deference. He spends long hours in his sumptuous rooms, planning great projects that never come to fruition . . . .'

'You have no conception of what he's trying to do.'

'That's true. I haven't. If that little quarterly that he and Nora have begun to produce in Paris is an indication . . . .'

'They're very proud of what they're doing and so am I.'

Ned made a gesture with his hand and said, 'I concede. I am not an aesthete. But I know the difference between a hobby and a profession. If a business does not support itself . . . .'

'Art is not business. At least not for artists. Art never supports itself.'

'As I say, I don't comprehend such activities. But since Jesse and Nora are well able to afford what they're doing I wish them well. I'm sure there is some satisfaction to be gained by investing time and money in what seems to be a noble cause. But from what I've seen I think they've taken a wrong turn. I don't expect there's a great audience for shredded prose passed off as poetry or for reproductions of paintings that seem to offer ugliness as their chief virtue.'

'God, but you're arrogant.'

'Perhaps you're right. I may even be ignorant. But I'm not a fool. I know a charlatan when I see one.'

'I assume we've come back to Jesse now,' Clara said.

'Yes, we have. I didn't quite finish my synopsis of his remarkable life.'

'His *bigamous* life.'

427

'That's correct. In Paris he has Nora and Valerie. Here in Northumberland as I've said he is the master. But more important he has *you*, the mother of his mistress, a duplicate in many ways of Nora. But with many attributes that Nora does not have. Patience, tolerance, imagination, intelligence, understanding . . . .'

'Are you describing *me*?'

'Of course I am.'

'How extraordinary I sound.' She smiled. 'What a wonderful wife I must be.'

'Not for me, I'm afraid. Not for any man you don't admire. You admire Angus and for some reason you admire Jesse. But you don't admire me. I suppose you did once. But that was a long time ago.'

After a moment she said, 'I don't think I like this conversation very much. I think we should call it off before we say things we don't mean.'

'I'm saying exactly what I mean.'

'I think we should call it off all the same.'

'Whatever you say.'

He sat looking at her, the wind punishing the trees outside their sitting-room windows, a shutter creaking somewhere in a far wing of the house. Her mind seemed to be sending signals to her body. The expression in her eyes said she had decided to stand up, say something healing and civilized, and go off to her bedroom. But she didn't rise, didn't speak, didn't move at all. She looked at her hands in her lap and at last looked up at him.

'I don't know what to say to you.'

'You needn't say anything. I didn't intend to discuss myself or our situation. I was talking about Jesse. If it makes you uncomfortable, I won't go on.'

'It doesn't make me uncomfortable. It makes me sad.'

'Yes, of course. I'm sure it does. Perhaps we *should* leave off. I suppose I've said all I had to say.' He paused. 'When I hear myself talking I think perhaps it's just envy that prompts me. I'm sure that's what Angus thinks. That I'm a man who'll soon be sixty competing with a young fellow my son's age. *Trying* to compete would be a better way of putting it. Trying to turn *unequals* into *equals*. We all waste a great deal of energy doing that. I'm a tall man. All my life I've seen how short men look at me and I know what they're thinking. Only a bald man knows what hatred can be inspired just by looking at a full head of hair. There's nothing harder to live with, I suppose, than a natural disadvantage. Makes no difference whether it's truly important or not. Doesn't even matter if it's real. If you *think* it's real then you have to live with it. Most of the things I've battled against all my life only exist in my head. But they *do* exist there. The things I hate most about myself are things that *I* created. I can look in a man's eyes, someone I've just met for the first time, and see him making decisions about me. I can see him withdraw, see him turn away. And I know as it happens that it's because of something I did or said to *keep* him from turning away. What does all this have to do with Jesse? I'm not sure. I can't say he's ever done an unkind thing to me. He's never ignored me or been condescending or superior. I said before that I was envious but I don't think that's the proper word. Resentful? Maybe. Because Angus likes him and Nora likes him and *you* like him. But the actual truth is . . . I *know* he's *likeable*. I *see* it. I knew it when I met him the first time. He's a genuinely likeable man. You know what I'm saying? It's not something he does, it's not some trick he's learned. It's just something he *is*. It's something that was handed to him. He's had it and he always *will* have it. That's what I can't deal with.'

It would be a mistake if we were to conclude that this particular dialogue between Clara and her husband was a turning-point in her relationship with him or with herself. In many respects it was a duplicate of countless discussions they had had through the years. One marked difference, however. On this occasion, under the guise of revealing something profound about Jesse, Ned had, in fact, revealed himself. And not accidentally, Clara felt. In all the time she had known him he had seemed to be saying, 'The world is in error. I am a singular man. Unrecognized and unappreciated.' Now, suddenly, he had swung full round and

429

was admitting, was at least coming as close as he *could* to admitting, that the flaw was in him. After spending his adult life singling out and castigating his enemies, he was confessing at last, it seemed, that the enemy was himself.

It was Clara's nature to meet a frontal attack with a corresponding positive response. In this respect she was, unquestionably, Angus' child. She was eminently capable of defending her position whatever it was. Conversely, she was quick to recognize true pain or weakness; she had no impulse to take advantage of a disadvantaged adversary. She felt no triumph in besting an unequal opponent.

Her relationship with Ned had settled, through the years, somewhere between those two poles. Although she was aware, from the first months of their marriage, of his low self-esteem, he made a great show of strength in relation to her, was self-assertive and stubbornly sure of himself in all family matters. If Angus and the outside world were determined to ignore his true value, he seemed intent on proving that he was, at least, the master of his own immediate household. The fact that Clara deferred to him, however, was a tribute to her kindness rather than his dominance. But she was careful to keep this fact from him.

Out of such a ferment, one might assume that when a man like Ned, for whatever reasons, finally let down the barrier, when he was able to admit, in even a tangential fashion, that the world's judgment of him might not be as inaccurate as he had previously insisted, it is reasonable to assume that a truly loving and generous woman such as Clara surely would respond with love and generosity. She might have been expected to say, whether she fully believed it or not, 'No, no. You were right before. You *have not* been properly appreciated. You *are* a valuable man.' Encouragement for the faltering. Kindness to the wounded.

No such impulse seized her, however. Too much time had passed. Too much erosion of what had once been true and lovely feelings. Too much listening to self-delusion. Too much absorption of foolishness. Too much saying yes when all her instincts and judgments said no. Too much given and far too little received. As she sat listening to Ned, when she heard him come as close as he would perhaps ever come to admitting that he had studded his life with false values and wrong choices, as she watched him slowly tumbling from the extremely modest throne he had struggled to provide for himself, as she waited for some ripple of emotion from inside herself, some smooth surge of love or, that failing, of compassion, all she felt was pity. And even that was of an inferior grade. Not the pity one feels for a person who has been brought down by circumstances but the sickening sensation that comes when a friend has gluttonized himself into obesity or drunk himself to cirrhosis.

That evening then, that conversation by the grate with the wind snapping outside, did *not*, as previously noted, open new routes for Clara and Ned. No decisions were reached, conclusions drawn, or patterns set. But a change did take place nonetheless. What had been a slow process of accommodation and adjustment and alteration became, abruptly, solidified and formalized. In Clara's mind at any rate. Ned's coming to terms with himself permitted *her* to see him and assess him honestly and without guilt, something she had not done before. She did not judge him. She simply observed him judging himself. It was as though the end of his self-deception brought an end to hers. She no longer had to pretend, no longer *could* pretend, that better days were ahead for them, that some miracle of their middle years would bring forth the light. She knew now, without question, that the emptiness of their past twenty years was an absolute; what they had had was what they would continue to have. It was not a poignant realization for her. It was a simple acceptance of circumstance. Standing in the rain without a coat.

Having crossed the line between uncertainty and certainty she did not then tell herself that ultimatums were the order of the day, that new rules were required, that each party must clearly understand now what each *other* party understood. Quite the contrary. She did not tell

431

herself that things had changed or *must* change between her and Ned. She simply accepted the fact that things would *never* change. This did not depress her. It gave her, instead, the incentive to *proceed*. Without guilt. It never occurred to her to end her marriage; she had no wish to do anything that would bring discomfort or pain to Ned. But she was quietly determined to get on with her life. 'If I'm fortunate enough to live as long as Angus, I have thirty more years to go,' she told herself.

A few days after her conversation with Ned she told her father she wanted to become more active in the family business.

'You're active already, it seems to me. You and Jesse have been a great help to me these past few years.'

'I'm glad you feel that way. But in future I want to accomplish more. I want to travel with you. I want to educate myself. I know there's resistance to me because I'm a woman. I've seen it in men's faces.'

'Well, we'll deal with *that*, won't we?'

'I mean I want people to see straight away that I know what I'm talking about.'

'Sounds like an excellent plan to me. But how does Ned feel about your trailing away here and there around the world?'

'He'll understand when I explain it to him. With Mother off in Newcastle most of the time, he knows I have very little to keep me occupied here.'

'Ned tells me he's anxious to have more responsibility. How do you feel about that?'

'I think you should give it to him. Why not let him work with the people in London? Go into the city two or three times a month. Let him feel as if he's on the inside. He's not incompetent, you know. Perhaps you could put him in charge of land acquisitions here in the north. He knows Scotland like his pocket. It could be a good choice, I think. And at the same time he could be made to feel . . . you know what I mean.'

'Yes, I *do* know.'

Was it all handled so neatly then? Were the interlocking

pieces shaken apart, shuffled about, and put back together in a new pattern that profited everyone involved? In some ways, yes. Angus was pleased, certainly, that his daughter had chosen to involve herself more profoundly in business affairs and Ned was delighted that he was being allowed, at last, to edge into the outside borders of the inner circle. But for Clara, ·who had made or had prompted all the choices, the process had been more intricate and disturbing than it seemed. It had all turned, not on Angus or Ned, not even on her *own* feelings or desires or ambitions, but on Jesse. Her calm demeanour as Ned had outlined his theory about her *sharing* Jesse with Nora had been in no way a reflection of the impact his words had made on her. She knew that her husband had stumbled on a sliver of truth, one she had concealed even from herself. Although he said that he believed the situation, the relationship, existed only in Jesse's mind, the thought that burned through Clara's brain was that it existed only in *her* mind. Having never acknowledged that fact before, she now could not avoid it.

Later that night, as she lay alone in her bed, she slowly opened all the gates and doors she had kept so carefully locked; she pulled down, stone by stone, the wall she had flung up between herself and the truth. She allowed herself to think of Jesse, to *relate* to him, in ways she had avoided for years. It was as though she realized that she could not win unless she surrendered. If her mind was to prevail at last then her senses must have their day. So she lay there in the dark, through those long hours between midnight and daybreak, and capitulated totally. No fantasy was forbidden. No shred of imagination was disallowed. She gave herself over completely to an aching physical relationship, the existence of which she had never acknowledged before, allowed it to consume her and carry her crazily through the night. Like a saturated alcoholic who at last can intoxicate himself with plain water, Clara took herself that night to places she had never been and where she expected never to be again. She told herself that when she awoke the next day, the woman who had loved Jesse

433

would still be sleeping and would not wake up again. She believed that was true. She believed she could make it true. And she did. When she saw him a few days later, when he returned to Wingate from Paris, she greeted him with warmth and tenderness as she always had and sat talking with him in the morning-room till tea-time. The servants saw nothing changed in her demeanour. Nor did Jesse. Clara was determined that no one ever would.

3

Nora had not been long in Paris, a year perhaps, when she was infected by a virus which attacks many visitors to that splendid city. In that seductive atmosphere of filtered light, violinists in every café, poets reciting on street corners, and painters at work in the parks and gardens, she decided that she, too, was inhabited by a creative spirit, that some hitherto unrevealed gift or talent lay hidden inside her and it was her responsibility to set it free.

All serious artists have patience. Instinct tells them and experience underlines the fact, that they have committed themselves to a long journey during which the delays and detours and stop-overs may be the most significant events. Haste is not important or valuable and may very well, indeed, make waste. A poem is, at foundation, one word or phrase. When a number of such are artfully joined, the result, if one is very lucky, is a poem. A painting likewise is not a grand conception. It is a process. A series of single brush-strokes that are persuaded to lie down together, both in passion and peace, and produce, at last, an harmonious entity. Chance made to seem inevitable.

Some vision of success, of achievement or recognition is the spur that speeds most of us along. No one is more impatient than a rug merchant or a man hawking potato-peelers on a street corner. A man going nowhere is always moving quickly. A painter or a poet, on the other hand, unless he deceives himself or feels driven to lie about his

434

prospects to his wife, realizes that his chances for recognition or reward are very slight indeed. So there's no need to rush. The road to self-fulfilment is lightly travelled while all roads leading to Babylon are crowded day and night.

Nora, feeling no creative surge inside herself but needing, nonetheless, to see immediate results, attempted to fuel herself by an act of will. Realizing that determination and discipline are a *part* of the process, she decided to make those two elements serve as the *whole*. Drawing a complex mathematical conclusion featuring apples and oranges, she theorized that since many of the gifted people she had met in Paris were notoriously non-productive, she would *force* herself to produce and out of the sheer volume of that productivity the precise nature of her gifts would be revealed to her.

When one has no restrictions or limitations, either natural or self-imposed, the problem becomes one of selection. Forced to choose one grape from a wagon-load, a person may well hesitate, whereas picking one apple from a company of two on a china plate presents no problem. Herein lay Nora's dilemma. Having chosen her objective which as nearly as she was able to express it to herself seemed to involve the pursuit of excellence, she was now faced with the problem of choosing a specific route. *And* a vehicle. Music was a mystery to her. She had been taught to play the piano and the violin but had been captivated by neither. She was able to read music but had no interest in trying to write it. So out of the broad spectrum of the arts that she saw around her – assuming that she did not want to be a theatrical performer, and she *did* not – it seemed that poetry, painting, sculpture, and the novel were the most accessible areas. Her schooling had given her a wide exposure to classical literature and of course to English poetry and fiction. And she and Hugh had been avid readers of American novels. An objective counsellor, therefore, would have steered her undoubtedly in that direction, towards what seemed to be her greater exposure, towards what would probably be her creative strength. If it is true that all great writers are also great readers, could

435

not the reverse, perhaps, be true? Or could it not be *thought* to be true? *No* to both questions. But all the same, in Nora's case, one might well have expected her, when she was fired with an urge to create, to pick up the pen.

She did not. At least not at the beginning. For two reasons. And valid or not they seemed extremely valid to her. Number one, she did not want to compete or to be seen as trying to compete, with Jesse. The prospect of their reading to each other from their separate works while a bottle of muscadet cooled did not excite her. Her second reason for steering clear of either the novel or poetry was in two sections. First, it seemed to her that there was an unacceptable time-lag between the finish of a poem or a story or a novel and its appearance in print. That disturbed her even more than the possibility that a given piece of work might *never* appear in print. She didn't allow herself to consider that.

Nora's chief aversion to writing as an activity involved the basic nature of the work itself. Knowing almost nothing about the habits of serious writers, she *had* learned one critical fact. Everywhere she inquired, everyone to whom she spoke, told her in no uncertain terms that it was a *solitary* activity. A poet named Kovacs explained it to her with particular clarity. 'In the morning, I have a coffee and a *pain chocolat* and a pastis. Then I go back to my room and lock myself in. At midday I eat bread and Camembert in my room. When I come out at dinner-time, I get drunk on armagnac at Kosmos and try to find a woman to sleep with. Whatever happens, I'm locked in my room again the next morning . . . working.'

'Don't you hate being by yourself all the time?' Nora asked him.

'Of course I do. But there's no other way to get the work done.'

So she arrived, after a process of elimination, at the door of an art school. She would learn to draw and paint, she decided. The fact that she knew nothing whatsoever about it may have stimulated her. Or perhaps the idea of a *school* attracted her, the activity, the ambiance. To Jesse she said,

'I like the thought of starting something new. It's like learning a different language. Going to a new country. I can't fail. Because no matter how little I learn, I will be one hundred percent further along than I am now.'

Failing to gain admission to the Académie des Beaux Arts, the Colarossi, and the Académie de la Grande Chaumière, she was accepted at last by a painter named Henri Pignot who lived in a run-down studio on rue Etex overlooking the Cimetière Montmartre and taught drawing to idle women and casual students.

M. Pignot was a constructivist and had previously been associated with the Dada movement in 1916. His background was sketchy. He was known to have been a morphine user and a brothel operator in Dijon. Rumours persisted that he had been in prison in Alsace during the war and his sexual habits were considered scandalous even in Montmartre. His credentials as an instructor in art were also suspect. He had had no formal training himself and he boasted to everyone, including his students, that he was unable to draw. 'But *you* must do exactly as I *tell* you. Then you will draw like a *maître*.'

The fact that her teacher neither knew nor cared about the principles of art was a boon to Nora. 'It's all an experiment,' he said. 'Do what you like. The only rule in this atelier is that you must not visit the Louvre or the Jeu de Paume and you must never do a piece of work that resembles anything you have seen before. Art goes forward only. When it looks backward it falls in the toilet. In 1913, a crazy Russian bastard named Tatlin came to Paris to steal ideas. He saw my collages and constructions, bought half a dozen to take back to Russia, and copied them. Then he announced to the world that he was a constructivist, that he had invented constructivism. I say *merde*. *I* invented constructivism. Ask Picasso. He knows the truth. Two other Russians – they're all drunks and crazy people, those bastards – copied Tatlin's work. Pevsner and Gabo. Then they said *they* invented constructivism. Crazy bastards. I am still the only constructivist who knows what he's doing. But it bores me now. So I don't do it. Everything bores me

437

once I've done it. Who wants to kiss his aunt? *Dada*. You know about Dada? People fall on their knees to Duchamp and Picabia and Schwitters, the German. But those men all followed *me*. When the war was still going on, in 1915 or 1916 I said all art is shit now. Death is the new theatre. Blood is the new art. So I invented Dada. Crazy art. At first I called it *Kaka*. Then some pederast critic, when he wrote about me, changed it to Dada. But it's still kaka to me.'

A few weeks after she began to work in Pignot's atelier, Nora took Jesse to meet him. They had an endless Hungarian dinner in a restaurant frequented by jugglers and acrobats from the Cirque Medrano across the street.

'Be prepared for anything,' Nora had told Jesse. 'He may get miserably drunk and throw food. God knows what he'll do.'

To her surprise, Pignot arrived in a rumpled suit, wearing a proper necktie, his thin hair plastered flat across his bald spot. 'So you're a writer,' he said to Jesse.

'I'm trying to be.'

'Don't try so hard. Automatic writing is the answer. Free association. Write in the dark. Whatever comes to your mind. The Dada people drank pastis and wrote all night. A man named Gilles – I never knew his last name – wrote a two-hundred-page *roman* in three days and three nights. Never ate. Never slept. When he finished five of us took turns reading his manuscript out loud at the Closerie des Lilas. When we finished we burned it in a bucket on the pavement of Rue d'Assas.'

'You burned his book?' Nora said.

'What else was there to do? Gilles had finished writing it and we had finished reading it. It was over.'

Pignot did not get drunk as predicted, did not insult Jesse, and was not argumentative. He drank quietly, used his knife and fork with a certain amount of skill, and conversed as quietly and reasonably as his prejudices would allow.

'Permanence is the enemy,' he said, 'that lunatic need for something permanent. We all know we're going to die

438

so we scurry around looking for something that *won't* die. Anything that's lived longer than we have is valuable. *That's* the song. I say *merde*. Does anybody give a damn for the Pyramids? *I* don't. *Old* means nothing. Old means *shit*. If they didn't have those crumbling churches all over the world, nobody would believe in God. Put a priest on some street corner, let him start babbling in Latin, and people will throw stones at him. Take the Mona Lisa out of the Louvre, sell it at a street market in Calcutta, and the man who bought it will burn it to heat water for his tea. I mean if something's not presented properly, if it's not in a proper building, if there's nobody there to tell you how much it's worth, then it's worth nothing. Just because something's built to last a thousand years doesn't mean it has value. Just because a man burns his work on the pavement behind the Closerie doesn't mean it wasn't a masterpiece. All the measurements are wrong. That's what I'm saying. And when they find *new* ways to measure, they'll be wrong too.'

They stayed very late in the bistro. Two musicians played on a platform across the room, a small double-headed drum and an accordion. People danced together and occasionally someone stood up on the platform with the musicians and sang through a megaphone. After Jesse paid the bill, when they were preparing to leave, Pignot hopped on the platform and picked up the megaphone; the drummer did a loose roll and a rim-shot.

'In a prison-cell in Alsace,' Pignot shouted through the megaphone, 'there was a man waiting for the guillotine. He'd killed his mother and father and two sisters. Every day he wrote on the wall of his cell with a black crayon. After they cut his head off, this is what they found written on his wall . . . .'

As he recited, the drummer played a soft wire-brush accompaniment and certain members of the audience who seemed to have witnessed this performance before, shouted out particular lines with Pignot as he went along.

439

I know my jailer. Every man does . . .
All of us live in confinement, dear.
Freedom is a myth.

Everything old is obscene and dank,
Everything new is worthless.
Rebellion is futile and stinks of rot
Youth is a pink cliché.

A man who swears that he loves mankind
Knows nothing of love at all
Only misanthropes can be trusted.

Fear of death – remember this
Breeds fear of life itself.
And fear of life, my foolish friend, *is* death
and nothing else.

Pignot stepped down from the platform with dignity, adjusted his black hat carefully on his head and without looking towards the table where Nora and Jesse sat waiting, marched stiffly out of the restaurant.

As they walked along Boulevard de Clichy a few minutes later, towards the taxi rank at Place Blanche, Nora asked, 'What do you think?'

'He's crazy,' Jesse said.

'He *is*, isn't he?'

'Crazy as a hoot-owl. But that's all right. Raymond used to say it's better to be a crazy artist than a successful dentist.'

Crazy or no, Pignot exerted a positive influence on Nora through the next three or four years. Teaching her nothing, offering no encouragement, cruelly criticizing what she thought were her best efforts, he, nonetheless, made her productive. Or perhaps he forced her to make herself productive.

Feeling hopelessly inept and out of place, surrounded by truly creative people, Nora compensated, as she had planned, with industry. In rue Cavalotti not far from

Pignot's atelier, she rented a studio for herself. The previous tenant, a Czech sculptor, who had been arrested by the Paris police for unknown reasons and shipped back to Prague, had painted on one wall in tall black letters, 'The first law of art is production.' Pignot, when he saw it, said, '*Merde alors*. The first law of art is indifference.' Nora, however, liked the sign, quoted it to all her friends, and left it there.

Using Dada as her springboard, she began at once to make assemblages. Sawing and snipping, cutting and gluing and nailing, she prowled the streets of Montmartre and the second-hand markets for *les objets trouvés*; rescued bent nails, rusty screws, and scraps of old wallpaper from building sites, collected shoelaces, combs, hair-pins, wigs, old cravats, old shoes, cancelled postage stamps, newspapers, journals and posters. She treasured bits of mirror, match folders, wine labels, and foreign bills and coins. She savaged old books for their engravings, their bindings, and their typography. Everything was valid, she told herself. Familiar objects could become in combination, a new and totally unfamiliar creation. 'It's all been done,' Pignot told her. 'We did it all before. All you're doing is collecting junk like some bum under the Pont de Sully. Throw it all away and do something you're good at. Cook a soufflé. Make a baby.'

All the same, activity, whatever its ultimate merit, had given her energy and confidence. Watching her hands at work she began to trust them. For the first time in her life she had rough callused palms and dirt and grease under her nails. She showed them to Jesse with pride and said, 'So far this is my best work.'

'But what does your master, Pignot, say?'

'He says "*merde*". He says the English can't paint or do anything with their hands. He says a woman can only be an artist when she's lying on her back.'

'What did you say to that?'

'I said, "If that's true, then why do you take my money?" and he said, "Because I *need* it. You like to give me money and I like to take it. What could be more perfect?" '

441

After almost two years of effort, Nora had accumulated thirty assemblages and collages and she was eager to exhibit them. 'I've never had a one-man exposition in my life,' Pignot said. 'Why should *you*?'

'Because I *want* to. I want to know what people think.'

'*I* can tell you that,' he said. 'I'm an expert on what people think. They don't think at all.'

'What about the critics?'

'The critics are pederasts and failed artists and fools. You pay them so much per line and they will write about your, work. But that doesn't mean they will like it. In your case, I guarantee you they will *detest* it. They didn't know what to make of Dada when it was new, when it was good, when it was *me*. These little experiments of yours, they will shoot down like game birds. They will hang you up and burn you.'

At last, however, he agreed to send her to a man named Cheval who had a small gallery in Avenue de Messine. 'He will try to crawl under your skirt but he's a cowardly man so you have nothing to fear. Simply say "non" very sharply and rap with your knuckles on his bald spot. He will weep then and be extremely apologetic and from that moment will give you no trouble.'

Cheval had performed as promised. But when he finished weeping he agreed to allow Nora to rent his gallery for two weeks in November to mount a showing of her work.

The posters for her show were well-designed, advertisements were placed in all the art journals, and the vernissage itself was a triumph. Nora's wealthy friends from Passy and Neuilly were there, and her artist friends came by metro from Montmartre and Montparnasse. They all mingled and drank wine, some of them were seen to exchange telephone numbers and addresses, and a few people actually *looked* at the carefully-hung collages and constructivist works. But no one inquired about prices from M. Cheval. And the critics, it turned out, were not persuaded.

'I told you they'd crucify you and they have. But you

mustn't pay attention. If they knew anything, they wouldn't be critics. Forget whatever they said.'

Nora respected this advice and tried to follow it. But one short comment, from the man at *Figaro*, stayed in her mind, like a child's prayer memorized. Twenty years later when she made laughing reference to 'My brief career as an artist', she was still able to recite it, word for word. 'This young Englishwoman has taught herself to be facile and to appear clever. Since cleverness and facility are the enemies of serious art, she has not arrived at a safe port.'

'It hurts my feelings,' she said to Jesse at the time. 'Plays havoc with my ego. But I can't honestly say I'm surprised. When the drayman brought my things from the studio to Cheval's, when I saw them for the first time on those cruel grey walls, I knew I was in for a bad patch. There's nothing quite so startling as being forced suddenly to be objective about something you've only been subjective about before. Naked in church. That was the feeling. But . . . what the hell. I had my fun. Now I can crochet and learn how to bake petit-fours.'

She cleaned out her studio, disposed of all those months of scavenging, and painted the place herself, walls, ceiling, and floors. But she made no move towards needlework or cooking lessons. Instead, using the Dada movement again as her springboard, she began to write; she attacked it with the same fearless energy she had used in her art work. She wrote free verse, doggerel, satire, political comment, critical pieces, and biographical sketches. And a thirty-page pornographic send-up of *Through the Looking Glass*. After fourteen months of such experiments, having shown none of her writing to anyone, not even to Jesse, she selected what she thought were her most successful efforts and caused them to be published, at her own expense, in a plain but beautifully printed edition of three hundred copies. Putting five copies in her strong-box at the bank she sent off all the others to her friends, each book accompanied by the following note.

These efforts of mine are being sent to you on the

specific proviso that you are *not* to read them. If you betray me I will cook you and eat you. That failing, I will simply strike your name from my guest list.

As her final salute to the spirit of Dada and as her farewell collaboration with Pignot, Nora, just after the collapse of the New York stock market in October 1929, produced, directed, and appeared in a chaotic concert at Théâtre Poche near the *gare*, just east of rue de Rennes in the Boulevard Montparnasse. Those who attended agreed that the time had come and gone for such performances. But those who had been involved in the original movement at the close of the war believed that this new effort, had it been presented just then, would have been a true reflection of the currents that were then running at that time in the *quartier Latin* or on the *butte*.

Jesse was in the audience of course. And Valerie, who had just celebrated her ninth birthday, was with him. When she described the performance to Clara during the Christmas holidays that year she said, 'It was really great fun. And quite artistic, I thought. Mama, of course, was superb. She was one of the principal performers. And the *only* pretty one. There was just *one* performance, you see. That was the intention. So only those of us who were lucky enough to be there that night are able to describe what happened.'

'Was it a proper play?' Clara asked, 'or was it more in the nature of *cabaret*?'

'Oh, it wasn't proper at all,' Valerie giggled. 'I'm sure that many people would have been shocked. There was a Chinese lady sitting astride a stuffed pony and she seemed to be wearing only riding boots. Also, a group of dogs wandered about the theatre and on the platform doing those nasty things that dogs do. But it was all quite amusing if you were there. When we went in, there were two large negroes painting the scenery and several dwarfs in boxing-gloves were punching each other on the stage. They seemed quite serious about it. In one corner a man was cooking hot sausages and two pretty ladies wearing

444

very short skirts passed out glasses of beer and wine along the aisle. It was like a grand soirée. Because a little band was playing all the while and the dogs were barking and everyone ate and drank all through the show and shouted at the people on the stage. And they shouted back. It was loud and smoky and hot. Jesse and I thought it was the most wonderful thing we'd ever seen. Nothing at all like a rehearsed play. Everything seemed to be happening for the first time. And it *was* of course. You wouldn't believe how loud Mama could yell. She sang crazy songs and danced with one of the dwarfs and screamed out the words of a long poem Jesse said she wrote herself. And then in the final part, three poets, two of them very old men, one with his leg in a cast, stood right at the front of the stage shouting advertising slogans all mixed in with quotations from the Bible. And everybody else, all the performers, stood behind them chanting, 'Da-da, da-da, da-da', and beating with wooden spoons on copper cooking-pans. What a fine noise it was. This part lasted for a very long time and while it was going on, the dwarfs were throwing make-believe apples and oranges and tomatoes at the audience. They looked real but they were made of papier-mâché. Everybody was laughing and screaming and the banging on pans got louder and louder and all of a sudden, those sweet little dwarfs were throwing *real* tomatoes and rotten oranges and eggs. And people started going crazy. Jesse got hit right on his new blue necktie with a tomato and the man next to him got an egg in his eye. And people were climbing all over each other trying to get out of the theatre. Right at the end, the little Chinese lady, the one with no clothes on except her boots, turned a hose on all of us. So then we really scrambled up the aisles to get out to the street. And that was the end of the show. It was wonderful, Grandmother. I'm sorry you weren't able to see it.'

'So am I,' Clara said. 'I expect I would be quite expert at dodging tomatoes.'

445

In the early autumn of 1930, just after *fermeture annuelle*, *Icarus*, a literary and critical quarterly, commenced publication in Paris, simultaneous editions in French and English. Listed on the masthead as publisher was Nora Bradshaw and as editor, Jesse Clegg Bradshaw.

'Is she his sister, then?' someone inquired. '*Mais bien sûr*,' was the sly answer. 'Sister of his thighs. *Mariée sans mariage.*'

When a French friend asked Nora, 'Why such a title for your magazine? To me, Icarus means failure,' she said, '*Exactly*. We are dedicated to impossible flight, inexhaustible hubris, and magnificent failure. Those are the hallmarks of genius, *mon vieux*.'

If Nora had been disappointed in the reception of her own creative efforts, her publishing of *Icarus*, a periodical designed to display and promote the talents of others, seemed blessed from the outset. Investigating a rumour that a popular quarterly, *Le Cri de Verlaine*, was about to collapse because of financial difficulties, she discovered that a second, more radical journal, *Les Brumes*, was also ceasing publication. Making each aware that she was about to take over the other, she then sat back and waited as the asking price for the assets of each publication plummeted. At last, when her *avocat* informed her that the selling price was as low, in each instance, as it was likely to go, she told him to inform both sellers that she was no longer interested. A week later, for no cash payment whatsoever, having agreed simply to pay off their debts, one franc for five, she owned both publications, total rights to their back issues, and whatever manuscripts they had acquired for future publication.

First, she dealt with the storage rooms filled with back issues. She called in a bookbinder and made arrangements to have all the previous quarterlies bound into books, ten or twelve issues to the volume. She then contracted to have these bound books sold in university shops all across

France. And she sold translation rights in Germany, Denmark, and Italy. Four months after her original acquisition, she said to Jesse, 'I think perhaps I am the eighth wonder of the world. I haven't published a single new issue and already I have made an obscene profit. I thought only *spending* money was fun. Now I see how delightful it is to *make* it. Angus will be proud of me.'

She was adroit also in the way she pulled Jesse into her *Icarus* project. She knew him well by now, knew that he abhorred long-range commitments, detested, in fact, commitments of any kind. Like many men who have absolutely nothing to do, Jesse was careful not to surrender any of his precious hours to projects that might be time-consuming. He seemed determined to keep himself free so that a worthwhile venture, when one came along, would find him ready and waiting.

Nora also sensed, however, that he was ripe for some transformation. He was no longer able to deceive himself about the significance of his phantom career. Too many years had passed. Too many failed plans, too much misdirected enthusiasm. Too much explanation and rationalization and nothing in the end to show for it. From her mother and Angus Nora knew that Jesse had displayed some skill in business. But she also believed, as did her mother and grandfather, that Jesse's mind and heart were elsewhere. He spoke of it seldom but when he did it was clear that he felt a permanent obligation to Raymond that predated his obligation to Angus. He measured himself every day by what he remembered as Raymond's standards. Prevailing in the market-place was not enough, he was sure of that. Skill in commerce would not suffice. He felt a continuing urge to *use* himself in some meaningful way, a need to bring himself into sharp focus.

Feeling anything but indolent, Jesse was struggling with a surfeit of ambition. He was desperately anxious to get on with it, to start moving ahead in a straight line, but all his efforts to turn ambition into achievement, however forcefully they began, inevitably lost speed, sputtered, and hesitated. And always in the same way. On close examin-

447

ation, no idea or project seemed grand enough or important enough.

This had been his pattern since returning to England ten years before. A sort of slow circular dance, without a partner and without musical accompaniment, a tedious and enervating wrestling match with great soft pillows, undangerous but suffocating, long swooping journeys to the far horizon and back again. Then a try at the opposite horizon. And always ending up at dead centre, safe on the starting marks, muscles taut and waiting for the crack of a starter's pistol that never came.

Nora sensed all these things in him, and was sympathetic in a way that was not characteristic of her. She had an instinct, had always had, for turning her own internal quandaries into objective combat. Isolate the adversary, if necessary create one, engage that adversary and win. And never fall into the error of imagining yourself, or some dark area of yourself, as the enemy. Instinct, or fear, perhaps, told her that those particular wars were unwinnable. One could bleed and suffer, charge and retreat, rage and despair, and find, at battle's end, that nothing whatsoever had been gained. Her self-discovered credo had always been, 'When you can't decide what to do, simply do *something*. When it's hopelessly dark inside, go outside.'

The fact that she felt this way and that she was able, when necessary, to *act* this way was sheer genetic good fortune and she knew it. Like having straight legs or white teeth. In Jesse's case, and Nora perceived this, he was not able to act first and sort it out later. He was so driven to thinking it through, tumbling it about, massaging and kneading it, then thinking it through again, that he was, more often than not, unable to act at all. And furthermore he had managed to persuade himself that such inaction was more creditable than an action that turned out to be less than perfect.

So he lounged in this perfect cocoon, had lingered there for years now, tapping his pencil against his teeth; he had learned to survive, it seemed, on stagnant, often-breathed air, had mastered the art of fending off difficult questions, of defending himself, and when all else failed, of consoling himself, with conviction.

But it was wearing thin. Nora sensed it and welcomed it. She knew that Jesse's attachment to Wingate Fields, his affection for that physical place, his dependence on those surroundings and those facts, all this had altered.

Louise, since her charity involvement in Newcastle was seldom seen at Wingate. Angus, also, was away more often than he was at home, sometimes for months at a stretch. And most recently, Clara, too, had begun to absent herself, very frequently. Only Ned remained a comparatively constant element but he, flushed with his new responsibilities and eager to present himself as far busier than he actually was, was no more enthusiastic about Jesse's companionship than Jesse was about his.

Unquiet as he was at times about the changing texture of his life in Northumberland, the area that upset Jesse most was the one that involved Clara. Returning to Wingate Fields no longer meant returning to her. When she was there, everything seemed unchanged. But she was seldom there now. For some time he pretended not to notice. He came and went as usual. Six weeks here, two months there. But more and more, the time he spent at Wingate Fields was time spent alone. 'How wonderful,' Nora said. 'Just think how much work you'll get done.'

But he did no work. His handsome study and antique writing-desk had no appeal. Without Clara to report to, without her as witness, as muse, as a silent collaborator, he had no interest in work. So bit by bit he persuaded himself that his future was in Paris.

The change was a slow one. It took place over a period of months, while Nora carefully monitored and recorded every movement. She sensed what was going on; as his trips to Northumberland became less frequent, she understood it more surely.

As she slowly drew Jesse into the operation of *Icarus* she knew she was arranging events to benefit herself. She needed his help if she was to organize and edit and publish and merchandise and distribute a periodical that would be

449

taken seriously. She needed his support, his counsel, and his energy. Also, she welcomed the opportunity to engage him in some continuing and demanding process that would keep him nearby. She had become increasingly disturbed by his absences from Paris. And, of course, there was Valerie.

'I can't get rid of you,' Nora said to Jesse. 'If I did, my daughter would murder me. Or she'd run off with you herself.'

'Not a bad idea. When she's twenty, I'll be forty-three. We should make a good match.'

'Over my dead body.'

'That won't be necessary. You'll be tired of me long before then.'

'You think so?'

'Of course. It's your nature.'

5

In November of 1932, just after Franklin Roosevelt was elected to the Presidency, Clara and Helen met in New York. It was just over thirteen years since they'd last seen each other, since they'd travelled to Liverpool together when Helen went there to board her ship for America.

They spent five days together before Clara, on her way home from a trip to Montreal and Ottawa, boarded a ship for England. They stayed in a suite in a splendid hotel just opposite the south east corner of Central Park, their sitting-room window looking west across the zoo and the lake and seemingly endless clusters of trees.

'We should have drawn up an agenda,' Clara said when Helen met her at the railway terminal. 'We have so much to cover we'll never manage it in five days.'

And they didn't, of course. But, recalling it later, it seemed to each of them as though they had talked incessantly, with only short intervals for sleep, through all of those five days. Contrary to her expectations, Helen listened more than she talked.

Coming east from Fort Beck to meet Clara, Helen had felt an exhilaration that was new to her. Remembering details of their hours together when she had visited Northumberland, she found it difficult to believe that they had not met in all the time since, difficult to accept that any mind-set or series of circumstances could have made such a separation possible.

As she sat in her rail-car drawing-room watching the fields of Ohio and Pennsylvania slide past outside the window she told herself that many of the disappointments she had experienced might have been avoided if only Clara had been nearby, if they could have seen each other and talked, if Helen could have had the benefit of a female viewpoint more stable than her own, or at least different from her own, if there had been someone to hear her without prejudice.

Not allowing herself to question whether she would have availed herself of such counsel and friendship if it had been available, not questioning her *own* role, past or present, Helen simply raced ahead of the train, hypnotized by the notion that this rendezvous in New York would somehow set things right; would make past events seem softer in outline and give some assurance that future trails would be clearly marked, routes and destinations in plain black letters on yellow backgrounds.

How could all this come about? This, too, seemed clear in Helen's mind. She would, simply, for the first time in her life, sponge the slate clean. She would trust someone enough, would trust *herself* enough, to tell the truth, to tell *all* the truth, to take whatever blame was properly hers, and to begin to forgive those who shared blame with her. She would come of age. Not in one meeting, not in one week or one month. But she would take the first step, have the courage to walk up to the edge and look over. 'I'm thirty-one years old,' she told herself. 'I'm able to do things now that have to be done. Able to trust myself. Not afraid to make mistakes. Able to admit at last that there's no

451

Raymond any more. And no substitute for him. There's just *me*. And a world full of people who didn't know him and who don't know me.'

She promised herself that there was no question of Clara's that she would not answer. She would tell the truth about her state of mind when she left England. She would tell about Hugh and the baby and what she had done and how she had tried later to remedy it. She would tell about her mother, what it had been like the last time she'd seen her and how Anna's death and her own still-born child had combined to rinse away every speck of self-esteem she had managed to collect.

And she would tell about Frank, a man Clara had scarcely heard of. It was critical, Helen believed, that she tell her about him.

Since her divorce, Helen had tried very hard not to review the events of that marriage. As orderly and civilized as their parting had been, she had come away from it with a taste of tarnished metal in her mouth that no wine or water could rinse away. She had lost her ability to select. She could not say, '*There* I failed, *there* I did not.' She could not examine the plus and minus. She could see it in only one way, as *her* failure. Soon, however, with Clara sitting across the table from her, she would be able to reopen her case, to deal with it, not with self-contempt, but with reason. She would simply present all the information, make no attempt to draw conclusions, or to influence Clara's conclusions, and once and for all, put the matter to rest. She would no longer have the sense that in her home, or in her mind, there was a sealed container threatening, at any moment, to explode.

As she rehearsed what she would say to Clara, both the thoughts and the words came easily. 'I made a ghastly mistake. I got married because I had lost all respect for myself. I chose a man who I thought would compensate for my deficiencies. I was desperate, of course. I see that now. I truly believed I was doing the only thing I *could* do, that I *had* to do it or suffocate.

'At the end, when we divorced, the thing that confused

452

people . . . was what went wrong. *Everyone* envied us. So they couldn't understand what he had *done*. Or what *I* had done. They couldn't see and I couldn't tell them, I couldn't even tell Frank, that it had almost nothing to do with him, neither the marriage *nor* the divorce. It was all *me* in relation to *me*.'

Now that she knew what she meant to say to Clara, the *need* to say it was overpowering. She was afraid she would blurt it all out the moment she first saw her at the railway station. Or certainly as soon as they were alone together at the hotel. But it didn't happen that way.

6

To Helen's eyes Clara looked exactly the same as before. She was scented by the same delicate toilet water and she talked to Helen as though they had last met only days before. After they had settled into their hotel, unpacked their luggage, and had some lunch, she began a detailed account of the Bradshaw clan, starting with Louise.

'She had us terribly concerned for a while. But now she's become *so* bizarre and behaves in *such* an extraordinary manner that we've simply decided to stop worrying. At first Angus wanted to protect her in every way he could but she was having none of *that*. So now he's decided that the officials of Newcastle, especially the churchmen, need to be protected from *her*. She's quite dotty, poor thing, but no one would guess it to hear her speak at a rally. She has the vigour of a woman of fifty – eyes sparkling and great rosy cheeks. When she marches with her followers up the steps of the cathedral, they say the bishop hides in his fine house and shivers in his slippers.'

'How old is she now?' Helen asked.

'Last month she was eighty-four. And she covers more ground in a day than *I* could. Her health, it seems, is no problem. But she's become . . . I don't know how to put it exactly . . . her doctor says most women her age lose

453

their hearing or develop arthritis. Louise, I'm afraid has gone a bit mad. So that's the situation, I'm afraid. All we can do is wait. Until she breaks a law or gets herself into really serious trouble, there's nothing else to be done. Eventually . . . I don't like to think about it, but sooner or later, she'll have to be where she can be looked after.'

Clara was equally candid about Ned. 'He's not a contented man,' she said, 'and he hasn't been for a long time. We are not a happy couple. It used to give me pain just to *think* that but now when I say it to you, it's as though I'm discussing someone else. That doesn't mean that I care nothing for my husband. I *do*. At one time I loved him very much. But . . . as you may know already, this peculiar thing we call love, whatever else it is, is not necessarily permanent. It changes colours and textures. It squirms around, slips away, comes back . . . it does all sorts of remarkable and unexpected things. And in many cases, more cases than we like to admit, it simply dies. And not just from neglect, either. Usually it dies, just as a person dies. Because it can't live any longer.'

In a letter from either Jesse or Clara, Helen had learned previously that Hugh was married. Now Clara gave her more details. 'She's a widow, a woman with five children whose husband fell down drunk in the river Oykel – at least this is the gossip Ned heard among the gillies – and drowned in two feet of water. It's not a distinguished family, I'm afraid, but they have a great deal of money. The father is an industrialist of some sort with factories in Glasgow. His wife is obese and the daughter, Helga, Hugh's wife, shows promise of following her mother's example. One doesn't ask her age but there's a sixteen-year-old son so we assume she's older than Hugh. But all the same, he seems quite taken with her. He's adopted all her brood of children and seems delighted to have them underfoot. They had a plain little family wedding in the church at Dornach and then a really lavish and vulgar party at Hugh's estate. The bride's father explained to everyone that although the party was being held in the groom's home, he, the father, was paying all costs. The whole affair

454

was totally without taste or restraint. An extraordinary number of drunken guests, most of whom had come up from Glasow. Some of them, I learned later, were still being discovered, in one guest room or another, five days after the wedding.

'During the party – this is what I started to tell you – the bride's fat mother confided to me that her daughter, after the birth of her fifth child, had seen fit to have herself rendered sterile. The mother kept saying, "Five is adequate. Five, in my view is certainly more than adequate." Since *I* was given this information I assume that Hugh also was not kept in the dark.'

'My son is a mystery to me,' Clara went on. 'And so is his sister for that matter. But Hugh, especially, has always been a surprise. And since he moved to Scotland, he's truly become a stranger to us. He seems warm and kind when we see him, but when I remember the way he used to be, wild and crazy and racing his horse across the fields, the young man I see now is like a fire that's smouldered out.

'I remember when I was a young girl, only ten or eleven years old, I used to hear Louise talking to our nanny about Raymond and me, and I used to promise myself that when *I* had my own family, things would be different. I would *understand* my children, and sympathize with them, and know how they felt and what they thought. Not only would I be their mother, I would be their best friend. I really believed such relationships were possible when I was a young girl. Now that I'm older I think it's a miracle if parents know their grown-up children at all, if there's *any* connection between them apart from that sort of automatic one where everyone has a family label and that's the extent of it.'

Winter was slow to come that year in New York. The autumn stretched on, crisp and clear and sunny, until the beginning of December. The days that Helen and Clara spent together allowed them to move about as they wished. No rain. No biting cold or sudden wind-gusts to capture their hats and sail them down Fifth Avenue. Both of them

455

excellent walkers, they prowled the streets and avenues, the parks and museums, from breakfast till sundown, following no prefixed schedule or itinerary, just strolling along arm-in-arm, and trusting their impulses. Lunch was a daily adventure. And each evening they dressed grandly, ordered a car and went to dine in the most elegant restaurants they could discover.

'We'll be enormously fat, won't we?' Clara said. 'We eat breakfast and luncheon and tea and dinner every day, snack a bit in between, and more often than not we finish off the day with some supper in our rooms. I don't see how we can avoid becoming huge creatures.'

'Not at all. We're walking ourselves thin. We're hiking ourselves into a marvellously slender condition. I'm sure of it.'

Helen had seen copies of *Icarus* in New York and was a regular reader of it. 'I think it's excellent,' she said to Clara.

'It's been taken up in London as well. And in Paris and Munich. Jesse says they're astonished that it's been so well-received. Only Angus has reservations. I suspect he's a bit put out because they went ahead with no advice or backing from him. He can't believe that any Bradshaw family venture can prosper without his wisdom. But it has all the same and Nora and Jesse deserve the credit. She seems a totally different person now. I think this is just a starting place for her. God knows what she'll come up with next.'

Of Nora and Jesse as a couple, Clara said, 'I don't know what to make of them. They don't seem to take each other seriously. But they continue to skate along. Sometimes I envy them. By not recognizing any of the problems that are supposed to exist for almost *any* couple, married or not, they seem to avoid them. They just *accept* each other. All very matter-of-fact and who-gives-a-damn. It's quite remarkable.'

Clara was particularly interested in the years that Helen had spent moving around the country; they discussed that a great deal, the details of that time. And Helen did talk about her marriage to Frank. But only in a general way. Clara seemed to sense it was a painful memory, difficult

456

to discuss, and Helen was satisfied to leave her with that impression.

Whatever promises she had made to herself on the train going east, however strongly she had felt about her decision to confide in Clara, Helen realized, before their second day together had passed, that she couldn't do it. She was simply unable to pass along those feelings and experiences that had been kept inside her for so long. When they parted at the embarkation wharves beside the Hudson river, Helen was sharply aware that she had said nothing about Hugh or the baby, had revealed almost nothing about her marriage, and very little about herself. She had promised to visit Wingate Fields again but had not said when. She had not told Clara where she would go when she left New York, because she didn't know. She had not discussed her future plans because she had none.

Chapter Ten

1

Since both Clara and Nora had been patient witnesses through the years to Jesse's efforts to define himself, to chart some straight-ahead course, it must have been astonishing to them that a single luncheon conversation at Chez Rosalie in Montparnasse could bring him into sharp focus.

It must have seemed extraordinary, also, to Jesse. After a chance meeting, on Boulevard Raspail, with Sidney Pence, a leisurely lunch, and a coffee later on the terrace of the Dome, Jesse knew what he wanted to do and how he would go about doing it.

He had first become acquainted with Pence at the time of Nora's exposition of her constructivist works, at the gallery of Paul Cheval. Pence was, at that time, in his late sixties, had been a London journalist all his life, but since 1911 had lived in France, reporting on cultural matters for the London *Daily Mail*.

'I know how I'm regarded,' he said to Jesse as they had lunch. 'I've always known. I am thought of here in France as a man who is more journalist than critic, someone who is careful not to bite the hand that feeds him. What is not taken into consideration is the fact that I was a working journalist for twenty-five years before I became a critic. I came to it with a different point of view. I believed, and I continue to believe, that the work being considered is the important thing. Art, even second-rate art, is a fact, an entity. Criticism at best is only opinion. And the world of opinion is hazardous. The wise man's vocabulary is also available to the fool. And since any audience is more likely to respond to foolishness than to wisdom, a critic must give careful thought to what he writes.'

'But they don't, do they?'

'Of course not. For many reasons. Some of them are simply envious or vindictive. But many others are trying to make their mark. They convince themselves that art is secondary to the art of criticism and that criticism, by definition, must be destructive. The public also has come to believe that. Words that destroy are more stimulating than words of praise. We imagine that we detect real truth in an attack, whereas compliments are always held suspect. *Reason* is not an appealing commodity except to reasonable people and they are always a minority.'

'If you feel that way I'm surprised your work doesn't reflect it.'

'I'm not saying what I *feel*. I'm telling you what I've observed. There is truth and there's pragmatic truth. They bear no resemblance to each other. Pragmatism exists in isolation. It resembles nothing except itself.'

'Let me put it another way,' Jesse said. 'If you were a very young man, just beginning your career, do you think you would approach it differently than you have?'

Pence smiled. 'I remember my first job, on a newspaper in Bristol. Like most young men I was more involved with myself than I was with the work I was doing. I felt that I would leave an indelible mark on any newspaper I graced with my presence. Monumental ego of course. But without ego, there's no ambition. And I was extremely ambitious. What I'm saying is that if any editor had put the weapon of criticism in my hands I would undoubtedly have savaged everything in sight.'

'But by the time you came here . . . .'

'By the time I came here I had witnessed all sorts of human failings. Many of them in myself. It gave me a kind of humility I hadn't had before. Some of us are not fit for life on earth till we realize the moon is not available to us. What I'm saying is that by the time I came to Paris I had begun to see my profession for what it was. I was willing

459

to serve it rather than insist that it serve me. I had stopped trying to build a monument to myself.'

'I suspect you're being too severe on yourself.'

'Perhaps I am. But my point is this. When I began to judge other people's work, when it became my job to pass such judgment, I'd been forced to acknowledge all sorts of deficiencies in myself. So I was not surprised to discover similar deficiencies in other people. From there it was a logical progression to discover that dissonance can enhance a piece of music, that a corrected passage in a painting can give it vitality, and that one awkward, angular line can have a power that brings an entire poem into sharp focus. Having painfully discovered that human beings are never perfect I was better prepared for the realization that perfection isn't art.'

'What is it then?'

'I don't know. Nobody does. Because it changes all the time. Mondrian once told me, "Art is what artists do." That's either the best definition of all or it's a joke, depending on your own sensibilities. One thing I'm sure of. All the words don't change anything. The good stuff is good and it *stays* good. It's what's on the canvas that matters. And that's *all* that matters.'

When they were sitting at the Dome later, the afternoon suddenly grey and foggy, Rodin's statue of Balzac just visible across the intersection, Jesse said, 'If a bright young fellow wanted to be a serious critic and came to you for advice, what would you tell him?'

'Bright young fellows don't ask for advice. And if someone gives them advice they pay no attention. However, if such a young man did come to me, I would know that his *real*, perhaps his *only*, objective was to make a name for himself. Just as Shaw did in England, as Mencken and Nathan have done in America. So the only advice I *could* give, certainly the only advice that would be listened to, would be of a tactical nature. Procedural matters. Tricks of the trade. I would tell him that the simplest formula for gaining a reputation is to *attack*. Everyone and everything. The more imposing your targets, the more brutal your criticism, the greater your reputation will become. When I was still in Bristol, a fellow I met there – he was just two or three years older than I – did that very thing. After several months of research, he did a series of destructive critical pieces about the Brontë sisters. He ripped and tore his way through their books, their values, their lives, and found nothing of worth anywhere. He was clever and thorough enough to have his facts right. So he could not be dismissed as an illiterate boob. But his literary judgments were a scandal across England for many months. Critics wrote lengthy rebuttals in all the journals and scarcely a day passed without an angry letter being published in *The Times*. And all the while my friend lay low in Scotland preparing a series of articles that would be as destructive to Jane Austen as his first series had been to the Brontës. The upshot of all this furore was that at the end of the year his name was known throughout England. At first he was thoroughly hated but as always happens in controversy, certain people sensed they could attract attention to themselves by taking his side. So bit by bit he became an established literary figure. His views and his articles were solicited by the literary journals. He spoke in all the major cities. And his books were published with regularity. Since then, whenever things have seemed too peaceful, whenever he began to feel bland and accepted, he has simply published a diatribe against some sacred cow in the British literary meadows. Dickens, Thackeray, Galsworthy, and countless others. He has a house in Sloane Square now and a handsome cottage in Surrey and he's invited everywhere. He is neither thoughtful nor intelligent. And he has no charm. He is simply well-known. From one clever and audacious notion he has fashioned an extraordinary life for himself.'

'And people forgave him for his trangressions?'

'It wasn't a question of forgiveness. They were mesmerized by his notoriety and began to mistake it for achievement. On certain levels of society it is only necessary to be known. Mere repetition of a name can begin to give it importance. But once again, my friend was clever. Having

461

attacked writers who were loved by all, he then made attacks in areas where he knew he would have British sympathy. He attacked the French. Beginning with de Maupassant, Proust, and Zola, he moved ahead to Ingres and Renoir, questioned the courage of the French military, and concluded with a six-part article in the *Observer* about French life in general. Their cuisine, their public toilets, and their penury. Just as we can make friends quickly in Paris by defaming the English so are the English always eager to hear or read negative judgments of the French.'

'So your friend was loved and hated in turn.'

'Exactly. But, more important, he was always in the public eye. He reached a point at last where he was able to publish what were meant to be reasonable and informed critiques. But since he is neither reasonable nor informed those pieces had a kind of vulgarity all their own which delighted his followers while continuing to offend his enemies. He seemed to be fashioned for success. Because he was, in essence, a man without qualities, his pitiful failures were almost indistinguishable from his hateful triumphs. Wanting, above everything else, to be noticed, he has succeeded in that ambition and failed in all others.'

During the next several days, as he struggled to find a subject for his occasional critical piece in *Icarus*, Jesse found himself returning to his converation with Sidney Pence. It had titillated and excited him. And it continued to. He sensed there was a window there which, if the proper pressure was applied, could be made to swing open. Sitting at his desk he felt a sudden aggressiveness that was new to him. He found himself neatly drawing arrows on a file card. He was fully prepared to follow Pence's formula, to find a victim, either an artist or his work, and take him or it apart with surgical precision. But no target presented itself.

At last, with the printer's deadline almost upon him, he shut himself in his study with a stack of recent art journals and literary sections from the Paris and London papers with the intention of doing a pot-pourri of activities and reactions in both capitals. But as he read the articles and critiques, Pence's words continued to jog his memory. On the last day before his copy was due at the printer, he got up at five in the morning, went to his desk in dressing-gown and pyjamas, and wrote the following headline at the top of a sheet of paper: THE CRITIC AS ASSASSIN, and followed it with his opening paragraph.

'The time has come for all of us in the critical profession to abandon the senseless cult of self-importance we have established for ourselves, to forego intellectual arrogance and to dose ourselves with a liberal portion of humility. The efforts of the poets and painters, the novelists and composers, are the centrepiece of culture and creativity. The rest of us are beggars at the table. We make no contribution to the history of art and in truth we confuse more often than we enlighten.'

He went on to castigate, specifically and personally, several prominent critics and closed his long article with attacks on Sir Arthur Thurman-Jones and Jean-Marie Briac. Thurman-Jones had recently published a monograph about Keats in which he had dissected *Ode on a Grecian Urn* line by line, word by word, and had established, at least to his own satisfaction that, 'although Keats is arguably a poet of the first rank he is in no way deserving of the God-like status he has been accorded.' Briac, in a series of pieces in *Le Figaro*, maintained that Delacroix was in all respects a superior painter to Rembrandt. He was particularly critical of the painting of the horse in Rembrandt's Polish Rider, the implication being that Delacroix was superior as a painter of horseflesh, therefore he was a more gifted artist. To conclude his attack on Briac, Jesse wrote, 'Briac has used imperfect reasoning to arrive at an idiotic conclusion. By his standards, Rosa Bonheur must be considered a greater painter than Delacroix. By those same standards Briac must be categorized as a handicapper of horse races rather than a critic of art.'

Of Thurman-Jones, Jesse wrote, 'Not only has he not proved his point, he has demeaned himself by his entire research. Perhaps, in literature, there are few examples of absolute and irrefutable genius. But however few they are,

463

no truly informed person would deny that Keats belongs on that small list. A temperate man, one who expects to be taken seriously, does not question the heat of the sun in summer, nor the presence of salt in the ocean. In his unwise attempt to re-evaluate a genius, 'Thurman-Jones labels himself as a man to be ignored.'

When the next issue of *Icarus* was published, *Le Figaro* printed the full text of Jesse's article plus an angry rebuttal by Briac. In London, the *Observer* also reprinted the article; they defended Jesse's point of view if not his conclusions. They did not include an answer by Thurman-Jones. In their next issue however, they featured a counter-attack by the chief editor of Faber and Faber, who had published the Thurman-Jones monograph.

There was a heavy postal response from readers of *Icarus*. Jesse's supporters and detractors seemed almost equally divided. Nora detested his article and the notoriety it brought. Even Sidney Pence, although he took delight in his own role in the affair, felt that Jesse had gone too far.

One thing was certain, however. Jesse Clegg Bradshaw had become in a short period of time, a new and raw critical voice, the sort of literary assassin he had excoriated in his essay.

2

When Helen had gone to Maine in the autumn of 1919, she had stayed alone as we have seen, had taken a house by the ocean near Hedrick and had lived, to a large degree, an isolated life. Apart from occasional trips to the bank in Damariscotta, to the grocery store in Hedrick or to the Bristol area library, she kept to herself. She was cordial to the tradesmen and to the workers who made occasional repairs to her house but she made no attempt to exchange confidences or make friends. Only Opal Feaster had tried to befriend her.

They had seen each other first at the general store in the

464

village of Hedrick. After that it seemed that Opal was in the store whenever Helen came there to buy groceries. Each time they nodded and said hello but Helen resisted longer conversations. One morning, however, Opal followed her out to her car, smiling and cheerful and impossible to dismiss.

'I don't know your name but I know you're living in the Dunstan house down by Brown's Cove. It's a pretty house, my husband says. He did some work there once when somebody forgot to drain the pipes and all hell broke loose with their plumbing. My name's Opal Feaster. Isn't that an awful name? My dad named all us girls after precious stones. Ruby, Pearl, and Garnet. I was the youngest so I got stuck with Opal. Not that any of the others are much better off. I can't stand parents who give their kids cute names, can you? My mother had a cousin who named her boys after whatever city they were born in. One of them was named Belvedere and the other one, Keokuk. People thought he was an Indian till they saw him. Then they saw he was as pale as an albino. I guess maybe he was an albino. He had sort of pink eyes and hair as white as a sheet. Anyway, my husband's name is Bud and he's seen you driving in and out of here in your Packard and he thinks it's the prettiest car he ever saw. We live across the street there in that old three-storey house. Looks like a barn but it used to be a hotel when people came up from Boston all the time on cruise boats. One toilet in the whole place. Can you imagine a hotel with only one toilet? My mother told me when she used to go to parties and dances in Sweden – that's where she lived when she was a young girl – nobody ever thought of going to the toilet from the time they left home till the time they got back. Can you feature that? I can't. Bud says I got no bladder at all. He says it's a straight shot from my gullet to the potty. Isn't that awful? He's funny, though even when he makes you mad at some of the cracks he makes. And I *do* pee a lot. I can't deny it. We drink a great deal of beer and it seems like I'm always on the move, either coming or going. "There she goes!" he yells out, whenever I leave the room.

465

No matter who's there. And when I come back he says, "Look who's here." I used to get all red-faced and not know how to act but now I just pass it off like nothing and let him have his fun. He's got a good heart, God knows. That's why a person can't get mad at him. He was in the war. Or at least he would have been. But an army fire truck ran over him and messed up his back when he was down at Fort Dix so he's been on full disability ever since. He still works at his plumbing sometimes. He's only twenty-five years old and I guess he'd go nuts if he didn't have something to get him out of the house once in a while. But he can't do heavy lifting like he used to. Can't put in a full day with the tools or work outside when it's cold. I've seen his x-rays. They let him take them along when he finally got discharged from the army hospital down in Boston – and I tell you his back is a fright. Like a plate of macaroni. They say it's a miracle he's moving around at all. So I say thank God for that. He can walk and he can still work some and we've got that United States Army government cheque coming in every month.'

As she drove home, Helen realized that Opal hadn't asked her name and she hadn't volunteered it. That night, in the diary she kept all through the months of her pregnancy, she wrote:

I met an odd young woman today. Couldn't tell her age. She could be any place between twenty and thirty. Closer to twenty, I suppose, but her eyes say she's older. I would guess she's had some exposure to life's surprises, whatever her age is. But she's open and friendly like the girls I grew up with in Illinois. Makes you feel she has no secrets. And if she *did* have they wouldn't be secret for long because she'd tell everybody. She could be pretty if she'd just wash her face and let herself alone. But she wears too much make-up. Powder and rouge and lipstick and mascara and eye-shadow The whole works. Like the girls who sell tickets at carnivals. And she has her hair dyed some crazy colour. A kind of carrot red. I guess she has a

466

nice figure but it's hard to tell because she was wearing men's outdoor clothes and it looks as if she's twenty pounds overweight.

Three days later a small delivery truck pulled into Helen's driveway. Opal got out and knocked on the kitchen door. When Helen opened it she said, 'I'll bet you're surprised to see me. Don't worry. I'm not coming in. I just baked a batch of banana bread and some cranberry cake and I thought you might like some. It could make you fat – look at me – but it's guaranteed to taste good.' As she turned and started back towards the truck, Helen said, 'Don't you want to come in?'

'Thanks anyway. But Bud's up in Rockland and he may be calling home. So I'd better stick by the phone. See you later.'

As the weeks went by, as the two women met and talked occasionally at the grocery store, Helen got the impression that for all her warmth and non-stop monologues Opal was no more eager to start an intimate friendship than Helen had been. When Helen thanked her for the cakes and said, 'Come by some day for your plates,' Opal replied, 'That's all right. I've got a cupboard full of dishes. Just leave them here at the store if you want to and Harlan will keep them till I come in. He might even trot 'em across the road to me if he thinks he'll get a glass of beer.'

After several weeks, reluctant to simply leave the plates at Harlan's store, Helen returned them to Opal's house. There she was persuaded to stay for lunch.

Bud, it turned out, was as gregarious as Opal. The two of them stumbled and sprawled about in their kitchen like two quilted bears, laughing and drinking and contradicting each other. If she told a story, he retold it, then they screamed and yelled and told it together. Like Opal, Bud was free with information about himself but asked no questions whatsoever about Helen. He simply declared her welcome at his house any time she wanted to drive into town and he appointed himself her emergency engineer and man of all work.

'This is Maine, for Christ's sake, and we're edging into winter. Ain't no house ever built can go through these winters up here without some kind of aches and pains. A kerosene lamp you can count on. Long as you don't run out of matches and kerosene. But anything else, you have to figure it will do something peculiar between the first of December and the middle of April. If you really get in trouble, we'll have the snow plough pick you up and haul you over here. We'll put you on a cot in front of the fireplace and give you a big jug of elderberry wine to keep you company.'

Sitting at home alone later that day, remembering the warmth of Opal's kitchen, the good smells, the hooked rugs and comfortable chairs, some instinct inside Helen caused her to rejoice. She had met two hospitable and receptive people. They seemed to be offering her friendship, advice, and assistance if needed. With no strings attached.

Having told herself from the moment she decided to come to Maine that it was an ideal choice because no one knew her there, she realized from the moment she moved into her house by the sea that she had a lonely time ahead of her.

Lonely or not, however, she was convinced that she must remain stubbornly on the rails, and move ahead one day at a time, by herself.

Now, however, an alternative had been presented to her. Without surrendering her privacy, without revealing any secret corner of her life, she was being offered, it seemed, the gift of companionship.

Until it had been presented, until she sat in the Feasters' kitchen with those two people so unlike herself, until she found herself totally distracted for two hours, she had not admitted to herself how lonely she had been these past weeks.

Sitting by her fireplace, hearing the ocean pounding on the rocks outside she told herself that perhaps she could have it both ways. She could stay for the most part inside her cocoon, and still give herself the occasional companionship of Opal and Bud Feaster. She felt very fortunate.

As she cleaned up her kitchen after dinner she listened to the gramophone Clara had given her; she played her favourite records as she sat in the half-dark then in front of the fire. As she read in bed later her eyes kept wandering from the page. 'I'll never sleep tonight,' she told herself. 'I'll be awake all night, smiling like a fool.'

As soon as she turned out the light, however, she went to sleep. But a few hours later she was awake again, staring at a moon-spot on the ceiling and wondering where her exhilaration had gone. When the sun was barely up across the ocean to the east she sat in her bed sipping coffee and writing in her diary.

You had your lovely hours of self-deception. Now it's over. You can't play make-believe with Opal and Bud. You can't accept what they have to give and offer nothing in return. Very soon it will be clear to everyone that you're expecting a baby. You can say nothing to strangers but you can't smile and tell lies to people you've accepted as friends.

For a week she stayed inside her house. Avoiding Hedrick, when she needed something from the store she drove to New Harbor or Bristol. At last, after ten days had passed, she sat at her desk and wrote a note to Opal.

I feel like a fool as I write this but I hope you will understand what I'm struggling to say. You have been very kind to me, both you and Bud, and I appreciate it more than I can tell you. I can think of nothing nicer than seeing you both on a regular basis and having you come here to my place.

Unfortunately, I am going through a difficult time. I have problems that I can't share with anyone and I guess I wouldn't even if I could. For a few months I simply must be by myself, *all* by myself.

Please understand. This has nothing to do with *you*.

469

It's my personal, idiotic battle and I have to fight it in some personal and idiotic way.

So please don't be angry with me. Some other time I hope circumstances will be better and I'll be able to show you that I'm not crazy after all.

She mailed the letter in Damariscotta that afternoon. A few days later she received a postcard from Opal.

Thanks for your letter. I'm sorry you've got troubles. Ain't we all? If something goes wrong with your house, call up Bud. He can fix anything. Good luck. Opal.

In the remaining months before she left Maine, Helen didn't drive into Hedrick. She did her shopping in Damariscotta and when anything went wrong with her plumbing or her lights, she contacted her landlord who sent a man over from Wiscasset. Occasionally she would pass either Opal or Bud driving along the road. Recognizing her car, they would sound their horn and wave. But she never spoke to them again before she left Maine to return to Fort Beck.

As she travelled around the country in the next few years, however, she thought of them often. It surprised her that they stayed so clearly in her memory.

She began to send postcards to Opal every month or so, pictures of courthouses and rivers and parks in whatever city or town she had chosen to spend some time. Occasionally, when she had given her return address she would have a card from Opal with scrawled messages such as, 'We're making home-brew. Having a helluva time,' or 'I've got the flu and ugly Bud is taking care of me. He's a terrible nurse,' or 'You should be glad you're not here. We're in snow up to our hobs.' And once she wrote, 'I hope your troubles went away.'

In the winter that preceded Helen's marriage to Frank Wilson, after she had visited her mother on Staten Island, when she decided to go to Maine to see Dr Kilwinning at the adoption centre, Helen sent a wire to Opal.

I have to go to Portland. I'm not sure how long I'll have to stay. Can I see you while I'm there?

When she found out she'd have to wait several weeks for her meeting with Kilwinning, when she called Opal in Hedrick, Opal said, 'Come on up. We've got more room here than we know what to do with. Bud even insulated the place last summer, all except the top floor. So we don't have to sleep in our socks any more.'

When she walked into their house it was as though the day they'd had lunch together had been just the day before. Bud's face was a bit more weather-beaten and Opal bulged more noticeably inside her clothes but otherwise nothing seemed changed. Smoked sausages and rings of braunschweiger hung on hooks all around the kitchen, a wheel of cheese and dark pumpernickel loaves in a basket sat out on the long table, and jugs of home-made wine and corked half-gallon bottles of home-brew stood in rows along the walls.

'We've got a new stove,' Bud said. 'Look at that sucker. Burns anything you throw in it and I've got it piped to heat the whole damned house. Opal skips around here naked as a bird some winter mornings and not a goose pimple on her.'

Bud was helping two of his friends instal a new heating plant in a church in Thomaston where the boiler had blown up one Sunday only twenty minutes after the morning service was over. So he was gone every work-day. When he got home, red-faced and blowing on his hands, they drank home-brew and carrot wine, ate cabbage and sausage and apple cobbler with heavy cream on it and listened to Amos and Andy and Guy Lombardo on their new Atwater-Kent radio.

During the day however, Helen and Opal were by themselves sitting in the kitchen or working together, making special dishes for supper.

It reminded Helen of the Bardoni kitchens in New York or her mother's kitchen on Staten Island. Also, the long morning hours at the table, talking and drinking coffee, brought back those times in the breakfast room with Clara. Safe and closed-in and warm, snow piled on the window-sills, the wind crying as it struggled to turn the corners of the house, and the orange cat, its fur matching Opal's hair almost perfectly, sleeping on the rag rug behind the stove.

There was no atmosphere of the confessional about their talks. No long autobiographical revelations. They simply dealt with whatever subjects came up. Little by little, however, they told each other a great deal about them-selves. Helen learned, for example, that Opal had spent all of her thirty years in this immediate vicinity.

'I've been to Portland a few times, and Brunswick. I studied beauty parlour work over there for a few months after I quit high school, but I never really got started at it. I hated Brunswick. Too far away from home for me. Bud and I are both stay-at-homes. He was born here in Hedrick, just north of town, actually, on the road to Waldoboro, and I was born down Pemaquid way, below Pumpkin Cove, almost down to the point. We played around the lighthouse there every day practically when I was a little snot. I could see that light blinking every night before I went to sleep. And hear the horns bawlin' like a pasture full of cows when the fog was in. Bud's travelled around some, with his work and the army and all, but he's got his can full of it now. He's like me. Don't want to go any place more than a few hours drive from this kitchen.'

Gradually, without having planned what she would say, feeling as warm and solid in that brick-walled, plank-floored kitchen as if it were her own, Helen, too, told how things had been for her, where she'd been, who she'd seen and known, what she'd done.

She told about her childhood in Fort Beck and New York. As she talked about her mother and father, some things about them came clear to her, not clearer than before, but clear in a different way. Her childhood and young womanhood presented itself to her now as a series of facts

472

and she told it that way. Low-key and dispassionate, conversation in the kitchen. And she talked a great deal about Jesse.

'I don't know how I felt about him. I'm not sure how I feel about him now. I guess he's just somebody permanent in my life and it doesn't really matter how I *feel* – *now* or five years ago or ten years from now. I read someplace that anybody who has the power to hurt you, to *really* hurt you, to hurt your feelings, I mean, is somebody you're probably never going to get away from, not completely. Even if you don't see them they'll still be there, loafing around inside your head, making you miserable sometimes.'

She hesitated about the Wingate Fields part of her life, thought twice about telling that whole story. But she found, as they talked day after day, that she couldn't leave it out and didn't want to leave it out. What she did avoid was the money and the splendour and the luxury. The Bradshaws became simply an English family living on a big farm, raising sheep.

'We've got some of those sheep farms out west of here,' Opal said. 'Russian people mostly. A whole colony of farmers whose ancestors came from over there. Settled right in the centre of the state. Inbred, a lot of them, my dad used to say – he travelled through there selling tools and fence wire – clannish people. Sticking with their own kind, marrying into their own families as often as not. Some strange-looking kids stumbling around, wall-eyed and simple-minded. It's sad.'

Helen never questioned that when they reached, in their conversations, the time when she had come to Maine before, she would tell Opal the truth. She had no impulse now to hold back. She was almost relieved, in fact, to tell someone, some isolated and sympathetic person who knew no one else in Helen's life, knew nothing about the child, about what she had done, how she had felt about it at the time, and how she felt now.

When she finally told Opal, however, she didn't tell her about Hugh. She did not identify *him*, either by name

473

or by relationship, as the father of her child. Something prevented her, still, from including *that* part of the truth. So she made up a story; she had made it up, in fact, long before, but had never told it. Not till now.

'He was a young man, just a boy, really. I met him on the ship coming from Liverpool to New York. He was my age or close to it and he was travelling with his father. I was upset about everything that had happened in England, sad and confused, angry at Jesse, not sure how I felt about myself or about anything else. So it was pleasant to meet such a nice young man. I could tell he liked me. Very sweet and kind he was. So we spent our days on the ship together, took long walks on the deck and played bridge and shuffleboard. And after dinner every evening we danced and drank champagne. It was all very festive and carefree, the way things can be on a ship. But then, one night, we were three days away from New York, we drank a lot of champagne and he was holding me very tight when we danced, and when he took me back to my stateroom I let him come in and . . . you know . . . things got out of hand. Maybe I *wanted* them to. Or maybe I just didn't care, but anyway, it happened. I wasn't sorry but all the same I didn't want it to go on so I stayed away from him for the rest of the trip. I mean I knew it was just something that . . . how can I say it . . . we didn't really know each other and there was not much chance that we would even see each other after the ship docked. He lived in Seattle and was going to start college there as soon as he got home. So . . . anyway, when I found out I was going to have a baby there was no question of my getting in touch with him. It never even occurred to me. I knew I'd have to figure things out for myself and that's what I did. That's when I came to Portland and then up here to this area.'

Her story was not totally untrue. There had been a young man on the ship. He had been from Seattle and he had been travelling with his father, but aside from those facts, the story she told Opal was a fabrication.

After Opal drove her to Portland to see Kilwinning,

474

Helen told her what she had found out. 'I feel wonderful now,' she said. 'At least I know *something*.'

Three days later, she left Maine. 'Just remember, we've always got a place for you,' Opal said as she put her on the train in Portland. 'You've never been up here in the summer. That's the prettiest time. Once the blackflies have gone, middle of June, Hedrick's as nice a place as anybody could find to spend the summer.'

'I'll be back,' Helen said. 'I promise.'

But she hadn't gone back. She had returned to Elkins where she had stayed till May, then back to Fort Beck. And at the end of summer she had married Frank Wilson. Through the next four years she had corresponded sporadically with Opal, writing frequently when she felt good about herself, less frequently during the difficult times. But always the memory of those splendid days she had spent at the Feaster home, those hours in that warm kitchen, had stayed with Helen like a fragrant recipe for contentment.

After Clara's departure to England, as Helen stayed on in New York, not sure just what she might do now or where she might go, she found herself thinking more and more often of Maine, of the Feasters. She spent long afternoons shopping for Christmas gifts for her half-brothers and sisters, Anna's children; she told herself that perhaps she would spend Christmas with the Bardonis. But as the day came near, she had all her gifts delivered by messenger.

On Christmas Day she ate dinner by herself in her hotel room. That evening, however, she called Opal and they talked on the telephone for forty minutes. Two days later Helen was on a train heading north.

This time, Bud and Opal met her at the railway station in Portland. As they headed out of the city on the road that borders the ocean, Opal said, 'We'll have another Christmas dinner now that you're here. And on New Year's Eve we'll have a little party. An army buddy of Bud's is up here now.'

'Crazy Chet,' Bud said.

475

'Chet Comiskey his name is,' Opal said. 'You'll like him. Everybody likes him except his wife.'

3

On January 14, 1934, two days after Jesse's birthday, an occasion he had celebrated at Fouquet's with Valerie and Nora, Valerie asked him, 'Are you vain about your age?'

'Sure, I'm vain about everything.'

'I mean are you trying to keep your age a secret?'

'Why would I do that? I'm practically the same age as you.'

'I'm fourteen,' she said.

'Like I said . . . I'm a little bit younger than you.'

'I asked Nora how old you are and she said I should ask you. So I decided that either she didn't know or she thought you didn't want anybody else to know.'

'Lots of people are sensitive about their age. My dad never told anybody how old he was, not even my mother.'

'That's what I'm talking about. Are you that way?'

'Not at all. I'm thirty-seven. Born January 12, 1897.'

Valerie considered that for a moment, then she said, 'If you'd been born five years earlier, you'd be three times as old as me.'

'That's right.'

She reflected again. 'But when I'm twenty-two you'll be only twice my age.'

'You're brilliant. And if you live to be a hundred we'll be practically the same age.'

'Do you know how old Nora is?'

'I'm not sure. Do you?'

'She's thirty-three. On May tenth she'll be thirty-four.'

'And I'll still be thirty-seven.'

'May I ask you a personal question?' she said. When he smiled she said, 'Did I say something amusing?'

'Only a little bit. I've never heard you ask permission for anything before.'

'Of course you have. I'm well brought up. I'm extremely polite.'

'Not when you're digging for information.'

'Maybe not. But this is particularly personal.'

'Fire away.'

'Do you have any children?'

'Just you,' he said.

'I'm not your child. I'm your sweetheart. I mean real children of your own.'

'Don't you think you'd know about it if I did?'

'Not necessarily. You were twenty-three years old when I was born. You could have had ten or twelve children by then.'

'How do you figure that?'

'That's what the books say.'

'What books?'

'Biology books, hygiene books. They say that a male human is fertile from age twelve. Some of them younger than that.'

'In that case I'm twenty-five years behind because I don't have any children.'

'You could have some without knowing about it.'

'Is that what the books say?'

'No. That's what Nora says. We've had quite a few talks about these things. My father's tried to tell me some things too. But he doesn't know half as much as Nora does.'

'You have a very smart mother.' He smiled. 'To answer your question . . . I don't think it's likely that I have children I don't know about.'

'But if you didn't know about them . . .'

'I knew you'd say that. But all the same, it's unlikely.'

'Wouldn't you like it?' she said then.

'Wouldn't I like what?'

'To have a bunch of children.'

'Like *you*, you mean?'

'*Nobody's* like me . . . .'

That's true.'

'You said so yourself. Many times.'

'That's right. I did.'

477

After a moment she said, 'You didn't answer.'

'I don't *have* an answer.'

'You don't know if you'd like to have children or not?'

'I guess I would. And maybe I will. But I don't spend a lot of time thinking about it.'

'I know,' she said. 'It's something women think about more than men.'

'Not necessarily. That depends on what man and what woman you're talking about.'

'In general, I mean.'

'Watch out for generalizations. They'll turn on you.'

'That's what you always say.' Then, 'Do you think you and Nora will ever have a baby?'

'We can't. We're not married.'

'Don't be a boob, Jesse. I'm not three years old. You two could get married tomorrow if you wanted to. And even if you *didn't* want to, you could still have children. Do you know the worldwide statistics about children born out of wedlock?'

'No. But I'll bet you do.'

She nodded. 'They're extraordinary. And becoming more extraordinary every year. The war started it, they say. At least in France and England. Lots of war babies. So people got used to the idea. Girls in my school ask me all the time if my parents were married.'

'What do you say?'

'Different things. Depends on what sort of mood I'm in. I don't see anything wrong with being a bastard. It's not like having a terrible mole or a wart on your forehead. I mean it doesn't *show*, being a bastard. History's filled with illustrious people who just incidentally happened to be bastards.'

'Did you ever discuss this with your mother?'

'Which part?'

'Did you ask her if she expects to have more children?'

'Sure. Lots of times,' Valerie said.

'What did she say?'

'Don't you know?'

'I could probably guess. I think she said no.'

'That's right.'

'Did she give you a reason?'

'She says she doesn't want to spoil her record. Having had one perfect child she doesn't want to settle for something less.'

'She might do even better the second time.'

'That's what *I* told her,' Valerie said, 'but she says no. Personally, I think she has other reasons but she never says what they are. It seems to me that if she could have a baby with you she'd be crazy not to do it.'

'Thank you.'

'I'm serious. You'd be a terrific father. You *are* a terrific father to me.'

'I'm not your father. I'm your sweetheart.'

'You know what I mean,' she said. 'And I'm not saying anything against Edmund. He's very handsome. Like a picture in a book. And he's ever so nice to me. But he's not the most stimulating man in the world. He says so himself. I mean he's not as smart as you are, for instance. And he's not cuddly like you. You know what I'm saying?'

'No.'

'I'm saying that I think Nora is crazy if she doesn't have some children with you before she's too old.'

Later that night, as Jesse and Nora sat in her bedroom talking, as they did every night, and having a cognac, he said, 'Valerie gave me a long lecture today. She thinks you and I should start having kids.'

'I know. I've heard all that. She's learned all about the process from books. Now she wants to see it put into practice. I think she sees us as a pair of laboratory guinea pigs.'

'Well, you know what they say.'

'No. What do they say?'

'Educators, I'm talking about. They say that curiosity is the wellspring of intelligence. Very important for parents not to stifle a child's curiosity.'

'I see,' Nora said.

'All the questions must be answered, even the difficult ones.'

'What are you saying?'

'Nothing personal. Just citing some informed opinions.'

Nora leaned over and kissed him. 'Are you saying that you and I should have a baby as a favour to Valerie?'

'Not as a favour exactly.'

'How would you describe it then?'

'Seems like a small thing to do to satisfy a daughter's curiosity. Perhaps we owe it to her.'

Nora gave him a long slow look. 'Let me think about it,' she said. Then, 'I just thought about it.'

'And . . . ?'

'I think not.'

'Whatever you say. But your daughter's going to be disappointed.'

'She'll get over it. She might even be pleased. I think she really has you picked out for herself.'

'I hope so,' Jesse said.

'She's lucky. Most girls her age have frantic crushes on their fathers. But Valerie not only has beautiful Edmund, she has you . . . a scrumptious live-in man who sleeps with her mother. Very romantic. I'm sure it keeps her awake at night.'

'Poor thing. Have you told her that men like me are hard to find?'

'*Easy* to find, I told her. Hard to get rid of.'

'There must be an answer to that,' Jesse said. 'There's an answer for everything.'

'There's *no* answer for *us*. We're stuck with each other. But Valerie's answer we'll see any time now. She'll come home with some untidy French boy, one with bad skin most likely and smelling as if he wants a good wash. And that evening at dinner she will announce that she's in love. From that moment, *you* will be used merchandise. A tiresome uncle. An older person. She won't be interested in whether or not you and I have a child. Her main concern will be how she can avoid having one herself.'

From the time Valerie learned to speak and understand, Nora had always related to her as an adult. She had been witness to adult discussions as well as adult passions and

480

frustrations. When she was old enough she had been told the reasons for her parents' separation. And Nora had never attempted to conceal the nature of her relationship with Jesse. Valerie knew, had always known, that they were not married, that they had no plans to marry, that they simply lived together as man and wife and seemed to enjoy it.

Valerie was delighted with the arrangement; when she was old enough to see that her school friends lived in circumstances that were quite different from hers she was particularly delighted. She loved being an intimate partner in something that was uncommon. If it scandalized certain people so much the better. She was, in many respects, Nora's child but there was also a direct genetic gift from Clara. Along with her mother's passion for taking flight and soaring she had a foundation of good sense that had skipped one generation and had come to her direct from her grandmother.

She was particularly obsessed with telling the truth. As a small child it had been instinctive with her. As she grew older it became a programme. She explained it in detail to Jesse one afternoon when she was nine years old. 'It doesn't make me angry when people play games with the facts. I know that most people can't say three sentences without telling a lie. Nora says it's a social necessity and maybe she's right. But I think it's foolishness. It's too time-consuming for one thing. Who can remember on Thursday all the lies they told at the weekend? If nothing else, telling the truth is a stabilizer and my tutor, Mr Plante, says people need all the stability they can get. It's like keeping your room neat. It makes it easier to find things.'

Her mother, however, took no pride in Valerie's relentless honesty. 'My God, one thing I don't need is for someone to tell me the *truth* about myself. I already know *that*. My main purpose in life is to *conceal* certain truths. I think it's true of everybody. I like things to be attractive and comfy and sweet-tasting. I never remind people of their shortcomings just for the sake of being truthful and I certainly don't welcome an excess of candour in their

481

remarks about me. So how did I end up with a daughter who tells me exactly how I look at any particular moment, where the flaws are in both my personality and my wardrobe, and what she feels I should do to give my life real meaning? And *that's* if I don't ask her a direct question. When I'm foolish enough to do *that*, she really lets me have it.'

Nora exaggerated, of course, in speaking of Valerie, as she did in most things. The fact was that her daughter, although she seemed bent on presenting the facts as she knew them, was slow to volunteer information. She did not gossip or betray confidences. Like many children whose parents live apart she had learned that in broken marriages there are at least *two* truths and often many more. She discovered very quickly that a man cannot be enlightened about his former wife just as that wife is permanently deaf to explanations of her ex-husband's virtues.

So whatever her convictions about candour, Valerie, in relation to her parents, had learned to substitute silence for truth. Only when she was pressed, as she was very often by Edmund, did she tell him things she thought he was eager to know but which when revealed left him less satisfied than he had expected. When he said to her, 'I think if I were you I would prefer living here at Bick House to life in a crowded and dirty city like Paris,' she said, 'But I love Paris. It's exciting. And after a time one doesn't notice the dirt.'

'You'll be the mistress of Bick House one day,' he told her. 'All these rooms and all these lands. You'll see then what a pleasure it is to live in a great house with a fine staff to take care of you and look after things.'

'We have only four servants in Paris. And we manage quite well. I shouldn't like it if I had *nothing* to do. My governess told me that a true lady never asks her maid to do anything she's not able to do herself.'

When Edmund said, 'I suppose your mother is happy there in Paris. She was always fond of parties and balls and cabarets,' Valerie replied, 'She's very happy. But we don't entertain a lot. And she's not out as many evenings as you might imagine. She works very hard as publisher of her magazine. Oftentimes when Jesse and I go out for a walk after dinner or to see a motion picture, Nora stays at home and works in her study.'

When her mother inquired about Edmund, which she did very seldom, Valerie said, 'I think his life is probably not much different from how it was when you were there.'

'That's a pity. I would hope it had improved. If I had stayed at Bick House I would have been confined long since in a home for the deranged.'

'But he likes it there. I suppose it's his favourite place in the world.'

'Do you think he's happy then?'

'I can't be sure of that,' Valerie said.

'I'm surprised he hasn't married again. It's more than ten years . . . .'

'I don't think he'll ever marry again.'

'Of course he will. He's still a young man.'

'You didn't let me finish,' Valerie said.

'I'm sorry.'

'I don't think he'll marry as long as *you're* not married.'

'Did he say that?'

'No. It's just something I believe.'

'But why in the world would what *I* do affect what *he* does? There's never been any chance that he and I would get together again. It makes no sense . . . .'

'I didn't say it made sense. But I think you'll see that he won't marry until you do. And if you *don't*, I believe he won't.'

'How odd. That seems dreadfully odd to me.'

'I don't think it's odd at all,' Valerie said.

With Jesse, of course, Valerie was able to be as free as she wished. With her wishes, her fantasies, her words, her judgments, her secrets. They related to each other with total trust. From the time when she was four or five years old Jesse had managed that most difficult feat of all in adult-child relationships. He had simply treated her like a grown-up and an equal. Consequently, when she was fourteen they connected as simply and honestly as they had when she was four. When she behaved like a fool, he said, 'You're an ass, Valerie. You are behaving like a consummate ass.' When she began painting herself with make-up at the age of thirteen, he said, 'You're a good-looking kid. Why don't you let yourself alone?'

'I think I look great.'

'You do. You look like a baby-faced *poule* outside the Gare de l'Est. If that's what you're shooting for, you made it.'

'You're bourgeois, Jesse. You're starting to sound like someone's father. Like a man who operates a shop in the rue de Rennes.'

'All right. Let me put it this way. If I were looking for a girl outside the Gare de l'Est and I met you under a strong light, I wouldn't take you.'

'Why not?'

'Because you look like a ten-year-old who got into her mother's make-up pots.'

'*Ten-year-old?*'

'That's it, Coco.'

'You're saying I shouldn't wear *any* make-up. Is that it?'

'No. I'm saying you should do what you want to. Just don't expect me to tell you you look great.'

Jesse seldom gave her advice, seldom counselled her, and never tried to serve as a conduit between her and her mother, never, in short, attempted to function as a parent, as an uncle, or as a figure of authority. When she asked a serious question, however, he answered it. When she made sense he told her so. When she didn't, he told her that. But nothing between them was ever made to seem final or profound. One could be a fool or a failure and suffer no consequences. Tomorrow would come no matter what. And tomorrow he would be there and so would she. It was a relationship without rules or definition but it brought each of them great joy. Only Jesse at last came to be disturbed by it. It reminded him of Helen.

4

In the summer of 1934, when Hugh Causey drove down from Sutherland to meet his mother in Edinburgh, it was four years since they had seen each other. When he came to her hotel suite she put her arms around him and said, 'I have to be here for five days. Can *you* stay two or three days at least?'

'As long as you want me,' he said. 'I'm your captive.'

She had a series of meetings arranged with bankers and land brokers and Hugh accompanied her to all of them. And when she was free they went to the zoo and to art galleries and had long, sumptuous meals together. 'This is how I used to hope it would be,' she said one afternoon. 'I thought you'd be involved with the family business. I thought you'd stay on at Wingate Fields or settle nearby and we'd see a lot of you.'

'I'm not a businessman, Mum. I have no head for it. And no stomach either. The genes didn't travel.'

'You don't miss us then?'

'Of course I do. All the time. It's my nature to detest what I have and to long for what I once had.'

She smiled. 'You're not telling me you dislike your home in Sutherland, are you? You never leave there.'

'I know I don't. But that doesn't mean I don't detest it. If I came back to Wingate Fields I would certainly detest being there and long to be back in Sutherland.'

'I think you're teasing me.'

'No, I'm not. It's the precise truth I'm telling you.'

'But you love your game forest, you love to shoot and fish and you love . . . .'

'I haven't taken a stag or a boar in more than three years and I can't remember the last time I hooked a salmon in the Oykel. I rarely go outside. See how pale I am. Mostly I play cards with my man and drink wine in my study and look out of the window at the gardens.'

'Are you so unhappy?'

'I'm not unhappy at all. I wasn't trying to tell you my

485

state of mind. I was simply saying what I *do*. I sleep late every morning and stumble through the day somehow. Then I dress for dinner, clean myself up, splash on the bay rum, and dine like a prince.'

'That's nice,' Clara said. 'It's a fine habit. Most men who live in the country let themselves go to seed a bit.'

'Oh, I've gone to seed all right. The brain has practically ceased to function. But I do dress for dinner. Perhaps that's why I do it, because I know very definitely that I have gone to seed.'

'You certainly don't look that way to me. You're quite elegant. I'm proud to be seen with you.'

'What a kind lady you are. My father is a fortunate man.'

'I don't think he shares that view.'

Hugh sipped from his brandy glass and smiled. 'He'd better or I'll have him whipped.'

'Let's get back to you,' Clara said. 'I'm sure your wife appreciates the fact that you dress for dinner.'

'I'm not sure she notices. I suspect I could come to table in a dog suit and she would be totally unruffled.'

'I doubt that. When a woman has gone to the trouble of carefully dressing herself . . . .'

'Ah, but she doesn't,' Hugh said. 'She complains of the damp, you see. Suffers quite a lot from the cold. Shivers in the garden even in midsummer. Has catarrh all year round. Her nose is usually red and swollen a bit. It's like a water-sprinkler from one season to the next.'

'What a pity.'

'Yes. She is truly pitiful. But to answer your question, she does not dress any differently for the evening meal from how she does at breakfast. Lots of warm skirts and petticoats and sweaters and shawls. Sometimes only her eyes are visible. She looks very much like a cart of used clothing being trundled into Shepherd's Market.'

His mother laughed. 'You haven't changed a bit, have you? You're as dreadful as ever.'

'Of course I've changed. I am now wistful and rueful and wry. A jester in tears.'

486

'Her children must adore you. Do you make them laugh?'

'I make them miserable,' he said. 'They think I'm wretched and I think the same of them. They were angry and resentful when their mother tore them away from filthy Glasgow and brought them to Sutherland and they remain angry and resentful to this moment. They live in my home like captives and they think of me as their captor. If they were either resourceful or courageous I'm sure they would have done away with me long since.'

After a moment, Clara said, 'Am I supposed to take you seriously?'

'Of course not. I am telling you the wretched truth but it is not to be taken seriously. I certainly don't take it seriously. I don't think about my situation at all. I mean I spend no time striving for contentment. Only a cow is totally contented. I never expected to be happy and I'm not. So I'm a perfectly fulfilled man. My expectations and my achievements match perfectly. My father, your husband, our Ned Causey, always talked endlessly about the importance of happiness and look at him.'

'Why did you happen to mention him?'

'It wasn't part of a plan. He just popped into my head and I served him up. Did I say something wrong?'

'No, I just thought . . . have you heard from him lately?'

'He writes quite often,' Hugh said, 'but there's never any information in his letters, only platitudes.'

'Does he write about me?'

'He only refers to your health. His diagnosis is that you are fine.'

Clara studied him carefully. Then, 'I'm asking these questions because . . . one reason I wanted to see you . . . I mean there are some matters concerning your father that I thought we should discuss.'

'I hope you don't want my advice. Whenever I give someone advice I always advise them not to take it.'

'Are you drunk, my dear?'

'Only a little. Later in the day I promise to do better.'

'I've never seen you the way you are now.'

'How do you mean?'

'I can't put a name to it. If I took you seriously . . . .'

'You mustn't do that.'

'I know. But I do all the same. If I listened to you carefully and observed you closely and took very seriously what I heard and saw, I would be extremely upset. Either you have given up caring about your life and yourself altogether or you have chosen for some reason to give me that impression.'

Hugh looked at her, calmly and almost sweetly, with no message in his eyes, but he did not answer. At last she went on. 'I talked to Nora about this the last time I saw her and I thought this trip would be a good opportunity to talk to you. I feel as awkward now as I did when I spoke to your sister. I asked her not to write to you. I thought it was something you and I should discuss face to face. Will you ask the waiter to bring us more coffee?'

She seemed to welcome the short silence while their coffee was being served; it seemed to help her in coming to the starting marks. As soon as the waiter left, she asked, 'Would you be frightfully upset if I told you that it's very likely your father and I will separate?' Before he could reply she said, 'Please don't give me a flip answer. Don't tell me that nothing in the world surprises or upsets you. I want a considered reaction. And an honest one. Anything else is of no value to me.'

After a long moment he said, 'If I thought it was something that would upset *you*, then it would upset me.'

'Ned will be sixty-two next month and I will be fifty-nine. I remember when we first knew each other, we thought that was a great signpost for happiness, that we were born in the same month.'

She paused. 'I know that many young people are shocked and embarrassed to find that their parents still have an emotional relationship long after their children are grown and married and have children of their own. And I confess I am shocked myself when people who have lived together for forty years suddenly discover they're incompatible.'

'I'm not embarrassed, Mum. I won't be embarrassed whatever you do. And not shocked either.'

'There's no war going on between Ned and me. Nothing like that. Perhaps it would be better if there were. It's more like a battle that has not begun and may never begin but which keeps everything and everybody else waiting. There's a vacuum waiting to be filled and when Ned and I decide to fill it, *if* we do, it will mean that we won't be together any longer.'

'Are you together now?' Hugh asked.

'Good question. No, we're not. Not really. And we haven't been for a long time.'

'So if you separate, it's merely a formality.'

'No, it's more than that. There are all kinds of alternatives in people's minds till someone says the final words. *That's* the difficult moment. Closing the door and locking it. Not least of all, it's an admission of failure and that never comes easy.'

'Are you angry with each other?'

'No. He's angry with himself and he has been for a long time. And he's angry with me, I suppose, for being a witness to all his years of floundering and frustration. Ned suffers from a disease that can't be cured. He thinks the world has ignored him. And maybe it has. But it ignores most of us. His problem is he can't *see* that. Or *if* he sees it, he won't accept it. He doesn't know that a marriage ages just like a person ages. It's all a process of gradual loss. You lose things that were once of great value. If you can replace them with *other* things then you keep moving ahead. But if you tell yourself you've been left with nothing, then that's exactly what you *will* be left with. One spring you look out at the garden and the bulbs haven't come up. You can either close the shutters and weep or you can go outside and plant new flowers. But you can't do nothing. Life won't permit that.'

The following evening, as they sat at dinner in their hotel dining-room, Clara said, 'We Causeys have made a bad record, haven't we? Nora's marriage came to a sad end, your father and I are on the verge of giving up whatever

489

it is we have left, and if I can penetrate that cloud of sarcasm and cynicism you surround yourself with, it seems that you're no better off.'

'We're an odd lot, all right.'

'At least Jesse and Nora seemed to have worked out some sort of arrangement that makes sense. It disturbs your grandfather, I think, but he keeps hands off as he should. If I'm to trust what I see, and if I listen to Valerie's judgments, which are many and detailed, those two have found that marriage isn't necessary. They seem to *feel* married, so they are. They are certainly committed to each other. And that, I suppose, is what it's all about. With your sister, however, I'm never sure. She's like a drop of mercury on a moving surface, apt to be anywhere at any given second. Most of us try to learn something about life as we go along. Nora seems to be inventing it for herself, cutting it to her own dimensions. But perhaps I'm wrong about that. She was admirably calm and domestic the last time I visited them in Paris. They'd just bought a splendid old house on the Ile St Louis and she had great crews of workmen refurbishing that. I expect they'll be moved in by now.

'Angus was furious when I told him about the house. He says it's a stupid time to buy property in France, what with all the foolishness that's going on in Germany. You know how angry he gets about Churchill but he thinks the man is right when he calls Germany a threat to peace. He also says the alliance between Hitler and Mussolini is a nasty development.'

'I don't think about things like that.'

Their last morning together, Hugh said, 'You haven't mentioned Helen at all. I thought you'd bring her up when you were listing the marital mishaps of the Causeys and the Bradshaws. Didn't you say in one of your letters that she was divorced?'

'Yes, I'm sure I did. And I must have told you that I saw her in New York two years ago.'

'You said you'd seen her but you gave no details.'

'That's because there weren't a great many details to

490

report. As I recall I did most of the talking. She told me a bit about her marriage and the break-up but it all seemed quite misty to me. Perhaps it was like that to her.'

'Did she look well?'

'She looked lovely, I thought. Very little changed from when she was here. But she was only eighteen then so, of course, she's a proper young woman now. But truly lovely and a joy to be with. We had such a good time together in New York, I hated to leave her there. Pleaded with her to come to England with me and she said she'd come as soon as possible. But no mention of it since. She's a true Bradshaw, I suppose. A lot below the surface that doesn't get seen. How old is she now? She must be thirty-three. I can't believe it. The years fly past. When I met Helen the first time I was a child in my early forties. I've often wished she'd stayed on at Wingate Fields when she was there that summer. I have a feeling she would have had a better life. More direction to it. More foundation. It seems she's done a lot of drifting since she went back. Not sure where she wants to be or what she wants to do. She still goes back to Fort Beck, of course, where she lived with Raymond. And she seems to have friends in Maine. Her last few letters have come from there. She mentioned a man she'd met, I think his name was Comiskey. I don't know if that means . . . I don't know what it means. But maybe she's thinking about getting married again. If she does we'll all fly to America and celebrate with her. How does that sound?'

'I think she can get married without me. I'll stay in Sutherland and celebrate there.'

When Hugh drove her to the railway station, Clara said, 'I hope you won't forget what I said when I first saw you the other day. I wish you could come home to Wingate. I need you. I really do. Poor Angus thinks he'll live to be a hundred but he won't. And as I told you I don't see Ned sometimes for weeks at a time. I know you say you're not a businessman but you've got a good head. And now that Jesse's seldom there, I can see a day very soon when all the decisions will be mine.'

'I'm a married man, Mum. I can't pack up that whole

491

brood and ship them down to Wingate. You wouldn't want them there even if I could.'

'From the way you were talking the other day, I thought . . . .'

'That I might like to just pack up and leave by myself? That's right. That's exactly what I'd like to do. But I'm not going to do it. You raised me like a proper gentleman. I made a bargain. Now I think I'd best stick with it.'

'I admire your sense of honour but I think you're dotty.'

'How so?'

'You have a long life ahead of you. You can do anything you want.'

'You've hit the key point right there, my darling, there's nothing at all I *want* to do. I certainly *don't* want to help count the Bradshaw money. I wouldn't be good at it. I don't even care about shooting and fishing any longer. Apart from drinking a bit and an occasional burst of witty conversation, I'm useless and happy to be. So in spite of my descriptions of my current home situation, in spite of the face of my dreary and untidy wife and her repellent squad of youngsters, they perform a service for me. They distract me. They provide a certain amount of commotion and a hateful level of noise about the place. If nothing else they give me a reason to go into the library and lock the door behind me. I have some fine books in that room and an inexhaustible supply of claret.'

'You won't be serious, will you?'

'I'm deadly serious, Mum.' He leaned over and kissed her. 'I'm so serious it brings tears to my eyes.'

'You're a bit crazy, that's what you are.'

'Of course. But we've all known that for years.'

5

For all her professed bewilderment about her daughter's impulses, Clara had been remarkably accurate in at least one observation about her. Nora, from childhood, had believed that her own instincts were more reliable, for her purposes and objectives, than the total knowledge and accumulated experience of the centuries. Nothing stimulated her energies and her creativity so keenly as a rule that couldn't be defied or a law that mustn't be broken. A state of total independence seemed to be her prime objective. And defiance was the carriage that would take her there.

This is not to say that she was argumentative or socially militant. She was not. As we have seen she was acutely aware of the subtle politics of power. She sensed that some battles must be lost. Or at least one must appear to have lost them. As a young girl she had concluded that in any circumstance she could envision she would need a man as an ally, a man who could be charmed, persuaded, manipulated, and at last, controlled, so that *her* objectives would become his objectives.

Her instinct told her, also, that as her objectives changed, new allies would be needed until at last she would reach a point where she would be able to rely totally on her own skills and her own resources. She theorized that once a person became flagrantly free and capable and magnificently independent, when there was no need to call on anyone else for help or instruction or guidance, then all things would be freely offered.

'It's human nature,' she explained to Hugh when she was thirteen years old. 'To give most freely to those who have no need. Anyone will lend money to a wealthy man. Fat people get plenty of dinner invitations. The finest dress designers are delighted to give away their gowns to ladies with splendid wardrobes. And a woman who is surrounded by men will soon find that she is surrounded by many *more* men.'

Sensing her own needs at an early age, Nora had practised on her father and Angus and Hugh. Her experience with them convinced her that her theories were correct. A clever and dispassionate woman with clear objectives and reasonable patience could go wherever she chose and *be* whatever she chose. It helped, of course, if one was

493

beautiful but that was not a requirement. Vitality could be substituted for beauty and the same ends could be achieved. 'Energy is more important,' she told herself, 'than large eyes or pretty skin.' Such conclusions were easy for her, of course, because she knew that she had both beauty *and* vitality. Indeed no listing of her own attributes, however self-critical she pretended to be, ever lessened her self-esteem.

This very confidence however, this feeling that she was predestined to be whatever she chose to be, this almost fanatic passion for far horizons, this conviction that no person or event could slow her or block her, this element that she thought of as her principal strength, had turned against her twice. First when she discovered that Jesse was capable of making independent judgments which might have no relation at all to her desires, and second, when she realized that her marriage to Edmund was destined to be something altogether different from what she had planned and imagined. In the first instance she had patched herself back together by abandoning Jesse and marrying Edmund. In the second instance she had divorced Edmund, put Northumberland behind her, and moved to France.

Valuable time had been lost, however, and damage had been done to her sense of self. She had hoped that the mere fact of life in Paris would perform a miracle cure but it had not. Circumstances had demonstrated her fallibility and those memories stayed with her.

After leaving England, as she busied herself with her new life in Paris, as she celebrated each day the fact of a ménage that was hers and only hers, as she marched strongly forward to a cadence that she alone had chosen, she told herself repeatedly that this was what she had always longed for. This rhythm, this autonomy, this sense of waking each morning and knowing that every hour was hers to dispose of as she saw fit. But for all this emotional house-cleaning, for all her efforts to sweep away the memories of previous situations that had restricted her, cobwebs of doubt remained.

494

If nothing else, she longed for conflict. She sensed that she had nothing to rebel against now except herself and her own choices. As she gorged herself with freedom and independence from a menu of infinite variety she found that the seasoning was not always to her taste. She made trips to Italy and Switzerland and Holland and Denmark, sometimes with Valerie, sometimes alone, sometimes with a carefully-chosen man. She hired new decorators, engaged a new cook, bought new cars and changed her hair-style half a dozen times. She moved from one social circle to another, then to still another, and back at last to the first. She entertained with style and splendour and impressed everyone who met her as a young woman of wit and intelligence. And her beauty, of course, was a fact that no one questioned; even the women who envied her and gossiped about her made no effort to deny her beauty.

So Nora had, indeed, all she had longed for since child-hood. And it was permanent. She would have it, she knew, for as long as she lived. But all the same, the thrill of battle was gone. All her dragons had been slain, all prizes seized, all lands claimed. Perched on the rim of the horizon she had sought for so long she could only look back. And looking back she saw Jesse.

Jesse's return gave her an armature she had missed since coming to France. Not just the presence of a man, not that at all. Nora rejected any notion that a man was required to complete her life. 'I love men,' she had said once to Hugh. 'I think they're grand and silly and sexually indispensable. I also love elephants. But I don't need to own one. I've never met a woman who really enjoyed having a man underfoot all the time.'

She was stimulated, also, by the fact that Jesse's return to her was gradual. At the beginning, as we have seen, he came to Paris on a very irregular schedule, and when he did come, stayed sometimes for only a few days. Although Nora told herself that such a rhythm was perfect, she soon found herself, in small ways that surprised even her, contriving to make his visits more frequent and more lengthy. When he was there she discovered, usually, that

495

there were events some weeks hence which had to be called to his attention. 'You probably won't be here, but if you are, a fine Fauve show is opening at the Grand Palais.'

When she sold her first apartment in the Boulevard de la Grande Armée and bought a much larger one in Passy, there was no suggestion that Jesse should abandon his usual practice of staying at a small hotel nearby. But some weeks later she said to him, 'My decorators are at a loss. There's a great barn of a room in my new place that seems to have no function whatsoever. If you like I'll have it made into an office for you, a place where you can work when you're here in Paris.'

Jesse said, 'Yes, of course. That would be nice.' He almost always said yes to Nora. He knew her well by now. He knew it was important to her to be in charge. Or at least to appear to be in charge. He knew, long before she admitted it to herself, that she wanted him to stay in Paris, that she wanted them to live together. He also knew that she was unable to approach the subject directly. Nor would she have been able simply to agree if such a suggestion had come from him. So he watched her back and fill and crab-walk her way slowly to the place she wanted to reach.

It was not until the birth of *Icarus*, however, that Nora felt all the pieces were in place. She had achieved, at last, what she could never admit to herself she wanted. One man, and only one man, in her house, in her arms, in her bed, in her life. Having fled from an engagement, having fled from a marriage, she was now, more than ever, *married*, not by law nor in the eyes of the church, not even in the eyes of her family or her friends or her servants or her daughter. But in her own mind she knew that the wild creature inside her who had longed always for freedom, had prized it above all other things, had now given it up. And she felt very good about it, very fine indeed.

None of these feelings were expressed, of course, between her and Jesse. It was as though they had formed a pact not to label or define whatever it was they shared. Having begun their relationship long ago with a formal engagement and an elaborate announcement of their pending marriage, they now resisted any impulse, whether it came from them or from their friends, to explain the nature of their present lives or to project what it might become in future. Nora pretended to believe that Jesse would never marry and Jesse pretended to believe that Nora had no desire to marry again. 'Why should they get married?' their friends said. 'Why spoil a perfectly good liaison? They're having a jolly time.'

This is not to say that their arrangement was in any way a matter-of-fact, coolly-managed affair. It was not. It lacked neither tenderness nor passion. 'Why can't I get enough of you?' he often asked her. And just as often she replied, 'It's just the other way round, *mon vieux*. You are the hors d'oeuvres trolley. *I* am the glutton.'

With no pressures from without, and none, it seemed, from within, it was not surprising perhaps, that they felt no need to discuss a future together. There was no reason to imagine that their future would be anything other than an extension of the present.

Even Nora, who was as quick as a ferret to see a shadow on a stone or to sense some movement in the grass, could not find anything to make her unquiet. Their lives together had been carefully mortised, piece by interlocking piece, and tested day by day for more than ten years. Although they did not talk about themselves they talked about everything else. They held no private views, concealed no secrets. They were bound together by a great and growing body of experience and opinion and common exposure. They shared the Bradshaws, they shared their work, and they shared Valerie.

On her thirty-fifth birthday, the morning of May 10, 1935, Nora felt more elegantly in possession of herself than she had when she was twenty-five. Standing naked in front of her bathroom mirror, studying herself closely for flaws and failures of the flesh, she could see none. 'You're doing all right, Miss Nora, my dear. Everything properly in place and functioning smoothly. And always something to look forward to. Every day a challenge and a pleasure and every night a joy. You have everything you've ever wanted and a lovely daughter as well. And you have Jesse. What a fine surprise. Odd, unpredictable, irreplaceable Jesse. What more could you want?'

There truly was nothing more she wanted. And surely Jesse was as contented as she was. When he told her about his conversation with Valerie, when he reported that her daughter was most anxious, it seemed, to have a baby sister or brother, they laughed about it. Each time it came up, they laughed together about it. But it kept coming up. And one day Jesse said, 'Maybe it wouldn't be such a bad notion after all. We could even get married. It probably wouldn't hurt at all.'

Nora caught herself just before she said, 'Too late for that, my dear. I mean the baby part. One of the first things I did when I came to Paris was to spend three days in the hospital in Neuilly. I had decided I would be content with just one child. And since I never expected to marry again . . . .'

Just as she hadn't said it then, she didn't say it later. She told herself it wasn't a topic they would be discussing endlessly. But she didn't fully believe that. She told herself that Jesse was thoroughly satisfied with things as they were. But she began to doubt that too.

6

The first evening Helen met Chet Comiskey, as they sat talking in the Feasters' parlour just off the kitchen, he said to her, 'Don't make the mistake of falling in love with me. I'm old enough to be your father for one thing. I was fifty years old this year. I've also got a wife and a daughter floating around someplace in California. And besides that I'm dying. Two years to live. Three or four at the outside. Not a good bet for any woman.'

He spoke without arrogance or cynicism. No sense of performance. They had, in fact, been discussing dogs, what sort made the best pets, and his tone and manner did not change in any way as he switched from that topic to the subject of himself.

Chet was not a tall man, no taller than Helen. His face was lined and weather-beaten, his brown hair was streaked with grey, and his body looked as though it had never enjoyed the luxury of an extra ounce of flesh. The rest of him seemed, in fact, to be a complex extension of his hands. Those hands were all bones and knuckles and angry tendons. Broken nails and thick pads of calluses on palms and fingers. And the grease from a thousand motors had been ground through the surface of the skin to a level no soap could reach. His denim jacket and his chambray shirt, however, and his corduroy trousers, were worn but clean. And the eyes in his hard face were as soft and brown as the eyes of an Irish setter.

'What makes you think I might fall in love with you?' Helen said.

'I don't *think* that. I sure don't expect *anything* like that to happen. I was just laying out the facts. Getting the record straight. The reason it came to my mind was that I was sitting here looking at you and I couldn't help thinking about what a cuckoo pair we make. I mean just the two of us sitting here talking, waiting for supper to be ready. If somebody looked in that window over there, they'd say, "What are those *two* doing together?" '

'Do you think so?'

'No question about it. When you go to the zoo in Cincinnati, you don't expect to see the peacock and the hyena in the same cage.'

'Which one are you?'

He didn't answer for a moment. Then he said, 'I'm the peacock. What do you think?' Then, 'On the other hand, you never know. Once in a while you find a crazy hyena who really goes for peacocks. That's why I was giving you all that other information.' He smiled. 'So you wouldn't get your hopes up. So you wouldn't start thinking I'm something better than what I am.'

When she'd first been introduced to him late that afternoon, Helen felt as though there must be very little to

499

know about this plain and angular man that Opal hadn't already told her. On the drive north from Portland, with additional comments from Bud, Chet Comiskey had been her only subject.

'He and Bud met in an army hospital down in New Jersey. I told you before how Bud got himself racked up in that fire-truck accident. Flat on his back for weeks.'

'Then I was in therapy and rehab for a few months while they tried to decide if they wanted to discharge me or not,' Bud said. 'Chet was there waiting for a discharge, too, so we got to know each other.'

'He'd got himself gassed, poison gas, in some battle in Belgium or France or wherever it was they were fighting that day,' Opal said. 'He got shot too but the gas was the terrible part. They didn't know how bad it was till they got him into a field hospital over there and really went over him.'

'For several weeks he couldn't see,' Bud went on. 'Blind as a bat. Then his hearing went on the blink and he lost his voice. He was a mess. So they shipped him home, sent him from one hospital to another, did some experiments on him, pumped him full of all kinds of chemicals, and little by little he got better. When I met him, they'd decided he was cured and he was just waiting around to get mustered out, same as me. But it didn't work out the way the doctors thought. Chet went back to New Mexico where his wife and little girl was. And he got his job back in the garage where he'd worked before. He's a cracker-jack mechanic. They were tickled to death to have him back. But a year later he was in a military hospital again. And that's the way it's been ever since. In one hospital and out of another one. I guess he's lost count of the times they've opened him up. Last time, a little over a year ago, they took a tumour off his lung. He's had a rough time of it.'

'And that crummy wife of his hasn't made things any better,' Opal said. 'She ran off to California and left him that first time he had to go back in the hospital. Took their daughter and got on the bus there in Lincoln, New Mexico, where they lived, and didn't stop till she hit San Diego.

She had a girl friend there that worked in a canning factory so that's where she settled. Till Chet got out of the hospital. Then she came draggin' back. And that's how it's been ever since. She comes and goes. He's married but he's not. When he needs her, she's gone. Billie, that's his wife's name. I've never seen her, except her picture, but Bud met her a time or two.'

'Chet had told me something about her so I was expecting a flashy number with peroxide hair and spike heels on her shoes. But she doesn't look like that at all. At least she didn't then, that's almost fifteen years ago. She was kind of a mousey little thing. Brown hair and freckles and talking so soft you could hardly hear her. But the way she *looks* ain't no indication at all of the way she *is*. Or so Chet says. And I've got no reason to think he's lying to me. She's got some idea she got short-changed by the world and she's out to get even.'

'And it seems like she's got her daughter thinking the same way she does. She sounds like a real pill.'

'Anyway, it looks like he finally got smart. He says he's gonna settle here in Maine. Build himself a house in the woods, get a good dog, and do some serious hunting. He's got his disability cheque coming in regular and he can work whenever he wants to on car motors or boat engines. These lobstermen up here are always having trouble with their boats. So he'll get along fine, just like we do, and maybe he'll have a little peace for a change.'

'What about his wife and daughter?' Helen asked.

'He finally got his can full, I guess. And high time, too. His daughter's in her twenties now and married to some surveyor in California. And God knows what his wife's up to. I guess Chet got tired waiting for them to show up in New Mexico or to call him in the middle of the night asking him to send money. So he sold everything he had except for his tools and his truck and drove up here. Left no forwarding address, he said.'

The morning after Helen met Chet for the first time, when she and Opal were alone in the kitchen, Opal said, 'What do you think of him?'

501

'You mean Chet?'

'Of course I mean Chet. Who do you think?'

'I like him. He's nice,' Helen said.

'What did you talk about?'

'A little bit of everything. Mostly we talked about dogs.'

'Did he tell you anything about himself?'

'Not much. He just said I shouldn't fall in love with him.'

'You're kidding me,' Opal said.

'No. I'm not. That's what he said.'

'What did *you* say?'

'I didn't say anything.'

'It didn't make you mad, did it?'

'No,' Helen said. 'I thought it was funny.'

'That's good. 'Cause that's the way he is. He's got a funny mouth. Just like Bud. He'll say anything that comes into his head. You'd think with everything he's been through he'd be sour and mean as a snake but he's not. He's not mad at the army. He ain't even mad at his wife. He don't seem to hold a grudge against anybody. Bud says he just wants to live one day at a time, get drunk once in a while, and have some fun.'

'He told me he was dying. Is that the truth?'

'Well, I don't know,' Opal said. 'I guess he'll die sometime. Everybody does.'

'He said he'll be dead in two or three years. That's why he said I shouldn't fall in love with him. Did he tell you that?'

Opal didn't answer for a moment. Then she said, 'Yes, he did. He told me and Bud. But I didn't think he'd tell you.'

'Why not?'

'Because he doesn't talk to most people about himself. Anything private, I mean. He gets mad as hell when somebody feels sorry for him. So he's got so he don't tell anybody anything.'

'Well . . . he told me.'

'I'm sorry,' Opal said.

'I'm not. I'm glad he told me.'

502

'Just don't let him catch you feeling sorry for him.'

'I won't. In the first place I don't *feel* sorry for him and if I did I wouldn't let him catch me at it.'

Helen had planned to stay in Maine for only two weeks but she stayed on till the middle of February. When she told Opal she would definitely have to leave at the end of the month, Chet, the following morning, walked with her down to the docks where the lobstermen tied up, and said, 'Bud tells me you're heading south.'

'That's right,' she said. 'I don't want to wear out my welcome.'

'I don't think that's liable to happen.'

'It's nice of you to say that but when March comes I'll have been here for two months. That's a long visit.'

'Yeah, I guess it is.'   •

As they walked back towards the house he said, 'Opal told me that once before when you were up here, you rented a place for yourself.'

'That's right, I did.'

'Couldn't you do that again? Then you wouldn't have to worry about being a visitor. You wouldn't be putting anybody out.'

'I suppose I could do that. But I don't think I will.'

'If it's a question of money . . . I've got a little put away.'

'It's not a question of money,' she said, 'but it's nice of you to offer.'

'I'm not being nice, I just don't want you to leave. I can't give you any good reason, I guess, but I wish you could stay around. How's that for a speech from a grown-up, broken-down guy? I sound like some kid askin' for money to go to the movies.'

'No, you don't,' she said. 'I know what you're saying. I'm just remembering what you told me the first time I talked to you. You said you were old enough to be my father and you had a wife and daughter floating around somewhere.'

'That's right.'

'You also said you were dying.' When he didn't answer

she went on, 'You said you weren't a good bet for any woman.'

'I still think that. But all the same I don't want you to leave. I tried to figure out what it would be like not talking to you every day and I decided I wouldn't like it much.'

Helen smiled. 'Does that mean you're getting used to me?'

'That's right.'

'That's the most complimentary thing anyone's ever said to me.'

'I'm not any good at that stuff,' he said. 'I never made out I *was*. I'm not saying you *ought* to stay. Matter of fact, I'll be surprised if you do. I just wanted you to know it would mean a lot to me if you did.'

When Helen told Opal she'd decided to stay in Maine a while longer, Opal said, 'That's terrific, kid. We really like having you here. Bud says you're like family, only better. And he's right.'

'That's nice of you. I like it too. But I've decided I'm going to rent a house like I did before.'

'That's crazy, honey. We've got loads of room here.'

'I know you have but I really want a little place of my own.'

'Well, I don't like *that* part of it but I'm tickled you're staying on. Bud will sure be glad to hear it and so will Chet. Did you tell him yet?'

Helen nodded. 'That's the main reason I'm staying. He asked me to. He said he didn't want me to go.'

'I could have told you *that*,' Opal said. 'Anybody in Hedrick could have told you *that*. You said that was the main reason. What's the other one?'

'The other reason is I didn't *want* to go.'

Chapter Eleven

1

There are certain forest creatures who appear to be gentle. When they are attacked, however, or when their young are threatened, they become suddenly vicious and will meet any challenge. There is also, of course, a class of predators who attack indiscriminately. And a category of victims whose only recourse is flight or death. Then there is a small but cunning group whose genetic inheritance seems both bizarre and unpredictable. These animals, although they are generally thought to be harmless, are capable of turning into instant assassins, capable of killing and devouring their mates, their offspring, or any other available victim.

How can such behaviour be explained? For centuries, zoologists concluded that such animals become rabid as dogs do. That they suddenly behave in a manner that contradicts their nature and their species. After twenty years of study, however, Dr Friedrich Greuninger of the Dresden zoo concluded that there is a far more sophisticated explanation for such behaviour. He theorizes that these animals *anticipate* danger; they believe they can *sense* a threat before it becomes overt. The result is that they strike out in self-defence before they have been attacked. 'Either such creatures have extraordinary, almost surreal powers of perception or they are truly pathological. If the latter is true, then we must conclude that paranoia is no longer to be found only among primates.'

It would be both unfair and inaccurate to draw a parallel

505

here with Nora. All the same, in one respect, there is a resemblance in spirit. Nora truly believed that she could sense when circumstances were turning against her, when promises were about to be broken or offers withdrawn; some gypsy instinct told her when a confidence had been violated, when a friend had ceased to be loyal. She did not have to be told. She *knew*.

In her years with Jesse, through all the time she had lived in Paris, those jungle sensibilities had been seldom used. They had been of little value to her. Since she controlled every element of her life, since she had the power of selection and rejection in all areas of that life, she needed to trust only herself and her choices. If she felt she had made an unfortunate choice, she had only to make another one. It was she, always, who chose. She did not allow herself to *be* chosen. This process meant that she could never be rejected or discarded. She had structured a wall of security around herself and her feelings that no ammunition could penetrate.

There were two exceptions, of course, to this self-protection formula she had devised: Valerie and Jesse. She was certain that they, of all people, would be the last to injure her, to lessen her self-esteem, to damage her in any way whatsoever. Their impulses towards her were as benevolent, she knew, as were hers towards them. So how did she suddenly become apprehensive about Jesse?

She did not, by any means, experience a moment of revelation. It did not come to her suddenly that he was not as safely inside the fold as she had presumed him to be. She did not hurry to a conclusion. Rather she simply began to have doubts.

It was an inductive process. She began to notice certain circumstances and relationships and reactions; she began to observe more closely, to see differently from the way she had before. From those observations she did not come to a decision, however. She simply continued to be watchful.

Since she was not eager to prove something to herself, since she was, in fact, intent on disproving it, for the first

506

time she could remember she scoffed at, and tried to ignore, her own instincts. But all the same she grew wary.

Most of the circumstances that disturbed her took form in her mind as questions, each one harmless in itself, but taken together . . . she didn't know if they could or should be taken together, but when they were, there was a cumulative weight there that she could not ignore. Did the servants now defer to Jesse more than they had before? Or had they always done and she had just begun to notice? Had Jesse influenced the printer and the editorial staff and the distributors to the point where they were hesitant to act on Nora's orders alone? Was there a kind of laughing and free communication between Jesse and Valerie that did not exist, had perhaps never existed, between him and Nora? Was it possible that he really was intent now on having a family of his own? Did all the jokes and teasing on that subject conceal something deeper and more serious? And what effect had his new and quite remarkable success as a critic had on him? Did he feel now that he was truly his own creature, that he could leave Paris and *Icarus* and Nora as abruptly as he had left America and later left Wingate Fields? Did he believe he would now be warmly received no matter where he chose to go?

Whatever her other failings, Nora was not ingenuous. On the other hand she was not eager to carry bad tidings to her own door. Consequently, she told herself that the questions she asked herself about Jesse could only be sensibly answered in one way – in the negative. So she did the sensible thing. She exonerated him and set her own mind at ease.

The feeling of relief lasted for two days, perhaps three. Then the questions came back. These questions, however, unsettling as they were, did not alter the rhythm of her days. No one who knew her questioned her peace of mind, least of all Jesse. Their life together was unchanged. If anything it was improved. To smother her doubts, to conceal them from Jesse as well as from herself, she became more tender, more loving, more considerate and pliable and ardent.

She had no impulse to try to articulate her feelings and suspicions to Jesse. They were too misty and ephemeral to be explained or discussed. She knew she must do the thing that was most difficult for her to do. She must calmly inhabit her own lair and wait.

Like the animal who anticipates danger, who responds to attack *before* the attack occurs, she was unable, however, merely to wait. She was unable, also, and unwilling, to go to the lists with Jesse. So she looked for outlets for her combative energy in other areas.

Having always been, particularly since her involvement with publishing had begun, a cyclone of energy, she now intensified her efforts and seemed to triple her number of activities. She had earned a reputation as a benevolent publisher, one who was both generous and flexible in her dealings with writers and painters; now, however, she began to be more demanding. Her staff and her contributors were advised that deadlines would be firm now, that publication dates would be met, that a firmer editorial policy, regarding both quality and content of material, would henceforth be observed. To document her seriousness of purpose, she hired new printers in both Paris and London, and discharged her production manager. She also contracted for new distributors in both England and America, ordered the format and the cover of *Icarus* redesigned, and for the first time, established a schedule of rates to be paid for poems, articles, stories, and drawings, rates that were markedly lower than she had previously paid.

'I think you're making a mistake,' Jesse said. 'We've had a good relationship with our contributors because we've been generous with them.'

'That's true. But now we have more contributors than we know what to do with. Every first-rate writer I meet wants to be published in *Icarus*.'

'So why tamper with success? We have an old saying in Illinois – "if it ain't broke, don't fix it." '

She smiled. 'Angus has a motto I like better. "If you spend more than you take in, you're out of business." '

'We're not talking about *business.'*

'*I* am.'

'Since when? Since when are we out to make a profit? We almost broke even last year. That's a miracle for a literary magazine. We're publishing good writers nobody ever heard of before, printing reproductions of unknown painters.

'I know that. But it's beside the point.'

'It's the *only* point,' Jesse said.

'Not for me. I don't want to be thought of as a patron and a dilettante.'

'We *are* patrons. We *are* dilettantes. We have money. We don't *have* to work for a living. And since when does it matter what anybody thinks?'

'It matters to me.'

'It never did before.'

'Maybe not. But it does now.'

In the next few weeks, Nora succeeded admirably in her efforts to redefine herself in the literary communities of London and Paris. She rejected a biographical sketch by Gertrude Stein, a long poem by E. E. Cummings, and critical pieces by Aldous Huxley and Malraux, as well as two drawings by Juan Gris and a posthumous tribute to Signac. In the following months she continued to participate vigorously in all editorial decisions. The gossip among artists was that her judgments were arbitrary and capricious but no one questioned their firmness. And contrary to Jesse's predictions, no one except Huxley publicly disassociated himself from her magazine.

In the other areas of her life, Nora seemed equally determined to redesign, reprogramme, and refurbish. It was at this time that she sold her apartment in Passy and moved to the house by the Seine. When she moved she bought an entirely new wardrobe, sleek and trim outfits, many of them styled in a manner that resembled gentlemen's coats and suits. She also bought a new car and hired a new staff for her house, keeping only Claudine, the housekeeper who had been with her since Valerie was a small child.

When Clara wrote to her that Angus thought she was

509

foolish to buy property in France at this time, Nora wrote back, 'Tell him I respect his judgment but in this case I think he's wrong. Not only do we now have a fine old house on the Seine, I have just bought a country house on another lovely river, the Marne. This time, however, it's all Jesse's fault. He drove me out to Villers' Cotterets one Sunday, then back through Forêt de Retz, and there, quite by chance, we found this gorgeous fifteenth-century house perched on the river-bank just at the edge of the forest. It was for sale so I bought it. It wants a lot of work but it will keep me occupied, as if I didn't have enough already to keep me busy.'

From the time of her own efforts to be a painter, from the contacts she had made during those brief semesters of her life, Nora had retained her interest in the plastic arts, painting in particular. Her experience with *Icarus*, the opportunity to meet young artists and see their work, her attempts to form some value judgment of their pictures before other public judgments had been made, all this further stimulated her interest and her eagerness to participate. Not as an artist herself but as a patron.

Soon after moving into the house on Ile St Louis, stimulated perhaps by the great foyers and heroic wall-space there, she began to collect paintings. Mostly she bought canvases by young French and German and Italian painters, artists she had met and whose work she had seen as publisher of *Icarus*. Many of them made their first sale to her. She did not make them rich, not by any means – she drove hard bargains – but she gave much-needed encouragement and more important, having made a purchase, she talked about the painter and his work wherever she went in Paris and London, sent other buyers to his studio, and caused other sales to be made. It was no secret among her close friends that she saw herself as a slightly latter-day Gertrude Stein, a person who appreciated, supported and encouraged artists who had previously found appreciation, support, and encouragement hard to come by. One of the reception rooms in her new home was hung as Stein's had been – paintings from floor to ceiling.

In addition to the canvases she bought from unknown painters, she anchored her collection with some truly fine works by men who were or would become acknowledged masters but whose paintings in the 1930s were still bought and sold simply as handsome pictures. They had not yet become items for investment or long-range speculation. Among others, she acquired a Beckmann triptych, a Gauguin flower painting, a Matisse nude from the Fauve period, a Juan Gris that was reputed to be his first cubist experiment, a Kirchner figure painting that would later be acquired by the National Gallery in London, and a haunting Münch self-portrait.

Since she approached collecting with the same energy she brought to all her other activities, Nora soon found that she had filled all the available wall-space in both her Paris home and the house on the Marne. Unwilling to have her hunger for acquisition stifled by something so tiresome as a shortage of space and appalled at the thought of hiding beautiful works of art in dark storage rooms, she bought a picture gallery in rue de Seine. There she began to sell paintings with the same enthusiasm with which she had bought them.

As though there were not enough demands being made on her time she instituted a Thursday evening salon at her home which quickly became known among poets and intellectuals as *Jeudi Nora*. Later, it was freely admitted by all, even by Nora, that the original lure of her salon had been food and wine. Poets who lived in cold rooms, ill-paid journalists and Sorbonne scholars, came to the great house on the Seine to get warm, to gorge themselves with food, and to drink, some of them, until they dropped.

As time passed, those evenings continued to be occasions for over-indulgence, but they also became what they had been intended to be, true cultural events, where Pound or Eliot or Auden or Anouilh might be seen, where one could hear them read from their latest works, where serious critics tried to defend themselves against angry painters, where pale and earnest men and women attempted to find the links between God and art, tried to determine if

511

politicians served anyone other than themselves, and if parenthood was the definitive creativity after all. Picasso did a surprisingly graceful dance there one Thursday, accompanied by a mouth-organ and a guitar. Chevalier sang a lullaby in Italian. Kiki was nearly always there. And Man Ray. And Raymond Duncan often whirled about in his robes and explained in detail that it was he who had taught Isadora to dance.

Almost always, on those evenings, just after the first wave of guests had arrived, Jesse and Valerie strolled out through the servants' entrance, crossed the bridge to the Left Bank, and spent the evening in a cinema or a café. When they returned home some time after midnight, the wine still flowing and the discussions continuing at full intensity, it became a ritual for one of them to say to the other, 'You see, nobody noticed we were gone.'

Nora noticed, however. But for many weeks she didn't mention it to either Jesse or Valerie. When it came up at last, it was in the tangential style Nora favoured when she was annoyed by something but was anxious to conceal that annoyance.

'A fine friend and colleague you are,' she said to Jesse one Friday morning at breakfast. They were sitting up in bed, their coffee and croissants and *pain chocolat* on trays across their laps.

'What did I do?'

'It's what you *didn't* do. Do you think I don't notice that you're never around for my Thursday evenings?'

'I'm *always* around,' he said. 'I'm here at the beginning and I'm here at the end. I just take a bit of a breather in the middle.'

'For three or four hours.'

'Perhaps. You know how I am about time.'

'And you take Valerie with you.'

'Correction. We take each other,' he said. 'No force is applied on either side.'

'No loyalty in my family.' She leaned close to him and kissed him. 'They leave me to fend for myself.'

'That's because you fend so well. Valerie and I were just praising you the other day.'

'Seriously, Jesse . . . .'

'Oh-oh. I'm in trouble. *Serious* at breakfast.'

'It makes me feel odd,' she said. 'When everyone else is here, when everyone in Paris is dying to come here on Thursdays, and *you* can't wait to escape.'

'I wouldn't call it *escape* exactly.'

'Whatever you call it, you're not here on the premises, she said. 'I can't understand it. When these weekly affairs first started, you thought they were quite splendid.'

'That's right. I did.'

'You said it was a grand idea for all these gifted people to have a place to gather. To talk and argue and theorize . . . that's what you said.'

'I still say that. I still think it's a grand idea. I have just come to question my participation in it.'

'Why in the world should you? You're well-known now. At least in Paris. People read your articles and critical pieces. You must know that.'

'I *do* know that. And that's the problem. My idea of a pleasant evening is not sitting around defending my opinions. I'm not a masochist. I don't want some lunatic I've never laid eyes on before throwing his drink in my face.'

'Maybe that's the price of fame. You should have expected that.'

'I'm not famous and you know it. Hardly anyone knows who I am except people whose work I've criticized.'

'*Attacked,* I think, is a more accurate word. And you must realize by now that those people make up quite a long list. You can't expect them not to respond if they have a chance to take you on face to face.'

'I *do* expect them not to respond. I criticize their work, not *them.* If they want to criticize *my* work, that's fine with me. Lots of people have done it. But not to my face. That's too boring.'

'It's not like you to run away,' she said then.

'Of course it is. Everybody runs away from something.

513

And intelligent people run away from all kinds of things. When you can't reason with a man you have the choice of knocking him down or avoiding him. It's easy to knock people down. I used to be good at that. But I prefer to avoid them.'

'So you avoid my salons?'

'Let's just say I keep my appearances brief. To minimize the lesions on my sensibilities.'

She poured more coffee into their cups and added hot milk. Then she said, 'Do you think we're all right, you and I?'

'How do you mean?'

'I mean has anything gone wrong with us?'

'That's odd,' he said.

'What's odd?'

'I saw a film the other night – Valerie saw it too – and Carole Lombard said those exact words to the actor who was playing her husband. She said, "Has anything gone wrong with us?" '

'And what did he say, the actor who played her husband?'

'He said, "I didn't think anything had gone wrong until I heard you ask that question." '

After a moment Nora asked, 'And is that what you're saying to me?'

'No. I was just telling you about the movie.'

'And so much for that,' she said.

'What do you mean?'

'I mean you have just dropped the subject. Correct?'

'Not if you don't want me to,' he said. 'I'm having a good time. It's nice and warm here in bed, I'm having an elegant breakfast, and you look beautiful in your blue nightgown.'

'Of all the men I might have picked, I had to choose a clever one. Clever and elusive.'

'I don't have to be clever to see that you look sensational in your blue nightgown.'

'You know what I mean.'

'Sure I do. But you're wrong.'

'What I was really trying to say,' she said then, 'is that we don't seem to see each other as much as we used to. And I guess that's my fault.'

'No, it's not. It's nobody's fault. You're a busy woman.'

'Busier than you are?'

'Oh, sure. Much busier than I am,' he said.

'I don't *have* to be so busy, do I?'

'Sure you do. It's your nature. Sustained effort. Continuous production. People like you keep the world humming.'

'Sounds dreadful.'

'No. It's admirable,' he said.

'And you admire me?'

'Of course. Everyone admires you. You're a dynamo in a blue nightgown.'

'And what about you?'

'Spasmodic worker. Fits and starts. Apt to shilly-shally. The mind wanders. That sort of thing. Liable to spend long hours staring. Always ready to doze off or wander away to the zoo. Very much at home with animals. Ill at ease with people. Awkward with human beings.'

'I've never heard such rot. You have the greatest social gift I've ever seen. Everyone says so.'

'It's all acquired,' he said. 'Not a native trait at all. Just an ill-fitting garment I'm able to slip on to disguise myself.'

'Usually I'm glad you're not an Englishman,' she said then, 'but sometimes I wish you were. When you ask an Englishman a serious question you get a serious answer. With you I never know what sort of answer I'll get. Is that because you're an American?'

'I don't know.'

'Are all American men like you?'

'About as much as all English women are like *you*, I suppose.'

'Let me start again,' she said. 'Do you think things have changed between us?'

'I hope so. Nothing stays the same. Why should it?'

'You won't stay on track, will you?'

'Sure I will. I just don't want to be boring.'

'Is that what *I* am?'

'Not yet. But you're getting warm. There's nothing more tiresome than two people explaining to each other that they will make any changes in themselves that are requested. That doesn't happen. It *never* happens. Love doesn't *change* anything. Sometimes it doesn't even make things better. It just makes things *different*.'

'God, that sounds cynical.'

'The truth always sounds cynical. The fact is that none of us are as flexible as we think we are or as we'd like to be. Love is ten percent passion and ninety percent *acceptance*. If you're asking me seriously if there are some changes we should make, I say no. Changes happen but they can't be *made* to happen. I have no desire to turn you into a different kind of woman than you are. If I did have such a desire, I wouldn't do it anyway. You're what you *are*. And thank God for that. That's why I'm *here*, sprinkling crumbs in your bed.'

'I don't think you know me at all,' she said. 'I could be all sorts of different people if I decided to.'

'No you couldn't. If I said to you that I thought we should get rid of this house and the country house, sell the magazine and the art gallery and all the paintings and trappings we've accumulated and go live in a cottage in Devon, or if I said I really have a yen to spend the rest of my life on a chicken farm in Nebraska, what would you say?'

She laughed softly. 'You really are a wild man. Do you know that?'

'What would you say?'

'If it meant something to you, if it was something you really wanted, I wouldn't hesitate. I'd say yes.'

'Then you're crazy.'

'No, I'm not.'

'Yes, you are. You could *never* do that. You could never *live* like that. Any more than you could live in Northumberland or Cumberland. You have to stay close to the flame. You have to feel the heat. I *know* that about you so I would never *ask* you to go clumping off to some plain place.'

'But if you *wanted* it . . . .'

'It doesn't matter. It so happens that I *don't* want that sort of life either. But if I did, I'd have to find it for myself. Without you. Or I'd have to find somebody else who wanted it as much as I did.'

'You're really starting to depress me.'

'Don't blame me. You wanted me to be serious so I got serious.'

'I didn't want you to be *that* serious.'

He pulled her close to him in the bed so her cheek was against his. 'We're serious all the time. We've got a serious thing going here. So we don't have to *be* serious. We don't have to consider serious questions. All we have to say is "Well, now, I think this is very nice. I'd like to have a lot more of this." *That's* it. That's all there is to it. When somebody says "This isn't so nice any longer. I don't think I'll have much more of this," then it's all over. All the words and the promises and the worries and the plans don't mean anything. If it's good, it's good. If it's not . . . .'

'I'm glad to hear you say that,' she said, 'because I've had enough.'

'No, you haven't and neither have I.'

'How much more time do you think we have?'

'Lots.'

'How much?' she asked.

'As long as that blue nightgown doesn't wear out or get lost, we'll be fine.'

2

Just after the first of the year in 1936, Jesse went to London to meet Angus. The day before he left Paris he had a note from Clara.

Angus tells me he'll be seeing you in London. So I think I should warn you that he's changed. In just a few months he has slipped badly. He's quite thin and

517

unusually quiet. Seems to stay very much inside himself. He still goes through the motions of working, still travels a great deal, but there's no spirit in him now. Perhaps it's a healthy sign that he wants to see you. I hope so. I've always felt he was indestructible, no matter what my head told me. It kills me to see him fading away.

Angus was staying at his club in Brook Street and Jesse booked rooms at Claridge's just down the road. The channel train was delayed in Dover so Jesse didn't reach the hotel till almost eight in the evening. He rang up Angus at once and they arranged to meet in Claridge's dining-room for dinner.

Having been prepared for a change in Angus' appearance, Jesse was not as taken aback as he might have been. Angus was thinner, no question of that, and some of the high colour had left his cheeks, but he walked strongly across the dining-room to Jesse's table and his voice when he spoke, although it lacked the heavy resonance that Jesse was accustomed to, was still full and vigorous. The disheartening thing was not his appearance or the way he spoke. It was the tormented tone of the things he said. Like a mortally wounded soldier he seemed to be flailing about with his sword, determined to take as many of the enemy with him as he could.

'You don't look well, Jesse,' he said as soon as he was seated. 'Have you been ill?'

'No. I've been fine.'

'I'd see a physician if I were you. Before you leave London would be my advice. I'm sure the people here at the hotel can direct you to a good man. Or I can send you along to Dr Fletemyer just down the way in Grosvenor Square. The only problem with Fletemyer is he's sicker now than most of his patients. Surly as hell. Not anxious to take on new people. Damned shame, too. He was a top-notch diagnostician. I'm sure he'd look you over if I insisted but you might be better off with a younger man. How old are you now, Jesse?'

'My birthday's next week as a matter of fact. I'll be thirty-nine.'

'Well, that's not so far along. But you're not in the full flush of youth either. A man never knows what to expect these days. Take my solicitor and dear friend, Charles Tremont . . . you know him.'

'Of course. I hope he's not . . . .'

'No. He's fine. Healthy as a stag. But his son ticked off last year of some odd blood disease. And two weeks ago his grandson fell dead at an ice-skating party. Damned fine lad he was, too. Smart as a whip. And only twenty-three years old. So take my advice and have a good doctor take a look at you. I don't like the way your eyes look. And your face has no colour in it. Maybe it has something to do with your bad leg. Has it been giving you trouble?'

'Not a bit. Like I said, I feel fine.'

'They tell me that chemistry's the thing we have to beware of. It's all around us, they say. In the food, in the air – everywhere except in the whiskey. And I expect they'll find a way to produce *that* in their bloody test-tubes before long. I'm not a scientist of course. I make no claims to scientific knowledge. But I know for sure that you can tamper with nature just so much. Then it turns on you. And I believe it's already happening. Everybody I know is either sick or already dead. Clara doesn't look well to me, my new driver's in hospital more than he's out these days, and Ned Causey's like a corpse walking around. Ned can't be more than sixty-four or sixty-five but compared to him I look like a stripling. Not that I see him that often. Either I'm away or he's away. I don't know where that man spends his nights but wherever it is, it doesn't agree with him. He looks to me as if he won't last out the year.'

When they met again the following morning, Angus had changed his topic but not his tone. 'They say no man understands his wife. I used to scoff at that but now I believe it as surely as I believe anything. More than sixty years I've spent with Louise. At the beginning I thought I knew every single thing there was to know about her. But by the time I was fifty I had decided there were things I

519

didn't understand after all. And by the time I was seventy I knew there were only a few things I *did* understand. Now I realize I don't know her at all and I never did. She knows me, though, knows me like her diary, but I don't know a damned thing about her. All I know is that I feel sorry for her. She just wants to die and she can't. Everybody else is dying, people who want to live, but Louise can't die. I went to see her a week ago and she looks better than she did thirty years ago. She looks like one of those seventeenth-century peasant women who stood at the window in their aprons and swore they saw Christ himself looking in. Her eyes are clear as the sea, her cheeks are pink and full and there's not a line on her face. She sits there with a little smile on her lips and her hands in her lap and doesn't make a sound. She seems to listen when you talk to her but it's hard to tell because she never answers.'

'You mean she won't talk to you?'

'Doesn't talk at all. She's like a mute.'

'Are you saying she *can't* talk or she won't?'

'The doctors say she *can't*. I say she *won't*.'

'Why would she do that?' Jesse said.

'Why does anybody do anything? I think she's doing it to get even with me.'

'For what?'

'God knows. Raymond did the same thing years ago. After he'd seen that young woman die in their hotel room in Holyhead. He didn't say a word to any of us from the time that girl died till the time he ran off and went to America. Vengeance, I guess you'd call it. That's what it was in Raymond's case. And in Louise's too, I think.'

'Where is she now?'

'She's in a home in the country just west of Newcastle. A convalescent home, they call it. Except no one ever seems to convalesce there. They just go there and stay there and die there.'

'Sounds awful.'

'Actually, it's a beautiful place. But beautiful or not, it's where she must be. She told her doctor in no uncertain terms, "I will *not* go home." And he said we shouldn't force her. So there she sits. She eats well, walks around in the gardens, and listens to classical music on her radio. She's taken care of and made comfortable and that's all she wants, I expect. But as far as I'm concerned, I'm sick of the whole business. For years she's been trying to make somebody pay for what happened to Raymond and I suppose that's what she's still doing. I said before I felt sorry for her but I don't. Not really. Since I've been travelling so much these past few years I've seen a lot of wretched people. *Old* people. As old as Louise and me. Old women still struggling to take care of their children and their children's children, trying to keep a fire going and put some sort of a meal together. No time to get sick or sad or to feel sorry for themselves. Their only life is trying to *stay* alive. That's a big percentage of the people in the world, Jesse. *You* know that. And so does Clara, God bless her. But then I see people like Louise and Ned and Hugh and Nora who've had everything provided for them, whose only problem has been to find some way to pass the time . . . I mean they don't have to produce or compete. All they have to do is stay out of jail and enjoy themselves. When they can't *manage* that, I don't find great tears of sympathy in my eyes. Spoiled people are like spoiled venison. There's no recipe that will accommodate them. No seasoning that will cover up the rot. Nobody gets through life without disappointments or bad experiences. But only spoiled people believe that one bad experience is an excuse for a lifetime of self-pity.'

From London, Angus was going to Southampton to board a ship to Cape Town. On his departure morning, Jesse went to the station with him. They had breakfast in the station restaurant while they waited for the boat train to be announced.

In all the hours they had spent together in the past days, Jesse had been unable to silence the tolling bells of Angus' judgments. There was no subject, no area of life, it seemed, that he had not studied and found wanting. All roads, in his new frame of mind, led to the abattoir, all streams disappeared in foul marshes.

521

When Jesse said, 'I thought when you asked me to meet you here in London that I was scheduled for a lecture,' Angus replied, 'Not at all. I've never lectured you. Why would I begin now?'

'Because I deserve it. I haven't seen you for some time and I feel guilty about that. It's more than six months since I've been to Wingate Fields.'

'And *I* wasn't there. Isn't that correct?'

Jesse nodded. 'Clara said you'd gone off to Milan.'

'So there you are. I'm the one who's been remiss. *That* is the reason I asked you to meet me here in London. So we could spend a bit of time together. No recriminations permitted on either side.'

'That's very nice of you, to take the blame yourself, but my schedule is more flexible than yours. I should have made more of an effort. I've been no use at all to you and Clara these past two or three years.'

'It doesn't matter, Jesse. You were useful when you could be. Now you have other things to keep you busy.'

'All the same I feel as if we had an agreement and I haven't held up my end of it.'

Angus smiled, for the first time since he and Jesse had met in the dining-room of Claridge's. 'We have only one agreement,' he said. 'You agreed to be my son and I agreed to be your father. I've never had a reason to regret that decision and I hope you haven't either.'

'I haven't. But I'm aware that a son has obligations. Business affairs don't run themselves.'

'At one time perhaps that was true. But no longer. In the past eighteen months we've restructured the whole operation so there's nothing for *me* to do, nothing for *Clara* to do, and nothing for *you*.'

'Somebody has to make the decisions.'

'Only the legal people and the bankers now. We are no longer in the business of aggressive acquisition. There's a war on the way and we've sold all our foreign property. We hold only Wingate Fields now, some other sheep farms in Scotland, and our buildings here in London. Everything else was converted to cash and is now invested in conservative bonds and securities. There's nothing more to acquire, nothing to sell, nothing to administer.'

'Then why are you still working so hard?'

'I'm not. I'm not working at all.'

'Why all the travelling? Why are you going to Cape Town?'

'I travel so people who know me won't realize that I have nothing to do now. And it gets me away from Wingate Fields.' He held up his hand. 'I know what you're thinking, what everybody thinks, that Wingate is my whole life. That used to be true. For most of my life it was true. I'm not even sure when it *stopped* being true. But it did. Now that old place is just a repository of bad memories. Nothing more.'

'I can't believe that.'

'It's true. Everything that held me there has either disappeared or changed. Even the servants are strangers to me. My butler died last year. My dear old driver the year before.'

'But Clara's still there.'

'Not as much as you may imagine. She's as uneasy at home as I am. Both her children are gone. She seldom sees her granddaughter. Her husband comes and goes like an itinerant rumpot and her mother doesn't recognize her when she goes to visit her.'

'God, I didn't realize . . . .'

'It's a gallery of ghosts, Jesse. In twenty years all the windows will be broken and the wind will whistle through the empty rooms.'

'I don't believe that and neither do you.'

'I not only believe it, I *predict* it. I think it's inevitable.'

'Don't you remember the first summer when I came to visit? You spent hours telling me the history of the Bradshaws, counting the generations that were born and lived and died in that house. You told me the house *was* the family, that they were inseparable. You said, "Continuity is everything." Do you remember saying that?'

'Of course I do. I believed it then.'

'And you're saying you don't believe it now?'

'It's not a question of belief. It simply isn't true any longer. I'm not a blind man, Jesse. I can see the world dissolving around me. I've seen my own family change. And I feel the change in myself.'

'I can't tell you how rotten it makes me feel to hear you talking like this. I come from a country where everything seems to flip-flop overnight. If you have a problem you change your address, change your job, change husbands, change wives. It's everybody's solution to almost everything. It used to bother me when I was a kid. It still bothered me when I was a young man. But I never knew exactly *why* till I came here. Till I met you. When I spent all those hours talking to you, I felt as if I was brushing against a piece of history. It gave me a new outlook on things. I began to see that commotion and movement weren't always necessary, that something important could take place in silence and isolation. I saw that there were ways of growing that couldn't be measured or hefted. Mostly, I guess, I saw what had made Raymond the way he was. He had it all inside. He didn't have to dance for pennies or follow the fashion of the season. He knew exactly who he was and where he came from. God, how I admired that. I envied it. Raymond was a specific person from a specific place. Wingate Fields was the place. If you hadn't made it possible for me to be a part of your family I would have begged you just to let me come to work for you. I would have done anything to make it possible. I developed such a connection to those rooms and hallways, the gardens and fields, that I began to believe I'd been born there.

'After I came there for the second time, when Clara had that beautiful work-room fixed up for me, I know it seemed to her, and to you, probably, as if I was looking out the window all day. And I *was*, for at least part of the time. But mostly I was sitting there soaking it in. Celebrating my presence there. I couldn't believe I'd become a permanent part of that chain of life and tradition you had once described to me. Now I can't believe that you're taking it all back. Are you saying the Bradshaw name doesn't matter and never did matter? Are you telling me it doesn't make any difference if Wingate is a house with people living in it or an empty ruin collapsing on the moors?'

'I'm saying that one man by himself can't keep *anything* alive. Not a marriage. Not a family. Not a home. Not a tradition. I used to think it would be a great tragedy if the Bradshaw clan disappeared from Northumberland. Now it's an idea I can accept.'

Just before Angus boarded the train, Jesse said, 'I promise you there won't be any broken window-panes at Wingate as long as I'm around.'

'You don't owe me any promises.'

'Maybe I don't. But I'm giving you one anyway.'

When they put their arms around each other, Jesse could feel the sharp bones under Angus' coat. And his face as he waved to Jesse through the compartment window, looked pale, suddenly, and very old. Jesse stood there on the platform till the train steamed slowly out of the station and disappeared. Minutes later he was still standing there.

3

Helen rented a small shingled house on a point of land that encircled the north edge of Hedrick harbour. From her bedroom she could look out on Muscongus Bay and the scattering of offshore islands that protected the harbour from the ocean. From her kitchen she could see downshore across the harbour mouth. And from her living-room window she looked west past the wharf and the refrigerator shed where the lobstermen pulled in, past the little restaurant and summer residents' cottages to the village, the Feasters' house in full view, Opal Feaster clearly visible if she was hanging out clean washing in the side yard or weeding in the vegetable garden.

As soon as she'd moved in, Helen wrote to Clara, enclosed Kodak snapshots of her new home, and told her she had decided to stay on in Maine for an indefinite period of time. When Clara answered she wrote:

Never mind descriptions of your fireplace and your bedroom and your kitchen cabinets. What about this gentleman friend of yours?

In her next letter to England, Helen told Clara she had read her letter to Chet and he told her to say that he was no gentleman at all.

And he isn't, of course, not by any popular definition of the word. He doesn't own a suit of clothes or a necktie. His entire wardrobe, in fact, except for his winter coat, would fit into one canvas duffel bag. He wears heavy work shoes when he's outdoors and when he comes inside he takes them off and pads about in his sock feet. He doesn't read books, he's never been inside an art museum, he's never heard a symphony orchestra, and he's never owned a car that wasn't a truck.

So what am I doing with such a man? I don't know for sure. We've known each other a very short time but I'm very attached to him. How does *he* feel? I can't be sure of that either. He doesn't admit it but I think he needs me. And I hope he loves me. He says he's not a gentleman and I suppose he's not. But he is the gentlest man I've ever seen and I adore him.

Opal's questions were not so easily answered. Early in April, six weeks after Helen had moved into the house across the harbour, Opal said, 'I guess it's none of my business but since Bud says I think *everything* is my business, I'll ask you anyway. What are you and Chet up to? You've got that nice little house all to yourself and he's still living here with us. Now it turns out he's buying five acres in the woods on the road to Brown's Cove. There's the running gears of an old house still standing on the property and he says he's gonna put it back together again.

526

Keep it pretty much like it once was but make it fit to live in.'

'That's right. That's what he says.'

'So now you've got a house, *we've* got a house, and Chet is fixing to have a house, too.'

'It'll be nice for him,' Helen said.

'I don't see how. I'll tell you the truth. When you said you were going to stay on here in Hedrick, Bud and I figured you and Chet had made some plans. We thought you'd probably be moving in together.'

'Why did you think that?'

'I don't know. We just did. You're both grown-ups. And when a grown-up man and a grown-up woman start spending a lot of time together, talking soft and laughing a lot, you don't have to be too smart to figure out what the next chapter will be.'

'Maybe we just want to be friends. Did you ever think of that?'

'I've thought of it but I've never seen it happen. In every case that I know of, people want to get to the kissy-kissy business first. Then they get to be friends later. I know men and women been married twenty years and they're not friends yet. You're a terrific-looking kid. I can't imagine any man not being all over you like a wet shirt if you gave him half the chance.'

Helen smiled. 'I guess Chet doesn't agree with you. Maybe he sees me more as a sister.'

'Bull. According to Bud, Chet's a real bird-dog. When they was still in the service, he says Chet had women coming out of his ears. Nothing wrong with Chet in *that* department.'

That evening, when Chet came to her house for supper, Helen said, 'We've got Bud and Opal very mixed up. Did you know that?'

'What are they mixed up about?'

'Opal says they thought you and I would be living together by now.'

'What did you say?'

'I didn't say anything at first. Then I said maybe we just

527

wanted to be friends. I said you probably see me as a kind of sister.'

He smiled. 'You don't believe that, do you?'

'I've never really thought about it. It was just something I said to Opal.'

'I'll tell you the truth,' he said then. 'I know some people like to talk a lot about stuff like this. Like to really chew it over. First one way then the other. And maybe that's all right for those people. Gives them something to do. But I don't like it much. My dad was a dumb bastard. Couldn't stay sober and couldn't make a living. But I always remember one thing he told me. "It's not what you *say* that counts, it's what you *do*." That was funny coming from him. Because his mouth was always flapping and he never accomplished *anything* that I know of. He fathered three screwed-up kids, made my mother miserable, and managed to get falling-down drunk just about every day of his life, but *that* was *it*.' He paused. 'If it sounds like I'm feeling sorry for myself, I'm not. I'm not mad at my old man either, not any more. I used to hold it against him because he never showed me how to use tools or throw an in-curve or shoot a rifle. But I got over all that. There's only one thing I've got against him now and that's not his fault. If I'd have been smart I'd have left my wife a long time ago. Nobody's fault. We was just a bad match. It took me a long while to figure out that the only reason I was staying with her was because I didn't want to be like my dad. If he'd been in my shoes I know he'd have left her in a minute. But I didn't want to do something I thought *he* would have done. So I stuck around. Dumb move on my part.'

'I don't think so.'

He tapped his forehead with one forefinger. '*Very* dumb. You don't know *how* dumb.'

Later in the evening, just before he left to go back to the Feasters, he said, 'I don't know why we're not living together either. I'd like it if we were. I mean I didn't want you to stay here just so I'd have somebody to talk to and eat supper with. I don't mind a one-night stand or a two-week shack-up or anything else if that's what it comes to. But that's not what I want from *you*. I mean I don't want to start a big thing with you just to say we did it. If you're not going to be around for a while . . . I mean I don't want to get myself jerked around to where I'm *counting* on something . . . .'

'I'm not going anywhere.'

'I know you're not. At least I know you *think* you're not. What I'm trying to say is, I don't want you to think I'm something I can't be. I don't want you to expect something I can't deliver. I know I'm not like anybody you've been around before. But maybe you like the way I am. I guess you do. The trouble is – there isn't any more where that came from. Some people like steak and potatoes every time they sit down to eat. Never get tired of it. I had an uncle that lived on bread and milk. But most people go for a little variety. Different cooking. Different-tasting stuff. Isn't that right?'

'I guess it is.'

'That's what *I* don't have,' he said. 'I'm not down-grading myself. I'm just telling you the truth. I'm the same now as I was when I was twenty years old. Same as I was when I was in the army. Ask Bud. He'll tell you. And I'll be like that I guess, from now on. So if you're gonna get tired of me I hope it happens now, or pretty soon, at least, before I've swum out so far I can't get back.'

'I could say the same thing to you.'

'No, you couldn't. It's not the same and you know it. You've been a lot of places I can't go to.'

'Maybe so. But I like it here better.'

'You mean here in Hedrick?'

She smiled. 'That's part of it.'

'This is a great place all right. But people get tired of it after a while. Most people just come here in the summer when the weather's nice. When it starts getting cold they don't like it any more.'

'This is my third time here and I still like it.'

All that spring and summer he worked on his house in

the woods, working slowly and carefully, putting it together, piece by piece, like wood sculpture.

'I told him not to be so fussy,' Bud said to Opal. 'The old timbers on that house are like iron, the floors are solid, and the roof beams will be standing there for another two hundred years. I helped him wire the place and put in new plumbing and he's got a wood stove that would heat a place twice that size. I told him all he has to do is put on siding, shingle the roof, set the windows in, and hang some new doors. I can put his insulation and wallboard in for him in no time. He could be living there by the fourth of July, snug as a raccoon. I told him that. But he just keeps plugging along at that snail's pace of his, planing and chiselling and sanding, fitting wood together like he was building something for a museum. Mortising and notching like a God-damned cabinet-maker. Never seen such a fool for detail. He'll stand there looking at a piece of lumber for ten minutes before he puts the saw to it. Strokes those boards with his bare hands like he was petting a cat. Damnedest thing you've ever seen.'

'I guess he just wants it to be nice.'

'It's a place to *live*, for Christ's sake. A place to eat and sleep. If Chet had built Noah's ark, all the animals would have drowned while they waited for him to finish up.'

Helen's reactions, as she watched Chet's house slowly develop and evolve, were far removed from Bud's. She was on the premises from the beginning, fetching and carrying and running errands in the truck, doing whatever she was capable of. But mostly she watched. Like a child seeing a sand-castle or a play-house come into being. She was witness to the labour and the sweat, the bruises, the strains, and the scratches. She saw the stacks of lumber, the bundles of shingle, and the kegs of nails slowly disappear, saw the rough structural carpentry come to an end and the fine, careful work begin.

Chet's painstaking rhythm that annoyed Bud so much was hypnotic to Helen. She had never been involved in sustained physical work, certainly in nothing so magnificent as the structure of a dwelling, a place where people

530

could sleep and prepare food and keep cats and dogs and songbirds if they chose to. She had always taken houses for granted. Fine rooms and staircases, bathrooms and kitchens and cupboards and porches and garages. Doors that swung open and shut, windows that could be raised and lowered. Water flowing from taps, hot and cold, light-switches and steam radiators, chandeliers and baseboards and banisters and railings. Now, for the first time she was seeing the interlocking puzzle of a house being simply, methodically, but magically pieced together.

Each morning she drove from her place to Chet's house to study in detail, before the day's work started, everything that had been done the day before. She touched every building-piece and every surface, memorized with her finger-tips the whorls and ridges in the wood, the surfaces of metal, of plaster, of stain and enamel. She helped carry field-stone for the fireplace and watched as each piece was cemented into place above the hearth.

The final days were half-excitement, half-sadness for her. With the windows and doors in place and the screened porch snugly enclosed, the trees and ferns and lilacs that through the spring and early summer had seemed part of the interior were shut out now. The woods had returned to themselves and the house which while building had seemed half-nature and half-man was now all man. It was all Chet. All his. Completed and polished and swept and scrubbed and perfect. Cupboards in the kitchen with dishes and cutlery, shutters at the window, rugs on the floor, towels in the bathroom and sheets and quilts and pillows on the bed.

Seeing it finished, prowling it, touching it, Helen remembered every detail of every day. How every beam had been shoved and punished into place, every peg inserted, every panel positioned. She could not articulate even to herself what the house meant to her, what the building of it had meant. Nor could she begin to measure what it meant to Chet. She only knew it was a living thing to her and she loved it like a living thing.

The day it was finally finished, during the last week in

531

August, when even Chet could find nothing more to pick
up or sweep away or tighten or loosen or smooth with
sandpaper, they sat on the couch in front of the fireplace
with their arms around each other and Helen said, 'Don't
tell me there's more work to do. I *know* there's nothing else
to do. It's finished, isn't it?'

'You never know with a house like this.'

'It's finished, isn't it?' she insisted.

'Looks pretty good, doesn't it?'

'That's not good enough. It's finished, isn't it?'

'That's right. It's finished.'

She held his face in her hands and kissed him.

'I love you,' she said. 'You're a wonderful man and you
built a wonderful house.'

The next day they moved all of her things from her
house to his. They ate and drank and slept and lived there
together from that day till Chet died.

4

Angus' wish that he would die on an ocean-going steamer
or in some foreign capital, was denied him. But at least he
was in motion. As he was being driven, one day in
December of 1937, from York to Wingate Fields, he fell
asleep in the corner of the back seat, tucked up warmly in
his car rug. When the car rolled up the long Wingate
driveway later and stopped at the west entrance of the
house, Angus had been dead for more than an hour.

Clara was in New York when she heard the news. She
telephoned Helen at once. 'I'm flying to London tomorrow
and I've booked a seat for you.'

'Oh, Clara, I'm sorry. I can't. I just can't leave now.'

'It would mean an awful lot to me. And to all the family.
You *must* come.'

To Helen's surprise, Chet agreed with Clara.

'I'm surprised at you,' Helen said. 'You've never been

inside a church in your life. You don't believe in *any* institution or any of the things institutions do.'

'Not for me, I don't. But you're different.'

'How so?'

'You were raised different.'

'I'll bet you've never been to a funeral in your life.'

'That's right. I haven't. But *you* have. So don't pattern yourself after me. Your people have different rules and customs than mine ever did. You liked this man, didn't you, the one that just died?'

'I loved him,' she said. 'He was my grandfather. And I feel terrible that I haven't seen him for all these years. But I can't make it up to him by going to his funeral.'

'You're right about that. He won't know the difference.'

'Then why should I go?'

'The only reason I can see to go to *any* funeral is to give a lift to the people that didn't die. To make them feel better.'

'But *you've* never done it. You said so yourself.'

'That's 'cause I'm not as well-organized as you are.'

She called Clara back a few minutes later and told her she'd meet her in New York. Chet drove her to Portland at midday and she took the south-bound train from there. The next morning she and Clara flew to England on the Clipper.

Memorial services were held in both London and Newcastle. In Parliament Sir Peter Newcombe of Blackpool spoke at length about Angus' life and accomplishments. But the funeral itself was held in the Wingate chapel. Only family and servants were there.

That night, at dinner in the great hall, the lights were turned up full and champagne was served. Jesse sat at the head of the table with Clara on his right and Helen on his left. As soon as everyone was seated, Clara rose and lifted her glass.

'I would like to toast my remarkable father, Angus Bradshaw.' After everyone drank and put down their glasses, Clara remained standing. 'It is difficult and heartbreaking to offer a toast at this table where Angus presided for so

533

many years. But I will do my best because he deserves the best I can give. Regarding this dinner, only strangers would question the propriety of a banquet on the night of Angus' funeral. Angus would have had it no other way. We have mourned his death and we will continue to, each of us in his own way, but tonight we will celebrate his life. All of us are in his debt in more ways than we can count. But we won't dwell on that, any more than we would be allowed to if he were sitting here. My father's accomplishments and his seriousness of purpose have been well-documented. Tonight let's remember him simply as a relative and a friend, as a member of this odd and magnificent household.'

Jesse and Helen, Clara and Ned and Hugh and Nora and Valerie were all at the table. Hugh's wife was said to be ill so she was not there. And Louise had not been permitted by her doctors to attend either the funeral or the memorial service in Newcastle. So she, of course, was not present.

For Helen, the shock of being so suddenly returned to Wingate was lessened somewhat by the public nature of her first few days there. She had welcomed the silence and the aloneness of the ceremonies. And the quality, very like anonymity, that sorrow placed on everyone. All individuals, their relationships, their viewpoints and their problems, seemed absorbed in the general atmosphere of mourning. She was able to see, to observe and re-evaluate, all these people she had known and at the same time avoid real contact with them. The nature of the event that had gathered them together permitted one to be as private and withdrawn as one chose.

Helen realized, however, that this dinner would mark the end of whatever special privacies Angus' death had given his mourners. The next morning, all family contacts would once more be in effect. There would be expectations and requirements. People who had not seen each other for many years would be expected to bring their autobiographies up to date and to listen with interest as others carefully explained themselves.

In her mind, Helen drew up her lists. She longed to talk to Clara. She hoped to talk to Jesse. And she was intrigued by Valerie, tall and lovely now, and seventeen years old. But she was not eager to talk to Ned, she saw nothing in Nora's face to indicate that a conversation with her was very likely, and Hugh, as she watched him marching ghost-like through the funeral days, seemed no longer a member of the family. Or of any family, perhaps. If he had been pointed out to her as one of the undertakers' assistants it would have seemed totally believable to her. He looked, most of all, like a creature bent on flight. His eyes never met hers and he spoke to no one but Nora. And always in hushed tones with head half-turned as though to foil any lip-readers who might be in the room. Whereas before one had sensed a surly vitality under his silence, he seemed now to be merely empty, like a dry husk after harvest time.

Because of this hollowness, this apparent absence of spirit, Hugh had begun, for the first time, to resemble his father. Ned Causey, who had always seemed well-muscled and well-fleshed, was now almost cadaverous. His cheeks, formerly ruddy from claret and stout, were still faintly lavender and pink from the web of broken veins that covered them, but there was an overall effect of greyness. And his nose which had once been angrily carmine now had the colour and consistency of putty. Ned's voice, however, unlike Hugh's which had diminished to a husky whisper, was more angrily contentious than ever, more challenging and insistent and argumentative. If respect was not to be freely offered him, he seemed bent on seizing it.

Nora, on the other hand, was like an electric fountain of self-assurance and goodwill. Her hair, though sleek and natural and its own russet tone, had been softly sculptured by some genius hand; her skin was clear and translucent and unmarked, it seemed, by either time or torment. She was properly restrained and sorrowful as the occasion demanded and the opulence of her mourning clothes was almost concealed by their sombre colours and severe design. But there was something in her demeanour, all the

535

same, that suggested that she, not Clara, was the true mistress of Wingate Fields.

She related to Helen, however, with simplicity and what appeared to be true affection. 'How stunning you look,' she said. 'You've completely captured my daughter. She thinks you're the most heavenly thing she's ever seen. You mustn't encourage her though. She's liable to stow away on the Clipper and fly to America to visit you.' Then, 'I can't believe we've let so much time go past without seeing each other. But I realize I must take most of the blame. I've absorbed the Parisian philosophy – "Why go anywhere else when you live in the most beautiful place in the world." Jesse, of course, gets about more than I do and Valerie shows signs of becoming a true gypsy. She loves to be on the move all the time. But I'm a stay-at-home. I rarely go further than our country house. And even *that's* just a short drive from Paris.'

'There's so much talk about war with Germany,' Helen said. 'If that happened, would you come home to England?'

'Oh no. I would never leave Paris. War or no war. And actually I believe things are more encouraging just now. It seems that Chamberlain has things well in hand. We've just signed naval agreements with both Germany and Russia. And Germany completed work on their Siegfried line last year. That, as everyone knows, is a defensive device just like the Maginot line. To me that's a sure sign the Germans intend to stay at home. But *whatever* they do I don't expect to change *my* plans. Not matter what happens, the French will continue to eat well and drink well and I will be there helping them do it. You must come to stay with us as soon as you can. We'll show you Paris like no one else could.'

Ned presented Helen with no problems. He seemed as unenthusiastic about talking to her as she was about searching for things to say to him. She tried, however, to be amiable and friendly whenever they were thrown together. But he was monosyllabic and barely cordial. When she mentioned this to Clara, Clara said, 'I know. I see how he is and I apologize for him. I certainly don't condone his behaviour but I suppose I've become accustomed to it. He's angry with the world, you see, and he's particularly displeased with all the Bradshaws. Angus' death has only made it worse. It galls him to see someone else sitting in Angus' chair. He's never been able to deal with Jesse. And I suppose he associates you with all that frustration he feels. If you hadn't brought Jesse here . . . .'

Helen smiled. 'As you remember, it was Jesse who brought *me* . . . .'

'It's all the same to Ned. He feels badly treated and in his mind all of us must share the blame. I would suggest that you just ignore his behaviour as I do. In a time of stress and sadness like this I've found that the good people get better while the not-so-good ones end up not-so-good. The irony is that Ned really *liked* Angus. He admired him and envied him and feared him. But he also liked him. And he needed him, I think. Now he'll have only himself to blame for his shortcomings.'

It is a popular misconception that tragedy tends to bring families together. The fact is that few family units survive after the linch-pin has been drawn. When a strong central figure is removed, very often family conscience and honour go with him. The vacuum that has been created cannot be filled. A solid kingdom is replaced by an unstructured cluster of fiefs.

It was this process that Helen sensed at Wingate Fields. Without Angus' presence, without him and his power to relate to, it seemed that all those present, with the exception of Clara, were nervously attempting to define themselves. Having lost an armature, each was in the process of concluding that he or she was his or her *own* armature, free-standing and indestructible. This conclusion gave each of them a certain patina of arrogance in relation to the others but it also left its own internal residue of uncertainty and fear.

Such were the elements that permeated the atmosphere at Wingate for those few days just after Angus' death. An air of unquiet and indecision and subtle competition that could be made to pass for sorrow but was in fact something altogether different. The commanding voice had been silenced. The unifying force had been removed. Now each person felt free to chart a new and independent course. But that freedom brought no visible joy to any of them.

5

When Helen thought about her son, although she carefully kept track of his exact age, she, nonetheless, thought of him as a child. It was a strange sensation for her, therefore, as she talked to Valerie, to realize that this gracious and self-assured young woman was, in fact, a few months younger than her son.

It was not that Valerie made an effort to seem older than she was, on the contrary, everything about her seemed to affirm her youth. But all the same there was something in her manner, some hint of wisdom or insight or experience that made Helen feel as if she were speaking to someone close to herself in age. And Valerie seemed to have similar feelings.

'Jesse told me, he's told me for years,' she said, 'that I remind him of you. So I've always studied your photographs whenever I was here at Wingate visiting Clara. But I never saw what he was talking about till I met you in person. And even now, I'm not sure what it is. But I do see there's *something*. Not a physical resemblance exactly. But some little chromosome in the Bradshaw blood was apparently passed along to each of us. We *are* cousins after all. And according to Nora, you might very well have been my aunt.'

'I don't see how that could have happened,' Helen said.

'Perhaps you never knew it. But Nora says Hugh was very taken with you. Quite stunned and shattered, she says.'

'I think your mother exaggerated a little.'

538

'Maybe. But I doubt it. She's a serious historian of other people's love affairs.'

'I assure you there was never a love affair between me and Hugh.'

'Oh, she didn't say there was. She just said there *would* have been if Hugh had had his way.'

When Helen smiled, Valerie asked, 'Did I say something funny?'

'No. Not at all. I'm just fascinated to hear things about myself that I didn't know.'

'I'm sorry. I didn't mean to be . . . I think I've said more than I should have done. I was just trying to explain why I've always been so anxious to meet you.'

'I understand. And I've been eager to meet you.'

'Also, I knew how much Jesse admired you, how fond *he* was of you.'

'And I'm fond of him. We were like brother and sister.'

'Nora thought it was more than that. She thought you two were going to get married. That's what she really meant, I think, when she said you might have been my aunt. Or my great-aunt, I suppose it would have been, since Jesse's my great-uncle.'

'If she'd have asked Jesse,' Helen said, 'I'm sure he would have straightened her out.'

'Maybe she *did* ask him. Maybe he was like Hugh. Maybe he never told you how he felt about you.'

Helen smiled again. 'Doesn't sound like him. He was never good at hiding his feelings.'

'I can't believe it. It's as if we're talking about two different people.'

'How do you mean?'

'Or else he's changed a lot. Because Jesse's quite expert at hiding his feelings now. That's something he's particularly good at.'

Helen felt as if there was some further question she was expected to ask but she couldn't decide what it was. Or perhaps she *did* know the question but was not eager to learn the answer. In any case she allowed the conversation to die there.

Helen stayed in England only four days after the funeral service for Angus. Much of that time she spent with Clara. But on the last day before she was to leave, Jesse followed her out of the breakfast room and said, 'How would you like to take a drive and have lunch with me? There's a great old tumbledown inn between Otterburn and Rothbury.'

'Sounds nice. Can I invite Clara?'

'Not today. I want you all to myself.'

It was an odd sensation for Helen, sitting in the car with Jesse, driving north across the sheep meadows towards Otterburn. She felt that their long separation had frozen him in her memory. It seemed that no time had passed and he was as he had once been. She felt easy and unthreatened. She was eager to learn nothing new about him, nothing vital at any rate. Nothing disturbing or destructive.

It was as though Jesse had read her mind. Although Clara had told him a bit about Chet Comiskey, he asked Helen nothing about her personal life and volunteered no information about his own. They discussed his work in great detail, its rewards and its frustrations. They discussed Clara and Angus and Louise, Chagall and Dos Passos and Amelia Earhart. Also, of course, they talked a great deal about Raymond. And as they drove home after lunch he told her about a letter he'd recently received from his father.

'How long since you've seen him?' Helen asked.

'A long time. You remember when I went to San Francisco after I got out of the army . . . .'

'That's almost twenty years ago.'

'Exactly. That's the last time I saw him.'

'Did you write?'

'For a while I did. When I first came back to Fort Beck. But he never answered. And neither did my mother. So finally I stopped writing except for Christmas cards.'

'How did he locate you then?'

'I sent him my address at Wingate Fields when I came back here the second time. But according to his letter he never received it. He said he read about me in one of the

San Francisco papers. It was a little article about *Icarus*. They also printed a picture of me so he got hold of a copy of the magazine and wrote to me in care of our New York circulation office.'

'Must have seemed strange,' Helen said.

'*Strange* is not the word. It was a real *hate* letter. He started out by telling me my mother died five years ago. The doctor said it was her diabetes that killed her. She'd had it for years. But Dad said it was *my* fault. He said she'd never been the same after I left Chicago. And after I went to see them in San Francisco he said she *really* began to fail. He said she spent the last years of her life in a wheel-chair. *That's* when he said he had no idea where to reach me when she died.'

'Maybe he really didn't get your letter with your address on it.'

'Of course he got it. I also used to put a return address on the Christmas cards I sent. He knew how to reach me, all right.'

'But if he never wrote before, why would he write now?'

'Like I said it was a *hate* letter. I think seeing my name, Jesse Clegg *Bradshaw*, was what got him in gear. He wrote a whole diatribe about people who are ashamed of their birthright, who try to disown their own families. He said it was a *hateful* thing to do. That's always been his favourite word . . . *hateful*.'

'You must have felt awful.'

Jesse shook his head. 'Twenty years ago I felt awful. But now I don't. I learned a lot from people like Raymond and Angus and Clara. I found out that when people really give a damn about you, they *show* it. Angus was more of a father to me in the first six months I knew him than my real father had ever been. My mother was another matter. I felt like hell about her. I always wanted things to be different between her and me. But finally I had to face the truth about *her*, too. She was like a whipped dog. She had no feelings of her own. She wasn't allowed to have. She took all her signals from him. I tried to talk with her that last time I saw her in California. I tried to get through to

541

her. But it was impossible. When he was around she *couldn't* express herself and when he wasn't around, she *wouldn't*. If *he* was angry with me, so was *she*. Even if she had no idea what he was mad about. He'd turned her into a wind-up toy and she'd let him do it.'

'What about your brother and sister. Doris, was it?'

Jesse nodded. 'Doris and Leo. Grisly news there, too. And most of it is my fault according to my dad. Leo was in prison in Indiana for five years. Now he's in prison in Michigan. Won't be out till he's fifty-two years old. Doris I'm not sure about. She's shamed the family, Dad says. Whatever that means. He says she lives in Mexico now, in what he calls a bad section of Tampico, and has a baby every year.'

'What's wrong with that?'

'You have to read between the lines. He means she has a *Mexican* baby every year. My father only likes people with white skin. No tan. No brown. No yellow. No black.'

'God, he must be an unhappy man.'

'You'd think so, wouldn't you? But I don't think he is. There's nobody happier than a lunatic or a bigot. And bigots are the happiest of all. They never run out of people to hate. And everybody they hate gives them one more reason to love themselves. I'm sure he kept a copy of the letter he sent me so he can read it once in a while and make himself feel good all over again. I kept it, too.'

'Why, for God's sake?'

'So I can read it through and remind myself how lucky I was to get away from that son of a bitch.'

Earlier in the day, as they'd sat in the inn having lunch, Jesse had asked, 'Do you think about Raymond much?'

'All the time. How about you?'

'I don't know if I *think* about him. I mean I don't sit down in a room by myself and try to see how much I remember. But he seems to be always hanging around. Keeping an eye on me. Either he wants to make sure I'm not acting like a jackass or he wants to make sure I'm having some fun.'

'A little bit of both, I expect.'

542

'I don't worship him, you know. I used to think I did, but I don't think that now. Is that a rotten thing to say?'

'No,' Helen said.

'I mean the older I get the more I see there's no such thing as a perfect human being. Nothing close to it. Am I right?'

'No question.'

'The surest way to destroy someone is to deify them. There *aren't* any two-legged Gods. None that I've ever met anyway. I know a maniac poet who lives in Munich. He says we are only capable of worshipping someone who fulfils our immediate needs. He says that's why Christianity is sure to die. What do you think? Is he crazy?'

'Yes.'

'Anyway, Raymond didn't want anyone to worship him.'

'Not at all.'

'But he did want people to *like* him.'

'That's true.'

'Is that a weakness?'

'Sometimes it is,' Helen said. 'But not in his case.'

'Why not?'

'Because Raymond wouldn't give up anything just to be liked. He *wanted* to be liked but he didn't *need* it.'

'Have you read W. H. Auden?' Jesse asked.

'A little bit.'

'He said all writers want to be successful, but he's never met a serious writer who wants to be *popular*.'

They drove along in silence then for a few miles. At last Jesse said, 'Do you think people go up to the clouds when they're dead and sit there playing harps and watching us all making fools of ourselves down here?'

'No.'

'Neither do I. So we agree that Raymond hasn't been spying on us with binoculars. But what if he was still around, what if we'd stayed closer to him than we have to each other, what kind of marks do you think he'd have given us?'

'I don't know. I've never thought about that.'

543

'Sure you have. The Germans say, "Everybody has a schoolmaster in his life, someone he needs to please." Raymond may not have been *your* schoolmaster but he was certainly mine.'

Helen smiled. 'If someone overheard this conversation they'd think we were a couple of ten-year-olds.'

'I'd be flattered. Rilke said, "Genius is the ability to re-enter childhood at will." '

'All right, genius. What kind of marks *would* Raymond give us?'

'A conditional pass for you,' Jesse said. 'A *flunk* for me.'

'Why do you say that?'

'No good reason. It's just a feeling I have. He used to write on student papers. "You haven't begun to come up to your potential." '

'Is that what you think about yourself?'

'Not at all. I think I've probably *exceeded* my potential such as it is. But I don't think Raymond would agree with that judgment. What do you think?'

'I don't think he'd give us any marks at all. I think he'd say, "It's all up to you. It doesn't matter what *I* think." '

'You're no help,' Jesse said. 'I can stand up under anybody else's criticism. The tough part is when I have to take a hard look at myself. The only grade I can ever give myself is an *incomplete*.'

'There's nothing wrong with that. I'll settle for an *incomplete* any day. That means all the doors are still open. There's still time to get your ass out of the fire.'

Jesse looked at her and grinned. 'Where did you pick up *that* expression?'

'I've got lots of them. I hang around with rough people now. I wear hob-nailed boots and flannel shirts and long johns in the winter. I can clean a fish and skin a squirrel and drive a truck on an icy road. I can even change a tyre by myself.'

'I'm impressed,' Jesse said.

The following evening as her plane headed west across the Atlantic, she felt as though she had picked her way through a hedged maze and had found the exit at last.

544

Everything behind her seemed complex and disturbing. Obfuscation as a device, detours at all the crossroads, and vines clogging every path. At last she leaned her head against the plane window, felt the cool glass against her cheek, and began to cry. She told herself she was crying for Angus and she didn't allow herself to question the truth of that. She wrapped a blanket around herself and wept softly in the dark until she went to sleep.

6

If she had been totally candid with Jesse when they talked together that afternoon a few days after Angus' funeral, Helen would have said, 'My life is not nearly so random as it may seem. It is certainly not what I expected it to be, that's true. But that is because *I* am not what I thought I would be. If my history so far is an indication, it seems that I am a person who *reacts* to events. I seem to skate along smoothly enough until something I can't avoid or ignore changes my course. Then I'm off in another direction. There have been times when I've hated myself for that. I was convinced that it was a sign of failed courage, lack of foresight, or some other character flaw. But now I know it's part of me and I've come to accept it. When I say I *react*, that doesn't mean that I'm unable to make sensible choices on my own, because I *am*. What I'm *not* able to do, it seems, or what I am *unwilling* to do, is to chart a course and stick with it, to decide where I want to be or what I want to be doing a year from now or five years from now, and then plough straight ahead. Raymond used to tell me it was important to have faith in the future but I think I took him too literally. Even when I'm in a bad period, when I'm convinced I've made a wrong turn somewhere, I still feel that there must have been some reason behind it all. I never feel trapped. I never think there's no way out. I always expect things to work out somehow in the end. And if they don't . . . you see, I'm not an optimist . . . I'm a fatalist. I used to think that was a pose, just an excuse for indolence and inactivity or sloppy planning, but now I feel differently. Now I believe you can control or design only the surface, only the day-to-day pattern. You can *decorate* your life but you can't *construct* it. The major events are all outside your control. They will happen according to some schedule of their own and all you can do is accept, try to understand, and try to survive. If that's true, then it's an advantage if you don't have a rigid life-plan, structured of steel. If you're flexible, if you can bend, then you have a better chance for survival. Like those tall buildings they're putting up now that are designed to sway a little when the strong winds come.'

This is not to say that Helen thought herself the slave of circumstance. She did not. She was able to respond to emotional signals even when she had no clear reasons for that response. She did not expect always to understand herself. She was able to *wait*. She could answer, 'I don't know,' to almost any question without a sense of failure.

She knew, for example, had known from the beginning, that her life in Maine was a tributary to the main stream of what she was, where she came from, and where she was capable of going. She had gone there the first time to escape, and each subsequent trip there had been some variation of that original impulse. By any objective calculation, she was surely out of place there. Her speech, her thinking, her background, all those things set her apart. Her closeness to Opal and Bud was an attraction of opposites. Goats in the zebra cage, a mule with the giraffes. She felt at times that the principal ingredient of that friendship was a sense of wonder that it existed at all.

These doubts, however, existed only in her mind. Her emotions were another matter. Her feelings about the Feasters, about Hedrick, and about herself being there, rang as clear and true as a tuning-fork. Each time she entered Opal's kitchen she had a sense of returning to herself that was indescribable. And outside, the smell of the sea, the engine noises of the lobster boats, the creaking sound their hulls made in the tide swell, all these sensory truths had settled into Helen's consciousness in a dark corner that is reserved most often for childhood memories. She truly felt at times that Hedrick was her birthplace. When she walked along the road and passed the church-yard, she almost expected to see the names Bradshaw and Bardoni chiselled on the eighteenth-century headstones.

So she lived with two truths, the truth she told herself and the truth she felt. It was not a competition, however, and if it had been, it would not have been a fair one. Once she had passed Portland heading north, once Brunswick and Bath were behind her, the logic of Fort Beck and New York and Wingate Fields was also left behind. She gave herself freely to the salt smell and the sigh of the pines, fixed her eyes on the rocks and the sea and the narrow roads twisting through the trees and made no further plans.

If she had allowed herself to measure Chet in the same way she measured coastal Maine and her presence there, she would have witnessed, undoubtedly, that same war between reason and feeling, between sense and sensation. But with Chet, with him and her together, she used no such measurements, allowed herself no judgments. From the day the two of them hauled her belongings from her rented house on the harbour to his house in the woods, from before that day actually, but certainly from that day forward, she fastened herself to that house and to no other place, to that strange, angular man and to no other person.

The first morning they had breakfast together there, they sat on the screened-in porch watching the squirrels and the chipmunks scurrying about, and the early-morning rabbits nibbling grass at the edge of the clearing, and the jays and cardinals and finches flashing through the sun-shafts to the bird feeder.

'It's very important to have a screened-in porch,' Chet said. 'It puts you right out in the brush and the brambles with the rest of the animals. They get a good look at you and you get a good look at them. And the closer you look the more you see it's dog-eat-dog. All those beautiful little devils are trying to out-manoeuvre each other. *Food.* That's it. That's all they're after. Finding it, *getting* it, eating it, and then finding some more. And God help anything that gets in their way. They talk about men making war. We're all pikers compared to those little bastards in the woods. If they're gonna live, something else has to die. What's the prettiest bird we got out there? The cardinal, I guess. Did you ever get a close look at a cardinal through a pair of field glasses? If you ain't done it, my advice is . . . *don't*. You'll never think they're so pretty again. They look like killers, like hangmen. A black mask around their eyes and good-night nurse. I mean they are really ornery-looking. Even that chipmunk. He's a vegetarian. But you get him in the glasses and he looks like he'd pick your pocket.'

'There must be some *nice* little animals, aren't there?'

'Only the rabbits as far as I know. They're not mad at anybody. They just keep chomping away and keeping themselves out in the open so nothing can sneak up on them. They have pretty good faces too, when you see them close up – not a worry in the world, you'd think to look at them.'

'Bud says he likes possums. Used to have one as a pet.'

'Bud's nuts. Get him in an argument, he'll always take a contrary view. If he had a possum it was just 'cause somebody didn't *want* him to. You can count on that. Did you ever get a good look at a possum? They look like a rat. They're related to a rat, I'd bet money on it. Just like a fat rat. You tell Bud, next time you see him, I'm gonna catch a possum and put it in his bed. We'll *see* how much he likes a possum then.'

In the weeks before the weather was due to turn bad they spent long days in the wood behind the house, Bud along with them sometimes, locating fallen trees and cutting them up for firewood. They trucked the wood back to the house and stacked it in long, five-foot-high walls just off to one side of the screened porch.

'You can't stack it against the house,' Chet told her. 'Did you know that?'

'No.'

'Lots of people stack wood right up next to the house

548

and when spring comes they find out their siding's started to rot. Or they've got bugs and mice and rats and every other damned thing in their under-beams.'

One evening she asked him if he'd grown up on a farm. 'Opal asked me and I said I didn't know.'

'No, I didn't. My folks was always town people. Blacksmiths, storekeepers, carpenters, that kind of work. They lived in Kansas City and El Reno and all over west Texas, but I was in Lincoln, New Mexico from three years old till I went in the army. But all the time I was just waiting for this. A house in the woods. I've had it in my head since I was knee-high.'

'Did you have me in your head, too?'

He shook his head. 'No way I could. I'd never seen one like you.'

'I'd never seen one like you either.'

'I'll bet you didn't. You got to go through a lot of second-hand stores before you find one like me.'

One early evening in September, as they sat outside on the screened porch having a drink before supper, Chet said, 'I'll bet you think I drink too much, don't you?'

'Why do you say that?'

'Because I *do* drink too much. And even if I didn't, most women think their men drink too much. Opal's the only one I know who guzzles as much as her husband.'

'But you'd never know it. She's still going strong when Bud's asleep on the floor.'

'That's these cold winters up here. Makes tough women.'

'You think I'll be tough if I stay here long enough?'

'Depends on how long you stay, I guess.'

'I plan to stay till you throw me out,' she said. Then, 'You didn't answer my question.'

'You're tough already.'

'No, I'm not. My feet get cold at night and I keep getting blisters on my hands even when I wear those work gloves you got me.'

'My idea of tough,' he said, 'is somebody that don't feel sorry for themselves.'

'I always feel sorry for myself when my feet get cold.'

'Never mind. You know what I mean.'

Later that night, after supper, when they were sitting in front of the fireplace, he said, 'The first night I met you I told you I was sick and I wasn't gonna get well. Do you remember that?'

'Yes.'

'I don't want to talk about it much. But I think maybe I owe it to you to tell you something.'

'I already know a little bit. Opal told me quite a while ago. Right after I met you.'

'What did she tell you exactly?'

'She didn't know too much. She just said you'd been gassed during the war and you spent quite a bit of time in the hospital. And she said you'd been back since then.'

'It all started with the poison gas, she's right about that,' he said. 'I got a tumour on my lung and they opened me up and took it out. They tried to tell me it was because I'm a heavy smoker but they didn't fool anybody. Since then it's been one damned thing after another. You've seen the scars. First they'd always tell me I was a goner. Then they'd pump me full of some kind of chemical crap and cut me up a little more and the next thing I knew I'd be cured. Till the next time. Every few years some jazzbo doctor would tell me I was a dead man so I got used to it. I was drinking all the booze in New Mexico and smoking a carton of Camels every two or three days and I thought, "What the hell . . . I'm having a pretty good time for a guy who's supposed to be dead." And that's the way it went till about a year ago. Then all hell tore loose. I'd never broken a bone in my life but in the space of six weeks I b..ke my wrist and my collarbone. Then my kidneys went on the blink and the next thing I knew I keeled over in the street and they had me in the hospital in Roswell. From there they took me down to the army hospital in El Paso where I'd been a half-dozen times before and the doctors there gave me the word. Multiple myeloma. You ever heard of it?'

'No.'

'Tumour in the bone marrow. They can't operate. And they can't cure it any other way either. But they said if I

550

stopped boozing and smoking and if I came in there to the hospital once a week for radium treatments or something like that I might live two years. I said thank you very much, went back to Lincoln, sold everything I owned except my truck and my tools and came up here. I've decided I'm gonna live till I'm eighty but if I don't, I *won't*. Now you know as much as I do. Can you handle it?'

'Yes.'

'Good. You and I are going to have a nice time here in the woods. We don't have to *think* about any of that crap and we sure as hell don't have to *talk* about it. Right?'

'Right.'

'What a lucky girl you are,' he said. 'It must be nice to have somebody who tells you exactly what to do. I mean you never have to worry about a thing. Or make any plans or do anything except eat and sleep and have a good time. That must really be nice.'

'Yes, it is.'

7

The men and women who made up the British colony in Paris in the 1930s were, for the most part, a resolute lot. Some of them were still in one department or another of government service. Many more were retired from posts in Africa, India, Singapore, or some other far-off corner of their country's empire. They had been witness to revolution, insurrection, fire, flood and famine. Through every sort of calamity and upheaval, they had stood solid. Their very choice of France as a home revealed an inclination to maintain a certain level of inconvenience and discomfort in their daily lives. There was less danger of succumbing to boredom and senility in a country where the simple purchase of a postage stamp was always a challange and often an adventure.

Even the younger English people who had come to Paris to study painting or to write poetry or simply to squander

551

their monthly stipends at a benevolent rate of exchange, were not, by and large, inclined to let fear or trepidation influence their decisions. Nor were that other group, the English men of commerce who had chosen to settle in France for reasons of profit, discouraged by factors other than fluctuations *in* that profit.

All these people were essentially English in one respect. They were slow to let outside circumstances interfere with their personal objectives. They were accustomed to staying with a sinking ship. Nonetheless, by the end of 1938, many of them had begun to re-establish family and professional contacts in England, some children and small animals had been sent there, certain bits of furniture and art had been crated for shipping, and while no man admitted that he or his wife intended to exchange Paris for some tiresome and predictable refuge in Kent or Surrey, the atmosphere was unquiet and the unrest could not be hidden; the exodus had begun.

Certain events could neither be ignored nor explained away. There was full military mobilization in Germany. Hitler's troops had marched into Austria and had occupied Sudetenland. The French had called up their reservists, Hitler and Mussolini had publicly embraced in Rome, and pogroms were being reported from Germany. Anthony Eden had resigned in protest over Chamberlain's policies of appeasement and Churchill was making daily predictions of chaos.

And most alarming of all to many people was Roosevelt's solemn announcement that the American ambassador had been recalled from Germany and all diplomatic relations ended.

Nora, however, although she felt she understood every nuance of what was happening in Europe, saw no reason why it should interfere with her own activities. 'Of course I can't predict the future,' she said, 'but I don't think Paris will be destroyed in any case. It has survived for centuries. It will survive now. People will dine and dance and write poetry. Children will go to school, men will paint, and books will be printed and sold. Life will go on one way or

552

the other. There may be difficult times but I see no reason to transplant myself just because of that.'

Although Jesse was neither as specific nor as vocal on the subject as she was, Nora had every reason to believe that he agreed with her when she said, 'A lot of people depend on us. Not for their bread and butter, but because we *stand* for something. I don't think there's going to be a war but if there is, it's more important than ever for poets to have a place to publish and for people to be able to read the best new things that are being written.'

When Valerie went back to England to enter Cambridge a few weeks after Angus' death, Nora had objected. 'It's madness. All your schooling has been here in France. Why uproot yourself now? There's no place better than the Sorbonne. Or if you want to get away from Paris, you can go to Grenoble or Lyons. You'll be a stranger in England. You'll be miserable there with the codes and rules and all the rot about class distinctions.'

'Maybe you're right,' Valerie said. 'But I have to do it anyway. I'm English, after all, and I need to see what it's like to *be* English. I'm not abandoning France. I couldn't if I wanted to.'

'People will think you're just like a lot of the others over here. Running home to England to be safe.'

'I don't care what they think and you mustn't either. I'm not trying to be *safe*. When the war starts . . . .'

'*If* it starts,' Nora said.

'It's sure to start, Mum. And when it does, people in England will be no better off than people in France.'

In May of that year, to honour Nora's birthday, she and Jesse drove to Beaune, stayed at the Hotel de la Poste there, and had an elegant celebration dinner, roast duck with a fine local burgundy. And with dessert they drank a great deal of champagne.

'We'll be very tipsy and out of control, won't we?' Nora said.

'Of course. It's your birthday.'

'It's a long time since we've had a birthday dinner by ourselves. Do you miss Valerie?'

'Sure I do.'

'So do I. But I also like having you to myself.'

'You're a selfish wench.'

'Selfish and possessive and ferocious. And don't you forget it.'

As they started their second bottle of champagne, Jesse took a small velvet box out of his pocket and put it on the table in front of her.

'I love presents,' she said as she untied the ribbon. 'I particularly love *your* presents. You always give me special things.' When she opened the box and peeked inside, she said, '*This* is *really* special.' She took the ring, an emerald-cut diamond, out of the box and tried it on. The band was too large for her small finger and too small for her forefinger. When she slipped it on her third finger she said, 'It's really lovely.' She held it up to catch the candlelight. 'But I can't wear it on this finger. People will think we're planning to be married or something indecent like that.'

'That's what they're supposed to think.'

She sipped from her glass, still concentrating on the ring. When she set down her glass she said, 'But we *can't* be engaged to be married. You've never proposed to me.'

'I don't have to. We've been married for years. Now we're just going to make it official and legal and respectable.'

'I don't *want* to be respectable. Do you?'

'Not necessarily. We'll be married and disreputable if you like that better.'

She sat very still then, looking at him. 'I think you're serious,' she said.

'I *am* serious.'

'You mean you really *want* us to get married?'

'Yes.'

'When?'

'The sooner the better.'

'Why?' she said.

'Why not? It's not so unusual, is it? People get married all the time.'

'*We* don't.'

554

'We haven't *yet*,' he said. 'But that doesn't mean we *can't*. Some of our best friends are married.'

'But they're not like us. We're different. People *envy* us. If we told our friends we were getting married, they'd probably hold a wake.'

'They can do whatever they want to. This is all between you and me. It doesn't concern anyone else.'

'How long have you been thinking about this?' she asked then.

'Off and on for quite a while. And the last few months I've been thinking of it a lot.'

Again she studied him over her glass. 'Since Angus died, you mean?'

'No. Before that.'

'You mean it's just something you've always had a yen to do and now you think we should do it.'

He smiled. 'I wouldn't put it in those words exactly. But that's close to it, I guess.'

'What if I said no?'

'Why would you do that?' he said.

'I don't know. But what if I did? What if I gave you a good reason.'

'We're not exactly strangers. We know each other pretty well. I think if you had some good reason I'd already know about it.'

'What if I told you I love you more than anything or anybody in the whole world and that I never want to be away from you for a day if I can help it but that I don't really want to get married? Then what?'

'I'd want to know why.'

'Suppose I just don't *like* being married. Isn't that a reason? I mean I don't like the *idea* of marriage. I tried it once and didn't like it. Not only did I not like it, I *hated* it. I felt as if I'd left my soul at the altar. I felt diminished and terrible. And I didn't feel good again, didn't feel like *myself* again, till I was divorced and solitary.'

'We've been together for fifteen years. Do you call that *solitary*?'

'No, I call it wonderful. But I don't call it married.'

555

'Do you think going through a ceremony would change anything for us?'

'No, I *don't* think that. I didn't think it with Edmund either, but it happened.'

'I'm not Edmund.'

'I know you're not. I'm *not* comparing you to him, God knows. Mostly I'm talking about *me*. I love the way *we* are. I love the way *I* am. I don't want anything to change. I want everything to stay the way it is. I don't need the word *wife* stencilled on my forehead. Or *husband* on yours. We're beyond all that, Jesse. We're not part of some great institution and we don't *need* to be. We're just *us*. Isn't that good enough?'

He studied her for a long moment. Finally, he said, 'Sure it is. Let's forget it and have some more champagne.'

'I can't. I'll be drunk as a monkey.'

'It's a perfect night for it. We'll both get drunk.'

'You're mad at me, aren't you?' she said then.

'How could I be mad at you? I *never* get mad at you. I just want to celebrate your birthday a lot.'

'I know you,' she said. 'You're mad as hell at me. All of a sudden.'

'No, I'm not. When I get mad I run away and hide. When I'm happy I order more champagne.' He looked over his shoulder to find the waiter.

'Are you sure?'

'I'm sure.'

'Good. Then do me a favour. Let's have some champagne sent up to our rooms. Then I can put on my nightgown and my new ring and we can drink and stay up late and be irresponsible.'

When they went upstairs ten minutes later, a magnum of champagne was cooling in an ice-bucket in their sitting-room. Jesse turned the bottle in the crushed ice while he waited for her to change. When she came into the room in her nightdress and dressing-gown he drew the cork and poured each of them a glass.

'Here's to us,' she said.

'Here's to *you*. Happy birthday.'

She sat down in the soft chair facing him. 'You're absolutely certain you're not angry?'

'Absolutely certain.'

'Can we finish our discussion then, the one we started downstairs?'

'I thought it was finished,' he said.

'I don't think so.'

'I said I wanted to get married and you said you *didn't* want to. Doesn't that complete the circle?'

'Not quite. Not till I understand why all this is coming up just now. Why not before?'

'I don't have an answer for that,' he said. 'When I was in college the sociology books said there comes a time in most men's lives when they decide they want to get married and have a family. I don't know if that's always true but . . . .'

'Wait a minute. This is a new development. Are you saying you want us to find a little cottage somewhere and have a little *family*? Is that it?'

'I have a feeling we shouldn't talk about it. Not tonight.'

'I *want* to talk about it,' she said.

'All right. Let's talk about it.' He refilled their glasses. 'I'm not talking about changing your life or mine. I'm not talking about moving into a cottage. I said I want us to get married. And if we get married I'd like it if we had some kids. It's a common occurrence.'

'I don't want to be common.'

'You know what I mean.'

'*Some* kids. What does *that* mean?'

'A kid. *Two* kids. I don't know.'

'I'm thirty-eight years old, Jesse . . . .'

'What difference does *that* make?'

'Think it over.'

'Some women have children when they're fifty.'

'*Some* women do all kinds of things. We're talking about *me*. Do you really think a few little toddlers running around the house wouldn't change my life at this stage of the game?'

'I'm *sure* it would and I think you'd like it.'

557

'Then you're not thinking straight. I wouldn't like it at all. I like my life the way it *is*. I don't *want* to change it. I don't want to have a ten-year-old child when I'm fifty. Or a twenty-year-old when I'm sixty. And you're three years older than *I* am. I can't believe you haven't thought of that.'

'Of course I have. That's why I don't want to wait any longer.'

'Are you saying that you're going to have a family come hell or high water? That if I'm not willing you'll find someone who is?'

'Do you *think* that's what I'm saying?'

'That's what it sounds like to me.'

'Then I think we'd better get off the subject.'

'I don't want to get off it,' she said.

'Then we'll talk about it later when we're both sober.'

'I don't want to be sober. This way I have the courage to say what I think.'

'Suit yourself,' he said.

'I'm not mad at you. Do you think I'm mad at you?'

'No. But I think you're going to have a sensational hangover tomorrow and you'll blame *me* for it.'

'I'll worry about that tomorrow. Now I need to find out what brought on this sudden change in you.'

'It's not so sudden. I've brought it up before.'

'Only as a joke. Always sort of off-hand, like a joke.'

'I wasn't joking.'

'But you weren't serious like you are now. Now you're dead serious. And I want to know why.'

'I can't tell you,' he said. 'Don't have the answer.'

'You *won't* tell me but I think I know anyway. It came back to me when I was changing my clothes just now. I remembered what I thought when I saw you sitting in Angus' chair at the dinner we had after his funeral. I thought, "There's the new head of the Bradshaw family." Was that going through your head too?'

'No. I've never felt like the head of the Bradshaw family.'

'Well, you *are*. Whether you feel like it or not.' She leaned forward and poured more wine into her glass. 'You're the last male Bradshaw just like Angus was. And if you don't have a son, or adopt one as he did, the Bradshaw name is *kaput*. That would be a damned shame, wouldn't it?'

'Yes, I think it would. But that has nothing to do with what you and I are talking about.'

'Of course it does. I'm not stupid. You'd be surprised how much I know. I know that Angus never really liked the idea of us being together. I know he didn't want us to get married.'

'He never said anything like that to me.'

'Maybe he didn't *say* it but he made sure you *knew* it. You don't have to admit it. I *knew* Angus. I *know* how he felt. So maybe that explains why all of a sudden you want to get married. You don't have to worry now that maybe Angus wouldn't like it.'

'You're not making sense.'

'Oh yes, I am,' she said. 'You may not *like* it but it makes perfect sense. It *all* makes sense.'

'I feel lousy. Let's give it up for tonight.'

'Not yet. It's my birthday. We need more champagne.'

'No more for me. It's too late.'

'Never too late,' she said.

She stood up, walked to the call button, rang the waiter and ordered two more bottles of champagne.

'Never too late when it's your eighty-third . . . .' She started to giggle. 'What did I say?'

'You started to say it's your eighty-third birthday.'

She kept on giggling but talked through it. 'When it's your *thirty-eighth* birthday was what I meant to say. Never too late on such an occasion.' She sat down again. 'I'm seeing things very clearly now. That little disappearing act you pulled with Helen. Into your car and off for the day across the moors, that last day before she went back to America. What was that all about, I asked myself? Renewing an old acquaintanceship? Making plans for the future, perhaps? Why not? If things don't work out with Nora, why not keep it in the family? Pure Bradshaw blood wherever you turn. *You* have the Bradshaw name but you

559

need a Bradshaw brood mare to keep the blood-lines authentic.'

'What the hell are you talking about?'

'*You* know what I'm talking about.'

The waiter returned then with two bottles of wine in a large silver bucket. He opened one bottle, filled their glasses, and left. Nora drained her glass and filled it again.

'I don't want any more,' Jesse said. 'I'm going to bed.'

'You *do* that. I'll just stay here and tidy up the wine. Or maybe I'll go down to the desk and treat the night porter to a few beakers.'

'You're really going strong. I've never seen you like this.'

'That's because I've never *been* like this. You're seeing me at a crossroads. Responding to unfamiliar stimuli. Sorting things out, as they say. Trying to measure up the profit and the loss. Asking myself where I go from here. Or if I go anywhere. All good questions. Good and vital questions. Just normal everyday questions that a young woman asks herself.'

Jesse walked across the room, knelt down beside her and put his arm around her shoulders. 'I wish you'd come to bed. You're really going to get yourself upset.'

She turned to look at him. Her eyes suddenly filled with tears. 'I always get upset,' she said, 'when people underestimate me, when someone looks me straight in the eye as you're doing now, and tells me the earth is really flat. When they do their little dance and shake their little bells and tell me stories about the elves and the trolls.'

'I don't know what you're talking about.'

'Yes, you do. Do you think I was ever deceived by that brother and sister act you and Helen put on when you first came to Wingate Fields? Not for a minute. No one else in the family knew why she ran back to America as soon as she found out you and I were going to get married. But *I* knew. I wasn't surprised she left. I'd made off with her gentleman friend and she was . . . .'

'We're both drunk, Nora. Don't say a lot of stuff you'll want to take back tomorrow.'

'I'm not taking anything back. Everything I'm saying is the truth.'

'No, it's not. If you're telling me that Helen and I . . . .'

'Don't lie about it,' Nora said. 'There's no point to it. Not now. You think a woman can't *tell* when she sees two people together? You think I couldn't *see*, that first day I met you, that there was something going on between you two? I didn't see anything wrong with it. I just couldn't figure out why you were so anxious that nobody should find out.'

'There was nothing to *find* out.'

'I know. I've heard it all before. She was like your sister and you were her brother.'

'It's the truth,' Jesse said.

'But you're *not* her brother any more than you're Clara's brother or Valerie's uncle. You have all the privileges of family membership but none of the restrictions. Why shouldn't you have your eye on Helen? Even if you insist she's your sister I guarantee you she doesn't think of *you* as her brother. So there she is. Willing and available. A perfect cottage type, it seems to me. A cottage in Devon. Wasn't that what you told me once? Helen could provide you with all the children you want in Devon. Probably even learn to fetch your daily paper. Bring it to you in her mouth like a springer spaniel.'

'That's enough, Nora.'

'No, it's not. It's not nearly enough. I'm doing you a service, you know. I've rebuffed you and I feel bad about it. I've rejected you and I feel guilty. If I'm not willing to provide this new bourgeois life you've decided you need, the least I can do is help you to find an alternative. Not feeling inclined to marry myself, I will function as a marriage broker. As I see it, it's a kindness. I am performing an act of kindness.'

She stood up, weaving a bit, filled Jesse's glass and her own, and sat down beside him on the couch. 'Very few women would be as selfless as I am in this situation. I could be angry or petulant and think only of myself but instead I'm thinking of you. Don't you realize that?'

561

'I don't know *what* you're doing and neither do you.'

'Of course I do. I'm being mature and wise and unselfish. If your life has taken a new turn, if you have needs that I am either unwilling or unable to gratify, then I feel obligated to point out that Helen might be a good choice for you. And if that doesn't work out, why not consider Valerie?'

'Jesus Christ, Nora.'

'Does that shock you? It shouldn't. Can you honestly tell me that such a thought has never occurred to you? I can assure you it has occurred to her.'

'What kind of mind do you have? Valerie's your . . . .'

'I know who she is. She's my daughter. *Every* young woman is somebody's daughter. But I've never imagined that she wouldn't someday select a man for herself. And since she was sixteen I've been aware that the man she would select would be you if you were available.'

'That's ridiculous.'

'No, it's not. And if you're honest with yourself you'll *admit* it's not. She's very conscious of the fact that you're not *really* her uncle. She knows you're not related to her at all. You're just a nice, attractive man who sleeps with her mother . . . .'

'She doesn't feel that way and you know it.'

'Let me finish. Do you really think that if you and I split up or separate or whatever they call it these days that you and Valerie would never see each other again?'

'Of course not. But that's a different matter.'

'In your mind perhaps, but not in hers. I was a young girl myself and not that long ago. I know how they think. I know how *I* thought. If you think Valerie wouldn't come rapping on your door if I was out of the picture, then you don't know much about women. And you know nothing at all about my daughter.'

'If *I* don't know her, who does? I've been with her almost every day for the past fifteen years.'

'Exactly,' Nora said.

'So I think I know her pretty well. I'm very fond of her and I know she's fond of me.'

'Wrong. You're fond of *her*. But she's *wild* about you. Why do you think she ran off to England to go to school?'

'I *know* why she went.'

'No, you don't. She went to get away from *you*. To get away from *us*. To stop feeling like the second woman in the house.'

'You're not making any sense.'

'Oh, yes I am. I am not an expert in all areas but in the science of male and female relationships I am an eminent scholar. I knew my mother and Ned were dead in the water long before *she* knew it. Some people can read tea leaves or forecast the weather. I can take one look at a man and a woman and tell you what's going on between them. Or what's *not* going on. That's my talent. And I trust it. You can spend the next five years telling me there was nothing between you and Helen but you won't convince me. Because I know how *she* felt. I also know how Valerie feels. She's weak in the knees every time she sees you. When she started quizzing you and me about why we didn't have a baby, that was because it was slowly dawning on her that *she* was old enough to have a baby. Didn't you *understand* that? All of a sudden she saw herself in a new light. And she saw *you* in a new light. It's not so unusual. Lots of girls her age have a crush on their fathers. But in Valerie's case it's not just a crush. And *you're* not her father.'

'What an imagination you have.'

'It's not imagination. You're just dumb about women. Most men are. They *look* but they don't *see*. They think they're experts but they don't know anything. Let me ask you a question. Do you think you can tell when a woman is interested in you?'

'I don't think much about that.'

'Of course you do. Every man does. When you first came to Wingate Fields, when you and I were having our little frolic together, when we decided we were going to get married, you certainly knew that *I* was interested in you, didn't you?'

563

Jesse smiled. 'As I remember, we were both very interested in each other.'

'Wrong,' she said. 'At that time I didn't give a damn about anybody but myself. At first I didn't even *like* you. Then I began to see you as a way out of Northumberland. That was the most important thing in the world to me. I thought if I married you it would be the start of a different life for me. *That's* what it was all about. It's what *I* was all about. Does that surprise you?'

When he didn't answer, she went on. 'It *does* surprise you. I can see that. Now I'll give you another surprise. What about Clara?'

'What about her?'

'How do you think *she* feels about you?'

'I *know* how she feels about me. In many ways she's the closest friend I've ever had. I respect her and I trust her and I like her and I know she feels the same way about me.'

Nora smiled and waggled her forefinger at him. 'I hate to tell you, but you're wrong again. That's the way she felt about you when you *first* came to Wingate. But by the second time, everything was changed. Helen was out of the picture by then, *I* was married, and Ned and Clara had stopped trying to pretend they still liked each other. Also, it's important to remember that at that time, Clara was only a few years older than I am now. Do you follow me? All those days the two of you spent together may have inspired trust and respect and affection in your heart but Clara saw it differently. My sweet lady mother was ga-ga about you. If you'd asked her to go away with you, for a week or a year or for the rest of her life, she'd have been packed up and ready in an hour.'

'You really *are* drunk, aren't you?'

'Not me. I'm not nearly as drunk as you think I am. And not half as drunk as I'd like to be.'

'I don't know what you'd call it then. All of a sudden these fantasies are bubbling out of you . . . .'

'It's not all of a sudden. I've known all these things . . . .'

'No, you haven't,' he said. 'Just saying whatever comes

into your head doesn't make it true. What makes you think you can see. . . .'

'Because I'm a witch.'

'No, you're not. You're a baby. You thought I was mad at you before and now you're trying to get even with me . . . .'

Suddenly she was crying. 'Don't tell me how I feel! Don't tell *me* what I'm trying to do. Just because I've never said anything before doesn't mean my head was a blank. I've been jealous of Helen since the day I met her. For years I was jealous of Clara. How do you think I felt when you were slingshotting back and forth between Paris and Wingate? Me here and Clara there. It used to drive me crazy. It *still* drives me crazy. Now I'm jealous of my own daughter.'

'I told you before . . . that's ludicrous. She's like my daughter, too.'

'That's right. She's *like* your daughter, I'm *like* your wife, Clara's *like* your mother, and Helen's *like* your sister. But none of us are exactly what we seem to be. We all have a piece of you but none of us knows how much. I'm not *blaming* you. I'm not saying it's your fault. I'm just saying that a strange situation exists and I don't see how it can do anything but become more strange.'

After a long moment, he said, 'You're really sick.'

'Don't tell me *I'm* sick. You're the one who's sick.'

The next day as they drove towards Paris, Jesse said, 'Well, you can't say we didn't celebrate your fête.'

'No, I certainly can't. My head is reminding me. What time did we finally go to bed?'

'Very late.'

'I think I drew a blank,' she said. 'I remember coming upstairs and changing into my night clothes but after that everything is quite spotty. What happened?'

'Don't ask me. We were drinking and carrying on and I vaguely remember a long discussion about something or other but all the details escape me.'

'What *were* we talking about?'

'That's what I don't remember. Do you remember?'

565

She shook her head. 'Big blank.'

He pretended to believe her and she pretended to believe him. It was an elaborate charade but a necessary one, they felt. If they pretended to have forgotten, perhaps in time they would truly forget. But one couldn't be sure. So from that morning on, neither of them allowed themselves the luxury of planning ahead. They simply attached one day to the next and hoped for the best.

Chapter Twelve

1

Although Helen never doubted that at some time she would tell Chet about her son, it was not because she felt an obligation to tell him. She had long ago concluded that this was a circumstance that concerned her and the child and no one else; she told herself she felt neither guilt nor shame. Nonetheless, she went through periods of torment over what she had done and for things she felt she had failed to do.

Strangely, perhaps, she never questioned or regretted the impulse that had taken her into Hugh's bedroom that night. That was hidden somewhere in the tangle of her emotional history and was not available for dissection or review. The choices she had made later, however, the decision to give up her child, to turn him over to strangers with no hope of seeing him again, *that* part of the experience could not be resolved or explained away or forgiven. Not in Helen's mind. Nor in the mind of anyone else, she suspected.

So she did have trepidations about telling Chet. But they were overpowered by her *need* to tell him. It was not that she expected approval from him. He was simply the only living person she felt she *could* tell.

It all came out one Sunday morning as they sat on the screened porch after breakfast. Starting with Raymond's death she described in detail everything that had transpired between then and the time she had the baby. All through the long story Chet said nothing. He glanced at her occasionally but mostly he looked out across the clearing to the wall of trees that marked the beginning of the woods.

'That's some sad tale,' he said after she finished. 'I've been sitting here trying to figure out why you're telling it to me.'

'Because I wanted you to know. That's all. I've never told anybody else the whole truth but I wanted to tell you.'

'I feel like I ought to be giving you some kind of advice but I don't know what to say.'

'That's not why I told you,' she said. 'I don't *need* advice.'

'I'm not so sure about that. You're not saying you're happy about the situation the way it is, are you?'

'It's not a question of being happy.'

'What's it a question of, then?'

'I don't know, but it's not that. I'm not trying to *change* anything.'

'Why not?' he said.

'Because I tried everything I could think of and I didn't get anywhere.'

'What were you trying to do?'

'I just wanted some information I guess. Where he is now. What his name is.'

'And what did you find out?'

'I found out I have no rights. That's what they told me. Any rights I had as a mother I signed away. I even went to a law firm in Portland and they told me the same thing.'

'Everybody has rights.'

'Not me. Not as far as Floyd's concerned.'

'Who's Floyd?'

'That's what I call my kid.'

'Is that his name?'

'I'm not sure. Maybe it is. Maybe it isn't. They wouldn't tell me definitely. Anyway, it doesn't matter so much now. I mean it *matters*, I guess, but there's nothing to be done. I gave up a long time ago. Wherever he is he'll be twenty years old next year. He's grown up. There's not much I can do for him now.'

'That's one way of looking at it, I guess.'

568

'It's the *only* way. I drove myself crazy with it for years. Now I just don't let myself think about it any more.'

'Are you telling me there's no way on God's earth that a woman can find out what her own kid's name is and where he lives?'

'I told you. I have no legal rights.'

'I don't give a damn about *legal*. You're talking about *information*. *Somebody* knows what you want to know. Quite a few people, probably. Clerks and secretaries and the like. So why are you the only one who can't find out? I don't care what kind of a paper you signed. There's a file on you at the agency in Portland. There has to be.'

'Of course there is but what good is it if they won't let me see it?'

'Just because they won't *let* you, that don't mean you can't. You're talking to a man who spent a few years in the army. And a few more years in army hospitals. *Everything's* a secret when you're in the service. You're lucky if they tell you where the latrine is. But my experience is that anything that's written down has to be stored someplace. In a box or a file cabinet . . . someplace. And there's always some sad-assed citizen who looks after those boxes and keeps track of where everything's put. The trick is to find that bird and figure out something he *wants* that he doesn't *have*. That way you get what you need. I always knew the results of my medical tests before the doctors did. I knew if I was being shipped home or transferred to another hospital two weeks before they got around to *telling* me.'

'What has that got to do with . . . .'

'Everything,' Chet said. 'I guarantee you there's some stenographer or file clerk or cleaning lady in that agency in Portland who can lay hands on your file and tell you what you want to know. But . . . .'

'But what?'

'If you gave up on the whole idea already, I guess there's no point in going to a lot of trouble.'

'It's a needle in a haystack.'

'That's right. But we know where the haystack is and

we know for damned sure there's a needle in it. So we're halfway home.'

'I just don't see how we could ever . . . .'

'That's *my* problem,' he said. 'I'm an old hand. I'll talk to my friend, Bud. He has all kinds of cronies in Portland. We'll do a few manoeuvres. Turn the two of us loose, there's no telling what we might come up with.'

2

Near the end of February in 1939, six months before France would declare war on Germany, Nora, leaving a small staff of servants in both her Paris house and the house on the Marne, left France and moved, not to England but to New York. Denying that the move was an escape, that it was in any way a refutation of her former statements about staying put, she said, 'I'm not fleeing from the war. There *isn't* a war in France. I'm simply making a professional decision. All my writers and artists have gone, many of them to America. So I am forced to follow along if I intend to continue with *Icarus*. Leger and Beckmann and Duchamps are all in New York. And dozens more. Feininger's there and Kokoschka's in London. Half of our poets are in Greenwich Village or Brooklyn Heights now as well as Milhaud, Bartok, Stravinsky, Hindemith and almost any other progressive composer you can name. So we're off to spend some time among the cowboys and the redskins, eating wild turkey and hominy grits. But before too long we'll be back home in Paris and happy to be.'

Nora's decision to leave, as the year progressed, seemed wonderfully prescient. In addition to the declaration of war by both Great Britain and France, other telling events were to take place. Germany renounced her naval agreement with England, signed a non-aggression pact with Russia, and a ten-year alliance with Italy. Conscription began in England, women and children began to be evacuated from London, and 150,000 British troops were sent to France.

Poland was invaded by both Russia and Germany, and Franklin Roosevelt, while proclaiming the United States neutral, asked Congress for half a billion dollars for defence.

Because she rode well, drove fast cars, and invariably dived into bathing pools from the high board, Nora had always thought of herself as fearless. But gradually, in the last months before leaving Paris, she discovered that she was restless by day and sleepless by night. She was raw-nerved and short-tempered and found it difficult to concentrate. It was a new experience for her, an unfamiliar feeling. For weeks she tried to explain it to herself, tried to resolve it and lose it. But when it finally was defined, she found it impossible to explain away. She realized suddenly that she was afraid, that for the first time in her life she felt physical fear. It annoyed her and embarrassed her but she couldn't push it back.

At her Thursday evening salons, refugees from Poland and Germany and Italy began to appear, some of them hoping to settle in Paris, others, more far-sighted, using it as a way-station to England or America. Nora was, as we have seen, well-informed. She prided herself on it. Thoughtful journalists from *Le Monde* and *Le Figaro* were among her close friends. So she missed very few of the stories behind the headlines. Tales of atrocity and torture and religious persecution were not unfamiliar to her. But these soft-spoken, first-hand revelations in her own home, the visible and invisible wounds, were quite another matter. An awareness of suffering was very little preparation, she discovered, for seeing the results. When they learned she was English, none of these people asked her if she was leaving France, they simply said, 'You must go. Don't wait. Go now.'

She didn't go, of course. She wouldn't go, she told herself, until she was quite ready. And then it would be for her own reasons, as publicly stated. But whatever the range of her reasons, and they were several as well as complex, she was unable to escape the truth of her fear. It stayed with her long after the war. Wherever she was. But

571

especially when she was in Paris. It never totally left her. Once the fighting and killing were over, she found other things to fear. And later in her life her fears needed no definition and no name. But they were persistent and permanent all the same.

The timing of her departure from Paris was carefully planned. Once she had made her decision to go she was determined not to delay until circumstances might prevent her from reaching New York.

Any thought of returning to England was anathema to her. Whatever her trepidations about remaining in France she told herself that anything would be preferable to life at Wingate Fields. Or even London. She had enlarged her disdain for her home county to include even that heroic city.

Not paramount in Nora's decision to move from Paris to New York but nonetheless always present in her subconscious as she listed plus and minus factors, was the climate between her and Jesse. Since her birthday the previous year, since that singular night at the hotel in Beaune, she had waited for what she assumed was some inevitable consequence. It never occurred to her that they would survive that night, those words, *her* words, that they would pick up the scattered pieces, somehow mould them together again, and proceed. She felt as if it was almost *necessary* that they part now, that no matter how hard they struggled, the residue of that birthday night would cling to them forever.

She was well aware that her normal instinct would have been, when anticipating catastrophe, to unbuckle her sword and take the initiative. But in this case the price was more than she was willing to pay. She told herself she was prepared for the eventuality of Jesse's leaving her but she was unable to take the first step herself.

Knowing she had wounded him, knowing she had *mortally* wounded *them*, she could not believe that there would not be, at last, a bill to pay. Still, if there was a chance in a thousand that she was wrong she did not want to precipitate what might, by some miracle, never be. So

572

she waited as she assumed he was waiting, he to swing the mace, she to take the blow.

All the same, it was agonizing for her. Waiting always had pained her. And in this instance, where there was truly something at stake, the situation was particularly severe, made more so by her frequently reminding herself that she could have averted it all. If she had had the courage to tell the truth – or perhaps it was her pride that had stood in the way – the subject would have been closed. There would have been no discussion and no idiotic listing of her fantasies and jealousies, they could have talked it through and there would have been no need for them to pretend, the following morning, that they had been too drunk to remember the details of their conversation.

If she had simply said, 'I *can't* have children, Jesse. I had a stupid operation years ago. When I first came to Paris. I was upset about my marriage and my divorce and I thought I was doing a clever, grown-up thing. Now I'd do anything to take it back, but I can't.' Just a short and earnest statement, saying what she truly meant, and everything would have been accepted and understood. But some impulse had stopped her. She hadn't done it.

Nor could she tell him later. Wishing she had told him that night in Beaune, she found herself unable to do the next best thing, to tell him afterwards. She could not risk being pitied, she could not present herself as a woman who was *unable* to do something. *Unwilling* was as far as she would allow herself to go. It was as though she had a fear that she had never articulated, even to herself, the fear that having offered and given *everything* it might prove to be not enough. She was chemically unable to be a victim. If she was destined to lose something of value, she was determined, she *needed*, to play some role in that process of loss. Her imperfection was her armour. Her unwillingness to give *everything* was her guarantee that there would always be something left for *her*. Something to nourish her and keep her warm, some nugget of self-worth to hold onto in her bed at night.

In her most positive moments Nora told herself that if

573

Jesse planned to leave her he would have gone by now. Nearly a year had gone by since that drunken performance in Beaune and he had never referred to it in even a casual way. Nor had the subject of marriage come up again. It was as though that discussion had never taken place or having taken place had been totally forgotten.

As much as she would have liked to believe all this, however, Nora could not. In a situation where she had no intention of leaving Jesse and could not bear the thought of his leaving her, the pain of not knowing *what* was going to happen was even more unbearable.

Her decision to move to New York, then, served multiple purposes for her. One purpose was specifically connected to Jesse. If he had been waiting for some circumstance that would make their separation seem less painfully personal, she concluded, *this* one would be ideal.

Some part of her said she was a fool to force his hand this way, but another more insistent voice said that nothing could be worse than the shapeless anxiety she had experienced in the past months. She hated the thought of living apart from him but she came to believe that the pain would be lessened somewhat if she could tell herself they had been separated by circumstances. The war, for example.

When she told him about her plans she made no effort to make them sound either sensible or inevitable. In her efforts to avoid seeming to persuade him, she made it appear that she was acting almost on a whim. 'I have no doubt that we could ride out whatever may happen here in Paris,' she said. 'And if for some reason we couldn't, the logical alternative would be for us to go back to England. But I have a feeling that I might like living in New York just now. So I've decided to close up here and move there. What do you think?'

His agreement had been as casual as her question. He hadn't hesitated. 'Why not?' he said. 'Why not try it for a while? I think you'll like New York.'

'But what about *you?*'

'I've *always* liked New York.'

If she had imagined that his agreement to go would give

574

her some feeling of reassurance, she was mistaken. The thing that stayed in her mind was not that easy agreement but a particular sentence he had said. It echoed in her head for the rest of the time they were together and when they parted at last she still heard him saying, 'Why not? Why not try it *for a while?*' It sounded ominously temporary to her.

3

As England became totally involved in the war, Helen began to receive long and frequent letters from Clara. In one of them, just after the near-disaster at Dunkirk she wrote:

I hope I don't smother you with my rambling letters. They are not a product of idle hours. In fact my days are fully occupied, from dawn till bedtime. But tired as I am, sometimes I can't sleep. All sorts of beasties in my head. The tiny lights we're permitted aren't bright enough for reading, so I write letters. And almost always I write to you, not just because my list of correspondents grows shorter every year which it does, and not just because I seldom write more than a note to either Hugh or Nora, but because, as you and I discussed at the time of Angus' funeral, we seem to have some kind of connection that is supposedly common among family members but which is, in fact, quite rare. When I have either good news or bad news to share with someone it's you who comes first to my mind.

Also, without having seen with my own eyes where you live in Maine, I feel, nonetheless, that you live in a kind of isolation there which is similar to what the war has brought us. So we're kindred spirits. Solitary apes.

As you surely know from your newspapers our little

island is going through an ugly time. The Dunkirk evacuation was a disappointment and a set-back. We are strictly rationed for all necessities, and the bombing raids on London and our other cities seem to grow more fierce each week. Also, the German submarines are becoming very active and their land attacks continue all over Europe. Since they have now invaded Holland, Belgium, Luxembourg, Denmark, and Norway, and since the newspapers predict they will occupy Paris within a month, that means all our close European neighbours will be in German hands.

Still there are encouraging signs. Churchill has replaced Chamberlain and most people feel it was a necessary change. Angus is doubtless spinning in his coffin since he thought Churchill a pompous fool. But for these times I feel he is the best we have. He has courage and foresight and he seems able to encourage and inspire people with his ideas and his words.

Our navy too, seems to be giving a good account of itself. And our little air force has done a miraculous job against the German bombers, often bringing down scores of them during a single raid. And now the R.A.F. has begun retaliation bombing over Germany. We are encouraged too, that your Congress has acted to conscript soldiers.

Ned is a leader for this area in the recently formed Home Guard and I am as active as our petrol allowance will permit in half a dozen support organizations. Hugh, as I told you in a previous letter, can not enlist because of some difficulties he had in the navy during the last war, but he has gone to work in a munitions factory in Glasgow.

As you see, we're all buckling down. In a country the size of ours war is very visible. There are no places to hide and wait for it to go away.

As I have said, both Ned and I are so occupied that we spend little time together. But from what I *do* see, the good and necessary work he is doing has transformed him. Or perhaps the death of Angus liberated

576

him in some way. Whatever the reasons, he is a changed and improved man. He seems proud of himself for the first time in a long time.

Since I work hard, eat less than usual, and have no time to fret about myself, I am in excellent health. It's hard for me to believe that I will celebrate my sixty-fifth birthday this year. And I *will celebrate* it. There's something to be said for living sixty-five years. So please drink a toast to me on July 24 (or whenever you get this letter), and I will toast you and your Chet with sherry and biscuits. How fine it is that you two can be happily together when so much of the world is coming apart.

4

'I feel guilty,' Helen said to Chet after reading Clara's letter.

'Why is that?'

'I don't know. Maybe it's *not* guilt. Maybe I just feel lucky. So much craziness going on. Cities burning. People without food and no place to sleep. And here I am, warm and comfortable and happy. So happy I don't know what to do with myself. I can't help feeling guilty about it sometimes.'

'Let me tell you something,' Chet said. 'I'm not overly smart but two or three things I'm sure about. One of them is that you should never feel bad about feeling good.'

'It just doesn't seem fair to me.'

'Of course it's not fair. Nothing's fair. I just mean that nobody has it good all the time. So if you're smart, you'll appreciate it and enjoy it when the cards are falling for you. Nothing sadder than some dumb bastard who's got the world by the short hair but doesn't know it till it's all over.'

'You're saying the good stuff never lasts forever. Is that it?'

'No, I'm *not* saying that. You may still be dancing around

577

with that silly grin on your face when you're a hundred years old. But for the most part all of us end up with a little good and a little bad. Chances are you drew a first-rate guy like me out of the bag just because you'd never had that kind of good luck before. Just like I got *you* because I had such a wonderful wife before and the Lord decided it was time for me to suffer a little.'

'You can't hurt *my* feelings. I *know* I've got the world by the short hair.'

'Me, too, kid.'

Later that day, as they were driving home from Damariscotta, Helen said, 'All of a sudden, there are lots of kids in army uniforms. At least they look like kids to me.'

'They *are* kids. Kids make the best soldiers. They still do what they're told. They don't *own* anything yet so they're not as scared as they will be later.'

'You think we're going to get into the war in Europe?'

'You ever heard of a country getting ready to fight and then changing its mind? *I* never have.'

'It's all so senseless.'

'That's right. But it keeps going on. People have to fight. If they don't have any reason to, they make up a reason. Like the birds on our feeder. There's plenty to eat for all of them. But they still keep squawking and pecking at each other. You hold up a gun and there's always some young guy ready to grab it.'

'Did you want to go the last time?'

'Me? Couldn't wait. Johnny-on-the-spot. I was there waiting when they set up the enlistment booth.'

'Why, for God's sake?'

'I'm a patriot. God, mother, and the flag. I believe all that stuff.'

'Are you serious?'

'Sure I'm serious. All poor kids are patriots. Farm kids. The ones whose fathers work in factories. They think if their country wins, *they* win. If the country's making money and winning wars they'll get a raise and be able to buy a Ford. If it wasn't for poor people there wouldn't *be* any wars. There couldn't be. Poor people want to protect

578

their country. Rich people want to protect their money. So the government has to keep the whole thing in balance. That's why they start wars every now and then.'

'You don't sound like a patriot to me.'

'You just say that because you've got all that money tucked away in the bank and you're mad because I won't let you spend it on *me*. You're mad as hell because I force you to live in the woods like a share-cropper. Washing clothes, scrubbing floors. Getting calluses on your hands like a yard-bird.'

'That's right,' she said. 'I'm sick of it.'

'I don't blame you. But that's what I meant before. You don't have anything to feel guilty about. When we get into the war and some smart-aleck asks you what you're doing for the war effort you just belly up to him and tell him you're taking care of a disabled war veteran, an old codger who fought in the big *dirty* war. That'll shut him up.'

'I don't take care of you. *You* take care of *me*.'

They lived an ordered life. But not by design. They simply found themselves doing the same things, the things they enjoyed, on the same days, at the same time every day. They did indeed live on his disability pension and the money he made as a mechanic for the lobstermen because that money more than paid for whatever they needed. But when Helen said, 'Let's go stay in a hotel in Portland for a week . . . my treat,' or when she made a great show of driving him to Rockland or Brunswick or Bath for an expensive dinner he always said, 'This is the life I was cut out for. A fancy man. Plaything for rich women. Let's never go home. Take me to Honolulu and we'll live in a pink hotel.'

To Opal, however, their life seemed indescribably staid. 'What do you do with yourselves? I thought we'd be seeing each other all the time. But as it is we hardly ever lay eyes on you.'

'Sure you do,' Helen said. 'Every Friday night we eat supper at your house and on most Sundays you eat with us.'

579

'That's right. But when *that's* said, it's *all* said. Outside of those times, you're invisible. Where *are* you all the time?'

'Well, we sleep late in the morning. Then we take a long time eating breakfast. And a little after noon Chet goes to the lobster dock and works on whatever engines need attention till five or so. When he's gone, I do chores around the house or read a book while I keep an eye on whatever I'm fixing for dinner. Or I play with the cat and pick ticks off the dog. Lots of interesting stuff like that. Then when Chet comes home he takes a bath and while he's getting dressed, *I* take a bath.'

'Then you play mama and papa on the bathroom floor.'

'Sometimes,' Helen said. 'But usually we go downstairs and have a drink.'

'According to what Max from the package store tells me you do *that* a lot. He says Chet hauls the Four Roses out of there by the truckload.'

'Not quite,' Helen said, 'but he *does* like to drink. We all know that. And he's teaching me to be a pretty good toper too.'

'So you sit there and get swiggled every night. No wonder we never see you.'

'No. Not just that. We eat our dinner and we listen to Amos and Andy and Lum and Abner and the A & P Gypsies. Chet loves the radio. And we play euchre or casino and just sort of kid around till we get sleepy and go to bed.'

'The same thing every night?'

'Pretty much. Sometimes we drive into Damariscotta to go to the movies. But not very often.'

'How's he feeling?' Opal asked then.

'Fine, I think. Full of beans. You see him every week. Don't you think he looks good?'

'He looks good to me. But you can't always tell by looking. The important thing is how he *feels*.'

'As far as I can tell, he feels great. He eats well and he sleeps like a baby and he has twice as much energy as I do.'

'I read someplace the other day that a woman in Syracuse, New York, had been given up for dead by two different doctors four years ago. Incurable, they said. But six months ago she checked into a hospital and some other doctors looked her over and told her she was all right again. A remission, I think they called it. Wouldn't it be swell if that's what's happening with Chet?'

Helen nodded. 'That would be terrific. And I wouldn't put it past him.'

5

Valerie had not been enthusiastic about leaving Cambridge and moving to New York with her mother. At first she had simply refused to go. 'I'm too old to toddle along after you. I have my life here at school. I've made commitments to myself and other people.'

'Yes, I've heard rumours about some of your *commitments*,' Nora said.

'You needn't settle for rumours. I'm not trying to keep secrets from you. I'll tell you anything you'd like to know.'

'Not necessary. I respect your privacy. But if I knew all the details, I suspect I would not respect your judgment.'

'I'm part Bradshaw, Mummy. I'm a fallible creature. I'm in the process of being educated. One always runs the risk of making errors. Don't you believe that's true?'

'I can't answer that,' Nora said. 'But I do know you're an intelligent girl. Not the sort of person who allows accidents to happen to her. So if you've fallen into a pattern of little scandals, anyone who knows you would conclude that you're doing it for a reason.'

'What reason could I possibly have?'

'I don't know. But I get the feeling it has something to do with me. There's something vengeful about you, something I haven't seen in you before. It's disappointing and definitely not attractive.'

'Do I have some reason to feel vengeful towards you?' Valerie asked.

'Not that I'm aware of. *Do* you?'

'Not that *I'm* aware of. You say you have respect for my privacy and I appreciate that. I hope you'll have the same respect for my desire to stay here in England rather than go skipping off to America.'

'I won't *force* you to go if that's what you mean.'

'Oh, I realize that. That would be difficult in any case, wouldn't it?'

'If you're trying to hurt my feelings . . . .'

'But I'm not,' Valerie said. 'I'm just disagreeing with you about what's best for me. I would think you're going to New York because you feel it's best for *you*. And you say Jesse is going along?'

'Of course he is.'

'Of course. *Also*, I expect, because he thinks it's best for him.'

'I would assume that.'

'Then you surely understand when I say I *don't* think it's best for *me*. I think it's best for me to stay just where I am. In England. At Cambridge.'

Valerie's discussion with Jesse on the subject, although it had a different tone from the conversation with her mother, had, all the same, a cool and distant quality that surprised him.

'Are you speaking for yourself,' she said, 'or do you come as an emissary from Mama Nora?'

'If you feel nasty today, there's no reason we have to talk about it at all.'

'I don't feel nasty at all. I feel exceptionally well. I just wanted to have it clear in my head if you are representing a group of two or if you're talking to me as single solitary person.'

'I don't recognize you when you're in this snotty frame of mind. I think we should drop the whole subject.'

'So do I,' she said. 'That sounds like a good plan.'

After a moment, he said, 'Are you in some sort of trouble?'

'At Cambridge, you mean?'

'Anywhere. I haven't seen you for a few months and you're a whole new exhibit.'

'I'm always in some sort of difficulty at school. Little oversights. You know what I mean? Departures from the norm. Open conflict with the norm. Bloody assassinations of the norm. But my work, of course, is brilliant. So they've been tolerant with me up to now. Not forgiving or understanding but reasonably tolerant. Willing to wait and see. Willing for the most part to look the other way when I stamp my pretty foot and assert my will.'

'One of your masters wrote that you seem to be *trying* to be expelled.'

'Not true. But it serves my purpose that they should *think* that. It means they will *never* drum me out. The perversity of *academe*. Never punish those who *want* it.'

'I wish you'd stayed in Paris,' Jesse said then.

'Why do you say that?'

'Because I feel as if I've lost a friend.'

'I'm not your friend. I'm your step-daughter once removed or your foster great-niece or the daughter of your lady friend, but I'm *not* your friend. It's all too intricate and baroque for simple friendship. I love you but I'm not your friend.'

'Whatever we call it, I've never seen a time when we couldn't talk to each other.'

'We're talking now,' she said.

'We're *talking* but the lights won't go on. Since I saw you last you've built a fence around yourself.'

'That's true. That's exactly what I've done. I'm glad it's visible. You know what it's like . . . distance and time and perspective . . . all those great therapeutic tools. I got away from the old homestead on the Seine and I began to see things differently. Everything I'd believed about friends and families didn't make sense to me any longer. I saw that behind the façade, all the people I knew were looking at different blueprints, everybody was working out his own menu, his own wardrobe, his own destiny. Making a few contradictory noises here and there, performing an occasional selfless act, but mostly heading straight down the road towards some particular, personal rainbow. Altruism and kindness and love for mankind floating through the air like incense, but the real activity was people trying to make things happen for themselves.'

'That's the way it's always been.'

'Of course it has. But I was too naive to see it. When I *did* see it, I said to myself, "Valerie, my darling, it's time to readjust your sights. Pick your goals. Define your purpose." So that's what I've been doing these past months. If I seem unfamiliar to you and Nora it's because I *am*. I am a newborn moth, flying all about, visiting various gardens and having a splendid time. Better to reject than to be rejected. That's my new motto.'

'I don't know what in hell you're talking about.'

'Of course you don't,' she said. 'I *know* you don't.'

'And I don't think *you* do either.'

'I know how you feel. But some day when I'm a big girl, when I'm out of university and out of patience, I will tell you all the things I know that you don't *know* I know.'

When Nora had concluded at last that Valerie was not coming along with her to New York, when the departure date was less than two weeks away, she received a cable from Valerie.

Better late than never. Decided to help you discover America. Aided in decision by dean of my college who believes I am too naughty to stay at Cambridge. Also my favourite young man has been both expelled and conscripted. So here I come. See you in Southampton on departure day.

6

Nora, whose expectations had always dominated her emotional life, had learned to accept the fact that reality was inevitably a disappointment. Even the delightful areas of her life, when examined closely, proved always to be something less than she had envisioned. Knowing this about herself did not cause her to dream less but it did temper the disappointment that presented itself when the true experience replaced the expectation.

Later she would tell herself that the joy she had experienced her first two years in New York was due to the fact that she had expected so little. Knowing almost nothing about the city she was going to and feeling heartbroken about the city she was leaving, she assumed that however brave a front she put up, however rational her reasons were for going, the result had to be a let-down. Only Balkan refugees still believed the legend of New York. To leave Paris was to regret it. She was sure of this. To expect anything grand or triumphant in the new world was to court disaster.

Another facet of her nature, however, was her fascination with the unfamiliar. She shared with Angus his enthusiasm about finding himself suddenly in strange world capitals, surrounded by buildings and people he had never seen before. Knowing this about herself, she drew on it heavily during her last days in Paris and during the sea voyage. And when their ship steamed through the narrows and turned up-channel towards the craggy New York skyline crowding up from an island that seemed too small to support the weight of the city's buildings, she said to Jesse, 'My God. I'm staggered. These immigrants have built a proper city after all, haven't they?'

From that first viewing, the city captured her. When she walked down Fifth Avenue for the first time she felt fired with energy. Although she was unprepared for the variety, the vigour, and the great up-reaching buildings, she felt at the same time, surprisingly at home. After the intricate maze of Paris and the ponderous grimy weight of London, she was fascinated by this city that was less than a mile wide, with great rivers flowing on either side. And most of all she was impressed by the vitality. In that respect it was the only place she had seen in her life that seemed to echo her own inner rhythms. 'I think I'll do well here,' she

585

told herself. 'I have a feeling I could be remarkably contented here.'

And she was, of course. She gobbled up the city like a starving animal. She revelled in the fact that one never had to sleep, that there was no hour of the day or night when she could not eat out or drink or dance and hear music. Or take a taxi to Harlem or the ferry to Staten Island. There was even a furrier, she was told, who would meet you in his vaults at four in the morning and help you to select a silver fox or a sable or an ermine wrap that swept the pavement as you walked.

She was a child at the fair. Racing, laughing, spending, and buying. The expensive stores she loved came to love her too. And they loved Jesse. They were both loved also, by famous bartenders and restaurateurs and doormen. They were seen to be something fresh and beautiful and rich. A strong but pleasant man who limped slightly and a lovely lunatic of a woman with a delightful English accent and the ability to slide, when the occasion required it, into flawless Parisian French or blistering Bastille argot. They were truly splendid. Everyone wanted to capture them and they were captivatingly willing to be captured. *En plus*, it was soon revealed that they were also productive people, practically famous in certain quarters, she as a reckless and original publisher and patron of the arts and he as an editor and critic whose scathing reviews were quoted in the salons and coffee houses.

When Jesse displayed his contempt, in scorching details, for *Watch on the Rhine*, *You Can't Go Home Again*, and *Finnegan's Wake*, even people who disagreed with him or felt they *should* disagree with him, said he was a courageous chap. When he said that Saroyan was a true American genius, and that O'Neill's *A Long Day's Journey Into Night* was the finest of all American plays, almost no one agreed with him, including Nora, but the people who collected opinion-makers hungered to meet him.

Nora re-established her evening salon and all the French and Spanish and Italian painters who were living now in New York quickly found her and helped to make the great old house she had bought in lower Fifth Avenue an important place to be on Thursday evenings. No one who had known the Mabel Dodge ménage, and who was later invited to Nora's home, publicly compared the two, either the hostesses or their parties, but they were, all the same, reminded of that other time and those other evenings when the beautiful, the gifted and the controversial mingled and danced and drank gin with those who were merely rich and restless.

Valerie attended none of these salons. She had lingered for less than a week in New York before taking a train north to Bedford, Massachusetts where she enrolled herself in Tufts College. 'I thought you'd given up higher education,' Nora said.

'Not at all. Cambridge gave *me* up. Now I've decided to be serious and responsible. I plan to show these colonists an inquiring English mind in action.'

When he put her on the train, Jesse said, 'You didn't have to pick a school so far from New York.'

'Yes, I did.'

Before he left her compartment he put his arms around her. But she pulled back and said, 'Better not kiss me. I think I'm catching a cold.' When he stepped down on the platform he walked along the slowly moving train to her window. But the blinds were drawn. He strolled back into the station then and had a rye and soda in the station bar.

7

The day after Christmas in 1940, the snow stopped after three days' steady fall. Chet strapped on his snow shoes and slogged his way out to the county road sixty yards from the house. Climbing into his truck which he'd left at the edge of the paved road, he drove into Hedrick. He had some coffee with Bud and Opal, then he borrowed Bud's pick-up with the snow plough in front, drove home and ploughed out a lane from the road back to his house in the

587

woods. Helen came to the front door and called out. 'Just in time. The radio says it's going to snow again.'

'I don't think so. Bud called the weather station down at Pemaquid and they said that front's sliding past us to the west.'

'Come in and get warm.'

'I'm fine. Let me take Bud's truck back first. I'll be home shortly. And listen . . . I think I might have some good news for you.'

'What's that?'

'I'll tell you when I get back.'

Driving towards Hedrick in Bud's truck, Chet felt nauseous suddenly. The road ahead of him blurred. He pulled over and stopped, rolled down the window, and breathed in the cold dry air. He smoked a cigarette and waited till his vision cleared. Then he drove the rest of the way into Hedrick. When he was sitting in Opal's kitchen he said to Bud, 'Stick a couple fingers of bourbon in this coffee and see if we can make it fly.'

'That's the ticket,' Bud said. 'Winter medicine.'

'If you two start drinking any earlier in the day, somebody'll have to bring it to you in your beds,' Opal said.

'That's *your* job. That's what wives are for. I'll bet you Chet don't get neglected at home the way *I* do.'

'Don't kid yourself,' Chet said. 'It's nothing but grief. Morning to night.'

'You're spoiled rotten, both of you,' Opal said. 'That's your trouble. You don't know when you're well off.'

Bud sat down at the kitchen table and said, 'You think I'm well off, Chet?'

'Compared to me, I suppose you are, but that's not sayin' much.'

Opal came over to the table then, carrying a cup of coffee for herself. When she sat down she said to Bud, 'Pour some of that rot-gut in here. If I have to listen to you two feeling sorry for yourselves I need something to prop me up.'

As he drove home in his own truck a while later, Chet's vision seemed normal again. And the whiskey had settled his stomach. But he began to feel sharp pains in the small of his back.

'Do you feel all right?' Helen asked when he came into the kitchen from the mud room.

'Sure. Don't I look all right?'

'I guess you do. But your eyes are a little funny.'

'I had some booze with Bud and Opal,' he said. 'Booze for breakfast.'

'I don't know how you do it. If I had a drink in the morning, I'd have to spend the afternoon in bed.'

'Nothing wrong with *that*,' he said. 'I've spent lots of afternoons in bed.'

'I'll bet you have.'

'You *know* I have. You're the policeman around here. You're the one who keeps telling me I have to get my rest.'

'That's right,' she said. 'I take good care of you.'

'You take good care of yourself, you mean. Every time I lay down on the bed, you're right there with me.'

'Of course. I have to look after you. Have to make sure you don't suffocate or roll off on the floor or something. I'll bet those army nurses didn't take as good care of you as I do.'

He looked up at her and smiled. 'If you think I'm going to answer *that* one, you're crazy.'

Later, when they were having lunch, Chet asked, 'Did Opal talk to you about Bud's birthday?'

'We just decided the four of us would get together.'

'Well, now she's decided we should drive down to Portland for a couple of days. She wants to stay in the hotel down there and carry on a little.'

'Is that all right with you?' Helen said.

'Sure. I don't see why not. His birthday's the sixth of January. We'd go down the day before and come back the day after. If we're still able to navigate.'

'Sounds good to me. We'll have a real party.' Then, 'Did you forget about the good news?'

'What?'

'You said you might have some good news for me.'

'That's right. It floated right out of my head. Remember

589

when you told me about your kid and I said maybe Bud
and I could find out something for you?'

'I thought you'd forgotten about it. It's been quite a
while.'

'I told you it might take some time. And it could take
some *more* time. But at least we've got our foot in the door.'

'How do you mean?'

'There's this guy named Herman Cherry lives in Portland. Runs a bar with a galloping poker game going on in
the back. Herman's not crooked exactly. He's just casual.
His legs are too short and his arms are too long and he's
a little cock-eyed. Looks like he got put together wrong.
But everybody likes him. Nice and easy-going, crazy about
women, and a soft touch for anybody who's broke. But he
takes no crap off of nobody. He's a damned fine guy. Bud
knew him in the army and I met him when I first came up
here. Anyway, Herman's the guy we talked to about your
problem. Well, yesterday, he called up and said something
might be opening up. It seems that Herman's got himself
a new girl friend – Fay, I think her name is – and she has
a sister who just got a job at this agency that found a home
for your boy. This woman, Fay's sister, is just kind of a
typist now but they told her she could work up fast till
she's a stenographer or a file clerk or something. She's
sharp as a tack, Herman says, and once she learns the
ropes in that office, gets the lay of the land and sees where
things are kept, he thinks she'll be able to get hold of what
you need. Bud told Herman it would be worth a couple
hundred to us and she was tickled to death to hear that.
She's got two little kids and no husband so she's hot to
make some extra money.'

'Do you really think there's a chance?'

'Sure I do. More than a chance. I told you before, that
information has to be on file there someplace and I'll bet
this woman – Grace, Bud said her name is – will locate it.
It may take a while but I'll lay you three to one she'll sniff
it out. I gave Herman your name and the dates you told
me and he passed it along to her. So she knows exactly
what she's looking for.'

590

'I can't believe it. After all this time.'

'That's because you didn't know *me* before. You didn't have a couple of sharp-shooters like me and Bud on your side. That's not to say that something couldn't go wrong. This Grace could meet a Greyhound bus driver tomorrow and go wailing off to Florida. Lots of things could happen, I reckon. But I've got a good hunch about it.'

When they went to Portland to celebrate Bud's birthday they took the train. 'I don't expect to draw a sober breath for two or three days,' Bud said. 'And if *I'm* half-crocked I expect everybody else to be too. So we don't want to be worried about drivin' ourselves in a ditch or up a lamp-post. If I remember right there's a cocktail lounge in that hotel, a saloon next door, and a package store on the corner. And Herman Cherry's establishment is only three blocks away. So there's no way we can miss. Ain't nobody gonna go dry on *this* trip. If I don't age five years before I get home here, I'll feel like a coward.'

The morning they arrived in Portland, Chet stumbled and fell as he got off the train. He bumped his head on the edge of a baggage cart and sprawled flat on the platform. But he got up and brushed himself off and they joked about it in the taxi heading for the hotel.

'Jesus,' Bud said. 'The man hasn't had but a drink or two and already he's ass over tincups all over the deck. You'd better switch to root beer floats, old buddy.'

'Never mind, you bastard. When they carry you upstairs tonight, I'll be the one that goes ahead to unlock your room. The day I can't out-drink you is the last day I drink anything.'

While they were standing at the registration desk at the hotel, Chet collapsed. Helen, turned half-away talking to Opal, felt his hand on her arm. As she turned back to him his eyes rolled back white and he slumped, soft and heavy, to the floor.

He was in the Portland hospital for almost five weeks. The morning of the day they released him, Helen had her final meeting with his doctor.

'I have nothing new to report to you,' he said. 'His

591

situation has not changed in any meaningful way, and I don't expect that it will. As I've explained to you there is no cure for his disease. He knows that already. He's known it for a long time. He also knows that he must follow the regime we've prescribed for him. He must be here for treatment one week out of four. He must take his medication and injections at home on the schedule we've laid out for him. He must follow his diet, must *not* use tobacco or alcohol, and he must rest in bed except for the four to six hours each day when he's allowed to sit up in his chair.'

'I'm not sure he can live like that,' Helen said.

'Then he won't live at all.'

'How long can he . . . .'

'It's impossible to say. He has a strong constitution. If he follows orders and if he responds at all to the treatments here, the process might be slowed down so he could live for two more years. Perhaps as long as three.'

She took Chet home in a private ambulance. She sat beside him and the nurse sat in front with the driver.

'This beats hell out of riding that crummy train,' he said. 'Nice and smooth. Put you right to sleep.'

'Are you sleepy?'

'What do you think? Before I left the hospital they gave me a shot that would put a horse on his back.'

'Don't fight it. Go to sleep if you feel like it.'

'I couldn't fight it if I wanted to.' He closed his eyes, then opened them again. 'That screwball nurse won't be staying with us, will she?'

'Don't you like her?'

'She's looney. She's a Seventh-Day Adventist and she's been trying to convert me. I don't want her around the house.'

'Don't worry. She just came for the trip and to get you settled in at home. You don't need a nurse once we're there. You've got *me*.'

'That's right,' he said, 'and you've got *me*. We're a pair of lucky ducks.'

That evening, alone in their house in the woods, he insisted on making a fire in the fireplace. 'This is my six hours out of bed,' he said. 'You make yourself a nice supper and I'll have my pills and tap water and we'll sit here and listen to the radio and watch the fire. All those weeks in the hospital, *this* is what I was looking forward to.'

When they went upstairs to bed, she said, 'Did you take your sleeping pill?'

'I don't need it tonight. I feel like a bear heading for hibernation.'

'You promised me you'd do what the doctor said.'

'I will. But not tonight. I don't think I'll wake up till noon but if I do I'll take a pill. I promise.'

Lying beside him in bed, hearing his regular breathing, Helen felt as if the accumulated anxiety of the past few weeks was slowly draining out of her. Just one evening at home, the two of them, quiet and alone, had cleared the tangles in her head. All the projections and predictions she'd been listening to, the grim faces and heavy pronouncements, all of it seemed unimportant now that they were back inside their house. As she slid slowly into sleep she realized she hadn't really slept, not deeply and peacefully, since the night before they'd left for Portland.

Some time in the night she felt Chet get up. Then she felt his cheek next to hers and she heard him say, 'Don't wake up. I'm just going downstairs for a few minutes. I'll be right back. Go to sleep, kid.'

When she woke up again it was early morning. Grey light bled in around the edge of the window-blind. She lay there with her eyes closed until she sensed, suddenly, that he was not in the bed. She switched on the lamp and struggled into her dressing-gown as she crossed the room to the bathroom. The door was open. He wasn't there. She hurried down the stairs then and quickly looked through all the rooms. She ran to the windows and looked out across the clearing behind the house. There was a light snow cover on the ground and heavy flakes were still falling. But she saw no tracks in the snow. And when she looked in the mud room, Chet's boots and sheepskin jacket were still there.

593

As she stood in the centre of the living-room, faint coals still glowing from the ash-heap in the fireplace, as she trembled from the chill, some flash of something she had barely seen, had half-seen, had sensed more than seen, in her barely-wakened state, came back to her. She ran upstairs again, to the bathroom. There by the sink were Chet's two prescription bottles, one of them for pain, the other to induce sleep. When she opened them, both bottles were empty. She looked up then and saw her face in the mirror above the sink, her eyes flat and expressionless. She turned, crossed the bedroom, and walked slowly downstairs. This time she went directly to the heavy oak door that opened to the screened porch.

Chet was sitting straight up in the redwood armchair. He was facing the snowfields that stretched to the edge of the woods, his hands in the pockets of his dressing-gown, an empty whiskey glass on the table beside him. Under the glass was a slip of blue paper, torn from the pad she used for grocery lists, on it a few lines in his awkward scrawl.

I'm sorry, kid. I'm not cut out to be an invalid and you're not cut out to be a nurse. Just remember that nobody ever had it as good as we did. It's the only part of my life I can remember.

8

When Valerie graduated in June of 1941, Nora had made elaborate plans to attend. She and Jesse would drive up for the ceremony and afterwards the three of them would have a celebration dinner in a private dining-room at the Parker House. When the day came, however, Nora was in a hospital in New York and Jesse attended the graduation alone. Instead of a lavish Boston dinner, he and Valerie ate together in a small Italian restaurant in Medford.

'How dare anyone break one of Nora's bones,' Valerie

said. 'I thought she didn't tolerate such inconveniences. I've always believed she was unassailable.'

'Nobody's unassailable in New York. She was getting out of a taxi and a bicycle knocked her down and broke her ankle.'

'That's terrible.'

'She was lucky. It's just a crack. She'll be in a walking cast in two or three days. She felt awful that she couldn't be here today. She was afraid you'd be mad at her.'

'Am I crazy? Do I get mad at people because they get broken bones? And besides, who can get mad at Nora? She's like the weather. Sometimes you enjoy it and sometimes you endure it. But it's lunacy to get mad at it. I love her. She knows that. We understand each other.'

'She just thought this was a special day.'

'Not for me it isn't. I put in my time here. I went to my classes and learned my lessons. And when you do that they give you a piece of paper with fancy writing on it and a gold seal. Mostly it's for the parents. To reassure them they didn't spend all that money for nothing.'

'Don't pull that cynical act with me. I saw your marks. You worked very hard.'

'No, I didn't. I took courses I liked and they were easy for me. If I'd fooled around with chemistry and physics and trigonometry and astronomy I'd still be plodding through my second year.'

'What now?'

'Right now I think we should have another bottle of Oruieto.'

'That's not what I meant.'

'I *know* what you meant.'

He called the waiter and ordered another bottle of wine. Then he said, 'Since you side-stepped that question I'll ask you another one. How would you like to come down to New York and go to work on *Icarus*?'

She didn't hesitate. 'I wouldn't like that. It's nice of you to offer but I wouldn't like that at all.'

'Any particular reason?'

'All kinds of particular reasons. For one thing I have no

595

desire to return to the womb. Also, I hate New York. And I don't like *Icarus* much any more either. I think it's become a snotty, self-conscious little magazine. Too careful and too pretty. Culture for the rich folks.'

'I agree,' Jesse said. 'Come to New York and we'll try to make it like it used to be.'

She shook her head and smiled. 'Sorry. You're inviting me to be earnest and sincere and nothing could be further from my mind. And besides, Nora *likes* the magazine. So unless you're planning to break one of her bones every month and keep her out of the office, I expect *Icarus* will remain pretty much as it is.'

'You give up too easily.'

'No, I don't. But I'd prefer not to wage daily war against my mother.'

The waiter came back with the wine then, opened it, and poured some into their glasses.

'I wasn't suggesting that you should live in Nora's house,' Jesse said then.

'I hope not.'

'It's not a bad place, however.'

'For you it's not. For me it's disaster. Too much traffic. It's Paris all over again.'

'I thought you liked Paris.'

'I do. But on *my* terms. On a smaller scale. Not so much noise. Not so many people. A couple of sleepy cats and a nice old dog who's not nervous. That's my style.'

'You can have all that in New York. We'll find you an apartment in Greenwich Village and stock it with all the dogs and cats you want.'

'Sorry, mister. The lady's not buying.'

'You're not coming to New York at all?'

'Not at all.'

'Any other plans?'

'Nope. See how American I'm getting? I go to Gary Cooper movies and I say *yep* and *nope* whenever I feel like it. Wait till Clara hears me. She'll faint.' She sipped from her wine glass. When she set the glass down she said, 'What about you?'

596

'What do you mean?'

'You're so curious about *my* plans. What about your plans?'

He smiled. 'I don't have any plans.'

'See. You're just like me.'

'Not quite. I'm not twenty-one.'

'Neither am I. Not till October.'

'All right. Then I'm not *twenty* with my whole life ahead of me.'

'Maybe not. But you're forty-four with your whole life ahead of you. Forty-four's a lucky age. Did you know that?'

'How so?'

'It's divisible by eleven. Twenty-two, thirty-three, forty-four, fifty-five . . . all lucky ages. This should be a lucky year for you.'

'I don't believe in luck.'

'That's because you're lucky,' she said. 'Lucky people *never* believe in luck. *Unlucky* people believe in nothing else.'

'Which one are you?'

'Lucky. Very lucky. You want to know why? Because I like little things. Simple things. Things I can hang on to. I don't need the moon. I don't even *want* it. I don't expect to spend my life chasing trains I can't catch.'

'What do you plan to chase?'

'Nothing. I expect to play the waiting game. The *still hunt* they call it. You pick out your prey. Then you sit and wait for it to come to you.'

'What if it doesn't come?'

'Then you wait some more.'

'Is one allowed to ask what you're waiting for?'

She laughed. 'One can ask but one must not expect an answer. No one is more silent than a still hunter.'

'Have you had too much wine or is this the way you are now?'

'It's the way I am, always was, and always will be. Lovable and scrumptious and no plans at all.'

'Staying right here in Medford for the rest of your life. Is that it?'

'Correct. At least partially correct. Staying here for now but not for the rest of my life.'

'Is there a young man in the picture?'

'In the sense that you mean . . . no. I have *not* chosen to stay in Medford to be with some particular young man. If you're asking if there have *been* young men in the picture, the answer is *yes*. If you're curious to know if I am still a blushing virgin the answer is *no*. I am neither blushing nor a virgin. When I marry I will be neither innocent nor ignorant.'

'And when will the wedding be?'

'God knows,' she said. 'That depends to a large degree on the success of the still hunt.'

'You've really become something of a lunatic, haven't you?'

'Not really. Actually I'm becoming quite normal. As you must remember there was a time when I felt I was going to marry *you*.'

'Yes, I remember.'

'Counselled you rather seriously as I recall. Gave you quite a lot of advice, didn't I?'

Jesse nodded. 'Marriage and family. That sort of thing. Children and pets and warm comforters on the bed.'

'Exactly,' she said. 'I remember. I still think it's good advice.'

'You plan to follow it yourself?'

'To the letter. When I say I have no plans, that only means I have no *immediate* plans. My long-range plans, on the other hand, are very clear. When the war is over in England I am going to go to Wingate Fields, take up residence, and become a county lady. Everything that Nora hated is what *I* want. Everything that delights her has no value at all for me. This is not meant to be a judgment of my mother. It is simply a little genetic surprise. Nora needs to own the world. I want a very small piece of it. I expect to make somebody extremely happy and to be very happy myself in the process.'

'I'm thunderstruck.'

Of course you are. You fancy sophisticated folks never know what to make of simple creatures like me.'

'One thing you're *not*, my darling, is a simple creature.'

She smiled. 'Not yet, maybe. But I *will* be. And you will be, too, I suspect, once you get off the carousel you're on.'

'Then what would I do?'

'That would be up to you.'

'I used to think *I* would end up at Wingate Fields.'

'I know you did.'

'But I guess I've changed a lot since then.'

'I'm sure you have.'

'I'm not sure I'd be a good county man.'

'You probably wouldn't,' she said. 'You'd have to want it a lot. You'd have to want it as much as I do or you wouldn't be much good at it. And it wouldn't be good for you.'

'You're pretty smart, aren't you?'

'Not smart. Lucky. I know what I want.'

9

Early in November of 1941, one night when he and Opal were already in bed, Bud Feaster had a phone call from Herman Cherry in Portland. When he came back upstairs twenty minutes later and told Opal what the call was about, she said, 'What did you tell him?'

'I told him the God's truth. I told him I couldn't guarantee him anything about Helen. I said she hides back there in the woods from one week to the next and we most of the time never see her. I can't tell if she's decided to drink herself to death or what. But whatever it is, she's doing it by herself.'

'She's had a tough time, Bud.'

'I know that. I know how hard it was on her. But times like that is when most people need their friends. She acts like she don't want anybody around.'

'Different people take things different. She's not mad at

us and you know it. We've seen her some. But she's not good at talking about things yet. So she's been keeping to herself.'

'She sure has. That's just what I told Herman.'

'But things will be different now. This kind of news is just what she needs to snap her out of it. It's like a miracle after all this time has gone past. Do you know how long she's waited for something like this to happen? As long as we've known her.'

'Well, all I know is she seems switched around to me. So she may not take this the way you expect her to. Like I said, I told Herman I couldn't guarantee nothing.'

'Well, *I* can. I'll go see her first thing in the morning. I can't wait to see her face when I tell her.'

Helen's face, however, revealed very little as she sat at the kitchen table next morning with Opal. 'I was so excited,' Opal said, 'it was all I could do to keep myself from driving over here in the middle of the night.'

'It's hard to believe,' Helen said. 'After all this time.'

'That's what I told Bud. I said you've been waiting and hoping for something like this to happen ever since I met you.'

'That's right. I have. But now that it's happened it doesn't seem to mean much to me.'

'Oh, yes, it does. It just hasn't sunk in yet. You'll sit there for a while and the next thing you know you'll be jumping up and down and clapping your hands together.'

Helen smiled. 'I don't think so, Opal. I waited too long. It's too late now. That little kid I've been thinking about all these years is a man now. He was twenty-one last March.'

'What difference does it make? He's still your kid.'

'I know,' Helen said. 'That's what I've been telling myself all this time. But it looks different to me now.'

'No, it doesn't. How could it? How can something that was so important to you turn into something you don't give a damn about?'

'It's not that I don't *give* a damn. I just feel differently about what I should *do*.'

'Nobody's saying you have to *do* anything. Once you've got the information you can burn it if you want to. But at least you'll *know*. You'll know his name and where he lives so you'll have something to go on if you decide you want to get in touch with him later.'

'Maybe you're right.'

'You know I'm right. We know how you've been feeling since Chet died. But you won't feel this way forever. You have to live your life. You're a young woman. You can't just bury yourself back here in the woods. You can't just suck your thumb and pass up this chance to find out about your kid. You have to go down to Portland and look at that file while you've got the chance.'

'What do you mean I have to go to Portland?'

'I told you what Herman told Bud. The girl can only get the file for an hour. She'll slip it out on her lunch break and meet you someplace so you can copy down the stuff you need to know. Or Herman said you could meet her at his place and he could have some of the pages photostated at the office supply store next door to him. It's all set up for next Tuesday. I'll go down on the morning train with you and we'll come back on the four o'clock.'

Helen sat staring at her coffee cup. Finally she said, 'I can't.'

'What do you mean?'

She shook her head. 'I just can't. I can't go to Portland. Maybe if they could send the information up here . . . .'

'How could they do *that*? The girl's taking enough of a chance as it is. She could lose her job if they caught her.'

'I know it doesn't make sense to you,' Helen said. 'And in six months maybe it won't make sense to me.'

'It *won't*. That's what I'm trying to tell you.'

Helen started to cry. 'I can't do it. I just can't.'

When Opal told Bud what had happened, he said, 'What's the matter with her?'

'She's a little crazy right now.'

'She'll be a hell of a lot crazier if she doesn't get out of that house and do something with herself.'

'*I* know that. And she knows it too, I think. But she just can't cut it yet.'

'Herman's gonna think we're all nuts. For months we've been trying to set this thing up. Now it's all set and we say "no soap". He'll think I'm the world's champion horse's ass. I don't know what to tell him.'

'Tell him I'm coming instead. I'll look at the file and get the information.'

'What good is that? We lay out two hundred bucks for something Helen doesn't even want.'

'She'll want it when she gets it. Just 'cause she's crazy now doesn't mean she'll be crazy forever.'

10

On Saturday, November 22, Jesse received a telegram from Helen.

Please meet me Monday, November 24. Hotel Touraine, Boston. Urgently need your help.

'What's that all about?' Nora said.

'It's a mystery to me.'

'You don't have any idea why she *urgently needs* your help?'

'How could I? We haven't heard from her for more than a year.'

'*We* haven't heard from her, but . . . .'

'*I* haven't heard from her either,' Jesse said. 'We sent her that sympathy card after Clara told us Chet died and I wrote her a couple times after that but I've never heard a word.'

'Clara says she hasn't heard anything either. So what's the big commotion all of a sudden?'

'I don't know,' he said.

'Why don't you call her up and find out?'

'I tried that as soon as the wire came. They said her phone was disconnected six months ago.'

'The mystery woman,' Nora said. 'Maybe she's decided her period of mourning is over and she urgently needs you in Boston to help her celebrate.'

'Not funny, Nora.'

'Not hilarious maybe, but reasonably amusing. At least I think so. But then you've never had a sense of humour where Helen is concerned.'

'When somebody sends a telegram and says they need help . . . .'

'Ahh. . . but it's not just *somebody*, it's Baby Helen. Your ward, your protégée, your lifetime responsibility.'

'What's the *matter* with you?'

'Nothing. I'm in fine spirits. I find all this very droll.'

'I know you do,' Jesse said. 'But *I* don't.'

'Of course not. You've heard the call to arms. A cry of distress. And you are very susceptible to ladies in distress. Do you realize that? I think you were born several centuries too late. I seem to be the only female you're not eager to rescue.'

'You can't be rescued. You've never been in distress in your life.'

'I will accept that as a compliment. Do you think Helen would think it's a compliment?'

'I have no idea.'

'I don't think she would. *Distress* seems to be her stock in trade. I suspect that she would not like to be thought of as self-reliant. Fragile and dependent, that's her style.'

'Lay off, Nora. She's no threat to you and she never has been.'

'Not true, my dear. Women like Baby Helen are a threat to *all* other women.'

That night they went to the theatre and then to the Algonquin for a late supper. It was almost two o'clock when they got home. 'I hate to have dinner so late,' Nora said. 'Every time we do it I promise myself it's the last time.'

603

'You'll snap back,' Jesse said. 'Tomorrow night you'll be rearing to go again.'

'Remember how nice it was in Paris? We used to stay home a lot.'

'About one night a week is the way I remember it.'

'I'd settle for that,' she said.

'It's very simple. You just have to learn to say no.'

'Maybe I'll try that.'

'I'll believe it when I see it.'

'All right. You think you're so smart . . . here's what I'm going to do. We're supposed to have dinner with the Ackermans tomorrow night. I'm going to call Sylvia first thing in the morning and tell her I'm sick as a dog. We'll stay in our pyjamas the whole day tomorrow. We'll eat grilled cheese sandwiches and sit around all evening with our feet up reading Barney Google.'

'I won't be here tomorrow night,' Jesse said. 'Remember? I'm taking the three o'clock train to Boston.' '

'No, you're not. You have to stay home and eat grilled cheese sandwiches with me. I'm depending on it.'

'*Next* Sunday we'll do it.'

'You're not serious, are you? You're not really going up there?'

'Didn't we already have this discussion?'

'We sort of talked around the edges of it. But I don't remember anything about a three o'clock train.'

'That's because I hadn't checked the timetables when we talked before.'

'Let me get this straight,' Nora said. 'Are you telling me that all that little fool has to do is send you a telegram and you're on the next train to see what's ailing her?'

'Since this is the first time it's happened in twenty years it doesn't look like much of a pattern to me.'

'Don't you feel a bit like a horse being put over the jumps?'

'No. Not at all.'

'It doesn't make you feel odd, trailing off to Boston like someone's footman?'

'No. I'd feel odd if I didn't go. If it wasn't important she wouldn't have sent that telegram. I can't just sit here and pretend I never got it.'

'You tried to call her. It's not your fault if she's living in a wigwam without a phone.'

'What's the difference? I wasn't calling to say I *wouldn't* come. I was calling to say I'd be there.'

'What kind of hold does she have over you? Will you tell me that?'

'If you're going to get all steamed up about this, I think we should drop it.'

'I don't *want* to drop it. I want *you* to drop it. I want you to come to your senses and tell me you're not running up to Boston just so Helen will have a shoulder to cry on. Or whatever it is she's planning to do with you.'

Jesse put his hands on her shoulders and said, 'You know what's nice about us? We're a nice civilized couple. We don't stay up half the night screaming at each other. We don't leave marks on each other and we don't make threats. I think that's very nice.'

'Maybe it is and maybe it isn't. *I* don't feel so civilized at the moment. Maybe we *should* leave some marks on each other. And there's nothing wrong with a threat if you really mean it.'

'I'm telling you . . . you're getting yourself all worked up over nothing.'

'If it were *nothing* to me,' she said, 'I assure you I wouldn't be getting worked up. We're not having this discussion because I think it's fun. I am simply trying to tell you that there's something at stake here.'

'What? What's at stake?'

'A lot. You're putting me in a position where I have to fight back whether I want to or not.'

'I'm not putting you in *any* position.'

'What would you call it then? You know I have a lunatic sensitivity about *her*. Maybe it doesn't make sense to anyone but me. But to *me* it *does* make sense. It *means* something to me when you say you're chasing up there to see her. It makes me *jealous*. It makes me *crazy*. It makes me question things about you and things about us. It makes my foundation shake. It makes me feel the way I felt before when you ran off to America after her. Do you know what I'm saying?'

'I know what you're *saying*, but it doesn't . . . .'

'Don't tell me it doesn't make sense. I already said that. This isn't a logical discussion. I'm not trying to sell you a new overcoat. I'm trying to make you see how I *feel*. If you think that *she* may need you in Boston, can't you look at me and see that *I* need you *here*?'

'I'm not *choosing* Helen over you, for God's sake.'

'Yes, you are. That's *exactly* what you're doing. You're telling me that you're going to Boston whether I like it or not. No matter how much it bothers me . . . .'

'Why *should* it bother you? That's what I can't understand.'

'I don't *know*, but it does. I remember that other time.'

'If you remember it, then you must remember that you were mistaken. . . .'

'Oh, no, I wasn't. I don't know what went wrong between you two when you got back to America but . . . .'

'I didn't even *see* her for almost a year.'

'That wasn't your fault. I remember you waited around till you *did* see her.'

'That's right. I did. And then I went back to England. And by then you'd been married for six months.'

'What did you expect? I knew I'd seen the last of you.'

'No, you hadn't,' he said. 'You were wrong then and you're wrong now.'

'No. I'm *right* now and I was right then. She has some hold on you and you know it. You think that hasn't been in my mind all the time you and I have been together? I knew the phone would ring some day, or a letter would come, or a telegram, and you'd be off on the next train. What kind of a feeling do you think that is? How would you have felt if you'd known that all Edmund had to do was whistle and I'd go straight back to him?'

'I've never had a thought like that.'

'I know you haven't. That's my point. But *I* have. I've never stopped thinking about you and Helen. She had you first and I knew it was just a question of time till she'd find a way to have you again.'

After a moment, Jesse said, 'I don't know what to say to you.'

'Of course you don't. There's nothing *to* say.'

'I mean I don't know what you want me to say.'

'It doesn't matter what I want and you know it.'

'Of course it matters. Why do you think we're having this discussion?'

'It's not a discussion. It's a fight. You've decided to do something I don't want you to do and you're *determined* to do it no matter *what* I say. No matter how I *feel*.'

'This is too complicated for me. Let's go back to the beginning. Just tell me what you want. In simple language.'

'You don't *care* what I want.'

'If I didn't care I wouldn't ask you.'

'I think you already know.'

'Maybe I do. But I think it's important that we both understand exactly what's taking place here.'

'I understand already,' she said. 'I understand perfectly. But I'll put it in simple language. This isn't like the night at Beaune. I'm not drunk tonight but I wish I were. I'm telling you that this is extremely important to me. More important than you will ever realize. You say you don't understand me. Let me make it clear. I'm saying that if you can go to Boston tomorrow, knowing how I feel about it, if my feelings mean so little to you, then *I* don't understand *you*. Or maybe I *do* understand and I'm trying *not* to. Either way . . . .'

'Either way what?'

'I don't know. I'm tired. Tired of all the words. Just tell me whether you're going or not.'

'I have to go.'

She smiled and sat down. 'And the bell in the steeple tolled three.'

'Meaning what?'

'Meaning nothing.'

'If I go, I shouldn't bother to come back,' he said. 'Is *that* it?'

607

'I didn't say that.' She smiled again. Very sweetly.

'You didn't have to,' Jesse said.

11

'His name is Floyd Simison,' Helen said. 'It's all there in those photostat pages you're looking at. The people who adopted him and raised him are named Lowell and Ruth Simison.'

'Indiana,' Jesse said. 'According to this, Mr Simison's a teacher at Wabash College.'

'That's right. In Crawfordsville. When they first took him, they were living in Wisconsin. But they've been there in Indiana since 1928. Or so it says.'

She had planned to tell Jesse the truth about Hugh. About everything. But when they met in Boston, when they sat down in her hotel suite, she told him the story she had told Opal, about the young man from Seattle, the one she'd met on the ship as she came home from England. In every other respect she stuck to the facts. Her interviews in New York with Reverend Galston and in Portland with Dr Kilwinning. She went through every detail of the adoption process, her doubts about it, and her ultimate decision. She told him about those months in Maine in the house by the sea right up till the time when she left and came back to Illinois.

When she finished talking, Jesse sat studying the pages in front of him and didn't say anything. Finally he looked up. 'Now I know where you were all that time I was waiting for you in Fort Beck.'

'Now you know.'

'Who else knows about this?'

'Outside of the people at the agency, just Bud and Opal know. And Chet knew, of course.'

'I'm surprised you never told Clara.'

'So am I. But I didn't.'

Jesse slid the pages back into the envelope and placed it on the table by his chair. 'Now what?'

'I don't know. As I told you I've been praying that *someday* I'd find out . . . I mean the information in that envelope is what I've been desperate to know for more than twenty years. But now . . . I don't know any more.'

'Let me ask you a question,' Jesse said. 'All those years you were trying to find out about your son, what did you plan to do if you *did* locate him?'

'I didn't have any *plans* really. I knew how slim my chances were of ever finding him. But I. . . I just wanted to *know* about him, to know where he was living and what he was doing. And of course I wanted to *see* him. I had this fantasy about sitting in a car across from his house and watching him play in the yard. Or seeing him come out of his school. Crazy things like that.'

'Did you have some idea of trying to get him back? Did you want him to come and live with you?'

'Of course I did. I mean I *wanted* that. But I knew it wouldn't be fair to him. Or to the people who had adopted him. I really didn't want to disrupt his life or theirs either. But at the same time, I wanted to *see* him and know about him.'

'You never planned to tell him who you were?'

'I don't *know*, Jesse. I don't know what I planned. There was nothing rational about it. I just felt some need to complete the circle. As it was, it all seemed so arbitrary and painful. I just wanted to make some connection with him. Even if *he* never knew the connection had been made. Does that sound idiotic?'

'Not to me, it doesn't. If I had a kid I'd never seen, I think I'd do anything to see him or talk with him or at least to find out all I could about him.'

'That's it exactly. That's how I felt.'

'All right. That brings me back to my first question. Now what?'

'I told you. I don't know.'

'Well, it seems to me you have three choices. You can leave things the way they are, or you can try to find him

609

and see him and get as much information about him as you can without identifying yourself, or, if you locate him, you can tell him you're his real mother and take it from there.'

'I'm losing my nerve just talking about it. It scares me to death.'

'Then that solves the problem,' Jesse said. 'Let things stay the way they are.'

'I'm afraid that's all I *can* do.'

'It's up to you,' he said. Then, 'I can't figure out why you bothered to send me that telegram.'

'I don't know what I was thinking.'

' "Urgently need your help." That's what the telegram said.'

'I don't know. I was in a panic. I *still* am.'

'All right, I'll tell you what *I* think. I think you've got yourself tied in such a knot you can't see straight. You have to stop *thinking* about all this and *do* something about it.'

'That's what I *can't* do.'

'Yes, you can. Your first instinct was right. You should locate your boy and find out all you can about him. Try to see him if you can without letting him know who you are. *Then* you can decide if there's going to be a next step.'

'I don't know how to *do* that. I wouldn't know where to start.'

'I'll show you,' Jesse said. He stood up, walked across the room to the telephone, and dialled the operator. 'This is Mr Bradshaw in suite five-eleven. I'm calling Information in Crawfordsville, Indiana. Thank you. I'll wait.' With his hand over the mouthpiece he looked across the room to Helen and said, 'Don't worry. I'm not going to talk to anyone. I just want to see if there's a listing for Simison.'

When the operator connected him with Crawfordsville he said, 'I'm calling a Mr Simison. Lowell Simison. Can you give me that number, please? I don't know the address.' He waited. 'I see. Is there *any* listing under the name Simison? All right. Thank you very much.'

As soon as he hung up, Helen said, 'They're not there after all.'

'Can't be sure,' he said. 'Maybe Simison doesn't have a phone. Or he might have an unlisted number. Or it might be listed in his wife's maiden name.'

'Or they don't live in Crawfordsville any longer.'

'That doesn't matter. If your boy grew up there, that has to be the best place to get information about him. If he's *not* there now, somebody in Crawfordsville will know where he is.'

'But if we can't call Simison, who do we call?'

'We don't call anybody. We have to go there. There's a night train from Boston to Chicago. We can be in Crawfordsville tomorrow afternoon.'

'I can't just pick up and leave like that.'

'Sure you can. You said you wanted help. I'm gonna help you.'

12

Jesse and Helen came down from Chicago to Crawfordsville on the Monon railroad. As soon as they'd checked into the Montgomery, an old frame hotel in the town square, Jesse went to the office of the telephone company. He asked to see local directories for the past ten years. Working backwards from 1941 he found Lowell Simison's name in the fourth one, the 1938 book, and in each of the preceding ones. *And* his address – 413 Sycamore Street.

The young woman at the desk said, 'You follow the signs to General Lew Wallace's home and you'll see that Sycamore Street butts right into the south side of it. It's a pretty block. Big old maple trees on both sides of the road. Nobody knows why they called it Sycamore Street when all they've got growing there is *maples*.'

Forty minutes later, Jesse and Helen were standing across the street from number 413. It was a two-storey white house with grey shutters at the windows and a low hedge bordering the front yard. 'Is that the kind of yard you imagined him playing in?' Jesse asked.

'I don't know what I imagined. I'm so nervous I'm shaking. What do we do now?'

'We go to the door and inquire about Lowell Simison.'

'I can't do that. What if he's there?'

'He probably won't be. But what if he is? He doesn't know you any more than you know him.'

'Maybe not. But I still can't do it. I'll wait for you down at the corner.'

Before he rang the bell, Jesse heard a radio playing inside. When a young woman carrying a baby came to the door with another child clinging to her skirt, he said, 'Excuse me. I'm looking for Lowell Simison. I believe he lives here.'

She shook her head. 'Nobody here by that name. My husband, Wayne Doggett, bought this place three years ago September and we've lived here ever since then.'

'Do you remember who you bought it from?'

'My husband dealt with a real estate man named Arthur Long. Has an office just cat-a-corner from the courthouse. The house was empty when we took it. We never knew the people that lived here ahead of us.'

'Maybe I should talk to Mr Long, then. I'm anxious to find out what became of Mr Simison.'

'You don't have to go that far. There's an old woman named Mona Teasdale lives right over there in that mustard-coloured house. Wayne says she's been here since Crawfordsville was an Indian village. And I promise you she's got her nose in everybody's business. If your friend lived here she'll know all the whys and wherefores. I guarantee it. Probably tell you how often he changed his underwear.'

The following afternoon, Jesse had a meeting with Dr Applegate, the dean of the faculty at Wabash.

'Are you a close friend of Professor Simison?' Applegate asked.

'Not a close friend. But I admire him, I met him some time ago when he was teaching in Wisconsin.'

'At Warburton?'

'Yes. I met him then and haven't seen him since. But I've heard he was here. So since I was driving through . . . .'

'You know he's no longer teaching here.'

Jesse nodded. 'I went to his house yesterday and I was told he hasn't lived here for more than three years.'

'He left Crawfordsville in March of 1938. In the middle of a semester. Went home one day saying he didn't feel well and that was the last we saw of him. A few days later, a big out-of-state van came and took every stick of furniture out of his house and next thing anybody knew the place was up for sale.'

'And nobody knows where he went?'

'Somebody in Crawfordsville may know but nobody here at the college knows.'

'He must have had friends on the faculty.'

'Only colleagues. No close friends. He was a fine teacher but not quick to confide in people. I was probably the closest thing to a friend he had. I brought him here from Warburton. But I was never inside his house and he never came to mine. He was amiable enough if you happened to see him on the street but he simply wasn't a sociable man. And his wife was the same. A nice woman but very private. Some of us felt it was because they were both in their fifties when Lowell came here to Wabash. By that age, most teachers have tenure and they're just cruising along waiting for retirement. But not Lowell. He had tenure at Warburton – he was the senior man in their history department – but he left all that to come here. He was devoted to teaching. Seemed to have no other interests really. I've never heard a man lecture on American history the way he did.'

'I remember he had a son. He was only four or five years old when I met him.'

'Yes. Floyd was his name. He went to high school here in Crawfordsville. Grade school, too, from third grade on. My wife always had the notion that it was difficult for him as he was growing up because the Simisons seemed old enough to be his grandparents. When he was fifteen they were both in their sixties. The way things turned out there

613

must have been something wrong between Lowell and the boy because when Mrs Simison died, Floyd left home. He was due to graduate from high school in four or five months but he just picked up and left.'

When Jesse told Helen about his interview with Applegate she said, 'Now we're back where we started from.'

'I don't think so. I think we're getting warm.'

'If nobody knows where Simison went and nobody knows where Floyd went . . . if they're not even together . . . .'

'We still have to concentrate on Simison. When we locate him we'll locate Floyd. And I have a hunch that Mrs Teasdale is going to tell me what I need to know.'

Mona Teasdale, it turned out, was eager to talk about the Simisons. Or about any other subject, Jesse suspected. He told her he represented an insurance company, that there were unpaid monies due Mr Simison from a policy he'd held on his wife. 'Our company lost track of Simison after he left Crawfordsville.'

'I'm not surprised at that,' Mrs Teasdale said. 'Strange duck, Mr Simison. And after his woman passed on he was stranger than ever. When he left here he took pains to see that nobody knew where he was headed. Even the local man that sold his house for him didn't know how to reach him. He was told to send the cheque along to some bank in Indianapolis and that's what he did.'

'Maybe Simison's in Indianapolis then.'

'Not very likely. Even before I *knew* where he went, I never thought it was Indianapolis he'd gone to. Too close to Crawfordsville, I figured. And I was right.' She eased back in her chair then as if she was waiting for a direct question from Jesse. But Jesse, sensing that Mona Teasdale would divulge information only when she was *ready* to do so, simply smiled and said, 'I see.'

'I'll tell you the truth,' she went on. 'If you're looking for somebody who's anxious to do a favour for Lowell Simison you're not likely to end up with a long list of names. Not in this neighbourhood at any rate. The fact is he wasn't a neighbourly person. And from what I hear he was no different over at the college. Stand-offish. Kept to himself. Lived across the street there for just under twelve years and I never had a conversation with the man. He managed to nod his head and go through the motions of tipping his hat but that was about the size of it. So when you tell me there's money due him it don't make me want to celebrate exactly. I mean I've got no reason to want to put a dollar in *his* pocket. But on the other hand I felt different about his wife. She wasn't likely to wear out her welcome anyplace either. But she *would* talk a little if you caught her out in the yard or if you bumped into her at the grocery store. She was a timid woman, it seemed to me, but I liked her. Felt sorry for her. It was me that called the doctor when she was taken. Right across the street in her driveway. I was on my front porch and she was sweeping leaves. And all of a sudden she dropped. Not a sound out of her. Just slumped down on the gravel like a bean-bag. Dr Holliday said she was dead before she hit the ground. Heart just stopped, according to him, like a busted clock. Sweeping leaves one minute and dead the next. Not an old woman either. Still in her sixties, I'd guess. It was a sad thing to see. Two months later the boy took off and then after a while the old man skedaddled. Never said goodbye, kiss my foot, or nothing. Just out the door, down the street, and gone. First it made me feel sad, seeing a little family come apart like that. Then I got sore. And the more I thought about it the madder I got. "Who does he think he is?" I thought. Skipping off and not bothering to tell a soul where he's gone. So I decided to do a little snooping around on my own. First I called the college but nobody over there knew anything. Then I asked Ralph Biggs, the letter-carrier. But he said there'd been no forwarding address left. He said all the Simisons' mail, what little they got, was being returned to sender.

'Then one day a big moving-van pulled in and started to load up everything from the house. I sat there watching and I thought, "That van has to be headed someplace and chances are, that's where Lowell Simison is." So what did I do? I walked across the street with a plate of sugar doughnuts and a pot of coffee and had a little snack there on the back steps with the moving men. One of them was an awful nice black fella. From Memphis, it turned out. And the other one was a skinny little devil from Toledo. I mean they trucked out of St Louis but Missouri wasn't where they came from or grew up. Anyway, we had a nice visit, the three of us, while we drank our coffee, and I didn't ask them one question about their business, where they was headed, or anything. But just before I came back across the street, I said, "Well, you have a careful trip now. According to the radio there's some tacky weather out there in Denver." The skinny one gave me kind of a funny look. Then he said, "We're not heading for *Denver*, lady. I wish we was. We're haulin' this load up to the Dakotas." I kept after him. I said, "Well, that's a surprise. I was informed that the Simisons had relocated to Denver." He came right back at me and said, "Maybe they *did*. But this furniture's going to Yankton, South Dakota." '

As soon as he got back to the hotel, Jesse called information in Yankton, they gave him a number for Lowell Simison and he placed a person-to-person call. He heard a man's voice answer and the operator said, 'I have a call for Mr Lowell Simison.' When the man replied, 'This is Mr Simison,' Jesse cut in and said, 'Cancel the call, operator. I'll call later.' Jesse turned from the phone then and said to Helen, 'He's there.'

13

Yankton is positioned on high ground, in the south-east corner of the state, with Nebraska just to the south across the Missouri river. Lowell Simison's house, in a cluster of cottages at the edge of town, perched on a bluff that looked out across the river.

In Crawfordsville, Helen had chosen to stay in the background, had preferred to have Jesse gather whatever information he could and pass it along to her. For this interview with Simison, however, there had never been any question that she would be present.

Lowell Simison, when he answered the door, seemed to be a contradiction to everything that had been passed along to Jesse from Applegate and Mona Teasdale. Expecting resistance and suspicion and hard edges, Jesse and Helen were met with gentle hospitality. When Jesse said, with a sober face, 'We represent the agency in Portland, Maine, where you adopted your son,' Simison replied, 'Yes, of course. Please come in.'

He was a small and slender man with silky white hair. His old-fashioned suit was carefully pressed but shiny with wear and he wore a grey pullover under his jacket. His shoes were polished and his tie carefully knotted. He ushered them into the parlour, a square, bright room with heavy upholstered furniture and the walls lined with books. 'Will you have some tea?'

'No, thank you,' Jesse said. Then, 'I hope we haven't caught you just as you were going out.'

'Not at all. I seldom go out.' Then, 'Ahh, of course, I look as if I'm just off to the lecture hall, don't I? Since I first entered college almost fifty years ago, and all the years since, I've put on a proper suit every morning of my life. It's a habit that's hard to break.' He seated them on a sofa and sat facing them in a wing-back chair.

'I assume you're here because I've been remiss in some reporting I was expected to do.'

'You left no forwarding address when you moved from Crawfordsville so the agency has been unable to contact you.'

'I realize that. But since Floyd is twenty-one now, I assumed . . . .'

'I believe we've had no communication with you since 1937 when the boy was seventeen.'

'As you may know, my wife passed on in 1937 and some of the details of my life have not been very well-handled since then.'

He told them then, about his wife's death and his

617

decision to leave Wabash. 'It was a foolish thing for me to do, I can see that now, but at the time I wasn't thinking clearly. My first teaching job had been here at Yankton college and I thought . . . I don't know what I thought. I suppose it represented some sort of haven for me. When it seemed there was no longer anything to keep me in Crawfordsville, I simply came back to South Dakota and I've been here ever since.'

'When did you come here?' Helen asked. 'What was that date?'

'It was 1938. In March. Floyd's birthday was March twentieth. He was eighteen that year. I left Crawfordsville the day after his birthday.'

'And Floyd came here with you?'

'Oh, no. He'd gone off two months before. His mother died in November of 1937 and Floyd left me the following January. You see, we had never told him he was adopted. It was a source of disagreement between me and Ruth all the time the boy was growing up. When we decided to adopt a baby, when we first contacted your Dr Kilwinning in Maine, we agreed that at some time, when the child was old enough to understand, we would explain to him that he was adopted. We thought it was the fair thing to do. But not long after we brought Floyd home – I know it was before his first birthday – Ruth said to me, "*I'm* his mother now and *you're* his father. We're the only parents he'll ever know. There's no reason we should tell him he's adopted." I disagreed with her, of course, as I've said, and we discussed it frequently when Floyd was small. But as the years passed by, as I saw how attached he was to my wife, the subject came up only occasionally. At last we settled it by a sort of tentative agreement that we would tell him on his eighteenth birthday. But as I've told you, my wife died in November of the preceding year and Floyd left the following January.'

'*Before* his birthday,' Helen said.

'Yes.'

'Then you never told him?'

'Oh, yes. I *did* tell him,' Mr Simison said. 'During our

semester break for the holidays, when Floyd and I were alone in the house I decided that the time had come. That decision has tortured me ever since. But all the same, I still believe it was my responsibility to tell him the truth about himself. Whether I selected the proper moment or not is something I suppose I'll never know. I suspect that his reaction would have been the same no matter when I told h..m.'

'What *was* his reaction?' Helen asked.

'At first he didn't believe it. But when I finally convinced him, he was upset. And angry. First he wanted to know why he hadn't been told before. Then he asked why I'd told him just now. And at last he said he wished I hadn't told him at all. I answered all his questions honestly. I told him the truth just as I'm telling it to you, but he wasn't satisfied with my answers. He had some idea that if Ruth were still alive . . . I'm not sure *what* he thought, but it was clear that he blamed me for his disappointment.

'At last, I suppose it was two weeks after I'd told him, he sat across the breakfast table from me one morning and said, "If you and Mom weren't my real parents, then who *is*?" He said since I'd decided to tell him the truth about himself he wanted to know the *whole* truth. But, as you know, I couldn't tell him. When I explained that we knew only that his parents had been two healthy, normal people, that we had no information beyond that, he refused to accept it. When I showed him the papers from your agency he made it clear that he thought there was something I was withholding from him. We said some bitter things to each other, I'm afraid, and a few days later, when I came home from my day at school, he was gone. He left a note saying he wasn't angry with me but he just needed to spend some time by himself.

'A week or so later I had a postcard from him that had been mailed in Pittsburgh, and not long after, another one, mailed from Boston. Early in March of that year I heard from the police in Hartford, Connecticut. They were holding Floyd on suspicion of car theft. I arranged for his bail through a lawyer in Crawfordsville and I took a train the next day to New York. When I got to Hartford, however, I was told that Floyd had disappeared and the bail money I'd paid was forfeit. During that train ride back to Indiana I decided to leave Crawfordsville and go back to South Dakota.'

'Since no one at Wabash knows where you've gone,' Jesse said, 'I assume that Floyd can't contact you either.'

'Oh, no. *He* knows where I am. Sometimes I feel as if he's abandoned me but I've never wanted to abandon *him*. When I came home from Connecticut there was another card from him giving me a post-office box number in Richmond, Virginia. He said I could always reach him there. So as soon as I moved up here to Yankton I sent him my new address.'

'Does he still live in Richmond?'

'I don't think he ever did. He must know somebody there who sends his mail along. Because when I had postcards from him he always seemed to be in a different city. Mostly in the south. Mobile, Memphis, Jacksonville . . . he seems to have been all over.'

'It's three years now since he left home?'

'More than three. He was seventeen last time I saw him. This past March he was twenty-one.'

'And you haven't seen him in all that time?'

Simison shook his head. 'I felt bad about it for the first year or so. But now I think maybe it's for the best.'

'Why do you say that?' Helen said.

'He's a changed boy, I'm afraid. He was in some kind of trouble from the time he left home. Sometimes I heard about it but most of the time I'm sure I didn't. I always helped out if there was anything I could do. Or if he needed some money. But I began to feel there was no real connection between us. Not any more.'

'That's a shame,' Jesse said.

'Yes, it is. But he felt cheated, I guess, and he had to take it out on somebody.'

'Do you know where he is now?'

'If you'd have asked me that a year ago, all I could have told you was that post-office box in Richmond. But since

620

July I've known exactly where he is. He's in California. He came before a court in Asheville, North Carolina for passing bad cheques. The judge gave him a choice of going to jail or enlisting in the service. So Floyd joined the navy. He wanted submarine duty but they found out he's handy with a paint-brush so they put him in a camouflage unit stationed in San Diego.'

Just before they left Mr Simison's house, as the three of them were standing just inside the front door, he asked, 'Are you his real parents?'

'Why would you think that?' Jesse said.

'I just decided the two of you might be Floyd's natural mother and father.'

'I told you. We're from the . . . .'

'Yes sir. I know what you told me. But I've seen quite a number of people from that agency in the past twenty years and none of them looked anything at all like you folks.' When neither of them answered, he said, 'Don't misunderstand me. You're fine-looking people. I was hoping maybe you *were* his parents. But if you say you're not, then I'm sure you're not. I'm a man who's spent most of his life reading books. My imagination gets out of hand sometimes.'

That evening when he and Helen met in the hotel dining-room, Jesse said, 'Did you have a nap?'

'I tried,' Helen said, 'but my brain wouldn't stop whirling. So I ran a bath and had a good soak instead.'

'How are you feeling? About today, I mean.'

'I don't know. Some good. Some bad.'

'We set out to find him and we did it. You must feel good about that.'

'I feel good about it and terrible about it. I wasn't ready for so much information at one time.'

'Have you thought about the next step?'

'I've tried to.'

'What do you think?'

'I'm not sure there should be a next step.' When he didn't answer she said, 'Why are you grinning like a monkey?'

'Because you just said what I was hoping you'd say.'

'You think I should give up?'

'I wouldn't call it "giving up". Besides I think you should do whatever feels right to you. No matter what anybody says.'

'But . . . .'

'But I think there's a situation here that can't be sorted out by just throwing your arms around someone and saying, "I'm your mother and I love you." Floyd sounds to me like an angry kid.'

'I guess I'd be angry, too,' she said.

'No doubt about it. So would I. But the question you have to ask yourself is whether your showing up will make that anger go away or simply redirect it. Don't think I don't have sympathy for him. I do. But I am much more concerned with what happens to you. If it were left to me I would not be willing to sacrifice *your* well-being for someone else's, not even Floyd's. Especially when we have no idea whatsoever as to what his reaction to you might be. Judging from his treatment of Mr Simison I would not be optimistic, if I were you. Am I talking too much?'

'No. I *need* to talk about it. My head's in such a muddle I can't add two and two.'

'Then I think you should take your time. You know where he is now. You don't have to make an instant decision.'

'Yes, I do, Jesse. If I let myself weigh the pros and cons endlessly, I'll drive myself completely bats. And once I've made a choice you have to help me stick with it. Promise?'

'I'll do my best.'

When he took her to the door of her hotel room after dinner she said, 'I've decided it's too late, Jesse. Whatever's been done to Floyd can't be undone now. You say you care about what happens to me. I don't care about *that* at all. But I care very much what happens to him. And I'm afraid that at this stage in his life my showing up might do him more harm than good. My first reaction was that I *had* to go to California. Right away, I told myself. But now I know I *can't* go there. I'm afraid to.'

The weather was clear and very cold the next morning as they travelled on the local train from Yankton to Omaha. 'We've had an easy time of it so far this winter,' the conductor said, 'but now we're almost through the first week in December and it's coming right at us from out of the north-west. You're lucky to be travelling now. A week from today, these tracks could be drifted over with five feet of snow.'

As they settled into their seats in the lounge car, Helen said, 'Don't be mad at me if I fall asleep. I was awake most of the night and I feel like the walking dead.'

She did fall asleep. Or at least she sat with her eyes closed through most of the trip to Omaha. At last, however, she opened her eyes. 'How much farther?'

'A half-hour,' Jesse said. 'Maybe a bit more.'

The porter brought them coffee and they sipped it in silence. Finally she said, 'Last night I made you promise to keep me on course today.'

'Don't worry. I will.'

'No, you mustn't. I want you to forget that promise.'

'Not a chance. I understood you then and I . . . .'

'Shhh,' she said. 'You must let me talk now while it's clear in my head. I'm nervous and crazy and exhausted and frightened but I finally know what I'm doing.' She sipped the last of her coffee and set the cup down on the table by her chair. 'For the past twenty-one years the most important thing in my life has been that child. I've lived in various places and I've become attached to various people. I've been married and divorced. And I suffered through Raymond's death, my mother's death, and Angus' death. So I should have been prepared for Chet's death. I knew it was coming. I knew it could not be avoided. But when it happened I wasn't prepared. Not at all. I haven't recovered yet and I don't expect I ever *will* recover. But all the same, through those painful times, the *continuing* pain I lived with was Floyd. That never left me. At the back of my mind was a conviction that I would somehow manage to find him someday. Not for any *reason*. Not for his benefit or mine. But simply because it was something I *had* to do. It seems incredible to me that only two or three nights ago I had no clue as to how I might begin to find him. No information, no hint or hope. I only knew it was something I was destined to do, that I was absolutely determined to do.'

'That's not true, Helen.'

'You promised not to interrupt.'

'I have to. You're selling yourself a bill of goods. When I met you in Boston, you had none of this determination you're talking about. I had to talk you into coming out here.'

'You're right. If it had been left to me I would probably have done nothing. But not from a lack of will or desire. I just . . . it's hard to explain, even to myself, but during these last months, since Chet died, I've been living like a sleepwalker, tucked away in my house, functioning on such a low level of energy that I had almost lost the *ability* to function. Then, all of a sudden, this information about Floyd was dropped in my lap. I didn't even have the gumption to go to Portland to get it. Opal did that for me. And even when I *had* it, when I was reading the pages I showed you, I had no idea what to do, no confidence that I could do *anything*. All I could think of was to call on you. Without *you*, I'd still be sitting in a chair someplace staring into space. But you got me going. Slowly, I admit. In Crawfordsville I felt every minute as if I was about to run away and hide. And even yesterday, last night at dinner, I was only operating on about half-power. But sometime during the night I sat up in bed, turned on the light and said to myself, "My God . . . what is the *matter* with you? Do you really think you can turn back now, that you can crawl into your bed on a train, go home to Maine, and *forget* what you've just learned? Can you forget all those years of wondering and hoping and praying for some little piece of information that might help you find your child?" '

'I think you're forgetting the things you said yesterday, after we talked with Mr Simison.'

'Of course I am. Because they don't matter. I won't let them matter. If I find I have a bitter, angry son, then that's the son I've got. If he hates me then I'll just have to hope he gets over it. I mean first I have to make him exist. First I have to see him and he has to see me. Until that happens, everything else is just words and theories and stupid fears. He won't really be born until I see him. You know what I'm saying? I will never be his mother till he sees *me*. That's all that matters. *That's* what I've dreamed about all these years. Those things have to happen first. Then there'll be all sorts of time to deal with other things. Why *I'm* the way I am, why he's the way *he* is. It's all a mystery. It could turn out that we detest each other. But I won't know till I see for myself. So that's what I have to do. That's what I'm going to do.'

Jesse sat looking at her. Finally he said, 'Maybe there's some argument against what you just said but I'll be damned if I know what it is. I wouldn't let you go back to Maine now if you begged me. We'll just turn our hats around and head for San Diego.'

'Not *we*, Jesse. Just *me*. I'm going by myself.'

'Nothing doing. I signed on for the full trip. A first-class detective like me never goes home till the job's done.'

She shook her head and smiled. 'It *is* done, Jesse. And *you* did it. I couldn't have done it by myself. But now it's personal stuff. Now it's between me and Floyd. I have to do the rest myself. I *need* to do it. It's my mess and I have to clean it up. Or maybe it won't be a mess after all. It may turn out to be nothing but ice-cream. If it is, if I'm *that* lucky, then I don't want to share it with anyone, not even *you*. Is that selfish?'

'Probably,' he said, 'but that's all right.'

Her train heading west was scheduled to leave Omaha two hours before his train would leave for Chicago. She boarded early and he sat in her compartment with her as they waited for departure time.

'God, I feel marvellous,' she said. 'I feel as if a lifetime

625

of cobwebs has just been swept out of my head. I feel as if my whole grown-up life has been jittery and half-cocked, waiting for me to make this one decision. But now it's all fixed. Now I fully expect, when I wake up tomorrow, to see flowers growing out of my ears.'

'You sure as hell look different than you did last night.'

'I *am* different. The caterpillar turned into a butterfly.'

Jesse smiled. 'Are you telling me you're in control of your life?'

She shook her head. 'God, no. Nothing as grand as that. I've never been in control of my life and I never expect to be.'

'Do you remember a conversation we had a long time ago? When we were leaving Fort Beck to go to England that summer after Raymond died?'

'I hope you're not going to remind me of something asinine I said.'

'I *have* to remind you,' he said. 'I promised I would. You said you'd never be dumb enough to love somebody who didn't love you . . . .'

'I was wrong about *that*, God knows.'

'You said you expected to always be in full control of your life . . . .'

'Wrong again.'

'And you said in twenty years you'd be an old lady.'

'How long ago was that conversation?' she asked.

'Twenty-two years.'

'Well, I was half-right. Yesterday I felt like a very old lady. But today I don't.'

Just before he got off the train, they put their arms around each other and he said, 'Good luck, kiddo. I'm proud of you.'

'I'm trying to be proud of myself.'

'That shouldn't be too hard. You just have to stop loving people who don't love you back.'

She pulled his head down and kissed him. 'That's the worst advice you ever gave me,' she said. 'I'll never stop that.'

After Helen's train disappeared down the tracks, Jesse

626

walked back along the platform to the station bar. He sat by a wide window looking across the interior of the terminal. Settling deep into a leather chair, he tasted his whiskey and lit a cigar. Making no effort to come to conclusions or manage his thoughts, he simply sat there, feeling like a man without restrictions or obligations.

It was an uncommon sensation for him, one he would have expected to find abhorrent. But on this particular day, during these particular moments, all known rules and standards seemed suddenly invalid. He felt empty and the feeling stimulated him. The silence in the near-deserted bar, his aloneness there, made him sharply conscious of all his senses. The feel of leather, the scent of smoke, the muted colours of the station waiting-room seen through the thick plate glass.

Jesse was aware of his breathing, of his heartbeat, of his weight on the chair cushion. Like a victorious distance runner he felt an intoxicating mix of exhaustion and exhilaration. He was about to begin a journey but his instincts told him he had completed one. All the destinations he had reached since first leaving Chicago seemed like mere stop-overs on the way to where he sat now. At point zero. At the nowhere centre. Nothing to repeat or complete now. No place to go back to. No calls to answer. No demands to be met.

He realized suddenly that he could stay where he was if he chose to and not board the east-bound train. Or he could select another train going in another direction. He could do or not do, leave or not leave. He could simply be. Or he could *begin*. He could commence something, reach for something he wanted.

The awareness of what he wanted had not come to him suddenly. He had stored it inside himself for a long time. His *acceptance* of it had come even more slowly. Only after he left Omaha for Chicago did he totally accept it. And only when his train pulled out of Chicago on its way east, did he allow it to come to full life.

15

On Monday, December 22, 1941, eleven days after Germany and Italy had declared war on the United States, Jesse and Valerie were married in a civil ceremony in Medford, Massachusetts. The following year, on November 12, four days after forces from England and America had landed on the beaches of Oran, on the Mediterranean coast of Algeria, and in Morocco, Valerie gave birth to a son. His name had been agreed upon months before. He was christened Raymond Angus Bradshaw.